True Love Lost

By Morgan Kelley

"They that love beyond the world cannot be
  separated by it Death cannot kill what does not die."
                              ~ William Penn

"You live on earth only for a few short years
  which you call an incarnation, and then you leave
  your body as an outworn dress and go for
  refreshment to your true home in the spirit."
                              ~ White Eagle

**And so begins Desdemona's story and the
journey of Callen Whitefox...**

Dedication:

To all those that believe in love at first sight.

To all those that have loved and lost.

To all those that were driven mad by love.

To all those that have yet to risk their hearts for their 'one true love'.

And to all those who never gave up and searched for that true love despite the odds.

To my mom and dad; a shining example of love never getting lost.

To my girlfriends who let me bounce ideas off them at all times of the day, and put up with my craziness in the pursuit of writing this book.
                    Wine is on me!

~ Prologue ~
Six Months Earlier

The mirror didn't lie, as beauty was in the eye of the beholder. Indeed she was a lovely woman, taking pride in her appearance. The main reason was her true love. He always enjoyed that she took time to make herself look just right. As she brushed her long blonde hair, she ran her fingers over the long silkiness, a smile crossing her lips.

"Tonight will be so special," she said, to no one in particular. "I can't wait until we start our evening together, lover." It would be a night they'd never forget.

There was nothing like spending a quiet evening in with the love of her life. It made her giddy with excitement at the prospects of what was to come. "I wonder what color lipstick I should wear for you tonight," she said, as she picked through the various colors in her makeup kit. "Perhaps a red would be perfect," she whispered giddily, as she puckered up and smeared it on her lips and then inspected the outcome.

It should have taken little thought, but yet there was that doubt and fear pushing into her mind. Finally, she made the decision.

"No, I think not. My lover's right. I look too trashy. I know how you don't like me to look like a whore. I guess I'll pick a new color, Lover," she stated to the empty room. Gently she picked up a tissue and began blotting the color from her lips. When it left a red stain behind, she felt herself becoming angry, rubbing harder and with more force. "No! This won't do," she snapped, desperately trying to remove the offensive color from her lips. Red was for whores and sluts. Not women in a committed relationship, and she knew that!

The love of her life was very particular. There were a few things that she'd learned to avoid when he was around. The first being, he liked his woman to be a lady. Not some crass, vile, trash bag that had no manners. Women you brought home to marry weren't gutter whores who acted like perverse tramps.

Once before she tried to play the sexy vixen and crossed the line, only to discover her lover's temper. That was a night she wouldn't ever forget, as it played back in her mind like a horrible nightmare. The anger from him was incredible and the strike to her face left a mark that took days to fade.

That mistake wouldn't ever be made again.

She thought about that night not long ago, and her heart pounded furiously in her chest. So much effort went into that evening to impress him. The perfect dinner had been planned, as he came home from a demanding day at work. Making his favorite food was tricky, because if it was too hot or too cold then there would be anger. He liked to eat promptly at six p.m. and not a second later. As he walked into the house he wanted a cold beer, his woman looking perfect, a clean house, and a hot meal. After all it wasn't too much for him to ask of her.

Rubbing her cheek, she remembered the moment it started to unravel. When she placed their dinner, a pan of lasagna in the oven, she inadvertently forgot to turn it on and the well timed dinner was going to be late. Maybe he'd forgive her and be in a good mood, or maybe he'd punish her and make her night hell.

Either way it was a craps shoot. Damned if she did and damned if she didn't.

As she waited for him to arrive home, she had a brilliant idea. She would dress in something sexy, possibly distracting him with her body for thirty minutes before dinner. Then he wouldn't even notice that the food was late coming to the table.

Men loved sex and food, and she was praying that the art of seduction would save her from getting hurt. If there was one thing she disliked, it was the quick snap of his temper when she did something horribly wrong.

It scared her.

NO! It terrified her.

Running around the house, cognizant of the clock on the wall and the alarm in her phone, she knew she only had so much time remaining before he'd arrive. Checking the details, she rushed into the living room just to assure herself that she wouldn't screw anything else up.

The remote was on the arm of his chair ready for his use.

There were three cold beers in the fridge, ready for his consumption through the night.

Even the pillows were in just the right spots on the couch, fluffed and ready to impress him with their perfection.

Lastly, she checked off the final item. The mail was in a pile ready to be read and on the little table beside his chair.

If any of these things weren't exact, there'd be anger and hell to pay. She knew that from experience, but that was her fault. He had rules and she needed to be obedient and observe them, because he was the man.

Now that the little details were handled, she could now manage the big issue at hand. The late dinner and why she'd screwed it up this badly. This would be her third warning, and the first one had been scary enough. Yet she didn't learn her lesson. The screaming frightened her, but still she made the error again. The second time, punishment was she'd been struck. If he got to the final warning, she was unsure what would happen. There was a part of her that dreaded knowing what he would do to her on the third mistake when he found out.

Shaking her head, she pushed it out of her mind, praying her plan would work. As she checked the clock again she took a seat at her vanity. It had been a present from her true love, and he expected it to be used. No slovenly women were allowed in his house. Women were to be arm candy, making their men look good. It was her job in life. She was his concubine and his representation out in the world, and when they were in public. Because he had chosen her there were benefits. He paid her bills, gave her a roof over her head, and loved her.

He really loved her…

As she hastily picked makeup out to impress him, she had that sinking feeling that the plan wasn't going to work. A silent prayer was said, and a promise that this wouldn't ever happen again, if she just survived this one mistake.

"Please God let me pull this off," she whispered.

Just one more chance and she'd be the perfect woman for him. After all she was still learning.

Digging through her dresser drawer, she found the one slutty outfit she owned. It wasn't one she ever wore with him before. Part of her was afraid of how he would react. There were times when they had sex, and he wanted her to be a filthy whore, making her do the vilest things, and other times where he couldn't perform unless she appeared chaste and pretended to not enjoy it. Either way, he loved her and that's all that mattered.

Crossing her fingers, she hoped she could distract him enough with her womanly wiles, and that he'd be in the mood for raunchy sex.

As she finished dressing, she slipped into a pair of heels that she owned before moving in with him. It was one of the rare pieces of her past that she'd kept. He didn't like her remembering anything before him. The men, the fun, the sex… But she couldn't resist the red shiny patent leather pumps. They were her secret happiness, and she just couldn't leave them behind. Checking the garters and looking in the mirror she heard his truck pull up to the outside of the house.

It was now or never! The show was about to begin.

Grabbing a beer from the refrigerator, she leaned sexily against the counter, waiting for him to enter. The only thing she could hope was her face didn't show the fear and terror that she was feeling inside if this didn't work.

The lock clicked.

Her heart pounded.

"I'm home, baby," he hollered, his back to her as he closed the door.

In her head she counted the steps through the mud room to the kitchen. Five, four, three, and she popped the beer tab and it made the hiss.

"I see you have my…" He stopped short and his mouth hung open at what was waiting for him in his kitchen. Surely he was in the wrong house.

"I thought we could have some fun before dinner," she said sweetly, hoping the act was believable.

Silence.

"I'll be the appetizer." She tried again, hoping and praying it worked.

Then she knew that the line had been crossed. The handsome features twisted into a sick rage, as the keys to his truck were slammed viciously onto the kitchen counter. The 'thunk' made her jump in her heels, and she knew then it was going to be bad. "Baby, wait! I can explain," she begged, holding out the beer in hopes it might calm him down. It wasn't like she forgot everything he liked.

"Explain?" he roared. "You can explain why you're dressed like some piece of trash and standing in my kitchen like this?" He motioned up and down her body with his hand.

She stuttered, "Ba-baby, I forgot to turn on the oven and dinner is going to be late tonight, and I didn't want you to…"

There was no time given to explain. The beer went flying, as he knocked it out of her hand and stepped dangerously close to her body.

"You didn't want me to be angry?" he hissed. "Well you have a funny way of avoiding that," he snapped at her viciously. "I warned you about trashy women in my home. It's forbidden!"

When he moved at her, she braced for the hit and fully expected it. It spun her head and knocked her off balance. The heels that she loved so much didn't help her, as they twisted making her fall backwards. Everything stopped, as she felt her legs going out from under her, and it was all broken as her head hit the corner of the counter.

Shaking her head to pull out of the memory, she refused to think about it anymore. That was then, and this is now. Her lover was waiting for her out there, and she was going to give him the best night of his life. One he'd remember until he died. One last check in the mirror, a spritz of perfume, and she was ready to go and face him.

"Here I come, baby," she called, as she exited their room they shared and crossed through the house. Looking around, everything was perfect. It was a job well done, and she congratulated herself on perfecting the task.

Entering the attached garage, she felt her breath catch in her throat. There he was, and he was magnificent. There was no doubt that she was indeed the luckiest woman in the world. As she approached him, she could tell he wasn't feeling well. His skin was gray and his breathing shallow.

"Lover, are you not feeling well?" she asked, as she looked down at him lying on the table in the middle of their garage. Her fingers traced down his body, avoiding the manacles and the chains lying across him to restrain him. "Don't worry love, after our evening together you'll find that you'll feel vastly better," she grinned, coyly.

Unbuttoning his shirt, she noticed his eyes were open.

"Where am I?" he slurred. "I don't feel well."

"You're at home with me, lover," she smiled lovingly at him. "We are about to have a nice romantic night together."

"Who are you?" he asked, as his eyes suddenly began to focus on the person standing above him. "Wait, that's not right. Oh my God!"

"Oh, you know who I am, lover, but I think you've asked enough questions," she said, as she ripped off a piece of duct tape.

"Wait, get away from me!" He began struggling to get free.

"Now, now lover. It's time for our date to begin," she whispered, grinning seductively, and then slapped the duct tape over his mouth. When she placed a kiss over the tape covered lips, he began screaming muffled words. "I promise, tonight will be a night to remember for you. She winked and moved to his feet.

The restrained man felt violently ill, like he was about to vomit. There wasn't any alcohol involved. Only a cup of coffee. Then it started coming back to him, and he fought harder to escape.

"Now lay still while I take off your shoes and socks, Lover. I need to get your handsome feet ready for the evening's festivities."

Removing his dress shoes and his socks, she seductively she ran her fingers over the arch of his strong feet. She knew when she saw him; he'd be the perfect donation. "I'm impressed, lover. You have such strong bone structure."

He fought hard to get through the chains, and when he saw the hacksaw being pulled from the tool chest he started begging into the duct tape. Next came the tears that started filling his eyes as the cold metal touched his skin.

"Lover, fret not my pet. I swear that this is all necessary. It's for us, my love. Trust me. I know what's best for us now."

There was more screaming as he struggled violently to pull his restrained legs from the hacksaw.

"Don't worry lover, it will only hurt for a little while, and then the pain will all go away, and there will be peace. I promise." She batted her eyelashes and patted his leg reassuringly, right before she began humming to herself. "Here we go."

The first slice was vicious. It cut through tendon and nerve and the teeth of the hacksaw scraped against the bone and made a sickening sound. He screamed, and howled from behind the duct tape, struggling nonstop, as each slice of the hacksaw was punctuated by the sound of bone being sliced at the ankle.

The room swam sickly, as he felt his heart pounding. The pain was so acute, that he knew he'd be passing out from the intensity of it all. The gray was now white, and the edges were slowly going black. As the next wave of pain hit, he prayed to go unconscious.

With his last scream, he fell into the darkness.

Willingly.

She flinched as the blood squirted from the artery onto her face and neck. "Damn it lover! You got blood in my hair," she said horrified, as she looked over at his prone body. "Just one more slice." With those words, she made the final cut and completely severed the first foot.

"Don't worry my love. I forgot about that artery. I won't get sprayed with the next one," she said, patting his unmoving leg.

The man screamed no more, as the blood in his body spurted from the decapitated limb with every pump of his heart. Soon there'd be little to no life left in his body, as all of his precious fluid ran into the drain in the garage floor.

Even when she began sawing at the second leg, there were still no screams. Life leached from him like the blood, and there were no thoughts but one, as he left his existence and became one of the dead.

Thank God the pain is over.

Three months later

She struggled to remove him from the truck and into the abandoned building. He was heavier than he looked, and now he was nothing more than dead weight. There was going to have to be a diet in her lover's future that was for sure. The love of her life seemed to put on weight since three months ago, when she carried him to their secret spot. It was time to stop baking him cakes and cookies, or he'd be as big as a house. Not that it'd matter. She'd still adore him unconditionally.

After all, you loved who you loved.

Dragging him seemed so cold and impersonal, but honestly he was heavier than she could manage on her own. If only he'd stayed awake and walked on his own, it would have been so much easier and quicker. Sadly, he couldn't stand the sight of blood, and once it flowed, he was gone to the world.

Down into the dilapidated building she pulled him, carefully avoiding him slamming his head off the door jam. After all, she didn't want to hurt him, and give him a wicked headache in the morning. Then he might be cranky and not enjoy their evening that she had planned for them.

"Oh look lover," she said, looking around at his company. "It looks like you have some friends to keep you busy while I go home and clean the house."

Placing him against the one wall, she patted his cheek. "Now, I promise to have dinner ready for you, after I clean the house and go pick up some beer. I do know how you like your beer cold and your dinner hot."

She blew him a kiss, before waving to his companions.

"Gentlemen, make sure you get him home safely, and you don't keep him out too late at night. You don't want to make me angry," she said giggling, as she tossed her long blond locks over her shoulder.

"Oh darn, you got me dirty," she wiped at the stain on the front of her sweater. "I don't think blood will come out of fleece. Darn it!" she paused, looking worried. "Oh, don't worry lover. I won't be late with dinner because I'm out shopping. I will just toss this out and make sure I'm presentable for you when you get home."

She stopped, as if listening for some conversation only she was privy to hearing. Tapping her chin, she gave it great thought before finally answering him.

"We're having lasagna. Your favorite, lover!"

And then she walked away giggling.

She was so lucky to have him in her life.

Two weeks ago.

The woman stood in her basement in front of the jars lining the wall, gazing at her collection. Each jar held part of her lover and once the collection was complete, she'd begin to reconstruct him and complete her mission in life.

Piece by piece…

And then she'd find someone to help her give him back what he was missing. That would take someone skilled with helping people, and it may be hard to pull off, but she'd figure it out. Anything was possible if it was done for the right reason.

LOVE

Every night she came to the basement and stood in front of the shelves to admire her work. It was her own little hideaway, found when construction had begun on the house she called home. She told no one when the construction crew came to her with the unsealed entrance to the ancient canning cellar. From that day, she kept it a secret and had plans to use it as her place to hide. Every woman needed a place to think. This was her special place.

It was a sanctuary of sorts. When her lover was with her, there were no places in the house she could call her own. Now it was different, and she was sure when he came back that there would be the allowance of her secret spot.

He'd give it to her out of gratitude.

Help her fix it up.

Tell her he loved her for being faithful, even though a normal partner would have given up hope of his return.

For now it housed her most important treasures. As she ran her hands lovingly across the big and small jars, she began to feel excitement. Soon she'd be able to completely put him back together again, and everything would be perfect.

Soon her true love would be back and there would be no more worries. It was hard being alone, and she didn't like it at all. Without a man in her life she felt incomplete. There was no one to please or wait on hand and foot. She turned the jar containing her lover's new foot and laughed at her own little silly joke.

Yes, she was incomplete just as he was, and once she completed him, she too would be whole again.

It would happen.

It was coming.

She could feel it.

Planning her next evening alone with him became the priority, as she moved towards the rickety stairs. "Good night my love," she whispered over her shoulder, as she pulled the chain on the dangling light.

"Until we meet again."

~ *Chapter One* ~
Monday Morning

Doctor Desdemona Adare stood in the kitchen of her newly furnished home, and had her second cup of coffee for the morning. The view from the window was one of cold winds and dreary weather. Mid-winter had everything in its icy grip, and all around her new home was dead and barren. Maybe it was just her, but winter wasn't something she enjoyed. The layers upon layers of heavy clothing, the sting of seasonal depression come January, and the slippery driving conditions. When she lived in Virginia, there were days when the roads were horrific, but never as bad as out west. When a big storm came, it came with a vengeance and tried to crush all living things.

Mother Nature was being bitchy this winter, and she was tired of the crankiness.

Just last week it took her two hours to dig out from the snowy free-for-all. It wasn't something she ever thought she'd like or adjust to either. Snow should fall in inches and not in feet. That was unjust punishment from Mother Nature. Back home in the bayou there was never snow, and as a kid she was jealous and wanted to see the fluffy white stuff. Now she was sorry she even thought that it might be fun. It wasn't at all. In fact, she could say without a doubt it sucked.

As she looked at the big stone house behind hers, protectively surrounded by the privacy fence, there had to be a good six inches of new fallen snow on the crest. Crap! That meant it snowed more last night.

That was it! Nature won, and she was going to do the smart thing and hire someone to plow her driveway and sidewalks. Even if it cost a fortune, it meant not having to freeze her ass off. That alone was worth it.

Desdemona laughed, as she'd once had the same thoughts about the sweltering heat of the bayou. Packing up her little car to head off to college, she swore she'd find a place with more than one season- HOT! Now she was thinking maybe it wasn't the location, and it was really her being overly picky.

Maybe she missed her family, and she was just trying to make an excuse to sell the house and run again.

Desdemona Adare watched the smoke from the stone chimney on her neighbor's house and thought about her family. There weren't many people left to call her own. Her mother disappeared years ago when she was just a small child. One day Trinity Adare went out into the swamp to gather roots for her grandmother and never returned. It didn't matter that there was a swamp wide search for her, or that they put up posters. She had gone 'POOF'!

Some said she ran off with a young man that grand'mere wouldn't approve of, and some said she fell into the swamp only to become a snack for the gators. Either way, Desdemona lost her desire to be from the bayou the day her mother disappeared.

Then there was her sister. Oh, she loved her with all her heart. Cordelia Adare was the spitting image of her mother. Tall, lean and so achingly beautiful that Desdemona couldn't help but be jealous. Unfortunately she got the short end of the genetic pool, literally. Where her sister was light and sunny, she was dark and sinister. Okay, maybe that wasn't a good word to use, but she was a Medical Examiner, and she did like to wear a lot of black. As much as she wanted to be like her cherished sister, she was just going to have to let it go and be happy with being whimsical and kooky.

Desdemona did miss her grand'mere. The woman was her rock and stability. When she told her that she didn't want to stay, but move north for medical school, her grandmother supported her and helped her pay for the education. How she did it that was the big mystery. Whenever Desdemona asked her grand'mere, she was told to 'hush and not worry'. Maybe it was for the best, and what you didn't know couldn't hurt you. If you looked in the dictionary under the word 'bizarre', you'd find her grand'mere's picture. Desdemona was convinced she inherited her kookiness from that part of the family tree.

Going to college had meant everything to her. The academic accolades, the push through the best medical schools in the country, and graduating top of the class with honors. It all meant the world to her, because no one expected a bayou girl to make anything of herself. Proving them wrong was the best payback. Now she had the big house, the fancy car, and enough money to support her sister and grand'mere back home. Life was good.

Almost.

Desdemona left working on the east coast for one major reason. It wasn't for the money; she had already had a cushy job that paid well. She left because **HE** had found her again. As she dotted the country trying to stay one step ahead of him, she came into and left jobs that she loved. Now she worked for the FBI, and as much as a mystery caught her attention, it was the fact she could carry a gun that made the job the selling point. When being stalked, having a gun and working in one of the most secure buildings in the world offered a great deal of comfort.

It wasn't as if she didn't try to find out who it was harassing her. Desdemona tried and in fact, she'd filed reports, asked for help and then finally moved. Each time going to the authorities, and being patted on the shoulder and told it was her imagination.

It wasn't her imagination!

There was that sense of always being watched. One moment it would be fine, and the next it would be there. This awareness would come and go, and then when she let her guard down, the messages would start back up again. At first she went through all the ex's and tried to figure out if it was one of them and nothing. Each one moved on and had their own lives. Now it wasn't only a mystery, but a colossal pain in her ass. It was like the stalker wanted her isolated, alone, and scared. There were no friends to lean on, and no men to keep her safe. She'd had to forgo all of that in the attempt to keep herself and them safe from being a target.

It was a horrible existence.

Not to mention creepy.

Always looking over your shoulder and wondering if the person behind you was the one. It was making her paranoid and edgy.

"Great, I'm a creepy, paranoid kook," she muttered, taking another sip of coffee.

Creepy was one thing. Don't get her wrong, Desdemona always liked creepy, and always had a fondness for the things that went bump in the night. It was just her 'thing' in life. It even influenced her career path in life and the way she dressed. As a child she always wanted to know what came after death. Was there more? Now she was the death doctor, and it was her job to figure out how someone came to the end of their existence.

Desdemona laughed, as she thought about her life. The Medical Examiner who lived alone, dressed all in black and thought she was being followed.

How the hell did she pass the FBI psych profile?

Maybe the way she dressed was the outlet she desperately needed. In life she shrank from attention, but when it came to dressing, she enjoyed being center stage. Some called her clothing Goth, but she just thought it was fun and easier. Black was not only slimming, but easy to match to everything in a wardrobe. As for the big clunky shoes or the giant heels, they had nothing to do with fashion and everything to do with height.

At five foot five, she had to look up at her bosses and felt like she needed to be on equal footing. Her first week working with them, she went home with a wicked crick in her neck every night and decided enough was enough. Out came the heels and she'd at least lose the munchkin status in the workplace.

Ethan Blackhawk stood a whole foot above her and then his wife… She was a whole other story.

The first day she met Elizabeth Blackhawk, the only thing that she could think of was holy shit the woman was 'intimidating'. Everyone in the lab talked about their boss. There were plenty of warnings, some that worried her, and some that she didn't think would affect her.

Then she met her.

Elizabeth walked into the lab to meet her, and she wasn't anything that she expected. There were visions of a FBI suit, gun, black glasses and a serious attitude. Well, the toughness was there, but so were the Cowboy boots, a belt buckle and an Amazon woman standing at just six feet tall.

This was her boss? Oh boy.

Then there was the simple fact that when she stood next to Elizabeth, she felt like the ugly duckling. Desdemona wasn't unattractive, but she wasn't Elizabeth Blackhawk beautiful. All the men that she dated fell for her because she was unique and cute. It was the mix of black and red hair, and the green cat colored eyes. On a good day she was pretty, on a bad day Desdemona was a Goth-y mess. But her boss… Yeah, if she wasn't intimidated by the stories she heard, then she was by how gorgeous Elizabeth was in person.

Director Elizabeth Blackhawk seemed friendly enough, but the icy blue eyes seemed to stare right though you into your soul. As if she was measuring the person hidden beneath in some sort of silent assessment, and she was deciding if you were friend or foe. Yeah, inadequate wasn't far from how she felt around her.

Intimidated, nervous, and plain scared shitless.

In the four months Desdemona had worked with her, she tried to be friendly, but she just wasn't good at making friends. People who stand around with their hands deep in the guts of a dead body weren't exactly the people you wanted to hang out with and get manicures. Elizabeth just seemed unapproachable. Desdemona had even asked her supervisor, if the hardness was because Elizabeth was pregnant. Maybe it was some hormonal thing that she didn't quite understand.

Chris Leonard laughed at that, telling her that Elizabeth Blackhawk had been known to kick ass regularly, and that pregnancy actually mellowed her out.

So, Desdemona stopped trying to get to know the woman, and just hoped she'd stay under the radar and not do anything that would piss the bosses off.

Ethan Blackhawk was a totally different story. Yeah, he was something. The tan skin, the dark blue-black eyes and the smile were stunning. When he called to ask a question, there were little butterflies in her stomach. The sexy radar went off the charts, and then it promptly stopped when she remembered his wife.

Director Special Agent Ethan Blackhawk had a very deadly looking, ass kicking, body hiding wife that could drop kick all one hundred and five pounds of her back to Quantico easily.

Desdemona laughed out loud. Okay that was a definite exaggeration, but that's the impression one would get. There were rumors around the lab that Elizabeth Blackhawk wasn't to be messed with, and she believed each one of them.

Preservation demanded it.

As a scientist she was a firm believer in the theory of 'survival of the fittest'. Her survival depended on staying out of Elizabeth Blackhawks range and under the radar.

Walking through her house, she admired the grandness of it. Growing up as a kid she was poor. No, that's not true. She was three levels below poor. The Bayou wasn't exactly a place of riches and wealth. The people there were simple, and they liked it that way. When she worked for a few years, she realized that her career wasn't going to go away, and it was okay to spend some of her salary. When she moved to FBI West, and Doctor Leonard gave her the salary being offered for the position, she really relaxed. Yeah, the house was an investment, but at the time the stalker had been leaving her alone.

Damn it! Didn't she deserve to have something she loved? Why was her life so void of happiness and friendship? Deep down she wanted to trust, but in the same recesses of her heart where she longed to fit in, she also knew it was never going to happen.

Doctor Desdemona Adare was destined to be a loner. But now all she really wanted was to have a safe place to call home. She'd forgo the love and friendship to just be safe.

It was her secret hope and dream.

Running her fingers up the mahogany banister, she appreciated every single thing in her house and cherished it all. This was her home, and from the top of the line security system to the dog she planned on buying. She was going to feel secure.

One way or another.

Standing in her closet, she looked through all the clothes and settled on the most logical for the weather. Dressing she looked in the mirror and smiled. Yeah, her choice was a little silly, especially when you worked for the FBI, but it made her smile. And that's what mattered.

Life was too short to be what other's wanted you to be.

Desdemona Adare gave up trying to fit in, and now all she was striving for was to just find the one thing that she prayed was achievable.

Happiness.

Red River
The previous afternoon

Red River was a tiny town just outside the snowy mountains. Nothing earth shattering ever happened there, and that was what James Duffy liked most about it. As sheriff of the town, he could come and go as he wanted, and take the day off if he so desired. Red River was a living, breathing quintessential Norman Rockwell painting, and that's how he hoped it would always stay.

Strolling back into his office, after taking the morning off, he found that everyone that was supposed to be on duty was indeed there. Sheila Court, his secretary, was busy filing some reports that the deputies had completed earlier in the day. Julian Littlemoon was sitting at his desk, filling out his logs for the day.

"Jimmy," she said, nodding. "How was your morning off?"

Sheriff James Duffy tipped his cowboy hat and considered the question. "Well, I got wood hauled in, and I managed to sneak in a nap too," he said, grinning the good ole boy smile that always worked with the ladies.

"Lucky you," Sheila Court answered back, cracking her gum. Working for Duffy was a mixed blessing. There was the truly awesome part of having a hot boss to think about all day, and then there was the bad part. James Duffy was a skirt chaser. He'd chase, catch, sleep with and then move on to the next skirt. Where she liked her men to be a little more monogamous, and a lot less tag them and bed them.

Red River was a tiny town, and there weren't really any eligible bachelors worth the time or effort. The town bordered an Indian Reservation, and quite a few Natives worked in town. Not that she cared either way, but she didn't really find Indian men sexy. She liked them blue-eyed, blonde, and less smart than herself. That way she could use the fine art of manipulation.

Flirt, wink, and buy me a drink. It was easy and she liked easy. Native men took too much effort, and that was time spent not focused on her.

"Yeah, I guess I am lucky," Duffy answered, heading into his office. "I'm going to take care of some paperwork. Why don't you call it a day, Sheila. It seems pretty quiet here, and it looks like there might be some snow coming tonight. I think I can answer my own phone for the rest of shift."

"Thanks Jimmy. I think I will," she said, standing. "But if you need anything, you give me a call you hear?"

James Duffy knew why she'd want the call. Sheila was a good person, but she also was a tad bit on the gossip-y side. When she wanted to dig for information, she would find it like a pig on a truffle hunt. The Sheriff grinned as he thought about that analogy, and how it would get his ass kicked if she even got wind of it. So it was best to just keep it his own private joke in his head. The blonde was high maintenance and would shit a ton of bricks if she heard herself being compared to a pig.

"Night Jimmy," Sheila called from the other room. The minute the door closed behind her there was the sound of desk chair scraping the wooden floor.

"Thanks for sending her home," Julian Littlemoon said from the doorway.

James Duffy laughed. "Rough afternoon?"

"Oh yeah, it wasn't pretty here while you were gone," he answered, entering and sitting down in the spare chair. Julian Littlemoon liked his boss a great deal. Then again, he was pretty laid back for the only Native on staff. He rolled with just about everything, because he had to working there.

"What did Sheila do?" he asked, almost afraid to have to deal with it. Along with being a gossip, Sheila tended to be a bit… bitchy.

Julian Littlemoon was his eyes and ears when he wasn't around. He trusted the man completely. When it came to being a deputy, he just had that innate skill to be present but be unseen. The very dark brown eyes missed nothing. Julian Littlemoon was good at blending into the crowd and finding things that went missing. If you needed something tracked down, ask Julian Littlemoon.

He was your man.

The irony behind it all was that Julian was imposing in size and you'd think he'd be the center of attention, especially since he didn't really look like the rest of the community.

"The mayor called this afternoon, to inform us that there's been a few complaints about the abandoned boy scout camp off the river."

"Vagrants?"

"No, apparently there's a smell."

James Duffy leaned back in his chair. "Okay, and what did Sheila say to him, or don't I want to know?"

Littlemoon laughed. "You probably don't want to know. I did hear her tell him that he was more than welcome to come down Monday morning and talk to you personally about cutting the funding to the department." Julian snickered at the look on his face.

"Well shit that can't be good," he said, flipping through his missed call notes on his desk. "He called four times?"

"About that many I suppose. I was out on patrol for a few hours."

"Son of a bitch," he muttered.

"Yeah those words came up too." Julian saluted him and headed back out to his desk. He was off duty in less than two hours, and he hoped it wouldn't drag by like it usually did. What he wouldn't give for some excitement. Working on his Rez would be more exciting, than playing desk jockey on a snowy Sunday afternoon in Red River.

Sheriff James Duffy weighed his options. If he pretended to not know that the mayor called, he was going to have to discipline Sheila and deal with the mayor in the morning. If he went out to the camp and snooped around before it got too dark, he could save Sheila's job and a whole lot of bitching tomorrow.

Yeah, he better do the responsible thing and head on out to the camp. With a sigh, he dropped his hat onto his head and grabbed his flashlight from on top of the file cabinet. Chances are it was a dead deer or a bear carcass from a poacher, but he'd check just in case. There were mountain lions out this time of the year, and often they had a carcass turn up. Last week's warm up must have kicked up the decay.

"Julian, want to ride shotgun for the next hour while we go look for the stink?"

Two hours of boredom or an hour of looking for some decaying animal? Yep, he'd take the dead animal any day. "I'm with you, Sheriff. It has to be better than sitting here waiting for the snow to fall."

"Bring a shotgun, just in case we find some hungry animal that gets pissy that we're snooping around its dinner."

"Got it sheriff. I'll meet you out at the truck."

James Duffy wished all his employees were as easy going as Julian, or maybe the better wish would be that the other employees would just quit.

Either way it was a win-win for him.

The ride out to the old camp was a slow one. Now that nightfall was coming, it was making the roads freeze and the driving conditions treacherous. Maybe letting Sheila get shit canned by the mayor would have been a more favorable option after all. The fact they could die out on the road trying to find a dead animal rang of irony. Where had this day gone wrong? Oh yeah, he knew. It was when he came back into work.

"Shit, it's wicked out tonight, Boss."

Sheriff James Duffy agreed completely. "If this is some half eaten deer carcass, I swear I'm going to let Sheila tear the mayor a new one while I make popcorn and watch."

Julian Littlemoon laughed. "I'm pretty sure she won't allow popcorn, because she hates the smell," he added. "So you better pick up some snack item that she won't scrunch her nose up at. Perhaps water?"

The Sheriff laughed. "Okay, there's the main building. Let's start there and make the rounds," he suggested.

"Want to split up?" he asked.

"Hell no, there's only three buildings, and we have one shot gun. You think my pea shooter will take down a raging elk or a mad mountain lion?"

"Way to think about self-preservation," he answered, laughing and checking the chamber for shotgun shells.

"It's a proven fact that Nature goes for the white meat first."

Julian Littlemoon snickered. "It's your cross to bear since you stole our land. Get over it," he said, laughing.

"Come on, let's get this done and I'll buy you a beer in town, Julian."

"Works for me, Boss," he nodded, and walked with the man through the snow, hoping they didn't encounter a confused bear that came out of hibernation early.

Well, he did ask for excitement.

Two buildings later, they were wet and believed the complaints and the Mayor were full of shit. Nothing smelled out there, but the reminiscent stench of wasted time that could have been more productively used elsewhere. Maybe it was the breeze blowing by and carrying any stink away from them, or maybe it was just the fact that there was nothing there to smell unless you had the nose of a bloodhound. As they approached the third and final building, they were glad they were almost finished.

"Last one, Julian, and we get the hell out of here."

He looked around. "I think I finally smell something, Boss." He stopped and sniffed the air, and looked at the building. "Something's definitely dead in there."

"You must have a super nose my Indian friend. I smell pine, and now wet leather coat. That's all my nose is picking up."

"No boss, really. Something's dead in there."

Sheriff James Duffy approached the door and still nothing. "Let's get this done," he said, pushing the door open and shining his flashlight into the darkness. Before he saw it, he was assaulted with the smell of dead body. Oh yeah, something was decaying.

"Holy Shit," muttered his deputy, and then he saw the problem. Staring back at him wasn't the carcass of a dead animal, but the dead sightless eyes of five men.

Sheriff Duffy slammed the door. "About that beer, Julian."

"Yeah, better make it five. Suddenly one won't cut it."

Monday Morning

Elizabeth Blackhawk sat on the corner of her husband's desk and sipped her coffee. They had both just been in a budget meeting, and she was still feeling the after effects. Tedium and using the phrase 'bored to tears' wouldn't be too far from the truth at that point. What she needed was a good adrenaline rush, a trip to the field, and an assignment where she had to use her brain to find the killer and not add a bunch of numbers. That was pencil pusher bullshit, and she was a Special Agent for a reason. Her best skills were utilized in the field and not sitting on her ass.

As she watched her husband leaf through a few papers on his desk, her mind immediately began to wander. There Ethan was in all his Native American glory. Sexy tan skin hidden under his well-fitted suit, and it didn't even matter to her that he spent a small fortune on looking that good. The reward was all hers, since she was the one allowed to openly leer at her husband.

Then she noticed he'd even forgotten to pull his jet black hair back this morning. Oh yeah, what she wouldn't do to run her fingers through the silky strands right now. It wasn't lost on her that he was letting it grow in a little longer than he normally would. If she could just slip closer to him, then she could…

"Elizabeth, really?" he said, looking up.

"What?" She tried to feign innocence, but the look must have been all over her face. Mental note: perfect the poker face if you're going to think wickedly, dirty thoughts about your husband in the workplace.

Ethan Blackhawk grinned. "I can feel the lecherous stare from here."

"I'm sorry, but I'm a little distracted by the fact that you didn't pull you hair back today, and it's getting longer. It's very distracting, Mr. Blackhawk."

"I figured since I was embracing the return to my heritage; why not entertain my wife by growing it out." Since marrying Elizabeth he'd found ways to secretively drive her wild. Every now and then, he'd let his hair free of the staunch ponytail he wore. Then sometimes he'd switch up his clothes. He preferred suits and all black in the workplace, but every now and then he'd pull out a white shirt and jeans. It was all to get her hot and bothered.

"Yippee," she said, enthusiastically. "I do declare, Cowboy, you just admitted that your culpable in making me leer."

He laughed at his wife. "Yesterday it was the fact I didn't wear black to work, and the day before it was my new shiny boots.

I'm beginning to think if nothing changes, you'll blame my breathing." Who was he kidding? Elizabeth leering gave him a sense of security, and he loved every second of her attention.

Elizabeth shrugged. "Your wife wants you, however do you sleep at night," she retorted, grinning. "If I wasn't pregnant," she paused and he interjected before she could continue.

"You'd still be doing the same exact thing." Or so he hoped. It was silly, but there was always that little fear one day she'd realize she screwed up. Waking up and realizing marrying a simple Native from the Rez was a colossal mistake. The scars of the reservation still ran deep, despite the time he was away from it.

Now she laughed, because he was exactly right. It wasn't his or her fault that she was six months pregnant and the baby hormones were making her a sex fiend. "Well maybe for the next kid I won't want sex." Elizabeth threw it out there. "Livy told me for kids three thru five she didn't have sex at all." Then she lifted a brow. "That's thirty months of no sex. I bet you'd stop bitching about me leering if that happened."

Just the idea worried him. "Thirty months of no sex?"

"Think about that, Ethan." Now she was grinning, because she managed to successfully turn it back on him. Score one for the slower, pregnant wife.

Ethan leaned back in his chair, observing the woman perched on the corner of his desk. Yeah, she was beautiful, but the outside had nothing on the woman inside. She was kind, funny and so full of life. The woman before him was his salvation and so much more. They'd been married about nine months now, and every day was an adventure.

Elizabeth LaRue Blackhawk had run him over in Salem, where she had been sheriff, and she continued to do the same thing here too. As Co-Directors to FBI West, the second biggest FBI hub in the country, she always kept him on his toes and so did the job. When Elizabeth knocked him off his feet, it only took four days and he proposed to her in hopes she'd say yes. When she did, he became the luckiest man alive. Now nine months later they were sitting in his office, sharing a job, expecting their first baby, and having a really good start at life together.

"Now you're staring."

"I'm thinking about you being pregnant," he replied, smiling. The baby bump was now prevalent, and his wife was still sexy as sin. In fact, her being pregnant drove him even wilder, if that was possible. Now he had more of a reason to be territorial and possessive. She was carrying his child. Yeah Elizabeth still wore her low ride jeans, gun strapped to her hip, but the new addition he purchased her was personally his favorite thing. Many times he teased her about the t-shirt that said 'baby on board', but she always looked mortified and threatened to slowly torture him.

So, he went and got her right where he knew her heart lay-the belt buckle. For their anniversary two months ago, he had a belt buckle special ordered, and she wore it pretty much daily. It simply stated the truth.

Momma.

At first when she opened it, he wasn't sure if she'd ever wear it. His surprise was that she was rarely without it. Well, that and she burst into tears and cried for ten minutes over it. To this day he still wasn't sure if he did a good job, or the baby hormones took over.

"I am definitely that," she said, rubbing her hand over the bump lovingly. Gone were the button down shirts. Now she just wore stretchy ones that accentuated the life growing deep in her body. Fortunately for her and her ravenous appetite, baby Blackhawk was always hungry and she had only gained three pounds so far. With all the burgers she consumed, you'd think she'd be a bus, but she still was the same size. Maybe it was the fact she still forced her husband to run with her. Only he refused to let her do it outside, she might slip. Ethan had purchased them treadmills and they ran side-by-side every morning. It wasn't the same thing, but she knew her very overprotective husband just wasn't having it. The control freak had final say.

Elizabeth watched her husband and wondered if he was going to take what she was going to say next well or lose his cool.

"You have the look, Elizabeth. What's bugging you? You went from 'sex' to perplexed."

Elizabeth considered her options.

Blackhawk started to look concerned. "You can tell me anything, Lyzee baby. What's wrong?"

Honesty was the best policy, and they lived by that rule in their marriage. "At the last doctor appointment, they told me I'm completely healthy and the baby is doing really well."

"Yeah, I was there." He lifted a brow, something big was coming. Elizabeth looked worried and usually she just said anything she thought, and whatever exploded around her exploded. If she was leading in with the baby, there was the intent to soften him up. Baby Blackhawk was his one big soft spot- well next to his wife.

"I want to go back out in the field one last time before we have the baby." There it was said and put out there for him and the universe. What's the worst he could say?

"No!"

The only reason her husband was being a hard ass about it was because Thomas Mason, his crazy half-brother abducted her and tried to kill her and his unborn child. "Ethan, really. I need to do this, because I've sat here for four months being patient and a good Director. It's making me freaking insane! I feel like I need to shoot something."

He fought hard to not laugh. Yeah he could tell she was going stir crazy, only because he was too. "Downstairs is a target room. You can go shoot all the targets you want."

"Let's go out one more time. You and me!" Elizabeth Blackhawk wiggled her eyebrows. "The Cowboy and Indian can ride again. Come on, baby. You know you want to," she drawled, lecherously. "Take your wife out into the field and let her use her mind before the baby sucks all her brains from her head."

Now he did laugh, but still wasn't going to budge. "I tell you what, you forget that idea all together and I'm willing to bribe you with something that will keep you occupied."

Now she was intrigued. "What kind of bribe?" Immediately her mind went to sex.

Damn baby hormones. Damn sexy husband.

"I'll make sure you have burgers daily for lunch to start, and I won't make any comments about the fat and calories."

Elizabeth shook her head. "Nope, I get those now. If you refuse to buy me them, I can skip down to the cafeteria, or make a minion do the dirty work. As for the fat and calories, you heard the doctor. I can eat whatever I want. Baby Blackhawk is a big boy and he's sucking up all my food calories. Plus with our demanding jobs and still running, I'm underweight."

Okay, Elizabeth was going to play hardball and that meant something bigger than food. "I'll forgo the hair tie every day until you have the baby, and I won't cut my hair until you tell me to do it. So it can be as long as you want."

"Callen and Wyler long?" Elizabeth had a thing for her brother-in-law's hair. She was woman enough to admit it. Often she found herself just playing with it when Callen was near.

"Yep, that's the deal."

Oh yeah, that piqued her interest.

Immediately, Elizabeth Blackhawk started fantasizing about her sexy, long-haired, native man with all the tribal art tattooed on his body and maybe a few braids.

"Plus you can run your fingers through it whenever you want, and I won't look mortified that you're doing it. You know you like playing with it," he grinned, salaciously.

"Even in front of the staff?"

Blackhawk tried to keep a straight face. "Even in front of Christina."

Elizabeth weighed the options and was about to give her answer when she heard the voice in the lobby. "He's back!" she said excitedly, jumping off the desk and grabbing her husband's hand and dragging him to the door.

The tell-tale laughter meant only one thing.

The Blackhawk three were back together again!

~ Chapter Two ~

Callen Whitefox was home. It had been a long four months in training, and it had been brutal. The classes, the qualifications, and then of course there was the survival training. Arrogantly he believed he'd have the upper hand, because he was a full blooded Native. Boy had he been wrong. The instructors were ready for him, and ran him through the ringer on a daily basis. For a while he wanted to quit, but he kept telling himself Elizabeth would kick his ass. After all, she survived training and ranked top of her class.

It was a matter of survival and saving face.

His.

It was all worth it. He was now home and a full-fledged FBI agent with the shiny gold badge. It matched his brothers' and sister-in-laws' badges, and he could now work with the two people he respected and loved most in the world.

Whitefox kissed Ginny on the cheek, as she hugged him enthusiastically. Nothing had changed; the woman was still the same as when he left. She was effervescent, bubbly, and fond of any man in jeans. Callen Whitefox suspected the ass pat she just gave him wasn't an accident.

"I missed you too, Ginny," he said laughing, as she bounced up and down almost breaking his jaw.

"Callen! Welcome back! You weren't due in for another day or so," she replied, smiling up at him. Callen Whitefox was the second handsomest man in the building. He was only second to his brother. In her opinion it was pretty much a dead heat when it came to hotness. Both men were two levels above scorching hot.

"I hopped an early flight out of Quantico. I had people that I missed terribly," he said, and then he just knew she was near. Looking up, Elizabeth Blackhawk and his brother stood in their office doorway and her smile was huge. It definitely welcomed him home.

Elizabeth stood beside her husband, taking in the man hugging their administrative assistant. There was no doubt she missed him, and she knew that her husband did too. When he came back into Blackhawk's life and hers, he was immediately added to their circle of family. One they both guarded carefully.

"Elizabeth, oh my God," he muttered, walking toward her and pointed at her belly. In four months she went from no belly to baby belly almost overnight.

She laughed and ran at him, launching herself at him and trusting he'd catch her. When he picked her up off the floor and hugged her to his body he definitely was home. During his past with his brother, he'd betrayed him over a woman. As much as he would always be attracted to his sister-in-law and head over heels in love, he wouldn't sabotage having them as his family. So, he would love her silently and keep her safe, because she healed their family just by becoming a Blackhawk. It was moments like this he cherished, and felt the heat and want roll through his body.

"I missed you, Lyzee," he whispered into her hair. She smelled like home and family. The spicy calming scent gave him a sense of peace and belonging.

Elizabeth's feet were finally placed on the floor and she took his face in her hands. "Welcome home, Callen," and she planted a big wet kiss on his mouth. When she pulled back she took him by the hand and led him over to his brother.

"Callen, I see you're kissing my wife again," he said, grinning at his brother.

"Hey, she kissed me first this time. I didn't initiate it," and he laughed when she winked up at him. "I missed you Ethan," he said, moving towards his brother and embracing him.

Ethan hugged his brother as Elizabeth closed his office door. "I missed you too, Cal. Welcome home little brother. It wasn't the same without you."

Desdemona Adare stood by the coffee machine just off the lobby. She just witnessed the most amazing thing. Well, two of the most amazing things. One was Elizabeth Blackhawk smiling and laughing like a mere mortal. Running at a man that wasn't her husband and kissing him in front of Ethan Blackhawk and the staff. The second thing even more amazing than the first was the man himself. Holy shit the sexy radar was off the scale again. The bells were going off and so were the whistles. Maybe it was the sharp angular features that screamed Native American blood, or the delicious form packed into the well-worn jeans that covered his body. But hell yeah, he was hot. He was dressed almost the same as Elizabeth Blackhawk and until that moment, she didn't appreciate jeans in the workplace. Now she completely understood the lure, and may even start wearing them herself.

She grabbed her coffee and wandered out to Ginny who was on the phone ordering a welcome back cake for the man who just locked himself behind her boss's door. Desdemona waited, and when Ginny hung up she had to know.

"Spill it. Who was that, Ginny?"

Ginny laughed. "Doctor Adare, that man was Special Agent Callen Whitefox. He's just back from Quantico."

"Is he here to stay?"

"I sincerely hope so. He's our Liaison to the Native American Community." she said. "His office is right next to Elizabeth Blackhawk's office. Oh, Excuse me," she said, as the phone rang again.

Desdemona Adare took her coffee and started back down to her lab. She'd been wrong earlier thinking that Ethan Blackhawk was the sexiest thing she'd seen lately. Callen Whitefox now held that prize. Then it occurred to her, he was just hugging and getting a very friendly kiss from her boss. Well crap, it looks like Elizabeth Blackhawk had laid claim to all the sexy natives in the office.

Damn it!

Callen Whitefox sat on the couch in his brother's office. His sister-in-law sat beside him, leaning against him. When he first met her, he wouldn't have sat this close to her in fear that his brother would have kicked the shit out of him. But now, they had an understanding. There was nothing but love and trust between them. Elizabeth had protected the blossoming relationship between him and his brother, and in the process made herself an indelible mark in his life. She was his best friend in the entire world, even more so than his own brother.

Healing three generations of Blackhawks and weaving them back together was no easy task. All the Blackhawk men and including himself loved her to death and would take a bullet for her. The three men not married to her had gotten her initials inked in them, just in homage to the woman that fixed the unfixable. Elizabeth was their miracle, and she was treated as such.

"So how are you, Callen," asked his brother, as he sat on the corner of his desk. The closeness between his wife and brother didn't bother him in the least. He trusted the man completely, and he trusted his wife even more. Was there the possibility Whitefox had feelings for Elizabeth? Ethan was positive he did, but there was no chance he'd ever act on it. Callen was attached to her, and he couldn't blame him. Both men lost everyone they loved in life, and she was a constant for them. Growing up and losing their mothers early had scarred them both, and having a strong female in their lives again was of the utmost importance. Blackhawk was willing to share his wife's love with a brother he held locked into his own heart.

Family was vital in the Blackhawk clan. Blood wasn't only thicker than water, it was like glue. Now that they were all healed, they stuck, they loved, and they shared a woman that had the greatest propensity to love all four Blackhawk men completely; flaws and all.

"Glad to be home. It was brutal, and you both could have warned me."

Elizabeth snorted. "Hell no, newbie. You have to take your ass kicking just like the rest of us did," she said, patting his leg and laying her head on his shoulder. "We missed you. It's been quiet around the house without you."

"I missed you guys too and Elizabeth?"

"Yes?" She looked up at him.

"Pregnancy has made you even more beautiful. You look radiant and gorgeous." Whitefox was dead serious. She was a glow and looked happy.

"Kiss ass." His brother coughed into his hand and both men laughed.

"Hey now, Cowboy! You said the same thing yesterday."

Her husband was well aware. A happy wife was a happy life, and he wasn't willing to risk a pregnant woman's wrath.

"Great, the Blackhawk boys are back together again and now I'm a very happy girl."

Whitefox was technically a Blackhawk. Both men shared the same father. The only difference was that Wyler Blackhawk was married to Ethan's mother at the time of his wandering indiscretion. Whitefox was the product of that night. Growing up, Callen always knew he had a brother, and when Blackhawk found out the truth, they bonded in their youth. Granted it was over the hate of their father, but that was all in the past. The men both had decent relationships with the man that sired them now, and it was all because of the sweet woman beside him.

"We are, and that may or may not set off the entire balance of the universe and cause some scary FBI vortex."

Blackhawk laughed.

"Okay, we have to discuss the obvious," Whitefox said, laying his hand on her belly. "Wow, that's a big kid!" He teased her. Elizabeth Blackhawk before pregnancy was tall and lean, and now she was tall, lean and had a big bump of Blackhawk Baby.

"Yeah, you should see his uncle and father. I'm genetically screwed. I'm giving birth to a mighty Indian warrior."

It took him a second. "So it's official? Granddad was right? We're having a boy?"

Not only had their grandfather known she was pregnant before they did, but he accurately picked the sex of their baby. The man just had crazy mad baby premonition skills.

"Yes, yes, and yes. You're getting yourself a nephew and I think he's the size of a toddler already."

"Wow," he grinned, staring down at her belly. "Did the baby just move?" he asked incredulously, as her body shifted while she leaned against him.

"Yep, he moves all the time."

"It's his way of communicating," answered Blackhawk. "One foot here, and he's hungry. His fist over here, and he wants her to roll over."

"Next he'll be sending up smoke signals," she said, laughing. "Yeah, I just did go there," she answered the look on both of their faces. "What? It's been four months!"

"Good to see you aren't out of practice with the Native references," laughed Whitefox. "I was worried I'd missed all the good ones while I was away."

"Don't get her started," Blackhawk demanded, but even he laughed.

"You both want to feel?" she asked, looking at her brother-in-law and husband.

Whitefox nodded, and cautiously placed the palm of his hand over one side of her belly.

Ethan loved feeling his child moving below his wife's skin. He crossed to her, and both men sat there in awe, feeling the life in constant motion. "It's amazing, and I don't think I'll ever get used to it," he said, as his eyes filled with emotion. His child was alive in her body.

"I've never felt that before," Whitefox admitted, as he placed his one hand on his brother's shoulder and connected all three of them together.

Elizabeth patted both men on the cheek. "It's very amazing. I happen to agree with you." Before she could discuss the new Blackhawk baby more, her husband's phone rang.

"It's Gabe," he said, putting it on speakerphone. "Hello boss man. What can we do for you?" he asked.

"Ethan, we had a call into Quantico, there's a serial killer out at Red River. We have five bodies. All male and missing various parts. You need to send a team out to cover it and make sure to include an ME, they don't have access to one. Think small town and plan accordingly."

"Okay," he said, seeing his wife get really excited.

"Do you have the personnel ready to go out?"

Callen raised his hand. He was fresh in from Quantico and itching to take on an assignment. Why not rush headfirst into a serial killing.

"Put your hand down, Callen, this one's mine," quipped Elizabeth. "I'm going out in the field, Gabe."

None of the men spoke. White fox looked incredulous, Blackhawk looked wary and Gabe... He just sounded irritated. "Elizabeth, I have to protest," he said over the phone.

"You can protest all you want, but this is most likely my last time out in the field until I'm back from maternity leave."

"Ethan, you're okay with this?" he asked skeptically.

Blackhawk looked at his wife and saw the hope and excitement that he used to see when they worked as Agents in the field. Then he saw his brother and how he really wanted to get out into the field and start living the job. And then he had a solution.

"Callen is going to Red River today. Send me the files and I'll brief him." Blackhawk noticed the look on his wife's face. "I have the new ME on duty while Doctor Leonard is out in the field, and she's going with him. I think in this case, they both need to partner up and get an assessment."

"Good plan," added Gabriel Rothschild. He was technically their boss, but he was also their family. When he sent them out into the field last time, it culminated with Elizabeth being abducted. It nearly drove her husband crazy, and then the killer almost took their lives.

"Well, there's more. Callen is only going in to assess and report back. He's fresh out of the classroom, and I can't dump him into a serial killer's lap without backup. Elizabeth and I will be following behind them. Once I secure the paperwork and get lodgings handled."

"Are you sure about this?" He wanted them to be safe and think it through before doing anything dangerous.

Ethan couldn't ignore the smile on their faces, and he knew he wouldn't be able to say no. Technically he couldn't stop his wife from going. She had the same seniority as he did when it came to time in the FBI. Callen answered to both of them, and in the end, he really could only roadblock him. Hopefully this wasn't going to bite him in the ass.

Whitefox would be safe with them there, and Elizabeth would be safe with both men. It was like double the protection on both the people he cared about.

"Yeah, you'll have to cover my meetings, Gabe. Team Blackhawk is going looking for a serial killer," he answered tentatively and hoped he just didn't make the biggest mistake of his life.

Callen Whitefox was excited. There was a trip out into the field, and he was going to get to work on an assignment with his two favorite FBI Agents. When Elizabeth told him to close his eyes and took him by the hand, he had no clue what she was up to but it had to be big. She was vibrating in excitement.

"Don't walk him into the wall, baby," Ethan teased. "Watch out for that sharp pointy stick."

Elizabeth kicked the wall to screw with him.

"Good to see you two aren't above hazing the new guy. I will open my eyes," he teased back.

Ethan knew she was excited to show him his new office. As Liaison to the Indian Community, he didn't have to have a desk out with the other minions. He actually got to have an office with the rest of management. The job was that important, especially since tension between the natives and the FBI was always an ongoing thing.

His brother was going to have a difficult job, and Blackhawk knew his brother was the best man for it. He was one of the Natives to the bone. He loved his heritage and was always comfortable with it. Ethan Blackhawk was the opposite. Before his wife it only brought him shame. Now he was somewhere in the middle, and that was thanks to his wife bridging the span for him.

"Don't worry, Callen. I won't walk you into anything," reassured Elizabeth Blackhawk. She squeezed his hand and he instantly twined his fingers with hers. It was their thing, and it connected them together.

"I'm going down to brief Doctor Adare. Callen, head down when my wife is done with you," he said, grinning. Elizabeth had personally taken care of his office space, and he believed his brother would be impressed. There was nothing like family, and with his wife she loved completely. Elizabeth Blackhawk already claimed Whitefox as a loved one, and she would always have his back.

"Okay," he answered grinning, as he followed blindly.

"I promise, you're going to love it," she said, and honestly hoped he did. "It's not far, we're almost there."

Callen Whitefox squeezed her hand, and let her take him where ever. There were two people in his life he trusted completely and she was one, her husband the other. It wasn't only trust, but complete love and dedication.

Elizabeth stopped him in the middle of his office and continued to hold his hand. "Are you ready, Callen?" she asked, excitedly.

"Yes, I am."

"Open your eyes."

Callen Whitefox didn't know what to expect, but this wasn't even close to what he could have imagined. They stood in an office, the same size as both of theirs, but so completely different. "Where are we?"

"This is your new office. Because you're Liaison to the Native Community, you get office space. In case anyone comes here, they don't have to sit out in the bullpen." Elizabeth didn't have to tell him that both she and Ethan Blackhawk wanted him close to their office.

Whitefox walked in a circle and took it all in as he brought her with him, refusing to break that contact. The desk was the same as theirs, big and intimidating, but the rest of the room felt comfortable, especially if there was a native in the room. "Who decorated the room?" The walls were a peaceful color of pale blue, and hanging on them were Native American works of art, and in one corner was a small totem.

"We did." Granted most of it was her placing and her husband telling her what was appropriate to any natives entering into the space. "Dad made the totem. I hope you like it," she added, hopefully.

Callen ran his hand over the carving in the one corner. It went from floor to ceiling and held all their spirit guides. There was his grandfather the bear at the bottom, his father the bull standing on the bear. On top were a fox and two ravens. He was the fox and the two ravens were his brother and sister-in-law, and they flanked him protectively. "It's gorgeous. I've never seen anything more beautiful in my life." That was a lie, she topped the list, but the totem was definitely in second place.

"It's all the Blackhawks. All of us together on one totem," she said, grinning. "I wanted to give it to you for Christmas, but Wyler couldn't get it finished in time."

"I love this room."

"Did I do it justice?" she inquired. There were tenuous relations between the FBI and the Native community. Elizabeth wanted to strengthen the ties, and hoped the room would offer anyone that came there peace. Since marrying into the tribe, and carrying a Native child in her body, she had a vested interest.

"Elizabeth, you did it more than justice. It's really my office?" He was incredibly lucky, before his brother came back into his life; he'd been the Chief of Reservation Police and hated it. Just by his brother offering him this job, he pulled him out of the life he was trapped in and gave him a chance to have everything he always dreamed about.

"All yours, Cal."

There was a peace pipe, dream catchers, and various paintings of ravens and foxes all over and, making it his space. "I don't know exactly what to say," he stated. His heart was overwhelmed that not only did he get his family; he got an amazing chance in life and to find his way to happiness.

"I love the Foxes and Ravens."

Elizabeth grinned, because they were special to her.

"It reminds me of us," he said, looking over at her. His heart was so full of adoration for her; it felt like it would burst.

"I didn't go overboard, did I?" she asked. "Ethan told me to stop and leave it alone. We just wanted to have it be a huge surprise."

Yeah, it was perfect. "Lyzee, it's gorgeous," he answered, his grin said it all.

"I'm glad."

Callen pulled his sister-in-law against his body and hugged her close. "I love it, and I love you and my brother."

Elizabeth let him hug her, and she could feel his body filled with emotion.

"I missed you, Callen. Don't go away again. It was boring without you," she said, softly. "We missed having you with us."

"It was the longest four months of my life," he answered, truthfully. "I missed having dinner with you and Ethan, and I missed us just watching football on Sundays."

"Your chair is waiting for you."

Whitefox kissed her on the forehead. "I'll be sitting in it as soon as we get back from the assignment. I promise if I'm home I'll never be far from you or Ethan ever again."

Elizabeth looked up at him. "I was pretty sure you were going to escape for the super bowl," she said, grinning.

Whitefox sighed. The time away from them had been the worst part. All he wanted to do was come home to the two most important people in his life. As soon as he got word he passed Qualifications, he packed, picked up his gun and badge and flew the Quantico coop. "If I didn't have qualifications the next day, I would have been here. I'm not going away again for a long time. In fact, you have to promise if I have to go away, you and Ethan will be right there with me," he grinned, knowing she couldn't make that promise. He'd have to travel with his job and he only hoped it wouldn't be too far from them.

Elizabeth thought about it. "I promise," she said, knowing that she never broke her promises to the Blackhawk men.

He was touched, knowing she'd do anything to keep that promise to him. Callen was a really lucky man. His family was the center of his life, and now would forever be the one thing he cherished more than anything else. Elizabeth was the reason.

"We should probably head down to the lab. You need to meet the new Medical Examiner."

"Let's go." Whitefox dropped his arm over her shoulder. When she easily wrapped his arm around his waist, he just enjoyed being beside his best friend. Outside the door he noticed the name plate. It was the same as the ones outside their doors.

Callen J. Whitefox
Director of Native American affairs

"That's a pretty awesome title," he said, running his fingers over the letters.

Elizabeth grinned. "Wait until you see the paycheck attached to it," she said, laughing. "Well, in the field you're still a special agent, but in the office you get to be upper management."

"I can't wait." He kissed the top of her head. His day couldn't get any better. He was certain of it. "I like that my office is right next to yours."

"Me too. Ethan wanted you on a different floor."

That surprised him. "Really? Why?"

Elizabeth snickered. "Because he knows we are going to be raising hell, and he's obligated to keep us both out of trouble."

Callen Whitefox grinned wickedly and then dropped his voice. "I can't wait. When do we start working the old man up?"

Elizabeth and Whitefox fist bumped. "ASAP!"

When she looked at him with her blue eyes, he felt his heart skip. "So, I get the new ME?" he asked, refocusing on work and not the emotion that was overwhelming him at that moment. All he wanted was to just hold her and kiss her.

"Chris Leonard is out in the field on an assignment. He went out two days ago and isn't due back until next week. You get to work with Doctor Desdemona Adare," she said simply.

"What's she like?" he asked, curiously. There was something in her voice, and it was barely there, but he knew her well enough to know something was under the surface.

Elizabeth thought about it. A few times she'd had the chance to talk to the woman and try to get and know her. It wasn't an easy thing. The new doctor was either super shy or just didn't like her. Elizabeth didn't know why there was that underlying tension between them, but she wasn't anything like Doctor Leonard.

"Well, that's hard to say."

Whitefox hit the elevator button. "What's that mean?"

"I think she's either afraid of me or doesn't like me very much. When Ethan talks to her she seems fine, but when I talk to her I get the impression she wants to get far away from me."

"Maybe she heard the rumors," he added laughing, but then ran his hand up and down her arm reassuringly, sensing the hurt in her voice. "You tend to be balls to the wall with the tech staff."

"I don't know, but I do know she's smart, and her work is perfect. I personally like her, because she's not the normal ME."

Callen pictured her in his head. Old woman with lots of wrinkles, because who else would want to do that job all day long. "Not normal? Care to tell me more?" he asked.

Elizabeth laughed. "Nope, I think I need you to meet her and then give me you impression of her yourself."

"Your wish is my command, Boss," he said, laughing. "This should be easy."

"Cal, darlin' you have no idea!"

Ethan Blackhawk found her at her computer. She was checking files that had been flagged by Chris Leonard. Results were in on the toxicology reports for a few teams and she was busy updating the files.

When he first met Doctor Adare, he didn't know what to think of the woman. She was petite and completely gothic. Not in a scary way, but definitely in an unusual way. At first he thought it was a joke. The woman didn't look over twenty five, and he was having a hard time believing she had almost ten years in as an ME in the private sector. Then she just laughed and pulled out her driver's license and handed it over. After meeting her, and enjoying having a conversation with her, he told his wife all about it. Unfortunately, Doctor Adare didn't seem to be as friendly to Elizabeth, and he wasn't sure why. He'd even gone as far as asking Christina if Doctor Adare was happy in the position. Everyone on the tech team loved her, and they enjoyed having her around.

Elizabeth could be hard at first, especially on the techs, but to his knowledge she didn't even bark once at Doctor Adare. The woman was good at her job, efficient, and one of the smartest people he'd ever met. His only hope was she'd relax around Elizabeth and with them all going out in the field she was going to have to and fast.

"Hey, Doctor!" he called to her. When she swiveled towards him in her chair, he almost laughed at her choice in clothing. Doctor Adare was very unusual. Today she picked black and white striped socks that came to her knees, shoes that had a three inch heel, a black school girl skirt and a sweater with a skull on the front. He wanted to call her Doctor Death, but he didn't think she'd find it funny or professional.

"Hey Director Blackhawk. What can I do for you?" she asked, pointing at the other chair. "Something come up?"

Blackhawk took the seat and leaned back. "You doing okay without Chris around?" he asked, breaking the ice first. No point in dropping the field bomb, until he warmed her up. Not all ME's liked working out of house and away from all their equipment.

"I'm good, Director Blackhawk. I'm just cleaning up some paperwork. I finished the last autopsy in holding this morning, and the cadaver is ready to go out for the family. Toxicology has been shipped, and my schedule is clear if you need anything."

Desdemona was glad to see him when she turned around and not his wife. Director Blackhawk didn't intimidate her, and all the techs said he was awesome to work with every day. So far they were right. She liked him and not because he was great to look at, but because he had kind eyes. Her grandmother always told her to go by the eyes. They were the window into the soul and heart. His eyes were almost black, but they were very warm and welcoming.

"That's funny you should bring it up, but I need to ask a question."

"Shoot," she waited, dropping her glasses on the desk.

"How do you feel about going out in the field?" he inquired, waiting for her reply.

"You mean going out getting the body and coming back here?" She wasn't quite sure what he was alluding to by 'field'.

"More like two hours away and working in a small town out of a facility we find there," he elaborated.

Doctor Adare shrugged. "Doesn't really matter to me, Director Blackhawk."

He leaned forward. "Good, pack up everything you need to do an autopsy in the field, and get ready to head out. You're leaving to go to Red River in an hour."

"Uh, okay. By myself?" That made her nervous.

Blackhawk laughed. "No, you are going with an agent and tech team. In fact, he should be on his way down shortly. He's going to escort you there and keep you safe while you do the retrieval and assessment."

Desdemona Adare relaxed. "Okay then, what do we have?"

"I'll send you the dossier as soon as Quantico ships it, but it looks like five men, various body parts removed. Looks ritualistic, but we won't know until we get there."

"We?"

"Yes, we. You have an agent going with you at first, but you also get Elizabeth and myself as agents in charge arriving after." Blackhawk watched her whole demeanor change instantly. Something about him or his wife closed her up. "Problem with that?" he asked.

"No Director," she answered. Well the assignment was going to suck with his wife intimidating the hell out of her. How could this get any worse?

Blackhawk stood. "I hear Elizabeth and the other agent now," he said, turning.

Desdemona Adare spoke too soon. Not only was she trapped in an assignment with Elizabeth Blackhawk, Ethan Blackhawk, but she also got the sexiest man on the earth; Callen Whitefox as her escort.

Well shit. This was going to be the longest field assignment of her life.

Elizabeth and Whitefox exited the elevator together, and his arm was still draped casually over her shoulders. It entertained him how everyone that walked past them looked surprised at the Director and the smile on her face. Everyone expected kick ass, and few looked past that to the big softie below the surface.

"I think they all think I went crazy," she said, laughing.

"Yeah, I noticed. If they only knew what a pushover you are," he teased, and earned an elbow to his ribcage. Immediately her hand returned to the spot on his back that had her initials tattooed. It warmed his heart, and connected them more, as she lovingly ran her hand over the spot.

"Nice, abuse me the first day," he said, walking towards Autopsy. "Thank God you're madly in love with me or I'd be screwed."

"You haven't seen anything yet, Cal!" Elizabeth laughed, lowering her arm to his waist as they approached the door. "Remember, I need an assessment of the Doctor, and I'm warning you to not take her for face value. She's..." she began.

"Different. I got it."

Whitefox held the door open and they both walked through, and then he came to a stop. It was so fast; Elizabeth looked up at him to see if he was okay. Then she saw the look on his face, and just knew. Different didn't cover it.

Callen didn't know what to think. Standing beside his brother was this tiny woman, dressed like some Goth girl gone wild. Part of him wanted to laugh, and part of him had his interest peaked. She was certainly different, and that appealed to him immensely. It took him a second to get past the clothes and focus on her face. Her eyes were unusual, just like her appearance. They tipped slightly, giving her an exotic look, and were the most unusual color green. Once he got past that he noticed the hair. Lots and lots of black hair, punctuated with strips of a wild red color

45

that wasn't found in nature. Her face was clean of almost all makeup, except the red lip color on her lips. She looked china doll-esque and delicate and almost like a child. They had to be kidding, and she had to be a tech. This couldn't possibly be the new ME. She looked like she needed to be carded when she went into a bar.

Elizabeth pinched him on the back, to get him to stop staring and refocus. "Callen, I'd like to introduce you to Doctor Desdemona Adare," she said, pushing him forward as a signal that the woman needed to be greeted.

Callen was grateful for the pinch. "Hello, Doctor Adare," he said, walking forward, his hand out. His eyes flickered up to his brother to see if Elizabeth was indeed serious.

Ethan shrugged.

Doctor Adare didn't miss how the man had his arm over the Director's shoulder as he walked in, and it also wasn't lost on her that the woman's arm was around his waist.

Almost like lovers.

It was confusing.

Elizabeth Blackhawk was married, wasn't she? From everything that she heard from Christina and the tech team, Elizabeth and Ethan Blackhawk were madly in love. She'd seen it herself and yet Elizabeth and Callen Whitefox shared an intimacy that didn't seem to bother Ethan Blackhawk. He had even been playing absently with a piece of her hair in her ponytail, and she couldn't believe the badass boss was tolerating it.

She felt like Alice after falling down the rabbit hole.

Nothing was what it seemed.

Automatically her hand came out, and she accepted his handshake. Doctor Adare had to look up at him. Callen Whitefox was just as tall as Ethan Blackhawk, and now she felt like a munchkin in Oz. "Hello, Special Agent Whitefox," she greeted him, and forced a neutral smile onto her face. The minute they shook hands, she felt her whole body flush with warmth. Oh yeah, this field assignment was going to seriously suck.

Sexy agent plus scary boss and a few corpses. Great.

"It's nice to meet you, Doctor Adare. Elizabeth has told me a great deal about you," he said, warmly. The feeling of her hand in his was really nice. She was delicate, just like the china doll she resembled.

Elizabeth lifted an eyebrow and looked at her husband. They passed a look between them that was only theirs to understand. Yeah, it was going to be interesting out in the field.

"Callen, give the doctor about thirty minutes to pack up what she needs, and then meet her at the Denali. You can drive her to her house so she can pick up some clothes and you do the same. You both leave for Red River shortly." He wasn't sure either of them was listening to a word he said.

"My clothes are in the Denali," he answered, still watching the woman, as he stepped backwards to stand far enough from her. Doctor Adare was a puzzle, and he had questions for his brother and sister-in-law.

"We'll need to swing by my house," Doctor Adare said, softly.

"Pack for cold weather conditions," added Elizabeth. "Red River gets snow, and from what Gabe emailed me, the bodies are off the beaten path and in the outdoors." Elizabeth didn't need her ME getting frost bite in a skirt out in the snow. "There's FBI gear in the storage room for snow retrieval. Take it with you," she said, watching them both.

"Yes, Director," she answered and turned away. "I better get packing," she answered nonchalantly, despite how nervous she was inside.

"I'll see you down at the Denali, Doctor," Whitefox said, heading for the door, pulling Elizabeth back against his body with his arm over her shoulders.

"I'll be ready for you, Agent," she replied, knowing that was nothing but a load of bull shit. Nothing in the world was going to prepare her for that man and what was coming, she could just feel it.

Red River Sherriff's Station

James Duffy hung up the phone and looked at the Deputies standing in his room. Right now one of them was stationed out by the find, and the other two were in his office. They had followed procedure for the situation and called into Quantico for help. Their county didn't have an ME or a processing lab, and with five dead bodies they were going to need all the help they could get.

"That was Gabriel Rothschild out of Quantico. They're on their way," he said. "They want us to keep the site secured and just keep it as quiet as possible, so the killer doesn't come back and try to move the corpses."

"Great, how many feds are they sending," asked Deputy Bobby Lee Tills. Feds were nothing but trouble, and he didn't like how they came in and played God.

"I was told the first wave was going to be the ME, a Doctor Adare, and a Special Agent Callen Whitefox," he answered, reading their names off the paper he scribbled them on.

"Great another Indian to deal with," he muttered, disgustedly.

Sheriff James Duffy looked up fast. "Bobby Lee, I mean it when I said watch your mouth. Not only around the FBI but also Julian, and if you can't seem to handle that then you'll be off duty until this is all over. I don't plan on having you insult the FBI. There's nothing wrong with Indians," and he meant it.

Bobby Lee Tills was a good deputy, but he was a prejudice asshole at times. The last thing he needed was to have the man piss off the FBI and make the situation worse, and then there was his own Deputy Julian Littlemoon. He respected the man, and he wasn't going to have a war brewing in his station.

Bobby Lee stared at his boss, he might have to shut his mouth, but he didn't have to like the idea of working with the indian FBI man.

"They should be here by this afternoon, and I need you to cooperate." Sheriff Duffy pointed specifically at Bobby Lee, and not the other deputy. "Bobby Lee, I want you to head out to the site and relieve Julian off his shift."

"Fine," he said, dropping his hat on his head and leaving the office.

"This is going to be a mess," he said to the remaining deputy. "I certainly hope that Special Agent Callen Whitefox has really thick skin. If not, he might be bailing on this assignment before he even gets started."

Callen Whitefox leaned against the Denali and watched the woman cross the parking garage. She carried a field kit and a tote bag, and wasn't smiling at all. It was like this was going to be torture, and he didn't understand why. At first the three of them thought she was chilly because of Elizabeth Blackhawk, but she still had the same look on her face, and Elizabeth was nowhere to be found. Despite her iciness, there was something appealing behind the craziness of her apparel. He was looking forward to this assignment even if she wasn't. Being trapped in a car for three hours, he at least hoped she'd talk a little and maybe he could get to the bottom of the issue towards half of the Blackhawks.

"Let me get that for you, Doctor Adare." He took the bag and kit and placed them on the back seat of the Denali.

"Thanks, Special Agent Whitefox," she answered, hopping up into the passenger seat. "I talked to Christina; they're heading out in an hour or so. They just need to load up the trucks and get the supplies we'll need for a night retrieval."

"Thanks," he said, politely. "Want to input your home address into the GPS? We can swing by your house and you can grab some things, and then be on our way."

"Okay," she answered, doing what he asked.

"Elizabeth told me to make sure you brought weather appropriate gear, so I pulled a parka and boots for you," he added. "They're in the cargo."

Doctor Adare tensed. "Thank you, Agent," she said finally. It never occurred to her that maybe her boss disliked her attire on the job. Maybe that was her hint on the point of contention between them.

Whitefox pulled out of the garage. He could feel the tension.

"It's going to be great working with you Doctor Adare," he said, amicably. His brother had pulled him aside and asked him to break the ice before they arrived. Both men suspected the issue was with Elizabeth, and they needed to head that off before she arrived in the field.

"Thank you, Agent Whitefox."

He needed a new approach, or they were going to polite this to death. "You can call me Callen," he offered and noticed she relaxed slightly. "Since we'll be working together on this. Unless you aren't comfortable with using my first name."

Doctor Adare thought about it. "Okay, Callen." There was no doubt that the he could hear the pounding in her chest. "You can call me Desdemona."

Callen Whitefox grinned at her. "Othello?"

He caught her off guard, and he earned a smile. "Yes, as a matter of fact."

"I think it's a pretty name," he offered, trying to get her to relax. He noticed they were heading towards his brother's house.

"My mom loved Shakespeare," she added. "Most people don't know it's from that play, but think it's some Goth-y name I made up."

"I not only know it's from 'Othello', but I also know she was his traitorous wife who broke his heart." He grinned at her when she relaxed completely. "It's one of my all-time favorites." Apparently, literature was a safe topic for future reference.

"I'm impressed, Callen."

Part of him didn't want to push her on the problem at hand, but it was time to get to the bottom of the reason she was so tense. "You're going to have to forgive me for asking this, Desdemona, but what seems to be the problem between you and Director Blackhawk," he asked, and tried to watch her face. Immediately, the shuttered look was back, and Desdemona Adare was hiding again.

"I don't know what you mean," she answered. "I have the utmost respect for the Director."

"Well, it can't be that we're Native, because you don't seem to have a problem with Ethan, and you were just smiling at me. Then there's the fact that Elizabeth isn't of our heritage. What is it about Elizabeth that has you this stressed out?" he asked evenly, trying to inflect calm into his voice to ease her tension.

Desdemona was surprised that in five minutes he'd managed to read her so successfully. She licked her lips as they pulled into the development where she recently purchased her home.

"If we're going to be partners in the field, we need to have trust. I can't work without it," he bluffed, pushing her for an answer. If she refused, she refused. There wasn't anything he could do about it.

"She makes me nervous." Finally, she just spilled it. He was right, they were going to be partners for this assignment, and he seemed like a decent guy, even though he was rolling right over her and taking control.

"Why?"

"The tech staff said she's tough, ballsy, and she can kick anyone's ass," she added. "And she just makes me anxious." It was hard to believe she trusted him with this, and obviously she was an idiot. The man was just cuddling up with Elizabeth Blackhawk on the way down to her lab, and they had to have some sort of personal relationship.

"I've worked with her when I was Police Chief of the Reservation, and I'll be honest with you, Desdemona. She's no-nonsense when it comes to the job, but you shouldn't believe everything you hear."

"Great," she muttered. Which part of the 'everything' should she believe then?

"Elizabeth is really great, but you should just relax and not be so stressed. She can smell fear a mile away," he laughed, trying to get her to relax, as he parked in front of her house.

"You sound like an expert on her," she added, skeptically. "I think I just need to keep my distance from her, and then everything will work out better for both of us."

"I am an expert on her," he paused. "Elizabeth is my sister-in-law, and Ethan's my brother. As for keeping your distance from her, that's going to be almost impossible," he added, grinning. Now he was entertained.

Well that explained the kiss and Ethan Blackhawk not minding. Now that she thought about it, there was a similarity between the men. Something in her relaxed marginally with this new found knowledge. "Why can't I keep my distance," she asked. "Is it because of the assignment?"

He hopped out of the Denali and looked over at her. "Well, you can try, but you see that big house right behind yours? The one with the big white fence you can't see over that surrounds the property?"

She looked towards the general location.

51

"The really big stone one," he added.

"Yeah, I know what one you mean." And she did. She stared at it from her bedroom window every night before she closed the blinds on the window.

"I'm assuming you haven't met your new neighbors," he added, trying to not break into laughter, but the entire thing was seriously funny.

"No why?"

"Ethan and Elizabeth Blackhawk own the house right behind you."

Desdemona felt sick to her stomach.

"Welcome to the neighborhood." Now he did start to laugh.

Aw hell.
No double hell.

~ Chapter Three ~
Monday Mid-morning

Elizabeth sat in her office, her boots up on the corner of her desk, as she rubbed her belly with her hand. She was absently staring out the window and didn't hear her husband enter her office. Thoughts were plaguing her mind, and the predominant one was regarding her brother-in-law and his safety.

Blackhawk just sat and watched his wife massaging their child as it grew protected in her body. She'd told him that when the baby started getting bouncy, rubbing her belly helped soothe him. It still amazed and captivated Ethan that she was pregnant and by summer they'd have a little one of their own.

Elizabeth felt him near and looked over. "Hi handsome, were you there long?" she asked.

"Baby all hyper?" he asked, as he closed her door and walked over to her. "I haven't been staring at you long," he winked.

"Good to know I haven't lost my instincts," she answered. "Baby Blackhawk is really hyper today. I think he knows we're heading into the field and is all excited."

Blackhawk kneeled beside his wife on her chair and pulled up her shirt and gave the bump kisses. "Daddy loves you," he whispered to her belly.

Elizabeth's heart went all mushy, that her tough Indian warrior was kissing her belly and talking to their child. There would never be anyone she could love more than this man.

"We need to figure out a name for you," he whispered to her growing belly. "Or your momma will seriously call you baby Blackhawk all your life."

Elizabeth snorted. "I will not! Stop lying to the child already!"

"Want to tell me what you were worried about? I'm going to guess it's not about what to name our child. That only leaves a few more possibilities."

"No, I already have my choice for baby names. It's a done deal for me. I'm just waiting on your choice so we can figure it out."

Blackhawk rubbed her belly and felt his child moving again. "I have a few thoughts on that, but I'm not one hundred percent sure yet." He looked up at his wife. "What has you worried, baby?"

"I'm worried about Callen."

Ethan Blackhawk would like to be surprised, but he knew the two of them had a special bond. "What specifically?"

"We just sent him there alone until we get there, and that has me wondering if it was a good idea."

Blackhawk laughed and stood. The love he felt for this woman was immeasurable, that she'd be worried about his brother this much. "Don't worry momma bird; the baby bird is ready to fly the nest, and he's been trained to keep himself safe. As for Doctor Adare, Callen's a man and his natural instinct will kick in fast."

"Oh, so are you saying a man can protect a woman better than a woman can protect a man?" Elizabeth crossed her arms and rested them on the bump, daring him to pursue that line of thought. "I'm sure you didn't mean to make that sound as chauvinistic as it sounded, Ethan."

Blackhawk laughed and leaned down to kiss his wife on the lips.

"No answer and kissy-face. I guess that's my answer."

"I'm simply saying that my brother is a smart man, he's been trained, and he'll do the job. Have faith in him, Elizabeth."

Standing she tucked her shirt in and looked him in the eye. "My faith in your brother isn't at question here. I happen to believe the Blackhawk men are a superior set of individuals. What has me worried is a killer that is taking pieces of men."

"Callen will be perfectly fine. I know my brother," he said, pulling her against his body. "Come here, Mrs. Blackhawk," he whispered, before he kissed her long and slow. Her mothering instincts were out in full force, and she was even more protective than usual. She was a miracle to the men in that family normally, but now she was over-the-top protective. It was ironic, because that was usually his job. The role of control freak and worrier was generally all his.

When the baby began kicking like crazy, she broke the kiss. "Even he says no kissy-face in the office, and I think he's offended that you're kissing his mommy," she grinned, wickedly. "Baby Blackhawk doesn't like to share."

"Funny. I see it's now two against one, and he's going to have to share because you were mine first." He was about to comment more when her office phone rang. "Don't think you're getting away from me yet, Elizabeth," he winked lecherously. "Blackhawk," she said, answering the phone.

"Elizabeth, hey it's Gabe."

She put it on speakerphone. "Hi Gabe, what's up?"

"The files have been sent, and I handled the accommodations for you both, the doctor and Agent Whitefox. The tech team will be staying in a different location."

"Okay, thanks Gabe." Elizabeth was suspicious. "You didn't roach coach us," she asked him. "Did you?"

Blackhawk started laughing. Gabriel Rothschild was notorious for torturing his employees with really horrific accommodations. It was like a game to him, and they all knew it.

"If you did, I'm telling your wife that you're torturing a pregnant woman."

Gabe began laughing. Elizabeth Blackhawk and his wife were best friends, and there was no doubt that his wife would give him hell for pulling that stunt. "For the record, I go by the allotment that the bureau allows me."

"Right," muttered Blackhawk, not buying that line for a second. He too was in charge of finding his people accommodations, and Gabe was just sadistic.

"I heard that and I am still your boss Special Agent Blackhawk."

Elizabeth laughed at how he dropped the 'Director' portion of her husband's title when it suited the moment. "Where did you put us, Gabe?" If they were going to be in a roach coach, hopefully it wouldn't be too bad. She'd stayed in some scary places while working under Gabe.

"Because it's a small town, they only had one hotel. I appropriated the remaining rooms for the tech team. I managed to finagle a private dwelling for the three investigators and the ME. ONLY because it's owned by a friend of the Sheriff, and he's desperate for our help. He pulled strings to get it into budget."

"Thank you, Gabe," she said sweetly, winking at her husband.

"I've transmitted the information and you should have it by now. Forward it to Whitefox and the ME so they're prepared before they arrive in Red River."

"We're swinging home for clothes and heading out shortly," said Blackhawk, wiggling his eyebrows at his wife. Maybe he could even convince his wife for a pit stop in their bedroom.

When Elizabeth laughed, Gabe became suspicious. "What's so funny?"

"Ethan wants to have sex," she said laughing, and then she laughed harder when her husband flushed red and looked embarrassed.

"Elizabeth!" He couldn't believe that she actually said that to their boss.

"Blackhawk, this is exactly how I ended up with six kids and had to trade in my sports car for an SUV," he said laughing, as he hung up the phone.

"I'm never trading in my Mustang," he replied, and then looked at his wife. "Am I?" Now he felt sick to his stomach. He loved his car.

Elizabeth laughed and patted his cheek. "I'll take one for the team and get the SUV. I don't want to face your midlife crisis fifteen years from now and blame the loss of your beloved Mustang Mistress." She'd started referring to his car as the Mistress, when she caught him waxing her and talking to her like she was a real person.

"If he's trying to deter me from having a brood, it's not going to work. There's nothing wrong with six kids and you driving an SUV," he said, laughing and then offered his wife his hand. "Shall we head home and then out into the field, Mrs. Blackhawk?"

Elizabeth took his hand and grinned. "Absolutely, Cowboy. Look out Red River, here come the Blackhawks!"

Ethan dropped his arm around his wife's shoulders. "I'm sure the place won't ever be the same again."

Whitefox sat on the couch and waited for the woman upstairs, as she finished packing. He definitely liked her house, and he couldn't help but want to wander around and look at all the memorabilia. When curiosity finally won out, he meandered to the book shelf, and checked out the pictures and little trinkets. One of his secret pleasures in life was books, and whenever he saw copious amounts of them, he was immediately drawn to them.

First thing that caught his eye was the picture. It was of her standing with another woman. They looked to be the same age, but the other woman was taller and looked aloof, where Desdemona looked approachable and friendly. They were standing by what looked like a swamp and both women were wearing bikini tops and cut offs.

Whitefox was curious since it was the only picture there. He thought about his own table beside the bed with quite a few pictures of him and his family, then of Elizabeth's bookshelves covered in photos. To him it seemed sad and lonely.

Whitefox was charmed by the collection of miniature coffins and macabre items on her shelves. There were some skulls housed in plexi-glass boxes and even some antique doctor's kits that looked more like torture devices than tools of heal. Doctor Desdemona Adare had a very eclectic taste in collectables.

"I like unusual things," she stated, carrying her travel bag and suitcase down from the second floor. Her first instinct was to defend her collection, like she always had to with strangers. Just one more thing that made her 'odd' and a spectacle.

"I really like this one," he commented, feeling the tension in her voice. "It's odd but truly beautiful," he said, pointing to one small box.

Desdemona moved closer to see which piece he was discussing. "That's a Cyanide box." She informed him. "Doctors were sometimes quacks, and they prescribed treatment with the stuff." She stood beside him. "I like to collect all the different medical items I can find, and the more unusual the item the better. I find it fascinating to see where we once were as doctors, and how we progressed as technology also evolved."

Whitefox grinned at her. If he closed his eyes she sounded much older than she looked. Doctor Adare was indeed very smart.

"Do you collect anything?" she asked, wondering more about the man.

"I collect books," he answered, offering up the information.

"Then you'd like my reading room," she answered, laughing. "I seem to like them too. Growing up I had to hike miles to the local library, and when I was able to start acquiring books, I seemed to lose total and complete control of my ability to stop. "

He could appreciate that. Books were always a way for him to escape a life he hated as a child. He'd hide for hours in the stories of books, and then one day he connected with his brother and didn't need to hide. It still didn't diminish his love of literature, but gave him a close friend to share his books with too. When they weren't raising hell, they were reading all about it.

Whitefox noticed she'd changed. "You actually have a winter coat with tiny skulls on it?" He was grinning now. Something about this woman entertained him and fascinated him.

"Yes, I happen to like them. I collect kitschy clothing too. Obviously." Then she paused and considered it. "Is this inappropriate for a crime scene? Sometimes I forget that not everyone sees the humor in an ME wearing a jacket with skulls."

He laughed. "I think it's just the opposite, Desdemona. They seem very appropriate to me."

She chewed on her bottom lip.

"Is there something on your mind?" he asked, as he carried her suitcase to the door.

Desdemona wasn't sure she could trust the man yet. In her past she'd noticed that men would betray easily, and she didn't want to get burned. Something about the man made him likable and easy to talk to about things.

"We're going to be partners on this assignment, so you can trust me and share anything you wish with me."

It was like he read her mind. It freaked her out how astute he was with her.

"Really?"

"Yes, really." Something happened in her life that made her this distrustful and worried about what people thought about her. That was blatantly obvious, and now he felt the need to heal it for her.

"Do you think that Director Blackhawk doesn't like me because of what I wear to work?" She just spilled it, and hoped he wouldn't tell her what they discussed. "If my work attire is the issue, I'll wear the standard FBI attire to keep the peace between us."

He looked confused at her words. "I don't know why you think she dislikes you, Desdemona. In fact, she thinks you're smart and really good at your job." It was truth, Elizabeth said those words, so it wasn't betraying confidence. There was no way he'd tell the doctor that his sister-in-law was just as worried as she was about being liked. Protecting Elizabeth was priority one, she was his family and the love of his life.

"I just know that sometimes my clothing choices can be inappropriate. I just like whimsical, and when you deal with death all day long, you need to find happiness in something or you'll lose your mind."

Whitefox shrugged. "Elizabeth is pretty laid back about clothing. She doesn't particularly like stuffy FBI attire."

"I can tell."

Whitefox didn't tell the woman that Elizabeth could be very girly, and that she collected vintage nineteen fifties frilly aprons. It would shatter the illusion that she worked hard to promote that she was tough as nails.

Desdemona opened her front door and stopped moving. All the humor and joviality was sucked from her body is a quick vacuum when she saw it.

Shit!

"What's wrong?" he asked, as he nearly walked into the back of her.

Desdemona Adare bent over and tossed the red rose that was laying on her stone steps over into the snow. "Nothing," she answered, as she set the alarm, closed the door, and continued to the Denali.

Callen Whitefox saw the flower and immediately sensed her tensing again, and he was curious as to why. But now wasn't the time. If he pushed, she'd clam up and he'd find nothing out. Sometimes it was best to just observe and go from there.

"We'd better get going," she said over her shoulder. There wasn't a worst time to have a flower show up, and there wasn't a better time to have to leave the area. Her hand automatically went to her hip, where her ME badge, and her gun sat clipped. Yeah, it was a very good time to head out into the field and escape for a little while.

When she hopped in, she saw the acknowledgement in his eyes, and knew that it would eventually come up again. Until it did, she knew it would sit between them like a weight. A man like Whitefox wasn't going to let it go for long and already she could feel his questioning gaze, assessing her and the situation.

Whitefox started up the Denali and his smartphone beeped. "I have incoming messages. Can you see if they're the case files that we're supposed to use to be vetted?"

"Sure thing," she answered cordially, taking the phone from his hand. As her fingers brushed his, she felt this tingle glide up her arm.

Callen watched her carefully. The woman was definitely hiding something. Poker faces obviously weren't her strong point, and she looked like she was ready to jump out the car door.

"We're partners Desdemona, and for now you can keep your secrets. But if it means keeping us safe, you're going to have to trust me with them." Then he focused on the drive. Whitefox wanted to shake his head. Something made him feel empathy for this woman. The idea that she had no one in her life to trust bothered him, because he'd been there once in life too. Before his brother returned, bringing him his new best friend, Elizabeth.

Desdemona didn't want to like him, and she certainly didn't want to trust the man. He was Ethan and Elizabeth Blackhawk's brother, but something in her just wanted to have that one person she could confide in and maybe have as a friend. For so many years she'd been a loner, and all she wanted was the one thing that entirely eluded her.

A circle of people to call her own or just one to trust completely.

Desdemona Adare could figure out what killed someone, how their lives ended, and what caused it, but she couldn't master the ability to fit into a group. It was so foreign to her and so out of her reach that she wasn't sure how to make it happen. Even as a child she wasn't really good at making friends. Now she wanted to learn, and wanted that as her new goal. All her life she set goals and met them. Yet with this one she felt panic.

What if she failed?

"Relax Desdemona."

That was easy for him to say. He didn't currently have a boss that hated him, a stalker chasing him, and the world's sexiest man sitting two feet from his body, making him nuts. Desdemona tried to not breathe in the scent of his cologne, as she closed her eyes and prayed for some sort of control. Now she needed to control her brain, mouth and the rampant hormones that were telling her to do things she knew she'd regret.

Right then and there, she just knew the man was going to break her heart.

Elizabeth dropped more clothes into their suitcase. At one time in her life, when she was packing for an assignment there was just a small carry-on bag. She like her husband had been the job, but now they packed all their things together. It was nice to have found each other and work together as partners.

Blackhawk watched his wife from the doorway as she fastidiously arranged their things. It wasn't lost on him that she was smiling at absolutely nothing. As she stood there getting their belongings ready for the trip, he couldn't help but think she was still the sexiest woman in the world, and he was the luckiest man. He looked at his watch, and they had a few minutes to spend together. Once they were sharing a house with his brother and the ME, he wasn't sure he'd get any alone time with her. Sneaking over to her, he wrapped his arms around her and left kisses on the side of her neck.

"Know what I like best about you being pregnant, baby?" he asked, as he did incredibly wicked things to her ear and neck.

"Mmmmm… no, what?" Elizabeth was trying to focus on the suitcase, but it wasn't looking like it was going to happen. "That I'm easier to catch?"

He whispered something erotic and suggestive in her ear.

Elizabeth shuddered at the mere suggestion, and it still heated her blood that the world's sexiest man still wanted her- even though she was pregnant and wobbly.

"That you're easier to catch is helpful," he said, spinning her around to face him, just before his lips met hers in a scorching kiss. He explored the depths of her mouth, as he searched, fought, and did battle with her for control. Deepening it, he was satisfied when she moaned in pleasure first. Just the sound made his entire body clench with need and incredible want. Before she could protest, he flicked open her belt buckle and pulled her even closer to his body.

"You know we have an assignment," she whispered, as he did amazing things with his hands and mouth. "We should be getting ready to leave."

Ethan stopped and looked down into her eyes. They were clouded with desire and pleasure, and not for one second did he believe she wanted him to stop. "I guess we can wait until the assignment is over, Elizabeth." He started to release her and she grabbed him by the front of his shirt.

"I didn't say we had to stop, Cowboy, and if you stop now, I'm going to get pissed!" She kissed him back and her hands travelled the same erotic path his had across her body. As she unbuttoned his shirt, the tattoos that she loved came into view and the heat that was deep within her body bubbled to the surface. "Love that tattoo," she muttered, as she allowed her lips to leave a trail over the large raven tattooed on his chest. Her hands expertly freed him from his pants and boxers. "I think that my name under the raven gets me even hotter."

"Good," he answered, breaking the kiss and waiting while she finished undressing. Seconds felt like minutes as he got harder and harder. "I really think I need to have sex with my wife before I combust, so if possible can you get naked faster?"

She looked up grinning, and purposely slowed the entire process down.

"Baby, come on," he muttered, his entire body was beginning to tense. "In three seconds, I'm coming at you and clothes will be destroyed."

Elizabeth considered his words, and wondered if he'd actually do it. The look on his face spoke volumes, and she dropped the rest of her clothes, quickly.

"Come here," he ordered, brusquely.

Elizabeth obeyed, jumping up and wrapped her legs around his waist and continued to kiss her husband like she was starving for him. Her hand was buried in his hair, and she wouldn't let him break away. She couldn't. The kiss was like a drug and she was an addict. The pregnancy hormones were definitely making her a sex manic. All she thought about was jumping her husband.

Ethan was her choice of addiction; her very sexy Native drug. "You know that not cutting your hair is fighting dirty," she muttered into the kiss, as she buried her hands into the delicious silkiness that she loved.

"Had I known it would get me more sex with my wife, I wouldn't have cut it since meeting you," he replied, holding her wrapped around his body. "I'll never cut it again."

Elizabeth's body tightened at the mere thought, and she dove deeper into the kiss.

"Bed now," he practically growled, as he yanked the suitcase off and onto the floor and replaced it with his wife. Everything fell out in a pile. After laying her across their bed, he stripped off the rest of his clothing and dropped it to the floor in a frenzied rush to get free of the restraint.

Elizabeth watched him from the bed, her eyes admiring not only the fine male specimen her husband was, but the sexy tribal art that criss-crossed his body. Yeah, she just loved those tattoos more than words.

Just the way his wife watched him, the eyes full of greedy lust, and wanting to climb all over him made him crazy. There was something wildly alluring about his pregnant wife, as she lie on their bed, crazy wild hair spread out around her like a wave of silk. Just thinking about the way it would feel sliding across his body made him harder.

"Come and get me, Ethan," she teased, wickedly.

There were days when he felt completely possessive and much like a cave man. Sex was always explosive between them, but now that she was pregnant with his child, he just wanted to own her and dominate. Desperation was driving him as he found himself fighting the need to just take whatever he wanted at that moment. It was like she was giving off some crazy pheromone that just made him want her that much more, and that much more often. In general, he was a man of rigorous control. Everything in his life was built on the premise that he was a type A control freak, but lately because of his raven haired hellion he'd had none.

Her lush naked body called to him, and he focused on devouring her like some starved lunatic. He began kissing his way down her torso, paying attention to her already growing cleavage. Yeah, he absolutely loved this pregnancy thing- A sexy wife with more curves, deliciousness and an increased sex drive. Ethan Blackhawk was pretty sure it didn't get any better than this. As he focused on each nipple and teased her unmercifully she was driving him wild with her breathless pants.

"Ethan," she begged, writhing beneath his mouth and wandering fingers. Now her husband had the last thing removed from her body. The panties were gone, and she would be at his mercy. "Please," she begged. "I need you."

"I can't just yet. I need to savor this moment with my wife, I don't know if I'll have this moment again for days!" He said it with such possessiveness that it made him wilder and crazier. The mere idea that he'd have to be around her and not touch her was maddening. When he slid lower down her body and found the sweet spot, she moaned his name, and he was ready to explode right then and there.

The complete and total feeling of her husband tormenting her was enough to make her shatter into a million pieces, and still he continued to the point it was pain mixed with bliss. She couldn't take it anymore and pulled him up her body, her hands buried in his hair.

When their mouths met again, she muttered into his mouth, "My turn, Ethan," and she proceeded to have her fun. Nothing turned her on more than having her way with her sexy Indian warrior. There was just something about the tattoos, the tan skin, the sexy body, and the hair. God, she loved how he'd been letting his hair grow instead of keeping it clipped to his shoulders. As the strands slid across her flesh it made her all hot and bothered. "Love your hair," she whispered against his mouth, as she dove back into the kiss.

Like his tattoos, his hair reminded him of his past. Since finding his wife and coming home, he'd learned to relax into his heritage. Instead of running, he was embracing it, and now he was reaping the rewards. If he knew that his wife liked it this much, he'd start wearing feathers and war paint to get this response. Thank you Native roots!

Elizabeth was going to explode into flames if she didn't taste him.

Blackhawk was breathing hard already, as he fought for control of his mind and body. Just devouring his wife, made him ready to lose it right there, but when she moved down his body and her hand wrapped enticingly around his erection, it took everything he had to not break apart.

"Too much control, Ethan," she whispered, and then blew across his already rock hard erection.

"Baby, cut me a break," he muttered, as she stroked him a few times, before laughing that bewitching laugh that made him want to just take her harder and faster.

Control.

He just needed to remember his wife was pregnant and rough wasn't an option. The entire thought did the opposite. Pregnant wife made him harder, and then she found him with her mouth. Now he was thinking about her hot, silky, wicked wet mouth. Christ, this was a mix of bliss and torture all at once.

Elizabeth took her husband in her mouth and did all the things that she knew made him lose control. Lately their lovemaking was controlled, and she knew he was worried about the baby. Now she was going to teach him a lesson he wouldn't forget. Elizabeth was going to take her husband, one way or another, making him lose complete and total control.

This was her new mission in life.

When she cupped him and stroked him with her mouth, he was in heaven, and when she added teeth he didn't think he'd make it much longer, and then she did something she never did before. His wife began to hum, and just that alone caused the shaking in his body to begin.

"Oh God, Lyzee," he mumbled, as he arched up to meet her mouth in forceful thrusts. It was like nothing he ever felt before. "Killing me, I can't hold out much longer," he practically begged.

Elizabeth listened to the desperation in his voice, and knew she still had a few moments to enjoy tormenting her husband before he lost control completely. Then she heard the ragged breath, and his body stopped shaking. When she gazed up at him, she saw the pure unadulterated lust on his face and she just knew. Ethan Blackhawk was a man teetering precariously on the edge and about to lose control.

"Baby!" It was the only word he could get out of his mouth, as he pulled her up his body and rolled with her until she was beneath him.

"I want you, Ethan," she spoke softly, opening for him. Her body welcomed him and lured him in with the promise of complete bliss and pleasure. "You can't hurt me or the baby," she whispered, giving him permission to relax and just enjoy the intimacy of the moment.

Once she gave him the words, he couldn't think anymore. The instinct in him to claim his wife took control. All he knew was he had to have her, and he needed it now. It was beyond need, it was compulsion. Sliding deep into her body, she moaned and he couldn't breathe. All he wanted was a rough ride, and he planned on it. Blackhawk was completely out of control, and once again, his wife pushed him there. As he felt her clench around him, his arms braced on either side of her, he began his invasion. It wasn't gentle and it wasn't easy. What he wanted and needed overcame his sense of protectiveness for his wife and unborn child. All he desired to hear was her begging and then screaming his name. The pure unadulterated lust was now in control, and he slid all the way in her body and then out. Then he slammed back into her and knew he wasn't going to make it much longer.

"Ethan!" Elizabeth dug the nails of her one hand into his shoulder, and with the other pulled his mouth down to hers and plunged into the ecstasy. All she demanded was met and returned with equal need.

Harder he slid into her body, until a gasp and moan escaped her lips. When he knew he wouldn't make it much longer, he broke the kiss, looking down into her eyes. "God baby, now!" he hissed through clenched teeth as he waited until she began to quake around him. When she did, he slammed into her one last time, pouring hotly into his wife and joining her in the blissful stupor.

Elizabeth shattered and she felt herself relax into the free fall. It was perfect. Everything about their coming together was heaven. It always would be, because he was her true love.

When Ethan could breathe again, he remembered his wife was pregnant, and that he was practically laying over her and the baby. "Shit, did I hurt you," he asked in a panic, practically jumping off her body.

"Mmmmm, no cowboy," she answered, pulling him back down and curling against him. "Two more minutes to just enjoy this before we head out," she whispered into his ear.

When he realized she wasn't in pain, he relaxed and enjoyed the few moments they'd have before they had to leave for Red River.

"Ethan?" she asked, running her fingers over the tattoo on his chest.

"Yeah baby?" Blackhawk could feel his body regaining feeling again.

"Promise me you aren't going to make me wait until after the assignment to have sex again. It's not nice to torture a pregnant woman. I could snap and kill everyone around me in some hormonal rampage."

Blackhawk didn't know what he was expecting her to ask, but it certainly wasn't that. Once he started laughing, she joined him. He left a kiss on the tip of her nose. "I can't allow that to happen, Elizabeth. The odds are in your favor that I won't be able to keep my hands off you. I never can."

Elizabeth grinned. "Good to know, Mr. Blackhawk."

Desdemona and Callen had some pleasant conversation as they drove together to Red River. She didn't think they'd have anything to talk about, but he had an easy way about him. There was no pretense, and she didn't feel like she needed to be someone she wasn't. Somehow he managed to get her to be completely relaxed.

"So, you want to tell me more about you?" he asked, as the GPS gave off its next direction. "I'll tell you all about me and my brother," he offered, trying to lure her into spilling information about herself.

She considered it and had to admit she was curious about both men. "Okay."

"Want me to go first?" he asked, as he looked over at her. Callen Whitefox had been spending the last hour, trying to get the doctor to just relax and not be so knotted up. The woman was a nervous wreck and for some unknown reason it pulled at his heart. She seemed like a really sweet person, and he genuinely was enjoying his time with her. In fact, she was actually cute when she smiled at him. He felt the waves of protectiveness building in him.

"Okay, you go first," she said, smiling over at him. Desdemona knew he was trying his best to help her adjust to him, and to the idea they were being joined by her bosses. ,

"Well, as you can already see the obvious, I'm native and I grew up on a reservation. My brother and I both lost our mother's early. I think Ethan was thirteen and I was fourteen."

She looked over at him, and understood the pain. "My mom disappeared when I was ten, and I never knew my father," she said, simply.

"How did she die?" he asked, softly. This might be something she didn't like to talk about, but he'd ask anyway.

Desdemona thought about it. "One day she went out to pick some roots for my grand'mere, and she never came back," she answered.

Whitefox noticed it was said with no emotion, but her eyes gave her away. The pain was still there. Now that she gave him some information, he'd do the same.

"My mom was a single parent and really young when she had me. My father knocked her up, on a one night stand, and then went back to his wife."

"That had to be hard," she said, touching his arm lightly.

Whitefox enjoyed the feeling of her fingers on his arm, and his body began to warm. It wasn't the same reaction he noticed when Elizabeth touched him, but it still drew his attention. "It was hard when I was growing up, but I ended up with a terrific grandfather out of the deal, and then I got my brother too," he paused, and thought about what else to tell her. "My dad and I had a shitty relationship until a few months ago. Ethan came back to help me solve a serial killer assignment on the reservation and we reconnected with our father. I found out somethings that I wasn't aware of, like he honestly tried to get my mother to marry him, but she wasn't into starting a family."

Desdemona heard the anguish, and saw how his face tensed. "Did Ethan have a bad relationship with him too?"

"Yeah, Wyler wasn't exactly a great dad," he shrugged and continued, "but he ended up saving Elizabeth's life, and then getting shot in the chest protecting our grandfather. I guess it gives you perspective when you almost lose a parent."

"My mom wouldn't talk about my dad. In fact, I don't even know if my sister and I share the same father. I've asked her to submit to a DNA test, and she just refuses and tells me it's best to not know."

"My mom made it clear who my father was," he stated and then pushed on, "but she told me to keep it quiet, and I did for a long time. For a while I didn't believe that we really were brothers. I always thought back to my mom liking to party and sleeping around. It was always a doubt in my mind. I don't look like a Blackhawk and it weighed heavily on me."

"Did you do a DNA test?" she asked, purely from a scientific standpoint. Okay, maybe not all science and some curiosity.

Callen thought back to the killer that they had caught that was their half-brother. Elizabeth had the lab run their DNA, and that was confirmation that Wyler Blackhawk was really his father. After the fact, he confided to Elizabeth that it was always his secret fear they'd find out he wasn't a genetic match, and he'd lose the only family he ever had. Not even his brother knew he doubted his DNA all his life. The woman knew all his secrets and all his biggest fears, and she told him the outcome wouldn't have mattered in the least. He would have been part of **HER** family.

"Yeah, we did a test." Thanks to his best friend, he had confirmation. Thinking about Elizabeth made his heart skip.

"How did you lose your mom?" she asked, softly. "You don't have to tell me," she added quickly, worried she offended him.

Callen Whitefox reached over and patted her cheek. "Desdemona, don't be afraid to just be you and ask questions. If you want to survive around the Blackhawks you need to not overthink everything. You'll find that with all of us, Elizabeth included, we tend to be pretty blunt and to the point."

69

She nodded, and was well aware that he was right. If anything she was nothing but timid and scared, and her past did that to her. When he looked away, she touched her cheek where his hand had been.

Yeah, he gave her butterflies. Big ones that meant trouble.

"As I said, my mom was a party girl. One night she went out to have some fun, drank too much and had a drug bender. She never woke up from it." He was honest with her, and for many years no one knew what happened to his mother. Whitefox was pretty sure his grandfather, Timothy Blackhawk, had managed to keep it quiet on the reservation. The man didn't want the tribe hurting his grandson with speculation and gossip. Only the family knew the truth. As for the abuse, not even Elizabeth knew about it.

"That's horrible," she said, her heart aching for him. "Where were you?"

"About two years before that my grandfather took me away from her. My mother didn't really want to be a mom. There weren't movie nights and cuddling on the couch. Sometimes she forgot I even existed. I could wander away, and she wouldn't think to even come looking for me. One day I did just that, and one of the tribe happened to tell my grandfather, and he intervened. Timothy wasn't going to watch it happen."

"I'm sorry Callen," she said with sincere feelings. She couldn't imagine how that must have hurt.

"I'm not sorry," he answered sincerely, looking over at her. "My brother once pointed out something important. If she wasn't the woman she was, I wouldn't have been born, I wouldn't have had my brother, and I wouldn't be here right now. Fate matters," he stated. "I believe in fate and how it leads us to where we need to be, no matter how hard we fight it. Because she made horrible choices, I was given things I wouldn't have had. Family to me is the most important thing in the world. Elizabeth and Ethan mean everything to me and they always will."

"I never thought of it that way," she said.

"When my mother let me go, I was given a family. Now I have Elizabeth and a nephew on the way too. My circle grew because of fate, and I wouldn't go back and do anything differently." That was a lie. He wouldn't have betrayed his brother, but he wasn't going there with a stranger.

Because he shared his pain, Desdemona decided to share a part of her past. "There were rumors around what happened to my mom. Some people said she ran off with some man, and others said she fell into the swamp and was eaten by the gators."

"Wow," he didn't know which was worse. Mom abandonment or eaten by a reptile. Both scenarios seemed unpleasant.

"My grand'mere raised me and my sister," she paused. "She's... different." No one knew about her grandmother, it just wasn't something she spoke about. Not because she was embarrassed, but... Okay, because she was a woman of science and her grandmother was the complete opposite.

"Different?"

"Can I trust you?" she asked. "I mean really trust you not to say what I'm going to tell you to anyone else?"

Callen Whitefox couldn't imagine what she had to say that would be surprising. "Yes, I promise not to speak a word of it."

Desdemona watched him with cat eyes and contemplated it. "Pinky swear?"

He laughed caught off guard. "Yes, I pinky swear," he held his hand out and offered it up. When she smiled at him, he finally saw her relax. Her eyes sparkled, her smile was genuine, and he realized that she was finally being herself.

She took his pinky with hers. "My grandmother is a bayou witch."

Okay, that he wasn't expecting, and he found it entertaining. "That's pretty funny."

"I'm serious." She didn't think he'd laugh, and instantly she wanted to hide as the hurt began to surface.

"Desdemona, I'm not laughing at you or what you've just said. What I'm laughing at is my grandfather is a reservation Shaman. It's the same thing, different religions that's all. We have a lot in common," he said, reaching over and touching her chin and making her look at him. "I won't ever laugh at you, I promise. We're partners on this assignment, and I don't laugh at people I'm here to protect."

Desdemona's heart skipped a beat.

"I swear, Desdemona."

"I believe you, Callen, but just in case." She held up her pinky again and laughed.

Whitefox shook his head, and he was completely entertained by this little woman. Again he held up his pinky and made the oath. "Now, can I be honest about something?"

Desdemona Adare chewed on her bottom lip, debating if she wanted to hear what he was going to say. Part of her hoped it wasn't going to be that she was cute. She really hated being called cute or adorable. Kittens and puppies were cute. "I guess so, Callen."

"Not that I don't like your name, but Desdemona is a mouthful. I think you need a nickname," he smiled easily. "Do you have one that your friends use?" he asked.

"I've never had one," she answered honestly. "Well, I had one in college, but it's not really a nickname."

"What was it?" Now he was curious.

"Morticia. I guess it was because of the hair and the dealing with death all day long. I didn't particularly like it, so I'd prefer we forget that option."

"No other nicknames?"

"Sometimes I'm called Doc, but other than that not really." Desdemona opted to not tell him she didn't really have friends. The last thing she wanted from him was pity.

Whitefox grinned. "I tell you what. I think I'll call you Desi, because it's easier and we're friends. Things should always be easier between friends. We'll keep the Morticia thing just between you and me. How's that?"

"Deal," she leaned over and gave him a chaste kiss on the cheek. "Thank you, Callen, for being my friend." Then she sat back, realizing what she just did, and she hoped she didn't just make a huge mistake. Immediately she began praying that on the outside she was maintaining a nonchalant look on her face. On the inside her body was on fire and churning into a wicked brew of lust and crazy mad need for the man. Crap the man smelled so damn good.

Callen tensed when he realized she was going to kiss him. Granted it was a simple kiss, and one that meant nothing more than what it was, but he reacted to it. Hope grew in him that finally someone would find something redeeming in him. That the possibility that he was attractive to an outsider might happen, and he may have the possibility of a life like his brother. The kiss was sweet, and it touched his heart. Desdemona was a nice woman.

"You're very welcome, Desi." Right then he needed to change the subject; he was supposed to be a Director for the FBI, not a man looking for a woman. "Can you check my phone for me? I think I heard it beep before."

"It's on your belt," she said, pointing out the obvious. It meant reaching over, under his coat and pulling it free. That meant almost touching him, not that she wouldn't mind running her hands all over his body…

Oh crap where had that come from?

Whitefox laughed. "You just kissed me, and you're worried about removing my phone from my belt?"

The heat rushed her face. "I kissed you on the cheek, that's not really a kiss," she stated, trying to defend it.

Whitefox didn't want her to retreat but he couldn't help it. "Oh, so explain to me how that kiss was different from a 'real' kiss," he teased her, grinning the Blackhawk grin he'd inherited from his family. It always caught the ladies. After he said the words and grinned he realized what he was doing.

Completely inappropriate.

Assignments were work and the last thing he needed to be doing is flirting with the woman sitting next to him. She was his partner, not a date. "On second thought here's the phone, Desi," he said, thinking about his brother and Elizabeth. If they knew he was acting like this, his ass would be kicked. No kissy-face on duty!

Desdemona grabbed his phone, and clicked on the text message. She was profoundly grateful he didn't make her explain the difference because she didn't have a chance in hell of explaining it without sounding like a moron.

"It's from Director Blackhawk. He's instructed us to head to the sheriff's office first. They're an hour behind us and will meet us there."

"Okay, then I guess we better start prepping for the meeting. Do you want to start with the photo's the Sheriff's department took of the bodies and give me any information you can on them. I know it's not the same thing as seeing them up close and personal, but it'll have to do for now."

"I've worked with photos before I don't mind," she answered, as she pulled out the tablet that she used in the lab and pulled up the photos one by one. Studying them she stopped seeing the person, and in her mind they became something of science only. It was how she coped with the death every day and didn't go insane. They could never be people to her, but instead they were just a puzzle that needed solving.

"Before you start we should call my brother or sister, so they can hear your initial assessment."

She wondered if he noticed he referred to Elizabeth as his sister and not sister-in-law. They obviously had a very tight bond. "Okay." Desdemona was nervous knowing Elizabeth would be listening to the call.

"Speed dial one is Elizabeth and speed dial two is my brother."

Of course Elizabeth was number one, she thought, feeling envy, jealousy and so many things that she didn't have a right to feel. Obviously, he called her frequently, if he made her one on his phone list. On her list, it was her grand'mere.

Desdemona Adare nodded and pushed past the sick feeling in her stomach and made the call. She placed it on speaker phone and allowed him to take control of the call. Or hoped he would.

"What's up Cal?" Blackhawk answered on the second ring.

"Doctor Adare is about to assess the pictures you sent, and she thought you'd like to know what she sees as her initial impression."

Desdemona looked worried.

"Great, thank you Doctor Adare," Ethan Blackhawk said. "I'll put you on speakerphone."

"Elizabeth, you there," he asked, waiting.

"I sure am Callen. Hello Doctor Adare. We're ready when you are. Please proceed when you're ready," she answered, trying to be as easy going as she could be. The doctor and she were on shaky ground as it was, and she didn't need to exacerbate the situation.

Desdemona Adare forgot her nerves and did what she did best. She looked at the dead and told their story.

"Okay, we have five victims. All male and by looking at them, I can tell that they appear to be anywhere from twenties to possibly forties. Victim one," she paused to blow up the picture and isolate the wounds. "He is missing his feet. Both left and right were severed at the malleolus. In this picture I can't ascertain whether the cut went from the lateral malleolus to the medial malleolus or vice versa. Once I get him on the table I'll be able to tell when I see the cut marks."

It was Elizabeth that spoke. "Doctor Adare, we need you to do us a favor."

"Yes?" she paused.

"Look at Callen's face, what does it tell you?" she asked and hoped it was the same look that was on her husband's face.

"I don't know, he looks confused, I guess."

"Okay, here's the deal, and a little rule we go by here in FBI West. Dumb it down for us non-medical personnel. I know that you were discussing the ankle, only because I spent a lot of time with Chris Leonard and Tony Magnus. But you lost Ethan at malleolus, and I'm betting Callen too. If you keep it simple for us that aren't your caliber, you'll save yourself time having to repeat the basics."

"I'm sorry Director Blackhawk; I'm just used to doing my initial assessments into a microphone and not to you both. I convert it to layman's terms for the reports you both receive." Desdemona felt her skin flush, and then glanced down to see Callen taking her hand in his and squeezing it reassuringly. Something about the simple action touched her and made her heart skip a beat.

"No need to apologize Doctor. We love that we hired the smartest and the best. It's us that are sub-par, so break us in easy please," she said, gently. "And the other hard and fast rule is you can call me Elizabeth, the Director moniker is for the minions. You're pretty high up on the employee list that we're equals. When people call me Director, I think Ethan is standing right behind me. He's more the boss, and I'm the muscle."

Both men laughed. Wasn't that the truth?

Whitefox mouthed the word 'see', and was happy when she relaxed visibly. He made a mental note to kiss his sister-in-law again for just knowing when a light hand was needed. It was obvious to him and probably his brother that she was walking on eggshells for the woman. Elizabeth never did that for anyone.

"Okay, Elizabeth," she said, and looked back down at the picture, but kept holding Whitefox's hand for support. "Victim one had one of his feet removed at the ankle. From the pictures I can see staining of the bone and marrow, so that means that he was likely alive when the cuts were made."

"Great to know," Blackhawk said. "What else do you have?"

"Until I get access to his body under the clothing not much, but I can tell you that he's fully dressed, and he isn't bruised on any part his visible flesh," she paused and enlarged the screen. "Wait," she looked closer. "I see some red marks over his mouth in a square like pattern. I could guess and say it's tape marks, but just don't tell Doctor Leonard. It bugs the shit out of him when I make unsubstantiated guesses," she said deep in thought, as she stared at the man.

Elizabeth started laughing. It entertained her that the woman used the word 'bugs' and 'unsubstantiated' in the same sentence. This woman was a puzzle.

"I'm sorry, I didn't mean anything by that," she began to apologize, and Whitefox squeezed her hand again.

"No apology needed. We know exactly how tough Chris is when you're trying to dig for information. It's nice to have it offered for a change and less draining mentally," she laughed some more. "Frankly, I'm getting tired of manhandling the ME staff to get information from them."

Again Whitefox grinned and mouthed 'go on'.

"That's all I have on victim one," she said, flipping the screen to the next picture.

"We're ready," said Elizabeth, as she furiously entered notes on her tablet in her lap. Anything they had before the scene was going to help them out when they arrived at base.

"Victim two appears to be quite young," she stated, looking at the picture. "I'd say early twenties to late twenties. The killer has removed his hands at the wrists. Again, once I get him into autopsy I can give you more."

"Can you tell if he too had tape over his mouth," inquired Blackhawk.

Desdemona zoomed into the photo and studied it. "I can't tell. The quality of the picture is too grainy." She studied the rest of his face. "I can tell you that he suffocated to death."

"How Doctor?" asked Elizabeth, surprised. Chris Leonard would never have told her that just by looking at the picture.

She zoomed into the picture around the eyes. "Our second victim has petechial hemorrhaging in the whites of his eyes." Then she paused realizing she used big words. Certainly Directors in the FBI knew the basics. "Do you need that dumbed down?" She was being serious and all three laughed.

"No Doctor, that one we got," answered Blackhawk. "But thank you for offering. I'm not as smart as my wife, but even that one I knew."

"Okay, just making sure," she replied and then continued. "Again, I see blood staining on the bones where they're severed."

"He was alive?" asked Elizabeth.

"He was very much alive," she replied, enlarging the picture an drawing arrows on the tablet and then sending it to her boss. "See where I've indicated?" she asked, waiting.

"I do," answered Elizabeth Blackhawk.

"Those are staining of the porous parts of the bone. It likely means that his heart was still pumping when the cuts were made. Heartbeat means life- for the most part."

"Oh good," said Ethan Blackhawk. "I see that we have another person that likes technology and know how to use it. Now I really feel antiquated."

Desdemona didn't know if that was a cue to something she wasn't picking up or not. Panic started that she just insulted her one boss.

Callen Whitefox squeezed her hand and nodded, signaling it was okay for her to continue. Something about the woman piqued his interest. Here she was super smart, and yet like a wounded small child. Doctor Adare touched his heart, and he felt the overwhelming need to protect her and keep her safe. Someone had to, and he suspected no one in her past ever had before. Just the way she nervously interacted with Elizabeth, always apologized, and was timid proved to him that she was delicately balanced between being okay, and toppling over the edge into sheer terror.

"Victim number three is male and appears to be approximately around his mid-thirties, but I'm not seeing any visible wounds. There is staining across his dress shirt, so my assessment on his wounds is going to have to wait until I get him undressed. All his limbs appear to be intact and his face shows no sign of trauma."

Desdemona flipped the picture and studied it.

"What do you see?" asked Whitefox curiously, as she studied the picture.

"Elizabeth, did the sheriff mention if there was any blood on the scene?" she asked as she looked closely at the staining on his shirt. It was centrally located.

"No blood, just bodies. Why?"

"This blood pattern on his shirt is in one spot. Let's say, if you're standing and you're shot, the blood is going to run down your body."

"I've been shot a few times, so I can attest to that conjecture," she said, easily. "Blood definitely runs downhill, and that I learned from Newton's law of gravity."

Desdemona didn't know what to say to that, so she continued. "His doesn't. So, I'm going to say he was restrained on his back for most of the time, and then died in that position. There isn't any blood anywhere else," and then she thought about it. "Once he coagulated then he wouldn't bleed out either."

"So, our victims were restrained on their backs?"

"This one was, but as for the others," she paused. "I need to get them into exam and then figure that out."

"Ah, and here I thought we finally had an ME that liked to live dangerously on the edge and make wild assumptions and unfounded guesses," teased Elizabeth. "Do they teach you to hold out in ME school?"

Desdemona took a chance and opted to joke back. "There's actually a class that teaches us how to frustrate and irritate the lead investigators. It's mandatory to get our licenses." There was that moment of silence and she thought she crossed a line.

Elizabeth snickered. "Great, now we know what we're up against. I wish someone told me sooner, because this explains a lot." There was more laughter from her. The ME's were tough when they were asked to hand out information that wasn't founded. Getting anything out of Dr. Chris Leonard was almost impossible, but Dr. Adare was a bit more forthcoming with her assessments, and that she greatly appreciated.

Whitefox grinned over at her, noticing she looked more relaxed. Since he didn't get to warn his sister-in-law about the situation, he had to assume she figured it out on her own. Elizabeth was playing nice and being exceptionally gentle and that so wasn't like her at all. It was just more proof that she understood people and was good at reading the situation. It was probably why she was a really good agent and even better human being.

"Victim four, he too looks to be in his thirties," she said, zooming into his face. "He's missing his tongue."

"Can you die when the tongue is removed?" asked Blackhawk, as he shuddered. His wife had a thing about dead eyes, and his big yuck was a missing tongue. The gaping wound left behind freaked him right out. The whole premise just screamed horror movie death to him. To see mouths agape with a bloody void, it gave him the chills and goose bumps

"Yes you can Director. There's a main artery in the tongue. The lingual artery, and once it's severed there would be blood loss and the person would exsanguinate."

"And if that person was lying on their back?" asked Elizabeth, trying to put the pieces together. "With tape over their mouth?"

"They could choke to death, if that's where your train of thought is heading, Elizabeth," she tried out the name again, and when there was no protest she continued. "It's a painful way to go, and then to drown in your own blood no less. You couldn't swallow that volume of blood."

"How about our last victim?" asked Blackhawk. "What do we have?" He had to stop talking about the tongue death. It was literally making his skin crawl, and his wife must have figured it out. She was soothingly rubbing his leg with her hand.

"What we don't have is ears. The killer took them," she answered, analyzing the picture. "While there aren't any arteries in the ear, the External Carotid Artery is right there. If the killer hit it while removing the ear itself, the victim would bleed out. But again," she was going to state the obvious.

"Yeah we know. Not until you do the exam," added Elizabeth.

"Sorry, but I can only do so much with a picture," Desdemona apologized for not having more to give them, and for disappointing them.

"Don't be sorry, Doc. You gave us a lot. Great job," answered Elizabeth. "It's more than I could get from the pictures, and it's more than Chris Leonard would give me before personally examining the body."

Desdemona relaxed a bit more. Well tried to anyway. Whitefox was running his thumb over her pulse in her wrist, and it was making it difficult to concentrate. Really hard, as her blood pressure was elevating and soon her skin would be flushing.

"We'll see you in Red River," added Ethan. "The sheriff is expecting you both, and then you'll be escorted to the scene." He waited a second and then said it. "Callen, watch your back, and Doctor Adare's. We don't know much about the town and the killer, and you need to keep her and yourself safe. Clear?"

Whitefox grinned. "Don't worry, Ethan. I think I can manage to keep us safe for an hour. You do know I'm a grown man, and I do have a gun, right?" Now he laughed. His big brother was being protective. Frankly, he expected it from Elizabeth, because he was accustomed to her playing guardian angel for him.

"Doctor Adare, can you use that weapon," Elizabeth asked, knowing her ME carried a gun, and although Elizabeth found it odd, in this situation she was glad.

"Yes, I can, Elizabeth." She had taken classes and was sufficient. "I'm more comfortable with a shotgun, but I can hit the side of a barn if I have to with my Glock," she added. "People frown when I walk around toting a shotgun," she added, grinning at Whitefox. Both of them shared the same visual.

Elizabeth was glad she was loosening up, but this situation she took very serious. Her team and Callen mattered, and she needed her on alert at all times. Risking her family wasn't an option, cspccially sincc shc promiscd Timothy Blackhawk shc'd keep them safe.

"Doctor Adare, I hate to be the one to break this to you and far be it for me to scare you, but the good news is the barns in Red River aren't going to be trying to kill you. The bad news is the killer may once we move those bodies. Serial killers get particular and testy when you touch their kills. All joking aside, once we touch those bodies, we don the bulls-eyes."

Desdemona stopped smiling, and tensed at Elizabeth's icy warning.

"See you guys soon," interjected Callen Whitefox, cutting off the call to help calm the doctor down again. He couldn't blame Elizabeth for being cautious. They had a history with serial killers and the family being put in danger. She was only doing her job, but then again, the woman beside him was now freaked out.

"Don't stress it, Desi. Elizabeth has to warn us, it's why she's a Director and we aren't."

It was too late. Doctor Desdemona Adare was already beyond worried and now bordering on scared shitless.

Elizabeth cut off the call and thought about it. Something wasn't sitting right with the woman they hired as their ME. It wasn't like she was doing anything outrageously crazy by carrying a gun. She may just like having a firearm, and working for the FBI allowed that, but her gut said otherwise and now that her curiosity was peaked she needed to know.

"Baby, you have that look on your face."

Elizabeth knew she did. "How much do we know about Doctor Adare?"

Blackhawk looked surprised. "She passed the standard FBI test and background checks, why? You think there is something up with her?"

"Not up, just off. My gut is in a knot, and now I need to find out why. She comes across as the timid kind of woman, and yet she keeps her service revolver strapped to her hip. I rarely see her without it."

"So do you," he added, playing devil's advocate.

"Yeah, but I'm frequently shot at," she stated, grinning at her husband.

"Don't remind me."

Elizabeth leaned back in her seat. "I also don't walk around FBI West packing heat, Cowboy. I leave my Glock in the desk.

Something about her isn't adding up in my mind , and you know how I get with the details."

"Like a rabid dog after a small school child?" he stated, navigating the traffic.

Elizabeth shook her head and rolled her eyes. "Yeah exactly. Nice picture there. I like how she's the innocent school child and I'm the scary rabid dog in this scenario."

"Baby, I didn't mean it like that." It wasn't like his wife to be this sensitive about what others thought about her. She was genuinely upset by his analogy. That was surprising.

Elizabeth swallowed the intense feelings she was having, and brushed them off as baby hormones. It really didn't matter what the doctor thought of her. It was funny how she had to keep saying that over and over again.

"You okay, Lyzee?"

"Yeah, I'm okay. I get it. I can be rabid at times. Just be careful I don't bite you and you have to be put down, Cowboy." Elizabeth tried to brush it off as humor.

Ethan Blackhawk wasn't buying it. "Well, when in doubt, call Quantico and get a check on her done, quietly," he added. "We have the authorization to pull everything on her without her being aware."

"Yeah I think we need to do it." Elizabeth pulled out her phone, placed it on speaker, and dialed Gabe Rothschild's secretary. She wouldn't bother her boss with this as of yet, not until she had something substantial.

On the third ring it was answered.

"Director Gabriel Rothschild's office."

"Maddy, it's Elizabeth. How's it going?" she asked, getting all the chit chat out of the way first.

"Elizabeth! It's going well. How are you?"

Madeline Miller had been Gabriel's secretary for as long as Elizabeth could remember. She was the general that guarded the gates to the boss. If Gabe wanted to hide, Patton himself couldn't break through to see him. Everyone in the FBI referred to her as Joan of Arc. No one got past her, and she'd throw herself on Gabe Rothschild if he was on fire to put him out.

"I'm getting fat, Maddy, but other than that it's the same old."

"How's that sexy husband of yours doing?" she inquired. "If you're tired of him, send him on back to Quantico. I miss having him in the office."

Elizabeth enjoyed the look on her husband's face. He was horrified. Something about him not knowing that women found him innately sexy was astounding. To this day she still didn't get it or understand how that was possible.

"I'll never get sick of him, so you'll have to look elsewhere, Maddy. Nice try though. I'm not doing this parent thing alone. He's staying chained to my side."

"I met his brother and he's just as hot."

Blackhawk didn't know what to think. He really was surprised at the conversation going on between the two women.

"Yeah, he certainly is. I think it's a genetic thing, Maddy." Elizabeth covered her mouth so she didn't laugh. The look her husband was giving her was hysterical.

"It must be!"

"Maddy, I need a favor, and I was hoping you could help a girl out." Elizabeth was going to cut him a break.

"What do you need?"

"Our new ME, Doctor Desdemona Adare, I need a deep search done on her and anything you pull sent to either me or Ethan. I don't want the Doctor aware we're searching for anything."

"Uh oh, you think you smell smoke?" she asked, scribbling the information on the notepad.

"I don't know, but I like to make sure all my bases are covered. I don't want anything jumping up and biting me or my husband on the ass."

"Yeah, that would be a shame to take a bite out of Ethan's ass," she said, then laughed.

Blackhawk's mouth dropped open.

Elizabeth almost burst out laughing. "Email anything you find that's sketchy. If you don't find anything, then just let me know."

"Will do, want me to pass it on to Gabe?"

"Not unless you find some skeletons that aren't supposed to be there. Like I said, I'm just going on instinct and curiosity."

"Okay, Elizabeth. I'll handle it. Give your truly excellent husband a kiss for me," she said, hopefully.

"I will, Maddy. Thank you," she answered, and clicked off the phone, then started laughing.

"I'm just mortified."

Elizabeth laughed more. "Ethan, you're a sexy man, why are you so shocked that women think you're hot?"

The heat was creeping up his neck, and he didn't have an answer for that. Maybe it was his past and the way he always felt about his heritage. Until Elizabeth he wasn't comfortable with the man he truly was inside and out.

"I don't think I can ever look at that woman again, and not think about this conversation."

Elizabeth dropped her sunglasses on her nose and took her husband's hand in her own. "I wouldn't worry about it, Ethan."

"Why's that?" he asked curiously.

"Joan of Arc will have a bigger fire to put out if she even thinks about taking a bite out of my husband's ass. I will give rabid a whole new definition."

Ethan Blackhawk believed that to be absolute truth.

Monday afternoon
Red River

Callen Whitefox pulled up in front of a building and read the sign. The GPS had been right, they were indeed in the right place. This was the Sheriff's office.

The rest of the drive had been very quiet. Desdemona would talk to him when he asked her a direct question, but she suddenly wasn't very talkative, and he wasn't quite sure why. The minute the call had ended, she dropped his hand fairly quickly. Granted, he shouldn't expect her to sit there and hold his hand, they'd just met. Desdemona was purposely avoiding contact.

Part of him wanted to learn more about Desdemona Adare, and part of him wanted to say 'screw it' and jump into the deep end of the pool, just because she was his shot at a normal life off the Rez. There was a little piece of him warning him that he needed to think it out and be cautious, and he pushed it down, shutting his out the gut instinct. What he wanted most in life was the life his brother had built, and that meant finding and outsider, much like their Elizabeth.

Now, if he could only get her to open up and stop being super skittish around him. That was going to be the challenge. That and keeping her from being scared to death of a woman that was really super gentle and sweet once you got to know her.

Desdemona was having a wicked hot flash, and it all had to do with the man sitting next to her. The last thirty minutes of the ride, she wasn't able to even think let alone talk to him. It may have come across as her being cold, but when she was completely flustered like this, she said stupid things. And people then tried to get as far away from her as possible. Desdemona didn't think she wanted this man to run, she genuinely liked him. From his warm gentle smile, to the caring brown eyes, everything about him felt safe and comfortable. Then there was the fact that he was completely and totally gorgeous. The scientist in her wanted to run her fingers down the sharp angular planes of his face and cheek, and then the woman in her wanted to see if those lines ran everywhere. Yeah, he was very distracting.

"Are you okay?" asked Callen. "You didn't say much the last few miles," he stated, the look of worry on his face.

"I'm fine, Callen," she said, giving him a smile. Just the fact he even cared made her heart a little more mushy over the man. Rarely, in her past had any of the men she dated or slept with ever thought to ask how she felt. There was something special about him. "Are you okay?" she asked back.

"Yeah, I'm ready to head in and start this, but we need to have some ground rules," he said, grinning at her.

"I'm pretty good with rules, so I guess we can have a few." Desdemona smiled at him and knew he was trying to cheer her up and keep her safe. It just seemed like the kind of man he was inside. Caring and very protective- both she never had before in her life with another man.

"Okay, since we're here to scope out the scene and get the assessment, we need to observe more than interact."

"Okay, and that means?"

"That means, we don't know if one of the people in that building is the killer. Until Ethan and Elizabeth get here, we watch everyone, and we try and keep under the radar. That means we tell the sheriff nothing we know or notice until the Calvary arrives."

"I'm not sure if the tech vans are heading right to the scene to secure it and get any unauthorized personnel away from the bodies or meeting us here," she added, checking her phone for any emails from Christina. The lab tech in charge, Christina Hart, was her left hand girl. The woman was head of the tech team and from what she'd seen and heard, Ethan Blackhawk's go to girl. The woman was very good at her job, and she knew the scene would be managed and secured as soon as she rolled in to the area.

"You don't leave my side." He tried to not sound bossy, but when his brother warned him, it meant something. Ethan Blackhawk didn't just throw out warnings for no apparent reason.

Desdemona laughed. "Oh, you're serious."

"I'm very serious."

"Okay, Callen. I promise I'll stick close."

He was satisfied. "Then, get out your badge and get ready Doctor Adare. We need to head on in and meet the players."

Part of her wanted to take his hand again, not because she was afraid of death, but because the living were the ones most likely to hurt you when you least expected it.

Sheila Court sat at her desk and looked up when the two strangers walked through the door of the office. One was a large Indian man and the other looked like some woman playing dress up. The skull jacket made her look like she was ready for Halloween. Then take in the red and black hair, and it was just something that wouldn't fly in Red River. These strangers were going to be trouble. She'd bet her next paycheck on it.

Whitefox dropped his sunglasses onto the top of his head and scanned the room. The interior was fairly empty. There was a deputy working behind his desk, and a secretary who watched them like a cat after a bird for dinner. It was apparent that she was the guard at the sheriff's door, and already wasn't pleased by what she was seeing.

Yeah, Red River was a small town.

"Excuse me, can I help you?" snapped the woman. "You're not from around here."

Oh good. There was going to be hostility right off the bat. Most local authorities had issues when the FBI rolled into their town, and it appeared that this woman was about as angry as they came. It wasn't boding well for what the sheriff was going to be like, and he braced for the hostility.

Whitefox pulled back his jacket and flashed his badge and gun. "I'm Special Agent Callen Whitefox, and this is our ME, Doctor Desdemona Adare. I believe the Sheriff is expecting us."

The woman stared at them, and then stared at Desdemona. "She's a doctor?"

It was like she wasn't even in the room.

"I'm the Medical Examiner Officuim."

"What?" she snapped her gum. "Officuim? Is that some weird language?" she asked. These two were quite the pair. In fact, this had to be a joke. There is no way that the girl was the ME. They were old men, and she looked barely able to drink.

"It means on duty," she answered, simply.

"In what crazy language? Is that some Indian term?

Callen bristled; the woman was rude, angry and going to get her ass kicked when Elizabeth walked into the office. Then again, the way the woman was staring at Desdemona, he wouldn't mind seeing Elizabeth beat some manners into her.

"It's not a tribal dialect to the indigenous people found in the United States," she added. It bothered her that the woman threw out the word 'Indian' like it was a bad thing. Desdemona was accustomed to the negativity. Her own grand'mere disliked Native people, a great deal and she'd heard it her whole life.

"Yeah, well whatever," she shrugged.

Whitefox looked down at his partner and the silent message was passed as they both rolled their eyes.

On top of it all, Red River was going to be a giant bigoted mess.

~ Chapter Four ~

The man in the doorway watched the entire interaction. He hoped to beat Sheila to the FBI agents, but he'd been tied up with the mayor on the phone. Now he was forced to watch his administrative assistant ostracize and pretty much disrespect the people that were going to help him keep his town safe.

Well Shit. Now he needed to fix this mess on top of the one they turned up at the Boy Scout camp.

Callen was a pretty patient man, and very laid back, but there was one thing that he couldn't tolerate. It was blatant bigotry. This woman was going to push him right over the edge. "Can we please talk to the sheriff? If it's not too much of a bother for you?"

She shrugged and jerked her thumb at the man standing in the doorway.

"I'm the Sheriff," said the man, walking towards them. "Sheriff James Duffy, and please forgive my administrative assistant." He struggled for a lie. "She's just frazzled by the deaths and not herself today," he covered for her. He didn't know why he did it; maybe it was because he didn't like the peace to be unbalanced or maybe he just was a complete idiot.

"Hello Sheriff Duffy. As I was telling your Administrative assistant, I'm Special Agent Callen Whitefox and this is our ME, Doctor Desdemona Adare."

"Welcome, please come into my office. Can I offer you both some coffee?" he asked, hoping he could smooth the ruffled feathers. He led them into the room, closing the door.

"No thank you," answered Desdemona. "I had some on the ride up here.

"I'm good too, Sheriff Duffy."

Whitefox pulled out the chair and waited for Desdemona to sit. Then he placed his chair directly beside her and relatively close. He was pissed the administrative assistant had insulted her, and he really wanted to tell her to go to hell, but that was probably a bad idea. Especially since he was supposed to be the Liaison to the Native American community, and he couldn't keep his cool around the outsiders. Right now he'd bide his time and let

Elizabeth chew up the woman. That would be vastly more entertaining for everyone involved.

Sheriff Duffy sat, and contemplated the two visitors in his office. "I have to say, I expected more people. I don't see how you both are going to handle all of this once word gets out, and it explodes."

"We're just the initial team, Sheriff. The two lead investigators are on their way, and should be in town within the hour. I'm here to meet with you, and get your take on the situation. Doctor Adare is here to start the preliminaries. Mostly my function is to give her back up and keep her as safe as possible on scene."

"I completely understand, Agent. I meant no disrespect," he smiled at the woman. "I'm sorry Doctor Adare, you must get this a lot, but you look so young. Are you one of those geniuses that the FBI scooped up to work for them?"

Desdemona smiled at him. The man was trying to be friendly and the fact that he was being honest was a bonus. She preferred to have people ask a direct question instead of assume and talk about her behind her back.

"Well, Sheriff Duffy, I can promise you that I'm relatively smart, but sadly I'm considerably older than I look. It's just good genes. What I gained in appearance I sacrificed in height."

"Great things come in small packages, Doctor," he said smiling. The doctor had a sense of humor and was a pretty hot. This might not be too bad of a day after all.

Whitefox didn't like the man flirting with Desdemona. It rubbed him the wrong way and made him want to grind his teeth. He took a deep breath. "Can we discuss a few things related to why we're here?" Whitefox hoped it didn't come out the wrong way, or sound like he was angry. Although he was bordering on it at that exact moment

Desdemona heard the ice in his voice, gone was the sweet and gentle, and it startled her. When she looked over at him, he gently stroked her wrist with his fingertips, reassuringly that everything was perfectly fine between them.

"Sure thing, Special Agent." James Duffy kept a smile in place, and he didn't miss the displeasure on the man's face. It was a less than subtle hint that the doctor was off limits. Good thing he ignored subtle as much as possible when it came to the opposite sex.

"Doctor Adare is going to need a place to perform the autopsies. Is there a location that you frequently use? Or that your town ME uses?"

Sheriff Duffy laughed. "We don't have a town ME; we don't even have a hospital. Nearest one is in the next town over. I do have a suggestion for a location though. When this building was built, there were plans for a cafeteria in the lower level. There is a cooler unit there that has shelving that can house the bodies."

"What about a prep area where my team and I can examine the victims?" she asked. The cooler would be fine, as long as it could keep the bodies at thirty nine degrees Fahrenheit.

"There's a prep area and sinks. I believe the cooler has a thermostat that's adjustable too."

"I won't need the sinks; we can't let the biological leak into the ground. My team knows the proper procedures and we'll handle it. There won't be any need for concern, I assure you."

Whitefox wasn't sure if he liked the idea that Desdemona would be in the sheriff's department. Yeah, she'd be safe there, since there were lots of people, but the sheriff kept watching her like she was a big meaty steak he wanted to consume. "Thank you, Sheriff for being so helpful." Man that was painful to get that out with a smile on his face.

"What can you tell us about the location of the bodies, Sheriff," asked Desdemona. "How many people have come in contact with them?"

Duffy thought about it and leaned back in his chair. "I found them with my Deputy Julian Littlemoon. Other than that, we've keep the door closed with the exception to take the pictures for the guy at Quantico. He was really insistent."

"That's good, because less contamination means my job is going to be easier," she answered and smiled.

"Miss Adare, I aim to please." Duffy tipped his hat at the doctor. "I assume it's Miss," he added, he looked over at Callen Whitefox.

Desdemona could smell the testosterone rising, and she didn't like where it was heading. The Sheriff was baiting her partner, and that angered her. Callen Whitefox had been nothing but kind to her, giving her support and the most important thing; friendship.

"If you're asking if I'm married, I'm not Sheriff Duffy, but you knew that from me not wearing a wedding ring," she smiled sweetly. "If you're asking if I'm in a committed relationship," she added, tipping her head to the side before continuing, "that's a very personal issue, and I don't plan on bringing my personal life to work with me. So if you don't mind, let's go with Doctor Adare. It took many years to earn the title. Miss is too generic for me, and believe me when I say I earned every letter after my name and before it too."

Duffy grinned his good ole boy smile. He loved a woman that had spunk. Yeah, he'd investigate the woman later when the man wasn't around.

Whitefox was having a hard time with the man blatantly flirting with Desdemona, and then she must have noticed. This time her fingers stroked his wrist in reassurance, as she told the sheriff in her own way to back off.

Both their phones began beeping.

"Blackhawks?" asked Desdemona looking down at her own phone.

"Yeah, they're twenty minutes out. It looks like we need to get up to that crime scene Sheriff," he said, standing and offering the doctor his hand. At first he wasn't sure if she'd take it, but she smiled up at him and accepted his gesture willingly. When she gave his fingers a squeeze, he felt even calmer.

"Thank you, Callen," she said, smiling warmly at him.

These feelings of intense jealousy were surprising. When his brother had brought home Elizabeth, he felt jealousy, wanting the life his brother found with the outsider woman. But these feelings were more emotions he couldn't understand. Desdemona wasn't his to be possessive about, and yet it was still there. This was something he needed to figure out and soon. Forcing himself to focus on Elizabeth, he felt the warm curl of heat rise through his body. Next, he thought about the woman sitting beside him and he was filled with the intense need to take care of her. Everything in him knew that this woman needed someone to stand up for her, and he was that man. Why? As of that moment, he had no clue.

"I'll have my deputy bring you up, and I'll be up there shortly. I just want to make sure I have the basement room ready for the doctor and her team," he said, smiling at the woman. She looked like a kid, but when she spoke you could tell she was definitely a woman. The outrageous doctor intrigued him a great deal. From the wild hair, to the skulls on her coat, she screamed mystery.

"Thank you, Sheriff." Callen Whitefox nodded at the man as he led the Doctor out into the reception area. Safely tucked in his bigger hand was her delicate one, and he didn't want to let go. It took everything in him to drop her hand and be professional, but once she was free of his touch he moved his body closer to hers in a very protective stance.

"Julian, can you take the Agent and Doctor up to the crime scene and relieve Bobby lee?" James Duffy didn't want the hostile deputy anywhere near them. That just screamed bad idea. Bobby Lee was a loose cannon, and more offensive than even Sheila could be on her worst day.

"Sure thing, boss," answered the man, as he stood from his desk.

"I'll be up as soon as I can get the downstairs ready for the doctor." He went back into his office and called the maintenance crew. He was going to need them to get over there fast and make sure that everything he just promised the doctor was taken care of, or they were going to have to put the bodies out back in the snow bank. That really screamed hick town sheriff's department.

Whitefox escorted the doctor out into the cold air and observed the man beside them. He looked like he wanted to say something, but didn't know if he should or not. "Deputy, is there something you want to say to us now that we're alone?" he asked.

"Yes," he said, looking over his shoulder. "The Sheriff, he's a good man. Jimmy is fair and runs this town the best he can, but you're going to have problems here."

He helped Desdemona into the Denali to get her out of the wind. "What kind of problems, Julian?" He was pretty sure that he knew where this conversation was headed.

Julian Littlemoon measured the woman with them, and gauged if she could be trusted, after all she was Caucasian.

"I assure you that my partner doesn't have issues with Natives. Do you Desi?" he asked her softly.

"I've nothing but respect for the Native people that were here before the Europeans. I don't believe in Manifest Destiny gentlemen," she said, honestly.

Julian Littlemoon and Callen Whitefox both looked over at the term. Manifest Destiny was the belief that the Europeans had the right to steal the land Natives inhabited because 'God' wanted it to happen. It was a touchy subject between the native people and white man for many years.

Julian Littlemoon smiled at the woman. He liked people that spoke their minds and didn't pretend.

"Again, what kind of problems, Julian?" asked Whitefox.

"The problems that turn up with the white man," he nodded at the doctor. "No disrespect ma'am."

Desdemona smiled at him. "None was taken, Deputy."

"Who should I expect issues with?" he inquired.

Julian Littlemoon looked over his shoulder. "The deputy at the crime scene doesn't like anyone that's not like him, and he's pretty vocal about it."

"Anybody else?"

The deputy laughed. "How about I tell you who you won't have a problem with in town? Me and James Duffy."

Callen Whitefox could move Sheriff James Duffy back into the category of trouble, but he kept it to himself.

"Just watch your back, and your partner's," he said, and then walked over to his vehicle.

"Thanks for the heads up," Whitefox yelled after him.

"Tech team's here," said Desdemona pointing and drawing his attention off the deputy.

Whitefox ran over to the first one, and Christina rolled down the window. "Follow us up to the scene, we're heading there now to begin retrieval. The Blackhawk's are in route and twenty minutes out." He almost called them by their names, but in the field they preferred titles, and he knew how Christina had the boss lust for his brother. Why provoke his sister-in-law while she was pregnant.

"Sure thing, Agent Whitefox," she smiled brightly. "We're ready."

Whitefox hopped back up into the Denali and brushed the snowflakes from his jacket. "Snow's picking up, when we get up there, stick close, okay? Don't wander away from me up in the woods. It's wild animal season and something other than the Sheriff might decide to try and have you for a snack."

Desdemona stared at him with her mouth open. She wasn't sure which horrified her more. The comments regarding the sheriff or the wild animals.

"It was hard not to notice," he said, wishing he never brought it up.

"I was well aware of the sheriffs' innuendos and for the record Callen; he's not really my type. I don't go for 'good ole boys'," she added.

Whitefox was going to ask her what her type was, but decided against it. For his first day on the job he'd been kissed, held his partner's hand, almost punched out the Sheriff and was warned by the only Native in town to watch his back. Luck wasn't on his side today, and self-preservation of his ego kicked in, and he decided to let it go.

Somethings were left best unsaid even if the curiosity was going to drive him crazy for the rest of the day.

Elizabeth and Ethan Blackhawk pulled up to the crime scene and watched the tech team mill about like ants on a mission. There was one thing that was a constant on assignments. They had amassed the best group of techs that could be found in the country. After the assignment on the reservation that reunited Ethan and his brother, the bosses decided to promote Christina to head of the unit. She'd earned it with her constant dedication and her willingness to go above and beyond to get the job done.

Elizabeth knew why the woman gave it five hundred percent. It was because the tech had crazy, mad lust for her husband, but if it got the job done and kept them solving the assignments, she'd look the other way. That was until it crossed the line and became a problem with the dynamics of the team. For now, Christina was still scared shitless of her, and she wasn't afraid to use that to her advantage. Especially since now she was getting big and wobbly.

"Looks like they've gotten a good jump on it," commented Blackhawk. He noticed his team was setting up night lights. Which meant Doctor Adare felt it was going to take a while to remove the bodies. Blackhawk scanned the area and didn't like what he saw. It was an abandoned camp, surrounded by nothing but thick, dense trees with one road in and no other way out.

Elizabeth noticed the lines of tension around his mouth.

"Baby, maybe you should head to the house and make sure that Gabe isn't screwing with us," he said, trying to sound nonchalant. His pregnant wife out in the open and snow didn't set well with him, and if there was a higher power, he'd be able to convince her to listen for once.

Elizabeth grinned at him, and knew he was worried about her. It was just how it was going to be, and especially since their last time out in the field. Ethan was going to hover and there wasn't anything she could do about it. Instead of the constant fight, she tended to chill out and cater to his panic and fear neurosis. "Okay, baby," she said smiling.

"Really?" Did his wife just agree with him? It had to be the beginning of the apocalypse for that to happen. He looked out the window at the sky.

"What are you looking for?" she asked, almost afraid to hear the answer.

"I'm waiting for the horsemen of the apocalypse. Are you really going to obey me for a change?"

Elizabeth opened the Denali door laughing. "Keep looking for them," she said grinning, and then she hopped out. "And to answer you, no I'm going to blatantly ignore any directive you give me in an attempt to assure the end of the world doesn't happen on my watch."

"Damn it," he muttered, chasing after her. She may be pregnant, but she still moved pretty fast, and he planned on standing incredibly close to keep an eye on her.

The man approaching her had to be the sheriff. The coat and hat with the silver star on it, kind of gave it away. She could tell that he was assessing them, and probably even checking her out. Boy was he going to be in for a surprise when she took off the big bulky coat. If anything it was laughable, but as a pregnant woman, she'd enjoy it while she could. Soon she'd be as big as a bus and no one would find her sexy, well maybe one person might. Elizabeth could feel her husband slide up behind her protectively, resting his hand on her lower back.

"You must be Special Agent Blackhawk," he said, holding out his hand and grinning. Whew wee, the woman was a looker. As he took in her tall body, he couldn't help but appreciate the big beautiful eyes, and the mass of chaotic hair peeking out from the hood of the parka. She was going to make this even more interesting. Where the doctor was interesting to look at, this agent was sexy and going to be fun to work around.

"That would be me," she answered, holding out her hand. "It's actually Director Special Agent, and you get not one, but two with the same name." She looked over her shoulder at her husband. The thing about Ethan Blackhawk was he was the observer out of the two. Since it was his job to profile the killer, he watched everyone with a healthy dose of skepticism. Now he was measuring up the man before them, and the blank look on his face and sunglasses still blocking his eyes meant one thing. Ethan Blackhawk wasn't happy. Gone was basic courtesy.

"Two?" he looked confused. "I think I missed something," and he had. "When I spoke to Gabriel Rothschild in Quantico, he mentioned a Director Blackhawk, a Special Agent Whitefox and the ME."

Elizabeth laughed. "I'm sorry, maybe you misheard Gabe, but out of FBI West, we happen to have two Directors, and both just happen to be Blackhawks." She pointed at both herself and her husband. "We're co-directors, and we're married," she said filling him in, and she was sure she saw disappointment. "This is my husband Director Special Agent Ethan Blackhawk."

Blackhawk stepped forward, and shook his hand. It wasn't lost on him that the man looked like he wanted to swoop in and steal his wife away. The proprietary part of him wanted to knock his ass into the snow bank and beat the hell out of him, but the civilized part had adjusted to the entire situation. His wife was beautiful, and she garnered attention. It was fact and he'd come to live with it, but it didn't mean he couldn't secretly fanaticize about killing the man.

"Nice to meet you, Director Blackhawk," nodded the sheriff. Well shit, the woman would still be nice to look at, even if he couldn't cozy up to her. "I'm glad you both arrived safely," he said, pulling an envelope out of his pocket. "Here's the key and address to the house that Gabriel contracted for you and your team."

Ethan Blackhawk took the envelope and tucked it into his pocket. "Thank you, Sheriff." He pulled back on his gloves. It was ridiculously cold outside and the snow was starting to fall again. "What can you tell me about the site," he asked, pointing at the buildings.

"It used to be an old boy scout camp, and then they stopped coming up here when one of the kids fell prey to a mountain lion. No one really comes up this far into the woods unless they're hunting or trying to get lost. Beyond the camp is nothing but old Indian hunting grounds and no one goes there but," he paused hoping he wasn't offending the FBI agent staring at him. "Indians."

"Native Americans," corrected Elizabeth. She may refer to her family as Indians, but anyone else should be politically correct, especially if they were considered outsiders.

"I beg your pardon," he said, nodding at the man.

She let it go. "Yeah, it was pretty treacherous getting up here," added Elizabeth. "Ethan, I'm going to go light a fire under the tech team. I want the scene cleared in two hours, before it gets dark and any mountain lions decide to come out for a night time snack." She whistled loudly, and as if trained the entire team stopped and looked towards the sound.

"Two hours team and it starts, now!"

They all started moving faster, knowing that if they were rushing a scene, there was a good reason.

"That's skill," the sheriff said, laughing. "Think she can teach my deputies to listen when I whistle?"

Ethan Blackhawk spoke, "That's not training. That's pure unadulterated fear. If they don't have the scene cleared in two hours, she then will start handing them their asses and they know it." Blackhawk kept his voice neutral. Already he didn't particularly like the man they were assigned to help. In his world first impressions were often accurate.

"Hey, whatever works," he said laughing, as he stood by the Director. He was glad calling him Indian didn't offend him. Now he was beginning to wonder if Julian Littlemoon had been offended all the times he'd made that error, or if the female FBI agent was just riding him.

Somehow he suspected the later.

Elizabeth found Callen and Desdemona in the building that had the bodies. She couldn't help but notice the look on Whitefox's face as he watched over the woman inspecting the bodies. Yeah, she'd seen that look before on Ethan's face when he looked at her. Her brother-in-law was developing a thing for the ME.

Elizabeth pondered that.

It wasn't like she disliked the woman, but she didn't really know her well enough, and when it came to Ethan and Callen, she'd promised their grandfather that she'd take care of them both. That meant that she now needed to learn everything humanly possible about Desdemona. Something deep down made her wary, but she brushed it off as hormones and nothing more.

Timothy Blackhawk wasn't going to be fond of the idea that his other grandson was chasing a non-Native woman. Since Ethan Blackhawk was only half Native, he'd given up trying to keep the bloodline pure. When he first met her, there was that moment of tension until she won him over. But Callen was pure Native blood, and Timothy wasn't going to like this at all. Her heart broke for her brother-in-law, and she knew she was going to have to intervene and help him out. She'd face down the elder patriarch, so Callen could catch a break.

Yeah, he was watching her the same way. Oh boy, things were going to get interesting.

"Callen, everything okay," she asked, grabbing his attention.

Immediately, he heard the voice and relaxed. His brother and Elizabeth were here, and he could just focus on the doctor and keeping her safe. "Lyzee," he approached to her, hugging her. "I'm so glad you both arrived safe," he said, leaving a kiss on her lips.

"Your brother was driving, so it took us longer."

Desdemona glanced over at the Director and Callen and the easy nature of their relationship, and she was envious. How she wished she could walk into a room, especially one with corpses and command someone's attention like that. Really, there were dead bodies all around them, the room smelled like death, and still Elizabeth Blackhawk had his full attention and the intimacy of a lip kiss. That was skill. Then there was the jealousy of the closeness between them, and it was something she didn't understand. Not often in her life did she feel jealousy, but now it seemed to be there eating away at her.

"Director," she said, nodding.

Elizabeth nodded. "What do we have, Doctor?"

"Well, I can tell you what we don't have," she said. "We don't have time of death, since the bodies are frozen solid. We don't have any identification on any of them," she continued, "and we have no chance of autopsy until tomorrow when they thaw out."

"Great, and here I thought it was going to be hopeless," she said, grinning.

"Bodies are all stiff, but I can't tell if it's because they're popsicles or if it's because they are in the rigor mortis stage. I need a good eight hours in the chiller to defrost them." Desdemona leaned down and tried to move an eyelid. "Even their eyeballs are frozen," she said, sliding the skin over the solid orb.

Elizabeth turned into Callen's body and his arms came around her automatically. She could handle anything about a corpse but the dead eyes. They really freaked her out, and had since the day she lost her partner in the field and watched him die, his eyes never leaving her face.

"Drop the lid, Desi," Whitefox said, softly. He knew it made Elizabeth squeamish. "It's okay, Lyzee. I have you."

Desdemona did what he asked, and looked over at her boss. Was it possible that the woman with brass balls that scared the tech team was afraid of corpse eyes? That amused her, and she tucked it away for future reference.

Whitefox whispered in her ear and she turned, squeezing his gloved hand tightly. Callen kept her against the front of his body protectively. Deep down he hoped Doctor Adare didn't make a production out of it. Not many people caught Elizabeth at her weakest moments, and he didn't want her big fear made into a joke at her expense.

"Sorry, Doctor. What do we know, since we seem to have a great deal of unknown?" She changed the subject fast. It didn't sit well with her that the doctor had just seen her cower in horror. She had a reputation to uphold with her tech team, and if word got out, her credibility was shot. Leaning against Callen, she felt icky feelings drift away, as he hugged her against him protectively.

"We know that the killer is only taking one piece of each person. There are no other visible external wounds."

Elizabeth moved over towards the victim with the stained shirt. "This is victim three right?"

"Yes, and I can't tell you what he's missing. When I pulled back the shirt, there's an incision of some sort, but its frozen solid. If I go digging around before he's thawed, I may lose evidence and risk us being able to figure out the weapon or knife used."

Elizabeth nodded. "Do we have a place to thaw the corpse-cicles?"

Whitefox answered. "The Sheriff offered us a room in the basement that has a cooler. We've yet to see it, but he guarantees it's adequate."

"It'll have to suffice. We'll dump them there overnight and go from there," added Elizabeth.

Blackhawk wandered into the building. "Wow, and here I was hoping to eat again one day soon. I guess that's just not going to happen."

Elizabeth snorted. "Two hours and you'll be eating something. Who are you kidding?"

Blackhawk laughed. "Yeah, probably." Turning he put his focus on Doctor Adare. "Nightfall is coming soon, Doc. How long will it take for us to pack this up and get away from this abandoned feeding ground for mountain lions?"

Desdemona stared at her boss with big eyes. "What? Mountain lions? Where?" Granted Whitefox mentioned wild animals, but she thought he was just being sarcastic because of the sheriff.

"Oh yeah the sheriff just mentioned it, so the less time here after dark the better off we are." He shook his head and patted his brother on the back. The man was staring at the doctor, and he knew that look. It was the one that spelled out trouble. Woman trouble, specifically and since he'd recently been there himself, he knew what was coming.

"Give me an hour to get the trace contained and then we'll be ready for transport back to the sheriff's station."

Blackhawk was good with that and nodded. "Callen, can we talk?" he jerked his finger outside.

He didn't want to leave either of the women alone.

"We'll be okay, Callen," said Desdemona, smiling brightly at him.

He followed his brother out and glanced over his shoulder at the two women. When his eyes met Elizabeth's, she nodded and he knew they'd be fine for a little while without them. "What's up, Ethan?"

"What's your initial assessment on the sheriff?" He didn't want to be biased, and he was since the man had hit on his wife, right out the gate.

He almost told him how he didn't like him because he was leering at Desdemona, but then he decided that probably wasn't the kind of assessment he wanted. "I think he's pretty laid back, and he's genuinely trying to be accommodating. His staff, that's another story."

"What happened?" he asked.

"In the first five minutes the secretary was abrasive and insulting, and then the native Deputy, Julian Littlemoon gave me a heads up about the other Deputy, Bobby Lee Tills. Apparently, he isn't fond of anyone not of his ethnic origin-specifically we 'Indians'."

"Well, I'm not surprised. We tend to run into a great deal of bias. Elizabeth had to correct the sheriff when he dropped the Indian word."

"That's funny," he said, snickering. "Did she use it in the very next sentence to taunt him?"

Now Ethan was laughing. "No but I'm sure it's in her game plan shortly. It isn't like her to not do it at some point. She actually sounded insulted."

"Nice. Deputy Littlemoon alluded that the town would be similar," he added, and looked back over his shoulder at the doorway. "So I'm sure Elizabeth will get plenty of opportunity to practice her PC skills."

"Or crack together a few skulls in the process." He waited for a reply, but Whitefox was staring at the doorway again. It wasn't lost on Blackhawk that his brother was in protection mode. He knew he was super protective of Elizabeth, since she was abducted, but he suspected this went further than just that alone. Maybe it was all about his wife. She was just leaning against his brother, and that meant something had to have happened. Elizabeth didn't get cozy at crime scenes.

"Ethan, I think we need to watch our backs," he said, shifting his focus back to his brother.

"That sounds like a good plan to me." If anything, he wanted his wife, brother and unborn child safe. "Here comes the Sheriff," he said, under his breath.

Both men stopped talking shop as the man strolled on over to them.

"How's it going, gentlemen?" he asked, stopping just short of the building holding the bodies.

"We'll be packed up and out of the elements in the hour," answered Blackhawk.

He nodded. "Works for me, I don't like freezing my nuts off out here."

"Sheriff Duffy, we may need an office space in your building. You know, to work out of while Doctor Adare is working on the autopsies tomorrow." Whitefox wasn't leaving her alone in that building.

Blackhawk lifted a brow, and analyzed his brother's request. They planned on working out of the private home as much as possible. It was just a safer option. He wasn't sure why he was asking for space.

"On top of the space for the ME?" he tried to figure out where to place them.

"Yes, I'll be working there when the doctor is conducting the autopsies." He met his brother's eyes, and the message was passed. Desdemona was not staying there alone.

"Anything you can provide would be appreciated, Sheriff," added Blackhawk, covering for his brother's request.

102

The man nodded. "Let me figure it out, and let you know tomorrow."

"Thank you," Callen said, walking back to where they left the women. Hell would have to freeze over first for him to leave Desdemona anywhere near Sheriff Duffy. That was like leaving the lamb to the wolves.

As far as he was concerned, it wasn't nearly cold enough outside.

Elizabeth watched as the last body had been zipped into the body bag, and she surveyed the scene. The tech team was collecting samples and stripping the entire place of any trace evidence. When she saw Christina, she motioned her over to her.

"Christina, here's the name of the place you're staying." Elizabeth handed her the GPS coordinates and an envelope. "There's only one hotel in town, so make the best of it, and try and be positive." That made her laugh. Christina Hart was always positive, bubbly and optimistic.

"Yes ma'am," she answered, smiling. "You all have an entire floor, and I'm putting you in charge of the situation. Same old rules apply. Keep it to a minimum, make no disruptions in the lives of the locals and don't do anything that will embarrass the FBI," she paused. "Or I will come over there and drop kick some techs off a cliff. Am I clear?"

Christina knew she wasn't kidding. "Clear as crystal, Director Blackhawk."

"Oh and Christina?"

"Yeah boss?"

"Good job on clearing the scene as quickly as you did. I appreciate not having to fill out paperwork on techs that were eaten by mountain lions," Elizabeth grinned and offered her a fist bump.

Christina laughed and took the fist bump willingly. Elizabeth didn't hand them out to just anyone. Usually it was something she reserved for her inner circle or closest friends. Getting one was paramount to getting a shiny star. The other option was an ass chewing, and they never ended well.

"Dismissed." When the woman saluted she nearly snickered, until she saw the ME watching her with the eerie cat eyes. "Get out of here," she said, nodding towards the tech vans.

"Thanks Elizabeth," she said, trotting off to the warmth of the van.

"Doctor Adare, you ready to roll and get out of the elements?"

"Yes, Director. I can keep an eye on the tech team at the hotel if you want," she offered. Yeah, Elizabeth Blackhawk was scary, and she couldn't wait until she was far enough away from her and could relax. The entire time she stood over her, she felt like she was going to fracture from the tension in her body. The woman made her incredibly nervous and envious at the same time.

"Not going to be possible. You're bunking across town." She pulled out her phone and messaged her husband that they were about ready to head out.

"I am?" She felt a little panicky. Staying alone in a strange town while the stalker could have followed her didn't sound like something that appealed to her common sense. Maybe she could find a tech to swap with and bunk where the team was going to be.

Whitefox strolled back in, and was relieved to see that they women were just fine. In fact he was happy to see that they were talking and getting to know each other.

"You're staying with us," she stated simply. The look of horror on the woman's face would have been funny if it didn't perplex her as to why it was there. "Is that going to be a problem?" she asked, watching the woman and still not getting it.

Whitefox heard the conversation and went to Desdemona's side and placed himself between the women. His hand automatically went to her lower back, offering her reassurance. He rubbed soothingly, all while watching Elizabeth.

"No, Director Blackhawk. I don't believe it's a problem at all." Except that she now wanted to vomit and just might still do it. Even with Whitefox rubbing his hand up and down her back, she still felt like the prey being stalked by the predator.

Elizabeth was about to continue the conversation, and ask the woman what the problem was with her. Had she offended her in some way, but the look on Callen's face told her to back off. The glare he was giving her said one thing. Desdemona Adare was off limits to any of Elizabeth's anger or questions. Her heart skipped in her chest at the hurt that slammed into her. This was the first time since meeting the man that he'd chosen sides, and it wasn't with her. Usually he was very protective of her, standing up to Ethan when there was a conflict.

Elizabeth took a deep steadying breath and let it out, keeping all the words she wanted to say locked deep within her. Her eyes never left his face, and she hid none of the emotion she was feeling. "Special Agent Whitefox, Doctor Adare, see you at the house," she spoke softly, as she turned on her heel. If she didn't move away from them right then, Elizabeth would say something sarcastic and over the top. Obviously Whitefox had decided that the woman he'd known for one day took priority over the woman he'd known for months and was part of the family.

Ouch.

Elizabeth walked past her husband and didn't say a word to him. At that point she couldn't or her temper was going to erupt from her. Patience wasn't exactly her forte to begin with, but the ME and her mystery issue with her was getting on her last damn nerve and now sucked in someone she loved.

"Elizabeth?" he asked, as she barreled past him. When she dismissed him with just a wave of her hand and a shake of her head, he didn't know what to think. Being the brave soul he was, he followed his wife to find out what had her all stirred up.

Desdemona turned and faced him. "I think I made her furious," she said softly. "No, I don't think it. I know it."

The worry deep in her eyes affected him. "It'll all work out," he said, brushing a hair from her cheek and letting his hand linger. It occurred to him that he was in a really bad position. Stuck between a woman he loved and owned his heart, and a woman that pulled at the innate need to guard and protect. It was going to come to a head; there was no doubt about that. He only hoped he wasn't going to have to pick sides. Five hours ago there was no doubt in his mind who he'd side with, and now he just betrayed his heart for God only knew what.

He was right. Today was a shitty day.

Elizabeth sat in the Denali, her eyes closed and her mind in a blur. As she thought back to all the conversations that they had, her and Doctor Adare, none of them would make the women dislike her this much. None stood out. Yes, she was tough on the tech staff, and some of them avoided her, but when it came to Doctor Leonard and Doctor Magnus, they all had a good working relationship. They worked well together and she prided herself on that. Elizabeth was tough, but she took care of her team and protected them. Now she was faced with what the hell she ever did to the woman who was managing to turn her brother-in-law against her.

She never thought this would happen. Callen was her best friend, next her husband. She loved him, and now she'd just had that handed back to her for no damn good reason.

Maybe it was just unrealistic to believe that every one of her staff would have a good working relationship with her. It was just driving her insane that she didn't understand why.

Then toss in the anger that Callen had immediately gone to her side and offered her protection, especially after all they'd been through as a family. Part of her felt betrayed, and maybe it was completely irrational, but family stuck together, didn't they? They were the Blackhawks and they were thick as thieves, and now suddenly... not so much.

Maybe it was just baby hormones.

Maybe coming back out in the field was a huge mistake.

Maybe it would be best if she avoided both the doctor and her family until she could sort this all out.

"Please let this be baby hormones," she whispered to herself. It hurt to think she needed to avoid him.

Elizabeth wiped the tear that slid down her face and tried to talk herself out of the funk that was surrounding her. If they were going to get through this, she needed to find her balance and work it out before it became too big of a distraction.

When she saw her husband coming towards the Denali, she pulled out her phone and began typing an email for Gabe to update him. The last thing she needed was for him to see her crying on an assignment. He'd pull her and himself off and have her committed to the nut farm. Yeah, that just didn't need to be happening. There was only so much she could brush off as baby hormones.

Blackhawk hopped up into the vehicle. "Hey, you okay?" he asked, concerned for his wife. Something was going on, and he wanted to figure out what it was and help her through it.

"Yeah, Cowboy," she said, smiling at him. Using the nickname he earned in the FBI for being cavalier and wild in the field made her heart lighten just a bit. It reminded her that it didn't matter what happened between her and the staff. Her husband would always have her back.

"You rushed off, are you feeling okay?"

"I'm great."

"Is the baby okay?"

Elizabeth leaned over and kissed him, gently on the lips. "Baby Blackhawk is perfectly fine too, really," she answered when she broke the light kiss.

No she definitely wasn't okay.

"We should go." Elizabeth fought to change the subject.

Now Ethan Blackhawk was on total alert. His wife was sitting in the Denali, hiding and now she kissed him on a crime scene? That was to distract him and sidetrack him from the issue at hand. What was bothering her so much she'd lie to him, and right to his face. In nine months, he couldn't remember one time when she ever lied to him, and that included the first day they'd met.

"Okay, are you updating Gabe?"

"Yeah, I figured I'd get out of the cold and warm up baby Blackhawk. I don't need him turning into a giant snowball," she smiled gently.

"That probably isn't a good idea."

"He's happier inside, now he's moving again," she added.

"Okay," he watched as the tech vans loaded up, and everyone started for their perspective vehicles. "You know that you can tell me anything, and I'll keep it between us." Ethan Blackhawk threw it out there, because he had a suspicion that it had something to do with his brother and the new ME.

Elizabeth looked over at him and punched him in the arm. "Ouch! What did I do?"

"That was for questioning that I tell you everything. I already do, Ethan." Her husband was a very smart man, and she knew he'd keep pushing until he figured it out, or she came out and told him. But right now, she just wasn't ready to deal with it. She was cold, tired, hurt, and hormonal. What she really needed now was to just get out of the winter gear, get warm and forget about the day.

"Okay Baby," he answered, watching her face. Her eyes gave her away, and he wasn't done with this yet.

"Thank you." Tomorrow would be a better day, it had to be, or at least Elizabeth could hope it would be.

While she finished her email to Gabriel Rothschild, her husband made the decision to just watch and wait. Eventually it would play itself out and his wife would let him know.

Blackhawk started the Denali and followed the directions on the GPS, he looked back in the rear view mirror and noticed his brother was helping Doctor Adare into their vehicle. The Sheriff was behind them.

Now it was time to get in out of the cold, and regroup until their next move tomorrow. He'd start working in his baseline profile, and focus on the assignment.

Even though all he was focusing on now was what was bothering his wife. There was this tiny nagging voice in the back of his head that was telling him that this was going to blow up and be a disaster.

A smart man would listen and avoid being put into the emotional crosshairs of what was coming.

Yeah it was a good thing he never claimed to be a smart man.

Whitefox started the Denali and glanced over at the woman beside him. She looked worn out, freaked out and completely out of sorts.

"Want to talk about it?" he asked, softly.

"I'm just off balance around her. That's all," she said it simply. It was the truth, Elizabeth made her a nervous wreck, and then toss in the nut job stalking her, and the man sitting beside her, everything was just making her a mess.

"Yeah, I can tell."

"I'll be okay; don't worry about it, Callen." Last thing she wanted was to drag him into her emotional mess. "You don't need to get involved," she said, softly.

Yeah, except he saw the look of betrayal on his Elizabeth's face, and he was already was neck deep. He just hurt the woman he loved, in an attempt to guard the one he felt like he needed to protect. What was bothering him now was not only how hurt Elizabeth looked walking away, but also why he just risked damaging his family for a complete stranger.

He must be out of his damn mind.

Now it was a little too late to not get involved. Callen just went all in on a very risky gamble.

~ Chapter Five ~
Monday Night

When Elizabeth and Ethan pulled up to the house the FBI had rented, they were actually surprised. Most times Agents out in the field had to stay in deplorable conditions due to budgetary constraints. But this time, Gabriel Rothschild had pleasantly surprised them. The house was actually very nice.

"This can't be it," said Blackhawk, laughing. "It has to be haunted or there are possessed demons residing here."

"Ethan!"

"Seriously baby. He's got to be screwing with us. The house looks normal, and you and I both know how sadistic Gabe Rothschild can be when he sends agents out."

Elizabeth laughed. "He isn't putting his pregnant family in a roach coach!" She knew he'd come through, especially since Elizabeth had no problem telling his wife what he did to her out in the field. Livy, his wife, was her best girlfriend in the entire world would ride his ass for a month if she got whiff that he put her in a roach coach. When she found out that he allowed her out in the field pregnant last time, he was in the doghouse. He knew better than to put her someplace shitty. All it would take is one call and the man would be sleeping on the couch for a week. They both knew it. Girlfriend code reigned in their world.

"Come on, let's check it out," Blackhawk said, smiling.

"Okay," she grabbed the keys to the place from the envelope the Sheriff gave her husband, and watched him carry in their suitcase. Once inside, there was even more pleasant surprises waiting. There was a fireplace, and the house was perfect. It wasn't as big as their home, but it was still big enough for the four of them to survive under the same roof.

Possibly, if Desdemona yanked the stick out of her ass and stopped making her insane.

Blackhawk carried the luggage upstairs, and picked the first room, no point exploring. A bedroom was a bedroom, and as long as he could bed down with his wife, he was happy anywhere. When he came downstairs, Elizabeth was making a fire in the fireplace. "Look at you with those crazy survival skills." He tried to make her laugh. "Who would have thought when an outsider gets impregnated by a Native they get tribal instinct by baby proxy."

Elizabeth couldn't help it, her husband cheered her up and she started laughing. "I wish. Your dad gave me a flint and taught me how the last time we were over his house." Wyler Blackhawk was hard core Native American, and at one time saved her life when a killer was hunting her in the woods. He wanted to make sure his daughter-in-law could survive out in the wild if she ever needed to again. "I was informed no daughter-in-law of his should be wandering around in the world without a way to make fire."

"Isn't that handy," he said laughing.

"I tried to explain that I married a caveman who could make fire if need be, but he wasn't buying that and insisted I needed to hone my Native American survival skills."

"More skill by proxy," he added grinning.

Elizabeth pointed at her baby bump. "I may not have a single ounce of Native blood in me, but your son does, and I'm not going to be one of those moms that doesn't practice what she preaches. Yes, a zippo would be easier, but it's not the way of the ancestors."

Now he was laughing. "I love you and you'd make a kick ass Native woman," he added. "Want to go back to my teepee and make fire together?"

"You just didn't say that did you?" Tears filled her eyes, she was laughing so hard. "I'm ignoring that comment. Anyway, I happen to think I would make a kick ass Native, as does Baby Blackhawk," she said, rubbing her belly. "Don't you Leroy?" Now she was going to torment him.

"What?" Blackhawk stared incredulously and wasn't laughing anymore. "You aren't naming my son Leroy."

"Our son," she corrected. "How about Heathcliff?"

Blackhawk honestly wasn't sure if she was teasing him or dead serious.

"Mick?"

"Elizabeth, it's not happening."

"Then I guess you need to get that very sexy Native behind moving on helping me pick a name, or it's going to be Leroy Heathcliff Mick Blackhawk IV."

"What? Where did the fourth come from?" Now he was starting to smile.

"That's so everyone thinks you, your father and grandfather all have that name when they meet him. Boy are they going to be pissed at you for saddling them with that atrocity."

Blackhawk started laughing. "Okay, point taken, baby," he said grinning. He was going to suggest a name, but he heard the second Denali. "Sounds like they're here."

"Terrific," she mumbled, all the humor leaving her face, and no more laughter filling the room.

Blackhawk assessed the situation. Yeah, his brother did something to jack their happy little group up. As soon as he got him alone he was going to kick his ass and make him fix it pronto!.

When the door opened Callen and the ME entered, one more hesitant than the other. "It's started snowing again," he said, brushing himself off, and Desdemona too. "Nice house, how did we score this?" he asked, looking at his brother.

He noticed his sister-in-law was starting a fire and wasn't looking at him, not even a glance. Part of his chest clenched. It was the part that held his heart. He knew he drove this wedge between them. All he wished was he could get her alone to tell her what was going on, but he didn't have that chance yet. Had he not hurt her, by now she'd be smiling at him, punching him playfully, or hugging him. God, how he hated the anger he placed between them.

"You can thank Lyzee. Apparently, she pulled the guilt and best friend code to keep us out of a roach coach."

Callen stared at Elizabeth, waiting for her to look up at him. All he wanted was one of her reassuring looks to know he still had her love. If he damaged them and couldn't fix it, there was no way he could continue to be near her. The pain would be too much.

Blackhawk looked in the kitchen. There were provisions sitting on the counter. Gabe was a lifesaver. "Gabe had food delivered, so it looks like we need to make dinner."

"Great. What's on the menu?" asked his brother.

"Burgers?" He knew his sister-in-law loved them, and he was

hoping to make her happy. When in doubt, bribe the pregnant carnivore with cow covered in bacon and cheese.

"Lyzee?" Blackhawk directed the choice to his wife.

She stood and watched the ME standing closely to Callen, and felt the tears building. "I'll pass, I'm not hungry," she said, her eyes meeting his. The tears were evident and she didn't care. "See you all in the morning," she said, walking from the room. Right now she didn't want to have a brawl in the rental house. With the way she felt, she was going to either punch her brother-in-law out for breaking the rules of family or weep at his betrayal.

When she found her way upstairs, the men looked at each other in surprise. Elizabeth wasn't hungry? That was a bad sign. Hell had just frozen over, and both men knew it.

Blackhawk pointed at his brother, when Doctor Adare wasn't looking and mouthed '*what did you do to her?*'.

Whitefox looked contrite. He now knew exactly how badly he'd screwed up.

He shook his head and wasn't even sure what they could do to patch this mess back up again. He should probably ask his brother what happened, but this was his mess to clean up. '*Fix it*', he mouthed, before turning his attention to the other woman.

"How about you, Doctor Adare," Blackhawk inquired. "Do you like burgers?"

"I don't eat meat. I'm a vegetarian," she offered. "Unless you have veggie burgers, but don't worry about me. I'm fairly self-sufficient.

Oh hell. Not only had his brother pissed off his wife somehow, but they had a vegetarian in the house with the queen of all carnivores. Someone was definitely going to be maimed. Maybe all four of them in the same house wasn't a good idea. Right about now, Gabe Rothschild was siting somewhere laughing his ass off over all of this at Ethan's expense.

All three sat at the table and ate dinner. It had to be the most uncomfortable meal any of them had in their lives. There was no laughter, just simple courtesy and nothing more.

113

Desdemona felt horrible. She knew the reason her boss went to bed was to get as far away from her as possible. She needed to face the cold hard truth. Elizabeth Blackhawk hated her. After they got back to FBI West, there was no doubt the woman would be getting rid of her in a heartbeat. There was no mistaking the look on her face when Callen came to her side at the crime scene. Elizabeth obviously didn't like the idea that she was moving in on her territory. This had to be the worst day of her life.

The entire time she was eating, all she could think was how grateful she was that her house was paid for, and if she had to sell it, it wouldn't financially break her. Part of her wanted to go upstairs and confront her boss, not in a bad way, but just to ask her what she could do to make them a better team. When she looked up at Callen, her heart skipped a beat. For now, he was being supportive, but when Elizabeth dropped the ultimatum, she was sure that the man would run screaming. There was no point in getting attached to the man at all. He'd stick with family and a woman like Elizabeth over mousy her any day.

Even if the chocolaty brown eyes made her feel safe and secure. When he held her hand she felt stronger and less alone, she had to face the cold hard truth. At some point, he'd run from the goth-y mess she was and regain his sense of sanity.

Callen Whitefox couldn't help but watch the woman across from him. Deep in his heart there was an ache for her, and how sad her eyes appeared. It was like she always expected the worst outcome. Part of him wanted to pick her up and carry her away to someplace safe and the other part wanted to stand her in front of a mirror until she saw the truth. Desdemona was a lovely woman, the only thing wrong with her was her view of herself. There was so much fear, and self-doubt that he wasn't sure he could ever find the real woman beneath. Yes, he'd seen bits and pieces, when her guard was down, and she was being herself, but around Elizabeth she was like some terrified animal. Callen understood about being helpless and weak, and that's why he felt the need to protect her.

Callen wished Desdemona would take the time to learn about the woman upstairs, and how sweet and gentle she was inside. That was the other part that hurt him, that the woman upstairs always protected them both. The way she killed their estranged brother to protect them both in the quarry was just one example of how she loved unconditionally. That day she left with blood on her hands and soul, to protect them both from the knowledge that they took their siblings life. Elizabeth stood in front of them, and at what cost?

The woman fought hard for the people she loved, and it crushed him that Desdemona didn't see that in her too. Yes, Elizabeth was tough, but that was just the outside. Inside she had a warm squishy center, and so much compassion and love. Look at the family she loved. The Blackhawk men were a mess, and she stood by each one of them and loved them fiercely. Elizabeth protected their grandfather, took care of their dad after heart surgery, and loved Ethan and himself with all she had in her heart. Elizabeth was his champion, and he cherished her.

Now she was hiding in a bedroom, and it was partly his fault. His only hope was she'd understand when he had the chance to tell her why he was standing between her and Desdemona. Elizabeth was tough and could take a hit to her armor. Desdemona had nothing to protect her, and he didn't want to see the debilitating blow break her. His fear was one battle of words with Elizabeth and Desdemona would be crushed. How could he explain to her that he was compelled to protect a complete stranger over her?

He loved Elizabeth, but he had the tiny whisper of attraction to Desdemona. At Quantico, they told you to always go with your gut, and his gut said that Doctor Adare needed him. He chose to ignore the part that was sending up the warnings. He had to stick, at least until she either turned him down or ran from him. Both of which he knew was a possibility. Deep down he trusted Elizabeth to pick him up and brush him off when it happened.

He could always rely on her to have his back. Then he remembered the woman he'd come to rely on for everything was the same woman he just betrayed. Whitefox betrayed what he knew was truth. Elizabeth was his true love, just forever out of his reach.

Blackhawk didn't know what the hell to say or do. First there was his wife, and she was stirred up about something big to skip dinner. When he tried to get her to come down, she had locked herself in their bathroom to take a bubble bath and didn't want to be bothered. He was pretty sure that Callen needed to fix this and fast.

Elizabeth had never hid before in her life. That just wasn't her style. She'd kick in a door and beat someone to their senses, but locking herself away didn't bode well for the assignment.

He knew that Elizabeth had some insecurity issues with Desdemona. His wife might be a hard ass and tough as nails, but the one thing that was a constant was everyone pretty much loved her. The elderly neighbor back in Georgetown had insisted he marry her after one day, her deputies in Salem loved her too. Strangers gravitated to her, just because she had a heart of gold, and then there was Doctor Adare. No matter how much his wife tried, the woman backed away, and that was driving Elizabeth insane trying to figure it out. She blamed herself.

But there was more.

Whatever Callen did greatly exacerbated the situation. His wife had an attachment to his brother. Not one that bothered him, but he honestly believed it had to do with her own brother being a killer, and having no family left. She'd been adopted by the Blackhawk men, and each of the four men loved her and protected her fiercely. Now there was trouble brewing between them, and he wasn't quite sure what had happened. There were few men he'd ever let near his wife, but his brother was one of them. His father and grandfather the other two. It warmed him when his brother felt comfortable around his wife, but now that warm had gone ice cold.

"I'll do the dishes," Desdemona said, standing. "Thank you for dinner, Director. I'll cook tomorrow, it's only fair," she said, trying to be friendly. Maybe if one Blackhawk liked her, then the other one wouldn't be able to fire her as easily. It was a silly hope to have, but it was her only hope at that moment.

"I'm going to go talk to Elizabeth," said Whitefox, tossing down his napkin and standing. He couldn't eat his dinner with this wedge between him and Elizabeth. He'd hurt her and he needed to patch it up.

"You may want to rethink that, Callen. Give her the night to calm down," Blackhawk warned.

"I need to talk to her. I'll take my chances. Isn't there a saying that you shouldn't go to bed mad at the people you love?"

Desdemona cringed inside, and almost wanted to tell him it was 'never go to bed mad at a spouse' and not loved one, but what did it matter? She pretty much understood that Callen defending her at the Boy Scout camp was a mistake. It was obvious that he was in love with Elizabeth, and she wondered if he realized it or not.

Blackhawk watched his brother go off, and wished him luck. What he was doing was either very brave or very dangerous. All he wanted was his family to be back in one piece again, so they could focus on Red River and not the family drama that they brought with them. It was hard to believe that all this turmoil stemmed from the little woman washing dishes in the kitchen.

Callen stood outside Elizabeth's door for a few minutes just staring at it. How did he apologize to the woman that gave him so much love and he'd wounded her heart as a thank you?

He'd have to figure it out.

Taking a deep breath, he knocked on the bedroom door. When there was no answer, he opened it, peeking inside. Elizabeth was inside and asleep in bed. He didn't know if he should leave or enter the room. Part of him wanted to walk out, but he needed to get it off his chest, whether she was awake or not.

He sat on the side of the bed, and watched her sleep. His heart skipped in his chest, and he remembered the first time he'd ever seen her. They were in FBI West, and he was there for her help. He'd always laughed at the phrase 'love at first sight', but on that day he fell hard for the woman. Callen lost his heart that day, and then had his dream shatter when he found out that she was married to his brother. God, weeks had passed and he still felt the same. Nothing made the ache of truth go away.

Once he'd betrayed the man downstairs over a woman, and he swore if he ever got a second chance that he'd keep them both safe. Despite what he felt inside for her, he wouldn't cross that line. If the man she married was anyone else, he'd be fighting to win her heart in a bloody battle to the death. Since it was his brother that she loved, he'd relegated himself to loving her from a distance. What he felt for her would remain in his heart and locked away, even though he was sure she already knew. Callen was sure it was one of his secrets she carried. Elizabeth was very astute.

"Lyzee are you awake?" he whispered, softly.

When she still didn't move, Callen debated again almost losing his nerve.

"I need to talk to you, and this is the hardest thing I've ever had to admit in my life. The first day I met you, I fell in love with you. Head over heels, because you're everything I've ever wanted in a woman. Then I found out that you were married to my brother, and I couldn't ever hurt him again," he paused, picking up her hand. "I won't ever betray him, despite what I feel inside for you. I know I'll never get over you, but right now I may have a chance to find happiness." Whitefox took a deep breath and prayed to get through it. "Anyone will always be second to what I feel for you. You're my true love, Lyzee."

"No one's ever protected me and loved me the way you do. For so long I believed I wasn't worthy of it. My own mother never felt anything for me, and then you showed up. You loved me unconditionally, and accepted me as part of my brother's life. You made me feel alive and valued. Granddad loved me, but when you hug me, or tell me you love me, it fills my heart enough to get through the cold moments. It's a different love from them. I've never felt anything like it before."

Callen brushed a curl from her cheek and gently touched her face. "Today I hurt you, because I didn't side with you. I saw it in your eyes, and it broke my heart. The day you married my brother on the Rez, I showed you the tattoo we all had done, and it means everything to me. Not only because you have my back, but because it's a reminder of who has part of my heart." He didn't know if he should continue. "You have half of me, and always will. No matter who comes into my life, you'll always live inside me. Maybe it's unfair to any other woman, but it's the truth. I'm still in love almost half a year later and it's not going away. I got the tattoo, Lyzee because I'm in love with you."

Whitefox wiped his eyes with his free hand. He wished she was awake to tell him it was all going to be okay. That she loved him, and always would even though he screwed up.

"You have to understand that Desdemona is a gentle soul, I can feel it. But right now she's broken in a million pieces inside and scared shitless of you. I took her side to protect her, and to keep her from being broken more. She doesn't hate you, she's afraid of you. Somewhere in her past she's been damaged, and that's something I completely understand. Before you I was broken into so many jagged pieces. There was no one to put me back together again. Then you knocked me over and fixed me. I was lucky. I had you to heal me. She doesn't have someone like you to fix the pain." Whitefox twisted the wedding band on her finger, wishing it was his. "She's alone and scared."

"Whenever I'm around her I feel like I need to keep her safe. I want to wrap her up and put her on a shelf where nothing bad can reach her." Whitefox brushed another curl from her cheek. "I need you to trust me on this. I look at her and see the fear and it crushes me. I know I have no right to dump more on you, but I need your help. I'm not good at the woman thing; if I was I wouldn't be sitting here telling you what an ass I was to hurt you." Whitefox lay beside her, facing her.

"I know you're carrying so much right now. Granddad has dumped us all on you. Wyler needs you to help him patch his relationship back up with Ethan and me. I'm a mess, and you've kept my secrets. Even ones that my brother doesn't know about, and now you're creating the next generation of men you'll still be carrying."

He took a deep breath. "You're the strongest person I know, and Desdemona needs strong now. As a favor to me, until I figure out where this is all going, can you just keep her safe? Granddad said you're the protective raven, sent to guide us and keep us on track. Can you bear to take one more lost soul under your wing? Can you help me fix her and keep her safe?"

"No one will ever be you, but it's as close as I'm going to get. If Ethan didn't find you first, this may have all been different, but it is what it is. I won't ever get to love you like I want, but I can try and love her at least with what's left of my heart and maybe it'll be enough."

When she still breathed evenly and didn't move, he sighed. "If it matters, if you told me right now you hate her, I'd walk away from her. I'd sacrifice anything for you, because I love you and trust your judgment." When she still didn't move, he leaned over and kissed her lightly on her lips, lingering longer than he normally would just to have the connection. He took the memory and buried it deep in his soul, vowing to save it for when he needed to feel.

"I'm sorry I hurt you. I hope one day you can forgive me. Sweet dreams, Lyzee. I love you," he whispered, again leaning over her to kiss her gently. One of his tears landed on her cheek, and he carefully wiped it away. "I'm so sorry. I can't do this without you," he said, voice choked with emotion. "I miss my best friend and need you to tell me it's going to all be okay, and that you still love me."

At least he said the words out loud. Maybe the universe would get them and deliver them where they needed to moved away from her to close the door, he didn't see the icy blue eyes open, and he didn't see the tear that slid down her cheek as the emotion overwhelmed her.

If there was any question in her mind if she loved the Blackhawk men, the conversation that Callen spilled while he thought she slept was exactly why. They loved completely and gave her so much of their lives. Now that he explained it all, she had no choice. He was more than forgiven. Elizabeth was going to do what she'd promised she'd do. Protect the men in her family at any cost, and if anything she would always keep her promise to the Blackhawk men.

It was the path she was meant to follow.

*   *   *

When the kitchen was placed back in order, Callen, Ethan and Doctor Adare all retired to their rooms for the night. No one questioned why it looked like Callen Whitefox had been crying. Nothing was said about what went on behind the closed door. It was obvious that the man was hurting and words wouldn't fix what was broken.

Only one person could do that.

Ethan climbed into bed with his wife, and immediately she moved into his body and curled against him.

"I love you, baby," he whispered and kissed her on the lips. "Take it easy on Callen. He looks like hell, and he may have done something stupid, but he didn't mean it," he whispered, hoping his family would be fixed and back to the way it was. "Don't let him suffer too long, he's been hurt enough in life."

When he closed his eyes and slept, his wife lay beside him awake and planning on giving him what he wanted too. Both men meant the world to her, and in the morning she'd protect them both with all she had inside her and figure out how to get through to a woman that wanted nothing to do with her.

*　　*　　*

Desdemona took the one room furthest from Elizabeth. It was a comfortable space, with a big bed and lots of pillows. She noticed there was a doorway that adjoined hers and Callen Whitefox's rooms. Just that thought made it hard to sleep. Looking around she tried to focus on anything else that would draw her attention. Oh look, there was a fireplace in there too, and she suddenly wished she knew how to light a fire like Elizabeth Blackhawk. Was there anything that the woman couldn't do? There was no doubt she could walk on water too if need be.

She wouldn't be surprised.

When Whitefox had gone up to her room after dinner, she was intensely jealous. When he came back down emotional, she wanted to storm up the stairs and fix it. It was after all her fault. The jealousy was something new for her. Even though she tried to not let it bother her, it was so hard to not feel the clawing at her heart. Yeah, it was irrational. Callen was nothing to her, but a friend. But sue a girl for wanting more. As she lay in the bed alone, she wondered what it would be like to have a man look at her the way both men looked at Elizabeth. Yeah, the green eyed monster was swallowing her whole and she wasn't proud of it at all.

There was a scraping noise, and Desdemona looked at the clock. It was almost three a.m. and there was no reason for anyone to be up. She listened for it again, and when it was there once more, she grabbed her gun and prepared to find the source. Panic filled her that the sound might be the mysterious stranger that was haunting her life. Maybe he followed her there. At the next sound she was definitely going downstairs.

Elizabeth lay in bed just listening to the even breathing, as her husband's chest rose and fell. She'd been lying there for the last few hours dwelling on the words that Callen had dropped in her lap. If she was going to be completely honest with herself, she wasn't going try to tell herself she was surprised. If anything, she knew people and had a way of reading the situation. How the man felt about her wasn't a shock, but when it was put into words and said out loud, it gave it a life of its own. Rolling to her side, she watched the man that lie beside her, and she thought back to what her brother-in-law had confessed while he thought she was sleeping. She put herself in his position and wondered if she, would she be as strong and honorable. If she was in love with Ethan Blackhawk, and he was married to someone else, would she be able to just love him from afar and never be part of his life?

Not likely.

Elizabeth did have feelings for Callen, but she was hopelessly, completely and totally in love with her husband. That didn't mean she wouldn't make a special place for him in her life. Out of love, she'd make room for him in her heart. If Callen needed this favor, she'd make sure it happened. Her heart was big enough to love all the men in her family, and like she promised Timothy. It was her job to keep them all safe.

As she lay there thinking about it all, there was this intense pain building in her body. It came hard and fast and stole her breath.

What the hell was that? she wondered. That was the first time in the six months of pregnancy she felt pain. Her heart started pounding in her chest. Gently, she rolled to her back, and away from her husband so as not to wake him. After taking a few deep breaths, the pain stopped, then again the wave rolled right through her again, and she felt her whole body tighten and then the baby literally go crazy and spin in circles.

She reached for her phone and realized it was in her jacket pocket, and her tablet was in her shoulder bag. Now she couldn't Google it, and see what was going on with her body.

Damn it!

Elizabeth slid carefully out of bed. If she woke her husband, he'd freak out and drag her to the nearest ER. Maybe some tea would help, and then she could sit and research it online. As she opened the bedroom door, it made a scraping sound and Elizabeth swore it was as loud as a gunshot. It surprised her that everyone didn't come running. When her husband didn't even move, she stepped out and closed the door. With the scraping noise again, she paused.

Still nothing.

She was almost in the clear. Walking slowly down the stairs, her hand protectively over the baby, she tried to massage him back into being calm. Whatever that pain was, the baby wasn't too happy with it either.

Finally reaching the kitchen, Elizabeth put the tea kettle on and leaned against the counter as the next wicked pain hit her. "Shit," she muttered, and she desperately tried to breathe through it. Yeah, right then she was wondering how her best friend Livy did this six times. Soon she'd be giving birth to her and Gabe's sixth child, and right now she honestly believed that the woman was more hardcore than a fleet of marines.

Elizabeth picked out a tea bag that Gabe had sent, and it slipped from her hand. As she leaned over to pick it up, she heard the noise and stood fast. Pointed directly at her face was a gun and shaking hand holding it.

"Oh my God, Elizabeth! I'm so sorry," said Desdemona, as she lowered the gun. Great, she just held her boss at gunpoint in the kitchen- A very pregnant woman that didn't like her. When Callen Whitefox and Ethan Blackhawk heard about this, she was going to be walking back to her home. It was going to be a long lonely walk back, where she could contemplate her recent unemployment.

Elizabeth felt her heart start to beat again, and she could tell the woman was about to cry. "Shhhhh. Doctor Adare, it's okay. Let's not wake the men." She felt another pain and almost doubled over.

"Are you okay?" she asked her boss, rushing to her side, and placing the gun on the island.

"Really bad pain," she muttered, trying to breathe through it.

Desdemona put her bosses arm over her shoulder. "Let's get you to the couch and have you lay flat. I'll check you out," she whispered.

"Okay," she practically growled from between clenched teeth. That's how bad it was, when she was going to allow her Medical Examiner to play OB-GYN on her while her very nervous husband could wander downstairs at any second.

Elizabeth let the woman help her to the couch. As she lay down, the pain subsided again and she hoped it never came back.

"Tell me what it feels like," Desdemona whispered. "Where is the pain?"

Elizabeth pointed to the spot on her stomach where it radiated from. "It feels like someone's running my stomach through a ringer."

"No bleeding?"

"No."

Doctor Adare ran her hands over her stomach and felt for the baby. Pushing in one spot, and then another until she got a response. "Is he moving a lot today?" she asked, as she continually checked her body. "Or barely moving?"

"He's moving a lot," she answered, her eyes filling with tears. "Is he okay?" Now she was completely freaked out. Maybe waking her husband would be a good idea after all.

"Yes, he's fine," I can feel his head over here," she took Elizabeth's hand and pushed it into the one side of her belly. "And here's his foot," she showed her with her other hand.

"Then what's the pain?" She was still nervous.

"Braxton-Hicks contractions. They start about twenty six weeks and will continue until the real ones start. They're supposed to get a mother ready for what's coming. Practice contractions," she said grinning.

"Well hell, if that was the pretend ones, I can't wait to see the real deal," she whispered back. "Thanks Doctor Adare."

"You're welcome, and I did a rotation in medical school in obstetrics. It was my second choice as a profession," she smiled. It looked like Elizabeth Blackhawk was human after all and could feel pain and fear.

"Can I ask Doctor, why ME then if you liked Obstetrics?"

"Pregnant women bitch and moan too much for me. I like my patients to be very quiet," she answered, jokingly. "Besides, expecting mothers get freaked out when the doctor walks in wearing skulls."

Elizabeth laughed.

"Let me make you some tea." Desdemona stood and started for the kitchen.

"Thanks Doctor Adare."

The woman took a chance. "Desdemona is fine Elizabeth," she waited to see what the woman would do.

"Thank you Desdemona. I appreciate it."

Adding water to the cup, she forgot to ask Elizabeth how she liked her tea. It occurred to her that maybe Callen had been right. Elizabeth wasn't as tough as she thought. After all, she had just seen the fear in her eyes when she was worried about her baby.

When she carried the mug back in it wasn't going to matter at all. Her boss had fallen asleep. Her wedding banded hand protectively over the baby in her body. Desdemona put the cup down beside her, and grabbed a blanket off the back of the couch. Tucking the woman in, she stared down at her.

Yeah, maybe the book can't be judged by its cover.

Morning came early, and Ethan rolled over to cuddle with his wife, and she was missing. He looked over at the clock on the bed stand, and it was barely six a.m. The house was silent, and then he got that sick feeling in the pit of his stomach, that something had happened to his wife. He rolled out of bed and was out the door and down the stairs in a panic. He rushed into the living and slid to a stop. His wife was asleep on the couch, tucked in and safe, and Doctor Adare was sitting in a chair across from her, reading the tech reports that she had received an hour ago.

"Is she okay?" he asked, looking panicked. Never had she ever left their bed to sleep on the couch.

"Braxton-hicks contractions," she whispered, trying to not wake her boss. "It was an uncomfortable night, nothing more."

The man looked completely horrified that his wife had been having contractions and somehow he managed to sleep through it. "Will she be okay?" he asked, sincerely scared for his wife.

Doctor Adare nodded. "Perfectly normal from now until the end." She looked up to see Callen rush down the stairs with his gun in his hand to stand behind his brother. All that went through her head was one word.

W*arriors!*

Wow!

She had to admit that when her boss came down, she was flabbergasted, as he rushed into the room in just his boxers. Being a medical professional, a naked person wasn't the shocking part. The truly amazing part about her boss was the tattoos covering his shoulders and chest. The Director seemed so straitlaced, but across his body were a giant raven and his wife's name underneath it. Then she got round two of shocking. Callen rushed in too, same state- boxers and very shirtless. Yeah, half naked it was clear that they definitely were brothers. Both men were a genetic match when it came to body and form plus the matching tattoo around their biceps.

Holy shit times two.

That answered the questions that had been plaguing her mind, if he was all angles and lines underneath his clothes. He was, and he too had tattoos. On his very defined abs was a tattooed fox. Desdemona felt the room getting very warm. Both men had the same matching tattoo around their bicep of their left arm, and she only hoped she wasn't leering.

"What happened," Callen looked around, and then he noticed Elizabeth asleep on the couch. "Is she okay?" he looked over at Desdemona, his eyes full of worry for his sister-in-law.

Unable to speak thanks to the hot flash she was currently having, she simply nodded. Whitefox was a very sexy man. He and his brother both hit the genetic jackpot. They were two tattooed sex gods and she prayed she wasn't staring like an idiot.

Oh crap, thinking about her boss like that was probably some cardinal sin, especially while Elizabeth lay in the room asleep.

"Elizabeth was up in the middle of the night having Braxton-Hicks contractions. I stayed up to just make sure she was fine. I got some tech report reading done." Desdemona smiled at both men, trying to sound professional. It occurred to her she could be talking very fast.

126

Whitefox began calming down and noticed a couple of things. The first thing being that Desdemona Adare was wearing glasses to read, and they were sexy black schoolmarm ones that immediately heated his blood. The second thing was that he was partially naked and Doctor Adare was staring at both men.

"Uh, we should go get dressed." Whitefox punched his brother in the arm, trying to give him the hint that neither were dressed appropriately to be standing in front of the doctor. If it were just Elizabeth, he wouldn't bat an eye, because it was a normal thing, but with the ME, that was crossing the line of comfort even for him.

Ethan just realized that he was partially naked himself. "Good idea," he said, as both men made a hasty retreat.

Desdemona watched them both walk up the stairs, and both men had tattoos all over their backs too. Oh wow!

When both men were out of range, Desdemona let out a breath.

Elizabeth started giggling. When she opened her eyes, they were filled with laughter and understanding.

"I should probably apologize for ogling your half naked husband and brother-in-law," Desdemona said, wondering if the laughter was the calm before the storm or if she was truly entertained. "But really they weren't easy to ignore."

"They're something, aren't they?" she said, sitting up.

"Yeah, yeah they are, but I'm not sure that the word 'something' covers it. That's a lot of tattoos between them," she said, fanning herself with the tech report.

"For the record, you don't really ever get used to it. They walk around our house like that all the time. It can be distracting."

"Great." She made a mental note to avoid any situations where both men would be topless. Then she realized how insane that would be. Who avoided naked perfection?

Elizabeth stood and stretched. "Thanks for not letting Ethan freak out," she said, finally. The fact Desdemona was checking out her husband didn't bother her, but what intrigued her was the flush of heat that she could see across her face.

"You're welcome." Doctor Adare knew she was still blushing.

"Which one got you all hot and bothered?" she asked, watching the woman's face carefully. She'd interrogated a lot of criminals, and could spot a lie a mile away.

Desdemona flushed further, but felt like she needed to answer. "Callen," she said honestly, and then blushed more, finally changing the subject.

"When I first saw them together, shirtless in just jeans, they were working on the tree house in our back yard; I almost had to take a cold shower. From behind without the tattoos they're identical."

Desdemona laughed. "I would have needed one definitely."

The woman seemed to be relaxing a little more around her, and that was probably a good thing, since she was going to go out on a limb and take one for the Blackhawk team. "It's one of my fondest memories of all time. Topless Natives doing yard work."

"They are definitely brothers. The matching tattoos were hard to miss."

Elizabeth laughed. "Yeah, they certainly are brothers. I like the ones on their arms, but the Raven on Ethan is my favorite."

Desdemona noticed she didn't mention her favorite one on Callen, and she suspected it was the heart with her initials on his back. Yeah, it was hard not to notice the beautiful script inside the heart, and she needed to change the subject, as she felt a wave of jealousy. "Thanks for not telling them about the gun in your face last night."

"Girlfriend code strictly prohibits me telling the opposite sex anything like that." Elizabeth let it hang there in the air between them. She opened the door and was giving the Doctor a chance to walk through it or walk away. It had to be her choice, and she figured the woman deserved a shot. It wasn't only for what she did for her, but because she'd walk on glass for Callen Whitefox, and he asked her personally to keep the woman safe.

Desdemona didn't know what to say. In all her life she never had a girlfriend, unless you counted her sister. "Thank god for the girlfriend code," she said, standing and joining her new friend.

"Coffee Desdemona?"

"Absolutely, Elizabeth."

She stood in her secret hideaway and admired the collection. Lying behind her was the love of her life. He was silent now, and saying nothing, but that would come to an end soon. Shortly, he would be back to his old self, and then everything would be perfect again.

When she leaned over his body, she patted his dried cheek. No longer were there the horrific smells of decay lingering. His body was past that stage, and soon he'd be ready to be put back together again.

Piece by Piece. Part by part. Limb by limb.

"What should be next, my love?" she asked, and waited for his reply.

"Excellent choice, darling. I shall find you some eyes, so you can gaze into my face and see how much I love you.

Elizabeth and Desdemona Adare stood in the kitchen together drinking coffee. Both women were dressed, but completely different. Elizabeth was a creature of habit. Today she was wearing a black stretchy top that was tucked into her well-worn low rise jeans. At Elizabeth's hip was her gun and badge. She brought her cowboy boots, but wasn't sure if she'd wear them or not. Something about the boots just gave her a sense of security, and always had since leaving home for the FBI. It was like carrying a piece of home with her everywhere, and she didn't want to ruin them. It may be a snow boot kind of day.

Desdemona was going to be in the lab all day working, and she wanted to be comfortable. She was wearing tights with tiny little skulls across them, and a little pleated plaid skirt and simple black sweater. For shoes she went with Mary Janes, only because they had the biggest heel, and she didn't want to feel too short standing beside Elizabeth.

Whatever had happened last night between them was monumental. It was as if she fell down the rabbit hole and landed in another dimension. She was still hesitant, but she was pretty sure that Elizabeth was no longer going to be an issue. Already she felt comfortable around her, and welcomed into her circle.

When Ethan wandered into the kitchen, he was surprised to find two women bonding over a tech report.

"Ethan!" She smiled and rushed at him, happy to see her husband. When she went into his arms he hugged her close to his body.

"Lyzee, are you feeling okay? You can stay here today and we'll head in," he offered, and she just smiled up at him.

"Nope, I'm feeling great." Elizabeth kissed him slow and deep. Yeah, she knew there was someone in the room, but she loved him so damn much. After all, he rushed into the room in his boxers to save her from some imaginary bad guy.

"I guess you are," he said laughing, after she broke the kiss. He hugged her close to his body and felt calmness wash over him. "Morning Doctor, How are you today?" he asked, politely.

"I'm well, Director."

She sat up all night watching over his wife and the least he could do is help heal the group a little. "Please, call me Ethan."

Desdemona smiled. "Then lose the Doctor title. Desdemona is fine by me." She sipped her coffee. That's when she noticed him. Callen Whitefox stood in the doorway and his hair was still wet from the shower. He too was dressed like Elizabeth, but in a white shirt and the same worn jeans.

"Is that coffee," he asked, and then stole Elizabeth's from the counter.

"Hey!" She sucker punched him in the side when he walked past her. "You better hope pregnancy never becomes contagious," she teased, and winked at Doctor Adare. "You're going to look silly with a baby bump."

"Nice, but I don't think I can pull off pregnant and still be this damn sexy," he teased back, and noticed that Desdemona was smiling and laughing with them.

"What's our plans for today, team?" Elizabeth asked, pouring another cup of coffee.

Desdemona raised her hand. "Five autopsies."

"I'm on missing person reports and AFIS as soon as the Doctor gets me some prints," said Whitefox.

"I'm going to be monitoring the tech team to make sure they're taking care of everything," answered her husband. "What are you doing?" he asked her. Whatever it was, he hoped it involved staying inside and safe.

"I'm planning on hounding the ME until she gives me what I want."

"You're going to wish that room had a lock on the door. Doctor Leonard locks her out all the time," offered her husband.

Elizabeth looked over at her very sexy husband. "You seem to forget who you sleep with, Darlin'," she drawled.

Callen grinned at her, loving how the southern came out expectantly.

Desdemona shook her head. "You can harass me all you want. I'm fine with it. I can use an assistant in autopsy today. You can record the data as I do the processing. It's faster if I don't have to keep ungloving to type in info and fill out the sheets. I don't want internal goo all over my new tablet. My boss won't requisition a new one for me."

"No, she really won't," she said, laughing.

"You going to be okay dealing with autopsy? You looked a little queasy at the scene yesterday, Elizabeth?"

"What? Are you okay?" Blackhawk nearly choked on his coffee. Elizabeth had an iron clad stomach. She never got queasy in autopsy.

Whitefox laughed at his brother's response. "Ethan, it was an eye thing," he said, covering for Elizabeth. He noticed the women were playing nice, and he was hoping it would be a better day, but he'd learned his lesson and wasn't going to betray Elizabeth with giving away too much information. It was her not well known Achilles heel. Callen would protect her secrets as well as she carried his.

"Oh, okay." Blackhawk visibly relaxed.

"You have a thing with corpse eyes?" Desdemona asked, curiously.

Both men looked at her, unsure what she'd say.

Elizabeth weighed all the options and looked over at her husband and brother-in-law. Both were offering her the same look.

She didn't need to share anything she was uncomfortable with. "Two years ago my partner and I were on a stakeout, and we were both shot. He died in the car, and one of the last things I remember about the entire thing was him staring at me as he died. Since then, dead eyes freak me out."

Desdemona nodded, understanding. "My big ick is when I have to take the scalp off and do the cranial exam. Creeps me out every time," she admitted. "So I get that. I promise no dead eyes."

"Deal. I'm okay with scalps and skulls, if you want to walk me through it. It may come in handy if Callen keeps stealing my coffee."

The man snorted. "Just try it, and yours goes too, beautiful."

"Then I'll have to kick your ass," added Blackhawk laughing. "I married her because of that hair."

"Yeah, that's the only reason you married her," Whitefox snorted, knowing what lured his brother in, because it was probably the same thing that caught him.

"We should clear this up once and for all," said Elizabeth. "He married me for the sex."

"Jesus, Elizabeth!" Blackhawk choked on his coffee. "Really?" Now he gave her the look.

Yeah, that's pretty much what Whitefox thought, as he gave her a fist bump for tormenting his brother so easily. Ethan Blackhawk was very straight-laced, and if he was sleeping with Elizabeth he'd hire a sky writer. They were complete opposites.

Desdemona was thoroughly entertained by the three of them. They obviously had a good relationship. They teased each other, but were incredibly close. If she didn't know better, she'd swear she was married to both of them, equally. That was the vibe they gave off, as one working unit. Yeah, she was jealous as hell.

"Back on topic, please," suggested Blackhawk.

"I'll take the help, Elizabeth, and then this should only take eight hours instead of ten," she laughed, placing her cup down. "I'll go get my things ready," she said, and headed out of the room.

"Okay, Desi," Whitefox answered.

As he went to take a sip of the coffee, she timed it just right. "I spit in the coffee today, Cal." She started laughing when he choked on it and his eyes watered.

132

Blackhawk kissed her on the head and walked away. "God, I love you," he said grinning, and then whispered in her ear. "It was absolutely the sex and how mean you can be."

Elizabeth winked at him. She was well aware.

It looked like his family was back to normal again. "While you two torment each other, I think I'll go call Gabe and get him to push the lab people." He picked up his coffee and carried it with him just in case she wasn't just teasing him. From the difference in energy in the room he figured everything was better, but they needed time to work out the previous evening.

"Evil," Whitefox stated laughing, as he wiped coffee from his chin.

"I try," she replied, grinning at the man.

When Callen reached for her, she didn't evade. The hugs they shared were a common occurrence between them. Elizabeth truly loved him, and when Callen picked her up off the ground, she whispered in his ear and caught him off guard.

"You have part of my heart, and I love you too, Callen. I promise to keep her safe, just for you. There's plenty of room under my wings right beside the men I love."

Whitefox froze. She'd heard everything he'd said to her and she understood. "Thank you, Lyzee," he whispered, burying his face in her hair and neck, as he just held onto her. He meant what he said. Elizabeth Blackhawk would always live deep within his heart. She was magic and he was lost in the spell.

"She's mine now too, Cal. If this is what you want me to do, I'll do it. Nothing is going to happen to her and for the record," she continued whispering. "You definitely have my blessing. Don't walk away from her because of me. I wouldn't ever forgive myself if I caused you to not to take a chance at happiness. I love you too much to ever ask you to do that. I support you, and am here for you no matter the outcome."

He looked in her eyes and his cheek twitched. "I'm an idiot to believe I have a chance. She isn't Native and granddad will have a stroke. He gave me everything I ever had in life, and I can't disobey him. It's the one thing he always made me swear. I promised Lyzee, and I can't break a promise to him."

Elizabeth stroked his cheek and braced his face between her hands before giving him a kiss on the lips. "Do you trust me, Cal?"

"You're my best friend next to my brother, I trust you with my life," and he did. He also trusted her with his heart, and she was probably the only woman that he ever would one hundred percent. Truth be told, Callen knew that Elizabeth was the one, but reality reminded him that boat had sailed.

"Then you leave Granddad up to me. I have your back," she said, patting him right over the tattoo on his shoulder. "Take your chance Callen, and worry about the rest later. Let me carry this one for you," she offered, leaning against him and wrapping her arms around his waist and resting her head on his shoulder. "I want you to be happy and fill the rest of your heart with more love, and I really like her." And she did.

Tears filled his eyes, and he fought back the overwhelming need to let the emotion escape. She had no idea how much she meant to him, and how much just having her by his side mattered. "Thank you," he whispered, a tear slid down his cheek. Whitefox sensed they weren't alone, and he looked up at his brother standing in the doorway.

Elizabeth wiped the tear away with her thumb, and looked over her shoulder at her husband.

Ethan observed the two most important people in his life, and his heart clenched. Something was obviously bothering his brother and his wife was working on healing the wound. Some men would be insanely jealous to have their wife hugging another man, but his wasn't just some other man or woman.

This was his family and he trusted them both.

He closed the distance between them, and threw his arms around them both. Whatever the pain, he was willing to help shoulder it, even if his brother wasn't ready to share it. When his wife was abducted his brother kept him sane, comforted him, and kept him focused, until she was back with him.

Elizabeth wrapped her arms around both men's waists and just held them together. They were her family, and she'd do anything to keep them intact.

Callen allowed the emotion to swamp him, and his brother and sister to stabilize him. With them he was stronger. "I love you both," he whispered, choked by the emotion. "So damn much."

"We love you too, Cal," answered his brother. "You'll never be alone again," he added, dropping his forehead against his brother and wife's. Together they were strong and they'd fix whatever was hurting his brother. "We can work through anything as long as we stick together."

"I need you both," he said, unsure if he was going to be able to carry it alone.

"We're here, Cal," Elizabeth said, kissing him on the cheek. "Ethan and I will help you, I promise."

Blackhawk braced his hand on the back of his brother's head. "Anything you need is done, Callen. I've got you."

Whitefox just nodded. If he spoke he'd break. He had to put his faith in them, and hope that they would lead him through what was coming. Inside he was a scrambled mess, and he had to believe they would help him clean it up and find his way to happiness. The tears were also for the guilt. The feelings he was having towards Ethan's wife ate away at his soul.

Desdemona Adare stopped just outside the doorway, hidden in the shadows of the other room. She watched the three family members as they hugged in the kitchen. It was beautiful and poignant, and wondered if she'd ever have that kind of happiness and people to always have her back. Desdemona watched the three embrace and offer strength to Callen Whitefox. Although she was lost as to what was the burden he was obviously carrying, it wasn't lost on her that he wasn't carrying it alone.

Everything she'd heard in the rumor mill was both wrong and right about her bosses. The Blackhawks were an unstoppable force, and that was true. What wasn't true was they were cold. These three people were probably the warmest people she'd ever met in her life. Just watching them close rank around the part of their family that was struggling proved it. Emotion was shared between them easily and again she felt the closeness of that of a single couple.

Desdemona stepped back, and gave them the privacy they deserved, even though she wanted to run in and join in the warmth they were so easily sharing.

God what she wouldn't give to have a family of her own. In that moment she believed she'd give up anything to be part of their circle. Desdemona would sacrifice love to just be part of what they shared.

Family.

They drove into town in one Denali, and left the second one in their driveway. Elizabeth and Ethan Blackhawk sat in the front, and Callen and the Doctor in the back, as they discussed the incoming tech reports. They needed a jumping off point to focus the investigation, and before they rolled into the sheriff's department.

"Did they find any trace?" asked Elizabeth.

Callen Whitefox leaned into the papers sitting in Desdemona's lap and scanned the information. "Blonde hairs."

"They put a rush on it to FBI West to find the DNA, and as soon as we get the results later, I can tell you sex. But with long blonde hair, I think we can assume woman."

Blackhawk looked up in the rear view mirror. "Female serial killers are a possibility, but honestly they don't happen often," he added, throwing it out there.

Desdemona considered his words. "I had to do the psych rotation in medical school, and I remember some of that." She was having a hard time focusing. Callen Whitefox's leg was brushing hers and he smelled incredible.

Elizabeth leaned back in her seat. "Did you start your base line profile, Ethan?"

Blackhawk nodded. "I need some more information before I can call it official. It's going to come down to whether the men we found were sexually assaulted." Part of him was infinitely grateful that the killer wasn't going after women. At least his wife would be safe.

The papers resting on Desdemona's lap slid off and Whitefox caught them, and he placed them back on her lap. The entire time he was beside her he was completely aware that the

136

doctor smelled really good, and he wondered if it was her perfume or hair.

"Thank you," she said to him, looking at him from behind her glasses.

Callen smiled warmly at her.

"I'll get that information for you within the first hour, Ethan," she answered. "The tech team would have started the preliminary if they noticed signs of assault."

"Thank you." He glanced over at his wife. "If there's no sexual assault, I'm going to say female killer. But if Desdemona finds any sign of it, it may be a man that is preying on other men. Like Dahmer or Gacy."

"Was the blonde hair found only on one victim? Or multiple?"

Desdemona scanned the papers, and took the one she needed and dropped the rest on Whitefox's lap. "Multiple. In fact, the team retrieved ten hairs in total. They were on their clothing and possibly transferred in transit."

"Any other trace?"

"The usual trace was found. There were fibers, linen ones, cotton ones and a gray one that appears on all of the victims. I'm sure they're isolating it as we speak. Christina is very thorough."

Elizabeth laughed. "Oh she is something alright."

Blackhawk looked over. "Elizabeth," he warned.

Whitefox snickered from the back seat. "Don't stir Ethan up. He has to go work with her today, and you know he gets flustered."

Elizabeth turned and fist bumped her brother-in-law. They both enjoyed tormenting her husband over the tech that had a bad case of man lust for him.

"I don't get it," Desdemona answered.

"Christina lusts after my husband, and she and I have a little game between us. She tries to check him out covertly, and I try to catch her."

Christina never mentioned that she lusted after her boss maybe that was why she told her all about Elizabeth, and how tough she was to work with. "Really?" She looked over at Whitefox for confirmation.

"She speaks the truth," he answered. Just by watching her eyes, he could see she was contemplating something in her mind and weighing all the information carefully.

This was all interesting information. She stored it away for later mulling.

"Christina is an excellent tech. That's why she runs the lab. I just let it go because I can't kick every woman's ass that looks at Ethan," she shrugged. Did it bother her? A little bit, because they were married. But she had to choose her battles. There was part of her worried now that she was fat and wobbly her husband wouldn't find her attractive anymore and find someone else.

Ethan took her hand and squeezed it, and Whitefox put his hand on her shoulder. They knew her well enough, to pick up on the emotion in her voice.

Desdemona noticed again how they protectively came to the weaker of the three and offered support and reassurance. First it was Callen Whitefox in his time of need, and now Elizabeth Blackhawk. It was automatic, and she didn't think they realized they even did it. Obviously Elizabeth wasn't as tough as everyone thought, and her family knew the truth and were going to protect her any way they could.

"We're here," he said, pulling the Denali into the visitors spot.

Everyone piled out and walked up the snowy walk way to the door of the Sheriff's department. The wind was whipping wickedly and blowing the snow around.

Desdemona contemplated her clothing options for a brief moment, and then remembered the scrubs that she brought with her. Yeah, thank god for the scrubs.

Entering the building, the men stood behind the women. Elizabeth took point and then Callen noticed the Administrative assistant. He probably should have stood in front of the women and drew her attention. Already he could see that Elizabeth was going to be the focus of the woman's attention.

"Yes?" Sheila asked, icily.

She unzipped her parka and pulled out her ID. "Elizabeth Blackhawk to see the Sheriff."

"He's on a call, he'll be right out," she answered checking out the woman before her. She was tall, and looked more like a model than an FBI agent. Then she noticed she was pregnant. "Have a seat." Sheila Court pointed to the row of chairs and went back to her gum chewing.

Deputy Bobby Lee Tills wandered over to the administrative assistant's desk and leaned down. "What's with the two Indians, the knocked up model and Morticia Addams?" he snickered and Sheila joined him. "The FBI must be hard up for good employees."

Elizabeth noticed that Desdemona flinched and she could only imagine the response with the men behind her. As her blood pressure shot up at the derogatory comments, she knew she'd had just about enough of the town and the bigots.

"Oh crap," whispered Whitefox, as he saw the look on Elizabeth's face as she stood.

It was about to get ugly fast.

Chapter Six

It took a moment for the rage and anger to pass, but Elizabeth Blackhawk had one major rule in her life. She didn't like bullies, and she certainly didn't like the way the man said 'Indian', tossing it out there like it was a dirty word. Compound it with the way it hurt her ME, and she wasn't going to take it sitting down.

Literally.

Assholes were a problem in their job, but she wasn't going to let them hurt her family or friend.

"Hey Doctor?" Elizabeth glanced at the woman beside her, smiling reassuringly. Yeah, hurt was on her face and she didn't understand why, but it was there. Mental note, being called Morticia was a big no-no with the Doc.

"Yes Director Blackhawk?"

"What's with the redneck hillbilly and the walking bottle of peroxide? I guess they don't school them out here. It's Native American and not Indian. I mean come on, we learned that in what? Third grade?" The burr hit its mark, and both Blackhawk and Whitefox snickered.

God they loved her.

The good and bad thing about Elizabeth was that you never knew what was going to come out of her mouth. This was case in point. When she was defending her family, she'd back it up with an ass kicking if the words didn't accomplish shutting the offending party down.

Sheila Court looked outraged, and stood while the deputy turned red with rage.

Desdemona was entertained. She didn't know what to say to that, but she couldn't help but smile at her boss.

"Who the fuck do you think you are?" the deputy snapped viciously, moving forward.

Elizabeth didn't back down. She placed her body protectively in front of Desdemona. After all, she made that promise to her brother-in-law.

"I'd back up if I were you, Deputy," growled Blackhawk. If the man thought he was going near his pregnant wife, he was going to be in a world of hurt.

"Don't do it," warned Whitefox, as he moved closer to Elizabeth, pushing Desdemona behind him protectively. "Unless you want to get hurt, that is."

The deputy assessed the situation and wisely backed up. The look he threw out at the pregnant bitch spoke volumes. He'd teach her a lesson and the freak behind her too. He'd get the last laugh.

"Hey, is there an issue?" interjected Sheriff James Duffy, as he left his office. His worst case scenario was Sheila and the deputy greeting the FBI, and this was exactly why.

"No issue, Sheriff," drawled Elizabeth. The southern came out in her voice, and that only happened when she was extremely pissed. "I was just becoming acquainted with your staff. Let me say, delightful individuals," she added, sarcastically.

"How about we head down to the room I told you about, Agents?" he tried to defuse the situation. "I think it will work for you," he continued.

Blackhawk and Whitefox kept their eyes on the deputy. They were ready if they had to be.

"That would be wonderful," answered Desdemona. Her body was pressed against Whitefox's protectively. It wasn't lost on her that Callen's hand was protectively placed on Elizabeth's hip.

"Great!" At that moment he just wanted to get the four FBI agents away from his staff, and then he was going to rip his deputy and administrative assistant a new one when he got them alone.

Everyone followed the Sheriff down the stairs to the basement and to the location he had promised them. There were a few of the tech staff milling about, and prepping the bodies for autopsy for the doctor.

"I hope it'll be sufficient," he stated, as he watched the woman wander through the workspace and drop her bag of tools on the table.

"I can definitely work here," she answered brightly. It was ten times better than she hoped, and she could utilize the space.

"I'm glad, Doctor. If you need anything else, here's my cell phone number. We don't have an intercom down here so just call me directly," he handed her the paper and winked at her. Desdemona blushed.

Whitefox's cheek twitched and Elizabeth grinned at her husband. Oh, this was going to be interesting to watch unfold. For once she and her husband were going to be on the sidelines enjoying the festivities unfold.

Blackhawk patted his brother on the shoulder in support. "Meet you upstairs Callen," he headed for the door. "Sheriff, how about that work space for us now?" It wasn't lost on him that the man was checking out the doctor, and he was going to help his brother out and run interference.

"Oh, yeah. Let me take you there," he said, watching the woman over his shoulder and almost walking into Whitefox. "Sorry Agent," he said, tipping his hat. The testosterone battle was going to be brewing for a while.

Elizabeth was going to give them some space, and she wandered over to Christina to harass her about trace.

"Stay inside, Desi," he said softly, as he moved towards her.

She looked up at him when the tone of his voice changed. "Okay, Callen," she answered.

He took the paper from her fingers and ripped it in half, and pulled the pen that was tucked into her wildly pulled up hair. He scribbled his number on it and tucked the pen back into the chaos, and then leaned down to her ear. "If you need anything, you call me." His lips were millimeters from her ear, and he answered his own question. It was her hair that smelled so damn good.

Desdemona was sure her eyes were huge. In her entire dating career, never had a man been that blatantly forceful with her.

"Promise me Desi," he said vehemently, determined to have his way on this one and strong arm her into compliance.

She felt like she had no choice and it stole her breath. "I promise, Callen."

Whitefox stepped back from her body, and it was torture. The idea that the Sheriff had any notion to move in on Desdemona fired everything deep inside of him. It wasn't happening. Whitefox glanced over at Elizabeth and a silent message was passed between them. She'd keep Sheriff James Duffy at a distance in his absence.

Now he could focus his job and believe that the woman would be safe from other poaching males in the station. Specifically ones that went by the name James Duffy. There were few he'd trust with the woman, but his sister-in-law's promise was good as gold, and he silently gave her a fist bump in gratitude.

"Elizabeth, the usual for lunch?" he called over his shoulder.

"Yeah, thanks Cal," she answered, moving towards the woman, smiling.

"Desi, I'll pick you up lunch," he stated, not giving her an option as he walked from the room.

Desdemona didn't know what to say. She looked over at her boss and the look must have said it all.

Elizabeth dropped her arm over her shoulders reassuringly. "I don't think I've ever seen him act like that before with anyone," she said, smiling. "Looks like Callen is staking his claim," she started laughing at the look of horror on her ME's face.

"I'm not territory." Desdemona managed to get out in abject horror, but part of her was incredibly turned on by the man and his possessiveness. "Is Ethan like that?" she had to ask, and hoped Elizabeth wouldn't be offended.

"Let's just say it's a Blackhawk gene thing, and the more you try and escape it, the more it will follow you and wear you out," she warned. "I say just accept it, go with it and enjoy the ride. It's a really awesome ride." Elizabeth pushed to help Callen out.

"I honestly don't know whether I should be angry or …" She didn't even have a word for it, but she was stuck on the phrase 'enjoy the ride'. It conjured up so many ideas in her mind, and none were appropriate to be having in autopsy or with her boss.

"Doc, here's my opinion. Once they set a goal, both men are pretty diligent in reaching it. They have bossy, sexy man syndrome. It takes less energy to just go with it."

Desdemona sighed.

"If this helps, picture them in their boxers with all the tattoos," Elizabeth suggested. "Whenever Ethan makes me really mad, I just go with that technique and believe it or not the anger just disappears."

Desdemona started laughing. "That I believe."

"See?"

"Maybe we should start the autopsies," she muttered, as she tried to regain focus. Yeah, something like lust was sitting deep inside her, urging her to just go for it as she pictured both men half-naked and covered in tattoos. Then came the jealousy that Elizabeth was close to both men equally.

"Good Idea," Elizabeth answered patting her on the shoulder. "Let's get started because now I'm thinking about sex in an autopsy room, and that's just creepy and very wrong."

"I'm with you there." Desdemona kept dwelling on the situation with Callen. For some reason she believed everything Elizabeth said.

Whitefox wasn't going to give up the chase.

Callen found the room that his brother had absconded, and taken over as their own. He was busy unpacking a white board, and setting it up for his wife. On the team, Ethan was the profiler, and Elizabeth was the one that took all the pieces they found and put it together to create the big picture.

Both Agents worked well together, and Whitefox was just glad he could learn from both of them, and be part of the team. He dropped into one of the chairs and dropped his boots on the edge of the table.

"You okay?" asked his brother. Callen had the distinct look on his face, and he'd seen it before when they were growing up and when he met Elizabeth. It was the look of woman troubles.

"Yes. No. I don't know."

Blackhawk laughed. "Here's the tech finger print reports. See what you can find out. Check AFIS, and we'll go from there." When his brother wanted to talk, he'd spill what was bugging him. He slid the laptop over to him, and a stack of papers.

Whitefox began entering the data and pulling information from AFIS to see if it would match any of the victims. Well, minus the one that didn't have fingers to print.

"Do you think I have a snowballs chance in hell?" he asked his brother after a few minutes, and he wasn't talking about finding a fingerprint match.

"Depends," his brother said, turning around and sitting on the corner of the table. "What are you looking for?" he asked.

When he'd taken the risk with Elizabeth, he didn't know they'd end up where they were today. In his heart he didn't believe he was worthy of her and their love. She'd convinced him otherwise and he'd fallen in love and fast. Now he couldn't imagine a single day without her in his life.

"I don't know." And he was telling the truth.

He reached into the wealth of knowledge he had as a profiler and as the man's brother. "I look at Doctor Adare, and I see that she's afraid. I don't get what's scaring her, but something is making her want to run. She's hiding things, Cal."

"I get that feeling too."

"Elizabeth ran her."

Whitefox looked up and was a little angry that they ran Doctor Adare behind his back. "Why?"

"Uh, shut it down, Cal. We're her bosses and we can run our employees. In fact, you're our employee too."

Whitefox didn't look any less pissed at the reasoning.

"Hey, Elizabeth loves you and so do I. We didn't find anything out of the ordinary, but what I did notice is she packs up and makes a break for it every year or so. Doctor Adare doesn't stay in one place very long."

"Maybe she just likes to move around…" But he knew otherwise. The red rose kept popping into his head, and he didn't know if he should tell his brother or not.

"Her last job was working in a lab doing forensics for a private company. She was making almost four hundred thousand dollars a year."

Whitefox almost fell out of his chair. "Holy Shit, seriously?"

"Yeah, and she came here to the FBI and took a big salary cut. Almost half. Why?"

His brother had a point, it did indeed look shady.

"I think that if you're going to invest the time and effort into her for the long haul, you need to find out what will make her bolt. If she's going to bolt in a year, and you're in love with her at the time, you'll get your heart handed to you. Plus you need to see if she's 'the one'."

Ethan suspected his brother couldn't truthfully say that.

Whitefox nodded. Desdemona wouldn't ever be 'the one', but he believed she could come close. Then the guilt returned over his feelings for Elizabeth and the betrayal of his brother.

"Then there's the real problem in all this. If she breaks your heart, Elizabeth will track her down, skin her and laugh while doing it."

"She's not native." That was all he had to say, and his brother's face softened.

They were both American Indian, but Callen Whitefox was full blooded and expected to keep the bloodlines pure. Their Grandfather was old school and hard core. The only reason he accepted Elizabeth was he had a dream, and she was the one he thought was sent to heal their family.

"Cal, you have to do what's right for you here." Blackhawk put his hand over his chest. "I get the whole native-white man issue that granddad has, but you know what," he paused. "What if she's the one that will make you happy? What you need to ask yourself is if it's worth waiting for a woman that's native and only brings you half the happiness. Is that the sacrifice you're willing to make? Maybe she won't be the one, but why shut out the option, because she's not Native. Why don't you just relax and enjoy the fact you might have found a woman you happen to have an interest in and have fun with it?"

Callen was torn. Family obligations or a legitimate chance at a future not tied to his past. Maybe his brother was right. It wasn't like he had to spend the rest of his life with her, there was dating.

"Think about it, and then decide. Besides you have one thing in your favor."

"What's that?" he asked.

Blackhawk laughed. "Elizabeth has the men in this family wrapped around her fingers. If there's a way to get granddad to accept her, and welcome her, Lyzee can do it."

He laughed. "She said as much."

"Then I say you forget the whole Native American clause granddad threw out there and just start living and decide after the fact. Her heritage and yours shouldn't matter."

He was curious. "If granddad hated Elizabeth what would you have done?"

"I would have had children with her, built a life and lived happily ever after off the Rez and away from the old man. Granddad made his choice, and I had to make mine. You're heart wants what it wants." Blackhawk grinned. "Mine wanted a bossy, bold, gorgeous woman who could kick my ass."

He laughed because so did his and ironically they were probably picturing the same damn woman; Elizabeth.

"I've never been happier, and you need to focus on the happy and forget the bullshit that's holding you back."

Whitefox felt a little better. Maybe his brother had a point, and then he recalled what they were discussing. Desdemona was running from something, and he was going to have to vanquish that demon before he could get her to stay in one place long enough to get to know him.

He ran the fingerprint reports, but his mind was downstairs on the unusual woman that caught his interest. Now he just had to trap her and lock her down.

Elizabeth sat on a metal counter top and watched the doctor work. She was fastidious, meticulous and did her job impeccably. As she did the internals, her voice went monotone, almost cold and emotionless. It had to be a coping mechanism that she developed in medical school or in her past. Currently her hand was stuck in the third victim, and she was fishing around for organs. They'd retrieved all of them but the stomach.

"Just the stomach missing?" she asked.

"I'm almost around all the bowel, just give me a sec," she answered as she carefully felt around by memory. If she pulled out the intestines, she'd have twenty five feet of slippery organs to replace in a tiny cavity. It wouldn't be easy, fun or pretty. Especially if it perforated and all the goo oozed out all over her scrubs.

"I don't know how you do it," commented Elizabeth. "Seriously."

"Ever kill anyone," she asked, nonchalantly.

"I've been known to take a life or five when the time is at hand," she answered, without any regret whatsoever.

147

"We all have a propensity for certain things in life. This is my thing. I like to work backwards through a person's existence and see how they lived. Then I can tell you how they died. " At least Elizabeth wasn't judging her.

"So, when the bleached blonde upstairs called you Morticia, why did you flinch?" If the woman was going to get cozy with Callen, she needed to know.

"When I was in Med school during my ME rotation, there was this one girl in the class, and she hated me" She began stitching up the Y incision. "People tend to think I'm obsessed with death because of my choice in clothes and my hair."

"I think you hide behind the clothes so no one sees you, and they focus on the outside and not the inside."

She looked up over her glasses and stared at the woman. Elizabeth Blackhawk was too smart to bullshit- so why try. "Perhaps. Anyway, this girl had it in for me, and she used to bully me."

"Why didn't you kick her ass?" Elizabeth would have just taken her out and beat the hell out of the woman. Nothing beat a good old fashioned ass kicking to shut up a moron.

She laughed. "You're more the 'ass kicker', and I'm more the 'cower in fear in a corner' kind of woman." Desdemona didn't mind the truth. She wasn't as tough as Elizabeth.

"If it matters, I happen to like your hair," she looked at the red highlights and was intrigued.

"I wear black because it's slimming and easy to match things to, and I happen to like red and black together."

Elizabeth thought about it. "I think you should be proud of being called Morticia."

Now she looked at her like she was crazy.

"Morticia Addams was the coolest woman ever. Look how she had her husband so smitten with her that he couldn't keep his hands off her. Then look how she commanded a room," Elizabeth grinned and got ready for the final part of her heart healing dialog.

"You think?" Desdemona never thought of it that way.

"*Normal is an illusion. What is normal for the spider is chaos for the fly,*" said Elizabeth, as she stood when her phone rang. It was Timothy Blackhawk.

"That's an awesome quote," she said smiling. "Who said it?"

Elizabeth answered the phone. "Hold on, granddad," she said, and then looked over at her new friend. "Morticia Addams said it. Be the spider Doc, and the flies will be running scared."

Desdemona decided that maybe she was right. After all, Elizabeth commanded a room. She had her husband's attention and Callen's easily. Of course Elizabeth was more 'Morticia' than her, but she could try and fix that.

Elizabeth wandered out to the corridor. "Granddad! How is the real love of my life doing?" she said enthusiastically into the phone.

"Elizabeth my precious raven, I am fine. How are you? That's the question." Timothy Blackhawk loved his granddaughter. She was a blessing and he believed sent to heal his family and take over as matriarch when his time was done on Earth.

"We're out on assignment, but doing well. Baby Blackhawk is kicking up a storm and Braxton Hicks contractions just started."

"You be safe, sweetheart, and finish growing my great grandson."

"What's bothering you granddad?" Elizabeth knew it wasn't going to be a social call. The eighty-eight year old man just had some Indian voodoo that gave him insight to everything. If he was calling, there was a good reason.

"I had a vision, and it involved Callen. He isn't answering his phone. I called your office and they told me you were in the field together."

"He's probably with the techs working on the murders."

"Who is the woman, Elizabeth?"

And so it began.

Honestly, she didn't expect him to call her, and Timothy caught her off guard. Despite that, she wasn't going to lie to him. "Her name is Desdemona Adare."

"In the dream she was this little doe, and she was running and hiding in the thicket. The fox was chasing her and when she was trapped in the brambles, the fox was trying to save her."

Elizabeth didn't say anything.

"She isn't native is she, Elizabeth?"

"No granddad, she isn't." Personally she thought it was some stupid antiquated thing that Timothy should let go of, but he was old school and who was she to tell him what to do.

"Callen knows how I feel about that."

"Granddad, I love you, but you really aren't part of the relationship and should butt out." Her husband would be horrified if he had heard this conversation. "Let Callen find a woman on his own. There shouldn't be outside influence from you, Ethan or me."

Timothy roared with laughter. "You are the only one that will stand up to me. I appreciate that greatly. When you come back, I demand to see her and my favorite granddaughter." Timothy began coughing.

"Are you still sick granddad?" she asked, worriedly.

"It's only a cold my sweet, protective raven. Stop worrying and come see me when this is all over."

"I love you, Granddad."

"I Love you, Granddaughter," he answered, hanging up the phone.

Now Elizabeth had to figure out how to get a stubborn patriarch to accept a timid outsider, find a killer that liked parts of men, keep her husband from freaking out, and grow a baby. Damn this womanhood gig was demanding!

"Anything on fingerprints?" asked Blackhawk, looking across the table at his brother who was watching AFIS do its thing.

"This is the final victim, and so far nothing. I don't think they're in the system," he started but then heard the beeping. "Wait!" He spun the laptop around. "We have a name on victim five. The one that was missing the ears," he said.

"Patrick Payne, and he has an arrest record." Whitefox scanned the screen and read the information. "His home address is outside of Red River. Our victim didn't live here, but about eighty miles from here."

"Read me the stats. I'll send the info down to Lyzee," he had his tablet out and began inputting information as his brother read the information. After typing in the address and basics he hit send.

"Doctor Adare was pretty close. Age thirty nine, and has a history of white collar crimes. He's never done hard time, but he did do a six month stint courtesy of the state in a minimum security detention facility."

"Okay, well one down four to go."

Blackhawk was about to comment when his phone beeped. It was the chime he set specifically for his wife. He read the message.

> *Got info thanks! Baby is starving and granddad called about Callen and the 'woman' in his dream. Give him the heads up that he's aware. I'm handling it.*
> *You smelled really great today, want to make out tonight?(Callen if you're reading this I meant with my husband.)*

Ethan laughed, especially at the last part. His wife was something. He'd better tell his brother what was going down. But it would have to wait until after he confirmed making out with his wife. He furiously typed and sent it, only then looking up at his brother.

"Why are you smiling like an idiot?"

Blackhawk passed his phone to his brother and watched his face go from amusement to horror that their grandfather was already worried about the 'woman' and then back to amusement. "Well hell now I'm doubly depressed. Granddad knows and I don't get to make out with Elizabeth tonight."

"Oh you can make out with her," he said, pausing.

Callen knew not to get his hopes up, and he waited for it. He'd give up his arm to have one big make out session with Elizabeth.

"That is if you want to die a painful death right after."

"Do I get a head start after?"

His brother snorted. "No," and then punched him.

"Then I guess I'll decline."

"Very smart man. Let's take a break and go get the women some lunch, including the baby," he patted his brother on the shoulder. "It'll all work out, Cal."

Whitefox only hoped he was right, and then he only hoped Elizabeth could convince the eighty-eight year old patriarch that controlled everything to let him break the biggest rule he'd set in his entire life.

Yeah, wasn't looking good. There were only so many miracles one man could get in his life. He'd had his share; his brother returned, and he found a woman to protect his heart. Getting another was going to be slim to none.

Doctor Adare rolled her neck to work out the kinks that were forming. It had been five hours of looking down, and she felt like her neck was going to be stuck that way forever. She pushed the cart with the man's body into the makeshift cooler and froze. There was someone standing in there with a mask and long knife. She backed out of the cooler and her voice was frozen.

"I'm gonna cut you bitch," he hissed, angrily.

That set her voice free. She screamed.

Elizabeth jumped off the counter, and her head jerked up at the blood curdling sound coming from her new friend. When her eyes registered what caused the fear from Desdemona, she did what any pregnant FBI agent would do. She charged the man.

It didn't occur to her to shoot him. He was relatively close to the doctor and waving around a wicked looking knife, and that meant getting him unarmed.

The first hit knocked him back, drawing his complete focus. When he lunged for her, Elizabeth did what she was trained to do. She fought hard to save her, Desdemona, and her child.

And once she figured out what was going on, she neutralized the problem as painfully as she could.

Just because she was pissed off!

Callen and Ethan were almost at the burger place, when his cell phone beeped. He looked down and panicked. Desdemona sent him a message.

HURRY BACK NOW! EMERGENCY!

"Ethan, get us back to the Sheriff's station. Something's happened!" Whitefox held on as his brother whipped the Denali around and hit the lights. A million things were going through his mind, and he was sure his brother's too.

"Call them," Ethan ordered, as he passed out all the cars in front of him. If something happened to his wife, he'd never forgive himself for leaving her alone.

Whitefox hit dial and started calling Desdemona's phone, and it was dumped right into voicemail. Now he furiously punched speed dial and waited for Elizabeth to answer her phone. She always answered his calls, and now the nausea was crawling up from his belly.

"Nothing, Ethan," he said, and then stared in horror at the Sheriff's station parking lot. There were three ambulances with lights on flashing ominously. "Oh my God," he mumbled. Every horrible thought went through his mind. Since Desdemona sent the message, he started to think something had happened to Elizabeth and the baby. This many ambulances meant something bad had happened, not a simple slip or paper cut. Whitefox began to panic, and worry about Elizabeth.

The brothers bailed out of the Denali, charging the sheriff's station, and searching for the rest of their team.

Ethan was scared shitless, hoping his wife and child were safe. Running headlong down the stairs to the makeshift morgue, he rushed the door, practically knocking the sheriff off his feet. When he got close, his heart finally began beating again as he heard his wife tearing someone a new one.

"Are you out of your fucking mind?" she yelled, pointing at the man lying on the gurney. "If I pulled my gun, you'd be going out of here in a God damned body bag! We're the FBI; we don't shoot to maim idiots wielding knives! When I pull the trigger I'm planning on standing over your damn body!"

Elizabeth looked up and saw her husband and brother-in-law rush through the door.

"What happened?" he asked, looking around. The lab was a mess, and it looked like there was a brawl.

"Deputy Asshole decided it would be funny to hide in the cooler in a Halloween mask and fake plastic knife, trying to scare Desdemona. Then I kicked the shit out of him and could have killed him!" she said, pointing at Deputy Bobby Lee Tills.

Both men lunged, much like rabid dogs looking to chew on a victim. The only thing that stopped them was the EMTs that blocked their patient from getting more injuries.

"You are fucking dead," growled Blackhawk, as he reached for the man's throat, almost getting his hands on his neck.

Callen glanced over at Desdemona, and she looked scared to death. He went to her, and pulled him against his body. "Are you okay, honey?" he asked, stroking her hair as she buried her face in his shoulder.

"I think so," she mumbled. "Elizabeth got bumped in the face during the fight and won't let the EMT's check her out."

Both men moved towards Elizabeth.

"I'm okay," she said, touching her lip and scowling at Doctor Adare for ratting her out. "I bit it when I caught his elbow to the chin."

Blackhawk touched her lower lip, and then pushed her towards his brother to keep safe, while he killed the deputy.

Callen pulled her against his body and immediately began inspecting her lip. Since the serial killer on the Rez, both men were super protective of Elizabeth. He held both women tight and dropped a kiss on her injured lip.

Sheriff James Duffy interjected himself between his deputy and the FBI agent, Understanding their anger. "We'll work this out," he said calmly, as he tried to stop Blackhawk from killing the deputy strapped to the gurney.

"Work it out?" Blackhawk raged, looking over the shoulder of the Sheriff at Bobby Lee Tills. "The man came after my pregnant wife, and in my world that means I kill him now," he growled. "And worry about the little details later."

Deputy Tills jumped when Blackhawk lunged again.

The only thing that calmed Ethan down was his wife wrapping her arms around his waist from behind. Blackhawk turned, pulling his wife into his arms to check her for any additional injuries she wasn't telling him about. When he was sure she was unscathed, he glared over at Deputy Tills. Elizabeth had beaten the hell out of him. His face was swelling, and he looked like he had a broken nose. "I'm going to cut your fucking balls off Tills and feed them to you!" he growled, pointing at the man, as he held his wife protectively.

"I'm sorry about this, Agents. Sincerely sorry for my Deputy's behavior, and what he's done. It's inexcusable, and he'll be reprimanded. I promise."

"Reprimanded?" Whitefox was appalled that the Sheriff thought it was going to end there. He'd tried to scare the women, and that was just unacceptable. "We both know that's not good enough, Sheriff Duffy."

Desdemona clung to his side, and she was finally starting to feel her heartbeat return to normal.

"He tried to assault two FBI agents. That's a federal offense, and I'm going to throw in the weapons charge for shits and giggles," added Blackhawk.

"It was plastic," whined Tills, "I just wanted to wipe the smug look off the bitch's face for calling me a redneck hillbilly!" He realized it was a bad choice of words.

Both men lunged again, but this time the women held them back.

"I'm going to kill you after my brother does for calling her that!" Whitefox growled at the man for using derogatory words to describe Elizabeth.

Tills looked nervous.

"When he's patched up, Sheriff Duffy, he's being transported back to FBI West and charged with felony assault with a weapon, because he's a smart ass and likes making comments, I'm tossing in felonious stalking and lying in wait for the women."

"You can't do that!" objected Tills.

Blackhawk was seething and feeling homicidal. "You could have hurt my wife and child! You're lucky I'm taking you in at all!"

"Get him out of here," motioned the Sheriff. "Quick, before we have a homicide on our hands."

Immediately, Ethan's attention was on his wife and the baby growing in her belly. Gently he stroked his child as he gazed into her eyes, seeking the truth. "You didn't get hit in the stomach did you baby?" he asked his wife, concern overwhelming him. "I'll kill him if he even touched our child." And he meant every word of it.

"No Ethan, Baby Blackhawk is completely safe," she said wrapping her arms around his neck and nuzzling his cheek. He was vibrating with anger, and she just wanted to alleviate some of the tension. "It's okay, Ethan," she whispered in his ear, until his body relaxed marginally.

"Can we get out of here for a while," whispered Desdemona. "I think I need to just get out of here and regain my bearings. I feel really unsteady," she said, softly.

Elizabeth looked over, worried about her friend. She was pale and shaky.

"Come on," answered Whitefox, as he bundled her into her coat. "How about we go get you some tea?"

"I think I need a bourbon."

Ethan Blackhawk helped his wife into her parka. "When I get back, you better have him ready for transport, because if not, I will arrest you for interfering with a federal agent's duty in apprehending a criminal." He wasn't screwing around. This was way past crossing a line.

"Can we talk this through Agent?" he asked, hoping to keep his deputy from going to federal prison. "Go get lunch. There's a diner down the road. 'Cup of Joe', they serve alcohol too. I'll meet you in my office. We can all calm down and talk this out rationally."

Blackhawk was already calming down now that he knew both women were safe. "We'll be back in two hours, Sheriff." He was back in control and in Director mode.

James Duffy nodded, and walked out of the room frustrated as hell wondering how he was going to fix this.

Now he had even more of a mess to contend with in town. Two FBI agents ready to beat the hell out of his deputy, a wrecked basement, a killer on a rampage, and a brewing migraine. Today was a really bad day to be Sheriff of Red River. Maybe if he was lucky, the mayor would let him resign.

Yeah, probably not. Who'd want to take over this mess? Nobody in their right mind would want to deal with this hassle.

Apparently, he was crazy.

In the Denali, no one spoke.

156

Both men were a frazzled mess over what could have happened if Elizabeth wasn't really good at protecting herself and those around her.

Elizabeth sat beside her husband and was still holding his hand, reassuringly. What she really wanted to do was roll her shoulder, because it hurt like a bitch. The last face shot she gave Bobby Lee Tills cost her. Now there was an ache beginning in the joint, and moving down her arm. Elizabeth hoped he didn't think to ask about it or Ethan Blackhawk might lose his damn mind.

Desdemona sat practically in Callen Whitefox's lap, as he held her close and stroked her hair. Being close to him was cathartic and maddening at the same time now that the adrenaline was dissipating.

Finally Ethan Blackhawk let out a deep breath. "I'm afraid to ask because it's going to get me angry again, but I guess I'm obligated to request the details. What happened?"

"I know that sigh. That's the 'Elizabeth can't I leave you alone for an hour' sigh. I want to go on the record right now and say in my defense, that I was sitting on the counter reading a tech report. I didn't leave the building, I didn't provoke a stranger, and I didn't even think anything was going to happen. Desdemona was finishing an autopsy. We were just working and minding our own damn business."

"And?"

Desdemona continued. "I just finished the fourth autopsy. My neck was killing me from staring down for five hours straight, and I wasn't paying attention. I pushed the cart into the cooler, and there he was. He came out at me swinging that knife. There was no way we could know it wasn't real."

"And then?"

"Your wife jumped in front of me to protect me, and beat him up."

Elizabeth snickered until her husband looked over at her and lifted an eyebrow in displeasure. She knew what he was thinking. His face said it clearly.

A pregnant woman should have a little more common sense.

"You should have shot him."

Elizabeth stared at her husband. "He was wielding a foot long knife, and Desdemona was blocking the way. I'm an excellent shot Ethan, but even I can make a mistake. What if I hit her?"

Whitefox pulled her closer. Just the idea made him sick to his stomach. He cradled her cheek with the palm of his hand and offered her comfort. Then he felt more sick that Elizabeth risked her own life.

"Okay, so you couldn't shoot him. I'll buy that," said Blackhawk, watching his brother in the rearview mirror. "Please continue Desdemona."

Doctor Adare licked her bottom lip as she tried to focus. "Elizabeth ran at him and knocked him away from me, and she had all his focus from there on out. She's pretty fast for a pregnant woman."

"Thank you."

Blackhawk looked over at his wife and gave her the look.

"I was doing my job." And keeping her promise to Callen, but Ethan didn't need that piece of information.

"When he went at her, she booted him in the gut, and that's when he clipped her in the face, but it was completely a lucky shot."

"Yeah it was," she mumbled.

"Elizabeth countered with this super painful looking thing with her elbow to his throat, punched him in the face-twice, and then I think when he still wouldn't go down she kicked him in the groin." Desdemona was now starting to laugh. It was that laughter you got when your adrenaline finally stopped and you came down off the fear high.

Elizabeth cracked her knuckles and tried to not snicker. "What?" she asked innocently, when her husband stared at her again.

"I don't think the deputy expected her to have cowboy boots on, and the shot to the groin was the one that took him to the floor."

Both men cringed. A family jewel shot was painful, but one with cowboy boots on had to be doubly wicked.

"Then," Desdemona continued, "on his way down he smacked his head off the counter, and she stomped on his solar plexus. But I'm rather sure the groin shot was the end of it all, but

158

getting the wind knocked out of him twice was probably to prove a point."

Blackhawk ran his hands through his hair not sure if he should be laughing or yanking it all out.

"That's when he started crying and begging."

Now both women were snickering. "He wept like a baby," added Elizabeth. "It was very gratifying."

"Today I earned my first gray hair," commented her husband. "You and Desdemona aren't allowed to play together anymore."

"Hey!" interjected Elizabeth. "I was just doing my job. Nutjob, knife and damsel in distress."

"Callen and I managed to work alone in a room and no one called ambulances or for help once. In fact, we even managed to safely exit the building to get lunch. Again, you two are not playing together alone anymore."

Whitefox laughed. "In theory you'd think that plan was going to work, but there's going to be a huge problem with keeping them apart, Ethan," he said to his brother.

He looked up in the mirror confused.

"Know the house right behind yours that you can see from your bedroom?"

Blackhawk shrugged. "Yeah, what about it?"

Whitefox pointed at the woman leaning against him.

"Hi neighbor!" she said brightly, hoping they wouldn't be disappointed.

Elizabeth turned and grinned at her new friend. "Nice," she smiled, offering her friend a fist bump. "I have an accomplice next door."

Desdemona accepted it, laughing and relaxing.

"Great and here I always thought home was the safe place where nothing can happen." Blackhawk started laughing. How could he not?

"Spiders and flies," she said, winking at her friend.

Both women burst into laughter at their private joke, and the look on Ethan and Callens' faces.

Both men were pretty sure the women had lost their minds.

Sheriff James Duffy sat in his office with one bitch of a headache. There were five dead men, a deputy that tried to assault two women, and two FBI agents that were on the warpath. Literally. When his phone rang, he seriously contemplated not answering it, but then duty won out and he figured it couldn't possibly get any worse.

Then he realized how wrong he'd been. It went from bad to absolutely horrible in the matter of minutes.

It was the hospital. His deputy had told them he needed to pee and escaped out a window. No one thought to monitor a deputy, because he was the law.

He had to be asleep, and at any moment he was going to wake up and find out that this had all been a big nightmare.

Duffy rattled around in his desk until he found the bottle of pills. As he popped two pills to dull the ache in his brain, he tried to mentally prepare himself to tell the FBI agents that the man they wanted arrested was gone.

The shit was going to hit the fan.

That should go over real well. He was picturing Ethan Blackhawk losing his damn mind. Now he needed to do something proactive to counter act the hospital's stupidity.

"Sheila," he bellowed.

The woman came running at the tone of his voice. It wasn't like him to raise his voice. Sheriff Duffy was pretty laid back. "Yeah, Jimmy?" she was frazzled over what had gone on at the station. She was pretty sure the women deserved the scare, and they were just bullying a small town deputy.

"Call in Julian Littlemoon. I have a special assignment for him," he said, swallowing two more pills. "Tell him it's going to involve tracking and to dress warm."

"Yes Boss," she said, backing out of the room.

Good. Now if Julian did what he did best it might appease two angry FBI agents. If not, he might luck out and Blackhawk wouldn't kick the shit out of him in lieu of his deputy.

Although his wife was the wild card and just might.

Callen was stressed. The text message he received from Desdemona made everything in him go stone cold. Now that she was beside him and was safe, he felt a little better, but he could still see she was nervous and that disturbed him. He was trying to comfort her the best he could, but he was trying to keep from crossing the invisible line. They weren't a couple, and he didn't know how she'd react if he acted like they were.

Something in him warmed at the thought. Yeah, he wouldn't mind being a couple with her. Desdemona Adare would be an adventure. Callen thought it through, and Doctor Adare could be a good partner through life. Next to Elizabeth, she was a sound choice.

"Still want that bourbon?" he asked, running his hand up and down her back, reassuringly.

Desdemona was trying to relax, but the man beside her was making her completely insane, and running his fingertips up and down the most sensitive part of her back. Callen Whitefox was giving her the mother of all hot flashes. She was flushing red, she was sure of it. "No, no bourbon. Thank you," she answered finally. That's all she needed to do. Get buzzed and do something incredibly stupid like jumping the man and kissing him until she got it out of her system.

Crap, more heat crept up her body.

"Let's order lunch," suggested Blackhawk, as he waved to a waitress and waited for her to meander on over.

"Yeah sugar," she said, snapping her gum and smiling at him while she fluffed her bleached blonde hair.

"We're ready to order."

"Okay, whatcha gonna have handsome?" she inquired, winking at him. "There's waitress on the menu today if you're interested."

Automatically he placed his hand on his wife's leg, in case she tried to jump up and kill the woman. Even if he was single, after his ex-girlfriend, blondes turned him right off. He liked out of control, raven haired hellions that kept him on his toes.

"Three cheese burgers, bacon on all of them and for one of them extra mayo," he looked over at Desdemona.

"I'll have a veggie burger please, no mayo just plain. Whole wheat bun please," she smiled at the woman sweetly, feeling bad for the woman. Elizabeth was glaring at her like she

161

was right. She was on the menu- dead waitress, with a side of kicked ass and her body to never be found again.

"Sounds good." She walked around the counter and the sweaty bald man behind the counter slapped her on the ass. She didn't protest, even though it grated on her last nerve. She needed the job and she refrained from hitting the man.

"I would have broken his arm off and beat him to death with it," added Elizabeth, taking a sip of her iced tea. "Although, she hit on my husband, so she's on her own and my sympathy is all dried up."

"Ah I love a violent woman," said her husband. "A violent, vindictive woman with a wicked temper that likes to hurt people and carries a gun."

"Lookee here cowboy, that describes me. How do you feel about fat and wobbly?" she asked, laughing.

"I happen to find fat and wobbly very sexy." Blackhawk leaned over and kissed his wife lightly on the lips.

"Good answer to avoid the violent, vindictive woman with a gun."

Everyone at the table laughed.

Desdemona watched her bosses and smiled. It was amazing how different they were once you got to know them. She was surprised they were the same people. In the office they seemed aloof and distant, but when they were off duty they were really normal people. Apparently, they were a very happy couple.

"Are you done with the autopsies?" Blackhawk asked pulling Desdemona out of her private thoughts. .

"Unfortunately no, I have victim five to complete yet, and then I can call it a night," she answered. "After lunch I'll get him done. I've noticed that all the victims have one single wound and that's it. The killer has intent to remove one part and discard the rest. Nothing else is damaged on the bodies."

"You're seriously going to autopsy after you eat?" Elizabeth was horrified. "Count me out. I want to keep my burger down. One of the men will have to pony up and ride that rodeo with you. If I wasn't pregnant I could pull it off, but Baby Blackhawk doesn't like autopsy post feeding."

Both men laughed already aware of what was coming.

"That's why I don't eat meat," she answered, and Elizabeth almost dropped her iced tea.

Blackhawk caught the glass and placed it back on the table, as the laughter ensued. Elizabeth simply stared at her blankly, like Desdemona Adare was talking a foreign language.

"Are you okay?" asked her husband, still grinning. Eating meat was his wife's holy grail. People who didn't were foreign to her and possibly alien and not of this planet.

"Maybe the deputy did hit me, my hearing must be going. Maybe I should see a doctor. Did Desdemona just say she doesn't eat meat?" Her face was dead serious, as she looked over at the men.

"Yes, she's very serious and told us last night."

"Not even bacon?" she whispered, horrified at the thought.

"Nope." Desdemona laughed at the look on her friend's face. It wasn't one of judgment, but one of genuine disbelief. "They do make a really good tofu bacon that I like."

Now she looked completely horrified. "Tofu bacon?"

Desdemona found the look on her face funny as hell.

Callen patted Elizabeth's leg and laughed. "Breathe deep. You can do it beautiful."

Desdemona ignored the nickname Callen had for her boss, or the jealousy would take over. "Elizabeth, I've been an ME for ten years. At three autopsies a day, that's nine thousand bodies I've had to cut into and wade around in to find the grossest things. To me, the human body is like meat. I just can't do it."

"Well when you put it that way, it kind of grosses me out now too," she said, as the waitress put the big greasy burger in front of her. Elizabeth looked at it and thought about it.

Both men grinned at Elizabeth.

"No meat huh?" she asked, eyeing the veggie burger in front of her friend, and then the meat burger sitting in front of her. One was bland and stuffed with things it shouldn't be, and the other had cheese and bacon sitting on it, calling to her.

"No meat," she answered, dipping a french fry in ketchup. "Not to mention if I ate the way you do, I'd weigh four hundred pounds. I'm not blessed with your metabolism. Even pregnant you're still thin"

Elizabeth began weighing the pros and cons.

Ethan Blackhawk watched his wife and was entertained. She was genuinely contemplating the options on eating the burger in front of the doctor.

Finally hunger won out. "What's that baby?" she asked her belly, and garnering laughter from the three others at the table. "Uh huh. Okay, I agree." She shrugged, picking it up to take a bite. "We're over it," she answered and smiled as her husband started laughing. "Sorry Doc. Blackhawk bossiness wins out once again."

Sheriff James Duffy was waiting for his deputy when he knocked on the door. The man was full Native, and one of his big talents was tracking. If they had a missing person, call in Julian Littlemoon. The man just had mad skills when it came to finding the lost. He was either very lucky or the powers that be had granted him a genuine gift. Once when a child had wandered away, Julian Littlemoon had found him in under four hours.

"You needed me, Boss?" he asked, dropping down into the chair in front of the desk.

"While you were off, we had a little incident," he told the man what happened with Bobby Lee and the female agent. He expected amusement, but what he didn't expect was the full-blown uproarious laughter.

"She beat him down, huh? I'd like to feel bad for him, but every racist bigot has his day, and he deserved it. I think I may like to shake her hand," he said still laughing. "It's pretty sad when a pregnant woman can kick your ass. He should retire and contemplate not tossing around the word 'Indian'."

Well that answered his question. Elizabeth Blackhawk had apparently been correct. Natives didn't like the word 'Indian'. "He's going to jail if I don't talk the FBI agents down from the cliff."

Littlemoon shrugged. "If some knife wielding wacko came at my woman, I'd kill him or want him in jail too. I can't blame the FBI agent."

Sheriff Duffy sighed. "I have a problem that needs your finesse."

"You want me to hold him down while they beat the hell out of Bobby lee? Sold. Sign me up and I'm ready. I'll do it without pay too."

"No, I need you to find him. When they transported him to the hospital to be patched up, he made a break for it. Once I tell Director Blackhawk he's going to kick my ass instead."

"You're telling me the pregnant FBI agent beat him up that bad that he needed hospital care?" Now he was laughing hysterically again.

"Julian, listen. He escaped and the FBI agents are going to be downright pissed when they get here. I need you to track him, find him, and bring him in for arrest."

Julian would do it, because his boss was in a bind, and because he really disliked the deputy. It would give him pleasure to track him and drag him in to get arrested. "I'll handle it, Boss," he said leaving, but he didn't plan on wiping the smile off his face. This was like a late Christmas present. The biggest staff bigot was on the lam.

Priceless.

James Duffy sat there rubbing his temples as his deputy left his office. The headache wasn't easing in the least. If he were lucky Bobby Lee would turn himself in, or Julian would find him. Then it just might appease the FBI agents.

"What do we know for sure? Let's recap it before we head back into the office. I want to make sure we can update the sheriff with as much information as possible. I don't need him crying to Gabe that I was uncooperative after his deputy tried to assault two of our team." Blackhawk had calmed down, and was now willing to play nice, as long as Tills was going to be handled by the sheriff.

Desdemona went first. "As I said, all the bodies had one injury and each one had a role to play in their death. The victims with the missing hands and feet-the cuts were from a saw that was manually controlled. Not a power one."

"How can you tell?" asked Whitefox.

"Uneven strokes. It was like the killer started and stopped, and then started and stopped numerous times. I can also tell you

165

the bodies were definitely on their backs restrained. I found ligature cuff marks on the men with hands and feet, and the bodies without the appendages, I found strap marks running across their torsos." Desdemona drew an imaginary line across Callen Whitefox's chest to demonstrate.

"So they weren't dead, they weren't able to escape, and they were alive."

"One victim asphyxiated on his own blood. Victim four." She thought back to it. "He had blood in his lungs, and his eyes were definitely blood shot. When I opened him up, he had hemorrhaging in the lungs too, and that's another sign."

"So the killer took out his tongue, and then duct taped him?"

"What the killer used is still up for the techs to determine. They took samples of the adhesive and they're running it now."

Elizabeth sat back in her chair. "Any sexual assault?" She really needed a baseline if this was a man or woman.

"On one thru four, nada. I can give you my answer on the last one when I finish up the autopsy."

Elizabeth looked over at her husband. "Okay, so what do you have in the ways of a profile?" She knew he was only in the beginning stages, but he'd point her in a direction.

"Since there isn't any sexual assault, I'm going to go with female. It's my gut to go the other way, and I don't know if it's because more men are killers than females, or if I'm just bothered by a woman being a predator."

"A woman as a killer bother's me too," added Whitefox, struggling to accept it.

"Why?" inquired Elizabeth.

Whitefox shrugged. "Women are the delicate ones, the gentle ones and I don't like to think of them as killers."

Elizabeth looked at him and didn't speak. She'd taken a few lives in her time. The man that was trying to kill her best friend Livy years ago, her own half-brother and would have been her victim if she could have. Then there was the illegitimate Blackhawk that was going to kill the men in her life on the Rez. She'd taken him out and not thought twice. This obviously spoke volumes about how 'delicate' she seemed.

Blackhawk cleared his throat, signaling to his brother that this was a bad avenue to take. He knew after killing his half-brother that she had blood on her soul, and did it for the men in her life to protect them and carry the burden.

Whitefox finally realized how his words were misconstrued. "Lyzee," he said, reaching over and taking her hand off the table and holding it in his own. Their fingers twined together in second nature. "I didn't mean that the way it sounded. There's a difference between a stone cold killer, and someone that's had to kill for survival and the law."

Desdemona Adare watched the interaction. She'd heard the gossip in the lab about the last few assignments and what had gone down. Those rumors must have been all fact. She glanced down at Whitefox's hand holding Elizabeth's. It was such an intimate act, one that lovers would partake in easily. It was a mix of love and support. When she glanced over at her other boss, he too was holding her hand. Again, the men were offering her some comfort and they seemed to blend the lines between them.

"It's okay, Cal. I know what you meant," she said, softly. If she had to take it all back and do it over she'd do the same exact thing. Her family was her priority. Yeah it hurt her heart, she was human after all, but losing her husband or Callen Whitefox would have hurt more that day. Then almost killing the man that murdered her father, there was very little remorse there.

Both men gently kissed her cheeks in reassurance.

"Back to the profile," Ethan Blackhawk redirected to draw the attention off his wife. "Okay so female and I'm going with Caucasian. She isn't killing anyone ethnically diverse, and that means she is relating to the men in some way."

"Help me understand why women kill," asked Whitefox, still holding Elizabeth's hand. "I'm the newest at this, and I'm here to learn from you both."

Blackhawk nodded. "Okay, women are basically going to kill for a few common reasons, Abuse is the big one. Then you can follow it up with monetary gain, a woman scorned, because she wants what another woman may have or to change her lifestyle and social status."

"When you're looking for a predator," Elizabeth said, "most of the time a criminologist will tell you that men are more likely to be the killer. Women make it personal; it's rarely a sexual thing."

"Exactly," confirmed Blackhawk. "If a woman kills, it's generally people she knows, or who are around her in her social circle. A man will lure, hunt, and stalk his prey. Rarely are women the perpetrators of serial killings. It happens, but not as often."

"As an investigator, Callen, our next logical step is to look at the victims," said Elizabeth. "We need to figure out what they all had in common to catch her eye. If women kill who they know, or pick up in a bar, then these men will all have one thread in common."

"Yes."

"We also have the blonde hairs. They're out for DNA, and they'll confirm male or female," added Desdemona. "Toxicology is out too, and should be back tomorrow."

Blackhawk stared out the window. "I have to admit that I'm having a serious problem with this being a woman. The victims were fairly large. Almost our size," he pointed at his brother and himself. "Elizabeth couldn't carry me, and she's," he almost used the word big, and caught himself when she lifted an eyebrow. "Tall for the average woman."

Desdemona chimed in, "I couldn't carry you either, and I'm the height of the average sized woman. Most females max out at five foot five or five foot six. I'm five foot five and one hundred five pounds. So I would assume that she's between my size and," she looked over at Elizabeth. "What's your height and weight without the boots?"

Both men gasped that Doctor Adare asked a pregnant Elizabeth her weight. Both men braced for the backlash on the question. Jokingly they once asked her and she ended up with one in a headlock and the other on the bottom of the pile arm across his throat. There were threats and promised of scalping and painful death if it was ever brought up again.

Elizabeth didn't bat an eyelash. "I'm five eleven and at my last doctor appointment one hundred forty five pounds."

"How come she could ask your weight, and you didn't just drop kick her into next week?" asked Blackhawk laughing. "Like you did with us."

Elizabeth grinned at her husband. "One- she's a medical professional and could have probably guessed my weight just by looking at me. She stares at naked dead bodies all day."

"I could have guessed," added Doctor Adare. "I would have said no more than one hundred forty. I bet the doctor's scale was off. I'm really good at guessing weight."

Elizabeth took a sip of iced tea. "Then there's the whole thing about it relating to a case. She wasn't asking to be nosey like you both did. Desdemona was asking to get a baseline to the killer and that's my job. I'll spill my weight to keep more bodies from turning up. You both know I'm far from vain enough to worry about what you all think."

"It was completely scientific and nothing more."

Blackhawk shook his head. "This woman thing has too many rules and sub rules. I'll never figure it out."

Whitefox laughed. "I give up. Just elbow me when I say something wrong. It's easier."

"I plan on it," she said laughing and squeezing his hand.

"Don't give her permission to hit you! Then she's going to hit me now too," threw out her husband, laughing.

"Lastly," continued Elizabeth, ignoring their banter. "I'm not overweight even six months pregnant. If I gained sixty pounds rule one and two are immediately forfeited and no one at this table would know my weight and live to tell about it."

"Technically for the gestational time and the length of pregnancy already completed, Elizabeth is underweight. You should eat more," she added laughing, sliding her fries towards Elizabeth.

"That boys was part science and part girlfriend code." Elizabeth popped a piece of gum in her mouth and offered Doctor Adare a stick. "I'll pass on the fries, why tempt the metabolism gods." Before she could move her hand from pushing them away, both men attacked them. "This is why I don't gain weight. They handle that for me," she shook her head, laughing.

"Thank you," she said accepting the gum and watching the men consume the greasy bounty. "Anyway, is it possible she has help? Could we have two women killing together? What we just discussed showed that if it's one killer, she's more bad ass than Elizabeth."

Blackhawk thought about it. "That makes it even less likely, and not because Lyzee isn't the pinnacle of badass. We'd have to examine the trace and see if more DNA pops, but honestly this feels like a single person job to me."

Elizabeth drummed her fingers on the table. "So what you're saying is we think it's a woman, who is going to be super strong, and a blonde. Hey, I bet it's a Viking!" she said, winking at Ethan Blackhawk. She knew he had to be stressed about the assessment and wanted to lighten the clouds brewing in his eyes.

"I believe I read that Vikings like the mountains. How hard could it be to find a strong, tall, blonde who is wearing a skull cap and horns wandering up by the boy scout camp?" added his brother, laughing and winking at the women at the table.

Blackhawk finally broke and started laughing. "When one turns up, don't be surprised. We attract the oddest things!"

.

Desdemona stood over the dead, and was thinking about the living. One living man in particular. She could feel his eyes on her as she worked, and it was super distracting. Right now she was praying to just get the autopsy done and stop her heart from pounding in her chest. Callen Whitefox stirred up a volatile brew in her body, one begging to boil over.

After they had lunch, the team returned to the autopsy room. Whitefox wouldn't leave her alone, and he could easily work from his laptop while keeping an eye on the doctor. If Elizabeth didn't opt out, he would have asked her to step in anyway. He wanted to spend some time alone with the woman, and this was the perfect opportunity to see if she'd fit into his life.

She stripped out of her street clothes, and slipped into scrubs, and he had to admit, they were sexy on her. When she was out of her monster sized heels, she was tiny and petite. He felt like he towered over her, even if he was only one foot taller. She looked delicate, and made of something breakable and at that moment he wanted to wrap himself around her and keep her safe. Aw hell, this was uncharted territory for him, because he wanted to keep her safe.

"Everything's here," she said, stepping down off the stool she had been standing on to look down into the body. "All present and accounted for."

"Well that's good for him, but not us," he said smiling. Autopsies weren't his favorite thing. It wasn't because he was super squeamish. The smell just bothered him. "How'd he die?" he asked moving over to her side. She was still wearing her little black glasses, and he was going crazy because of them.

"The killer took the ears and severed the External carotid Artery. Want to see?" she asked, slipping on a pair of fresh gloves.

"Yeah, show me." Whitefox assisted her up onto the stool with his own gloved hand, and he continued to clutch it in his.

"Right here," Desdemona pointed and leaned over the body, bracing herself on the table.

When he leaned forward, his hip hit the table, and it shifted, and unfortunately she started to fall. Whitefox moved fast and pulled her towards him, catching Desdemona against his body. Just having her this close to him was intoxicating and a very dangerous thing. He hoped she'd help him forget what his heart kept screaming to his brain. Callen was smart enough to know his heart was in denial about who he wanted to be with.

"Oh," she said, as he held her against his body, his lips weren't far from hers.

"I apologize Desi," he said.

"It's okay, it was an accident," she replied, looking right into his eyes and she wondered how long could she stay motionless, just held against him. If she moved he would certainly put her down.

"No, this wasn't an accident," he said softly, and brought her lips to his in a gentle kiss. It wasn't filled with wildness, but sweet and offering heat and enjoyment. His brother's warning kept bouncing around in his brain, and he pushed it down, choosing to ignore it. She may have had a propensity to run, so he would keep it easy and keep her here. He dropped her feet back on the stool, so he could place his hand on the back of her neck, and keep her locked in the kiss.

Desdemona didn't just smell delicious, she tasted like heaven. Peppermint from the gum she'd been chewing. As he kissed her deeper, he felt her arms touch his shoulders at first tentively and then firmly. Yeah, this wasn't an accident at all. Completely on purpose and he loved every second of it. It was nice to know he could distract himself with an attractive woman.

Desdemona had never been kissed like this before. Yeah, she'd had men and lovers that she'd been with, but this man's lips should be registered as illegal. The kiss started as soft and then deep. Just when she thought she was going to completely combust in his arms, he pulled back and looked into her eye. "That wasn't and accident or a mistake," he whispered, watching her for any sign of fear.

She didn't know what to say, but she managed to not yell '*DO IT AGAIN*!', so there was a small miracle. Desdemona just nodded at his words and agreed. Something about this man sucked out her brain, and she was willing to follow him into anything, like making out next to a dead body. In her brain she heard the little voice warning her she'd always be second, and she chose to ignore it. Being near him felt too good.

"Callen," she said softly.

Whitefox shook his head. "It's going to happen again." Right there he threw down the challenge. He was going to get what he wanted, and that was her. Forcing her to see how it was going to be didn't matter to him. When it was all done, he'd be victorious.

She wasn't sure what to think. Part of her wanted to do a cartwheel and part of her wanted to escape far away.

He helped her step down. "Let's wrap this up here, and then go find Ethan and Elizabeth. We should head out of here soon."

She nodded, and went to go get the lab techs. "Stitch him up, and store him in the cooler. I'll finish my report tomorrow. Ship out the samples to the lab at FBI west, and mark them urgent and then head out for the night," she said to the techs in the next room. Desdemona hoped they didn't just see her making out with the sexiest man in the world. On second thought, she hoped they all did. Kudos for her!

"Why are you laughing," he asked, as he lifted a brow.

"Today has been the weirdest day of my life. I was frightened by a deputy dressed up as a killer, my pregnant boss kicked his ass, and then I just made out by a corpse with a sexy Native American. Possibly what is most disturbing is I'm beginning to believe that I'm the only one that finds this the least bit out of the ordinary."

Now he started laughing. "Your best bet is to just accept and roll with it." Part of him was secretly thrilled she wasn't laughing at the moment they just shared, because it felt monumental for him.

It wasn't lost on Desdemona Adare that she'd just gotten the same advice earlier from Elizabeth Blackhawk.

"Give me twenty minutes to get changed back into normal clothes." She needed to escape from him to just catch her breath.

"I'll wait for you right here," he watched her walk away, and immediately felt her retreat. His brother had been right. She'd run in a heartbeat. Desdemona was going to bolt the first chance she got, and he was going to do everything in his power to stop that from happening. Someone should have told Doctor Adare that when you play hard to get, it just makes the man want to hunt you down that much more.

Protectiveness kicked in, as she needed that from him. He needed a way to move forward in life, and he'd offer that in exchange for being her guardian. Deep down it felt wrong, even as he tried to rationalize it, but he shut off the inner voice.

"Start running, Desi, I'm right behind you," he whispered. Yeah, right behind her and willing to run a very long marathon.

*   *   *

Those two bitches were going to pay. First they came to his town and made him look bad in front of his co-workers, and then the one ambushes and breaks his nose. She was just lucky the mask got in his way, or he would have beaten her into a pulp, pregnant or not. She just got damn lucky.

Now he had to make a run for it, and get back to his place and get some things. First he was going to break into their house and teach those women a lesson, and then he was going to head out of the state. His brother was in Canada, and he'd be across the border before they had any clue where he was heading. They'd never find him again.

Stupid, worthless, broads had cost him his job, and now it was going to cost them their lives, and the men following them around too. If he was going to jail, it was going to be for a truly heinous crime. Not just scaring two stupid women with a mask and play knife. It was time to teach them a lesson about what happens when women aren't kept in their place and made to mind their manners.

They ended up dead.

*   *   *

"I'm perfectly fine!" objected Elizabeth, as her husband was bullying her once again. "Wait until I'm not pregnant, I swear

174

I'm going to kick your ass," she stated, as he had her scooped up off the ground and into his arms.

"Just let Desdemona look at your shoulder," he replied, smiling. He'd let her kick his ass, if she'd just get checked out.

"Ethan, put me down!" she ordered and then saw her brother-in-law standing in the doorway. "Callen, please help me," she pleaded to the man.

"What's wrong now?" he inquired, walking in and laughing. She may have been mad, but the love they had was still evident between them.

"When she had her little fight this afternoon, she hurt her shoulder. I just caught her rolling it out. It has to be stiff."

"The one with the bullet wounds?" Whitefox asked.

"Yes."

"I'm perfectly fine, and the fact that you're carrying me around is making me angry, and that's going to exacerbate the ass kicking I give you when I get down."

Blackhawk laughed. "I'll stop holding you," he said, winking at his brother. "Hey Callen, catch," he said, tossing his wife to his brother.

It showed the complete trust between the men. Elizabeth was precious cargo to him, and he only trusted his brother with her.

Elizabeth closed her eyes and prayed he caught her.

"I got you, Lyzee," he said, kissing her neck and gently cradling her against his chest.

"Please Cal? Can I get down?" she asked, touching his cheek, trying to play the 'girl card'.

Whitefox grinned wickedly, knowing her game. "Sure beautiful." He tossed her back to his brother and when she screamed in frustration they both laughed.

Desdemona watched the game of catch from the doorway and smiled. There weren't many people that could manhandle Elizabeth Blackhawk, and these were probably the only two she knew that would get away with it. There was distinct jealousy at the intimacy they shared.

"If you willingly let Desdemona look at your shoulder, I'll put you down," said her husband. If he didn't lighten her anger by their little game, she'd kick both their asses without a doubt.

Already he could see the fire leaving her eyes and he kissed her, figuring it was safe.

"Sure."

"Liar," laughed her husband, as he tossed her to his brother.

"Will you let her?" Whitefox spoke, gazing at her seriously. "We're just worried about you." When Elizabeth looked into his eyes, he wasn't above begging. "I'm worried about you." He dropped his forehead against hers. "Please beautiful? For me?"

She sighed. "Okay Callen."

Blackhawk grinned. He had no doubt that she'd eventually cave, and especially if his brother gave her the wounded look. She didn't have a snowballs chance in hell against it. Elizabeth was a sucker for the Blackhawk men and especially Callen.

Desdemona came further into the room and was ready to check out her shoulder. She decided to ignore the way Whitefox cradled Elizabeth in his arms. Thinking back to the kiss they shared, the jealousy grew at how it wasn't the same. "Men out," she said, pointing. When they were gone, she smiled at her new friend, despite the raw feelings inside her heart. "Let me look at your arm," she helped Elizabeth out of her shirt and inspected the wound. "It has a little swelling on the joint. I'll give you some ice and then heat will make it feel better."

"Can you do me a favor?"

"You want to screw with them, don't you, Elizabeth?"

"Oh, yeah I do. Want to help me teach them a lesson?"

Desdemona smiled. "What can I do?"

Elizabeth whispered in her ear, and told her what to say and how to play it. "Can you pull it off?"

"Yes, and I'll enjoy every second it too."

Desdemona rushed into the living room and looked worried. Immediately she could tell both men sensed her panic.

"What's wrong?" Ethan stood. Gone were the laughter and the wicked grins from tormenting his wife.

Desdemona dropped her voice. "It's bad. Her shoulder it's a mess, she's in the kitchen crying, and you guys screwed it up tossing her around. You both better get in there fast."

176

"Shit!" They both rushed the door, entering the kitchen. Elizabeth was ready and waiting for them. Turning suddenly, she tossed a bucket of ice cold water on both men, drenching them completely.

"That's for thinking might is right," she said laughing, wickedly. "I'm smaller but not above fighting dirty!"

Blackhawk stood there soaked with cold water. To add insult to injury, his wife had opened the windows and back door so the room was subzero in temperature. "You are so going to get it now," he growled menacingly, as he started stalking towards her.

Elizabeth ran for the back stairs and headed up them two at a time, her very wet, laughing husband right behind her nipping at her heels.

Desdemona stood in the doorway laughing at the man remaining. "You're right, I like Elizabeth a lot, thanks for bringing us together," she said snickering, and then she saw the same look on his face. "Callen, don't do it," she warned, but it was too late. He already had her by the arm and was dragging her across the room and into his arms.

Whitefox was going to teach the woman a lesson, she was pressed between him and the kitchen counter, and he invaded like an advancing army. Callen wanted what his brother had, and his only frame of reference was watching Elizabeth and Ethan together. He followed suit, pulling her into the kiss. It wasn't gentle and he worked hard at conveying how he felt. He buried his hands in her hair and pummeled her mouth unmercifully. He took what he wanted and didn't care if she was going to protest.

Desdemona at first was filled with fear. The look on his face scared her, finally realizing he wouldn't hurt her. Callen may have looked scary in that moment, but his eyes stayed warm and gentle. It was her own fear of her past that had her frightened, and what she was going to do about the man pressed against her. Now he was invading her mouth and wouldn't let her free, and she was falling for him. Something about him just made her feel safe. When he picked her up and plopped her on the counter, never breaking the kiss, she felt her heart pounding in her chest.

Somehow he'd set her hair free from the clips holding it up, and he was running his hands through the long lengths, and continuing to swallow her whole. This warmth grew in the pit of her stomach, and her hands began to trace a trail across his shoulders and chest.

Wow, he had a really nice muscular chest.

"Desdemona, are you okay?" Came the yell, as Elizabeth ran down the stairs and slammed to a stop. Yeah, they had the worst timing ever, as her husband ran into the back of her.

Callen turned to look at his family and his face was flushed. His eyes met Elizabeth's as if waiting for some unsaid approval or disproval. When she smiled her beautiful smile at him, he relaxed.

"Um yeah, I'm fine!" She finally squeaked out, blushing red.

Both Blackhawks began walking back out of the room. "So sorry," she said, grinning at them both easily. "Night guys," she snickered, and hustled out of the room giggling with her husband on the way back up the stairs.

"Oh, that was the most mortifying experience," she said closing her eyes and covering her face with her hands. "Oh my God!"

Whitefox tried to not be hurt by those words, but they sliced at his heart viciously. It wasn't like they would care that she was kissing him. Both his brother and sister-in-law were pretty laid back about affection around each other. "I see," he said, and stepped away from her to put space between them. "I'll lock up," he stated angrily, closing the backdoor and refusing to look at her. Then he did the same with the windows, and the entire time he didn't say a word. He couldn't. He was that damn mad at her.

Desdemona stared open mouthed. "Callen, I didn't mean…"

Whitefox cut her off by shaking his head. "Have a good night, Doctor Adare." He walked out of the room alone, angry, and hurt.

What could she do? She wasn't mortified by him kissing her, but by her bosses catching her making out with their brother in the kitchen. Now she'd ruined everything. Then again, she wasn't surprised.

It was the story of her life.

* * *

Elizabeth heard Callen's door slam, and she glanced over at her husband. Next was the less audible click of Desdemona's.

That wasn't a good sign at all.

"Uh oh," she said, softly. Immediately, she was concerned for Whitefox.

"Don't get involved, Lyzee," he warned, and he noticed she wasn't listening to a word he was saying. "You're going to get involved aren't you?" he asked, sighing.

"I'll be back," she answered, kissing him on the lips. "I'll go talk to Callen."

"No bloodshed."

Elizabeth laughed. "I promise no bloodshed."

"Hurry back," he said, wiggling his eyebrows, lecherously. He had devious plans for his wife once he trapped her in bed with him.

Elizabeth snorted, sliding off the bed and out of the room, before her husband could pounce. At Callen's door she knocked, only to earn a growl of 'go away'. Of course she ignored it and opened the door anyway. Lying on the bed was her brother in law, his shirt was off, and he was barefoot and still in his jeans. His focus was on the ceiling. "I said go away!" And then he realized who it was, and his temper cooled instantaneously.

"Can I come in, Cal?" she paused, waiting at the door.

"Yeah, you can, beautiful. You're always welcome," he answered, watching her cross the room, as he patted the bed beside him. He'd be crazy to not let her crawl into bed with him.

Elizabeth hopped up beside him. "I'm sorry we interrupted you in the kitchen. We didn't know." She started, and he just closed his eyes.

"I'm not mad at you or Ethan."

Elizabeth rested her hand on the tattoo of the fox on his abs. "Want to talk about it?" she asked, gently. "I'm a pretty good listener."

Whitefox let out a breath he was holding and took her hand in his, twining his fingers with hers.

"Are you mad at Desdemona?"

"She has me all tied up in knots, and when I'm this tangled up I lose my temper faster." Whitefox looked up at her, and tried to

179

decide if he should continue. Here he was confessing lust to the woman he loved and wanted. Callen needed Desdemona to forget the truth.

"Cal, you know you can tell me anything and I won't tell a soul. You can trust me."

Whitefox knew he could. It was once upon an assignment when he told her pretty much the same thing that he was feeling now. "I'm beyond sexually frustrated." He left it at that.

Elizabeth laid beside him, and placed her head on his shoulder. "What can I do to help you?"

He started laughing at the words, knowing she didn't mean it the way it sounded. "You helping me would get me killed," he snickered. "But then again, it would be a great way to die." God, he wished he could take her up on that offer. His body tightened.

Elizabeth started laughing. "Nice! You're definitely hard up to want a wobbly pregnant woman."

Callen honestly believed she was still incredible while pregnant. If she wasn't married to his brother, he'd still be chasing her down.

When he didn't answer, she saw the truth in his eyes. Immediately, Elizabeth changed the subject. "Did she upset you?"

Whitefox shrugged. Upset, hurt, what was the difference at this point? Her denial of him was a big turn off for him. If a woman could deny him, then she wasn't what he needed.

"Want me to go next door and kick her ass for you?" she offered, smiling up at him. "I can promise she'll cry."

Whitefox hugged her closer to his body, and some of the tension lessened, and he didn't feel as angry as he was a moment ago. She always had that effect on him. "No, I think you've kicked enough ass today to cover it." Her frame curled against him relaxed his body and gave him peace.

"I think you like her."

"Yeah I do."

"More than any woman you've ever met before," she said, softly.

"No, not every woman." Whitefox alluded to the only other woman he'd ever loved, and she was currently pregnant with his brother's child and married to him too. That woman still had him tied up in knots and always would. "There's only one woman I'm crazy for in this world."

"Then that other woman is damn lucky to have such a role in your life and place in your heart. Don't think that it doesn't matter a great deal to her. It does."

He glanced at her.

"She also thinks that you have plenty of space in here." Elizabeth ran her hands lightly over his heart and continued, "for Desdemona."

"Yeah?"

"Yes," she answered, honestly.

"The other woman is very important to me too." Whitefox kissed the top of her head, and this was why she was the center for him. Elizabeth just knew and understood. "More than I have words to express. I hope she knows the truth."

He started playing with a piece of her hair, as he stared at the ceiling thinking about the two women.

"I told granddad to butt out of your life today and let you find any woman you wanted to be happy with." She waited for his reply.

"You didn't use those exact words, did you?"

"Yes, I most certainly did."

Only Elizabeth could get away with talking to the family patriarch like that. "What did he say? That couldn't have been good." Now he was definitely surprised. Her defending him to Timothy touched his heart, and he fell harder.

"He laughed and told me to bring the girl when we get back."

Whitefox kissed her on the forehead and inhaled the spicy scent of her perfume. He couldn't love her more. When he was hurt she comforted him, when he was worried she protected him. "Thank you, Lyzee, but it might have been for nothing at this point. I just might have ruined any chance I could've had because I was frustrated."

"Tell me what she did, and I bet I can help you patch it up."

Callen spilled it all to the woman lying on his shoulder. Not only was she the heart and soul to their family, but he trusted her to hold onto his secrets. It seemed unfair that he had help navigating love, when he knew he brother had to figure it all out on his own.

His life was messy, and still she never complained. He purged it all from the kiss in the Autopsy room to the fight in the kitchen, and the hurt he had felt at her words.

"It just hurt to have her deny me, like she was embarrassed by the man I am."

Elizabeth was well aware that both brothers were emotionally damaged. Ethan Blackhawk ran from his past and built a very attractive outer shell to keep life from hurting him. Callen Whitefox was completely the opposite. He wore life on his sleeve, and when he was hurt, he wore that too. Of the two brothers, this one was the more sensitive and more easily broken.

"It hurt to hear her say those words right to my face."

Part of Elizabeth wanted to kick Desdemona's ass for hurting one of the men she loved fiercely, but part of her completely understood. "Cal, she wasn't mortified by the kiss. Desdemona was busted by her bosses in the kitchen, making out with their brother. Not to mention on an assignment in a house work is paying for and it was her gut instinct."

"I know," he said, twisting the hair around his finger.

"I know it hurt you, and I'm so sorry that she wounded you." Elizabeth watched, as he thought it through. "What if it was reversed? You're at her house and her family walks in and catches you man handling her."

Point was taken. "I really hate how you're logical like my brother," he said, sighing. All the anger was now gone.

"Wow, I come in here to help you and you insult me by calling me logical. Nice one," she laughed.

Whitefox kissed her on the forehead and continued playing with a long curl. "How do I fix it, Lyzee? I'm not good with this kind of thing. You're my only frame of reference. I make you mad, I let you beat on me and we're good."

"Violence is the answer, my friend," she quipped, and then got serious. "Tomorrow you tell her you're sorry and the truth."

"Which is?" he asked.

"That she has you tied up in knots because you like her."

Callen stared down at Elizabeth and contemplated his words. "I've only loved one woman in my life," he said, honestly. "I haven't cared about a lot of people in my life." He spoke the truth because she would protect him. "Is it wrong to build a life with someone else when you can't give them your whole heart?" he asked, quietly. Life was seldom simple, and he'd learned that a long time ago. People were going to love who they loved, and it wasn't always going to end the way they wanted. Maybe being in love with Elizabeth wasn't the most logical thing in the universe, but he had to believe it was for a reason. It was completely out of his control. Deep down he knew the truth; anyone else was just a distraction from what he lost to her.

His heart.

"We can love lots of people in our life, Callen." Elizabeth thought about what he said. "I know you can too. Tell her you're sorry and try to enjoy life and live for the moment. You know what's in your heart, and you know how you feel. It doesn't make it wrong, if you honestly feel it. Love is unconditional, and that's how it needs to be. Not everyone fits into the same mold. There's nothing wrong with your feelings." Elizabeth patted his cheek.

Whitefox gazed directly into her eyes, believing her

"I wouldn't lie to you even if I'm the other woman. What we have isn't going to disappear if you open yourself for a chance. I'll still be part of you. We're a family and that's unbreakable."

"Thanks Lyzee," he answered, helping her sit up. "I love you," he said, grateful that she always had his back.

"I love you too," she replied, leaning back to give him a kiss. "Night Cal," she whispered, and then touched his cheek. "If you need me, you know where to find me. Come get me. Sleep is overrated, and I'm always available for you."

As she left, he found himself smiling. Yeah, he was pretty lucky to have her in his life. Maybe the love they had was the best kind. It was unconditional, and unclouded by a physical relationship. All he knew was she'd always be there, and help him get through all the things that tied him and tripped him up. Deep in his heart he knew he could love her and try to start a relationship. The love of his life just gave him permission to open himself up to the possibilities, and still have her to fall back on just in case.

He was a very lucky man to have found true love, as unconventional as it may be.

Now came the hard part. He had to fix the mess he made with Desdemona.

It was late in the night, and she just had no hope of sleeping. When she came back to her room, she could hear the whispers next door of Callen and Elizabeth. There was no doubt that he told her everything that happened, about their fight. She felt so incredibly stupid. There she was in the kitchen, making out with the sexiest man she'd ever seen, and she had to go and use the word 'mortified'. For some unknown reason, the man wanted her, and here she had to hurt his feelings. Callen and his family had been nothing but kind to her, and even offered her friendship, and she threw it back at him. What a complete moron.

In frustration, she climbed out of bed, and decided to go make a cup of tea. Maybe it would calm her down, and help he finally sleep. Granted, she didn't need much, but she still needed more than zero.

In the kitchen she stood, with her back to the sink, and drank her tea. A slight click drew her attention, and when she looked over, it took her a few seconds to register what she saw. Horror and fear filled her, as she saw the deputy that Elizabeth beat up earlier in the day, opening the previously locked door. Not only had he escaped, but he was in their kitchen, and the knife this time didn't look fake.

"You're coming with me bitch," he moved at her, and Desdemona screamed.

It had to be the loudest scream that ever came from her mouth in her whole life. It didn't stop the man from dragging her toward the kitchen door, and trying to get her out of the house. If he got her through that door, she was going to be dead. They'd never find her in the snow and dark. She began fighting, and fighting hard, as he dragged her across the room to the back door.

Bobby Lee Tills wanted her to stop screaming, so he hit her, just in time for the two men to race through the door guns drawn. He released the woman in a panic and headed for the snow covered yard.

"Desi," Whitefox rushed to her side and pulled her against his body, cradling her in his arms. There was a trail of blood from her lip to her chin, and he was scared shitless.

"I'll go after him," said Blackhawk.

Elizabeth ran in her gun out too. "What the hell?" She rushed to her new friend, and grabbed the towel off the counter, holding it to her lip.

"Both of you go, I'll watch the door," she nodded. "Hurry and don't let Ethan go alone," she whispered to her brother-in-law.

Whitefox contemplated it for a second, and she knew the woman would be safe with Elizabeth. "Wait for me!" Whitefox grabbed his boots and his jacket, and hurried after his brother.

Blackhawk nodded. "We can track him in the snow. Elizabeth, shoot to kill if he comes through that door!" Her husband ordered, as he slid into his parka and boots. "Keep the door locked."

Both men were out the door in under a minute and on the trail of a man that crossed the line a second time. This time they were going to find him and show him what justice really entailed.

Elizabeth sat on the floor with her friend lying against her and the baby bump. She hugged her, as she held the towel to her mouth. "Are you going to be okay?" she asked, softly.

"No," she answered, and then burst into tears.

Elizabeth wrapped her arms around her, and just let the woman sob. "Shhhhh, it'll be okay," she whispered and stroked the woman's hair with her gun hand. "You're safe now. I won't let anyone hurt you," she promised, as she watched the doorways in the room in case the Deputy returned and made another attempt to take one of them.

"I'm not a spider," she whispered through the sobs and tears. "I'm not like you!" All she wanted was to be like Elizabeth, for so many reasons.

"That's okay, Desdemona. Sometimes we all have to take a turn as the fly." Elizabeth knew she herself spent many scary moments trapped in the web.

Bobby Lee Tills ran through the trees and towards the road. He just needed to get to the main road and away from the FBI Agents that he was sure were chasing him through the woods. Damn that stupid woman, he almost had her out the door. She had to go and scream. Now the FBI would be searching for him with a vengeance. He'd tried to take one of their own.

Stupid!

Stupid!

Stupid!

When he finally hit the main road, he rushed out into the street and flagged down a vehicle going by and it actually stopped. This might be his lucky night. Then he saw who was driving, and he knew he was home free.

"Hey, you need a lift? Did your car break down?"

"Yeah, can you get me out of here and fast?" asked Bobbly Lee Tills.

"Sure thing," the driver answered, pulling away finally.

"Wow, it's lucky I ran into you out here."

"I was just getting out of work." There was a pause. "Hey you look cold, why don't you have some coffee. Pour yourself some in that clean travel mug. You look frozen to the bone."

"Shit, thanks. I am frozen solid," he said, pouring a big mug full and starting to drink. "Hey, just the way I like it- sweet, thanks a lot!" He was grateful to have run into a friend.

"Not a problem. Have another mug if you want."

"This is my lucky day," said Bobby Lee Tills, smiling smugly. Those idiot FBI agents weren't catching him tonight.

The driver laughed. "It certainly is."

Elizabeth helped a shaking Desdemona to the couch; she tucked a blanket around her, and made her some tea. Then she returned to sit beside her, arm around her shoulder and loaded Glock in her lap.

"I was so scared," she said, still shaking. "Being abducted is a scary thing." She drank some of her tea.

"I couldn't agree with you more," Elizabeth said, rubbing her hand up and down her arm. "I've lived it before."

"You've been abducted?" she asked, curiously.

Elizabeth nodded. "Serial killer took me, drugged me, and then hunted me through the woods to kill me and hurt Ethan and Callen."

Desdemona gasped. "How long did he have you for?"

186

"I think I was unconscious for about four hours, and then there was six hours in the woods trying to escape him. Ten hours give or take a few."

I don't think I could survive that," she said, softly. Yeah Elizabeth Blackhawk was tough. "When was this?" she asked, feeling a little better, knowing her boss understood the fear she'd just felt.

"Four months ago."

Desdemona put her head on her new friend's shoulder and closed her eyes. "I wish I was as strong as you," she said, softly. Who was she kidding? Desdemona Adare wished she WAS Elizabeth Blackhawk, and for a myriad of reasons. She was fearless, and she knew that her friend owned the heart of the man she desperately wanted to belong to her. All she could hope for was a sliver of his heart, and she'd be happy with that.

"You don't know how strong you are, until you have to survive. I personally think you're very strong."

She thought about it. "I screwed up with Callen tonight."

"He told me about it." Elizabeth wasn't going to lie to the woman, it was against the girlfriend code.

Of course he did. There wouldn't ever be anything he kept from her. She was truly his confidant and best friend. That was obvious to her. "How mad is he?"

"I'm pretty sure this will get him right past his anger, and he'll completely forget that there was even a fight." Elizabeth knew the men in her life.

"You guys are pretty close and have an interesting relationship."

Here it came. Elizabeth was waiting for this to come sooner or later. "We're incredibly close and I guess you could look at us and say that."

"I saw the tattoo on his shoulder. Are the initials yours?"

"They're mine. Wyler has them on his chest, granddad has them on his forearm, and Callen has them on his shoulder. They all got them after I saved them from their homicidal family member."

Desdemona was trying to not be jealous, and she relied on the fact that she knew Elizabeth loved her husband. But still. It just seemed unfair. How unlucky could one person get in their life? The woman had a man that loved her. Did she really need two? "I heard about that from a lab tech," she said softly, trying to let the jealousy go. Before knowing the woman personally, it was one of the reasons she was afraid of Elizabeth at the beginning.

"I need to know if Callen and my relationship are going to be a problem for you." she asked, waiting.

"If I said yes what happens then?" She wanted to scream yes very loudly. It did bother her, because she was green with envy. She knew pretending it didn't was wrong but still…

Elizabeth laughed. "Then you're going to lead a very stressed out life. I love Callen and we're very close, but then you have to factor in the rest. Callen practically lives at our house, and he and Ethan do everything together. The Blackhawk men are very family oriented. If you think you can fracture it then you're asking for a whole world of pain," Elizabeth warned her for her own benefit. She agreed to help Callen Whitefox, but she had no intention of lying to her friend.

Desdemona thought about it and figured it was best to tell a white lie. At least she was getting the closeness of the family out of the deal. After all, isn't that what she desired most? A family that welcomed her to be part of them. Right in that moment she made the sacrifice, because she believed in time, she could make Callen love her more. One day she could replace the feelings he had for Elizabeth. All it would take was time.

"No, I'm really glad he has you as family and that you love him like you do. He's a really sweet guy and you're both lucky to have each other as family."

Elizabeth didn't buy it for a second. "There's room in our family for more people," she offered, for Callen's sake.

Desdemona felt her eyes fill up with more tears, and she hid them from her boss.

If only that was a possibility, until the truth that lived in her heart finally escaped.

Both brothers backtracked and raced back to the house, where the women were holed up, and trying to remain safe. They'd tracked Bobby Lee Tills about a mile, until he hit the interstate, and then he was gone, like a ghost. Either he had a car parked there waiting, or someone picked him up and got him out of there fast.

He was fortunate, because he had two natives accustomed to tracking, chasing him through the trees and ready to end his life.

When they arrived back at the house, they were met by Elizabeth at the back door. "How'd it go?"

"Where's Desdemona?" questioned Whitefox, nervously.

"Sleeping on the couch. She took a Xanax and crashed. The asshole scared the shit out of her completely." Elizabeth hugged her husband, once he was free of his parka. "Are you going to call the Sheriff?"

"Yeah, the tech team can wait until morning, its dark out and the weather is turning shitty. We'll cut them a break until dawn. We already know who it was, so no need to make them work in the dark."

"I'm going to carry Desdemona to bed and make sure she doesn't wake up scared. If you need me, I'll be in her room," he said, waiting to see if either of them would make a comment.

"Night, Callen," said Elizabeth, kissing him on the cheek, and squeezing his hand in reassurance.

Ethan watched his brother leave. "He's going to make a move on the doctor."

"Yeah, he is."

Blackhawk thought about it. "It feels off to me, baby."

"Me too, Ethan, but we have to let Callen drive this one on his own. This is his journey not ours. We just love and protect him no matter what the outcome. Maybe we're both wrong."

Not likely. "I already told Callen to forget what granddad said, so I'm with you on defending my brother."

"I knew you would be," she answered, smiling. Ethan Blackhawk was extremely protective of his younger brother.

"I'll call the Sheriff while we climb into bed, you look tired baby."

"I am. This pregnancy thing is tough," she said, taking his hand.

Blackhawk grinned at her. "Want to get naked and roll around?"

Immediately she wasn't tired. "Okay," she grinned wickedly. "Race you upstairs?" she said, winking at him.

Blackhawk loved her so much; he let her have a head start.

Callen Whitefox laid Desdemona gently in her bed, and stared around the room. There was a chair off in the corner that would be suitable to catch some zzz's in while he watched over the ME. Then he thought about how uncomfortable that was going to be, and he looked at the bed. She was out cold, what would it hurt to just get comfortable. He was a light sleeper, when she started to wake; he'd slide out of bed and escape to the chair. Climbing in, he got comfortable, and started to close his eyes, and then it happened. Desdemona rolled towards him and put her head on his shoulder, arm across his chest and leg across his.

Everything in him clenched tightly. So much for sleeping in the same bed with the woman, and he should have known better from the start. The chance that he was going to get any sleep at all was slim to none. Here was a woman, with soft skin lying across his body, and her breath was on his neck. Now he needed to not focus on how she smelled or felt. Maybe he'd have a fighting chance.

He looked at his watch, and counted the hours until he had to be up, maybe if he just thought about crime scenes and dead bodies, he'd forget about her and find some sleep. No, dead bodies reminded him that she was an ME, and then he thought back to the kiss, and then…

Shit. How did his brother sleep next to a beautiful woman every night and not stay awake staring at the ceiling. Oh, yeah. He was having sex with her. That's right, he was getting laid.

Lucky bastard.

This was pure torture.

This was his karma for not sleeping in the chair.

* * *

She brushed her blonde hair and prepared for her evening with her lover. Right this second he was just resting, and soon they would begin their time together. Oh how she loved gazing deep in his beautiful blue eyes and whispering of her never ending love for her true love. What they had, it was special and unique and would never be matched by anyone else.

They were soul mates. She knew from the minute they met. It was a love that would cross time and distance.

Pulling her lipstick from her vanity, she picked the color pink, and tried it on to make sure it was just right. When she finished the task, she inspected the handiwork in the mirror and was impressed.

"This is perfect for a night in with the love of my life," she said, as she wandered to the kitchen to get them both a glass of wine. Hers came from the bottle on the counter, and his was the special mix she kept under the sink. Pouring a full glass of the thick liquid, she smiled seductively.

"I hope you don't get too drunk tonight, my love," she called to him in the other room. "I want our night to be completely memorable, and like nothing you've ever experienced before."

She tied back her long blonde locks, and carried their drinks into the garage to start the magic of their evening together. As she reached his side, she ran her fingers down his cheek, and he opened his eyes to look up at her.

There was nothing but horror from him, as he registered what he saw.

But she saw only love and adoration in his gaze.

"Here is your wine. Drink up." Quickly, she ripped the tape from his mouth and he screamed in pain, his body bowed from the tearing of flesh.

"Sorry my love," she giggled, and squeezed his cheeks until his mouth opened, and he was forced to swallow the sickly colored mixture.

"Why are you doing this?" he gurgled through the liquid. "Why?"

"Because I love you of course. We're meant to be together, and I won't ever lose you again," she said, as she ripped off another section of Duct tape from the roll. "Now hold still," she whispered in his ear, and then replaced the tape over raw bleeding skin.

He shook his head violently, and struggled to get free from the table. He didn't understand what was going on. First he was trying to abduct the FBI woman, then he grabbed a ride with a friend, and now… The wave of dizziness hit him, and he felt like he was drunk. Whatever was in the wine glass was numbing his body. He didn't think he could move.

"I see you're ready for me to look deep into your eyes and stare into your soul," she said as she pulled the tools from her pocket. "I promise, this shouldn't hurt too much," she whispered and kissed him on the cheek.

Bobby lee Tills saw the scissors coming toward his eyes, and he knew what was going to happen. He screamed as one eye went blind and the pain filled his body. When the second eye went blind he prayed for the pain to stop, and then it just did.

Everything stopped in his life, as it was simply gone.

She lugged Deputy Bobby Lee Tills through the snow, humming as she went. It was another great date night, and she owed it all to the man she loved. It wasn't easy to carry him, but she still managed. He seemed to lose weight since last time, and that had her worried. "I hope you're not sick, my love," she said, kicking open the door with a booted foot, only to stared in complete dismay and horror.

"They're all gone!" she whispered, and looked around the room. All her lovers were gone. "Where have you all gone?" she spoke softly, but anger began to build in her chest. Someone had stolen them right out from beneath her.

She dropped his body against the wall and kicked him. "You can never trust men," she hissed, and kicked him again and again. Until she heard the bones breaking in his side. "They always leave," she hissed in anguish and pain.

Slowly, she regained composure, and ran her hand down her jacket. "That's okay, I'm okay." Deep breaths followed and then a smile.

"I'll just have to make sure you know that I'm your true love. I think I'll have to come back and watch to see if you try to leave me too, lover," she sighed. "I wish I could trust you, but I just can't seem to trust anyone."

With that, she left the building. It was time to place his eyes with the rest of her love. Before long the hunt for the next part would begin.

But first she was going to get her men back and kill the whore that stole them away.

* * *

Desdemona slowly came awake, and something didn't feel right. There was slow steady breathing, and her head was moving up and down, as if it rested on a chest. Before opening her eyes, she assessed the situation. Her leg lay across a body, and her senses were being assaulted with a familiar scent. It was the scent of Callen's cologne. It was unmistakable. It was spicy and woodsy with a touch of patchouli. Exotic and delicious, just like the man himself. Well hell, she was in bed with the sexiest man alive, and her hand was inches from things that until now she could only fanaticized about. Her biggest fear was if she opened her eyes, he may disappear. Desdemona weighed her options. Run for her life or just jump in and enjoy the ride.

The sane part of her said run. The man was wicked as sin and was going to end up breaking her heart. A man like him wouldn't ever want to be with someone simple, unadventurous, and afraid of her own shadow. Then there was part of her that demanded she be that woman, take charge and surprising them both. Deep down she wanted to be Morticia Addams, just like Elizabeth. Maybe if she changed, he'd feel about her the way he obviously felt about the 'other' woman. It might buy her some time to change his mind.

She debated. Crap, hardest decision of her life.

"Good morning, Desi," he said, softly. He knew exactly when she woke. Her whole body gave her away. She went from relaxed and easy breathing to tense and rigid.

Desdemona opened her eyes and faced the music. The jig was up and she was going to have to decide fast.

"Morning, Callen," she answered, looking up at him, yet not moving her body. It felt too nice waking up with him against her.

"How did you sleep?" he asked, noticing she had the look of a trapped animal ready to run at the first given chance.

"Like a rock," she answered, honestly. It was the truth. She obviously didn't recall anything, or she'd know how she ended up in bed with the man and do it all over again tonight.

Whitefox wasn't sure if he should push her, or wait for her to come to him. He had patience, but he wasn't sure if he had that much patience. Again came the wave of protectiveness.

In the early morning light, she looked even younger. Her hair was completely down, and she had a lot of it. Most of it covered her pillow and his shoulder.

"Are you still mad at me?" she asked, forcing any emotion from her voice. Just in case he was going to hurt her.

"No, I'm not."

Desdemona debated and made a choice. "I'm glad," and she did what she never thought possible, she moved towards the danger and took control. She kissed him and for once in her life stopped overthinking and just dove into life.

The kiss was slow and warm until she relaxed into it, and he tensed for a change. When she broke the kiss, she didn't miss the surprise on his face. Somehow she managed to catch Callen . off guard.

He didn't expect her to make the move, and he wasn't ready for it. Yet now his body demanded more, and he wasn't quite sure he could hold it back. A woman in bed kissing him was a recipe for one thing in the male mind; sex. His brain shut off and he did what he did so many times before with the countless others, he dove into the sexual pool on auto pilot. It was time to conquer.

Desdemona was enjoying the look on his face, and then she saw the moment it changed, and her heart began to pound.

"You shouldn't have done that, Desi," he whispered, and then rolled until she was trapped beneath him. "I have very little control today. I've been awake all night with you lying against me. I'm in a very dangerous mood."

She looked up into his eyes. The look of predator was there plastered across his face, yet she believed she'd be completely safe. Well, physically she would. Emotionally she was going to be in danger, and had been since meeting him in the lab.

He waited ready to strike and wound so tight his body was beginning to vibrate in need and want. The sexual frustration he'd felt for months was boiling to the surface and ready to ignite. Since meeting Elizabeth it was on slow simmer, and he needed to release it somehow.

Desdemona ran her hand up under his shirt and across his ribs. Baiting the tiger and pushing her luck.

Whitefox stared down at her lips, partially open, soft and delicious, and when he felt her hand caress his ribs, he knew she'd signed her fate. It was open season, and he was going to catch himself a skittish ME and make her his.

Desdemona didn't see him move, he was so fast the only thing she could ascertain was the crashing of lips to lips, and then mating of heated tongues. The kiss was wild and out of control, and yet, he was careful of her split lip, tender but dangerous, wild but controlled. She let it sweep her away, into something she'd never felt before in her life.

Whitefox tasted her, taking more and more until they both surfaced, gasping for breath.

"If you have any intention of stopping me, Desi, now's the time to do it. I won't stop later," he warned her, just in case she planned on bolting as the morning progressed. In his mind he was already planning the next step. Part of him screamed that he shouldn't be plotting, but fully immersed in the act. Again, he ignored his heart.

Debate occurred and was pushed aside in Desdemona's mind. How often in her life was a man of Whitefox's caliber going to want to have sex with her? She wasn't giving this up for anything. This was stuff hot sweaty dreams were made of, and she was wide awake for a change. If she passed this up, she would need to make an appointment with a psychiatrist and soon. Only a complete nut job would pass up a romp with Callen ..

He watched her eyes, and they were clear of doubt. When her hand traversed up his shoulder and sunk into his own long hair, free from being tied back, he felt himself throb at the intimacy.

Desdemona pulled him back down, using his hair against him. The long silky brown hair was always pulled back in a long ponytail down his back. Yet more evidence the man was exotically native. She kissed him this time, and his hands began wandering, and she thought she'd burst into flames at any second.

Tentatively she did the same, until he broke the kiss and sat up, ripping off his shirt, and returning right back to where he'd left off. Holy crap! More naked man and she was on fire. When he began moving down her neck and to her throat, leaving kisses she felt bliss, and when he bit her shoulder, she gasped his name.

Whitefox just wanted to devour her, and he tried. When she moaned his name in that shocked breathy gasp, he was lost. He had to have her, all of her. Kneeling above her, he pulled her shirt from her body, and stared down at her. Yeah, she may be small and compact, but Desdemona had a nice body. She wasn't focused on his face, but looking straight in front of her at his hardened body, ready to find a home.

Something made her want to just touch him, and she reached out, and ran her fingers across the front of his jeans, to the bulge waiting for her. Just stroking him through the material excited him, and pulled a moan from deep within his chest. It called to her, and made her want to be bolder and wilder.

She flicked open the button and slid the zipper down.

Whitefox didn't know if she was a scared rabbit, or a feisty vixen. Just when he thought she would run in fear, she touched him tentatively. "More," he demanded, pleased when she obeyed.

She freed him, taking him in her hand. He was hard, silky and completely smooth against the palm of her hand. She tested the water, stroking him once, then twice, and then she did something so completely un-Desdemona like. She tasted him, licking him and then sliding him into her waiting mouth.

When she stroked him with her warm fingers, tracing patterns across his erection, he was a happy man. The warm wet slide of her hand and her tongue was making him crazy. Callen closed his eyes, and dropped his head back just to enjoy the way she was worshipping his body. So many thoughts flooded his mind, and he forced himself to think about the woman touching his body and no one else.

She could feel him shaking and enjoyed the moment. Never had she felt that free and uninhibited with a man before and it felt really good. Never had she wanted to feel this way with a man, Callen just brought it out in her and at the same time she knew the truth, and pushed it down for the time being.

"No control today," he muttered between clenched teeth, as she began stroking, licking and then sucking. He looked down at her, and just the visual was more than he could take. Something in him snapped and he pushed her from his erection and enjoyed the surprised look in her face. Ripping her FBI sweats from her legs, he enjoyed the fact she wore nothing beneath them. Less work for him to get to the part of her he wanted desperately. Frustration demanded he take what he needed from her. Now he wanted to just forget, like he had before with so many other women.

"Callen," she whispered, as he pulled her legs apart and took his place between them.

197

"No gentleness, Desi," he hissed in her ear, and felt her shake. He didn't even have the patience to remove his jeans. Whitefox was that desperate to quench the need in his body from months of torment at another womans' hands.

She swallowed and nodded, as he found her wet and ready and pushed into her hard and fast.

"Christ so tight," he muttered, as he had to take a moment to regain his control. He opened his eyes to see her looking up at him, still no fear present, and she too was breathing hard. "Ready?" he asked when he was finally able to regain the power of speech.

She couldn't answer, he was filling her to capacity, and it was the most delicious feeling she'd ever had in her life. Again, she just nodded, and her hands went to his shoulders, and then she lost the ability to think, as he started moving and there was just too much pleasure.

Desdemona was tight and like a satin lined glove. Slowly he pulled out, and slid back into place fast.

They both gasped and then came together again and again.

Part of him wanted to slow down, offer her so much pleasure, but the wildness in him was in control. He couldn't slow down, he wanted harder and faster. To the point it was merciless pounding of his body into hers. Now his mind wandered, and he let it, visualizing the woman her wanted desperately.

The breathless moans kept slipping from her lips, and when he switched the angle, and continued he found just the right spot. Light erupted, and shattered around her is such an explosion she couldn't breathe.

When Whitefox heard her moan his name, and then the tightening of her body around him, he wasn't going to last long. One more stroke, then two, and then on the third he slammed home, erupted hotly, and followed her into the white bliss.

Desdemona couldn't feel anything but him lying over her body, and then she could feel the room spinning and she was no longer on the bottom. Callen had her across his body, and his arms protectively around her.

"You okay?" he asked, when he could speak again.

She laughed.

"I guess that's a yes?" he looked down at her, and she had her eyes closed and a smile on her lips.

"That was most definitely a yes, Callen." When she opened her eyes, she could see the worry on his face. "What's wrong?" Immediately she began to worry, maybe he hadn't enjoyed it, or she did something wrong.

"Did I hurt you?" he asked softly, running his fingers over the cut in her lip. The guilt was now there, and not because she had a cut on her lip but because he was thinking of another woman while having sex with her. Callen pushed it down, praying it would just seep away.

It touched her heart. He wasn't going to tell her she sucked in bed, he was worried about her. She lost another part of her heart right there and then. "Nope, I'm perfectly content," she said running her fingers over the tattoo on his abs.

"I'm glad."

"Why a fox?" she asked, curiously.

Whitefox pulled the blanket up around them and thought about her question. "Ethan and I grew up very native," he answered. "When we both were young, we picked spirit guides. Our grandfather used to call us the Raven and the Fox. Ethan was the big brother that watched over us, and I was the fox, the one younger brother that managed to always find us trouble," he paused when she laughed.

"Yeah, you're trouble alright. So I think you picked the right spirit guide."

He grinned wickedly. "You wouldn't be the first woman that's told me I'm trouble."

Oh, Desdemona had no doubt about that. She didn't understand the whole 'Native' spirit guide thing, it always seemed silly to her as a scientist. Well that and her grand'mere scoffed at anything Native. In fact, if she knew about Callen, she'd lose it.

Callen noticed the guard coming back up, and the hard shell to protect her returning. He didn't understand why she didn't see what he saw. Everything in him wanted to make her feel better, after all he owed her that much.

"I may be trouble, but there's no one I'd rather be trouble with, Desi."

She looked at him wondering if he was being honest or not. Men said lots of things, especially after sex.

"I promise next time I'll take my time and prove it to you." And not think about another woman- or try.

Desdemona changed the subject. "So, what's growing up on a reservation like?" She was genuinely curious.

"Horrible, destitute, miserable, poor," he paused. "Want to visit it?" Now he was laughing. He was glad he escaped the Rez, and now he had a well-paying job, a life he loved, and a woman needed to persuade to stay with him. So he could build what his brother had in life.

She continued to run her fingers over the fox, tracing it, and enjoying the way his muscles rippled at her touch. "I'd love to visit it. Do you still live on one?"

"My cabin is on the Rez and not far from my brother's house. But I'm thinking of moving off it, once my grandfather is gone." Those words stung, but he knew he only stayed because of Timothy and obligation.

Desdemona heard the change in his voice.

"I'll take you to see it, if you want," he said, impressed she was curious. Also he thought back to what Elizabeth had said. The family patriarch demanded to meet her. If they were going to have a relationship, they were going to have to go back at some point.

"I'd like that," she said.

"What was the bayou like?" Callen Whitefox wondered if she'd tell him the truth about her life, or if she'd evade.

"Horrible, destitute, miserable, poor," she laughed, as she used the same words he used. "But my grand'mere made it tolerable. When my mom disappeared, she was all I had left and because of her 'unique' job, it was fun. There were the snakes, bugs, roots, and of course the gators. We didn't have a lot growing up, but honestly I never realized it. Everyone around us was in the same financial state. It was just the bayou."

Whitefox kissed her on the top of the head. "Will you take me there sometime?" he asked, wondering if she'd keep her past locked away.

"You want to go to a swamp?" she laughed. "Damn, maybe I am seductive," she laughed.

He noticed she didn't answer the question. "Nice deflection. How about you answer the question?"

Desdemona laughed. "I tell you what, if I ever decide to go back, I'll be sure to invite you along."

"You don't visit?"

"Not really. In ten years maybe three times." How did she explain to the man that whenever she went back the stalking became horrible. It chased her for months after, and eventually she made excuses to stay away. It scared her shitless to go back to the bayou, and it was a constant reminder of losing her mother. There really wasn't anyone to go back to there. It wasn't like she had a family circle that welcomed her. If she did, maybe she would go back more often or live there. What she didn't tell him was that her grand'mere would have a shit fit if she wandered home with an 'Indian'. Morgana Adare wasn't fond of Natives at all. No, she wanted to keep Callen as far from her family as possible.

"Deal," he said, holding up his pinky finger, waiting for her to swear.

Desdemona laughed, covering the lie. "Happy?"

"Extremely."

"We should get ready to work. I can hear Elizabeth downstairs, and they'll think we're…" She didn't know what to call it.

"Does that bother you?" Again he had a flashback of last night, and he fought to keep the anger down. Despite the conversation he had with Elizabeth, her being embarrassed by them together bothered him. What he wanted was complete acceptance from her.

"Callen." She touched his cheek. "Don't. Okay?"

"Don't what?" He was irritated that this had to be so damn difficult. Affection should be easily given, despite the situation.

"It's easy for you, because he's your brother, and she's your sister. You're comfortable with them and at ease." She almost wanted to add the part where he was obviously in love with Elizabeth, but she opted to swallow the jealousy again. "They're still my bosses. It has nothing to do with you and me, or us having sex. It just feels weird to be rolling around in a bed while your bosses are downstairs. That's all. Nothing more and that's what I tried to tell you last night. I'm not embarrassed by us being

201

together. I'm horrified that my bosses, the people that hired me, know I'm having sex with another co-worker a few feet away."

"So if we were at your house and they live right behind you?" he asked, posing the question.

"Close the blinds and then commence rolling. That's my house and they aren't eight feet below me."

He tried to laugh, as he pulled her up his body to kiss her. "Okay, I won't read too much into it," he answered after breaking the kiss, but still it bothered him. How could it not? He wanted a woman that wouldn't ever deny what they had. That was a deal breaker for him. Callen needed someone unashamed of him and his life. Right there he should have listened to his brain screaming the warning, but he once again pushed it down. He opted for the long shot.

"Good," she rolled off his body and shook her hair out. "I'm going to shower." Desdemona blew him a kiss. "See you downstairs."

Whitefox got the message. She was retreating to the shower to be alone again and dismissing him. Again he fought the anger, but this time opted to do something about it. When he heard the water turn on, he counted to ten, and slid out of bed. He knew he had to chase her down, and he followed her into the bathroom. Desdemona wasn't getting away that easily. If she thought she could escape at all, she'd use it all the time. Whitefox was cutting off all the viable escape routes, except the one that led straight to him.

When she yelped in surprise, as his hands wrapped around her waist, he grinned predatorily.

"I get the feeling you believed you were showering alone, Desdemona."

She stared at him. "I intended to, Callen."

He covered her mouth with his and refused to let her protest. The willingness she had to deny him, based on Elizabeth and Ethan nearby pissed him off. When Whitefox was a boy and he was told to not do something, it just made him want it that much more. It appeared the same thing happened to him as an adult.

This time he took his time and didn't care their bosses were downstairs. Now it was all about proving a point, to her and himself.

202

Elizabeth sat watching her husband across the table, as he read the tech reports that had just come in, and he looked distracted. His hair was down, and he had yet to button his shirt. Last night he chased her to bed, and then called the sheriff. That's all she remembered, because she fell asleep immediately. Part of her was worried that he was upset they hadn't had sex. Usually they spent the time before bed kissing and rolling around, but with this assignment and other people in the house, it wasn't happening. He wasn't talking, and that made her incredibly nervous.

Blackhawk could feel the questioning stare of his wife, and he was trying to regain his composure before they had the discussion that was bothering him. The previous evening's attempt on their lives had him worried that Deputy Tills wasn't going to stop until they found him. Soon he'd have to boss his wife around again to keep her and his unborn child safe.

"Are you mad at me because I fell asleep before sex?" she asked, softly. There were tears filling her eyes, and she was going to embark on the emotional pregnancy rollercoaster at any second.

Alarmed, he glanced up. "Baby, what?" He wasn't even thinking about sex. When he was stuck on the phone longer than planned, he noticed she fell asleep, and he smiled tucking her in. The pregnancy and the assignment was grueling on her body, he wasn't upset in the least.

"You look mad, and I didn't do anything else that I'm aware of to piss you off." A tear slid down her cheek.

"Oh Lyzee baby!" Ethan Blackhawk took her hand and pulled her up and into his lap. "I'm not mad at you, and I wouldn't ever be mad that my pregnant wife was so exhausted that she fell asleep. The baby and you come first." Blackhawk kissed the tear away and then found her lips, and kissed his wife, slow, long and deep. Her hands were buried in his hair and he felt his body coming alive. He was about to suggest going back upstairs, when his brother and Doctor Adare entered the room.

Callen stopped. "Sorry," he said, laughing and clearing his throat. Then he noticed Elizabeth was crying. Immediately, he rushed to her side. "Are you okay? he asked, glaring down at his brother and punching him in the arm. "What did you do to her?" he accused.

Blackhawk laughed at how protective his brother was of his wife. It should have angered him, but it just gave him a sense of peace that his wife was doubly protected and loved.

"Ethan didn't do anything," she said, standing from his lap. I'm just an emotional mess thanks to pregnancy hormones," she said, and it was completely true. Never in her life had she cried this much.

Whitefox hugged her to his body and kissed her on the top of the head, and whispered in her ear. "If he made you cry, I'll kick his ass for you. Don't cover for him, beautiful."

Blackhawk snorted. "I heard that, and you sincerely wish you could take me little brother," he grinned, looking up at Doctor Adare. "Good morning, Desdemona. Coffee's on." He could see she was flushed, and he knew why. He looked up at his brother and the smug look was there, and he laughed.

Elizabeth punched him on the arm and gave him the look, as she walked by him to go speak to Desdemona. "Leave Callen alone!" she demanded.

Whitefox enjoyed how protective Elizabeth was when it came to him, and he winked at his brother. "I am so her favorite!" And both men laughed more as Whitefox poached her coffee mug again.

"Callen, I swear to God, if you don't stop stealing my coffee…" She pointed at him as the cup was midway to his lips.

He took a sip anyway and ignored her and earned the yank on his ponytail.

"You know I like when you pull my hair," he grinned, teasing her.

Desdemona wished she had the easiness that Elizabeth did with the men. The camaraderie, the love blatantly obvious between them was something she longed for in her life.

"Did you sleep okay, Desdemona?" asked Elizabeth. She could see the whisker burn on her neck and knew why she was pink and flushed this morning.

"I did," she answered, nervously.

Elizabeth glanced over her shoulder and the men were discussing the tech report, and she took her chance. She leaned in close and whispered. "Hey, stop looking so damn scared. Ethan and I aren't going to bite because you're sleeping with Callen."

"Jesus, is it that obvious?" she whispered back. Now she was mortified.

"Yes, and I'm happy for you." She took her hand in hers and held it. "Really," she hugged her, and more tears filled her eyes. All she wanted was happiness for Ethan's brother, even if it meant swallowing what she already saw brewing. This was his journey to take, and Elizabeth loved him enough to back him up.

Desdemona hugged the woman back, and enjoyed having her as her friend. So this was what she'd been missing all her life. The closeness and the strength of the bonding was an amazing feeling. She noticed Whitefox and her boss were watching them closely. Part of her wanted to be nervous, the rest of her wanted to just belong, so she took a second risk for the day and whispered back. "It was absolutely amazing."

Elizabeth laughed and pulled away from the hug. "Don't I know it, Darlin'?" Elizabeth picked up her new coffee cup and clinked it against the doctors. "To the spiders," she said and looked over at the men, "and the flies."

Both women laughed uproariously at their private joke.

Whitefox hadn't a clue what he missed, but what he did understand warmed him right to his soul. He couldn't love Elizabeth more and he mouthed the words when Desdemona wasn't looking and earned an air kiss and wink back.

Elizabeth knew that Desdemona would need the reassurance, and she kept her promise of protecting the woman. "I feel so cheap," he said, smiling at the two women. Desdemona blushed, and Ethan pointed at his wife.

"Elizabeth, don't do it!" Blackhawk warned and then laughed. When she actually obeyed for a change he took it as a sign and quickly changed the topic. "Today the Sheriff is going to do a press conference discussing Deputy Bobby Lee Tills. When I spoke to him last night, he told me that he has his other deputy tracking him. It seems that Julian Littlemoon has a specific skill."

"No sign of him at all?" asked Whitefox. That made him nervous, since he already tried to abduct one of the women last night. If he was still out there, then that meant he could try again.

What if he went after Elizabeth? That made him sick to his stomach. Callen watched her smiling and he became more edgy.

"None. He's gone off the grid."

Elizabeth pulled Desdemona over to the table, and sat her down beside Whitefox. Easily she went and dropped into her husband's lap, trying to show the woman that easy affection wasn't something that had to be hidden. She was about to ask a question, when there was a knock at the door.

"Probably Christina, the tech team is assessing the outside of the house and collecting evidence to prove Tills was here last night."

Whitefox went over to the door and opened it. "Morning Christina," he said, smiling at the ball of energy.

"Morning, Callen!" She looked over at the table. "We're all finished, Boss."

"Find anything?"

"Tracks leading to and from the road, and then a red rose on your Denali," she said holding up the bag.

Desdemona froze and her coffee cup actually fell from her hand, and when she stood, the chair fell backwards.

Oh God, oh God, he found her there too.

Everyone looked over, as the woman backed up from the room, all color draining from her face. No one spoke; it was just too surprising to see the woman run from the room.

Elizabeth stood. "Let me, Callen," she said, leaving the room after her ME. She heard the bathroom door slam, and she followed her there, knocking on the door. There was no answer, only the sound of retching. Elizabeth checked the doorknob and when she found it open, she entered and locked it behind her. Immediately her heart broke for the woman. Something had her terrified so much, she was as sick as a dog.

"I'll be okay," she said, between vomiting.

Elizabeth held her hair back and knelt beside her, gently rubbing her back and trying to soothe her nerves.

When Desdemona emptied her stomach, she stood and rinsed her mouth out at the sink. In her mind she struggled to come up with a lie, or something to cover. The last thing she wanted to do was pack up and leave another job. She just found a friend, and a man that wanted her. Desdemona didn't know what to do.

Elizabeth sat on the side of the tub, and watched the woman. The trained investigator in her knew she was biding time, to cover for the reaction to something she viewed frightening. When Desdemona faced her she still waited her out.

"I'm sorry," she whispered. She didn't want to lie to her friend. For once she wanted to believe that she was worthy of someone shouldering this alongside her. She wanted a friend, and she wanted to believe she was finally accepted by a family.

"How about we try this," she said, patting the tub beside her. "You tell me the truth. We can't help you if you lie."

Desdemonas' eyes went wide.

"Yeah, I'm good at my job, Doctor. I'm also thorough. I ran you, so I know that you are running from something that has you scared. Now as I see it, you have two choices." Elizabeth patted the tub edge again, and reached into her pocket to pull out the keys to the Denali. "You can either believe that I'm your friend, and am going to have your back, or you can take these keys now, walk out that door and head back home to escape. I won't judge you either way."

Desdemona stared at the woman. It wasn't what she expected, and she caught the keys in the air.

"If you run, you leave a friend behind, and you leave Callen. Is whatever has you scared worth more than that?"

"Did you really run me?"

"Yep, you left a four hundred thousand dollar a year job in the private sector to take a civil service job with the FBI, when we pay half that. It's still a decent deal, but confusing as to why. I could say maybe you just wanted a change, but I looked at your records. Every six months to one year, you pack up and run. That screams one of two things. You're being chased or you're completely flighty."

Desdemona sat beside her.

"I don't think you're flighty since you just bought a very pricy house right behind mine. I know how much we shelled out for ours, and I doubt that yours was much less. Flighty people don't drop six figures on a house they plan on abandoning. It seems to me like you wanted to lay down roots, take a stand, and fight against whatever is scaring you."

It was the last part of her resistance that cracked. She broke down and began crying. Sobbing and falling apart in front of her boss.

"Let me stand up against it with you," said Elizabeth, as she wrapped her arms around her, and let the storm brew, crash and pass. When the tears stopped and the woman could breathe again, she handed her a tissue. "We can help you. If you just trust me, Ethan, and Callen. I promise you, Desdemona. We'll stand with you on this."

Desdemona wanted to believe. Desperately, she wanted to feel like she belonged.

"Girlfriend code," Elizabeth said, holding her hand. "Come out there and let us stand with you. Stop running, Desdemona, or at least let us run with you."

She nodded. It was time she trusted someone. "Promise you won't hate me once I tell you the truth? That you'll still be my friend?" Desdemona wanted a friend so bad.

"I promise. Well unless you're a crazed serial killer and then I'm kinda obligated to either shoot you or arrest you, but if it makes you feel better I'll visit you in lockup. FBI law sometimes will supersede some parts of girlfriend code. Not all, but some."

Desdemona laughed. "I think I'm ready."

Elizabeth stood, and took her hand. "I'll get you through this, I promise."

Somehow, Desdemona believed her. The woman looking down at her was a kind woman, and her eyes showed it too. If there were any people that she could trust, it was these three. She took a deep breath. "Okay let's do it. I don't want to run anymore."

Whitefox paced back and forth in the living room of the rental house. He desperately wanted to go to the door, knock and check on Desdemona. Worry filled his body, as he could only hope that Elizabeth wasn't making the situation worse by being alone with her. She tended to be a little harsher at times than most people.

"You know, she's pretty good with things like this," stated Blackhawk. "Don't underestimate her. Rarely does she kick a person while they're down."

The muscle in his cheek twitched, and then he thought back to all she'd done for him and there was an intense feeling of guilt that he was questioning her compassion.

"You should have some faith in her. If Lyzee knew you were thinking she was abusing Desdemona, she'd be crushed," he paused. "Then I'd have to kick your ass for upsetting my wife."

Whitefox was about to comment when the door to the bathroom opened, and Desdemona exited with his sister-in-law, their arms around each other's waists. One woman had tearstained cheeks, the other looked tough, and strong. She was doing exactly what he asked, holding up the weaker of the two and bearing the burden. Desdemona Adare was safe beneath the Raven's wings, and he'd been worried for nothing. Love overwhelmed him.

"We're ready to talk about it now," said Elizabeth, pulling her new friend closer, protectively.

Both men sat in chairs facing the couch, as Elizabeth pulled Desdemona down beside her, and took her hand in hers, offering her as much warmth and support as she could. "Come on Morticia, you got this," she said softly, whispering the quote to her friend.

Whitefox bristled. This was going to be a disaster.

Desdemona laughed, it was weak but it was still a laugh. "It all started in college. One day I was at class, and when I returned home there was a flower arrangement for me. Roses. I wasn't dating anyone, and when I read the card, it said 'watching you'."

Whitefox felt his blood pressure rise.

"Go on," pushed Elizabeth.

"I figured I'd be extra careful and just not go out alone, stay on well-lit trails, and I'd be fine. Then it stopped."

She finally looked up at her boss sitting across from her. His face was emotionless, as he listened to her. The Blackhawk glare was what the techs called it, and it was very intimidating. Then it occurred to her that she'd been very wrong. The scary one turned out to be the gentle soft one, and the quiet one was definitely the scarier of the Blackhawk bosses.

"Off I went to medical school, and one day a rose appeared. Then nothing." One day, I came home from a thirty-six hour rotation. Someone had been in my apartment. Little things were moved, like I was going crazy. Blankets flipped, shoes moved from one closet to another."

"That had to be scary," Elizabeth added, sympathizing.

"I really thought I was losing my mind. Then it occurred to me, take a picture. I snapped pictures of everything. Then came home after my next rotation and they were all moved. Everything was touched. I knew I wasn't insane and had a big problem."

Whitefox stood and started pacing, like a stalking tiger. The poor woman, no wonder she was a nervous wreck, she lived her life looking over her shoulder. The need to protect overshadowed everything else he felt for her.

"The breaking point was the night I came home and re-fixed everything. When I woke up eight hours later, everything was switched back. The stalker had been in my apartment while I slept," she shuddered.

"Did you call the police?" asked Blackhawk.

"This time no. All the previous times I alerted campus security and each time it was laughed off."

"Did you go to the real police?" He needed to see the reports if they'd been filed.

"No, what would I tell them? Some unknown unseen person was in my place redecorating while I was at class or that it was haunted."

"You should have notified the authorities, regardless." Blackhawk knew he was being hard on her, but someone had to be the tough one. She hid this from the FBI and it could cost anyone of them their lives. She should have been forthcoming. Full disclosure was required to work for the FBI.

Elizabeth lifted an eyebrow at her husband. She understood why he was being a hard ass towards the woman, but it was uncharacteristic of him. Usually she was the mean, hard one. She could see the look on her brother-in-laws face, directed at her husband. Trouble was brewing between the Blackhawk blood.

"Then it stopped. I thought I was safe," she sighed. "I started my first job at a hospital in Wyoming. I loved working there. It was quiet. I met people, finally started living and then the notes came back. They warned me that if I started a relationship the person would die."

Elizabeth was horrified.

"I ran. To save the people I liked, I bolted. I dumped a really nice guy, made excuses and ran."

"You can't run forever," interjected Elizabeth.

"She's right, you have to stand up and fight," said Callen Whitefox. "I'll stand with you."

Her heart skipped in her chest. The last piece of her heart was gone, he owned it. He was such a kind man, she had no doubt he'd stand with her and risk his life. She may never own his heart, but now he had hers.

"Please continue," requested Blackhawk, emotionless.

"I found a new job, and then again it happened. I kept running and someone kept following me. I've been in the clear the last four months."

"Why the FBI?" asked Elizabeth. "You took a huge pay cut to come here."

"I figured the person harassing me would be frightened away. Who stalks someone in the FBI?" She took a deep breath. "I got to carry a gun; I was in a secure building. I felt safe and bought the house I live in now. First time for me, I never felt like I could."

Ethan Blackhawk wasn't thrilled. The terror was in his own back yard now. He felt for the woman, but she should have been honest, and had all this documented.

"Now it's started again. Before I came up here, Callen was with me when I found a rose on my porch." It just felt like it wasn't ever going to end, and there was a sense of hopelessness. "The stalker must have followed me here."

Blackhawk stood and looked at his brother. "Outside. I need to talk to you, now." It wasn't a request, and everyone in the room knew it.

"I'm sorry," she whispered. "I didn't want to cause this."

Elizabeth patted her hand. "It's okay. We'll work through this together. You chose to stand and fight, and we make a stand together."

"I don't want them to fight!" Desdemona was alarmed that she had managed to cause an issue between them.

"They're brothers and fighting happens. I once saw them wrestle over the last beer, and it got ugly," she answered, trying to offer the woman some reassurance. It was bothering her that they were about to brawl too.

"Please go stop them," she pleaded.

"I'll go play referee."

Blackhawk stood outside zipping his parka and waiting for his brother to join him. Before Whitefox could even get his parka zipped he was ready to explode at the man.

"You knew?" he raged, pointing accusingly.

Whitefox was angry too. His brother had acted like the woman was a criminal and was ice cold towards her, and he found that unacceptable. He'd once been the weak and knew how that felt to be the prey. "Knew what? That all this was going on? Hell no! I saw the rose on her porch. She threw it in the snow, and I didn't question it. I'd known her ninety minutes. I didn't think I had the right to interrogate her over it."

"This whole situation is a bad thing."

"Could you be a little colder to her in there? Do you know the courage that it took for her to even tell us all that? The woman is scared shitless, and I didn't think you would be cruel to someone beaten down."

"Cold? You think that was cold? You're out of your damn mind. I wasn't cold, Callen. What I was being was the man responsible for all four of our lives, and the twenty techs we brought with us. It's called being the God damn boss!"

"You could have cut her a break."

"I won't cut a break to a person that knowingly breaks the rules. We work for the FBI. All of this should have been disclosed. The risk she put everyone at isn't something to screw with. My job, as shitty as it can be is to keep an open mind and keep everyone safe. This isn't a game and if we screw up someone is going back to FBI West in a body bag."

"We're safe!" He pointed out angrily.

"Callen, if you weren't sleeping with her, would you honestly believe that?"

"Yes I would!"

Ethan hit where it would hurt. "So if this stalker takes out Elizabeth as collateral damage, then you'd still believe we were completely safe and that had nothing to do with it?" If he said yes, he was going to seriously question his brother's judgment and sanity.

Whitefox lost it. Later he wouldn't know if it was because his brother was right or if he hit him with a well-placed blow to his heart. The one true love in his life.

Elizabeth was fucking off limits!

The mere suggestion that they could lose her ripped at his heart and rattled his cage to the point anger became fury that he'd even speak the words out loud.

The younger brother did something he would regret later. He rushed his older brother and swung, punching him in the face.

Ethan knew it was coming, and he moved with the punch and went down, taking his brother with him. The two men rolled around in the snow, trying to beat the hell out of each other. Blackhawk got an elbow in, catching his brother in the jaw and he fell off him. Immediately both were back on his feet.

More swinging continued, as Whitefox took a fist to the cheekbone and went back down.

"This proves what I said. You're emotionally attached to the situation and not thinking straight."

Whitefox was up again, and he spit blood into the snow. "Like you haven't been there? You started screwing your wife when you were supposed to be professional." The anger clouded his judgment and he said words that he knew were going to have a cost.

That one sentence was like poking the bear with a stick, especially the 'screwing' part. Blackhawk charged and took his brother down with a shoulder to the solar plexus. He pinned him, and had his arm under his chin on his windpipe.

"No, I wasn't professional Callen, and it almost got us killed. That day I almost lost my wife. I watched another man beat the hell out of her, wrap his hands around her throat and try to take her life. She ended up lying on a sawdust covered floor in hers and my blood. If you think that makes me proud as her husband and a man, then you have no place in my life!" Blackhawk blinked and regained his control. "My lack of professionalism almost cost me Elizabeth. I'm speaking from experience, and this is my point. If you think I'm busting your balls just because I have nothing better to do, then you don't fucking get it." He got off his brother and stared down at him, spitting blood into the snow now too.

"Actions have consequences and maybe you're willing to risk my family, but I'm not for a complete stranger that lied before. If she'd lie about this, what else is there out there?"

Callen closed his eyes, knowing his brother was absolutely right. He was emotionally attached to the situation. When he opened them again, his brother was gone.

"Shit."

Here he believed his brother was being a jerk, but the only thing he was doing was being a brother. When his brother threw Elizabeth into the mix it made his blood boil and his heart squeeze in his chest that she could get hurt.

Damn it!

Now his actions were going to likely have big consequences too- ones that involved his family.

~Chapter Nine~

Elizabeth stood in the doorway and watched the men kick the crap out of each other in the snow. If she got involved she'd just beat down both of their asses, and really… she might hurt them. This they had to do on their own.

Brothers being brothers.

She was saying it over and over to herself in order to not go out and pull them apart. It came down to trust in both men not to cross the line and hurt the other too much.

When he came in the kitchen, the mad was gone from his face, and the old Ethan was back. This was her proof violence did solve problems, and she would have pointed it out, had she thought he'd find it funny. Nothing fixed a problem like a good old fashioned beat down.

"Here's a tissue, baby." She held one out to him.

"Do you think I was being an asshole too?" he asked, softly, waiting for his wife to take his brother's side.

Elizabeth went to him and kissed him on the cheek. "I think you're being a man responsible for all our lives, and a brother worried about his younger brother, nothing more."

Blackhawk nodded and he relaxed knowing his wife supported him. "Where is she?"

Elizabeth pointed. "And then you need to change. You're wet and your shirts torn, honey." She watched him walk away. There was no need to follow him. Ethan Blackhawk was a gentle, honorable man. It was why she fell helplessly in love with him. Now that the anger was gone, he'd protect the woman in the other room. She'd bet her badge on it.

And all their lives.

Blackhawk walked into the room, and found the woman alone on the couch. She looked so lost and scared and part of him defrosted fast. Looking at her on the couch with her legs tucked up under her, and a scared look on her face made him think about what he'd do if she was his woman.

Anything to keep her safe, much like he'd do for Elizabeth.

"I'm sorry, Director Blackhawk," she said softly, and the tears were close to coming again. "You can fire me. I understand. I withheld information from the people that hired me and risked everyone's life. If you prefer I'll resign immediately and leave Red River."

"What will you do?" he asked, curiously.

"It doesn't matter. I can't let you and your brother fight over me. I'm not worth it."

Something in Blackhawk melted and he understood why his brother was sucked in. She looked like a broken child that needed a big brother to protect her.

"I broke the rules, I withheld, and this is all on me."

It was funny, that his brother didn't get that, but the woman who was the victim did. "I want a list of everyman you slept with, had a relationship with, lived with or thought about living with. Go all the way back to your childhood."

She looked up surprised. "I'm not fired?"

"Much like my wife, I don't kick people when they're down. You came to us, trusted us, and I'm going to help you get out from under this weight."

"Because I'm sleeping with your brother?" she asked, no emotion on her face.

"Despite that, Desdemona." He patted her knee as he knelt in front of her. "We take care of the ones we care about." Blackhawk let it go at that. He was absolutely doing it for Callen.

She saw his lip. "Did Callen punch you?" She was horrified.

Blackhawk grinned wickedly. "He sure did," he paused. "It wasn't the first time and it sure as hell won't be the last, but make sure you yell at him for it too," he laughed, standing. "Get me the list, and we'll start fixing this." Blackhawk left the room, and knew he did the right thing, but in the back of his mind, he hoped it would be enough. Now his brother's life was on the line too, because he knew he'd never walk away from the woman. He'd be honorable and act like a shield between her and a nut job hunting her for over ten years. Love or not, Callen would act the protector.

Damn it!

Elizabeth waited for Callen to come inside. She held a tissue for him too, and she was going to heal his lip then kick his ass.

"Safe to enter?" he asked from the doorway.

"Depends, I may beat you down just for shits and giggles." She pointed at him and then the chair.

Whitefox wasn't sure he could take her, so he opted to just sit and obey.

"Are you certifiable? You just attacked your boss, while on assignment in the field. Punched him in the face, and rolled around in the snow with him."

"Uh, he got a few shots in too," he sighed, pointing at his face and lip. "I was mad, ok?" Callen didn't tell her why.

Elizabeth sat at the table and took his hand in hers. "Your brother and I are responsible for everyone here. Our job is to find a killer, and get us all home in one piece. He's thinking like the boss, and you need to keep that in mind. That man would take a bullet for you, and so would I," she added. "But you have to remember that making it easy for a nut job risks us. Do you want to risk your nephew?"

He looked horrified that the woman he adored was at risk and now his nephew too. He'd never risk Elizabeth and the baby for anyone. The mere idea made him want to be sick.

"Trust your brother and cut him some slack. He's a good man, and that's the bottom line." Elizabeth handed him a tissue.

"I know I screwed up."

Elizabeth didn't acknowledge it, but yeah he did. "Your lip is bleeding too. It was a decent swing, but he saw it coming and when he went down it was to break the momentum. Next time switch it up, and when I say next time I mean with someone other than my husband. If it happens again, I'll take you out back and show you an old fashioned beat down." She leaned over and kissed him on his lip like he'd done for her the other day.

He laughed as the tension lessened in his chest. "I love you, Lyzee, and my lip feels better now too." The tingle shot through his body.

"I love you too." Elizabeth stroked his cheek gently.

Whitefox stared at her, and thought about what his brother had just said to him outside in the snow. What would he do if all this cost him her? He swallowed the lump in his throat and the tears that threatened to fill his eyes.

"What?" she asked, as he stared at her.

"Promise me that no matter what you'll keep you and the baby safe. Please put yourself first and don't get hurt."

Elizabeth looked over her coffee cup and into his eyes. The man looked rattled. "What's wrong, Cal?"

Callen looked right into her eyes and lied. "Nothing, just covering all my bases." It was one thing to risk his own life, but he had made her promise to keep Desdemona safe. Now he realized how stupid that was for him to do. Now that there was a stalker, by standing in front of her, Elizabeth was now carrying the target on her back. He'd just made the woman loved a possible victim.

She smelled a lie but let it go. It was only a matter of time before she figured it out, and then smacked him silly for not telling her the truth.

All this drama, and it wasn't even eight a.m. yet. It didn't give her high hopes for the day at all.

Whitefox found her sitting on the couch crying. It crushed him how dejected she looked. He would do anything to take away that sadness for her. "Desi, are you going to be okay?" he asked, softly.

She looked up, and saw the battle wounds on his face. "Oh Callen! What have you done?" she asked, standing and moving towards him. "Look at your face," she said, sniffling. Pulling him to the couch she pushed him down, and sat beside him, checking to make sure he was okay.

"Ethan and I had a little fun in the snow," he said, grinning.

Desdemona should have been mad, but it touched her that he'd fight his brother for her. His own flesh and blood, for a woman he just met. "Come here," she pulled his face towards hers, and kissed the mark on his check, and then left a whisper light kiss on his cut lip.

"Thank you," he added, smiling. It wasn't lost on him that her kiss didn't have the same affect, and the guilt came back and overwhelmed him again as his heart and mind waged war.

Just then his brother came back down the stairs; he'd changed and was ready for the day ahead. He looked at the woman. "Don't forget, by noon today if possible." He nodded at her and walked away, ignoring his brother. Granted it was beneath him, but he was still irritated that the man challenged him, oh and punched him in the face.

"Noon what?" asked Whitefox, confused.

"He wants a list of everyone in my past I had a relationship with, and he's going to help me get free of this mess," she answered. "You have an amazing family, Callen. Your brother is a really good guy and Elizabeth is pretty damn amazing too."

Whitefox, if possible felt like even more of an ass. Yeah, what an idiot he was today, especially towards his brother. The man he just accused of being cold was going to clean up the woman's mess, and he knew he would have done it despite the fact his brother was sleeping with her.

"Come on, let's get you into dry clothes, we have to get to work soon," she said, standing and offering him her hand.

Then he needed to talk to his brother and tell him how sorry he was to have doubted him, and risked their relationship. Now he could only hope his brother, who gave him a free pass off the Rez, was letting him love his wife, and be part of his life would forgive him.

Or he just lost everything that mattered in his life.

Ethan drove into the Sheriff's station with just his wife. Right now he wanted to give his brother some time to cool down, and figure out what end was up. Women could turn a life upside down, he knew that from experience. His wife had done the same to him too. Now she was turning his life upside down at every chance, and he suspected Callen's too,

"How mad are you at him?" she asked, as they pulled into the parking lot.

"I'm not. But sometimes you have to beat sense into the stubborn ones," he answered.

"Hell, if I don't know that," she said, grinning. "If I was included in those 'stubborn ones' comment, keep in mind you probably couldn't take me."

Ethan laughed at the visual.

When he parked the Denali, she paused. "Mr. Blackhawk?" she asked.

"Yeah, Mrs. Blackhawk," he looked over.

Elizabeth reached over and pulled him over to her, bringing her lips to his, starting to kiss him lightly, then gradually increasing the kiss, until he moaned in pleasure. When she broke away, both of them were breathing heavier.

Blackhawk licked his lips. "What was that for?" he needed to know, so he could keep doing it.

"That's for that sexy display of manhandling your own brother in the driveway, and the fact that you evaded that punch with some excellent skill and timing. Big turn on indeed, Mr. Blackhawk. Those were some crazy mad fighting skills. Turned me right on," she said, winking.

"Like sex tonight turned on?" he asked, hopefully. It felt like weeks since he'd been able to put his hands all over his wife.

Elizabeth leaned over and whispered in his ear.

"Shit! Really?" Ethan Blackhawk sat with his mouth open, as he visualized it.

"Really Mr. Blackhawk," she winked, opening the door. "Come on, Cowboy, we have work to do."

Ethan Blackhawk watched his wife walk up the walk to the front doors, and he couldn't help but hope the day went by fast, so when they got home he could be the victim of her manhandling.

*   *   *

She stood in the trees with her shotgun. If her lover tried to escape, she'd show him who was boss. If someone was trying to steal her man, she was going to protect her one true love no matter what.

A girl had to do what a girl had to do.

Watching the buildings, she prepared to make the shot, and put down the person that dared go near her lover.

Once she found the whore, she'd take her down with one clear shot. No one touched her true love and got away with it.

The best whore was a dead one.

*   *   *

Sheriff Duffy waited inside for the FBI to arrive. He needed to update them on the situation that had been brought to his attention. Deputy Julian Littlemoon was back from tracking, and he needed them to hear what he'd discovered.

When the female Agent entered the building, he moved toward them quickly, not wanting Sheila Court to make any comments to exacerbate the situation. They'd yet to find Deputy Bobby Lee Tills, and he knew it was priority one with the FBI. The man tried to kidnap one of the agents, and that was a big offense. His deputy was going to jail, and he couldn't stop it from happening. It was time to cut his losses

"Agents, can I see you in my office?" He rushed forward, ushering them into his space. Inside Deputy Littlemoon sat, in civilian clothing.

"Agent Blackhawk," he said, nodding and standing to allow the female agent his chair. She may be an outsider, but she was married to a Native, and he'd give her respect. Especially since the ring on her finger had the symbols and stones of her husband's tribe. Obviously she'd been claimed by their people too.

"Thank you, Deputy."

Blackhawk nodded at the deputy and his courtesy to his wife. "I'm assuming you want to give me some information on Deputy Tills? Have you found him?"

The previous night, Sheriff Duffy had received the call pretty late about the suspected abduction. Immediately, he called Littlemoon, and told him where to start looking for the man. "It is about him and sadly, he hasn't been found. Deputy Littlemoon was out tracking him, and he found himself back up by the boy scout camp again."

Blackhawk looked over at the man. "Julian, what did you find?"

"I tracked the man close to the house you're renting. He travelled from the hospital, up past the boy scout camp, and then down to your dwelling. Once he hit the road I lost him, but there were plenty of tracks at the camp."

221

"Okay." Blackhawk looked over at the knock at the door, and then turned back.

Whitefox walked in with the ME.

"I think that he might be hiding out up at the boy scout camp and using the buildings to lay low. We wouldn't think to look there for him," he said.

Elizabeth and her husband stood. "Then we need to get up there and search," she said.

"They don't make maternity Kevlar, Elizabeth," her husband said, as he walked past his brother and the ME. "You aren't going." Ethan Blackhawk wasn't even going to negotiate this.

Elizabeth followed him out, and wasn't going to listen to a single word he said. In fact, she watched the men getting ready and had a plan. "Desdemona, still have my keys?" she asked, keeping her eye on her husband.

"Yeah."

"Let me have them, and when he realizes I'm gone, tell him where I went," she said, walking out the door and to the Denali. She loved her husband, but just because his brother had him pissed off, he wasn't going to boss her around. She didn't have any intention of going onto the scene, but she would sit there and wait for him to arrive. At some point he'd learn that snapping orders at her was just going to cause more drama and pushback from her. Apparently, at month nine of being married, he still didn't realize that if he ordered her around, she was going to fight him.

Independent and stubborn were about to collide once again, and this time she had raging hormones in her favor.

Ethan Blackhawk had given out the orders to everyone that was heading to the boy scout camp. Everyone was to be in Kevlar, ear pieces, and to watch their backs. As he went to give his wife a kiss goodbye, he realized she was gone.

"Where's Elizabeth?" he asked, looking around at the people surrounding him.

Whitefox shrugged, but had a sneaking suspicion.

222

"She walked out the door ten minutes ago," added Desdemona. "What?" she looked at both men. "I can't blame her; you just barked orders at her. By now she has the entire scene cleared." She began putting on her Kevlar vest.

"Desdemona, You aren't going," said Whitefox, adamantly.

"Really? With the deputy running around lose you want me here by myself? That sounds like a horrible idea."

The look on his face was priceless.

Desdemona just laughed, walking away and channeling her inner Elizabeth.

"This is all your wife's fault," muttered Whitefox, suiting up. "She's a horrible influence on Desdemona. Just yesterday she listened to me, for the most part."

"I swear to God, I'm going to drag her home and…" He didn't think anything would stop his wife from being a complete menace to herself and his nerves. "Let's get out there, before my partner gets herself killed.

Blackhawk was pretty sure he felt like committing murder.

Elizabeth hopped out of the Denali, as she heard the snow crunching beneath tires. There was something new at the camp that had her attention. Above the buildings she could see the birds and hear the caws. In fact, there was a tree full of black birds "Shit," she muttered.

Blackhawk was at her side fast, and he wasn't happy. "Elizabeth, you're not going in there," he said, glaring angrily at his wife.

"Ethan, we have a dead body," she answered, pointing at the building. "Carrion birds," she added. "They've been having a snack, and we need to get in there and keep the remains from being destroyed further."

Blackhawk motioned to the ME. "Doctor Adare, we have scavengers. Suit up," he said, pointing to the birds sitting in the trees.

"Director Blackhawk, I need to go in first and see the scene in situ, wait for me." It was time to get to work, and she was pretty sure she knew what waited for her.

"Open the door!" He yelled over to the deputy. "Stay out until the Doctor gets in there first, but look in first to make sure we're cleared."

Julian Littlemoon pulled his gun and looked around the corner and visually cleared the room for the FBI Agents. When he looked back, he motioned the room was clear.

"What do we have?" Both Blackhawks moved towards the building, guns out.

"It looks like we can stop looking for Bobby Lee Tills. Right now he's lying against the back wall and pretty much same as the others," he answered. "Killers been here, and this time, he's missing eyes. We can thank the killer or the birds."

Whitefox walked behind Desdemona, his Glock out, scanning the area around the building to make sure she'd be safe. Behind him Blackhawk began dialing the tech team for retrieval.

Something about the birds drew Elizabeth's attention. Carrion birds were scavengers, and they were all looking down into the dilapidated building at the meal that was going to be out of their reach soon. All she could hope was they got there before the birds pecked apart the evidence too much.

Desdemona stood in the doorway, looking in at the deceased man, and she felt bad for him. Yeah, he tried to abduct her, but she wouldn't wish this end on anyone. As she stepped in the room, Desdemona noticed the glassless window facing the tree line. At least with the missing sections of the roof and open window there would be plenty of light to examine the body. She stepped in to get her part of the job done.

Elizabeth heard the telltale pump of a shotgun, and then the birds all taking off at the same time, cawing in alarm. She ran towards the building, alerting her team. "Down! Gun!" The team dove, as she slid into the building, knocking both Callen and Doctor Adare off their feet and to the snowy ground. The blast filled the area, then a second, before silence filled the clearing.

When there were no more shots, Ethan was the first to be up and moving. He motioned to Littlemoon, and they charged off into the trees to head off the killer. All the while he was worried about his family in the building, but he needed to do his job and trust his partner.

Elizabeth leaned over Callen and touched his leg, fear filled her heart. Both were lying motionless on the ground. "Cal, are you okay?" she asked, tentatively touching him.

Whitefox reached up and pulled her flat and against his body to keep her safe.

"Are you out of your mind?" he hissed into her ear. "You could have been shot!"

"Yeah so could you!" she answered back, her heart was still pounding in her chest.

"I'm wearing Kevlar, Lyzee. You're wearing skin. I would have been okay," he answered, exasperated. "I could have landed on you and the baby when you slid into us."

Elizabeth placed her hand over her belly, and was grateful that wasn't what happened. "Oh, well next time I'll wait and see how that thick skull of yours does against a shotgun blast."

"Are you both done fighting," whispered Desdemona. "Some of us don't do well in these situations, and you both aren't making it easier."

"Yeah, we're done." Elizabeth placed her hand on his cheek. "You okay, Doc?" she asked, looking over at the woman.

"Yeah, I think so, Elizabeth."

Callen turned his head and kissed the palm of her hand. He was grateful she was still fast on her feet and had no sense of self-preservation.

"That was close. If you didn't plow into us and knock us down, that wouldn't have ended well." She let it hang in the air as she looked over at the giant hole in the wall from the bullet.

"Close calls keep me on my toes," she said, joking.

Desdemona was shaking. "Elizabeth. I love you," she said, kissing her boss on the lips. "Thank you for saving us!"

Elizabeth laughed at the entire situation. She was the pregnant woman lying between two lovers, and was just kissed by her ME.

Whitefox snorted. "Ethan is going to be pissed he missed that kiss," he said, and started to stand. "Speaking of Ethan, I better go after him. Both of you stay down. Elizabeth you aren't vested!" He gave her the look.

"I know, I know."

"Keep down, until Ethan or I get back."

Elizabeth watched him run from the building. "Slide back against the wall, and keep your eyes on that window," she said getting into position with her ME. "Got your gun?"

"Uh huh," she said, her hands shaking. "How are you not completely scared and rattled?"

Elizabeth shrugged. "I'm just used to getting shot at and more so now that I'm pregnant." She patted the woman on her leg. "Or maybe it's a statement of my mental status. Possibly a little of both," she joked, trying to hide the fact she was badly rattled. Callen Whitefox almost didn't walk out of that building.

Desdemona didn't understand how the woman could be so blasé about the entire episode. It was possible she was completely insane. "Next time a field assignment comes up, I think it's Doctor Leonard's turn."

Elizabeth heard the crunching if snow, and elbowed her ME. "Get ready," she whispered. "Someone's coming." Both women lifted their guns. Elizabeth's steady and Desdemona's shaking. "Don't shoot unless you don't know who it is," she whispered.

"I'm good with a gun when I'm not scared shitless," Desdemona whispered.

"Elizabeth, it's me," her husband said, knowing she'd be ready to kill whoever came through the doorway.

"Hey honey, just hanging out with Desdemona and the dead guy," she said, pushing the ME's gun down towards the snow, so she didn't accidentally shoot her husband.

"Do you see why I didn't want you running around without a vest," he said, peeking around the corner.

"Yeah yeah, so you keep saying, but if I wasn't here there may have been a vastly different outcome."

Desdemona squeezed her hand. "I don't know how you knew the killer was going to shoot, but thank heavens you did."

"I heard the pump of the shotgun, and then the birds took off out of the tree." Elizabeth pulled her friend to her feet. "Did you catch the shooter?"

Whitefox appeared behind his brother.

"Whoever it was, they took off in a car," answered Blackhawk.

"I called the tech team, so we can start processing the scene and then get the hell out of here," he said, staring around the abandoned space. "I don't like working on scenes where people are shooting at me and my family, or my wife is playing cowboy."

Elizabeth ignored him and stared down at the man that just last night was trying to kill them. "Get to work Doc," she stated, patting her friend on the ass as she walked past her.

Desdemona laughed and felt a little less shaky.

"That was for the kiss," she replied, winking and walking past her husband.

"Wait, what kiss?" he asked, staring at his brother. "There was a kiss?" The tone of his voice was sheathed in unadulterated disappointment that he missed out on that.

Whitefox snorted. "Oh yeah, you should have seen it. Desdemona was kissing your wife and I got to watch."

"Son of a bitch. I hate this killer."

Wednesday Afternoon

Desdemona once again stood on her stool looking down into the face of death, and as usual she felt pity for the violent end to his life. Yes, he was a vicious man, who wanted to do her and Elizabeth Blackhawk harm, but in the end no one deserves to have their eyes removed or pecked out by scavengers. With her micro-goggles she examined the wounds in the orbital sockets for any trace or sign of what happened. Just as she was leaning over the body, she heard someone clear their voice.

"Excuse me, Doctor?"

Desdemona stood up and pulled the goggles off her head. "Yes, Sheriff?" she asked, preparing to pull the sheet over the man's body. He was one of his employees, and she didn't want him to have to see him before they cleaned him up.

"Can I see Bobby Lee?" he asked, softly. "I know he was a colossal asshole to you and the Agents, but he was still someone I knew."

She contemplated it.

"You can look, Sheriff, but you really can't touch. The tech team hasn't swept him for evidence yet," and she saw the look on the man's face and went around the table to him. "I'm really sorry for your loss."

He nodded and moved closer to the body. When he'd seen him at the crime scene his adrenaline had been racing, due to being shot at, and now he was back down to normal. It all just seemed senseless to him. Completely senseless for anyone to die this way. In defense was one thing but this was a travesty.

Desdemona took his hand and patted it. "The FBI will find who killed your friend and co-worker. You can trust in that." Desdemona smiled up at the man. "Have faith."

"After this week, I think I need a drink or two," he spoke to the tiny woman beside him. "Want to join me tonight for one?"

That caught her completely off guard and she didn't know what to say.

"Unfortunately, she's going to be very busy tonight, Sheriff. I'm afraid Doctor Adare is very unavailable." Callen Whitefox stood in the doorway of the make shift morgue and leaned against the wall with his arms crossed over his chest.

"Oh, I see," said the man. He suspected there was something between them, but he wasn't definitely sure until just that moment. Oh well, strike two with the feds. He'd have to find his companion out of the women in Red River.

"I hope you do," he answered, stalking towards them. Whitefox was very aware of their hands still joined, and he lifted a brow and shifted his glare to Desdemona.

She released his hand like it was a hot coal straight from a fire.

"I'll go get some work done," he said, tipping his hat at the doctor. It was a shame, she looked like she'd be a fun distraction for the evening.

"Doctor, the only hands you're going to be holding and drinking beer with are mine, am I clear?" He glared down at her.

Desdemona must have been staring with her mouth wide open. When he put his fingers under her chin and closed her mouth, she didn't know what to say to him. "Callen!"

Whitefox didn't care if she was outraged, and he planned on showing her. Leaning down, he pulled her face towards his and

228

kissed her hard and fast. When he broke away, the telltale dazed look in her eyes gave him a sense of possessiveness. "Am I perfectly clear, Desi? That's an order."

When her mind was finally unclouded, she nodded at him. There weren't any words left in her head at that point. The man certainly could kiss and distract a woman.

"Elizabeth and Ethan want the presence of your company in the room they're using. Seems they want a preliminary report and any data you've received on the other victims. I'll walk you up," he said, stepping back. After todays' events, he was on an adrenaline high.

"I think I can find my way upstairs," she muttered, grabbing her papers from the table. "Derek," she called over to a tech prepping some instruments. "Can you please put the deputy back in the cooler, until the team is ready to wash him down and check for trace?"

"Sure thing Doc," the young man said, smiling.

"Thank you, Derek." Desdemona started for the door and noticed the look on Whitefox's face. "Are you going to stare like that at every man that comes within proximity to me?" she whispered to him. "Even the techs?"

"Yep."

"Why?" She didn't understand what was bothering him.

Whitefox waited until they were out in the stairwell, and he took her by the arm. Desdemona stood on a stair ahead of him, and they were almost eye level. "Because I don't share what's mine," he practically growled, low in her ear.

The words and how he said them gave her goose bumps.

"I've found I've grown attached to you, Desi, and I've also found that men sniffing around you makes me very irritated." He loved the way she smelled, and he wanted to just grab her and take her home and do very insane things with her. Callen knew why it was happening, and again more guilt came and he bore it alone. Not even Elizabeth could help him carry this.

"Don't I get any say in this?" Desdemona was outraged, that he was taking control of her life and whipping it into a frenzy. Part of her wanted to stand up to him and defend herself. This was her life after all, and she deserved the right to speak her mind.

"No, you don't." He took a deep breath, trying not to focus on the black glasses perched on her nose, or the way she stared at him in outrage. "We better go, before I do something that gets us both embarrassed if we get caught."

Now she blushed bright red. "Callen!"

"Come on," he turned her around, and tried desperately to not watch her as she walked up the stairs. His body was hard and taut as he visualized the morning they spent in bed together. Then came the memory of Elizabeth saving their lives, and risking her own again. At that moment he was a volatile brew, needing an outlet to his ever growing frustration.

Desdemona rushed up the stairs, and prayed her face wouldn't give her away. Her skin was burning, almost like sunburn and that meant her bosses were going to know she wasn't only thinking about the dead man downstairs, but the very living one walking behind her. Maybe she was getting her wish and capturing his heart for her own.

Elizabeth sat perched beside her husband on the table in the little conference room they were working out of in the station. Ethan Blackhawk was talking to their boss on speakerphone, and giving him an update on the situation. Although they were Directors of FBI West, Gabe was still their boss. He was head of Quantico, and ran his divisions with an iron fist.

Blackhawk relayed all the information, and then told him about Desdemona Adare's situation.

"What?" he asked angrily. How did something like that get casually forgotten?"

Elizabeth looked up as Both Doctor Adare and Callen Whitefox entered the room. "It's my fault Gabe." She took the heat. "I had my ME interview and hire Doctor Adare. I take full blame on this one. I didn't vet the situation, and it's all on me. "

Desdemona didn't know what to do. Here her friend was taking the blame, because she didn't come clean and tell them what was going on in her life. No one had ever covered for her like that before.

Callen tensed, and he pulled the woman's body back against his, protectively. He wished he did jump her in the stairwell. Then she wouldn't be hearing this conversation. Deep down he wanted to protect Elizabeth too from her boss's anger. This wasn't her fault, and she was once again standing in front of them taking the heat because he asked her to do it.

Damn it!

"What are you going to do about it?" Gabe was a firm believer in making his Agents and his Directors, despite them being family, clean up their own messes.

"I'm handling it," answered Blackhawk. "I have a list of everyone she's had a relationship with, casually and intimately, and I'll work on it until I can eliminate the suspects."

"In your spare time?" he asked testily. "And off the FBI dime?"

"Yes."

Gabe Rothschild thought about it. "Handle it, but if this blows up into a hot mess, the blowback is going to be messy and exclusive of the FBI. That means if anything sketchy goes down, it can mean both of your careers. I can only look away so much, Ethan."

Desdemona felt sick to her stomach again.

"I'll take the consequences, Gabe," answered Blackhawk.

"As will I," added Elizabeth. "She's our employee and we'll take care of any mess that comes along with it. This won't touch the FBI."

"Make sure, Elizabeth. Next time do your own damn interviews. This was a bone headed screw-up and I expect better from you and your husband. This was a rookie mistake."

"Ethan had nothing to do with this. I told you this was all me. I'm owning it and taking full responsibility. Put it in my personnel file."

Blackhawk gave her the look, and he wasn't happy.

"I don't want excuses. I want resolution. Fix it or fire the Doctor. At this point you both need to learn to play by the damn rules."

Whitefox stared helplessly at Elizabeth and felt horrible that she was getting dressed down by her boss in front of all of them, and it was all because of Desdemona's actions and his request. He stared into her eyes and mouthed, '*I'm sorry!*'

Elizabeth sucked it up, and knew the route she was going to take. "You know me, Gabe. I play the game by the letter of the law and handle my own mess." Elizabeth pulled a card she'd held close to her vest for over ten years ago. When she'd been a special agent beneath Gabe, the woman he was in love with, her best friend was being stalked and almost killed. Elizabeth took care of it for the people she loved. "I'll clean up this situation, much like I've handled other stalkers. You won't be pulled into it."

Gabe Rothschild got the message, and immediately he softened. "Use the FBI resources, clean it up Elizabeth, and sweep it under the carpet."

Blackhawk was startled by the use of his wife's name. Usually Gabe called her by her nickname. Something big just happened.

"I owe you one look away, and here it is. I'm surprised it took you so long to claim it," he said. "Well played on that card Elizabeth."

"I learned from the master at how to play the game, Gabe."

Now Blackhawk looked over at her, wondering what the hell just went on. His wife was good but no one was that good. They were discussing something he wasn't privy to, and he was going to be privy and soon.

Callen knew Elizabeth was a miracle worker, but when 'The Dragon Slayer' just changed his tune that fast, it meant something. Now he was curious how she just pulled it off. If she had that kind of favor, the implications were huge.

Elizabeth changed the subject, knowing the woman was in the room and she didn't want to have to give away too many details to a secret she and Gabe shared. Already she could feel her husband and Callens' eyes on her. Family was one thing, but honestly, she didn't trust anyone outside of their circle with something so big.

"How's Livy doing?" Gabe's wife was on bed rest with her last pregnancy. It was a tough one, and both Blackhawks knew how stressed Gabe was worrying about his wife and unborn child.

"We'll take the kids if you want," added Blackhawk. "As soon as we're off this assignment, so you guys can get a break." Blackhawk took his wife's hand in solidarity. It would be chaos, with five little girls running around their house, but he didn't mind. "We can take them to the Rez and let them play in the treehouse."

"She's hanging in there. The doctor said she needs to hold on for another six weeks at least. I hope we get a boy, because she's already declared that one of us is getting fixed," he laughed, the previous conversation was forgotten. Business was business and personal was personal, and rarely did they intersect in Gabe's world.

None of the men in the room found it funny and they were betting Gabe wasn't either.

Ethan ran his hand over his wife's belly. "Kiss her for us, and we'll keep you updated." He hung up the phone and looked over at his agent and the ME. "A little birdy tells me we have more in forensically."

Desdemona nodded and stepped forward.

"You look nervous, Doctor," added Blackhawk. "Is something bothering you?"

"I feel really bad that you both are risking your jobs and covering for me with Mr. Rothschild," she said, pulling the chair out at the table and taking a seat.

"Desdemona, we cover for our friends," Elizabeth answered and glanced at her brother-in-law. "We protect the ones we care about and love, no matter the personal cost."

Whitefox wondered at what cost and if she just sold her soul for the favor he asked of her.

"Agreed. So, you can stop worrying about it. Besides, Elizabeth and I have a personal relationship with Gabe, and if he sounded irritated on the phone it was only because he's worried about his wife." Yeah, and his wife obviously had something over her boss that he was willing to mellow out that fast. It had to be huge and he was going to start digging.

"Livy is having a bad pregnancy and struggling. This is their sixth child, and apparently their last," Elizabeth added.

Whitefox felt really horrible that he'd had a fight with his brother. He covered for Desdemona, when he really didn't have to, and he owed him an apology. There should have been trust in his relationship with his brother, and that he'd do the right thing for the woman. Taking the seat beside the doctor, he let his leg touch hers, in the slightest act of reassurance.

"It'll all work out," Blackhawk added. "Let's get refocused on this assignment. Can you tell me what we have in the way of forensics that will help me profile this killer and begin to allow Elizabeth to put the pieces together."

Desdemona Adare nodded. "Certainly. I have yet to do the autopsy on the deputy. I can tell you my preliminary findings with just what I noticed," she paused waiting for them to signal they were ready. She opened the file on the tablet, and pulled up the pictures that the tech team had taken once the deputy was returned back to the lab. "Please note on your copies of the photo of his face," she clicked on her picture and it appeared on Elizabeth's tablet.

"I love technology!" Elizabeth actually giggled and Ethan glanced over. "What? Come on, that was fun," she added.

"Yeah, if you enjoy fun photo sharing of bloodied corpses."

Desdemona relaxed. "Look at the orbital sockets." She looked over to make sure they both understood the technology.

"We got it, where the eyes usually sit."

"Notice the bone around the eyes. Its scraped," she magnified the picture, and Elizabeth's did the same. "There was a tool used to get down beneath the eye and remove it. If it had been one of those big nasty birds, then there would be peck marks in the bone, and there weren't."

"It looks like they ate around the eyes," Elizabeth said, looking at the snacked on flesh.

"Ewww," Whitefox muttered. "Sorry, but that's really disturbing and gross."

Desdemona patted his thigh absently and then realized what she did. "Uh, yeah. I guess it could be construed as gross." She went back to the picture. "Elizabeth is right, there are peck marks from the beaks of the carrion birds. They began consuming the flesh that surrounded the open wounds."

"Do we have COD?" asked Blackhawk, needing cause of death to help profile.

"Not until I open him. I will tell you there is no sign of sexual assault. It all appears to be the same MO as the other deaths. Restraint marks around the wrists, and then the mouth was the interesting find."

"Whatcha got Doc," asked Elizabeth, leaning forward. Interesting to the ME was probably going to be a good thing.

"Remember the victim with the square mark around his mouth that I suspected was duct tape?"

"Yeah, was it?"

"Yes. We swabbed and it was the adhesive used in common duct tape. The silver stuff."

Blackhawk considered what she was saying. "But that's going to be a big swath of people. Everyone has duct tape. We have duct tape."

"On our deputy, there were the same adhesive marks, but it's what was on the inside of the tape. He ingested a liquid before tape was placed over his mouth."

"How do we know it was before the tape was placed over his mouth?" asked Whitefox. This was all new to him, and he was trying to learn on the fly. Everyone else in the room had a decade on him with forensics and the FBI.

"No stomach bile mixed in," answered Desdemona.

"Okay, you can stop right there, I don't need it explained," he said, shuddering.

She pointed to the mouth and the picture opened up and gave them a close up of his face. "Furthermore, the tape residue around his mouth give us the same shape and wound pattern of duct tape being ripped off the flesh. Duct tape is particularly nasty when it's ripped of flesh. I actually saw lips come off once…" She noticed all three agents were staring at her. "Uh sorry, that was not apropos to the assignment, and way too much detail for non-ME staff."

Elizabeth stood and went to the whiteboard. This was her area of expertise. In her hands were the pictures of all the victims. Some were yet unidentified. So they didn't have before pictures. As she started to place them on the whiteboard she began filling in the information beneath them. "Callen, you get any more victims identified?"

"We did get two more in this morning. I just picked up the report from Christina," he said, pulling out the report and opening it up. "Sorry, I'm not as tech savvy. My report is still on good old fashioned paper."

Elizabeth didn't even look at them when she spoke, "That Native American Indian on those public service announcements, to save trees, wearing the headdress just rolled in his burial ground," she quipped, absently.

Both men laughed at her comment.

"Anyway, victim number one, we have a name and a before picture from his driver's license. His name is Ryan Larkson, and he was on a business trip, according to his girlfriend. Which wasn't uncommon for him at all. When one of the techs notified her and questioned her, she stated she filed a missing person report six months ago. He left his apartment and drove north to his meeting. His boss called to find him when he never showed up at the meeting on schedule."

"So he was driving right through town?" she asked.

Desdemona pulled up a map on her tablet and shot it over to Elizabeth.

"Here was his final destination, and here is where he originated," Callen said, touching the screen. "Most logical route if he stayed on the highway would be this route," Whitefox highlighted the path with his finger.

Ethan studied his wife's tablet. "So he didn't drive through Red River."

"No, he wouldn't have driven through. He would have circumvented the town completely by about ten miles," but he paused. "Maybe he came into town. There isn't much outside of town but mountains."

"We can canvas and ask the local shop keepers if they ever saw any of the identified victims. There's a chance we'll get lucky and someone might have seen one or all of them. Maybe they needed a pit stop, a coffee, or a place to stay," stated Elizabeth.

"We'll hit the field as Doctor Adare does her autopsy." Blackhawk watched his brother's face for any reaction to being separated from the doctor, and he didn't flinch. Apparently, the Blackhawk poker face was genetically handed out to his brother too.

Elizabeth put the picture up on the board and wrote the information under the picture. "Who do we have next?"

"Victim number three, Torrance Delmar. No wife and no girlfriend. He was the one missing his stomach. The prints came

236

back when we searched the military databases. He was a discharged soldier, employment as a professor. He taught calculus at the local community college."

"Any missing person report filed on him?"

"Yep, three months ago by the college. Christina called on this one. Her notes say that they called it in when Professor Delmar didn't show up for class a full week. By that Friday, an irate student who was paying for the class and missed his calculus fix, called the school bitching and wanting a refund."

"Who actually misses Calculus?" asked Blackhawk.

"I liked it," added Desdemona.

"Yeah who here who didn't go to an ivy league college didn't miss it," Blackhawk said, smiling.

"For the record, I had it and I hated it," said Elizabeth. She noticed the look from the doctor. "What?"

"You went ivy league?" asked Desdemona. "That's surprising. I just took you for a bad ass inner city school that taught ass kicking as a requirement."

Whitefox cringed. That wasn't exactly a compliment, and he couldn't help but wonder if Desdemona knew it too. It felt like a cheap shot to him and from Ethan's face, him too.

Elizabeth laughed it off for Callen's sake. "Nope, Cornell, but had they had that class I would have taken it," she said, smiling. "Although I would have picked Harvard over Cornell, but they wait listed me for my major."

Whitefox stared over at his brother. "Do you feel grossly inadequate and suddenly not as smart as you were ten minutes ago?"

"You get used to it," he answered honestly. "I never thought to apply to Harvard, they would have laughed and burned my application," he said.

"Well hopefully Leroy Heathcliff Mick Blackhawk IV will be handsome like his father, and smart like his momma."

Whitefox choked on water he was drinking. "Please tell me that's not going to be my nephew's name. I'll still love him, but using his name is going to be painful." Then it hit him. "Where did the IV come from?"

"Don't ask. She's sadistic."

Elizabeth pointed at her husband. "I am, and that will be our child's name if daddy doesn't help me pick a name."

"Ethan, don't do that to a kid. Leroy? Come on; pick a damn name for my nephew. Hell, name him Wyler at this point."

"I'm working on picking a name. It has to have some meaning to the Blackhawk family. This is the first of his generation. My first son needs a special name that speaks volumes about our family."

"Poor Leroy Heathcliff Mick Blackhawk IV," giggled Desdemona. Watching the three of them play off each other was really entertaining. "I wouldn't worry about his name. It really won't matter."

"Why?" asked Blackhawk and Whitefox at the same time, looking over at her suspiciously.

"Have you seen this kid's gene pool?" she asked, laughing. "Look at his mother. She's absolutely stunning. Then look at the father. He's downright handsome," and she paused. "Then look at the uncle. The boy is going to be handsome. No woman is going to care what the hell his name is once he's an adult."

Elizabeth laughed at the point she was making. "So Leroy it is."

Blackhawk just shook his head in exasperation. "We'll pick this up in private, Elizabeth. No one gets to know the baby's name until he's born. There should be some surprise."

Whitefox coughed into his hand. "Control freak."

He ignored his brother. "Shall we continue with the assignment?" he asked, not even dignifying his brother's comment with a retort. Over his dead body was his son going to be called Leroy or Heathcliff, but then no one was going to know that for a few more months.

"Anyway," Whitefox continued. "A student called it in, and they called local police to his house. No one saw him for over a week. Finally someone came forward to inform the police he had gone hiking in the mountains."

"Did he come through Red River?" she asked, as she scribbled the information on the board.

"Nope, this time he traversed the other side of the town. But again, he may have stopped in for supplies. If he was hiking and needed water or even coffee, this is the closest town."

"If the killer is targeting this far a location around Red River, we're going to have a big problem, if we can't prove the victims came into town. The possibilities of how they were grabbed shoots up exponentially," she said, looking over at Whitefox when he and her husband were grinning. "I'm going to ignore you both."

"Smaller words, Lyzee," snickered her brother-in-law.

"Can you print me out copies of the routes they took? I want to add them to the board later," she requested. "How about Patrick Payne? We had his ID, but do we know what he was doing when he went missing?"

"He has an ex-wife. When he was arrested for white collar crimes, she bailed on the marriage and moved on with her life. She was called and stated that she hasn't spoken to him since she signed the divorce papers."

"So we have no idea where he was headed. We only know he lived eighty miles from Red River."

"Pretty much," Callen Whitefox closed his folder.

Elizabeth stared up at the whiteboard and took in all the information. Nothing about the victims was related; they appeared so far to be completely random.

Desdemona's phone began ringing. "It's the lab at FBI West," she answered it and spoke to the tech on the other end.

"We need a push on the rest of the victims," Elizabeth returned to the corner of the table. "Ethan, you know I hate to push you on this, but how's the profile coming?" she asked softly, to not pressure him too much.

"I don't have much, Lyzee."

"I have more to add," Desdemona said, hanging up her phone. "That was the lab, and they have tox in and the DNA profile on the blonde hairs we found on all the victims, well minus the deputy. The reports are on the way as we speak"

Elizabeth stood and went back over to her board, preparing to hopefully fill in more of the missing information and start to piece together a picture of what the hell was going on in Red River. "Okay, Doc. Make my day. What do you have?"

"We'll start with the whom. The blonde hairs are all female and they're all one woman. The team checked the DNA on them against each other, and they are all the same person. Before you ask if the DNA is in the system, it's not."

Blackhawk started mulling that over in his head. "So we have a female, and since she's killing men between twenty and forty that is the age range I'd put her at. Women killers tend to focus on familiarity."

"Unless she's a cougar and likes younger men," added Elizabeth. "My next husband is going to be younger. I'm wearing the older man out," she said, laughing when her husband lifted an eyebrow.

"Then you better assure that I'm completely dead, because if you only maim me and try to move on, bad things will be happening," he said, laughing at his wife. "He better be fast, very fast."

"Just keep in mind that Ethan is the OLDER brother, and I'm really fast," Callen stated, grinning.

Elizabeth fist bumped him and then his brother just punched him.

"Christ, don't bruise her next husband," muttered Whitefox. "Let her do that."

Desdemona tried to laugh, but the entire conversation made her angry.

Elizabeth started laughing, and then noticed the look on Desdemona's face. She was laughing, but it didn't reach her eyes. It was time to refocus on work.

There was nothing more in life that Callen enjoyed than teasing his brother and wife. Then he looked over at Desdemona, and wondered where she fell into the mix. Something in him felt very unsettled when he saw the look on her face. She was watching Elizabeth, but the look was very curious. She was joining in, but she didn't look thrilled.

"So, we have a female, twenty to forty."

"We also now have COD on all the victims but two."

Elizabeth got excited about that. It meant they had another avenue to focus on. "Spill it Desdemona."

"Victim four lost his tongue, he definitely bleed to death and choked on his blood. COD is suffocation by the tape and profuse bleeding. Victims one, two, three, and five were poisoned along with varying degrees of bleeding out from losing organs or appendages."

"Poisoned?" Blackhawk wasn't expecting that. "Poisoning is a very 'female' orientated crime. Men don't usually poison, but women will use that as their method of eliminating a victim."

"What was the toxin of choice?" asked Elizabeth.

"Ethylene Glycol."

"Antifreeze?" asked Whitefox, not sure if he was right or not.

Desdemona blinked at him with green eyes. "Yes, or something that contained enough of it to use it to kill the victims. It may be how they were incapacitated."

"Doc, what would the symptoms be of a poisoning?" Ethan Blackhawk inquired. "Or is it instantaneous?"

Desdemona pulled up a list on her tablet and shot it over to Elizabeth to add the information to the board. "First you'd feel drunk, dizzy, off-balance, much like if you drank too much. Then you'd possibly have seizures, and blackout. Coma is the next step."

"Can you recover?"

"Yes, but if you go past the thirty six hour mark, it's not likely. Renal failure and system shutdown is the outcome. In pets it's within a couple hours, but the human body can survive up to the twenty four hour mark as long as the kidneys are working at optimal output. Once they start to fail then it gets sketchy past that timeframe."

"They're drinking it?"

"Stomach content report isn't in yet, but I would imagine it's on its way. It's easy to mask in food and especially drink. Alcohol is the perfect medium if it's some fruity drink."

Blackhawk sat back. "That would explain how the killer is getting the victims subdued. If they're in a drunken stage and more willing to take help offered to them, she could have them walk to where ever they are being killed."

"True," Desdemona agreed. "They have no defensive wounds, and the lab is saying no other DNA but the blonde hair. So, the killer is at some point, gloving up. It's impossible to not leave some trace of evidence without taking some sort of precaution."

"So we have a blonde preying on men with food or drink?" asked Desdemona.

Elizabeth turned her focus back on the men sitting at the table. These two men mattered to her more than anything else in her life. "Both of you," she paused, when she had their attention. "Neither of you eat or drink anything while you're alone," She was dead serious. "If this killer is taking out men she finds in this town, then that makes you both equally alluring to a killer."

Callen Whitefox was touched that Elizabeth was so worried. "You have nothing to worry about with us," he motioned towards his brother.

"Yeah? Why's that?" Elizabeth crossed her arms and rested them on Baby Blackhawk bump.

"Blondes aren't our type," he said winking at her, and joining his brother laughing.

Elizabeth hoped by the end of this all, they were still laughing.

~ Chapter Ten~

Ethan Blackhawk dismissed everyone and sat in the conference room alone, reading and re-reading all the tech reports that came in on the trace evidence. A big part of him was relaxed, knowing his wife wasn't a target in Red River. Because of that simple detail he was able to breathe a little easier. Now the only thing that he was dwelling on, was his own brother. Part of him wished he could send him back home, keeping him busy with something else. Just thinking that he'd ever leave was comical. Where ever Desdemona was, he was pretty sure his brother would be right behind her or worse in front of her.

When he first met his wife, Ethan had been the same way, and was pretty sure his face held the same look of fascination. Falling for Elizabeth had been the best thing in his life, but now there were twin feelings of happiness and worry for his brother. Ethan was genuinely happy for the man, if this was what he wanted in life, but he was worried for his life. The killer and stalker made him feel very unsettled.

It wasn't hard to see that his brother had a 'thing' for his wife. Not that he didn't trust them both completely, but there was a little wave of awareness whenever he saw Callen Whitefox watching her. Part of him wanted to be angry and push the man away, and part of him wanted to pull him closer. There was this need to protect his baby brother over everything else.

He remembered being kids, when both of their mothers died. Blackhawk shouldered it like a little man and Callen crumbled, not because he missed her but because then he was alone. The two mothers were like night and day. Catherine Blackhawk was very maternal and doted on her son. Charlene Whitefox had the mothering instinct of a rock. She forgot often to feed her child, come home to him, and never once kissed a cut or made cookies.

That alone made Ethan want to do anything to protect his brother. He'd had plenty of knocks to the heart in his life. Of the two, his brother could be wounded more easily and struggle to come back in one piece. It was that fact that made him willing to share the love his wife had for them. Blackhawk would do anything to keep his brother from breaking down. Including giving him the precious gift of his wife's love and affection when he desperately needed it.

Yeah, Callen betrayed him in the past, but this was entirely a completely different thing. Ethan wasn't a boy anymore, and he wasn't thinking about his own needs solely. Family was paramount.

Blackhawk put the reports down and looked up. The awareness of eyes watching him drew his focus. As if he knew he was just thinking about him, Callen stood in the doorway. Again, the same shuttered look on his face, but he could see beyond it.

"Busy?" he asked, once his brother was focused on him.

"No, come in and close the door."

He did just that. The fact that there was an issue between him had the man off balance. When his brother came back into his life, he gave him so much. There was no other person he loved more in life than his brother, with the exception of Elizabeth.

"What's on your mind?"

"We are," he answered, sitting in the chair closest to his brother, and he could feel the tension there. It broke a part of his heart that he caused this between them. Before the fight they were fine, and again a woman came between them. Just not the one he always believed would. Go figure on that one.

"What specifically?" Blackhawk felt bad too. Not only had he punched his brother again, but he was gripped with tension over his wife and the man here before him.

"The fight we had. I'm sorry I got pissed and punched you in the face over a woman," he said, looking into his brother's eyes. "I was way across the line, and I wasn't thinking. You matter more to me, and I just need you to know I was way over the line."

"It's okay." Blackhawk sighed. "If the truth is to be told, I punched you back for the same reason." Where to even start with this? "Part of me is edgy about the relationship between you and Elizabeth."

Whitefox looked surprised. He didn't think his brother was angry. "I wouldn't ever cross that line, Ethan. I swore to you that it wouldn't happen. I gave you my word."

Blackhawk nodded at his brother's words and steepled his fingers. If he was going to trust him with something so precious, he at least wanted honesty. "So you aren't in love with her?"

Callen wasn't going to lie to his brother. "I am in love with her, but you're well aware of that and so is she."

"So Doctor Adare is going to be enough to help you forget how you feel about Elizabeth?" he asked, seeing the pain in his brother's eyes and already knowing the answer to that question.

Whitefox thought about what he was going to say, and he weighed it all in his head first, unsure if he should just say it or bury some of it deep.

"Man to man, Callen, and brother to brother, I think I deserve to know the truth."

"I'll always be in love with Elizabeth. I can't help how I feel about her, and it's the equivalent to me asking you if you can flip a switch and turn off love for her too. The first day I met her in your office before I knew she was your wife, I fell in love. I don't know why it happened, and I can sit here and apologize about it daily if it'll keep us on solid ground, but it's the truth. I fell for her the same way you did. The only difference is you found her first."

Ethan had to respect the man for not lying. They all were aware of his feelings, and it was the big pink elephant in the room when the three of them were together.

"What about Desdemona?" he asked his brother again. "Where does she fit into this?"

Callen leaned back in the chair. "I really care about her. I don't believe one is a replacement for the other. I'll be in love with Elizabeth for the rest of my life, but I still wouldn't risk the love I feel for my brother. Your wife is in love with you, she just loves me because she loves you. There's a big difference."

Blackhawk didn't believe that for a second. "She loves you because of you, Callen. Not because of me. If we're going to be honest, then let's be honest. My wife loves you too. Don't try to rationalize away the feelings we both know she has. "

Whitefox wanted to believe that in the worst way. Everything he was building in his life was based on the love he felt for her. She was his strength and knowing she loved him the same way gave him the ability to keep going.

245

"Are you mad because of it?" Whitefox asked, knowing his brother had every right to be angry over the entire discussion. When he came back into his life, he'd told him that his wife was completely off limits, and now he was giving him a chance.

"Honestly?"

"Yes, since you're big on honesty today."

"I should be mad as hell. I should be beating the hell out of you, but I don't feel threatened."

Whitefox didn't know what to think.

"Any man near her usually pisses me off and puts me into a rage, but for some reason I'm willing to stay calm with you."

"Why?"

Blackhawk thought about that. "I don't know. It just doesn't feel wrong knowing she cares and loves you." He didn't tell him it was all because of his brother's past and the wounds Callen had inflicted on his heart. The fact he always felt like an outsider because he was the 'bastard' in the family, or how his mother essentially threw him away for drugs and booze. "I'm trying to not look into it too much. Elizabeth is pretty logical, and I'm going to let her take the lead on this one."

"I'm sorry I punched you."

Ethan Blackhawk accepted that. "I'm sorry I punched you too," he said grinning.

"So we're okay, Ethan?" Callen couldn't believe his luck. Having a brother was a really great thing.

"Thick as thieves, bro."

It was a phrase their grandfather used frequently, when they were growing up. His eyes began to fill with emotion and unshed tears.

"Come here," Blackhawk said, standing. The protectiveness was back, and he would do anything to keep the man in front of him in one piece emotionally.

Whitefox stood and went to his brother, and they wrapped their arms around each other. He could feel the strength in the man he called brother, and he allowed himself to take some of it as his own.

"I'm glad she's your best friend, Cal. She's ours, and I'm okay with trusting my blood with the love of my life. I told you once before that she wasn't like the woman that broke us up. Elizabeth has so much love in her, that giving you half of it still leaves me with more than I deserve in this lifetime."

Those words meant everything to him. His brother was allowing him to relax and care about the woman that healed them without retribution. He let out a ragged breath.

"Oh look at this! It's a group hug, and I wasn't invited," said Elizabeth from the doorway.

Callen couldn't speak; he was too choked up as he looked up at her across the room.

"My two favorite men in the entire world are hugging it out, and I don't get an invite?"

Both men opened up for her, and she immediately went to them.

Elizabeth just had that effect on them. They were a family and a sturdy unit. They may fight and have their moments of stress, but when it came down to it, they were tight.

"I love you both," she said, trapped between them protectively. "But the next time you beat the hell out of each other over something so completely silly, I will hand you both an ass kicking for being idiots." Elizabeth willingly accepted the kisses on each side of her forehead.

"I wouldn't expect anything less," said her husband laughing.

"We're Blackhawks, and that means we have each other's backs." Elizabeth loved them both and trusted they'd work it all out. "Nothing breaks us. Nothing will pull us apart and at the end of the day, we go home together or we don't go home."

"Like the Three Musketeers?" asked Blackhawk.

Whitefox interjected teasingly, "I get to be the French one."

Elizabeth laughed. "I'm getting you that book for your damn birthday, because they're all French. And you call yourself a literary collector?"

Now all three were laughing and were glad no one could see them in their big group hug.

"I specialize in collecting Seuss," he muttered into her hair, as he felt the tears evaporating with just her being near.

Elizabeth laughed and stared up at her husband. She wasn't sure what he did, but it brought the emotion out in Whitefox and the tension there earlier was gone.

He smiled the famous Blackhawk grin, and was completely at ease with both of them. They were safe and in his arms and that's all that really mattered.

"Now we need to get out in the field," Elizabeth muttered into their shirts. It pained her to have to break up their little hug fest, but there was a killer to find.

Both men broke apart and started laughing. "You're not going out in the field," they said together.

"You know that the little conversation about you being my second husband wasn't regarding you being able to boss me around too, right?" she stated, pointing at Whitefox.

"Let's vote," suggested Blackhawk. "All those in favor of Elizabeth going out in the field raise their hands."

Elizabeth did just that.

"All those that are fervently against Elizabeth going out to risk her life, please raise your hand." Both Whitefox and Blackhawk raised both hands, and opened themselves up for two sucker punches to the ribs.

"You know, I'm not going to be pregnant for much longer, and as soon as I'm baby free, I swear on everything that's holy, I will kick both of your asses big time. I'm not an invalid."

Both brothers laughed as they rubbed their rib cages.

Desdemona wandered into the room blowing a bubble with her peppermint gum, she was about to head down to start the autopsy, and she wanted to see if anyone was joining her. What she found was the beginnings of a fight.

"Uh, I can come back," she paused in the doorway.

"No need," answered Ethan Blackhawk. "We were just planning the rest of the day, and who wasn't going out in the field.

"I'm going," Elizabeth said continuing, "and the reason I'm going is simply this. No one is killing women, but someone is killing men. I also excel at the details and you do not," she pointed at Ethan Blackhawk. "You are still a newbie and are inexperienced." Then she looked over her shoulder at the Doctor. "She has a body to dig through. The most logical choice is to go with me, so stop fighting me."

"I don't want to leave Desdemona alone."

"Hey!" she protested. "I'm a grown woman."

Whitefox started laughing and then realized doing that only worked for them and Elizabeth. The doctor looked pretty angry at his laughter.

Desdemona walked towards him and looked over her glasses at him. "For your information Callen, you may be bigger than me, but I assure you while you can only kill with that gun, I happen to know one hundred places on the human body that will kill a person and none of them take much force."

He didn't know what to say to that.

"Wow, looks the Doc has a brass set after all," snickered Elizabeth, fist bumping her husband. It was funny to watch the look on Whitefox's face.

"I'm only borrowing yours," she smiled at her friend. "I have ten lab techs downstairs, and all of them are armed. I'll be perfectly fine!" She spun on her heel. "I don't need a damn babysitter!"

Whitefox just stared after her, unsure what to say.

Elizabeth squeezed his hand reassuringly. "Callen this is where you chase after her and apologize and let her hand you your ass back," she said gently. "Go on, and fix it before we all go out in the field."

Whitefox kissed her on the cheek and nodded.

As soon as he was gone, she looked over at her husband. "Want to tell me what the little pow wow was about between you and Callen?"

Blackhawk shrugged. "He's tied up in knots over being in love with you, and I told him that its fine and I was willing to share your love."

Elizabeth hugged her husband. There was no doubt how hard that was for him. "You're a very good man, Ethan Blackhawk."

"Let's face it. The safest person for him to lose his heart to is you. You won't stomp on it and hand it back to him." He told her all about Callen's childhood and Charlene Whitefox. Just the look of abject horror on her face said it all.

"Oh god, poor Callen."

"Yeah, he had it pretty rough."

Elizabeth felt her own heart breaking for the man. "I'll keep his heart intact the best I can," she said, taking her husband's hand in hers.

"I hope he's not in over his head with the doctor."

Elizabeth nodded, understand what he meant. "Family sticks together, and we'll get him through whatever is coming," she answered, and led him to the door. "Now, where are the three of us heading first?"

"The diner, are you hungry?"

"Always."

Whitefox ran down the stairs and caught up to the woman. She was moving pretty fast, and he assumed she was furious with him. "Desi, wait!" She spun at his voice and looked up at him.

"I'm not a child! I'm a full grown woman and you need to remember that. I go where I want, and I do what I want. I don't think I need you to put an armed guard on me in the lab. The deputy is dead, and I'm safe." She pointed at him and had him backing up.

Wow, she was pretty pissed. "I just wanted to…"

"Zip it. I know why you wanted to do it. Let me just put this out there Callen, but maybe I don't like to be bossed around. How would you feel if I bossed you around?" she asked, now on the landing with him, and not far from his body. "Everyone assumes because I'm not an Amazonian warrior like Elizabeth Blackhawk that I'm harmless. I can take care of myself, and I can decide where I go and what I do." She looked over the top of her glasses at him. She was angry for so many reasons, and the pot picked now to bubble over. Most of it had nothing to do with his bossiness, but how he viewed her as less than Elizabeth.

Before he could speak, she walked up against him and grabbed him by the shirt and pulled him down to her lips and kissed him. Fury and anger came out in the kiss. She kissed him hard, deep and with everything in her body. Pressed against him and standing between his legs, she invaded his space and owned the kiss. It wasn't a meek, mild kiss; it was one of frustration, pent up aggression, and sheer lust. Callen let her control it, because he owed it to her. Slowly Desdemona broke away from the kiss and looked up into his eyes.

"I know I'm not Elizabeth, but I'll be fine." Desdemona wasn't sure what came over her. "Now, if you don't mind I'll go autopsy the deputy. See you later," she said softly, as she made her hasty retreat to dwell over what she just did.

Whitefox didn't know what to say and wasn't quite sure what she was alluding to either or maybe that was his guilt ridden conscious talking. He hoped the truth wasn't written on his face every time she stared at him.

The three agents rode in the Denali on their way to the diner. They figured it was as good a place to start questioning possible witnesses. There were lots of people coming and going and maybe they'd get a lead for the assignment. When Callen Whitefox's phone rang again and he ignored it, both agents looked back at him.

"Who are you dodging?" asked his brother.

"Granddad called again," he said, shrugging. "I'm not in the mood to have a confrontation regarding the woman I'm sleeping with," and then he snapped the gum and realized he gave it all away.

"Oh, look Ethan! Callen has taken up chewing blue peppermint gum. That seems familiar to me, and yet I can't quite place my finger on it," she teased.

"Well, let's back track. We hugged and I didn't smell peppermint did you?"

Whitefox started getting red.

"No. I smelled his woodsy cologne, your spicy cologne, and then soap. Pretty sure none of it was peppermint. Then in came Desdemona, and she was chewing that same gum. Now I guess we need to deduce how that gum went from her to Callen."

"Maybe it's magical jumping gum," snickered Blackhawk.

"Maybe I just wanted a stick of gum," Whitefox added, and starting to grin at how they were teasing him. "And she shared."

"Darlin' we don't doubt she shared, but the more likely reason is you kissed her so deep you ended up with her gum in your mouth," Elizabeth fanned herself. "I do declare that must have been some kiss!" Now she was teasing him unmercifully with her southern belle accent.

Callen yanked on her ponytail and earned a punch in the leg. "Shit that hurt," he said, rubbing his thigh.

"You bet it did," she said, winking.

"For the record she kissed me," he added, grinning. "But I did learn that kissing technique from someone in this vehicle."

"Don't look at me," said Elizabeth. "You've kissed me plenty but you've never ended up with my gum."

Whitefox snickered. "Can I try?" Just the idea caused his heart to pound.

Ethan pulled into the dinner and looked up into the mirror. "If you're alluding I taught you, I'm pretty sure I've never shared gum with you, Cal."

"Eww! Not you kissing me, you kissing the ladies."

Elizabeth lifted a brow. "Oh, do tell all, Cal."

"Callen, you're going get me killed. You're just giving her ammunition against both of us. Sit there and stare straight ahead and say nothing," he said laughing, as he earned a punch in his leg too. "Hey!"

"I get cranky when I'm hungry," she retorted, grabbing the files and hopping out of the Denali.

Both men followed laughing. When they hit the door, the humor was gone and back was the hard ass FBI agents on the job.

Elizabeth slid up to the counter and stared at the fat bald man perched behind it. It was the same man that was ass slapping his waitress the other day. Already she disliked him. "Excuse me, can you tell me who owns this place?" she questioned, civilly. Despite what she was feeling, she'd play nice.

"I do little lady. You interested in a job? You're a little chubby with that baby belly, but you can tote trays just as good as the rest, I guess."

Blackhawk went to move forward, but his brother put his hand on his arm. Elizabeth could chew this man up and spit him out in big meaty pieces and if she didn't, THEN they'd kill him for insulting her.

Despite his comment he looked up and down her body, lecherously. "Come on back to my office, and we can talk about the job requirements." He stood and started heading back.

Elizabeth knew her husband was ready to go shit wild and beat the hell out of the man. "I'll be fine, split up and start asking the waitresses if they saw the victims." The man was going to be sorry he called her chubby.

Blackhawk let out a breath. "I hope she rips his balls off," he muttered under his breath, and then moved his focus to the woman waiting tables. "Let's grab a seat, order, and then cage in the waitress," he looked back at the door his wife had gone through, and couldn't help but worry.

Elizabeth took the offered seat and took off her jacket. "I'm going to assume since you have the cushy digs, you're the owner." She looked around at the sparse office and the messy desk and looked back at the bald, fat man. Yeah, it suited him just fine.

A pig in his pen.

"I'm Joe Lemar. I own this place, so ask what you need to ask." It wasn't lost on him that she had a really nice set of curves on her and a great rack. She may be pregnant, but he'd still do her, in a heartbeat.

"Have you seen any of these men in your establishment before?" Elizabeth placed the pictures across the messy desk and waited for him take them all in.

"This one." He picked up the picture. "Wilma waited on him. I don't know much about him, just that."

Elizabeth picked up the picture of victim three. It was Torrance Delmar, and he'd definitely stopped into the town. "Anyone else you recognize from the pictures?"

"No sugar, no one interesting there, but I have to say," he looked at her chest and licked his lips. "You interest me a great deal."

"Trust me, Mister Lemar, you want to shut that down right now. Because one, you can't handle me and two, my husband out there will break every bone in your body." Elizabeth picked up the photos and put them back into the folder. "Thank you for your time, Sir." She turned and when he slapped her on her ass she sighed. "Oh Mr. Lemar, you're going to wish you didn't do that."

Blackhawk ordered his wife lunch, a big meaty burger with extra bacon and mayo. He figured she was going to be hungry and dead cow always made her very happy. After his brother ordered his lunch and something to take back to the doctor, he pulled out his file and read the name tag on the waitress's shirt. "Wilma May, can I ask you a few questions?" he smiled his smoothest smile. The one that charmed women and got him answers from the opposite sex. Usually he whipped it out whenever his wife wasn't around. If she caught him, someone would die and that meant paperwork.

"Depends on what you're asking Darlin'." She snapped her gum and slid the pencil into her hair. "You two boys police?"

"Yes the FBI, and we're here trying to find a murder. Can you look at these pictures and tell me if you remember seeing any of them in here in the last few months?"

Wilma May looked down at the very exotic man. Oh, he was delicious looking and his smile was sexy as sin. "For two sexy men, certainly," she winked at the man with the brown eyes. She'd always been a sucker for a brown-eyed man, although his partner was just as delicious.

"Thank you, Wilma May."

She studied the pictures closely, and then with a blood red nail pointed to the third picture. "I waited on him, flirted a little too, because he was a fine specimen too," she paused, "but not as sexy as you handsome," she tapped Ethan Blackhawk on the cheek "Or your friend here."

Callen wanted to snicker, but he knew his brother was in the middle of building a rapport with the woman. He was just infinitely glad Elizabeth was busy, or he could picture her dragging the blonde outside and punching her bloody.

"Did he say anything about what he was planning or if he was meeting someone?" Blackhawk kept asking the questions before his wife came back out, or he lost the woman's interest.

"Hiking or maybe camping? He ordered a large coffee to keep warm," she tapped her chin. "Yeah, tipped well, and was really nice. Sometimes you get serious assholes in here that treat you like shit because you're just a waitress."

Blackhawk smiled. "Wilma May, I'm betting you see everything, and you don't miss a thing. That's a valuable skill for a waitress or anyone else."

254

"I like you sugar," she said, grinning. She was about to offer her number until there was a horrible crash.

Both FBI agents stood, watching Elizabeth walk around the corner, carrying her jacket. Behind her out hobbled Joe Lemar. He was bent over and covered in something red.

"What the hell?" Wilma May muttered and stepped back to let the woman pass.

"Hi baby," said Blackhawk. "I see it went about as well as expected."

Elizabeth kissed him on the cheek and let him pull the chair out for her as she read the woman's name tag. "Wilma May, can you get Mr. Lemar an ice pack for his groin? Oh and I apologize for the state of his office."

"What did he do?" asked Blackhawk.

"Well, the groin kick was for slapping me on the ass and the cherry pie filling," she shrugged. "That was for calling me chubby. Baby Blackhawk was greatly offended at being referred to as chub."

Blackhawk was ready to kill the man.

Elizabeth touched his arm, and then stood back up. Glaring over at the hunched over man, she pointed and he backed around the corner and left for cover. Then she sat again.

Whitefox began laughing as Wilma May brought over their drinks.

"Can you teach me how to do that?" asked the woman in awe. "He's always slapping all of us on the ass."

Elizabeth pulled out one of her cards. "Next time he touches anyone that isn't attached to his own dick; you call me and put him on the phone. I think the sound of my voice will bring back the fond memories we had together. I know I'll never forget the look on his face."

Wilma May walked away with the card.

Ethan started laughing. "Come here!" He pulled his wife in for a kiss, and took his time. "I have never loved you more, Mrs. Blackhawk," he said when he broke the kiss.

Elizabeth laid her head on his shoulder. "The feeling is completely mutual," and then she saw lunch coming. "Is that a cheeseburger with bacon?"

"That it is," he grinned.

"Now I've never loved you more, Mr. Blackhawk."

"I told you Cal, she's just after me for the food I buy her," he laughed.

"Do you really care why she loves you? Because if that's the way to her heart, I'll claim buying her lunch to ease your conscious on this one."

"I'm ignoring you both again," she said, biting into her burger. "How did it go with blondie?" she asked, nodding towards the woman standing behind the counter. It wasn't lost on Elizabeth that the woman was staring at her husband and brother-in-law. With one look back, she had the woman glancing away. These men were off limits.

"She waited on him. He got a coffee, large to go and mentioned that he was going hiking or camping."

Elizabeth took a sip of her water. "Baldy said the same thing. Minus the chit chat with the victim, he wasn't privy to that. He was probably too busy slapping someone on the ass."

Whitefox ate one of her fries. "I'm betting you cured him of that affliction."

"Let's just say he won't be afflicting anyone anytime soon," she answered, grinning.

Whitefox gave her a fist bump and Blackhawk started laughing. "You realize you have all the fun, right Elizabeth? What if I wanted to kick him in the groin and dump cherry pie filling all over him for manhandling my pregnant wife?"

"That's not your style, Cowboy. Besides, it gets you all hot and bothered when I screw with the locals. I do it for you. It's a labor of love."

Both men snickered.

"Gets me all hot too," interjected Whitefox, and then he took a punch to the arm from his brother. "Hey! No fair!"

Blackhawk lifted an eyebrow and then gave his brother the look while Elizabeth laughed uproariously.

"Down boys, you both can be all hot and bothered, and return to your perspective sexual partners."

"Elizabeth, you're too much," her husband said, laughing.

Wasn't it the truth?

Desdemona stood above the deputy and made the last stitch in the Y incision. She had just tied the knot when she felt someone in the room with her. Looking up and putting down her scissors, she saw Sheila Court standing in the doorway. Immediately she threw the sheet back over the dead man's face and body. No one would want to see what the killer and the carrion birds left behind.

"I want to see my friend," she said, as she moved towards Desdemona and the table.

"I really think that is a bad idea, until after he's seen by the mortuary and cleaned up." Death was never pretty, but this death was exceptionally gruesome. A face without eyes was a creepy thing that one would never get out of their minds.

"I don't care what you think," she snapped, ripping back the sheet.

Desdemona took a step back, and felt bad for the woman. The sight waiting her was beyond horrific. The woman may be a bitch, but no one should be seeing what she just had her arms in up to her elbows.

"This is your fault," she snapped bitterly, as she turned on Desdemona. "You put him there on that table!" Sheila Court pointed at her friend, and then angrily swept her arm across the table, knocking all the tools to the floor.

Desdemona took another step back. It was ironic because just two hours ago she was demanding Callen Whitefox respect her ability to protect herself, and here she was wishing he would walk through the door and come to her rescue. Man, did she owe him an apology on this one. She wasn't close to being as bad ass as Elizabeth.

"It was a stupid joke, and you and your bitch boss got him killed!" She pushed the cart over with the samples waiting to go off to tox on them. "It was a damn joke!" The distraught woman threw a bottle of solution at the wall and it splashed everywhere.

"He made his choices, Sheila. He chose to scare us and then swing at Elizabeth Blackhawk, and then he chose to try and abduct me. I didn't make him do any of that, and you're right, it was a stupid joke, and he paid a high price. A price that no one should have to pay."

257

The woman began throwing things and breaking things, and then she turned back to Desdemona. "I hate you, and I hope you die for this," she screamed and then charged at her.

Desdemona braced for being hit, and then she heard her tech's voice and would have kissed him if Whitefox wouldn't have lost his mind.

"Hey!" shouted Derek Williams, as he stepped between the woman, and restrained her from touching the doctor. He held on as she fought.

"Let me go!" Sheila struggled and then started breaking down and weeping over her deceased co-worker.

"Take her upstairs, Derek to the Sheriff. Tell him what happened. I'll start cleaning up the mess, and redo the samples from the autopsy."

"Yes Doctor." He walked the wailing woman out of the room.

Christina came into the room, rushing to the woman's side. "Are you okay, Doctor?" she asked, and began helping pick up the mess.

"Yeah, but the samples are destroyed, so I have to reopen the deputy and start again," she said sighing.

"You do the autopsy, I'll get a few techs in here and we'll clean up the mess," she offered.

"Thank you. I'll re-sterilize the tools. Who knows what trace is all over this floor. Back to the drawing board," she muttered, collecting all her tools from the floor.

This was going to be one hell of a long day.

The three agents walked back into the sheriff's station, only to find the woman crying hysterically, their tech standing off to the side and the sheriff looking out of sorts.

"Derek, what happened?" asked Blackhawk, motioning his lab tech over to them.

"I was down working in the lab going over trace, and we heard these yells and screams. I went to go check on the doctor and the woman was destroying the lab, and almost got to Doctor Adare."

258

That's all Whitefox needed to hear. He went running down the stairs and to Desdemona. He found her standing on the stool and cutting the stitches in the Y incision. "Are you okay?" he crossed to her, and touched her cheek. "Did she hurt you?" he asked angrily.

"No, Derek grabbed her before she could get to me, but she destroyed all the samples. Once they hit the floor, I can't use them. Now I have to redo them over."

"Can I help you?" he asked, watching all the techs move through the room like ants, cleaning up all the wrecked supplies.

Desdemona considered it. "Okay, glove up, if you have the stomach for it," she said, and then noticed the bag in his hand. "Did you bring me lunch?" she asked smiling at him.

"I did."

Desdemona leaned over and kissed him softly on the lips. "Thank you," she said. "That was incredibly sweet of you."

"Well, that's me. Mr. Sweet."

Wednesday evening

Whitefox stared blankly at the whiteboard. He was pretty sure that nothing was going to come to him now, or twenty minutes from now. They'd worked everything that they could, visited a few local shops and no one but Wilma May remembered seeing any of the victims. It just seemed like the end to a very long and unproductive day. What he'd love to do now, is take Desdemona back to the house and get her all alone. Then he remembered they wouldn't be alone. Something just felt odd about it. Having sex with a woman he was having a relationship with, while the woman he was crazy in love with was in the next room. Why the hell couldn't his life be simple, cut and dried?

Ethan Blackhawk had plans for the evening and they didn't involve anyone but his wife. Back to the house, dinner and maybe some good old fashioned sex in their room. Honestly, he didn't care if his brother and the doctor knew what he was doing. He was a married man, and once this baby came, he was sure the sex

259

would slow down. Then he looked over at his wife and she was lecherously staring at him. So, maybe not. He wiggled his eyebrows and she winked. Yeah, they were on the same page, he just needed to figure out how to get her alone.

Elizabeth watched her very sexy husband sitting not far from her. He had unbuttoned his shirt down about two buttons, and she could see portions of his tattoos on his chest. She licked her lips, and watched the vein in her husband's throat throb. Oh what she wouldn't do for a few hours alone with the man. When she had his attention, she knew exactly what he was thinking. She mouthed the word 'Sex', and when he nodded her heart started pounding.

"So what's left on the agenda for tonight?" asked Callen Whitefox. Doctor Adare had just wandered into the room, and took the seat beside him.

"We need to see if the killer is picking up men in the bar," Ethan Blackhawk set it up, glancing over at his wife, and they shared a look.

"As much as I'd like a night of drinking and debauchery, I'm pregnant and the last place I should be is out drinking," Elizabeth patted her belly. "Unless you want your first beer, baby Blackhawk."

Callen looked over at Desdemona. It would be interesting to see her out of the work element and get to spend some time alone with her. "I'll go and watch the locals."

"You can't go alone, Callen," objected Elizabeth. "The killer is hunting men."

Desdemona wouldn't mind a few drinks and some down time. Besides, Callen might be fun to watch getting drunk. "I'll go; I could use a drink or three. Especially after being shot at, and had a woman try and kick my ass."

Blackhawk felt his pulse start to pound.

"But I need a shower first. I've been playing in death all day," she added.

"Elizabeth pulled her keys out of her pocket and tossed them at her brother-in-law. "Don't drive drunk, and at your age you don't have a curfew," she winked at him. "Go and have a good time. Director Blackhawk here is giving you a night off, just observe, relax and enjoy your date."

"Really? A full night off?"

Blackhawk grinned. "Yes, enjoy."

"Maybe we could get something for dinner." Whitefox started formulating a plan. "Would you have dinner with me?"

"That sounds perfect."

They both stood and left the room. Ethan started laughing at what they just managed to do.

"And this Cowboy is why we run FBI West."

"You, me, and wild out of control sex with a side of takeout, baby?"

"Just for the record you had me at wild and out of control."

"Always good to know, does that mean you don't want takeout? We can cut a good twenty minutes off the food foreplay and hope right into bed."

Elizabeth shook her head and slipped into her coat. "No way, Cowboy. I'm not that easy of a date. You still have to buy me dinner to get me to put out."

"Good thing I don't mind easy women or buying them dinner," he said, grinning, and dodging her swing, as she chased him out to the Denali.

Whitefox drove them back to the house, and was incredibly excited at the prospect of spending some down time with Desdemona. Just the idea of them getting to be themselves and hang out without his brother and Elizabeth watching them, gave him hope the woman would let her hair down.

"Give me about an hour, and I'll be ready," she said smiling. "What are we having for dinner?"

He probably should take her somewhere nice, but it was Red River, and that meant casual. "Well, if we were home there are a myriad of places I would love to take you, but we're in Red River, so I think they have one Italian restaurant."

"Perfect, I love Italian," she smiled. "See you in an hour?"

"Yes. I can't wait," he answered, grinning like an idiot, as she ran up the stairs. Then it hit him, he didn't bring the correct attire for a date. He pulled out his phone and dialed his brother.

Mr. Suit and Tie was about to become very handy, and when he answered on the third ring, he was eternally grateful.

"I need a favor."

Blackhawk would have given him his kidney to have him out of the house and some time alone with his wife- his very sexy, hormone ridden wife. "Shoot."

"I'm taking Desdemona to dinner, I need something more formal."

"I have plenty of black dress shirts, and pants. You can take anything you want. They're all hanging in the closet in our room."

Whitefox heard the desperation in his brother's voice. "Hey, you are trying to get us out of the house! You want to have sex with Elizabeth!"

"In the worst possible way, So wear what you want, grab the doctor and give me at least three hours alone to have sex with my very turned on wife."

"Wow, you're desperate," he said, laughing.

"You have no idea."

Whitefox laughed. "Thanks Ethan."

"No, Callen. Thank you!"

Desdemona was a serial packer. When she travelled it was never light, and she tended to bring the most insane things with her that she never needed, but swore she might need in an emergency. Right now noting thrilled her more than the way she'd packed. Desdemona was going to have a date with the sexiest man she'd ever seen, and only hoped she could grab his attention the way he had hers. Getting him away from Elizabeth was going to be a big victory for her.

As Desdemona stood in the bathroom blow drying her hair straight, she began to worry. What if she didn't pick out the right thing to wear? Or worse yet, what if Callen Whitefox wasn't thinking this was a date. Oh crap. What did she do now?

Elizabeth and her husband walked into the house, and they were well aware that both the doctor and Whitefox were still home. Keeping her hands off her husband the entire time home was one of the hardest things she ever had to do. When she climbed into the back seat of the Denali because she didn't want to climb all over him, he laughed at her. Then she told him what she was thinking about doing in the FBI vehicle, and he stopped laughing and told her to stay in the back and not move.

The directors of FBI West didn't need to be caught having sex in the company vehicle paid for by the taxpayers.

"They're still here, behave," he warned her, as he put the Chinese food down on the counter.

"Trust me, I'm trying to not think about sex," she muttered, not looking at her husband. "If you loved me, you'd tie your hair back right now, it's really distracting."

"Yeah, well you smell really good, so can you stand over there?" he laughed.

Elizabeth's phone chimed. "Oh Christ," pulling it out she crossed her fingers.

"Please tell me that's not work related, because if I have to go back to work, I'm going to quit my job and jump you in the Denali. Because I just don't care."

Elizabeth snorted. "Desdemona has a girl issue and she needs my help."

"Why is she messaging you?" he said, laughing.

Elizabeth would show him. She walked over to him, and slid her hands up his torso, making sure to have as much bodily contact against him and then she whispered in his ear what she wanted to do with him on the couch, then the chair, the kitchen counter, and finally in their room in front of the fireplace.

If it was possible, he just went dead, blind and dumb all at once. "You better be following through with that or it's just plain cruel, Elizabeth."

"I do try, Cowboy. Now think about me."

Oh, he absolutely was and would continue to think about her. He needed to get that fire started in the fireplace.

Elizabeth ran up the stairs, and stopped when she'd seen Callen. Never had she seen him dressed up. Yeah, at their wedding, but that was the family colors and not formal black like Ethan always wore. "Wow, you look amazing, Cal," she drawled, winking. "Very sexy, Mr. Whitefox. I'm incredibly impressed."

"Thanks, I may have to invest in some all black threads," he answered, grinning. "How do I smell?" he asked, moving close to her body.

Elizabeth sniffed him and the scent called to her and warmth flooded her body. "Since that's Ethan's cologne, I think you smell delicious. Personally I love it. He wears it because it makes me want to jump him." She offered up the truth.

"Well I have a few minutes free," he suggested, wiggling his eyebrows.

Elizabeth grinned and whispered in his ear. "I like more than just a few minutes, Cal," she teased, watching his whole body react.

"Unfair!"

"Probably, but you're planning on getting lucky tonight with the Doctor," she grinned. "One woman a night. Pace yourself!"

"Since you just turned me down, I'll have to follow up with my original plan."

Elizabeth went up on her toes and kissed him gently on his lips. "She'd be crazy to not fall head over heels for you. You're a definite catch, Mr. Whitefox. Good luck handsome." she patted him on the ass and took off down the hall laughing. Next she had to get the woman out of the house so she could climb naked all over the other sexy native in the house.

Whitefox watched the woman hustle down the hall to Desdemona's room, and his body was completely taut. He took a deep breath and tried to focus on his love for the woman and that alone. Then he thought back to the conversation he had with his brother, and relaxed. Having her love meant everything and he refused to be embarrassed about how his body reacted to her.

Elizabeth knocked on the door and was practically pulled into the room. "What's wrong?"

"Callen. Date. Clothing. No clue. Help," she said, punctuating each word and sounding like she was about to hyperventilate.

"Okay, relax. What do you have with you?" Desdemona led the woman over to her suitcase.

"Holy shit, how much did you pack?"

"Please, help me pull this off and I'll have your next kid for you, okay?" She practically begged.

"Half this shit still has tags on it!" Elizabeth pulled out some things. "Okay, first of all, your hair looks perfect. Wear it down. With all those streaks of black and red it looks sexy. Next go put some makeup on, and I'll handle the clothing."

Desdemona nodded and wandered back into the bathroom to obey. "I don't date a lot of men. I'm not good at this," she admitted. "I've had relationships, but they never felt like this," she added. "This is a date right?"

"Yeah, he's borrowing Ethan's clothes, so it's a definite date. Callen doesn't do dressed up for just dinner out. This has to be special in his mind. Plus he smells really good."

Desdemona wanted to ask why she was sniffing her date, but then realized she was standing half naked in front of the woman. Who was she to question anything at that point? "I hope I can pull this off," she said, suddenly.

"Okay, I'm going to say this, and then deny that we had girl chit chat, if you ever say I said it," she said, walking over to the door. "He's a man. Trust me, you could wear a bag and as long as you smile, smell good and flirt you're safe."

"Okay," she took a deep breath.

"Plus I just saw Callen, and he's got one thing on his mind. You have this in the bag."

"Thank you, Elizabeth."

She wandered back over to the suitcase. "Lyzee. You can call me, Lyzee. I'm particular with who uses that, but since I've seen your underwear, been kissed by you, and slapped you on the ass, all in one day, it just seems fitting."

Desdemona laughed and it eased up the stress.

"Okay, you want blow his mind and freeze your ass off outside, or do you want so-so and stay warm?"

Desdemona contemplated that. "I'd walk naked in the snow right about now for him."

"Okay then," she said, starting to pull things out and deciding. "This," she held it up, "and this," she said finally. "Those shoes."

"Okay," she said taking a deep breath.

"Wow look at this thing," she held it up. The bra was all sexy and stripper-ish all at the same time.

"There's a G-string to go with it." Desdemona thought about it. "I've never worn it, why don't you put it on and surprise your husband?"

Elizabeth contemplated it. "Deal. Wear the red one, Callen will choke on his tongue."

"Then it's good I'm a doctor and know the Heimlich."

Elizabeth snickered and started stripping. She was actually enjoying herself. Maybe having Desdemona in her life was going to be a really good thing. "Hey, if this thing between you and Callen doesn't work," she said, looking over at the woman.

"Yeah?" She didn't even want to think about it not working for a myriad of reasons, but now she just acquired a girlfriend and she couldn't imagine giving her back.

"You and me will still friends right? Despite anything else?"

Desdemona almost wanted to cry. The woman in front of her was offering her something very precious. Friendship with no strings attached.

"Don't do it! You'll start me crying and then ruin your makeup."

She sniffled. "Yeah, we will. It's in the girlfriend code. It matters."

Hell yeah it did.

~ *Chapter Eleven* ~

Elizabeth stood patiently with the men in the living room, and waited for Desdemona to make her grand entrance down the stairs. She was impressed with her own work. Yeah, they busted her ass about being less than a woman, more of a tomboy, but she could still pull it off. Just because she preferred jeans and cowboy boots didn't mean she didn't like to dress up once in a while too. When she left Desdemona, the woman was putting on some very sexy shoes with lots of straps and angles.

"Remember Callen. Relax, have fun and enjoy the night off," said Ethan Blackhawk. "We're not working, so you don't need to either."

"When Callen sees what she's wearing, he won't want to work. I picked it out." She was supremely proud of herself.

"Now you're playing fashion expert?" asked Whitefox laughing. "Is she wearing jeans, cowboy boots and a button down shirt?" he grinned. "Not that there's anything wrong with that," he added quickly. It was true, the first day he saw her she was in jeans and a white shirt and he was enamored instantly.

"I'll have you know, I can dress up. I do own dresses."

Ethan Blackhawk came to her rescue. "She absolutely does, and she paints her toenails girly colors too. It's a sight to see."

Whitefox snickered. "Sexy."

Elizabeth pointed at her husband and he lifted his hands in surrender.

There was the telltale clicking of heels down the hall, and to the stairs. At that moment she wished she had her phone out, to click that picture. Callen Whitefox looked like he indeed swallowed his tongue and was completely speechless.

"Told you so," she said, laughing.

"Holy shit," he muttered, as he stared. The woman looked completely different. Gone was the comical clothing and in its place was the clothing of a woman. She had worn a black form fitting pencil skirt and a low cut silk shirt that showed off cleavage and the shoes were wicked and completely erotic. Then there was the hair. She'd tamed it, managed it, and it hung straight across her shoulders and down her back in red and ebony waves.

Elizabeth pinched him to get him to focus.

"Wow, you look lovely."

"Thank you," she smiled and took his outstretched hand. It wasn't what she was hoping for, but obviously 'beautiful' was reserved for Elizabeth.

"Don't wait up for us," said Whitefox. He was completely distracted by the transformation before him. Desdemona Adare managed to catch him completely off guard.

"Oh, we won't," answered his brother. When they walked out the front door, he grinned over at his wife.

"Wait until they've left the driveway. They could always come back in, and then what?" she grinned, wickedly.

"Good point," he said, sitting on the couch.

When they heard the Denali drive away, Elizabeth pointed at the food. "You bring that, and I'll meet you up in our room."

Blackhawk watched his wife walk away, and he rubbed his hands together. The kids were out, and the parents were going to have a sex fest and then Chinese food naked in bed.

The night couldn't get any better.

Desdemona continually snuck little peeks over at the man she was going on a date with that evening. She was definitely sure he was the sexiest man in the world. The fact that he put on dress clothes and looked as amazing as he did was making her have a really hard time focusing.

"You do look great tonight," he said, driving. He was infinitely glad that he borrowed his brother's dress attire. She looked too good to be with a man in jeans, and right now he needed her to want to be with him.

"I think you look amazing," she said, and then she couldn't help it. "And you smell really good, too."

Okay, he was grateful he borrowed his brother's cologne too. "Thanks," he grinned at her. "I don't often get to go out with a doctor."

She laughed. "Well then I guess this is a first for me too. I've never had a date with an FBI guy before. Aren't I the lucky one?"

Callen Whitefox's entire body clenched. Yeah, she was sexy and she was making it hard to not just jump on her right there.

"Truth be told, after the whole stalker thing, I don't get out often with anyone." When he reached into her lap and took her hand in his, she swore she was going to break out in sweat.

"Well I think you should. You can't live your life in fear because of a nut job. You'll miss too much. "

"I haven't found anyone that I really wanted to go out to dinner with in a long time," she answered, softly.

"Until now?" he asked hopefully. If this was a boredom, mercy dinner, his mood was going to plummet a great deal.

"Yes. You win the date prize on this one, Callen."

He smiled and was glad to hear it. "We're here," he said, parking the vehicle. "Ready for our date?"

"I absolutely am."

Elizabeth was waiting for him on the arm of the loveseat beside the fireplace. "What took you so long, Cowboy?" she asked watching him walk towards her.

"Locking the door," he replied, sitting on the loveseat and pulling her down into his lap. "But now my very sexy wife has my full attention. I promise." Blackhawk began kissing her.

"Mmmmm..." Elizabeth moaned into the kiss.

Blackhawk almost lost it right then. It was just the sound of her moaning in pleasure while sitting on his lap was practically enough to put him over. "God, I missed touching you, Elizabeth." He returned back to the kiss, and her hands began wandering and unbuttoning the buttons on his dress shirt.

Elizabeth slid her fingers through his hair and shifted so she was straddling his body. "Nice touch with the fireplace," Kissing him had her attention again, that and running her fingers across his chest.

"I thought so," he answered, into their kiss.

Elizabeth moved to his throat. One of her very sexy husband's weaknesses was his ear and she used it to make him shudder and moan. When he dropped his head back against the loveseat she began torturing him more as her hands wandered lower to unbutton and unzip his pants.

"So amazing," he whispered, as he grew so hard it was almost to the point of pain. "The things you do to me." When she bit him he groaned. "Baby," he arched his lower body against her, just to feel some relief from the intense need rocking his body. Her fingertips were stroking him lightly, teasing him.

"You taste really good, husband," she whispered in his ear, running her one hand lightly down his chest and using her nails. When his muscles twitched under her fingers and at the junction of where their bodies met, she knew her husband was on his way to extreme pleasure. "Ethan?"

He opened his eyes at her using his name. "Yes baby?"

Elizabeth stood off his body and took a step back from him. "I have a surprise for you," she said as she untucked her shirt and flicked open her belt buckle.

"By all means, surprise me."

"I know how much you liked the cheerleading outfit, so I think you'll be pleasantly surprised," she purred.

Blackhawk thought back to seeing his wife dressed like a cheerleader, and it was making him break out in beads of perspiration. Just the visual in the tiny skirt made him all hot and bothered. Sex with his wife was never boring, and he wasn't sure she could top the cheerleader costume. But then again, this was Elizabeth, and she was a wildcard in life and the bedroom. Since her, his sexual bucket list had tripled.

Elizabeth dropped her hair down her back, and shook out the curls. They fell all the way down her body to almost her waist and then she began the unveiling. Pulling the shirt over her head she tossed it at him when he sat there mouth open. "I take that you like it?" she asked.

"Like it?" he repeated, when he finally got his voice back. The bra was black and had red lace over it, and it looked erotic and very seductive. It showed her pale flesh beneath it. Nothing was hidden, "I'm almost afraid to ask where you got that," he swallowed. "Please tell me there are more of them to come in the future."

"So you do like it?" she asked, running her hands over her breasts that were barely contained. Then she turned her back to her husband and drop the zipper on her jeans.

"Like isn't even close to how I feel right now. You look completely…" he didn't have words as she dropped her jeans and gave him a view of the lacy concoction from behind.

"Stripper-ish?"

"Uh yeah." He licked his lips, because they were suddenly dry. Then she slid her jeans down her legs, and he saw what else she planned for him. The G-string was ridiculously tiny and barely contained anything. It left nothing to the imagination, and that was worse. The red and black straps crisscrossed her back, inviting him to do wicked things to her.

Elizabeth turned and stalked towards him, enjoying the look on her husband's face. It was pure awe and pleasure.

Blackhawk felt his entire body start to burn, and she was the cause. He pulled her down onto him, so she was straddling him. Like a mad man he dove into her mouth trying to quench the fire that was building in his body. Gone was the gentleness and the ease of casual sex. Now it would be how he felt; wild and out of complete control.

"Ethan," she gasped, as his hands forcefully pulled the bra off her body and he began leaving a trail of bites and kisses across her upper body.

"I want you, Elizabeth," he said between devouring her and exploring her with his hands. She sat across his body and he wanted to do nothing more than pound himself into her with abandon.

"Tell me what you want, Ethan," she whispered seductively. "Tell me how to pleasure you, Mr. Blackhawk," she purred into his ear.

He groaned at her words and the implication that she'd do whatever he wanted. Right then he knew what he wanted and needed.

"Anything to please you, Mr. Director, Sir," she purred.

It took a second to form a complete sentence. "Use your mouth on me." He got the words out, and watched as his wicked wife dropped to her knees, taking him in her mouth. "Jesus Christ," he muttered, and dug his hands into the arms of the love seat as she began her torture.

"Whatever you want, Mr. Blackhawk," she complied and returned to her mission of driving her husband completely and totally insane.

Elizabeth slowly licked, sucked and enjoyed him.

The more he moaned the more she worked him. Hard then slow, and then hard again until his chest was struggling to get air. Ethan was breathing heavy like he was running a marathon.

"Please," he pleaded, as she lightly cupped him and rubbed. "Oh god, baby stop," he begged and looked at her with wild eyes. It was all too much for him. The outfit, the stroking, the way his wife was using his body to drive him completely insane. Elizabeth stole all his control and filled the empty space it left with nothing but lust and desire.

Elizabeth eased up on him and stared up at him with big icy blue eyes. "What next, Ethan? What do you want?"

"I just want to bury myself in you and…" He almost slipped and used the word, and he knew he shouldn't. This was his wife, and it was more than that.

"And what Ethan?" she ran her fingertips across his erection, and batted her eye lashes innocently. There was no doubt what he wanted, and now she was going to make him let go of the carefully constructed control he carried all day and just be himself with her.

"Elizabeth," he pleaded.

"Say it Ethan," she pushed, and then licked him with one long stroke, as if to punctuate it. "What do you want to do?"

"I want to fuck you!" He finally got it out, nearly choking on the words.

Elizabeth grinned as she finally broke his control. "Then fuck me, Ethan," she whispered back, as she licked him from base to tip.

Blackhawk lost control, he pushed up from the loveseat and grabbed his wife, dragging her to the bed and tossing her into the middle. First he ripped off the G-string and then he dropped his pants, and dove onto her, burying himself in her. "No control," he whispered, as he slid in as far as he could, and then back out. The scent of wife, the feel of her body wrapped around his was maddening, and he'd never get enough.

"You don't need control with me, Ethan," she whispered, holding on for the ride, while her very sexy Indian warrior found and gave pleasure.

Blackhawk felt the last restraint snap, as he started pounding into his very willing and bewitching wife. She arched to meet each stroke and was whispering so many things to him and driving him crazy with her words.

Elizabeth moaned his name, as she felt the heat building and bringing her to the precipice. She held on with nails and sheer will until she could tell that her husband was about to lose it.

As her body exploded, it forced his pace to falter, and he shouted her name as he slammed into her one last time. Ethan's entire body shuddered as hers milked his, and forced his release hotly into the only woman in the world that would ever have his heart.

She was his true love.

Elizabeth started giggling, as she lay trapped beneath her husband.

"Did I hurt you," he asked, without even looking over.

"No you didn't, but wow Mr. Blackhawk that was some pretty fantastic sex. It took me nine months to make you lose complete control, and it was so worth it," she snickered and bit him on the earlobe.

"I love you, Elizabeth." He finally had his breath back, and he rolled bringing her to his chest.

"Oh, I love you too. Very impressive," she laid kisses across his chest.

"I don't think I'm done with you yet Mrs. Blackhawk."

"Goodie."

Callen was enjoying dinner with Desdemona, and he was greatly turned on that the men in the place were staring at her. He didn't mind them looking, because tonight she was all his. Then the little voice in his head asked about what after that. What did he want after that with the woman? She was sweet, funny and filled a hole in his life. Just thinking the words brought back the guilt.

"Callen, you're staring, what's wrong?" she asked, beginning to feel paranoid, like she was doing something completely wrong. After spending most of her time with the dead, she'd lost practice with the living.

"I'm sorry, I was just thinking about you," he answered, taking her hand.

"I hope nothing bad," she said, softly.

"Oh no, there was nothing bad." He didn't want to scare her away, but he was thinking about what he was going to do about her when this was all over. Part of his mind was dwelling on the Rez and his grandfather, the other part on what she was wearing beneath that skirt and shirt.

"So, tell me about your life outside the FBI," she asked. Since it was a date, they shouldn't talk shop, or death for that matter.

"I'm pretty simple. I like to go hunting, and I like to hike and camp too."

She thought about it for a second. "I've never been hunting, and I think I'd pass on that one, but I've been camping and hiking."

"You have?"

"Why are you surprised? I know I don't look like the average woman who does normal things, but I assure you, Callen. I even watch TV once in a while too."

He laughed. "I don't own one. If I watch TV it's always at my brother's house and it's generally sports related." Then he thought about it, and took the first step to seeing if they could have more after this was all over. "Would you go camping with me when spring comes?"

She didn't even think twice. "My tent or yours?" she asked, picking up her wine glass and taking a sip.

"Your tent, my sleeping bag," he quipped, grinning. "I like to be fair."

"I think that sounds completely intriguing."

Whitefox grinned the infamous 'Blackhawk grin'. "That wasn't the word I was thinking of going with, but it works for me."

Desdemona laughed. "Then I think you have a deal."

When she laughed, his whole body tensed at the sound of it crossing his body. It was like silk stroking his nerve endings and pulled lust from deep within his body. Part of him wanted to go get a sleeping bag right then and there and drag her into it. He was about to suggest some other creative things they could do in the sleeping bag when there was a crash of glass and angry voices.

Both of them looked across the restaurant to a woman standing beside a table. The blonde woman was angrily pointing at the man and she was just about to throw her wine on him.

"You're a cheating bastard, and it would be shocking if you could stop staring at every woman's ass that walks past you in here, but you have no self-control." She dumped the garlic bread into his lap, as the waiter tried to calm her down. For his efforts, he received an elbow to his solar plexus.

"But Courtney, I just looked that was all! It's a guy thing!"

She dumped the wine in his lap and turned on her heel, but just before she gave him one last look. "Rot in hell, I hope someone cuts out your cheating, lying heart."

"Wow," said Desdemona. "That was something." She really couldn't blame the woman. She'd feel and probably do the same thing. Who was she kidding? Elizabeth would be ballsy enough to do that; she'd probably scurry away and hide. Then again she was finding that she was stronger than she thought she was and had a lot more in common with her friend than she believed.

Whitefox forgot it was supposed to be a date and was back on duty. "Yeah, we need to find out who that woman was, just in case the poor bastard is the next one on your table."

Desdemona just nodded and tried to not be disappointed that their dinner alone turned into a work thing again. There was this intense wave of sadness that she so easily lost his attention, and yet she wasn't surprised in the least.

"Yes, I suppose we should."

Elizabeth sat in bed with chopsticks, her husband and dinner. After rolling around in bed, her husband seduced her into joining him in front of the fireplace, where the love making was gentle, sweet and seductive. Blackhawk had taken his time and where the first time was fast and hard, the second was slow and achingly sweet. He whispered words of adoration, love and what was in his heart for her.

"I love you, Ethan," she said, touching his cheek.

Ethan grinned over at his wife. "I love you too, baby. Now come here!" He pulled her under his arm, and she began feeding her husband Chinese food while they curled together in bed and watched the flames flicker in the room.

"We need a fireplace in our bedroom," she stated.

He laughed. "I'll put it on my list of things to do," he said, "I'm still not quite finished working on the tree house for the back yard. It's just about completed."

Elizabeth thought back to the time they snuck up into his childhood tree house and had an incredible time. "What do you think is going to happen between Callen and Desdemona?" she asked suddenly.

"Worried?"

"Yeah, I am. I really like her and I hope if this doesn't work out between them she'll still want to be my friend."

Blackhawk knew that once his wife found someone she loved, she would collect them for life. It's how her heart worked and one of the things he loved most about her. "I think it'll work out."

"I miss having a girlfriend."

Blackhawk snickered. "You want a girlfriend?" he wiggled his eyebrows, lecherously and took a shot to the ribs because of it.

"You know what I mean," she laughed. "I miss Livy, she's so far away, and she's so busy with the kids. It's nice having a friend," Elizabeth said, honestly.

"You have us," he offered. He knew that she was close with the men in her family, but he could understand. A woman friend offered a different kind of friendship.

"You want me taking Callen lingerie shopping to buy things for us to use?" she questioned him, grinning. "Because he'll do it and enjoy every second of it too."

His earlier conversation with his brother came to mind, and exactly how willing he was to share his wife with him.

"Can I come shopping then too?" Blackhawk started laughing at the look on her face.

Elizabeth lifted an eyebrow. "You did just hear what I said, right?"

Blackhawk nodded and then figured he should tell his wife about the conversation he had earlier in the day, since it had everything to do with her.

Elizabeth listened to everything her husband said, and she wasn't quite sure what she should say to him. When he was finished she took his hand in hers. "I think you're an amazing man."

"I want to ask you something, and I need you to be honest with me, Elizabeth."

"Oh great, my first name and not Lyzee, so I'm sure this is going to be one of 'those' talks."

"Are you in love with my brother?" he asked, with zero emotion in his voice.

"I love your brother, but you know that."

"I mean are you attracted to my brother?" He tried another route to the answer.

"Ethan, I am attracted to him, because you two are very similar. You know that I think the Blackhawk gene pool is very alluring."

He thought about her words.

"Are you asking if I'm going toss over my husband and shack up with his brother?"

"I think I am."

"Nope."

Blackhawk looked into her eyes and saw nothing but honesty and he felt immediate relief.

"I think your brother is sexy and I love him a great deal. But I hope you realize that I married you for a reason, and that I wouldn't cheat on you behind your back," then she teased. "Besides, have you seen your wobbly wife?"

"I told him today I'm perfectly fine with you two being close." Then he contemplated his next words. "If anything were to happen to me, he'd take care of you. I know my brother would step up and make sure you were safe."

Elizabeth didn't like this conversation at all, but she listened because he obviously needed to get it out. It was beyond her comprehension how the night went from wild sex to talking about his brother. "I'm not worried about that, Ethan. You aren't going anywhere." Then it occurred to her this was all a segue to what he really wanted to discuss. "Are you worried about Callen?"

"Yeah, I am."

"Want to talk about it?"

Ethan accepted some Chinese food and chewed thoughtfully. "No, I think we've discussed it plenty for tonight. I just wanted to let you know that he and I had a conversation."

"Okay Ethan."

Blackhawk changed the subject.

"I do think you need to go shopping with Desdemona for some fun things," he wiggled his eyebrows.

"Well this was all her doing."

"Shop with her on a regular basis," he said, grinning. "In fact, spend lots of money on anything that resembles or reminds you of tonight's little outfit. In fact, I'm physically fit; my heart can take even more risqué."

"You're going to regret saying that."

Blackhawk thought about a big bill and lots of sex with his gorgeous wife. "Uh, yeah don't bet on that."

"Do you think I'm too much of a tom boy?" she asked, suddenly.

"Baby, where did that come from?" he asked, turning her face towards his and looking into her eyes."

"I don't know, but maybe I shouldn't be so…"

"Tough? Bad ass?"

"Yeah. Do you want me to soften up, wear dresses and dress more like Desdemona was tonight?"

At first he thought she was kidding, but the look on her face was serious. "I happen to like you just as you are, Elizabeth. If you want to change, do it for you not for me. I like that my wife comes across as tough and hard at work, and that she wears frilly aprons when she's making me breakfast at home."

She didn't look convinced.

"I get the best of both worlds. You in jeans is a thing of beauty," he said, lecherously. "Then you catch me off guard when I find out you've painted your toes pink. I like the little moments of femininity. It's a big turn on."

Elizabeth kissed her husband and cuddled against him. "Well then Darlin', I aim to please." Now she was thinking back over their conversation. Of all the conversations, this was the one she had to over think and figure out where her husband was heading with it.

Callen Whitefox could feel the evening going to hell in a hand basket, and he wasn't quite sure why. Something changed between him and Desdemona. They were laughing, flirting, and having fun, and then she put the wall back up between them, and he had no clue why. He kept replaying it over and over again in his mind, and then just went with safe topics. Like work.

"I see the Sheriff's here," he said, nodding to the bar.

Desdemona looked over and swirled the drink in her glass. "Yes, he is." She was definitely having a hard time being jovial and happy, when she realized this wasn't a date, it was a stakeout. She was just part of his disguise and that made her sad and angry all at once.

"And he looks awful cozy with that blonde woman," he answered, wishing Desdemona would come over and sit by him, like the blonde woman was with the Sheriff. Now he just couldn't figure out how to swing it. The 'available' sign was gone from her mood, and he was struggling to find a way back.

"Yes, he does. Maybe they're on a date," she answered blandly. "If you'll excuse me," she stood from the table and pushed in her chair. "I'm going to go check my lipstick." By now she assumed she'd need a touch up, not that he actually even kissed her. Desdemona walked away, and the tears were building and she needed a few minutes away from Callen Whitefox. Deep down she knew she shouldn't be mad, they were working, but part of her was hurt that he'd never see her for anything more than just the FBI Doctor.

Standing in front of the mirror, she noticed the blonde had followed her to the ladies room.

"Great shoes," she said, and smiled.

Desdemona smiled back. "Thanks. Great bag," she threw back the compliment.

"Thanks." The woman leaned her hip on the counter. "You work for the FBI?" She'd heard the gossip around town, and this woman was new around the bar. She needed to stake out the competition and see if it was long term or just passing through.

"Yes, I'm Doctor Desdemona Adare." She held out her hand. "I'm the medical Examiner for the FBI."

"Carly Kester. I own the bookstore in town."

Desdemona gave her a polite smile. "If you don't mind, my date is waiting." Dropping the lipstick into her purse, all she wanted to do was escape. Her mood was questionable, even to a stranger.

"Yeah, mine too," and she turned to go into one of the stalls.

Desdemona hustled out of the bathroom, and stopped at the sheriff's side. She leaned down in his ear, and whispered to him. Recognition dawned, and then he nodded but remained in his seat. Desdemona crossed the bar and took her seat, shaking her head

Callen Whitefox had watched the entire interaction. Part of him was completely jealous that she was smiling at the Sheriff and touching his arm. Part of him was curious what she could be saying. When she sat, he spoke.

"What did you tell him?"

"That a blonde was drugging men, and to be careful. I didn't want to see him on the table in the morning."

"That was nice of you," he said. "But he didn't want to hear it?"

"Nope. Hey, all in a day's work, Right?" she finished her wine. "I think we should go."

"Okay, Desdemona." He knew he did something, and this was more proof. The woman was ending the date. When she stood and put on her own jacket and headed for the door, he felt his stomach drop.

This answered the question of what would happen between them when this was all over, absolutely nothing. Desdemona just made it blatantly clear.

Callen Whitefox couldn't stand the silence any longer. She wouldn't even look at him, and was staring out the window. This was a bad sign, and it made him feel a little panicky. He was attracted to the woman, and he didn't want her walking away from him, not now and certainly not later. He already had a plan when it came to her.

"Why are you mad at me," he asked, carefully. Remembering the woman melting down in the restaurant and hoping she wouldn't follow suit.

Desdemona looked over surprised. "I'm not mad at you." And she wasn't.

"Well, we went from a great night to an okay night to a shitty one in the span of two hours. So, something went wrong and I have to assume it's something I did."

"I'm not mad at you, Callen. I'm mad at me."

Now he really didn't understand. How could she be mad at herself? They were having a really nice time, sexy woman, and then he thought to when it went downhill. The other woman, fighting in the restaurant, and talking about work.

She sighed. "I'm mad at myself because I actually believed we were going to have a date, and I dressed up, and it just wasn't what I expected."

Shit! Now he got it. "Desi, I'm sorry." Maybe he should have been a little more sensitive. Yeah, he needed to watch people for his brother, but he should have been focused on the most important one in the place.

"It's fine," she said, as he pulled up to the house. "It was insane to believe you'd want to take me on a date anyway. I'm just the ME." Desdemona hopped out of the vehicle and fought to hold back the tears.

"Wait, you think I wouldn't want to take you on a real date? Are you serious?" Then he saw the tears in her eyes. Well hell, he just needed to fix this. Desdemona really thought she wasn't worth his time. Here the entire time he was trying to protect her from Elizabeth, and he was the one that was going to hurt her.

"No one ever does, I'm completely invisible," she said finally, as she pushed into the house they were staying in. "Thanks for dinner, Callen. See you in the morning." She walked past him and to the stairs. Now she'd run and hide, and try to regroup to face them all in the morning. This was why she hid behind the goth-y clothing, because rejection hurt. She was insane to believe that sexy Callen Whitefox would ever see her as anything more than a one night stand. To her it was more proof of where his heart lived.

Callen watched her leave, and he had no idea how to fix her or the mess that just started between them.

"Seem to have a problem?" Elizabeth inquired from the kitchen doorway.

Whitefox jumped. "Jesus, Lyzee."

"Sorry, I was getting some tea." Elizabeth rubbed her stomach to calm the baby down. "Want to talk about it?" she asked, as he followed her back into the kitchen.

"We started out great," he said, then told her everything that happened. "I didn't try to screw this up," he stated in frustration. "And yet I managed to make it an epic mess."

"Ethan told you to take the night off tonight for a reason. He wanted you to have fun. Any woman wants to be the center of attention when a man takes her out, Callen." Elizabeth took his hand in hers and they twined fingers. "Doctor Adare isn't the normal woman you screw around with. Get them drunk, bring them home and forget their name after dawn."

"I'm out of my element here," he said hopelessly, spilling his heart to the only woman that knew his secrets and fears. If anyone could help him, she could and would. "I don't really romance women. The women I bring home aren't the type."

"What does she mean to you?" she inquired, softly.

Whitefox had trusted the woman before him with all his secrets, to the ones that involved her and anything else. He relied on that trust to keep him afloat when he was adrift in the sea of confusion. "I don't think I can love two people at once. Can someone be so hopelessly in love with one person, and then still have a relationship with someone else?" he asked her, because he really needed the reassurance and Elizabeth would tell him the truth.

"Absolutely Darlin'." Elizabeth believed that without a doubt. Love was a multilayered complex thing and couldn't be bound by normal rules. "I love your brother and I love you too. You can love two people if you really want to do it and it's meant to be."

Callen listened to her words and tried not to read into it too much, especially after talking to his brother today.

"I think she's a really special woman, and I'd like to see if I can fit her into my life. Something about her just throws me off balance, makes my head spin and I feel like I'm completely out of step."

"Sounds like the potential to be love."

Yeah, he was well aware what love felt like. Elizabeth gave him the same feelings, only ten million times worse. "What do I do now?" he asked, needing her help. "How do I fix this Lyzee? I don't want to screw this up any more than I have."

Elizabeth stood and went to his side. When he leaned against her and rested his head against her body, and the baby bump, she stroked and played with his hair. "You need to make it up to her, and give her a new date to replace the one that got ruined. Do something that makes her feel special and unique."

He nodded. "Thank you, Lyzee." He'd be lost without her, and this was why he loved her like he did.

"Don't worry, Callen. If it's meant to be, nothing will stop it from happening."

Whitefox stood up and pulled her into his arms, just relishing the feeling and scent. "I love you, Lyzee," he said, taking her face in his hands and kissing her softly on the lips. It was hard to not push the kiss too far, despite what his brother said to him.

Elizabeth felt the tone of the kiss change slightly. It wasn't odd that he'd drop a kiss on her lips, but this kiss was vastly different than the normal ones. Pulling away she looked up into his eyes, questioningly. "I love you too, Callen."

Whitefox allowed his fingers to linger and finally turned away, leaving her standing in the room alone, as he headed to his room.

Part of him had always been afraid of losing Elizabeth's love if he found someone else these last few months. Never could he live with the idea of replacing what he felt for her with another woman. Now he knew he didn't have to replace her. Elizabeth would stay firmly rooted in his life while he started to build a relationship with the woman upstairs. She'd always be there for him- never walking away.

Deep in his heart he locked that part that she owned up, saving it for the first woman he'd ever fallen in love with. It would always be there for the rest of his life. Now he was able to focus on Desdemona. Now he just needed to figure out how to make everything all right.

Elizabeth watched the man walk away and she was even more confused than before. Maybe it was all the pregnancy hormones. Man, she couldn't wait to have her emotions and body back.

Desdemona took off all her makeup, slipped out of the skirt and shirt and into a night shirt. As she climbed into bed, she could hear Callen moving around in the room beside hers. A part of her felt guilty for making him suffer with her. Just because she was completely unlovable and a lost cause, it didn't mean she needed to make him pay for it. She wished he'd find something redeemable in her and want to be with her for something other than sex. She wished Callen saw her the way he saw Elizabeth.

As she curled up in her blanket, the tears came. Her heart wept openly, because she'd fallen in love with him. His bossiness, his possessiveness, and now she'd pushed him away. Damn it, she was a hot mess that ruined everything. Lying in bed, she gave in to the tears and just purged it all.

Whitefox was getting undressed, and thinking about the woman in the room beside him. Come hell or high water, he was going to fix this and make it right. Then he heard it, the soft crying, and his heart broke. Damn what a mess he created. Work could have waited one night, how many times would he get a chance to have dinner with her and have her be his complete focus. Going to the door that connected their room, he gently twisted the knob and stepped into her room. She was lying in her bed, so small and broken by his blatant stupidity.

"Desi?" he whispered her name softly, as he walked towards the bed.

"I'm fine, Callen," she answered, as she sniffled.

At that moment he wasn't sure what to do, but he took the chance. "It doesn't sound like you're okay," he said, climbing onto her bed and lying beside her.

Desdemona froze. She was in no mood to have sex and she really was disappointed that he was thinking it was a possibility. Her whole body tensed.

Whitefox felt her freeze up. "Come here, Desi. I know when I'm hurt it helps to just not be alone." When she didn't move, he went to her, curling protectively around the back of her body. Slowly she relaxed.

When she realized he was just there to make her feel better, she welcomed it. Maybe he did understand.

"Go to sleep, sweetheart. I'll watch over you tonight," he said, leaving a simple kiss on the curl of her ear. "I promise."

Desdemona felt the anger floating away, and she closed her eyes. "Thank you, Callen." She felt a little better, as hope filled her. Maybe there was a chance, deep down he did understand that she was hurting.

"No problem, Desi," and he meant it. It was time to convince her that when this was over, the only place she was going was with him.

Home.

*　　*　　*

Angrily she brushed her hair in long vicious strokes to punish herself. In the tree line she had the perfect shot to kill the woman that was after her man. The perfect opportunity wasted, and then the other woman had to warn her. Damn them! They must both be after her men. There was no way she was going to let those cheap whores get to the love of her life. He was her true love, and a woman must do anything to protect what was hers.

ANYTHING!

She looked in the mirror and checked out her appearance. Why would he pick them over her? It was inconceivable. She'd done everything he'd asked and wanted of her, and even gone as far as offering him her heart and her soul.

After all, she'd given up her life for him.

*   *   *

When the phone rang, they both jumped at the sound. When a call came in the middle of the night, it only meant one thing. Something bad had happened and there was an emergency. Desdemona Adare quickly answered the phone, and it took her a few minutes register what it was all about. When it sunk in, she knew there was a possibility that she may get sick.

"I'll be there in a couple of hours, I'm out of town," she said simply, and then hung up the phone.

"Desi, what's wrong?" asked Callen Whitefox. They must have just fallen asleep not too long ago. He'd laid there listening to her easy breathing, making sure she slept first and keeping his promise to watch over her while she slept. Looking down at his watch, he noticed, it was three in the morning.

"I have to go, Callen." She hopped out of bed, and started to pack her suitcase. Her heart was pounding in her chest, and fear was creeping up her body, preparing to freeze everything into one solid useless mass.

"Go where, sweetheart," he asked. Part of him knew if she ran now, he'd never get her back, and that left two choices. Talk her out of it, or run with her.

"The police just called. My alarm company was alerted at my house. Someone broke in and wrecked the place," she said, ready to cry. They didn't have to tell her who did it, she already knew. The stalker that haunted every step of her life had accessed the one place that was sacred and destroyed it on her. Her home wasn't safe anymore.

"I'm going with you," he said, sliding from the bed. "Give me a few minutes to get dressed, I'll drive you." He was already moving to the door adjoining their room.

"Callen, wait, you have a job to do here. I'm finished until the next victim turns up, I can go. You can't." God, she hoped she couldn't talk him out of it. Inside her head she pleaded with the mystical higher powers to not let her push him away, even as her words did just that.

Whitefox walked back over to her, took her face in his large hands and looked down into those green eyes that intrigued him. "I'm going with you. I can't let you face this alone. I promised you Desdemona, so stop asking me to when it's just a useless waste of time and breath. I always keep my promises, because that's the foundation to everything in life. If you break those you have nothing."

"Callen." Desdemona said his name, as her eyes filled with more tears.

Leaning down to her, he kissed her delicately on the lips, no push, no hardness. Just gentleness that he thought she needed at that moment to keep her from shattering apart. "I'll meet you downstairs, and I'll tell Ethan and Elizabeth that we're leaving."

Doctor Adare nodded and watched him walk away. Hope bloomed; all the while terror began feasting at her heart and soul.

Callen packed his bag fast, as he clipped his gun to his hip and tucked in his badge. Next was trying to convince his brother that he had to go, and if it came down to it, he'd quit in a heartbeat and worry about the consequences later. Desdemona was going to take precedent over work, and he wasn't letting her do this alone. Tonight he screwed up, but he'd at least keep the woman safe.

Walking to his brother's door, he knocked lightly.

"Come in," came his voice.

Whitefox opened the door and immediately he noticed both Elizabeth and Ethan were sitting up, but his brother was still protectively around his wife. Just in case.

"What's wrong?" he asked, relaxing as his eyes focused on his brother before him. Whitefox had taken a seat beside his wife.

"Desdemona just got a call," he paused, linking fingers with Elizabeth, for support and strength. All he could hope was his brother didn't fire him. "There was an alarm at her house, someone broke in, and wrecked the place."

"The stalker?" asked Elizabeth, squeezing his hand.

"They didn't say, but who else could it be? Some random coincidence?" He stated in doubt. "She's packing to head back, and I'm going with her." Whitefox put it out there waiting for his brother to tell say he wasn't going.

"Head downstairs, and give us two minutes to get down there. I'll have the FBI tech team at FBI West go in and run it for prints and for any trace."

Callen loved his brother more than words would ever be able to express. Yeah he was his boss, but he just put brotherhood first. "Thank you, Ethan, for understanding."

"It's what family does, especially the Blackhawks."

~ Chapter Twelve ~
Thursday early morning

Desdemona lugged her suitcase downstairs, and she was surprised to find everyone waiting for her. Both Blackhawks and Callen stood having coffee and leaning against the counter in the kitchen. There was this little wave of worry that kept pushing at her and making her scared, but she knew she was an adult and needed to handle the messes that she found waiting for her. Telling her bosses she was leaving the assignment was probably going to be one of those messes.

Callen immediately took her bag and placed it by the back door. The Denali was heated up and they would begin their trip, as soon as she was ready to go.

Elizabeth felt sympathy for her new friend and poured her a cup of coffee, pushing it across the counter to her, noticing that she looked worried. "You'll need this," she added. "It's bitching cold out there."

"I'm sorry." It was all she could think of at that moment.

Elizabeth went to her friend and hugged her. "Hey, you didn't sneak to your house and wreck the joint, so stop apologizing."

Desdemona hugged her back, and knew that part of her would love this woman forever. She'd accepted her and offered her something no one else ever had. Unconditional friendship. "Thank you for understanding."

Blackhawk spoke up. "The other tech team is in en route to your house. They'll sweep for anything they can find and then run it."

"But this isn't FBI related!" Desdemona tried to object.

He knew it wasn't and again the curiosity rose to the surface of how his wife pulled it off. "You heard Director Rothschild. Elizabeth and I are going to handle this, so just give them the next two hours to do the initial sweep and then you can enter the house. Don't drive like maniacs to just be in their way." That was meant for his brother. "You have our house key. Take Desdemona there if the tech team is still busy working the scene.

Use the quiet there to crash for a while. You know the alarm code."

Whitefox nodded and went to Elizabeth. "Thank you," he rubbed her belly and his yet born nephew.

"Come back in one piece, Callen," she whispered back, taking his face in her hands and looking into his eyes. "Promise me."

He kissed her on the lips, and made the oath. "No worries beautiful. You keep an eye on my brother."

Elizabeth nodded, releasing his wrist.

Next he went to his brother and hugged him. "Thank you for understanding."

"Watch your back, Cal," he whispered in his ear.

"Yes, Sir!" Callen saluted, and his sister-in-law laughed.

"Come on, Desi. We'll go take care of this, and get back here before anyone knows we've even gone," he said grabbing the bags.

"Thank you," she said, following him out the door into the bitter night.

Both Blackhawks watched them leave, and he looked over at his wife. "Worried, baby?" he asked, noticing the look on her face.

"Yeah, Cowboy I am."

"Me too," he said, locking the door and pulling his wife away from the kitchen door. They had a few hours until they needed to be back at work. "I'm not going to be able to sleep."

"Me either."

"I think we need to talk." It was time. "We need to discuss how you got our boss to allow the FBI to foot the bill for Desdemona's problem." Blackhawk knew the minute his wife registered what he wished to discuss. Her whole body went rigid and tense.

Elizabeth's first instinct was to lie, but then she remembered who she was talking to, and couldn't bring herself damage the trust between them.

"Well Elizabeth?"

Again she didn't speak. She wasn't sure how to broach the conversation.

"How about we bring our coffee upstairs, I light a fire, and we discuss what you're hiding from your husband." Blackhawk knew tossing out the title of husband was playing dirty, but then again, keeping secrets was just as dirty.

Elizabeth grabbed her coffee and his. "Sounds good to me. I love a crackling fire," she answered, trying to keep it light and airy. Once she told him the truth, she might lose her husband and his respect.

Blackhawk led his wife up the stairs to their room, and he released her hand. He went to the love seat, and he noticed she chose to sit on the bed, placing distance between them. This had to be very bad sign of what was coming.

"When I was back in the FBI under Gabe Rothschild, my last assignment with Livy was a bad one. We were sent in to work on a serial killer assignment. It was one of my firsts. I had just transitioned from violent crimes into Gabe's department. When he was promoted, he pretty much took me with him."

Blackhawk sipped his coffee and just listened.

"The killer became infatuated with Livy," she paused, slipping back into her memories to find the secrets she'd buried so deep.

"Infatuated?"

"He was stalking and killing redheads. Maybe you remember the case. It was in Boston, 'The Irish Butcher'. Elizabeth watched the look on her husband's face. Ethan was the king of poker faces, and it was bad when his suddenly cracked, when the information hit its mark.

"That was your assignment?" he asked, incredulously. They'd all seen the dossier on it, because it was legend at Quantico, and not for a good reason. It was a big slipup that allowed the killer to get away, and all the victim's families were furious that the FBI screwed up and didn't get them justice.

Elizabeth laughed. "Yeah, I headed that clusterfuck."

Blackhawk didn't know what to say, but it still didn't answer why she was able to manipulate Gabe over it. If anything she should owe him, her name was never tied to it.

"The killer focused on Livy. The sicko began stalking her everywhere, and we contemplated using her as bait."

"Okay, I'm with you so far."

"Right about then, Gabe and Livy fell in love. She asked him to marry her," Elizabeth laughed. She remembered the day, and it still made her smile. Her boss was so stiff and rule orientated that Livy rocked his world upside down.

"Gabe told me that Livy proposed."

"Yeah, she didn't like to play by the traditional rules, and it's probably a good thing. Gabe tends to drag his feet on certain things, like living wild and crazy."

"You're stalling." He hoped it didn't come out hard, but he was starting to get a sick feeling in the pit of his stomach.

"Yeah I am, because what I'm going to tell you is that damn bad."

Blackhawk wanted to go to her, but she didn't seem to want the comfort, not yet.

"Anyway, this wackjob was getting more twisted, leaving presents for her, dead animals, nasty notes and then one night she called me. I couldn't understand the call, it was her whispering and it was garbled. I rushed over as fast as I could."

"What happened?"

"She went home to her apartment after work, Gabe was working late, and the butcher was in her place."

"Oh shit."

"Yeah, when I got there he had roughed her up and was going to kill her, but I interrupted." Elizabeth left it at that. The details weren't hers to share, and she hoped her husband understood that.

"Baby, I'm so sorry," he said, the emotion was clearly visible on her face, and he couldn't imagine what she was feeling.

"I called Gabe, and he was going to go after the guy."

"I don't blame him," Blackhawk stared at his wife. It was starting to all come together.

"I wouldn't let him. By that time in the case, Livy and I had a suspect, and when he came at her, we knew we could identify him, but it would mean her having to testify against him."

"He assaulted her, didn't he?"

Elizabeth felt her eyes welling up. When her husband went to move to her, she shook her head. "I need to get through this, and you can't sooth me. I don't deserve it."

Blackhawk sat back down. "Okay, Elizabeth."

"Ethan, if I tell you the rest of this, you're obligated to arrest me. I broke the law, and Gabe buried it."

"What did you do, Elizabeth?"

"I played judge, jury and executioner for my partner and my friend."

Ethan walked to the bed, took the coffee from her hand and placed it on the end table. "I'm guessing 'The Irish Butcher' didn't really get away did he?"

"No. The victims got justice, but the families never knew it."

Blackhawk's cheek twitched.

"If you want a divorce, I completely understand, and If you want to turn me in, I'm ready," she said, placing her hands on her child growing in her body.

His heart broke that she'd been carrying this alone, and honestly believed he'd see her differently. "I wouldn't ever divorce you." Blackhawk climbed on the bed beside her and pulled her into his arms. "Elizabeth, I love you, and you aren't some sicko killing random people."

"It's a fine line, Ethan. A gray one that once you cross you can't get back from. I'm not proud of it, but I did what I had to do to protect the people I loved. Livy couldn't sit in that courthouse and talk about it, and Gabe was going to lose his mind over the entire thing. They had a strong connection, but a yearlong serial murder trial that culminated with one of the lead investigators being raped and having to testify would have broken them. Love is fragile."

Blackhawk thought back to when his wife was abducted, and he thought she could have been assaulted. Just the idea made him willing to kill. He couldn't imagine what it would have been like had Thomas Mason sexually assaulted Elizabeth. That wasn't true; he would have been driven to murder.

Easily.

"I acquired an unregistered. I made the shot and he died." She finished it up, leaving out as much as she could.

"No one ever suspected?" he asked.

"To this day, the police in Boston have it as a cold case."

Ethan kissed his wife on the top of the head and pulled her tightly against his body. "Did you really believe this would change what's between us?" he asked, softly.

"You're an honorable man, Ethan."

He tipped her chin up to look into her eyes. "I also know that 'The Irish Butcher' was a vile, disgusting man and he deserved to die. I'm just sorry my wife had to be the one to do it."

Elizabeth shrugged.

"Anymore secrets?" he asked, hoping she didn't have anything bigger than this hidden in her past.

Elizabeth laughed. "I'm not as bad with a gun as Livy and Gabe let on," she added. "In FBI qualifications, I helped Livy, not the other way around."

"I suspected. When you took that shot between me and my brother at the quarry to take out Mason, it wasn't a shot that just any Special Agent would take."

"So you suspected huh?" She wiped her tears.

"Dead giveaway." Ethan kissed her slow. When he broke away, she had more tears. "I love you, Elizabeth. Your secret is safe with me."

Elizabeth was a lucky woman.

"I know you think it's your job to protect the Blackhawks, but we also get to protect you too. It goes both ways."

"We can stop worrying about this then?" she hoped. "You really can't tell anyone Ethan, including Gabe. I swore an oath that day. If this ever got out, I'm going to jail, so is Gabe and now so are you."

"It'll be okay baby."

"Ethan, if this does gets out, I'll do the jail time. You have to promise me that you'll play dumb and never, ever say you knew about this. We're having a baby and you can't get dragged into this. Someone has to make sure our son is taken care of and I don't trust anyone with our child but you."

"My lips are sealed," he answered. Now he was an accomplice just by knowing and neither one of them were going to jail. He'd protect his wife, just like Gabe had protected Livy. He owed it to the man. After all, if he didn't send him to Salem, he never would have met his wife, and had a chance at a real life.

Sometimes you had to look the other way when you had a debt to pay. This was one of those times. As far as he was concerned, his wife wasn't ever going to jail and neither was Gabe Rothschild.

"Want to get some work done?" she asked, wanting to forget all about her past for a while. Now she wanted to live in the present and future.

Ethan hugged her again. "Yeah, let's get some work done." Now he needed to regain focus and start thinking about the assessment at hand.

"I'll go get the files," she said, slipping off the bed. "Thank you, Ethan."

Blackhawk smiled as his wife blew him a kiss. Now that this big mystery was solved most of his thoughts were now refocused. Callen Whitefox was walking right into danger. He had that feeling again, that twist in his gut that meant that something bad was coming. There were a few times he felt it in his life, the day he woke in Salem to find his wife on their patio with a giant raven was one, and it almost cost them both their lives. The other time when they were trying to find a serial killer targeting pregnant woman on the reservation. Both times they survived to tell about it, but he only hoped his brother would be that lucky.

Something bad was brewing and he hoped his brother would be ready and not distracted by women issues.

Desdemona didn't know what to say to the man driving her back to her home. There was this uneasiness filling the Denali and she knew it was all her fault. She'd over reacted as they were on their date. Obviously the man with her was a good guy. It wasn't even dawn, and he was driving through horrible weather to get her back to her house and the waiting mess. There was no doubt what she needed to do.

"I'm sorry about last night, Callen," she spoke, quietly.

He was surprised. "You have nothing to be sorry about, Desi. I should have been more focused on you and me, and less making it about work."

"We're here on an assignment, I over reacted. It wasn't a date, it was a job."

Callen looked over quickly. "It wasn't a job. What I feel for you has nothing to do with the job. If you want me to quit to prove it, I will."

"What?" Now she felt panicked. "Why would you quit your job?"

"I'd quit to prove a point. The job is the job, and we were on a date last night. My brother didn't need people watched, yeah, it was helpful, but he wanted us out of the house."

She stared at him openmouthed.

"Yes. He wanted to have wild sex with his wife, and he wanted us to go out on a date and give them the house."

"I don't know what to think." Then she started laughing. Could she blame them? She would have done the same exact thing to get Callen alone if she was in their position. "They could have just had sex, I don't care if they do. They're married."

"Ethan's straight laced to a point. He wanted to focus on Elizabeth," he paused. "If you tell them I told you, I'll deny it," he added, laughing.

"I won't tell." She promised him and she'd keep it.

"Pinky swear?" he asked, holding up his free hand, and waiting for her to make the oath. When she laughed and did it, he kept her hand in his. "I know I may not deserve to ask this, but I want a first date re-do."

She didn't think she was that lucky in life, but apparently she was indeed.

"I screwed it up, and I want a first date to prove how serious I am about us. Twenty years from now I don't want you thinking back to the screw-up but to the re-do." Whitefox looked over at her and hoped she'd say yes. "Give me a second chance?" he asked seriously.

"Yes." Desdemona finally got it out. Twenty years from now? Her heart was skipping in her chest, and she may need to go to the ER. It was quite possible that she was having a cardiac incident. How could she say no?

"Good," he said, grinning. Now to just figure out how to dazzle her and keep her completely interested in him. He was a simple man, and he may need some help on this one too. "When we get to the house, let me go in first okay?" Whitefox didn't want her to see the place totally destroyed. If he could he'd bribe the

296

tech team to put it back together again best they could, and he hoped they were delicately sweeping for trace.

"Okay," she answered, shivering. Just the idea that this wackjob was touching all her things, it freaked her out.

Whitefox pulled into the development onto the street that held her house, and it looked like an invasion. When his brother sent in a team, he sent in a squadron. "Sit tight," he said, leaning over and kissing her fast on the lips. "I'll be right back." Callen Whitefox hopped out of the Denali and headed over to the police sitting outside of the house.

"Sir, you can't come on the property." The man moved to block the large man trying to gain access.

"I'm Special Agent Callen Whitefox, and this is my crime scene," he stated, pulling out his badge. "The team inside is mine, and the woman that owns the house is our Medical Examiner." He simply pointed at Desdemona sitting in the running Denali.

"Sorry sir, I didn't know. I was told to just keep anyone who wasn't supposed to be here off the property. Some bigwig from the FBI West building called my boss, and had us assigned to sit out here until the Agent in charge arrived. I think his name was Blackhawk."

Whitefox grinned. His brother would cringe at being called 'bigwig' and that entertained him. "Thank you so much, Officer. I can't tell you how much it means to me. Can you tell me what happened?" Now he needed all the details before he entered to see the mess.

"We got a call from the alarm company informing us of a breaking and entering at the residence. Apparently, someone went in through a window on the first floor in the office. They made one hell of a mess in there."

"I bet." Callen Whitefox's anger was palpable.

"The good news is, the call came in at two a.m. and we were here by two ten. So, the person or persons didn't have much time to get in there and do too much damage. It is mostly just books thrown all over the place, furniture knocked over and just a mess."

"Great. Thank you for all your help," he shook the officers hand. "I guess you and your partner can head out."

"It's a slow night; we'll sit here in the car and keep an eye on your crew until we get called to something else."

"Thank you so much. If you'll excuse me, I'll go check on the fingerprinting and sweeping," he said, and headed into her house and closed the door behind him. Yeah, the maniac did a number on her things.

"Director Whitefox, how are you?" asked the agent he'd never met before. The woman currently in charge of the scene was watching him with unblinking blue-gray eyes.

Whitefox noticed they bordered on a blue and appeared to see everything. Her red hair was pulled back and she wasn't wearing makeup. The call must have pulled her out of bed. He'd seen Elizabeth look the same during a few early morning calls.

"I've had better wake up calls," he said, and looked down at the badge. "What do we have, Special Agent Christensen?" He scanned the room, and there were ten tech team specialists milling around, gathering evidence.

"We have everyone gathering evidence. The person entered through the Doctor's office window. It was jimmied. From the wet footprints through the house, the intruder tossed this room first."

"You think it was tossed, because they were looking for something?"

Agent Christensen mulled it over. "I definitely think that the perp was looking for something. Let me show you, follow me please." She led him over to the desk. "See that book?" She pointed to an old book under a glass protective box. "That's a first edition William Shakespeare. Othello. A book in that kind of condition is worth my salary for the entire year and then some."

Whitefox stared at the book. "The intruder walked right past it? Maybe our criminal wasn't an avid book collector." He offered up that as an excuse, unsure if his brother and sister-in-law wanted anyone else in on what was going on in Desdemona's life.

"Yeah, and that's not all. Look at the wall behind us. See the doctor's diplomas?"

"Yes."

"On the black market, they're valuable. They are authentic sealed diplomas for Harvard. Know what they would get for those outside this country? Some wannabe doctor in Russia could open

298

his own practice and pretend he was trained here in the US if he had access to one of those beauties."

Whitefox nodded. He already knew the intruder was the stalker and wouldn't want the diplomas. He wanted to terrorize.

"Now, if you come out to the great room, this is the second place I believe the intruder came. The wet floor patterns show that he or she stopped in front of the bookshelf. All the doctors things are all over the floor, the books, her trinkets, and some of them look smashed, like the person stomped all over them. That doesn't scream random break in for me. The person that trashed her things was angry."

"Possibly because the alarm was going off?"

Christensen shrugged. "I checked. It's a high end alarm. It's silent and directs right to the alarm company. If the Doctor hit the button herself it would alert all her neighbors, but with the intruder jimmying the window, it sent it silent."

"Smart alarm."

"Exactly. Our criminal didn't know the cops were coming until they pulled up. The intruders anger was directed at Doctor Adare."

Callen knew that the fact her collectables were destroyed was going to crush her, she loved her odd little things.

"This looks like the intruder had personal knowledge of the doctor. If this was random destruction, and I was the intruder I would have gone for maximum cost. See the couches? Real leather, and with a blade done in three seconds with a few slashes."

She led him to the kitchen. "Doctor Adare, she's an interesting person, but when it comes to inviting in crime," she paused, pointing to the stack of papers sitting on the counter mail basket. "In here are two credit cards, unopened, a bank statement and then all her personal information she wrote in this little book."

Whitefox nodded. Yeah, that was pretty careless. Desdemona was making it easy for the stalker.

"I'm assuming none of it was touched, which again makes me believe that this person was looking for something. Doctor Adare has money, you can tell by her house, her things, and the person who came in here didn't touch a single thing worth value. So, the intruder was either an idiot, or it was someone here with intent."

Whitefox knew the intent. It was to terrify her and make her run. But where? "How about upstairs?"

"That's the funny thing," she led him there. "We found no damage upstairs, but the person did make it there."

Whitefox walked into the woman's bedroom and it felt like her, and then he saw it. On the bed stand was a vase of roses, and on the bed a single red one.

"Maybe someone she's in a relationship with did this, is she sleeping with anyone?" she asked. "He could be the first suspect we need to talk to about this."

Now Whitefox was angry.

"Doctor Adare is sleeping with me, and I can guarantee I didn't leave her red roses. I was on the same assignment, and we left three days ago to work in Red River with both Directors. Ethan and Elizabeth have the list of her past relationships, and he's working that angle already." Agent Christensen was very smart and very good at her job. Just by walking through, she'd come to the conclusion they were all aware of, and he knew evading the truth wouldn't matter. Now he had to trust the woman who was running this assignment.

"Ethan and Elizabeth huh?" Agent Christensen was entertained that the agent was calling the big bosses by their first name. She knew he was new to the division, but that took balls. "Just so you know, if they hear you calling them by their first name, you'll get your ass handed to you by the female one," she grinned at him. "I hear she's a ball buster and eats agents for breakfast regularly. You don't mess with the female of the two."

Whitefox grinned at how funny it was to hear Elizabeth described that way by people outside their circle. "Well, I've been calling Ethan by his name since we were kids and as for Elizabeth, she and I are on a first name basis and have been for a while. In fact, she's very fond of me. You can ask her. Elizabeth is crazy in love with me."

The woman looked at him like he'd lost it.

"Ethan Blackhawk is my brother," he said, laughing.

"Oh, and that makes the ball buster…"

He laughed even more. "My sister-in-law, but Elizabeth is more like a real sister." He saw her bristle. "Just so you know, she's busted my balls plenty, and if she heard you say it she'd agree. So relax, because she's pretty easy going."

Somehow she doubted that. She nodded and made a mental note to tell anyone in her area about this, just in case. "Thanks, anyway, I was told this was your entire scene. What do you want me to do now that you're Agent in charge?"

"Bag anything up you find and take it to FBI West with a rush on it. Then after the sweepers are done, I want a team in to put it all back together again. Or at least get the glass up off the floor."

"Okay, works for me," she answered, walking out of the room. "Really, she's fond of someone?" she inquired incredulously. Elizabeth Blackhawk was an enigma among the agents. She inflicted awe and a little bit of fear. Christensen had seen her on the firing range and watched in amusement, as she outshot her husband and the other males easily.

He laughed, "Yep and I'm pretty fond of her too and the baby."

Agent Christiansen was infinitely grateful she didn't make the spawning comment that she had planned on making. "Where will you be until the team is done?"

"I'm taking her to my brother's place. It's the house right behind this one," he followed her out the door.

"Give me your cell number; I'll call you when it's clear." Christensen took his card he handed her. "Talk to you later," she said, walking away to get the team ready to go from sweep to clean up. It wasn't their typical job, but if it came down from the Directors, they were going to comply and then do it fast.

Agent Christensen looked out the window at the big house behind the Medical Examiners. "Must be lucrative being Directors of the FBI," she muttered, and bundled up before heading back into the cold.

Whitefox went out to the Denali and climbed in, and Desdemona was anxiously waiting for him. Part of him wanted to pull her into his lap and offer her comfort, but he knew techs were milling around and he didn't want to make more of a scene. "Let's get to my brother's house and we'll talk about it," he said, stroking her cheek. "Okay, sweetheart?"

Desdemona nodded, and accepted his hand when he offered it. It gave her some strength just knowing that he was sticking with her. "While you were inside, I emailed Elizabeth the information regarding the two blondes from last night. I completely forgot about them, and didn't know if you told them."

"I didn't, thank you," he said smiling gently. He knew she was trying to take her mind off the entire thing. When he pulled into the driveway, she was inspecting the house. "We're here." Whitefox noticed she was taking in the entire house. "Not what you expected?"

"It looks like a castle, all the stone on the front of the house. It appears less imposing from the back,"

"From what I hear, Ethan picked the house."

Desdemona grinned. "I can believe that. It looks like something he'd like," she said, looking over. "You know, to keep the fair maiden safe from any pillaging armies."

Whitefox never thought about it that way, but it was probably a very accurate evaluation. "When we were growing up, we lived in this tiny cabin," he offered, sharing a part of his past. "We'd dream about what life would be like when we grew up."

"Is this what he thought his life would be?" she asked, curiously-not only about her boss, but the man beside her.

"Ethan always said he'd have the fastest car, the hottest woman and a castle to call his own."

Desdemona grinned. "Then I'm guessing the shiny black Mustang with the chrome is all his, and the bad ass looking jeep is Elizabeth's vehicle."

"Yep."

"It sounds like he got what he wanted. Elizabeth is gorgeous, and this resembles a castle."

Whitefox nodded. "He deserves it." There was still that guilt he felt for betraying his brother those many years ago.

"Hey, you okay?" she asked, touching his arm.

Whitefox shrugged. "I betrayed my brother once, and lost him for almost twenty years. I was just thinking about that," he said, turning off the Denali.

Desdemona wondered what he did, but she wasn't going to ask. If he wanted to share, he would. "How about you, Callen? When you were younger, what did you want when you grew up?"

Whitefox was surprised at her question. He was fully expecting to have to tell her what he did to betray his brother. Not what he wished for as a kid.

"You don't have to tell me."

"I wished for love." And he'd been fortunate too. When his brother returned he found it easily. Once when they reconnected and once with Elizabeth, but he kept it to himself.

It caught her off guard.

"Like I told you about my mom, she wasn't very maternal. I didn't ever have her love. I'm fairly a simple man. I like my cabin. I love my truck. I drink beer out of bottles, and I just wanted love."

Desdemona's heart skipped a beat, and she could feel the pain and see it in his eyes. She leaned forward and kissed him gently on the lips. "I hope you find it," she whispered, and then stroked his cheek, already knowing who he was talking about.

He was pretty sure he was on the right path.

"I hope you do too, Desi," he answered, looking right into her eyes and soul.

Desdemona knew she was already gone. It was just a matter of waiting to see if he caught up or walked away. Never had she felt this safe and protected with anyone, and she'd take that any day over love. The man with her right now was offering her his family and safety and that to her was paramount to the emotion of love.

"I'm ready to go inside."

"We'll crash here until the house is ready, and then we'll stay at my house on the reservation tonight. I think we'll be here a day or so, until we get everything taken care of," he stated, leading her to the door. He unlocked it and stepped in to turn off the alarm.

They hung their coats up on the coat tree, and walked into the house. It was silent and peaceful. Callen was accustomed to being there. He often stayed overnight if they had a family dinner, or if it was a holiday. He, his father, and grandfather all stayed for thanksgiving and Christmas. Being there felt like home, more so than his small cabin on the reservation. Then it occurred to him, maybe she'd hate his home. It was simple, small and essentially a lot like him, a plain man. Callen grew up with very little, as did his brother; he continued to live that way, where his brother went the other way to escape it all.

"It doesn't look like them," Desdemona stated, walking around and looking at the photos. "Elizabeth is tough, and Ethan is very quiet and mysterious. I pictured their home to be colder, and less, accessible."

He understood what she meant. He thought the same thing when he first saw their home.

"This is very warm and inviting," she said. "I love the colors. The red, green and chocolate brown make me feel all cozy. I may have to steal those colors for my house. My walls are sterile white. It's like a family lives here," she said, softly. What she wouldn't give to not be alone in her house, the big empty existence of her life.

"I spend most of my time here," he paused, "or my grandfather's home. When Ethan came back he accepted me into his life, and I was grateful. That's why I have a key- I'm here so much." It was funny. "I'm a permanent fixture here." Whitefox pointed to the recliner that his brother and sister bought him for Christmas and kept here at their house for him. To prove it was his and his alone, Elizabeth had bought him a pillow embroidered with his name on it and some of the tribal colors and symbols that matched the ones tattooed on his and Ethans' bodies.

"If you have your own furniture, I guess you are a fixture." She ran her fingers over the embroidery. "They match your tattoos."

"Yep. This one is the word 'Brothers' in our native language," he said, lifting up his shirt and matching it to the one on his back. "Ethan and I got them one day when granddad told us tattoos should mean something. Nothing means more to me than that."

Desdemona felt her body heat up, and forced herself to not touch the man's body, even though she wanted to run her fingers across the tattoo on his back. Then she saw the heart and everything cooled.

"Elizabeth is hell on details, and the chair and pillow are two of my favorite things in this room. Next would be the pictures."

Desdemona took that as a personal invitation to wander to the book shelf.

She picked up a picture and giggled. "Why is Elizabeth dressed like a pilgrim," and then she got it. The picture was of her standing between both men, and they were each kissing her on the cheek and had their arms wrapped around her waist. She ran her fingers over the words on the bottom of the frame.

Elizabeths' two favorite Indians.

"I thought Indian wasn't a word Elizabeth liked you both to be called," she asked, remembering how she corrected people when they used it around Whitefox and Blackhawk. She'd heard it plenty growing up from her grand'mere.

He thought about how to explain it. "I think it depends on how it's used. When Elizabeth calls us 'Indian', it's never derogatory. For her it's more just pointing out the obvious and being funny and showing propriety. From her it's a term of endearment. When others call us that, or when the deputy did, it was the way he said it that was offensive."

Desdemona wondered if she'd ever be so integral to his life that he'd have a chair in her home and be allowed to use the word as freely as Elizabeth.

Callen took the picture from her hand. He loved it with all his heart; he had the same one on his nightstand, and he looked at it every night. Thanksgiving was their first one together as a family. "We never celebrated Thanksgiving in our entire lives. The whole white man stealing our land thing, but we call it Elizabeth's Turkey bash. She isn't native, and who are we to take her holidays away, even though she's incredibly understanding about it. We don't do it on Thanksgiving Day; we do it on the first weekend of November. There was turkey on one day, and then my grandfather cooked our traditional foods the next day."

"It sounds really nice."

"We played football in the yard. Elizabeth and my dad were one team and we were the other. You'd think a nearly sixty year old man and a girl would lose, but Elizabeth plays dirty."

"Sounds like the perfect day, but the pilgrim outfit?" she asked.

"Elizabeth is probably the only woman on the planet that could pull that off with my grandfather. He's old school and he doesn't like outsiders. But the first day he met her, he fell in love with her, and he thinks her Indian references are entertaining. When she walked into his house dressed like that, it was funny. I think my granddad laughed for about twenty minutes, and then when she proceeded to take her gun out of the pocket and place it on the counter, it was just too much. When it comes to the four of us, she's very protective and very territorial."

"The pilgrim garb is pretty funny."

"The original Indians helped and protected the settlers. I think she decided to wear it as a statement. Payback if you will. The Pilgrim is now protecting the Indians."

It never occurred to her that Elizabeth's little actions were deeper than just humor. "That's pretty deep."

Whitefox nodded, wishing Desdemona didn't keep thinking Elizabeth was anything but intelligent. This was the second time she seemed amazed. "Everyone thinks she's tough and of average intelligence. I think only Ethan, you and I know that she has a degree from Cornell. She likes to come across less intelligent. It helps her control the situation better. People tend to respect people that are more like them, and see them working hard. Once she lets people see who she really is, Elizabeth is amazing."

"She's hard to not like." Yeah, it was easy to see how Callen felt about Elizabeth. Desdemona knew it was territory that she'd have to accept. Just the way the man was talking about her and holding the picture in his hand, she knew that Elizabeth was going to be a constant in his life, and that wasn't going to ever change. She and Elizabeth had the talk, and she wasn't kidding. Callen was hers in more ways than one.

"Every man in my family is in love with her. She's the only female Blackhawk and in our culture the family has a patriarch. My grandfather didn't hand it down to one of us, or even my father. He passed it on to Elizabeth and probably for good reason. I mean any woman who can get an eighty-eight year old man to get her initials tattooed on him is just pure magic."

She wondered if she were to meet the man if he would like her or hate her. Somehow she figured she'd not be accepted like Elizabeth was, because she was just… Elizabeth. Desdemona took a deep breath, trying to not be jealous of the woman that was now her friend. Her ONLY friend, but it was hard.

"We all have that picture. She gave us the frames and picture for Christmas along with some other funny things. Everyone thinks she's bad ass all the time, but that's just a show. Lyzee's pretty soft and gushy inside, and if you're a Blackhawk she's a puddle of love."

She picked up another picture. "Who's this?"

"That's my granddad, Timothy." He loved that picture of his grandfather. "It was taken the night Ethan and Elizabeth remarried on the Rez. He's the shaman, and did the ceremony." He ran his fingers over the picture and smiled. In the picture he was wearing his ceremonial robes, and had his sleeve rolled up showing his tattoo on his arm of Elizabeth's initials.

"Elizabeth told me all the men had the same tattoo," she said, and then looked over. "Sorry, I saw your back and had to ask."

Whitefox didn't know if that was a bad thing or a good thing. He did have another woman's initials on his body and usually a new woman was going to look at it unfavorably.

"Callen, it's okay. I can see that she's important to you." The look on his face was one of worry and nervousness, and she hated to see him suffer. Whether it bothered her or not, it wasn't going to wash off and what's done was done.

"I want to be honest with you right now, before what's going on between us goes further. Elizabeth has half my heart and she always will, Desi. I love my family, Elizabeth included and they matter to me."

She thought about it and then grinned up at him. "I don't have a lot of family, and who am I to try and make you live without the people that matter to you. I can see that you two have something special and unique together and I'm really okay with it. I happen to be fond of Elizabeth myself." Yeah, she was jealous again. But not only because he loved Elizabeth , and because he had an amazing family and she wanted to know what that felt like, to belong. God, all she wanted was a family like that to call her own. The safety appealed to her.

Callen could feel the relief flood through his body. The new woman would be accepting of the other woman. His chest loosened up and he genuinely smiled at her.

"This has to be your father. He's really handsome, and I see where you and Ethan get it from," she continued, picking up another picture and changing the subject. "It's funny, you look at Timothy and can see what your dad will look like eventually, and you can look at your dad and see what you and your brother will look like, well mostly Ethan," she said. The man in the picture had dark black hair, like the wings of a raven, and his eyes matched and were pure black. Ethan Blackhawk was going to be handsome even into his later years, but then again all the men in the family were attractive.

"Yeah, I look more like my mother's side of the family, or so I'm told. I've only met my maternal grandmother once and then she died and my mother followed." He kept the pain from his voice. "I only have my granddad, dad, Ethan and Elizabeth."

She knew how that felt. "I only have my sister Cordelia and my grand'mere, so I completely understand."

He led her to the couch. "You look exhausted. Why don't you lie down, and I'll make you some coffee, and something to eat."

When he tucked her into the couch, and covered her with a throw, she smiled at him. "Thank you," she accepted his gentle kiss, and then watched him walk away. She could see him moving around the kitchen, and when he put on an apron with flowers all over it she laughed.

"Are you laughing at me, Desdemona?"

"I am Callen, because of the apron and the fact you look lost in the kitchen. Do you need my help?" she asked.

"No, but if you want to come watch me destroy Elizabeth's kitchen, feel free. She's been teaching me to cook, and I don't know if I'm just a lost cause, because I really don't have to practice. She takes over when I start destroying everything around me."

"So cooking lessons and your own chair? Do you have your own bedroom here too," she asked, laughing.

"Yes."

Oh boy, he did practically live here.

308

Desdemona went into the kitchen and took the cup of coffee he offered her. "Why the apron?" She couldn't help but laugh. Here was this big sexy Native man wearing a gun and a flowered apron.

"He pointed up at the sign above the kitchen window. "I made the mistake of having my father carve it for her for Christmas and now it's law," he said smiling.

Desdemona read it.

'Lyzee's kitchen- Lyzees' rules'.

"You three are really close." It wasn't a question, just an observation. Yeah, he'd said it a few times, but the man donned an apron in Elizabeth's kitchen, and that said it all.

"Ethan's my blood. I'd die for him. Elizabeth and I just clicked from day one. Some people just wiggle their way into your life and stay there forever," he said honestly. If he was going to try and start something meaningful with this woman, she deserved the truth. "I'd do anything for her," he paused. "Three musketeers."

"Ahhh a literary reference. That I completely get," she said, winking. She wanted to remind them that they didn't have relationship. One night of sex wasn't a relationship or anywhere close to one, but why ruin the mood because she was dwelling on that one important fact.

"I'm very close to my family, and anyone that I having a relationship with should be aware of that and be able to accept it. I won't decide between them and love." Maybe he told her that as a warning, and maybe he told her to see how she'd respond. As he cracked an egg into a bowl he glanced over at her. "They're my foundation and I want the woman I date to be part of it."

Her heart started pounding in her chest. Just the idea of them having a relationship made her a nervous wreck. She wanted it more than anything. Just being near him gave her a sense of peace and she'd fallen in love with him. "Are you directing that at me, Callen? Are we having a relationship?" Now she held her breath and she only hoped he'd answer before she turned blue and fell backwards off her chair.

"I think we're already having one, unless for some reason you're not interested in starting one with me." He watched her face, first came the fear and then the calm that followed and he had to take it as a good sign.

"What about your grandfather?" she asked, he mentioned he didn't like outsiders.

"I wouldn't worry," he answered, smiling. The smile was a complcte front. Right now he needed to listen to his brother and pray his sister-in-law had the magic touch once more. Right now he was placing all his faith in her and laying it at her feet. The ball wasn't in his court anymore; it all came down to exactly how much influence Elizabeth had over their granddad.

"Sure you don't need my help?" she evaded.

Callen walked around the counter and lifted her chin in his fingers. "Answer me, Desdemona. Are you interested in being in a relationship with me?" Now he pushed harder.

Desdemona's breath caught in her throat. "I'm interested in beginning one."

Whitefox grinned, and brought his lips down to hers, possessively. The kiss was slow, deep and showed ownership. Callen was thinking about the next step in the plan. Finally he'd gotten her to agree to the first step and that was huge. She didn't bolt. Now he was going to lock her down and insure she never had the chance to run away. This would work. It had to work. He found he was desperate to achieve his goal. He may not get another chance to mimic what his brother had found.

Desdemona broke the kiss, and found herself pressed against his body and trapped. "I think I like the way this relationship is starting," she said, softly.

"You haven't seen anything yet."

Whitefox began planning their first date re-do, and he knew just what he was going to do. Elizabeth said do something special and he knew what would impress her.

"I can't wait," she answered, accepting another kiss and for a brief moment allowing herself to forget what was happening at her house across the back yard. Callen was good at making her forget.

Now she hoped he was just as good at keeping himself safe.

Elizabeth read the rest of the tech reports and looked up at her husband; he was reading something on his smartphone. "What's up?"

"Callen just got to our house. The alarms been deactivated," he said, putting his phone down. "At least they got there safe."

"Desdemona sent us an email," she replied opening it, reading it, and then passing it to her husband. "It seems they found two very angry blondes last night."

"Well what do you know. Looks like the Sheriff knows one of them personally. Maybe when we head into the station we should start there," he said grinning, and then he stopped when he noticed she wasn't smiling or listening to a word he was saying. In fact, she had the work look on her face. "What did you just figure out?"

"Something's been bothering me about the victims, and it's been nagging the crap out of me, but until now, I didn't figure it out."

He leaned forward and she had his full attention. His wife was really good at picking up the tiny details that usually solved the assignment. If it was bothering her, then it had to be important. Sometimes he wished he had her skill, and would swap the profiling job any day. It was incredibly stressful, but then again, so was having an entire assignment resting on her figuring it all out.

"What is it, baby?" he asked.

"We have five original victims, right?"

"Yes."

"We know all of them aren't from around here, so here's what's bugging me. Where are all the cars they were driving?"

This was one reason why he loved her. He hadn't even thought about that, and she picked it up. As a team, he was the definite lucky one to be her partner.

"If we figure that out, then maybe we can sweep the vehicles and find more evidence, and that may lead us to the killer."

"I think we need to discuss that with the Sheriff too, when we head into the office." Blackhawk stared at his wife and felt the overwhelming need to hold her. "Come here, Mrs. Blackhawk," he pulled her into his lap and kissed her long and slow. "Have I ever told you that I think your mind is incredibly sexy?"

"You've mentioned it a few times, but I think you're bullshitting me and thinking about my ass most of the time."

Blackhawk snickered at her blatant honesty. "Yeah, I am," he answered, and then kissed her some more, enjoying the taste of his wife before work.

Elizabeth felt her husband's body coming alive as his hands wandered her body and his mouth took all he wanted. "Mr. Blackhawk!"

"I can't help it, a smart woman who wears trashy lingerie is such a turn on," he stated swinging her up in his arms. They had a few minutes before work and he planned on showing her just how appreciative he was of her mind, her very fine posterior and the incredibly sexy lingerie.

He stood outside her home, holding her hand and preparing her for what may or may not lay waiting for them inside. He'd received the call from Special Agent Christensen, and she'd told him it was clear of techs and clean-up crew. Now he just had to trust that Desdemona wasn't going to get any nasty surprises.

"You don't have to do this, Desi. I can handle it."

"No, I have to do it, Callen," she said, squeezing his hand. "How'd he get in?" she asked. If she could she'd pack up and run away from the house, but she owned it. It was hers. It was home and because of it she now had ties with people too. If she ran she'd lose Callen and her new girlfriend.

Her **ONLY** girlfriend.

Desdemona could live without love, she had for such a long time, but she finally had a best girlfriend and that was an amazing feeling.

"Your office window," he answered, leading her into the foyer. Everything was righted back into its place and nothing was lying in their path. Score one for the tech team and clean-up crew. "Most of the damage was in there," he said, and noticed she looked horrified.

She dropped his hand and rushed to her office. Her heart pounded that her single-most important treasure had been destroyed. "I only have one thing in there that matters," she yelled over her shoulder to Whitefox.

He assumed it was the book. When she walked right past it to the book shelf, she burst into tears and dropped into the arm chair beside the bookcase and just began sobbing. "Sweetheart," he rushed to her and sat beside her. "What isn't here?" he asked, looking around.

"I had only one picture of my mother," she said between sobs. "It was her, me and my sister." He picked her up in his arms and carried her to the desk chair and sat with her in his arms until she stopped sobbing. "Honey, we'll look for it, maybe the tech team misplaced it. The entire room was tossed."

She listened to his reassuring words and the tears slowed and eventually stopped. "Okay," she whispered, believing that he'd tell her the truth and they'd find it.

His heart was breaking for her, and he wiped her tears, and offered her kisses to soothe the hurt, like she was a lost child. Slow kisses that drew her attention and made her focus on him and nothing more. Once he knew she was thinking about him, he deepened them, holding her mouth to his, refusing to let her pull away until he believed she was forgetting about everything around them. His own body suffered at the closeness and the way she felt sitting across his lap. He prayed for control and patience as he soothed her body and tormented his own, unmercifully. When he finally broke away her eyes weren't filled with tears, but hazed with heat and lust.

"Better?" he inquired, his voice barely there.

"Yes," she whispered, and licked her lips. They tasted like him and it kept her thinking about the man she was currently resting against.

Whitefox needed to think about anything else but the woman sitting across his body, or they were going to be clearing the desk and copulating right there. He prayed again for control, and then realized this was probably his karma for not being a saint for all those years and lusting after his brother's wife.

"At least your book is safe." Whitefox threw it out there, drawing her attention to the book.

"Yes," then she cocked her head, and looked confused. "Did the team put it on my desk?"

Now he was confused. When he toured the house with Agent Christensen, he was sure it was on the desk. They wouldn't have put it there. "It was there when I entered the house. Why? Where was it?"

She turned in his lap, and faced the book and the box. "It was beside the picture on my shelf. I bought that book a few years ago. It was an impulse buy."

"Sweetheart, a candy bar is an impulse buy. A hundred thousand dollar book is an investment," he laughed, and tried to cheer her up. "I hope you have insurance on it."

"I do," she answered, pulling open her desk and removing a trace kit she kept as a spare. Out she pulled gloves and she carefully lifted the glass lid to the box. "I don't ever touch this book. It's too rare and valuable. Oils and dirt on fingers would degrade the value." Now she noticed it was crooked on the little holder. "Someone touched the actual book."

Now he looked alarmed.

Slowly Desdemona opened the book, and inside was the picture of her mother, her and her sister. A sigh slipped past her lips. Then she turned it over, in her gloved hand, and there in angry red words were the warning.

COME HOME OR
I'LL KILL ANYONE YOU LOVE.

Desdemona dropped the picture and stood from Callen's lap. The stalker was now willing to hurt anyone she became attached to, and there was only one person she loved.

"You have to get as far away from me as possible," she whispered and rushed from the room. She felt sick to her stomach that she could be the reason the man she had fallen for would be pulled into his mess.

Whitefox watched hurry away from him. He read the message over and over. Part of him was worried that the lunatic was going to scare her away, and the other part of her was thrilled that she was worried about him. That meant one thing. She did have feelings for him, and he may have a chance with the woman. As for her going home, he was inclined to keep her there with him

314

permanently. If the killer wanted her there they were going to do the exact opposite.

Desdemona wasn't going back to the bayou.

EVER! At this point in the game he was going to forbid it.

The Team of Blackhawk and Blackhawk sat in the Sheriff's office and worked on getting as much information out of the man as possible. When they arrived in Red River, they had offered to allow the Sheriff in on the investigation, giving him the option to be part of the team. To their surprise, he told them to just handle it and update him when need be. That was relatively surprising, most law officials saw the FBI as a horde taking away control, but the Sheriff, he didn't want anything to do with it.

It was odd.

It was off-settling.

And frankly it pissed off Elizabeth Blackhawk to no end.

She'd been a Sheriff, and she knew what it felt like for the FBI to roll into town, and there was no way in hell she would have given over control of her town. Not even on a bad day. Every time she thought about it, it made her want to shake the man and see what fell out of his head.

Sitting there and listening to her husband update the man, she really was at a loss, and it took a great deal to render her speechless, and she was battling with herself for composure.

"I'm sorry, I have to interrupt. Sheriff, forgive me for being so blunt, but why the hell do you just look bored out of your mind when we come to update you?"

Blackhawk should have known it was coming. His wife was like a bloodhound and anyone that wasn't sucked in by the curiosity of the entire situation had to be a few bricks short of a wall in her book.

"I don't know what you mean."

Her husband gave her the look. It pretty much said 'don't piss off the locals-too much'.

"You just don't seem to care what happens to your town, or for your own well-being. Last night you were at a bar, getting cozy with a blonde. Were you not?"

Sheriff Duffy shrugged. "The FBI is good at taking care of these things, and I'm not. I'm fairly laid back, Director Blackhawk. Why get in your way. As for the blonde that was just Carly Kester. She owns the local book store. We hang out all the time, if you know what I mean."

Blackhawk jumped in before his wife slapped some sense into the man. "You are aware that there's a blonde woman killing men and leaving their bodies in your town. Right?"

"I do believe you told me that the other day."

Elizabeth just shook her head in disbelief. This man was a lost cause and she needed to take a new tact. "Okay, what do you know about Carly Kester?" Maybe that route would get them more information. Apparently, self-preservation didn't matter to the man.

"Carly is plenty of fun. I don't think she's seeing any one man specifically." He leaned back in his chair waiting for the FBI agents to get his meaning. When neither spoke he elaborated. "She gets around and just likes a good time."

"And you frequent her company?" asked Elizabeth.

"I do off and on. Carly is like a good pair of shoes. You don't wear them every day, but sometimes you miss them and try them on a few days in a row."

Blackhawk spoke fast. His wife was vibrating in her seat over the man's choice of descriptive endearments for a woman. Maybe it was a very good thing that the Sheriff had very little interaction with the team. He might be strangled by a pregnant woman in a rush of hormones. "Who else does she 'frequent'?" Blackhawk could see his wife getting ready to pounce.

"Well, I believe she and Bobby Lee had a few one night stands."

Elizabeth actually smacked herself in the forehead and laughed. Here was a sheriff, his deputy killed by a blonde nutjob, and here he had just had a relationship with the woman. "In most investigative circles, we'd call Carly a suspect."

He laughed. "Agent Blackhawk, I grew up with Carly. We've been hooking up since we were sixteen years old. I know she's not a killer. Carly is opportunistic, a man collector and possibly a nymphomaniac, but what she isn't is a killer."

316

Ethan knew it was a dead end. So he changed the subject before his wife had a stroke. "Here's a new topic. Has anyone reported any abandoned vehicles? The victims weren't from Red River, so that means they had to drive or be driven. Did anyone see any?"

Sheriff James Duffy thought about it. "If there were any vehicles left on the roadside or in private parking lots, they'd be towed to the impound lot."

"How long would they be held for?"

"That I can't tell you, you'd have to swing on over to the impound lot and ask for Randy. He's my brother, so he'll help you out, if you ask nice." He directed that right at Elizabeth.

Blackhawk patted her on the leg. "Do you know anything about a Courtney Brewer?" he inquired. "It seems that she had a domestic squabble in the middle of a restaurant last night."

"She's had it tough since her husband took off with his secretary. Courtney loved him to death, and then one day she just found the truth out. He loved dicking around with a younger employee." He leaned forward. "It makes you think to not hire younger secretaries," he added, laughing.

"I have a younger secretary," interjected Blackhawk, grinning at his wife. "I'm quite attached to my wife and wouldn't dream of cheating on her," he added, reassuringly.

"What a coincidence," added Elizabeth grinning back at him and not missing a beat. "I seem to have my own younger Administrative assistant, and he's native." She started laughing at the look on her husband's face. The fact she had Native eye candy in the office and it wasn't him drove him nuts. Why tell him the young man did nothing for her, when she could make him completely insane over it.

James Duffy had no idea what they were going on about and decided the agents had lost their minds.

"If you wouldn't mind, Sheriff, can you tell your brother we'll be swinging by?" he asked, trying to ignore the need to kill his wife's new administrative assistant. He knew her hiring a native admin was going to be a problem from the day she mentioned it. Then and there he should have crushed it.

"Sure will, Agent Blackhawk."

Elizabeth and her husband walked out to the Denali. "We have a few blondes to look at now at least."

"Good job on not being too insulting in there, Elizabeth." He laughed and took her hand, so she wouldn't slide on the snow. Fortunately she had the fortitude to wear snow boots, and not her cowboy boots.

"Ethan, if I seriously ever lose my mental capacities to that extent. Put me down with my own damn gun. Don't let me wander around making a jackass of myself."

Blackhawk grinned at her. "Yes dear and just so you're aware; when I get back to FBI West I'm putting down your native administrative assistant just for shits and giggles."

Elizabeth burst into laughter and almost pulled them both down into a snow bank laughing so hard.

So much for Native eye candy.

~ Chapter Thirteen ~

When Whitefox found her, she was sitting on her bed, and looking at the vase of roses. There was no emotion on her face, but the pallor on her face said it all. When he first met her, she was skittish, and if this didn't exacerbate the situation, he didn't know what would.

"Sweetheart, are you going to be okay?"

"I don't think I can ever stay here alone again, and I obviously can't go back home."

The look on her face showed fear and he was glad. This was serious and she needed to realize that. "We'll fix this together, I promise. I won't leave you alone."

"What about when the assignments over, Callen? Then what?"

"You can stay with me on the Rez if that's what you want to do. Or I'll move in here until we find who's doing this." They were in a relationship, and he'd protect her too. Elizabeth couldn't do it alone, and the woman before him made him want to care for her like she was a wounded child.

"You need to get far away from me. As long as I stay alone, no one will get hurt. I can handle the stalking as long as you're not going to get hurt."

He laughed. "Not happening. What happens when the stalker escalates to beyond just watching from afar? When you refuse to go back to the bayou and it intensifies?"

Desdemona looked at him with tears in her eyes. "Please Callen. Just go away. You and your family are going to get hurt if you try to help me or stay with me."

It wasn't happening and he didn't care what she said. He'd sleep in a tent in her back yard. Okay, he's sleep in his brother's house in her back yard, but he's stick regardless. Callen went to her, grabbed her by the arms and pulled her up to look him in the face. "I'm not running, and neither are you. There's safety in numbers and we're sticking together. Are we clear on that?"

Desdemona nodded.

"Under no circumstances are you to ever return to the bayou. Ever! Do you understand me Desi?" he demanded. "Promise me!" Her bottom lip quivered, and he felt terrible that he raised his voice to her.

But she promised, and held out her pinky. "I promise and I won't break it."

"Oh honey," he pulled her against his body, kissing the top of her head, as he took her offered pinky. "You're safe; I won't let anyone hurt you." Her arms were wrapped around his body tightly, and he could feel her shaking. "Desi, my family will keep you safe. You have nothing to worry about."

Desdemona clung like a scared child.

"Let's go to my place."

She nodded. "Okay. I can't be here anymore."

Callen led her to the closet, and pulled down a second suitcase. He needed to get her out of there as soon as possible. Desdemona was scared and he couldn't blame her at all. "Okay, Desi. Let's pack a big suitcase and you won't have to come back here for a while."

She released her grasp on him and walked towards the bathroom, grabbing hair supplies and other girl products. Desdemona reached into her medicine cabinet, pulling out everything she needed. The sooner she was out of the house, the better.

Callen began grabbing clothes from her closet. The only closet he'd ever seen with more clothes in it, had been is brother's massive collection of apparel. This reminded him of his- a great deal of black clothing and arranged to death.

"You're going to have to help me, Desi. I've never packed for a woman before." And he hadn't. Most women in his life were temporary. Like his mother, his grandmother, all the nameless ones he woke up beside. There were only two he cared to remember, and Elizabeth never needed his help packing clothes. If she did, it would be easy. Elizabeth liked to keep it simple like him. Jeans were the foundation of their wardrobes.

"Okay, I'll take over. I think I'm okay now. Can you throw the roses away? Shove them down the garbage disposal? I don't want them in my house."

"Absolutely," he grabbed the flowers, and left the room.

Desdemona continued packing as quickly as she could, grabbing bras, panties and even some perfume. Just in case. She was still throwing clothing into the suitcase when he returned.

"The deed is done; those flowers are nothing but pulp now."

"Thank you, Callen."

When she tried to lift the suitcase he laughed. "I'll get that sweetheart," he picked it up easily and grabbed her overnight case too. "Anything else you need me to carry?" he asked grinning wickedly.

"I could use a piggy back ride," she quipped, sarcastically, then laughed when he crouched down for her to get on his back. "I was only kidding because you were being all cave man."

"Come on, what is there to be afraid of now?" he asked, grinning.

"Oh, that you'll drop me on my head, and that I'll hemorrhage and forget how to do my job or that you'll fall on me and I'll bleed to death internally."

Whitefox laughed. "You've obviously over thought it. It's a piggy back ride. Elizabeth jumps on all the time and she weighs more than you. Stop being scared and making excuses instead of just jumping in and doing it without thinking first."

Screw it; what did she have to lose? If Elizabeth did it, so could she! Desdemona jumped up on his back and was laughing as he balanced her suitcase, her overnight bag, and her. As she looked over at her bedroom mirror, they looked silly. Like a small child getting a ride on some male's back.

"What do I get if I make it all the way to the car?" Whitefox inquired.

"A kiss," she offered back, trying to get the image and the irony out of her mind.

"Deal!" And he hustled down the stairs to the front door, where she whispered the code in his ear. After setting the alarm, he navigated the front walk through the snow and then dropped her to her feet beside the door of the Denali. Tossing her bags in the trunk, he returned to her side. "Well, pay up," he stated victoriously. "I'm not even winded."

Desdemona loved the sparkle in his eye. When she was around him she forgot all the things that scared her. He just had

321

that effect on her. This man just made her feel safe and like she was enveloped in his family. "I always pay up." She opened the vehicle door, and stepped up onto the running board, so she'd be even with his face, and she leaned into the kiss. It started tentative, and when she slid her fingers into the loose ponytail at the back of his neck she deepened the kiss, tasting him, enjoying him and forgetting everything around them. She forgot the snow, and the cold, and all she felt was him, and his mouth locked to hers.

His hands slid up under her jacket, and pressed her to his body, as her mouth did really creative things with his. Already his body was getting warm, and every muscle in his frame was going taut at the idea of what he'd like to do at that moment. It involved carrying her back up the sidewalk, into the house and right to her bed. Slowly, he felt her breaking away from kissing him.

"Good enough, Callen?" she asked, feeling lightheaded. There was no way she could beat that, kiss. Never had she kissed a man like that before, and she wasn't shocked he brought it out in her. Callen Whitefox brought out everything in her. "Winded yet?"

He grinned but didn't answer her. It was time to claim his plan for the night. "I want my re-do date today."

He caught her off guard. "Oh, okay."

"It's going to be something you never experienced before." She laughed. "Now I'm scared shitless."

Whitefox put his hand on the top of her head and ducked her into the passenger seat. "Just don't worry about it. I promise it will be the most exciting time of your life."

"Really? Because I grew up on the bayou, and would swim in crocodile infested waters for fun on the weekends."

He looked over at her and lifted an eyebrow. "I said most exciting time of your life. Not careless, reckless and most likely to get you eaten," he winked at her. "There's a huge difference there, although you are delicious."

Desdemona did something even more reckless, more dangerous, and completely unlike her. She made the first move by reaching over and taking his hand in hers. His fingers closed protectively around hers, again the image of her on his back popped into her mind. When he didn't twine their fingers together like he did continually with Elizabeth, she had to fight down the disappointment and jealousy. Once again, Elizabeth reared her gorgeous head in their private moment. *DAMN HER!* Desdemona forced herself to let it go, because he already warned her that his family was part of his life. They shared a bond that she and Callen didn't, and it pissed her off.

Callen felt her hand tense, as she adverted her gaze from him and their joined hands. "What are you thinking about?"

"I'm ready to be impressed by your date plans, Special Agent Whitefox." Breathing out she began channeling her inner Morticia. She could do this!

Whitefox looked down at their joined hands and wondered what he did wrong now…

Thursday Mid-morning

When they pulled up to the impound yard, there was a man waiting for them, and he looked very similar to his brother, just without the uniform. He was leaning against the fence and finishing up the tail end of a smoke.

"Hey, you both must be the Feds. My brother called to tell me you were coming, let me just finish this smoke up, and we can go on in to my office," he said, smiling at Elizabeth.

"Take your time, Randy. It is Randy, right?" asked Blackhawk, observing the man. He favored his brother in the looks department. They both had the same sandy hair and blue eyes.

"Yes, sir. Jimmy was named after my grandfather and me, well I'm named after my dad." He flicked the butt into the snow.

The two agents followed him into the building, where his office was housed. "Can I get you both some coffee?" he asked, looking over at Blackhawk.

"No thanks."

Elizabeth unzipped her parka, and the man was staring right at her belly. "Is something wrong?" she asked.

"No ma'am, I was just thinking about smoking in front of you and I hope I was far enough away. I've read stories on women and second hand smoke, that's all."

Elizabeth smiled. "I was downwind of the drift, no worries, Randy." It was nice that he was concerned about the smoke. At least he wasn't pointing out the obvious that she was pregnant.

He nodded and sat. "Now Jimmy said you had questions on cars I may have impounded?"

"Yes, we think that they may be linked to the dead victims we found up at the boy scout camp. So I'm going to need the last six month worth of impounds."

"Oh well, if that's all you need, I can print it right out for you Agents." Randy clicked a few keys on his computer and the paper began printing. "This I can give you, but if you want to see the vehicles, then we have a problem."

"What would that problem be, Randy?" asked Elizabeth.

"After three months, if the owner doesn't pick up, we retain rights and sell them at auction."

"It's okay, we really just need to ID the rest of the victims, and this will make it a little easier."

Randy handed them the paper. "I hope this helps. Is there anything else I can help you with or do for you?"

"How many people do the towing?" Blackhawk was looking at the paper and he saw all the victims' names they had already identified. He was willing to bet the rest were on the list. Since there were a total of twenty names he gave them, pulling up their picture ID and running it against missing persons reports should be easy.

"Just myself during the day and then one guy I have specifically for nights. Jeffrey Teller. Real good guy, I hope you don't think he had something to do with this," he looked concerned for his employee. "We're a small town. We don't get real busy here. Most of the calls we get are people breaking down on the roadside or outside of town."

"No, we're looking for a woman," added Elizabeth. But they both knew the woman could have an accomplice.

"Oh, well that's good," then he paused. "I didn't mean it to sound like I was glad there was a killer running around, so beg my pardon Agents."

Blackhawk nodded. "Not a problem, Randy. Thanks for the information." He shook the man's hand.

"If I get anymore impounds that are abandoned, should I bring them by the Sheriff's office first?"

Elizabeth shook his hand. "Just give us a call and we can come to you." Out came the card with her contact information, and she offered it to the man.

"Okay."

Both Blackhawks left the building, and outside Elizabeth spoke. "How's the list look?"

"We have our victims on here, this is going to get the rest, I'd bet lunch on it."

Elizabeth grinned. "I tell you what, Cowboy. I'll buy you lunch and you can buy me dinner."

"Deal."

Whitefox was getting nervous. Never in his life had he brought a woman home sober, and with the intent of keeping her in his house for more than some sweaty quick sex. Usually it was get drunk, pick a woman, bring her home, and hope she had the common sense to be gone when he woke up. Like his brother, there'd been a string of regrettable women in his life, and now he believed he found the one he needed to work on keeping.

It wasn't like he wanted that kind of relationship with women. He just didn't know how to relate to them. The only experience he had was what he saw growing up, and his mother was a pretty shitty example. Now he was watching his brother with Elizabeth and trying to learn on the fly.

Growing up impoverished, he and Ethan had been challenged early in life. They joked about the Rez now, but it wasn't funny as a child. In fact it was hard to swallow when he thought back to it. Their grandfather did the best he could, even when his mom would choose partying over working for a living. So, things in his life weren't elaborate even today. Granddad gave them stability, food, and clothing. The rest they had to work for, or 'appropriate' creatively. Now that he was bringing Desdemona to his home after just being in hers, he felt a little uneasy about what she'd think about it. As he pulled up to the house, his truck was in place, and everything looked exactly as it did as he left three days ago.

"We're here," he said, putting the Denali into park. "It's not as big as your home, but it's all mine." Whitefox tried to reassure himself, hoping it wouldn't be a huge disappointment to the woman sitting beside him.

Desdemona released his hand and hopped out of the Denali, she began wandering towards the house just taking it all in. There were trees surrounding it, tall trees that had been alive for many years. There was a porch, that sat facing them, and she wished she had the seclusion of trees around her home. When you grew up surrounded by nature, you missed it when it was replaced with concrete.

Whitefox quickly grabbed her suitcase and rushed after her.

Desdemona walked up onto the porch, and there was a table made out of wood, and she wished it wasn't winter. It would be the perfect place to just sit and enjoy the silence. All in all, she'd trade her house for his log cabin any day.

"Did you build it?" she asked, running her hands over the table and then leaning against the rail of the porch.

"I didn't build the house, my granddad had it built for me. When Ethan left the Rez and went off to the FBI, he sent granddad money to upkeep his home, and when there was more money than he needed, he built me mine. So I guess technically it's Ethan's house, but he wouldn't ever live on the rez, unless it was by gunpoint or the last safe place on earth."

"I think I'd live here in a heartbeat. I love the trees and the silence. It just feels safe and secure. You can think here," she said, watching him. "Why do you have that look on your face? Did I say something bad?"

His first instinct was to lie and cover the look, but he tried for something new with a woman. The truth. "I just wondered what you'd think of my home. Yours is very different."

"I like yours better. Want to trade?" she laughed. "Mine comes with a stalker- free of charge as an added bonus."

Whitefox laughed. "Yeah, we can trade but we better get you a tan so you blend in, you don't exactly scream Native American." He held out his hand for her. "Come on, I'll get you inside. It's cold out here." Whitefox unlocked the door and dropped her suitcase beside the wall and held the door open for her. Then it occurred to him, he was bringing a vegetarian who dealt with death into a house with deer heads, animal skins and… crap.

"Uh Desi, it didn't occur to me until now that there's animal heads on my wall."

"You mean someone snuck in and hung them there while you were gone?" she asked, laughing at him. "You should call the police and tell them there's a random serial decorator in your neighborhood."

That caught him off guard. "I mean," Whitefox actually blushed and continued, "You don't eat meat and here you have animals I hunted and ate, watching you."

She walked into his living space and like his brothers it was warm. It had lots of native American colors, patterns and yes, there were the animals. "Callen, I don't mind that they're there. You ate them; they didn't die just to be a trophy. People have to eat. I don't eat meat because of the job I do. Before I was an ME I did like meat. I still will eat seafood if need be."

He relaxed.

"Is that bear skin?" She pointed at the rug under his coffee table.

"Uh yes." He cringed as she walked over and knelt down to run her fingers over the fur. "I always wondered what one would feel like," she asked smiling. "You can't touch the one in the zoo. Apparently when they post the sign 'don't feed the bears' they mean it."

Her smile was enormous, contagious, and she was funny when they were alone.

"It's a little different when you've seen him running at you and you're his next snack, I guess. I didn't really think 'oh let me pet him'. I was thinking more 'don't get eaten by the big angry bear'," he laughed, as she wandered around his room. When she stopped at his wall with shotguns on it, he was curious to see what she'd do.

"May I?" she asked, before touching it.

He walked over and pulled the shot gun down for her.

Desdemona was accustomed to shotguns, the one her grand'mere had was similar. She popped it open to see if it was loaded. "Loaded gun on the wall, Callen?" Desdemona grinned up at him. "Living dangerously huh?"

His heart skipped a beat as he watched the sight before him. Here was this little woman, holding his shotgun and actually looking like she knew how to use one. "Are you familiar?" he asked, watching to make sure she didn't accidentally shoot him or her.

"I'm a better with a shotgun than a handgun, believe it or not," she smiled. "I'm a decent shot," she added.

This intrigued him. "Really?"

"You doubt me?" she inquired, laughing. "Do I need to prove it to you?" She loved a challenge. In medical school when the male students doubted her, it made her work that much harder.

"Well if you must you must." The good ole' boy grin said it all. Whitefox wandered to his fridge, grabbing a six pack of beer and six sodas in cans. "Ammo is on the shelf, join me outside."

Desdemona was laughing. "I hope we aren't shooting at the beer, that just seems like a horrible waste if alcohol."

"That's for drinking, the soda is for shooting. When we Blackhawk's target shoot, we like to live on the edge and mix beer into the situation. We're crazy like that." Now he was laughing too. "It's not much fun with Elizabeth being pregnant. She wins all the time when Ethan and I get drunk. Then again, she can outshoot me sober, so I guess it doesn't really matter."

She followed him out, and they both stood on the porch.

"I'll set them up. You just don't point that at me until I'm back." He ran off through the snow and set the cans up on a log he and his brother had just used a few weeks ago. "Okay," he trotted back. "Let the shooting begin!"

Desdemona grinned up at him. "You give your first dates loaded guns all the time?"

"No way! I usually don't know their names. I sure as hell don't want them to have a gun." He laughed and blushed that he actually said it out loud.

"Callen, relax and don't screw up the date. You don't get a re-do on a re-do," she laughed. "It would be the date that never ends!"

"The **official** date hasn't begun yet, but thanks for the warning." Being around her was easy. When she smiled at him, actually found himself grinning back. "Okay, six cans, you have two shots per load. First two cans are yours. If you miss, I get whatever I want."

She laughed. "Yeah, well I bet it's going to be sex related. I'm betting that's not the wager when it's you, Ethan and Elizabeth."

Callen's body clenched at the idea of that being the prize. He wished many a night it had been. "No, we go hardcore and shoot for cash, but for you the ante is sex." He winked at her.

"Okay, if I get them both?"

"Then I have to make the next two, or you get what you want?"

She thought about it. "You're going to go vegetarian for an entire week."

He looked appalled. "Seriously? That's a hardcore bet."

Desdemona sat on the rail of the porch and cracked open a beer, taking a long sip. "Hell yeah, Special Agent Whitefox. You aren't going to touch meat for a full week. I sincerely hope you like salad."

Callen was grinning like an idiot. "I've been hunting since I was ten. You are going to be putting out, Desdemona. On the first date too," he snickered and cracked open his own beer.

"That goes to show you. I already put out and wasn't even dating you," she answered, laughing.

Whitefox opened his mouth and then just started laughing. She had a point and anything he could say might be construed the wrong way. Again, zipping it to preserve the first date re-do.

"Callen, are you sure you want to do this?" she wanted to warn him and give him a shot to back out. "A full week without meat is a long time for a carnivore."

"No way, I'm looking forward to making you put out again, but this time naked on the bear rug." The idea drove him wild. Pale delicious Desdemona naked on the bearskin he hunted down. It made him feel like a caveman and primitive.

When she finished her beer, she placed the can on the table beside her and hopped down. If she lost the bet, she'd willingly have sex with him in a snow bank, who was she kidding? The man was sexy and he made her all warm and wild. But he didn't need to know that, and watching him eat salad for a week was going to be priceless.

Desdemona took the gun from him, and closed it. Aimed at one of the two cans in the middle, and took her first shot. It exploded and left a spray of brown all over the white snow. She looked over at him and grinned. "Lettuce, carrots and peppers-oh my."

IIc laughed and finished his beer, opening two more. It was funny that some outsider doctor was challenging a native in shooting. "One more shot, Desi. Don't miss, or you're going to be on top." He tried to rattle her, and hoped he did. Picturing her riding him was so erotic he felt his body tighten.

She aimed, and pulled the trigger. The second can exploded, like the first and flew through the air. "I don't miss, Callen." Desdemona opened the gun, popped out the cartridges in one fluid motion and took the two in his hand. "Your turn." Desdemona exchanged places with him, and couldn't help but watch his form. He was incredibly sexy, and she couldn't wait to climb all over him.

"What are you thinking about," he asked, as he took his first shot. The can exploded and fell off the log.

Desi waited for the right moment. "Thinking about being on top and enjoying the ride," she said innocently, just as he aimed and fired.

It missed the can and hit just below on the log.

Whitefox looked over fast. Unsure if she was teasing him to screw with him, or if she was completely serious. If she was serious, he didn't mind losing to her. It meant he'd still get the prize. The look on his face must have given him away.

"Very serious," she answered, and his reaction was priceless. Desdemona walked over, taking the gun from his hand. Standing really close to him, and ran her hand up the front of his body. Even with a jacket on, she could feel that Callen Whitefox was well defined.

"Don't tease, Desi," he stated, earnestly. He had their first date planned and sex was on the menu, but not until later. This was about seducing the woman and making her see that they were meant to be. He would put her first, even if it was complete torture.

Desdemona wasn't teasing, she felt brave. Reaching up, she placed her hand on the back of his neck, and pulled him down to her lips. "I was serious," she whispered, kissing him slow and smoothly. They both tasted like beer, and it was both erotic and enticing. When she felt him pressing excitedly against her body, she deepened the kiss. Then she felt the power she had over him, and it intoxicated her. The man really did want her. Now she had to not screw it up.

Whitefox pulled his lips away and his eyes stayed closed. God help him, his control was going to be tested

She giggled and took the gun.

When he opened his eyes, he stared at her. "You're up." It was all he could get out.

It was highly entertaining that for the first time meeting him, she managed to make him feel what she felt whenever they were together. Yeah, she could get used to this power. "Yes, sir," she winked and took aim.

Callen was going to play dirty. "You can shoot undistracted, but what if someone's trying to shake you up, Desi," he whispered in her ear and stood incredibly close to her body. He put his hand on her hip.

Desdemona blocked it all out, pictured the target and then thought about him eating lettuce for a week, she started laughing and then pulled the trigger and hit the can, immediately taking the next shot and taking it. When the cans flew she stood up and turned into his body and looked up at him. "Apparently, not a problem."

He grinned and leaned down to kiss her on the lips. "One can left."

"Doesn't matter, Callen." She took the shotgun shell from his hand, and loaded only one shot. I hit four out of six. You hit one out of six. I won this little game, and you're having salad all week."

A bet was a bet. "I will. You won fair and square, but I'll take my last shot." When he took the gun from her she wasn't finished.

"Oh, but can you take the shot distracted, Callen?" Desdemona pressed her body against the back of his and ran her hands around his waist and up under his jacket and shirt to his really defined abs. He sucked in a sharp breath, and she started exploring them while he tried to make his shot. "Make the shot and you can still have the sex," she whispered, and felt him flinch.

"Deal?"

"Promise," she answered and continued exploring.

He lifted the gun and aimed for the can, trying to not think about her hands running across his flesh. They were slightly chilly, and that made it more erotic, he had goose bumps and a wave of heat at the same time. "Desdemona," he muttered.

She pushed further, enjoying how his arm shook as he tried to focus. Then she flicked the button of his jeans open and when he quivered, she slid her hands into the front of his pants. "Make your shot, Callen."

Her hands were millimeters from stroking him, and he couldn't even see the can, let alone shoot it. Now his arm was cramping up as he held the gun aimed at something he couldn't focus on, and then she found him and he forgot everything, including how to breathe.

Desdemona slid her hands over him, gently, silkily and enjoyed the way he tensed and throbbed at her touch. His breath was coming harder and she knew he wasn't thinking about the target. Then he fired.

The can flew through the air and he turned fast, dropping the gun to the table, spilling his beer. He picked her up under her arms, and carried her to the side of the house.

Automatically she wrapped her legs around his waist, just as he pressed her against the house, kissing her.

Whitefox felt like he was going to catch on fire out on his porch. Her hands and body cast a spell, and he wanted to take her right then and there. Lust and need overwhelmed him. He kissed her and buried his hands in her hair, as he pressed her against the house and took all he wanted from the kiss.

Someone moaned.

Hands wandered.

Desdemona could feel how excited he was, he was pressed intimately against her and she wished she wasn't wearing so many damn layers of clothing. "Callen," she muttered into the kiss as the invasion continued.

Slowly he refocused, and realized this was supposed to be the first date, and he was going to do it right. Even if he burst into flames and died that very second.

"Desi, I'm going to put you down. Not because I don't want you, or want to take you right here and now. I'm planning to, but I want to do this right, and I have our first date planned. Don't think that I'm pushing you away," he said softly. He didn't want her to think he was rejecting her.

"Okay, Callen," she answered breathing heavy. He still didn't put her down.

"Promise you'll pick up where you left off later?"

Whitefox laughed hoarsely. "I can guarantee it."

Desdemona giggled.

"Damn it!" Whitefox took a deep breath, lowered her to her feet and backed away from her. "Go take a shower. I'll bring your suitcase in and put it on the bed. I just need you to get far away from me until I'm back in control."

"Okay, Callen." Right in that moment she felt powerful, that she had the ability to make him feel that chaotic. Desdemona thought back to what Elizabeth had told her. The quote by Morticia Addams was true. She was the spider. She made a mental note to thank her friend with a text message as soon as she could.

"Lock the bathroom door just in case I lose control," Whitefox grinned back.

Desdemona walked into the house laughing. "What do I wear Callen?"

"Go with something comfortable and relaxing."

When she walked away he walked over to the table and chugged an entire beer. This was his entire fault. Had he not screwed up the first date, then he would have carried her in an had his way with her right then and there. Now he was being forced to be patient.

Well hell.

Pulling out his cell phone he called and ordered a pizza, and because he promised he'd only eat veggies not meat, two salads to go with it. When he hung up, he planned on making the woman pay. He may be eating salad all week, but he was going to make her pay too, with lots of pleasure to get his mind off it.

* * *

333

Elizabeth and Ethan Blackhawk sat in the 'Cup of Joe' having something to eat, and reading printouts. When her phone beeped, she looked down at the incoming message and grinned.

"What's so funny?"

Elizabeth shrugged. Desdemona had sent her a text saying she was a spider, and she smiled thinking about her brother-in-law finally finding happiness. "Spiders."

Blackhawk shook his head and went back to the reports. "You have no intention of telling me do you?"

"Nope, it's girl talk."

"Good to know," he said, continuing to read. "I won't even try to decipher it then. It probably will make no sense to me anyway."

Focus shifted, as she felt eyes watching them. Wilma May watched them from the counter, and Elizabeth wasn't sure if it was because she manhandled her boss while pregnant, or if it was because her husband was sitting beside her looking as sexy as sin. On second thought, she knew the answer. Today Ethan Blackhawk was in a rare mood, and actually put on jeans. Although, come to think of it, his idea of jeans and hers were pretty much opposite sides of the spectrum. Hers were beat up and looked like something a cowboy would wear, and his were tailored and designer. The man had a serious clothing fetish. Go figure.

"Baby, you're staring in a public place." He looked up, grinning wickedly, and leaned over to kiss her, and casually rub his hand protectively over his child growing in her body. "Not that I mind," he whispered in her ear and followed it up with some innuendo.

Elizabeth swallowed, hoping she could keep herself in check and not jump him right there. "I can't help it. You're wearing jeans, and a white shirt. I don't know what to do with it," she stroked his cheek. "Wow," she looked under the table. "Boots and not dress shoes. I didn't even know you owned boots. You know it's cheating to buy cowboy boots already distressed. You're supposed to wear them down and have them be authentic."

He laughed. "I don't have time for that."

"I may have a casual clothes orgasm," she whispered. "What's with the clothes? Usually you like to dress up when we are out interviewing suspects."

334

"I just felt like living on the edge," he whispered something in her ear about what was going on underneath his clothing.

"Cowboy, keep talking like that, and we are so going back to the house to find out." Elizabeth put her hand on his thigh and planned on tormenting him when they noticed they weren't alone. In front of them stood a blonde woman and she was staring at her husband like he was a snack.

"My name is Carly. Jimmy said you wanted to talk to me." She pulled out a chair and sat down.

"Well, then have a seat, Carly," answered Elizabeth. Already she disliked the woman. One, she interrupted her sexy talk with her husband, and two, she was now moving from staring to leering, and she had a snow ball's chance in hell on acting out anything that was going on in her head.

"Thank you," she was focused on the man. She heard there was one or two hot FBI agents in town, and now she could confirm. Immediately, she checked out his ring finger. Oh well, didn't mean a married man wouldn't stray.

"We were coming to you next," answered Blackhawk.

"Well now I'm here."

Elizabeth pulled out her tablet and prepared to enter the information as her husband asked her the questions. He was the one she was focused on, and he might be able to get some information from her. Personally she wanted to take her head of blonde curls and beat it off the table. It was best if she just zipped it, and let her husband drive this conversation.

"So you have a relationship with the Sheriff?" he asked.

"It's a small town, we all grew up together. I've had a great deal of relationships, Agent. I like to believe that we all should enjoy life while we have it. Look at poor Bobby Lee."

"Yes, speaking of Bobby Lee. You also had a relationship of a sexual nature with him?" he stated, and then looked down at his file.

"I did. We'd hook up occasionally."

"The day he was killed, can you tell me where you were?" he asked, and felt his wife tense beside him, and didn't quite understand why.

"I own my own book store, you should swing by and see if you find anything you like," she smiled a big smile. "At night I

335

generally go out for a drink and some company. You can check at the bar. I'm sure they'll know if I wasn't there. I'm always around and available for a sexy man."

Blackhawk knew the woman was headed for an ass kicking, but he just pushed forward with the questioning. Ignoring how the woman was now taking off her jacket, and underneath was a white sweater that was cut way too low. If her intent was to distract him with her assets, it wasn't going to work. One- blondes were a big turnoff, and two- his wife's hand was on his thigh. That he was big on, and he wouldn't flirt in front of his pregnant wife even to help a case and get information.

Elizabeth felt her blood pressure rise. She played calm, but at some point, it was going to be hard to control.

"Have you seen any of these men before?" Ethan Blackhawk pulled out the autopsy photos, just because the woman was baiting his wife, and that pissed him off. He purposely left the Bobby Lee one in the pile to see her reaction.

She flipped through them, emotionless. Even the one with the man she was sleeping with and that spoke volumes about the woman. She was stone cold. Elizabeth watched her and made notes.

"This one," she said, pointing to the same man that Wilma May had picked out the day before. "I was in here, and he was getting coffee."

"Thank you, Ms. Kester," he said, not bothering to look up.

Carly pulled a card from her pocket and slid it across the table. "If you find yourself bored," she winked. "Give me a call and we can get a drink."

"I'm very happily married, Ms. Kester, to the love of my life."

"Yeah, since when does that stop men?" She leaned forward flashing the goods. That always worked with the guys.

Elizabeth had it. She was going to lean in and show her husband her chest then there were going to be repercussions for her actions. Elizabeth moved her hand fast, and the glass of vegetable juice tipped precariously and fell splashing on the woman and her white sweater.

Carly jumped up appalled. "This is angora!"

Elizabeth leaned back smiling. "It looked better on the rabbit, and for the record, the next time you plan on playing footsies under the table with my husband; you may want to make sure it's his foot and not mine."

That explained why his wife tensed, and he started to laugh.

The woman was almost as red as the vegetable juice, as she grabbed her jacket and turned to leave.

"Wilma May, can I get another juice?"

Blackhawk watched the woman storm away, "Nice one. I thought for sure you were going to beat her to a pulp, but the juice, that was a new one."

Elizabeth smiled up at Wilma May when she brought another juice. "Thank you." She wiped the spilled juice up and handed her the rag. No need for her to clean up her mess. "Violence is overrated," she said sipping her new juice.

"I love you, Lyzee," he leaned over and kissed his wife. "Very sexy how you controlled yourself until the very end. Well timed too."

"I try," she grinned. "So, what do you think about her other than her chest?"

This wasn't his first rodeo, and he wasn't falling for that one. "She had a chest?" Blackhawk said it with a straight face and earned himself a kiss a deep one that she normally wouldn't hand out in public.

When they broke the kiss his entire body was tingling.

"That's for not noticing she had a chest, and saving your pregnant wife's heart." She knew why he did it, and it was appreciated. Now that she was getting bigger and feeling more insecure, her husband was doing everything right.

"I only think about your chest. Specifically your chest in the number you wore the other night."

Elizabeth stroked his cheek and took a moment to just stare into his eyes.

"Do you both need anything else?" interrupted Wilma May.

Ethan Blackhawk was the first to look away. "No, thank you."

"If you don't mind me saying," she said, looking over at Elizabeth. "You two are cute together."

Elizabeth grinned at the woman. "I think you may be the first to ever say that to us."

"Well, you are and Carly's a bitch and deserved that juice. In fact, that juice that was on her is now on me. That was well worth seeing."

Now Blackhawk laughed. "Don't get my wife started."

"She has a nasty habit of looking for men that she has no business being with, and enjoying the thrill of breaking hearts. She preys on men that should be off limits like married men. To her it's nothing more than the thrill of the hunt."

Elizabeth nodded. She'd ass kick the woman to Siberia if she thought she could pull that off with Ethan Blackhawk.

"I like you, so watch your man," she said to Elizabeth before walking away.

Ethan could see the worry on his wife's face. "Want to talk about it?" he asked, seeing the emotion.

"I feel fat and wobbly." Elizabeth sniffled.

"What?" Ethan was surprised. "Baby, I don't think you're fat or wobbly. Ok, you're wobbly," he said, smiling gently when she gave him the look. "But definitely not fat. You're all baby and from behind you definitely don't look pregnant. Why do you think I spend all day walking behind you? Trust me it's a superior view, Baby."

Elizabeth fought to control the hormones and wondered if she should tell him what was bothering her. Finally she figured if she could share her worst secrets this should be nothing. "I know, I'm just an emotional wreck, and when I wasn't pregnant it didn't bother me when women hit on you in front of me, because," she paused and then continued, "I felt attractive at least."

There she said it.

Ethan lifted her chin and kissed her on the lips gently. "You're having our child. That's a miracle. I'm not my father, Elizabeth, so stop thinking I'll cheat on you." Blackhawk's voice was filled with tension that she doubted his fidelity.

Immediately her face said it all. "I didn't mean that you were." Elizabeth suddenly closed up. "I shouldn't have said anything," she said putting it all away. "It was a mistake. I'm sorry and I'll never bring it up again."

Blackhawk realized he made a huge mistake. She didn't doubt him, but herself. If she couldn't be open with him, who could she be open with. "I'm sorry. It's a touchy subject for me still. I don't want you to ever think I'd cheat on you."

"It's okay. It's my issue and not yours." Elizabeth changed the subject. "I think Carly could be a possible suspect. She had potential contact with one victim, is blonde and is known to be on the prowl for men."

"Elizabeth," he said her name wishing he hadn't brought up anything about his father. His wife was shutting him out, and he didn't know how to get her to open back up. "I'm sorry."

"Let's just worry about the assignment. That is why we're here. Nothing else should matter or distract us."

The topic was closed and she wasn't going to discuss it.

Blackhawk sighed. "I think she could be a suspect. When she looked at the death pictures, there was nothing there. No remorse or even shock."

"What's next?" she asked packing up the photos, unable to look at him, or she'd break down. She'd opened up and trusted him with her insecurity, and he didn't get it. Why would he? Ethan Blackhawk was sexy, had his body and wasn't fat and wobbly.

"I'm going to text Callen, and make sure that everything is okay there."

"Good idea. Then where to?"

He knew what might cheer her up. "Want to go to the bar, baby? I say we head to the bar and confirm her alibi," he looked at his watch.

"I feel so redneck and backwoods," she drawled, in her accent saved for when she was angry or upset. The fake happiness didn't reach her eyes. "Come on, baby daddy, let's go warm some bar stools at two in the afternoon."

Ethan knew he screwed up big time, dumping his issues on her instead of hearing what she was opening up to him about. Now he needed to fix her heart and be a better listener and husband. Immediately he started planning on a way to do just that.

*   *   *

Desdemona found the note he slipped under the bathroom door. It asked her to take her time while he set up for their date, and that he'd pick her up when he was done. She smiled like an idiot as she kept reading it over and over again. So she did just what he asked. After her shower she put on perfume, blew out her hair and got dressed. It wasn't like she brought a ton of relaxing clothes, so she pulled on a simple t-shirt and jeans.

When she ran out of things to do, she noticed he had books in his bedroom and decided to sit in the reading chair against the window and enjoy a book. Checking the selection, she reached for one she'd never read before.

It was hard to not be drawn to the selection of photos sitting on his nightstand. There was the Pilgrim photo that she'd seen at the Blackhawk house. There was a photo of Callen dancing with Elizabeth at what must have been the wedding on the Rez. One photo was of the two brothers dressed in turquoise and holding beers, their arms around each other. Then the last one was Whitefox kissing her on the lips and dipping low, again at her wedding. It was hard to not feel jealous. The man she was trying to have a relationship with was currently in love with another woman. The look in his eyes was obvious, but then she pushed it down. He'd already informed her. Family came first, and Callen admitted the truth, and she'd lied, saying it was fine.

Desdemona flopped down in the chair and got lost in the book. When she heard the door open she looked up, and he was standing there and he changed too. He was wearing flannel and he looked masculine and sexy in it.

"Find a book to read, sweetheart?" he asked, watching her from the doorway. His heart flipped in his chest, as he opened the door and saw her sitting in his chair, legs thrown over the arm and his book in her lap. There was no doubt, she'd fit in his life. They definitely could make it work. Now he only had two hurdles left. Make her see that, and his grandfather.

"Is it date time?" she asked, taking her glasses off and placing them on the book in her lap.

"Did I take too long?" he inquired, moving to her and taking the book and glasses and placing them on the bed stand. They looked right there together. Completely and totally right together as a little of him and a little of her came together and mixed with the people he loved most in the world.

Desdemona didn't miss how he meticulously fixed the pictures she'd just been inspecting, or how he reverently touched the one of him kissing Elizabeth, moving it forward in the group.

"No, I got lost in a book." Desdemona stood, and when he scooped her up, she laughed. "I guess you meant literally pick me up for the date."

"I did."

Desdemona didn't know what to say, when he carried her out into his living room. He moved all the furniture out of the way, and had a fire lit and a tent set up in his living room. Callen Whitefox was taking her camping. "Wow."

"So, you said you like camping, and I figured I couldn't go wrong then with camping for our first date."

She didn't know what to say. It took him hours to set this up. All for a first date. Suddenly, she wanted to cry. Yeah, she was completely in love with him. If he'd do this for her, when he knew he was going to get sex regardless, then he was most definitely a good man.

"Hey, are you okay?" he asked, turning her and wiping the tears that already fell. Now he was a nervous wreck. It couldn't be a good sign that she was crying. Maybe she hated camping. Well crap. Now what?

"Callen," she pulled his face down to hers and stood on her toes to kiss him, long and sweet. "This is amazing," she said looking into his eyes. "Thank you, I won't ever forget this, for as long as I live."

He relaxed and wrapped his arms around her. "Well, I screwed it up, and this is the date you deserved." Whitefox kissed her again, and didn't miss that she smelled like his soap and her shampoo and it turned him on incredibly. It was more mixing of his life and hers, proving they could move together seamlessly.

"Mmmmm…" she kissed him back. "Okay, before we make out all night, I'm ready to be impressed."

He grinned wickedly. "I ordered us dinner," he laughed at the look on her face. "It's meat free. I swear," he led her over to the fireplace. "But first, we have dessert."

She laughed. "Works for me," she took a seat on the blanket in front of the fireplace, and watched him open the wine, and pour it in two glasses. He sat beside her and opened a picnic basket.

"I hope you like chocolate," he teased, wiggling his eyebrows.

"Callen, I'm female, don't be silly. I'd marry chocolate and have little baby chocolates if that were possible."

He laughed and kissed her. When they were alone, she bloomed, and gone was the fear and trepidation. Out came the woman buried behind the shell. "How do you feel about smores?" He risked it, and hoped she'd like them.

"Love them!" Desdemona helped him set them up and was enjoying their time together. When it was all over, she wondered if this would continue. Packing up and leaving him would hurt.

"Me too." Whitefox put her marshmallow on a stick and handed it to her, then did his. Together they toasted them in the fireplace.

"I think I may never camp outside again. You ruined it for me with this date." Desdemona smiled and blew the flame out on her marshmallow.

"We can do this whenever you want," he said, watching her make her smore, and waiting to see if she'd acknowledge what he just said to her.

Desdemona took a bite of the gooey mess, and then held it out for him to take a bite too. "Best part is sharing the smore," she said, and then licked her finger.

"Agreed," he replied, wanting to say so much to her. "Desi?"

"Yes, Callen?" She took a sip of her wine.

"When this assignment is over, what then?" he asked, wanting to see what she planned on doing. He knew where he was going to be.

"What do you want to happen?" she asked, carefully.

"I think we should take it past dating and exclusively see each other and only each other."

Her heart skipped a beat, and her pulse quickened at how fast he was moving. "Then I think we should see where it goes, together."

342

Callen leaned over, kissing her. She tasted like chocolate and wine, and he was completely drunk on her already. His intent was to start the kiss, then pull back, but she pulled him closer, and he didn't think he'd have the control to back away from sex with her again. "If you don't stop now, I won't be able to," he whispered, as her hands went to his chest and she began unbuttoning his shirt.

"I don't want you to stop," she answered, and continued unbuttoning his shirt. "This is after all dessert."

"Good," he replied and moved towards her, laying her on her back on the blanket. He continued the kiss, even as she pushed his shirt from his shoulders and ran her fingers over the tattoos on his body. His heart began thundering in his chest.

"I like your tattoos," she whispered against his lips. "They're sexy."

"When you wear the little skirts and tights with skulls on them, it gets me really hot and bothered," he admitted, and when she laughed. He looked down at her, she was smiling at him. "And the little black glasses, they make me want to jump you right then and there."

Now she was giggling, until he pulled her t-shirt off and began kissing his way down her throat, and to the valley of her breasts.

Desdemona felt like he was lighting her on fire. His mouth was burning a trail across her body. She reached up, and set his hair free. Rarely did he release it. It fell around them and tickled her flesh and turned her on. When he reached her belly button, and swirled his tongue she moaned his name.

"I just want to spend all day tasting you, Desi. All day," he mumbled, and then continued on his exploration lower. When he met the button on her jeans, he flicked it open, just like she'd done to him. When he slowly slid her jeans down her hips, he wasn't expecting the erotic looking panties waiting for him. They were lacy and looked like sin, and immediately he hardened more, and was desperate to just taste her and see the prize waiting beneath. He pulled them off, and his body shook from what he wanted to do. He wanted to bury himself in her repeatedly, but he kept saying the mantra.

First date sex not everyday sex.

First date sex not everyday sex.

Finally he regained control of his body. But he was going to devour her, and he wasn't going to stop until he was satiated.

When his fingers slid deep into her body, and he began licking and tasting her, she arched at the sheer pleasure of it all. "Callen!" she gasped, when he did something creative with his mouth.

He was lost in the way she tasted and felt and didn't think of anything but giving her complete and total pleasure. Callen needed her breathless and exhausted beneath him. There was no way he'd let her leave him, and he'd make sure she couldn't live without his touch, and his hands on her body. As she started shaking beneath his mouth, he swirled his tongue, and when he sucked on the most sensitive part of her body, she exploded and buried her hands in his hair.

Desdemona couldn't even think, and he started working his way back up her body.

"You're delicious Desi," he purred into her ear. "This time you'll scream my name, and we'll keep going until you do," he demanded possessively. He only hoped he could handle it, and follow through.

Staring up at him, she would have done anything he wanted, since she still was unfocused. When he stood, and began unzipping his pants, sliding them down his body, she was mesmerized. As he stood in front of the fireplace completely naked, all she could think was how amazing his body was. No not just amazing but pillaging warrior amazing, all lean lines and perfection, meeting at delicious angles.

"What are you thinking, Desdemona?" he asked, dropping to his knees.

"Just how perfect your body is," she answered honestly. "I love everything about it."

He placed himself over her, and prepared himself. He wanted to watch her face as he slid home. This woman was going to be his. After years of searching he was finally going to lay claim. His heart and mind did battle over the entire situation. He kept trying to rationalize the lies he told himself in his mind.

Desdemona, opened for him, and wrapped her legs around his waist.

As he slid into her waiting body, he pushed hard, she was tight and he just fit, barely. He closed his eyes and prayed for control, especially after what he just said to her. Someone was going to be screaming, and it wasn't going to be him. Then he began moving and it took both of their breaths away.

"Callen," she gasped.

"So tight, Desi." Whitefox found his rhythm and kept going; not exploding first was going to be the hardest thing he ever had to do in his life. He leaned down to her ear, and whispered the words he was thinking. "No one's going to ever feel this with you again. I'm it Desdemona. No more men, and no more dates for you. I'm going to be the last man that you get naked with and experience this kind of pleasure with." Picking up the pace, he felt her tighten around him, and he prayed for control. "Am I clear, Desi? Me and that's it."

She nodded even though she was feeling out of control.

"I want to hear you say it," he whispered again, just as he felt her tighten down around his body. There was no doubt that she was experiencing as much pleasure as he could give her.

"Callen!" Desdemona felt the heat building and the overwhelming feeling like her body was about to shatter apart into a million pieces.

"Say it Desi," he ordered again, and as he saw the look on her face he started moving harder into her, until she gave him the words.

"Yes, Callen. Only you," she said, giving him anything he wanted in that moment. Maybe it was the sex or possibly the fact she believed he wasn't going to take no for an answer. After giving him the words, she fractured and arched into his body.

Whitefox barely survived that one, and he slowed the pace down, and gave her time to catch her breath. As he kept moving he tried to not think about how wet and warm she felt wrapped around his body. If he did, he was done.

Desdemona fought for her breath, and looked up into his eyes. This man wanted complete control, and she just decided to let him have it. She could trust him, and he was going to take care of her. Just the way he was now as they were making love in his living room. The man was trying to give her so much pleasure.

"More Desi?" he asked, starting to move harder again, into her body.

She didn't think her body could handle anymore pleasure. "Callen," she protested. "I can't!"

"Not until you give me what I want," he muttered, as the sweat beaded down his taut body. She was pulling apart his control, and he was going to get what he wanted, all of her. There wasn't any way he was stopping until he had her mind and body. If he could control that then he had a chance she wouldn't run far and fast. Maybe he was rushing it, but he needed to take charge and do what was best for them both.

"Callen, please!"

He shook his head, refusing to say anything more. If he did he'd lose his focus and be unable to remain in control.

Desdemona felt the heat building again, and it was tinged with lust, pain and the knowledge that he was going to keep inflicting pleasure until she gave him what he wanted. Part of her wanted to fight, and stand her ground. Everything was going too fast. She felt out of control and her mind was scrambled. The sane part of her mind tried to get her to rationalize; her heart told her who cared, as long as she had him. Desdemona's mind called her a liar, as she tried to rationalize everything going on around her.

Desdemona let her heart overrule her mind.

Digging her nails in his shoulders, she arched into him as he drove into her. His hair fell around them, and the feeling of it brushing her body and him invading was too much.

In the end, he won. She did scream his name right before she shattered and the light blinded her.

At his name on her lips and the way her body squeezed his intimately, he knew he was close and it was time. One more stroke, pushing past the resistance, he moaned extremely proud he'd achieved his goal, and getting what he wanted. The control was the prize, she had conceded, and he was victorious. Callen got exactly what he set out to obtain.

Desdemona submitted.

She couldn't move. Then she realized why. Callen was lying over her body. Then she thought about it, and instead of flushing with embarrassment she just began laughing.

Whitefox went up on his elbows and looked down at her. "After all that, you laugh?" He started laughing himself.

"What if I didn't scream your name," she said, still giggling.

"I wasn't worried. It was all part of the plan," he stated, kissing her, and was enjoying it, when there was a knock on the door. Whitefox looked at his watch. "Dinner," he pushed off her and slipped into his jeans.

"Wait! I'm naked!" She jumped up looking for her clothes and where he threw them.

"Yeah I know," he said snickering. "That's for laughing."

Desdemona grabbed his shirt, and quick buttoned it up. It smelled like his cologne and soap and she wasn't planning on giving it back. Not for a long time. She was laying claim on it just because it had his delicious scent all over it.

Whitefox paid for the take out and walked back into the room, and then he saw her and his heart just stopped in his chest. Here stood this little woman, wearing his shirt, and her hair wild and crazy down her back, and he pushed for more.

"What?" Desdemona looked alarmed. Maybe he didn't want her in his shirt.

"When this assignment is over I want you to move in with me." He wanted to see her in his house, in his shirt, and in his life forever. This was the life his brother had and he'd coveted. Now it stood right in front of him, and all he had to do was grab it and make it his.

Desdemona wasn't expecting what he just threw at her, and it wasn't what she was hoping for either.

And she still didn't have an answer.

~ Chapter Fourteen ~

Elizabeth sat at the kitchen table and her husband massaged her lower back. Twenty minutes ago the Braxton Hicks contractions started, and they weren't letting up. She tried to explain to her husband she was perfectly fine, but as usual he was over the edge about the pregnancy. He carried her out of the sheriff's station, much to her horror. When he placed her in the car and then started searching for the nearest hospital just in case, she'd had enough. When she pulled the keys from the ignition and threatened to swallow them, he finally calmed down and listened to her.

It was hard to get upset with him, and she'd even forgotten that she was upset from before. He was just being a doting father, and smothering her and the baby to death. Now he insisted on rubbing her back, even when she tried to tell him there wasn't any pain back there. Trying to remember the fear he'd survived when she was abducted, accommodating him as much as possible was her priority. When he kept looking at her with eyes full of concern she was helpless to not soothe him.

"You're going to be a great father." There was no doubt in her mind. The man was just so sweet and loving.

"I hope so." It was his secret fear, and the only two people that knew he was scared shitless were his brother and his wife. That was why he reacted incorrectly in the diner. The fear grabbed him and shook him every day.

"Hey, how about dinner?" she said, turning to face him.

"Okay, what do you want?" Now he was gently rubbing her belly. Suddenly the baby rolled and pressed against her stomach. "Is that a foot?" he asked, poking back at it.

Elizabeth laughed. "How should I know?" As her phone rang, he continued poking at his child and laughing when he kicked back.

"Hello Granddad," she answered, laughing.

"What's so funny, granddaughter?" he inquired.

"Your grandson is poking at the baby, and the baby is kicking back. I'm the evening's entertainment." Elizabeth slapped her husband's arm and covered the bottom of the phone. "Stop provoking the kid!"

He laughed and went back to rubbing gently and listening to the conversation between his wife and grandfather.

"Is everything okay, Granddad? You don't call in the middle of the week unless you're worried about something. What's bothering you?"

His Granddaughter was very astute. "I had that dream again, Elizabeth, and I know you will be the only one of the three that won't lie to me."

She put him on speakerphone. "Ethan wouldn't lie to you, granddad. He just doesn't like you to worry."

"Covering for him, my protective Raven?" Timothy inquired, knowing by now his boy would be listening.

"Absolutely," she answered. And he was very right. She wouldn't lie to him. "Now what was your dream about?"

"Callen and the Adare woman."

Elizabeth looked over at her husband. Was she shocked he was calling? No. He knew she was pregnant before she even did, and when she was abducted, he knew it was coming and tried to warn her.

"What is the status with the woman? Callen isn't answering my calls, and that isn't like him. I think I deserve to be told the truth."

"They're pursuing a relationship." She didn't want to rat her brother-in-law out, but she didn't lie to the Blackhawk men, especially granddad. He would be eighty-nine soon and was razor sharp.

"This time in the dream the fox was willing to die for her. Last time he was just protecting her, so something has happened."

Elizabeth just looked at her husband. He was of no help.

"Tell me what you feel about this woman. I trust your opinion. I know my boys would cover for each other, isn't that so Ethan?"

"Granddad, he's my brother." He gave up pretending to not be eavesdropping.

"I don't think you have anything to worry about Granddad. The doctor is a lovely woman, and I personally like her a great deal. You can tell how she feels about Callen when she looks at him." Elizabeth immediately switched to defending Whitefox.

"And she isn't native?"

Elizabeth sighed. "No granddad, but neither am I. I love you, but really, let the Native thing go. Can't you just cut him a break on it? What if she's the one, and he pushes her away because of obligation to you then marries a native that destroys his heart and life. You know he'd forgo love to keep his promise to you." Elizabeth sighed. "Please, as a favor to me. Let him out of this promise and let him find happiness. Maybe it's not with this particular woman, but let him have the freedom of choice to find his own way."

Timothy Blackhawk remained silent.

"I'll give you a brood of Blackhawks you can boss around, but Callen's heart can't take much more and if it breaks over this, it won't ever be the same."

"Elizabeth," he started to say.

"Please, for me granddad? Let it go and release him from this promise."

There was silence on the phone as Blackhawk watched his wife work her mojo.

"Elizabeth, this is why you shall head this family when I'm gone. You are their warrior who will fight to keep my boys safe," he paused, "Where are the boy and the woman?"

"Promise to not go all Native Indian all over her?" she asked. "Scaring her with the war bonnet and tomahawk?"

"I don't believe I own a tomahawk," Timothy answered, laughing.

"Want one?" she inquired, trying to keep her voice serious." Your birthday is coming up."

He laughed. "Are you trying to bribe me?"

"Is it that apparent?"

"I love you, my precious raven. I will be as welcoming as I was to you."

"Well, just shoot the poor woman then! Don't grill her on your house and your feathers," she added, and then thought about it. "Cal's either at our home or at his house."

"Both of them?"

"Yes granddad."

His granddaughter was a joy, and really the only one that would speak honestly with him about anything he asked. "How is my great grandson, and have we named him yet?"

"We're working on it, Granddad. I am leaning toward Leroy Heathcliff Mick Blackhawk IV."

There was a pause over the phone.

"Wonderful name," he finally said, laughter evident in his voice. "Who are you punishing Raven? The child or your husband?"

Blackhawk started laughing, knowing he was the intended victim in this atrocious crime.

"Is it that obvious?" she asked.

"Ask her why the IV, granddad," winked Blackhawk, throwing his wife under the granddad bus.

"Elizabeth, why are there Roman numerals at the end of my great grandson's name?"

Now she saw it was a free for all and she was on her own. It was time to reciprocate. "Since Ethan is dragging his feet, anyone that meets this child is now going to think he, Wyler and you are all named that."

There was a pause.

"I love you Leroy Heathcliff Mick Blackhawk the first."

Timothy Blackhawk roared with laughter. "I love you, Elizabeth, and for you I will willingly change my name. I will trust your judgment on the woman, but if she turns out to be a holy disaster it will be your entire fault and you will rectify it and do what needs to be done. Am I clear, my sweet raven?"

Blackhawk snickered.

"Yes Granddad, but I guess you'll have to disown me," she replied, laughing. "Bet that tattoo on your arm will be a bitch to get off. Looks like that train ride to crazy town just came back to bite you in your ass."

Timothy laughed more. "Ethan, pick a name for my great grandson already."

"We love you granddad. When we get home, we'll have dinner at our house with the whole family."

"I look forward to it, and if Callen picks a woman one third as well as Ethan, than I am going to be overly blessed. Be safe

351

sweetheart." Timothy hung up the phone to find his other grandson.

Ethan was still amazed that his wife yielded the power she did over his grandfather. The man was the head of the family and his boys all worried and feared him, but his pregnant wife wasn't worried in the least. "Think she'll survive meeting him? Granddad is intimidating."

"I think so, but I just have this feeling their entire situation isn't going to run as smoothly as ours did. Meet and four days later get married and have a kid. I just get this feeling that granddad and his dream is going to be right. This stalker thing worries me."

"Think he's in danger?"

"I think if he's anything like his brother, he'll die to protect the woman he loves. That means the bulls eye won't be on her, but on him. I just feel off about all of it."

Blackhawk thought about it. "Then I think we're going to have to help him keep her safe. Well, I am anyway."

Elizabeth laughed. "Let's have dinner, and then work on the profile and this assessment. I want to get home before something happens."

"Callen's new at this agent thing and that worries me most."

"Yeah, me too." She was very worried for her brother-in-law and now Desdemona too.

Deep down Elizabeth just knew this was far from being over, and she hoped her family stayed intact, including Callen's heart.

He wasn't going to move until she gave him an answer.

Desdemona looked like a deer in headlights.

No, he wasn't proposing, because if he dropped those words on her, he was convinced she'd rabbit fast and far.

At first he was going to try baby steps, but with someone as skittish as Desdemona, he needed to steam ahead. Callen was willing to push as hard as he needed to, in order to get the outcome he wanted.

Now he just had to get her to stay with him forever. If he took away her choice then everything would be fine. Like his brother pointed out, he had to keep her from running away a year down the road. And he had to buy some time to get his grandfather to approve of a marriage.

"Desdemona? I want us to live together."

She stared at him and took a deep breath unsure what to say to the man. It was so sudden and completely off the cuff that she was freaked out. All she could think of was to go with the obvious. "I have a nut job stalking me. Did you see the back of that picture, Callen? Just the idea that you'll be a target makes me sick to my stomach. I can't go home and I can't fall in love."

"Well, then I guess I'm completely safe unless you love me." He threw it out there. Hoping and waiting for her response.

"We can't live together!" She didn't want him to die.

He still refused to give up and was feeling desperate enough to say the words before he was ready. "It's too late. I love you." He said it, pretty sure that would work. The truth was written all over her face. "So whether you love me or not, I'm a dead man," he joked, and then realized he went too far.

Desdemona backed away from him, bottom lip quivering as tears filled her eyes. All she could do was retreat for his room, slamming the door and locking it. What had she done? Just being near him risked him, and she did love him, and if she lost him because of her past how could she recover?

As she lay on the bed, she looked to the nightstand and the pictured of him with another woman, and her heart ached. Could she love a man that loved another woman? Then she tried to find the positive in it, and went with that. It was family, and wasn't that what she always wanted? Plus toss in a friend to have all for herself. The tears overwhelmed her, and she wasn't sure what she was crying over.

There were so many reasons. Love was damn complicated.

"Desi, I'm sorry. It wasn't funny. Please let me in," he begged. Way to go on screwing up re-do date number one. When he didn't answer he got desperate and pulled his pocket knife out and popped the lock. Once inside he found her lying on his bed, face buried in his pillow and sobbing. "Oh sweetheart, I'm so sorry."

He pulled her into his arms, and kissed her tears away. "I didn't mean to upset you like this," he said, as she held onto his body and sobbed. Her tears ran down his bare chest.

"I have to get far away from you," she sobbed. "I don't want to see you get hurt because of me."

"You can't leave, and we're going to live together. Do you want to live here or in your house?" he continued, ignoring her words and forcing her to comply. When she was running it was best to yank her back and give her no choice. By taking her choice away, he'd keep her safe and give him the same life Ethan had built.

"Callen! You're not listening to me. If you stay around me, you'll get hurt."

"Stay with me and I promise you protection. Nothing will hurt you if you just stay by my side. I'll take care of you forever and love you."

It wasn't lost on Desdemona that he mentioned protection first and then love, but wasn't that what she always wanted? To feel safe for once and to belong? Callen had a pretty amazing family and just to be part of that warmed her heart and gave her hope. With time she knew she could get him to love her more.

"Stay Desi, and let's start something really great together."

Part of her was screaming to her, warning it was all too fast. The other part of her was taking in the man before her, and the amazing body he had. The sex was stellar and the family was loving. The pros outweighed the cons. So what if she didn't own his heart. What could possibly happen? Elizabeth was a happily married woman. Again her mind and heart went to war, and she was prisoner until it was decided.

Watching her face, he knew the minute Desdemona had come to a decision. "It's my life, I get to decide if I risk it for love or not. A life without love or a short life with love, and I choose love. I'm offering you protection and love."

"Where will we be safer?" she finally asked, laying her head on his shoulder. Her brain lost again, and her heart made the decision.

"After the assignment your house is safer. There are houses around it, it's in a more public place, and Ethan and Elizabeth are right behind us."

"Can we get a dog?" she asked.

Callen laughed. "Yes, we can get a dog. A loud barking one with very big teeth and that likes strangers for breakfast.

"Can we get a tall privacy fence like Ethan and Elizabeth have?" she asked.

"Yes." He kissed her on the forehead.

"Gun turrets?"

"What a coincidence. After Ethan finishes building the tree house, they're on Elizabeth's Honey-do list. I bet she'll share."

Desdemona laughed. "Of course they would be. I wouldn't be shocked."

"Now, how about we go have dinner and I try to salvage this date. Unless you plan on letting me have a re-do on a re-do."

She laughed. "You don't need a redo on this date. I think it's a pretty spectacular date. Great sex, camping and you told me you loved me. This is a really good date."

"I'm glad," he smiled, never noticing she didn't say the words back to him. Whitefox was just so excited he finally got her to concede. If she stayed, he could keep her safe. He led her out to the take out. "Do you want to sit by the fire or at the table?"

"Camping doesn't have a table," she replied, laughing. "What's for dinner?"

Whitefox walked over with a pizza and two salads. "Salad and pizza, there's no meat because I promised."

"I love you."

"Because I ordered a pizza and salad? We can have it every night for dinner if that's the case. " It was hard to not feel smug that everything was going as he planned.

"No, but because you're a really good man." Desdemona watched him sit in front of her, and never had she met a man so honorable, and one willing to protect her. "Because your family is amazing and because I happen to think bossy, Native American men are incredibly sexy."

"Stay away from my brother," he ordered, grinning.

Desdemona leaned forward and kissed him gently. "I will, but not because you're bossy, but because Elizabeth scares the shit out of me."

He snickered. "Here's the big secret. She's actually a pushover if she loves you. That's how I get away with all my shit," he answered, grinning. "She has a really big heart."

"I know she's been okay with me so far, and she says 'girlfriend code', but you just told me you love me and what if that doesn't make her happy, I mean…" She didn't know how to phrase it, and she felt really nervous because she knew who held the first part of his heart and always would. Desdemona thought to the pictures on his nightstand and swallowed the jealousy.

Callen looked at his watch. It was still early, and he pulled out his cell phone.

"What are you doing?" she asked, appalled. "Callen don't call her!" When he hit speed dial she just stared with her mouth open, as she heard it ringing on speakerphone. "Oh my God!"

On the second ring she answered.

"Callen Darlin', are you okay?" she asked, worriedly.

"Yeah, Beautiful I'm more than fine." Whitefox glanced over at Desdemona. "I just told Desi that I loved her, and we're moving into her house as soon as this is over."

There was a small pause.

Desdemona started to feel nervous.

"Okay, we can have dinner on Sundays. We'll have to have Italian since Desdemona isn't big on meat. Does she like Italian?"

"She loves it."

"Great, but I'm still making Ethan cook me meat, baby Blackhawk has control of my brain for now. I won't let my carnage contaminate her food."

Desdemona just stared. It was that simple to be accepted into his family? No questions asked?

"We're getting a dog, and a fence like yours. Can we put a gate in so I don't have to walk all the way around the development to watch the game with Ethan?" he asked, opening his salad.

"We should just make it one big fence and put in a pool. Desdemona, do you like swimming," she inquired, knowing the woman had to be right there. The call had to be more for Desdemona's sake, and not Callen's. He already knew she'd support anything he wanted out of love.

"Yes, Elizabeth I do," she answered, finally finding her voice. The woman just ran them both over. If she believed Callen

Whitefox to be a force to deal with, there was double trouble with Elizabeth and him teamed up.

"Welcome to the family Morticia," she said. "I told you Desdemona, spiders and flies!"

Desdemona laughed, finally over the horror of the situation, and forcing herself to not feel off balance at how fast it was all moving. Her sanity had to be in question. It was hard to believe she just met them all.

Callen was grinning, and grateful to his sister-in-law. Her open acceptance sucked some of the terror from Desdemona's face. "Okay beautiful, I'll email you later. I'm supposed to be on a re-do date and I'm pretty sure that calling another woman while on the date is a bad idea," he said, grinning at Desdemona.

Doctor Adare wanted to tell him that calling another woman beautiful was a problem too, but she swallowed it, unwilling to ruin the moment for either of them.

"I think when you're on a date it's acceptable, but during sex it gets questionable."

Blackhawk laughed in the background.

"Good to know," he snickered. "Love you, Lyzee."

"Love you too, Cal. Love you Desdemona," she added, and then disconnected the phone.

Desdemona didn't know what to do with all this. It was shocking enough to be plowed over by Callen, but now his family too. When she heard Elizabeth tell her she loved her, she almost burst into tears. What she found with these three people was something she never thought possible. This morning she woke up without a family, and now she had one. Talk about moving at the speed of light. The scientist in her was appalled at her lack of common sense, but the woman in her was swept away with the romanticism of it all. Again, she hoped love would grow.

"I'm sorry she calls you Morticia, I can talk to her if you want," he said, sympathetically.

There was uncontrollable laughter. "No way! Are you kidding? Elizabeth made me realize how amazing it is to be Morticia Addams."

Callen smiled and felt bad that he ever doubted Elizabeth. Now he owed her a big kiss for that one too. "Okay then, and spiders and flies?"

Desdemona touched his cheek. *"Normal is an illusion. What is normal for the spider is chaos for the fly,"* she said, quoting her new favorite quote in the world. "Morticia Addams said it, and I plan on embracing my inner Morticia Addams."

"I say go for it. I support you in your attempt to channel your diva of death."

Desdemona laughed. "And you thought Elizabeth calling me Morticia was bad?"

Whitefox grinned. "Yeah well, I have to be me and just for the record if my family is too much, we can stay here and give you some space from them." He offered it because she just seemed suddenly overwhelmed. "I love my family; I hope you can tolerate them." His family would either make or break them, because they were going to remain the same. It was his greatest hope to incorporate Desdemona into the fray seamlessly. Part of the plan was to spend as much time around them, not only for safety but so he could learn how to do this relationship thing. He needed a role model to navigate it seamlessly; Ethan was that model.

She took a salad from him and popped the lid of the container. "No, we'll stay there. You're family doesn't bother me; It's nice to have people around that care about you and want to just keep you safe."

Desdemona went quiet.

When she put down her salad, he looked over at her. "What's wrong? Did I upset you?"

"Can we eat later?" she asked, watching him carefully.

"Yeah, what do you want to do?"

Desdemona stood and went over into his lap and sat, kissing him. "I think I'd like to climb into our tent, and maybe," she whispered in his ear what she wanted to do.

Immediately, he pushed away the container. "I hate salad anyway," he said, scooping her up as she giggled in his arms. "I'm never taking down this tent."

And he wasn't.

Thursday night

358

Ethan Blackhawk sat on the couch with his wife sitting between his legs; they were lounging, relaxing, and checking out the incoming tech reports. They now had all the victims ID's and they could start tracking their last days.

"Tomorrow we need to have the tech team head to the impound lot and search whatever cars are remaining that belong to the victims," said Blackhawk.

Elizabeth wasn't listening; she was too busy reading the stomach contents reports that just came in from FBI West. "Ethan, I think we can safely say how they all died."

"We know they died of Ethylene Glycol."

"Yes, but now we know how the killer got them to consume it." Elizabeth pointed to the information on her tablet, and waited for him to see what she saw. The wheels were starting to spin in her head.

"They all had coffee," he answered, thinking back to what they'd learned. "The one victim stopped in the 'Cup of Joe'."

"We also have a blonde that works there." As much as she liked Wilma May, the fact was, they all died with coffee in their stomachs, one victim was seen there, and she worked for a man that disrespected her and every other woman he met.

"Tomorrow we need to head to 'Cup of Joe' and talk to the owner to find out more about Wilma May. I'll talk to her boss and get her work schedule. You stay far away from him."

Elizabeth laughed. "Okay, Cowboy. Then I need to meet with Christina. I know that Ethylene Glycol is in antifreeze but I want a list of everything else that it comes in, just so we can start looking at all the possibilities."

"I have to send Callen an email. The tech team found nothing out of place there, and he needs to head back. I need him here to help me double team Carly Kester. "

"Well if Callen isn't back, you're not going alone. She's a shark just looking for some juicy native flesh to sink her teeth into for a man-meal."

"I can't bring you, Elizabeth. I don't think she'll buy the veggie juice was an accident, and the minute she sees you she'll clam up."

Elizabeth snorted. "What baby Blackhawk?" she spoke to her belly. "Baby says it was an accident and that she can kiss his momma's..." Her husband covered her mouth before she could finish.

"I'll ground the baby if he's cursing in utero."

She laughed and bit his hand. "Baby wants a name, daddy."

Blackhawk sighed. "I know it's just so hard. I know we agreed we'd use the names of our family, but we have Charlie, for your dad, Timothy for granddad, Wyler for my father, and then we tossed in Callen and Gabe. If we have to teach our son five names and then Blackhawk by kindergarten this poor kid is going to have to learn to write his name at two."

"Well, do you want to see my choice?" she asked, looking up at him, as she leaned against his body.

"Yes," he answered and watched as she opened a file that had baby ultrasounds, names and anything that she researched for the baby.

Elizabeth showed him.

"I say go with that one since my choice is very similar, but with one difference," he said, typing it out and waiting for her opinion on his selection.

"I like this one too," she patted his leg. "I think we may have our name." She knew where Ethan was heading with it.

"I agree that we need a nickname," he said, kissing her neck, as he protectively placed his hands over her belly. "I love you, Elizabeth," he whispered in her ear. "I'm sorry about today."

Elizabeth looked up at him confused.

"Today when you were telling me how you felt, and I assumed it had anything to do with my father and the history of his infidelities."

"Oh." She'd genuinely forgotten about that, and usually did whenever they were alone together. Elizabeth was secure as a couple when women weren't staring at her husband like he was a snack.

"I want you to be able to come to me and tell me how you feel and not have to worry I'm going to accuse you of something."

Elizabeth remained silent on the topic.

"Want to talk about it?" he asked gently, holding her hand in his.

Elizabeth shrugged. "I told you, I feel fat and wobbly and when women hit on you it makes me feel insecure, because I'm obviously not what I was," she said, waving her hand down her body, holding back the tears. It was a touchy subject for her. "It has nothing to do with you and everything to do with me."

"You're right, you're not the same." Blackhawk felt her tense. "Elizabeth, you're so much more. You were just my wife before."

Elizabeth looked at him, and he got up from behind her and knelt before her.

"You were just a wife and now you're the mother of my son, and that elevates you to a status that no other woman can ever hope to achieve. I loved you endlessly before, but now I find that there is more love for the woman that is giving me such a treasure. We made a life together and that's staggering."

"I try to not let it bother me," she said sniffling, and then rubbed her hand over their child. "But I just don't feel like me right now."

Blackhawk kissed her on the lips. "You won't be pregnant forever," he promised. "Then you'll be the original you but still have the advantage of being the mother of my child. I'm in awe, in love, and hopelessly smitten with the bad ass wife I married."

"Okay, Ethan," she said, feeling a little better. "I can't wait until these hormones are gone."

"Want to go upstairs, and roll around in bed with me? Despite you thinking you're fat and wobbly, I can't seem to keep my hands off you, so I think it has to be you that makes me crazy."

"Are you kidding? Absolutely, Mr. Blackhawk," she stood and reached down to help pull him to his feet. "And, I'm crazy, stupid in love with you."

"Mrs. Blackhawk, I think I'm supposed to be taking care of you and helping you stand, not you pulling me up." He swung her up in his arms.

"Mr. Blackhawk, I'll always take care of you and have your back, when will you get used to it," she said, kissing her husband and running her hands through his hair until it made him wild, and he deepened the kiss.

"You can take care of me upstairs, and get the trashy lingerie out again," he whispered and then ravaged her mouth like a starving man.

When she pulled away her heart was pounding and she made a mental note to ask Desdemona where to get a year's supply of sexy stripper panties.

They were her new favorite thing.

Friday Morning

Whitefox woke up with a crick in his neck. They both opted to finish up the camping date by sleeping inside the tent. The good thing about that was the tent sex that they had randomly through the night, the bad thing about it was the hard floor didn't make sleeping all that comfortable. Yet, Desdemona made it the whole night without complaining at all.

Rolling over to cuddle with her, he found her space empty and her pillow cold. His heart began to pound in his chest, at the idea that she ran for the hills to escape him. Whitefox pulled on his jeans, and quickly unzipped the tent to hunt her down. Then he smelled the scent of coffee, and he was pretty sure she wouldn't make him coffee and then run.

Looking around, he noticed her jacket and boots were gone, and he went to the door, to see if the Denali was too. If she took off, he was going to be angry, mad, and incredibly hurt. Promises were very serious, and you didn't break them.

That's when Callen found her. Desdemona was sitting on the rail of his porch, staring out at the snow and the two deer that were eating some leaves. His heart calmed, knowing that he wouldn't have to wake up every morning and look for her, but trust that she'd stay.

Whitefox walked back over for a cup of coffee and then dressed to join her on the porch. When he was home alone, he often went to his porch to watch nature or the sun rise from that exact spot. Something about having her there to do it with him lightened his heart and soul. When he first reconnected with his brother, he wanted what he had. An outsider that loved him and would always treat him like his heart mattered, and now he believed he got his wish. Doctor Desdemona Adare would keep him from living a lonely existence, as long as he could keep her safe, he'd make sure they'd live happily ever after.

Maybe.

There still was the entire Timothy issue that loomed on the horizon. Where he may look past his grandson fooling around with an outsider, he didn't think he'd like the diluting of Indian blood with mixed children.

When the idea of kids came up, something in him went hot and then cold. Just watching Elizabeth walk around, with a baby belly, and bringing the next generation of Blackhawk into the world, and it warmed his heart. Maybe one day, he'd get to see Desdemona in the same condition.

Then he thought back to the one time he thought he got a woman pregnant, it was Kaya Cheek, and his warmth went cold. He'd forgotten to use protection with her, so he hoped she was either keeping herself safe, or she wasn't going to reject the idea of kids.

The icy cold crept further up his body towards his heart, at the idea that if she did get pregnant, the child would be just like him, a nameless bastard. His mood began going south, and fast. Callen fought hard to put a smile on his face, as he exited his house to join her.

Desdemona liked the silence of the woods surrounding his home and was glad he brought her here. When she bought the house in the development, she always wondered what was on the other side of the river and the gigantic trees sheltering their secret world. Nature called to her, and this was such a restful place; she actually felt better just sitting there. When the two deer left the safety of the woods to feast on the tender leaves poking through the snow, her breath caught in her chest. There was a large buck, standing protectively over the doe. Their bodies were touching, and it made her smile.

"You look happy," he whispered, joining her at the rail.

"Look how beautiful they are," she whispered back, leaning against him when he put his arm around her. "Do they come here often?" she asked, curiously.

"They come all the time. Sometimes it's just the male, and sometimes the female. She's pregnant, you can tell. When the male hovers like that, it means she's going to be giving birth when the weather breaks."

"He looks like he'd kill anything that came near her," she laughed softly. "It's like an Ethan deer."

"It's a male species thing. That protectiveness is just something we can't fight. When you fall in love, you want to keep your woman safe. Ethan will probably hover over Elizabeth just because, even though Elizabeth can take care of herself."

Desdemona looked up at him, and hoped he wasn't just referring to Ethan Blackhawk, but himself too. She knew he'd always keep her safe, and she prayed love went with that. Before she could ask him what was on his mind, they heard crunching of tires on gravel.

Whitefox stood protectively in front of the woman, and then saw the truck and relaxed. It was only his father. How Wyler Blackhawk knew he was around was beyond him, but it probably had to do with his grandfather.

"Hey son," he said, bounding up the stairs. He immediately went to his boy to hug him. Since his oldest son, Ethan had returned, the three of them were working on fixing the relationship he broke when they were boys. As he pulled back from the hug, he saw the little woman and smiled at her. This was the female that had his father all worked up in a tizzy.

"Dad," he stepped out from in front of her. "This is Doctor Desdemona Adare." He watched his father's face for any indication there was going to be coldness, because she was an outsider. When there was none he relaxed. It helped cement the man back into his life, that he didn't make Desdemona feel unwelcome.

Desdemona hopped off the rail and put out her hand, offering it. When the man laughed and pulled her into a hug, she wasn't sure what to think, but she was glad he was friendly. For some reason she expected him to be aloof like his son, Ethan.

"I've heard about you, Doctor. It's a pleasure," he smiled, releasing her. And boy had he heard about her. For three days now his father was nonstop blabbering, and it was nice to finally see what had Timothy pacing his house. She was tiny and unlike

Elizabeth, his other son's wife, she looked vulnerable and breakable.

"You must be Wyler," she spoke, smiling up at him. "Ethan looks just like you," she said, noticing that the man and his son were fairly close to a genetic replica. Then she turned towards Whitefox remembering how he always sounded so sad when he talked about being the 'bastard'. "You have your father's facial features, and the body structure."

He nodded, hiding the pain because he was used to keeping it locked deep inside with anyone other than Ethan and Elizabeth Blackhawk.

"Granddad sent me, son," he looked over at his boy, and he looked worried.

"I figured. What does he want?" Callen Whitefox wasn't going to let his grandfather run Desdemona away.

"Lunch, today." He knew he didn't need to say more, his son would understand that the family patriarch wanted to check the young woman out, and see if she fit or needed to go.

"I don't think we can make it," he replied evenly.

Wyler Blackhawk lifted an eyebrow. "That's the message you want me to give to your grandfather, the head of our family?"

Desdemona spoke up, she didn't want there to be this tension, but obviously she knew it had everything to do with her. "Callen, we can go," she offered, softly.

He glanced over at her and weighed the situation. "Tell granddad, that we have some things that are FBI related off the reservation today, and if we can make it, we'll be there." Right now he needed to explain to Desdemona what she was walking into and what the situation was going to be like. "She's also a vegetarian." Whitefox threw it out there as a heads up.

"So sitting her beside Elizabeth at the table would be a bad thing?" he smiled, trying to lighten the mood. Wyler felt bad for his son, so he went to him and hugged him, whispering to him. "Hang in there, we've all been there." He too brought an outsider home once and it ended badly, because of his philandering ways. At least he still had his sons. Stepping back he spoke to Desdemona.

"It was very nice to meet you Doctor, and I hope that I get to see you at lunch." He nodded and walked away whistling. He picked a non-native, his one son did, so why wouldn't he expect the same from his other son. Wyler really wished his father would let go of the stringent past beliefs and let his boys just relax.

Callen Whitefox watched his father walk away.

"What do you need to tell me, Callen? I can feel that you're all messed up over this," she said, softly. "You have this look on your face, and it's scaring me."

"From the day I was born, my grandfather has insisted I keep my bloodlines pure. Ethan isn't full native, his mother was an outsider, but my mother was part of the tribe. Timothy Blackhawk pretty much had one rule for us growing up. If we were to date, procreate or marry, that it be with a native woman."

"And I'm definitely lacking in that department."

"Yes." He hated that he even had to have this conversation with her. To him, her heritage didn't matter, and he didn't think his mattered to her. Wasn't that what it was supposed to be like? Unconditionally accepting of the other person after you finally found them and not being embarrassed.

"Is it going to cause problems for your family?" The last thing she wanted to happen was for him to be put in a position where he had to choose between her and his family. One- because she knew what they meant to him, and two- she didn't think he'd choose her. Why would he? They just met.

"Let's go inside," he said, offering her his hand.

"Want me to make you breakfast?" she offered. "Then we can discuss this."

Callen didn't know what there was to discuss, he was going to be forced to watch the old man run her through the ringer. "Okay," he led her into the kitchen. "Have at it," his mood was deteriorating quickly.

"Your smartphone was beeping before," she offered as she poured him more coffee.

"I better check it," he picked it up and saw the messages. One from his brother requesting him back in Red Rock later that day. "We have to head back tonight," he said. "Ethan wants to interview Carly Kester in the morning, and he can't take Elizabeth."

"He can't?" She was surprised. "You'd think Elizabeth would insist. She doesn't like attractive man-eaters around her husband, and I can't blame her." She didn't particularly like the idea of the woman around Callen either, Elizabeth included.

"It seems, Carly crossed the line and Elizabeth dumped vegetable juice down the front of her."

"Oh," she snickered. "Good for her. I want to be Elizabeth Blackhawk when I grow up."

Whitefox laughed. "Don't we all?" Then he tried to be serious. "Will you be okay with going back later?" he asked, flipping through his other messages. There were copies of lab reports from the FBI. They swept her house and found absolutely nothing that gave them any information.

"Yes, I don't mind. I just have to wait for the window repair man to fix the jimmied window frame and the alarm guy to re-wire the window. Then I'm clear." Desdemona whipped eggs in a bowl, and watched him without saying a word. She lost him, he was thinking about something else.

Whitefox was lost in the emails.

"When I'm done here, I'm going to go roll naked in the snow, or maybe have a very raunchy affair with Elizabeth behind both of your backs." She stated. "Then I thought I'd shave my head." Then she gave up, and just made him his breakfast. This whole grandfather thing had him rattled.

Whitefox looked up and into her eyes. "Yes on the snow, and you're not shaving your head. I happen to like your hair," he answered, grinning. "As for you and Elizabeth having sex, yeah I'm fine with that, but Ethan and I get to watch and take pictures."

Desdemona stuck out her tongue. She was pretty sure he was kidding, but there was that doubt in her mind. "Good to see you can multi task."

Callen was about to say something, when there was a loud explosion from outside his house. He jumped from his seat and ran to Desdemona pulling her down. "Stay here," he said, grabbing his Glock and running for the front door.

What waited outside astounded him. "Well holy shit," he muttered, pulling out his phone. He dialed FBI West. When Ginny answered the phone, he spoke quickly. "Ginny get the tech team to my house, someone just blew up the Denali, and I believe it's related to the Adare situation.

"I'll send them ASAP, Callen. Want me to call the Blackhawk's?" she asked already paging the tech team and transmitting his address.

"No, I'll call them, after I call the fire department." Desdemona touched his arm and stare in horror. "No Desi, don't even think it, you aren't running and that's the end of discussion. You promised me to stay, and I'm holding you to it!" Whitefox began dialing the reservation fire department. After explaining the situation, he knew he had to call his brother and he began dialing.

Blackhawk answered his phone on the second ring. "What's up Cal?" he said.

"The stalker just blew up the Denali, in my driveway."

"What?" He almost spilled his coffee. "Are you both okay?" he inquired, now he was beyond worried about his brother and doctor. Now it was life of death. The stalker was escalating and probably pissed that Doctor Adare was with a man.

"We're fine, we were inside. I called FBI West, Ginny is sending techs, and the fire department is coming." Then he told him about the note in the book.

"Try and keep the evidence uncontaminated, and just watch your back. I want you back here ASAP, do you hear me?" Ethan wasn't taking any chance with his brother's life.

"I have to see granddad and then I'm heading back."

"I want to know where you are hourly," he ordered. "The stalker is unhinged, and now you're tagged to be in the crosshairs. This lunatic now knows where you live. You aren't ever going back there, not until we find him. Pack all the things you need for an extended stay at our place."

"I'm aware and I will," he was answering cautiously. He didn't want Desdemona to hear the conversation. Already she was sheet white, and looked like she was going to run for the hills. "Can I bring a guest?"

Blackhawk got his meaning. "Yes, you can bring her."

"Thank you for understanding."

"See you tonight," he said, and then paused. "Callen, keep yourself safe, okay?" he added, softly.

"No worries Ethan, I'll see you at the house or sheriff's station before dark," and he would. If his brother was worried about him, he wasn't going to be focused on the killer and that would risk the team there. As he hung up he could hear the fire truck coming. "I have to handle this. I want you to make breakfast, get your gun and don't leave the inside of this house. Am I clear Desi?" he asked, lifting her chin so she was forced to look in his eyes. "I will chase you if you run, and when I catch you, I will be pissed. I take promises very serious, pinky swears included," he warned. "If I have to drag you back, the fight will be epic."

She was irritated he knew she was thinking of running from him. "Be safe," she whispered, her eyes filling with tears and then she threw her arms around his waist hugging him.

When he left the house, she started crying. "I'm so sorry, Callen. Please don't die instead of me."

Ethan was pacing as he dressed. When his wife exited the shower he knew she was staring at him. He just had to remain calm and hope his brother got back to Red River in one piece. This was the dilemma of working with family. It hit close to home. For now whoever was stalking the doctor wasn't to the snapping point yet. Blowing up a vehicle was one thing; a sniper hiding in the woods was another and he hoped it didn't get to that point.

"What happened?" she asked, already knowing something bad was brewing.

"Callen just got a nasty message from Desdemona's stalker."

"Uh oh. What?"

"The Denali was blown up." He knew she was going to be worried, and he didn't like stressing her while she was pregnant.

"Are they okay?" Elizabeth was sick to her stomach. All she could think of was the dream their grandfather just relayed to her.

"Yeah, they were in his cabin at the time."

Elizabeth started pacing, and rubbing her baby belly. "Did you tell them to get back here?" she asked, as she felt sick to her stomach.

"Yeah, he's heading to granddad's house, and then he'll head back here."

"He's new at this, he really isn't equipped to handle this on his own, Ethan." Now she wished they were there with him.

Blackhawk went to his wife and pulled her against his body. "Don't worry baby, Callen's a smart man, and now he knows that the stakes have been raised on this one. He'll watch his back, and keep Desdemona safe until he gets back here, and we can keep them both safe." Part of him wasn't thrilled at that prospect either. His pregnant wife and child were here, and that meant they could be caught in the crosshairs of the invisible enemy they now had to protect themselves from. Here he just allowed Desdemona into their inner sanctum, and was risking them all.

"We have to help her despite the risk," she said, knowing what he was thinking. "Desdemona doesn't have a chance alone now. If the stalker's blowing things up it's only going to get worse. It's escalating."

Blackhawk was aware. "Nothing is happening to them," he promised. "I need to shower and then we have work to do," he said, trying to distract her.

"Okay, I'll get ready." Elizabeth sat on the bed and was feeling panicky. Suddenly she needed to see if Callen was safe. She typed out a text and hit send, holding her phone and feeling the overwhelming fear beat at her.

"Please be careful, Callen," she whispered, as she closed her eyes and waited for his reply.

Callen Whitefox stayed out of the way of the fire department as they extinguished the flames on the Denali. When his phone beeped he checked the incoming message.

Please be safe and come back in one piece.
I love you -L

Staring down at the phone he knew how rattled she had to be over this. He dialed her number and she answered on the first ring.

"Please be careful, Callen."

"Hey beautiful," he said, hiding all the nerves in his voice. "Long time no talk. I need you to not worry about me okay? You're pregnant and the last thing you need is to be stressed over all this."

Elizabeth felt rattled. "We're both worried. Don't let anything happen to you. Baby Blackhawk needs his uncle."

Callen Whitefox knew that she was trying to stay calm and not show him too much emotion. "I promise I'll be back in time for dinner. I won't let anything happen to us."

"Promise?" she asked.

"You know how you never break a promise to a Blackhawk?"

"Yes."

"It's reciprocal. I promise."

Elizabeth believed him, he sounded completely assured. "If you let anything happen to you I'm so going to kick your ass and be mad at you for a very long time."

Whitefox grinned. "No worries, I love you, beautiful. Don't forget it."

"Bye Callen," she answered, feeling better now that she talked to him. Now she could focus on her day. When she disconnected she realized she forgot something. Banging out another text, she put her phone away and got ready for her day.

It was time to get her job done, despite where her mind was at that moment.

Callen Whitefox had just put his phone back into his pocket when it beeped again, pulling it out he read the words and his heart skipped a beat.

There was no doubt in his mind he loved her too.

~ Chapter Fifteen ~
Friday morning

Ethan Blackhawk and his wife were on edge, and as they sat in the conference room at the sheriff's station it wasn't looking like it was going to let up until Whitefox and Doctor Adare were back among the team. Elizabeth worked the white board, and prepared for the arrival if Christina Hart from downstairs. She needed more information, to add to the white board.

Blackhawk was emailing Gabe, informing him of the misfortunate incident with the Denali, and hoping he took it better than he thought he would. The stalker wasn't really the FBI's issue, but the destruction of federal property was going to piss him off and now officially make it FBI related. Even if Elizabeth finagled their boss to their side with the whole favor thing, it was a matter of time before it would have worn thin on Gabe and he pulled the plug on FBI funds and assistance. Now he really couldn't, if they could prove the stalker was the one that blew up Federal property.

Christina came to the door and knocked. Tentatively she entered the room, and waited until both Blackhawks were focused on her. She didn't want to bother them if they were working on case related work.

"Hey, Christina," said Blackhawk, not even looking up from his email. "Elizabeth needed to see you, and thanks for making time for us this morning. I'm sure you're busy with the trace evidence."

Even though she spoke to Ethan, she looked directly at Elizabeth. "It's no problem Director Blackhawk; I was packing up some things for transport to FBI West."

"Are you transporting?" he asked.

"Yes, I can leave and be back in a few hours. I don't feel secure leaving the bodies in the cooler downstairs. If Doctor Adare were here she would want them transported along with any trace. It's secure at home and really downstairs is just a basement," she said, watching the tone of her voice. She had a bad case of boss lust for him, and his wife was well aware of it. On a good day she wasn't willing to poke the tigress by drooling over her husband, but pregnant, uh no. That was suicide and all the female techs knew it.

"Send another tech to handle it. What about Derek? I need you here. We think we have some leads and may be processing some evidence. Today we're interviewing suspects."

"Oh, okay. Derek is on duty later. I can load up the van and have him take it tonight. He'll be back before dawn in case we need the equipment again. Hopefully another body doesn't show up, but in case one does, we'll be ready." She said, pleasantly.

"Christina," Elizabeth drew her attention to her and off her husband. She was well aware the woman was wary of her, and that was fine by her. They'd discussed it and drew boundaries. As of now, there were no issues and Elizabeth was glad. In fact, she liked the woman a lot, but she let her think she was dangerous. It was just entertaining. When her husband kicked her foot under the table she almost laughed.

"Yes, Director Blackhawk?" she asked. "What can I do for you?"

Elizabeth patted the seat beside her. "I need to pick your brain. Since Doctor Adare isn't here right now, you're the next smartest person in the room."

Ethan Blackhawk doubted that statement. His wife had an Ivy League education very few knew that, and she preferred it that way. It made everyone underestimate her, and that's how she tripped them up.

"Okay," she said, sitting. "Pick away."

Elizabeth gave her credit; she was keeping the nerves under control. "We know the killer is using Ethylene Glycol as the method of drugging and incapacitating the victims, and I know that it's in anti-freeze, but I need to know what other substances contain it. I could just Google it, but you're the best at the chemical-ese stuff, and I need the best."

Ethan was proud of his wife, she actually was being friendly, and he patted her leg. When they had been working the serial killing on the reservation, they'd had a disagreement over how friendly to be with the techs. Christina Hart was one of his techs, and had been for over five years, and when he had to watch how friendly she was with the doctors that she hired, it bothered him. Blackhawk was still wary of Doctor Leonard and Magnus, and Elizabeth wasn't thrilled with Christina. So for now they both agreed to be themselves, but cognizant of the boundaries.

"Well boss, Ethylene Glycol is everywhere in polymers and products."

"I think we need liquid form. We believe the killer is using coffee as the vessel for the poison. Or at least that's what we think." She slid the stomach contents report to the woman. "Are we correct to assume that?" she asked.

Christina read the output data from the content and scanned the information. "It's the only thing they all have in common, Elizabeth," and then she realized she used her name. "I'm Sorry, Director."

"In house use our names, it's okay," she reassured her.

"Okay, Elizabeth." She thought about it. "I can give you a few off the top of my head, the rest I'll need to run a list for you because it's that extensive."

"I'm ready," she pulled out paper. "Shoot."

"Anti-freeze is the most logical medium. It's relatively easy to find. Any grocery store that has windshield fluid usually carries Anti-freeze right beside it"

"What else?" asked Blackhawk.

"Without getting too complex with the description of the chemical, Ethylene Glycol is part of a family of chemicals. Off the top of my head, some stains for wood contain it, as does those products to fix flat tires, chemicals to develop pictures, herbicides, some adhesive products. Then you have paint products, caulk, and most ink and toner cartridges contain it too."

"So basically it's everywhere."

"Yeah, but in anti-freeze it's your most likely culprit. Ethylene Glycol is sweet and can be hidden in things."

"Thank you, Christina. I appreciate you helping us," said Elizabeth. Something was bugging her about that list. She had that little nagging feeling again in the back of her mind. Now she just needed to think, and she blocked everything out to do just that.

Ethan realized his wife was gone. She was deep in thought, and was done with the tech. "Let me know when you're sending Derek with the van."

"Sure thing boss," she said standing, and leaving the room, but right before she left she couldn't help one last look at him. Yeah, now she had her Blackhawk fix for the day. Now it was time to get the vans inventoried, loaded and ready to leave. Since Derek would be delivering to FBI West she might as well have him pick up anything they needed.

Blackhawk tapped his wife on the shoulder. "Want to share with those of us not in your head?" he laughed. "You have the look on your face."

"Photo developing solution."

"Okay," he said, still not quite there yet.

Elizabeth pulled up the list of suspects on her tablet and pointed at the three women. "This one," she pointed at Carly Kester's name, "she had contact with one victim, and then she slept with another. Then we have Courtney Brewer, she owns a photo shop and gift shop."

"Oh, photo developing solution."

"Yeah, and then we have Wilma May who had contact with the deputy, he lived here and certainly stopped in 'Cup of Joe', and then waited on the same victim that Carly identified."

"Okay so that's three suspects. All three could be the one, or involved."

"We have four. Then there's Sheila who has a violent temper, as we found out, knew the deputy, and she has access to supplies for the station. I'm betting ink and toner are hers to regulate and hand out."

Blackhawk didn't think about her. "So basically we have four women, all of which could have done it. And finding out what drugged them and was used to lure them in hasn't made it easier, but harder."

Elizabeth laughed. "Now, if we could appropriate ourselves some DNA evidence, we could run it against the blonde hairs we found, and then we can eliminate suspects."

"Oh and how will we be doing that, Elizabeth?" he asked. "We do have to follow the law, so you can't go yank hairs from their heads in a fight. Plus if it's one of them, and you match the DNA then it's going to be sketchy in court."

"If we can match one of them, then we can stake them out, follow them and see if she leads us to her next victim."

"Okay, I'll agree with you there, but again how? You still can't start a fight and pull out their hair."

"Yeah, too bad because I'd like to yank Carly Kester bald," she muttered, and then the look on his face made her laugh. He knew as well as she did, that if she had to slap some women around for DNA she'd do it in a heartbeat.

"You have a plan don't you?"

Elizabeth grinned. "I have a plan for each one of them, but I'm pretty damn sure you're going to hate each one of my ingenious schemes."

Now Blackhawk looked nervous. "Oh crap, if you're calling them schemes they're going to be shady."

"Remember, it's this or your pregnant wife has to have four fistfights."

"Shit. Okay, what do I have to do?"

"You're going to start smoking again, baby."

"What?" Blackhawk hadn't smoked in almost ten years, and he really didn't want to start up again. They had a kid coming and didn't want lung cancer.

"You're going to go out on a smoke break with Sheila, and have a smoke. When she's done smoking, and leaves you grab her butt," she pointed at him. "By butt, I mean cigarette butt, not her ass, or you have a whole other issue to worry about than smoking that will kill you faster than lung cancer."

"You know this is crazy, right?" he said, not believing that they were going to go there.

"Hey, you want me out there smoking with her or yanking hair out of her head?" She pointed at the baby.

"Why me?" he asked rhetorically, rubbing his forehead and already knowing the answer.

"She hates the women on this team, remember? It's you or Callen, and he isn't here. But I guess you can't handle it, so I'll just do it," she offered, baiting him.

"I am absolutely not having my pregnant wife lighting up on a nicotine break!" Blackhawk started laughing. "This may just work, and that makes me think you're either insane or some evil genius."

She thought about it, and it made him laugh even more. "I think I'm going to go with evil genius on this one and possibly plead the fifth for the last three. Although…"

"I love you," he said laughing.

Elizabeth sat back in her chair. "Wait until you hear what you have to do to get the DNA from the other three. Since you're not mad at me yet, I'll say I love you too now. In case it's the last time you want me to ever say it again." Elizabeth kept a straight face and had to fight to not laugh.

"Elizabeth!" Blackhawk suddenly didn't find it funny, because he didn't think she was joking.

"What?" she asked, innocently.

"I can't believe I'm going to do this."

"Me either. I figured you'd make Callen do it," she said, dropping her boots on the corner of the desk, laughing. "You know, haze the newbie."

Blackhawk looked down at his watch. He'd never make it back in time.

Damn it!

Whitefox wouldn't let her go back to her house; it just wasn't going to be safe. Instead he sent Special Agent Christensen. Asking her for a favor wasn't too bad, the woman seemed to understand that the situation had just upgraded from stalking to something more dire. Blowing up a federal vehicle was a big offense, and when the lunatic was found, it was going to be more than just stalking. Now they were dealing with federal jail time.

Desdemona didn't protest when he said she wasn't leaving his sight. She seemed willing to stick close to him, and that was a good thing. Right now he didn't need to have to chase the woman all over the country trying to get her back to his side. He wasn't above handcuffs and trumped up FBI charges to drag her back. Now they just needed to wrap up the personal aspect of their time on the Rez, and then head back to Red River to get to work.

"We don't have to do this," he said, more for her than for himself. He could handle his grandfather, but she shouldn't have to deal with his family's personal baggage. He'd seen more than a few women break down under Timothy's gaze.

"Callen, it's okay. I know what I'm heading into, and I'll be fine. What's the worst he can say? You can't marry me and have kids with me?" she paused, realizing what she said. "We're going to live together; you aren't committing to me forever, or giving me children."

Whitefox looked over at her. The only reason he didn't ask her to marry him was he thought she'd run, well that and he planned on just forcing her to marry him by wearing her down eventually. "Would you marry me if I asked you?" he needed to know.

"Callen we just met. I think we're rushing it, so no."

"I'd like to point out my brother married Elizabeth on day four and they are perfectly happy."

It irritated Desdemona that he was using Elizabeth and Ethan as his standard. She wasn't Elizabeth and knew she'd never be her. "Not until this stalker mess is over. I don't like risking you now; I won't risk my husband to a nut job. That's just sticking a big red bull's-eye on you. Screw that," she adamantly objected, burying her feelings. "It's not happening. I'm sick about living together, and putting your life at risk. I'm hoping to talk you out of it at some point."

"Biding your time are you?" he laughed, taking her hand in his. "I'm stubborn, so it's not going to happen." Part of him was thrilled that she would marry him if there wasn't a nutjob harassing her. At least she acknowledged it was going to happen after all this was over.

Desdemona sighed. "You are exasperating, do you know that?" Staring down at their joined hands, still there were no twined fingers. It lacked intimacy and still irritated her.

"You wouldn't be the only woman to tell me that," he paused. "Well the only difference is the other women didn't use such large words. Most the women before you weren't exactly doctors with their fancy vernaculars." Now he was teasing her, as he parked the replacement Denali in front of his grandfather's. It still impressed him that a simple native man managed to get a doctor to fall in love with him. Whitefox wondered if this was what his brother felt like when he managed to catch Elizabeth.

She rolled her eyes and then punched him in the arm.

He looked at the totem, and the new addition his grandfather had commissioned. Wyler had carved another raven and placed it at the very top, wings spread as if scaring off danger. It was completely Elizabeth and her addition to the family, and it suited the entire pole. Wyler even gave the black raven icy blue eyes, so there'd be no doubt that she was the protective Raven looking over them all. "You can still change your mind," he said, softly.

"Let's just face him, and go from there." Deep down she hoped he didn't see how scared she was that he was going to be talked out of being with her. "Just stay calm, Callen. We can figure it out." Desdemona leaned over and kissed him. "I promise."

When he looked over, he saw his grandfather waiting. "Let the show begin," he muttered. "I apologize in advance."

She gave his hand a squeeze and then bravely hopped down from the side of the Denali, making her way to the man standing with his arms crossed on the porch. Yeah, he was intimidating as hell, but she wasn't going to let him see her afraid.

"Hello, Mr. Blackhawk, I'm Desdemona Adare." Holding out her hand, she stared into his brown eyes, and understood why he was the patriarch. He was bad ass like Elizabeth. Even at eighty-eight years old, but she was ready.

"Hello, Doctor Adare. Welcome to my home." Timothy stepped backwards and held the door for her.

"Thank you, Mr. Blackhawk. I appreciate you having me over for lunch."

Timothy hugged his boy, and patted his back. There was nerves and worry written all over his face. It hurt his old heart that he was the cause of it. His grand daughter-in-law was right. It was time to trust his boys. After all, Ethan had found Elizabeth and that was better than if he had done it himself.

"Before we continue, let's stop the false pleasantries, if you don't mind and get down to the reason we are all here today and then have lunch. Please have a seat." It was a direct order as he pointed to the couch and nodded at his grandson too. Now his boy looked wound so tight, he was going to spring apart at any second.

"Certainly." She sat, and squeezed Callen's hand. They would survive anything he said to them.

"I spoke to Elizabeth, and she told me I'm a control freak who needs to trust my boys and let them make their own choices in life. I have decided to listen to her and butt out of this one. I trust Elizabeth to guarantee that Callen's choice is quality."

Whitefox looked surprised.

"She told me you're a lovely woman, and that you wouldn't do anything to hurt Callen. I believe her and have decided to forgo any of this judging you based on your heritage, and let Callen decide what is best for him. Who am I to interfere?"

Now Whitefox's mouth hung open. As soon as he got to Red River, he was going to kiss his sister-in-law. She managed to get him something he never thought he'd have. Freedom of choice to love anyone he wanted. Yeah, he loved her to death.

"Son, are you happy?" He looked over at his youngest grandson.

"Yes, I am." He squeezed her hand and felt the pressure release from his chest. This was the last step in his plan.

"Then consider yourself free of your promise that you made me years ago."

"I think I have to be dreaming," he said. "Desi, pinch me please. My stubborn grandfather just admitted he was a control freak and then willing let someone else make a decision."

"Are you sassing me son?"

Desdemona elbowed him hard.

"Young woman, I will say this. If you break his heart you need to run fast. I suggest the witness protection program. I will be sending Elizabeth to clean this up."

She nodded and swallowed. When he looked directly into her eyes she felt like he was staring into her soul and wasn't kidding in the least. The old Indian was dead serious. *Crap!*

"Now, I need to ask about great grandkids" he said pleasantly. "I want lots of Whitefox great grandkids."

Desdemona laughed, she thought he was kidding. "Uh, well we haven't gotten to that point in the relationship to even discuss that."

"There will be lots of kids," Callen tossed in there. "Don't worry. I plan on matching Ethan kid for kid. He plans on seven and I'm going for eight."

She looked over at him incredulously. "Excuse me? Shouldn't I have some say in that Callen? Since I'll be the one carrying, growing and giving birth to any children that we decide to create together?"

Wyler laughed from the kitchen, and so did Timothy Blackhawk.

"What's there to discuss. Do you like kids?" he asked, just so overjoyed that he was essentially getting his grandfather's blessing, that he was completely giddy.

"Callen, I love kids, but we aren't even getting married," she objected. "Don't you think children talk is a little 'cart before the horse? I refuse to discuss children at this point in our relationship unless you add the phrase 'WAY down the road'." Desdemona might be talked into living together, but having kids was a different thing. She was a product of who knew what kind of relationship. Her father was unknown, and her mother never married. Kids needed close consideration and more time than a week of knowing a person, as did marriage.

"Desi, we're going to get married and have kids."

Her heels were dug in on the kid thing.

"You're against marriage? Is it because of the entire situation where your life is at risk?" Timothy asked bluntly. "I will not be having any of my boys shacking up with a woman and having children outside of marriage. My great grandkids will have either Blackhawk or Whitefox as their last name. There will be no Adare children on the Rez."

Whitefox tensed at the idea they could even possibly have illegitimate children. There was no possible way he could let that happen- even if he had to drag her to a justice of the peace and make her sign the license. Better yet, he'd get Elizabeth to do it.

"Someone threatened to kill who ever I love!" She couldn't believe how stubborn this family was, and completely irrational. "Why does no one see the main issue here?" Now she felt herself heading into hysteria at being ganged up on over the topic.

Desdemona felt bullied, and it made her uncomfortable.

Callen dropped his arm over her shoulder and pulled her against his body. "She's being silly." He kissed her on the forehead. "Desi is absolutely going to marry me and soon."

Wyler came over and stood behind his father, placing his hand on his shoulder. He knew his father had been plagued with dreams and was worried.

"It doesn't matter, he's already risked. What is coming is going to involve you both, and you won't be able to run from it."

"He had a dream, Callen," added his father. They all took his dreams very serious. The man foretold Ethan Blackhawk's return, Elizabeth's abduction, and now this. "He already knew about you being hunted, Doctor Adare."

Timothy patted his son's hand. "The minute you met him, fate intervened young lady, and you can't push him out to stop it. Now it has to play out from start to finish. You were the deer in the thicket, and the fox was defending you, standing in front of you. It's already begun."

Whitefox touched her cheek, offering reassurance.

"You've already pulled my boy into this."

Desdemona's eyes filled with tears, and she couldn't hold them back any longer.

"Sweetheart, it's okay," Callen Whitefox tried to soothe her fear and sadness. "He didn't mean it that way," he said, as he gave his grandfather a look.

Timothy stood. "Wyler, please take Callen outside for a little while. I wish to speak to the Doctor alone for a few minutes."

"Granddad," he stood, objecting as he was terrified to leave her alone with him. "Please."

"Boy, unless you have Elizabeth in your pocket to talk me out of it, you need to show your elder some respect and get your behind out of my way. She is the ONLY one that has me wrapped around her finger, so move."

Callen weighed his option. He trusted that Elizabeth had handled it for him and it would all work out. Leaning down, he kissed her gently. "If you need me, I'll be outside. He's old. You can outrun him," he said trying to get her to relax.

Desdemona nodded and patted his cheek.

Timothy waited until his grandson was gone from the house, and he moved to sit in his spot. There was no way he could be hard on this girl. She wasn't tough like Elizabeth; he needed a softer touch with her and a great deal more tact. Taking her hand in his old weathered one, he looked into her eyes. They were an unusual shade of green. Deep in them he could feel the need to run, and he didn't doubt she'd try. The woman had a great deal of baggage, and he was beginning to question what Elizabeth saw in her. The woman's energy didn't feel right with his grandson's.

"Tell me about you," he asked softly, handing her a tissue.

Desdemona wiped her tears. "I'm from the bayou. My grandmother's a witch, my mom disappeared. I have one sister and I deal with the dead for a living." It said it all. "I'm the worst possible person for him, and I can't get him to see that. He's stubborn and won't run for his life."

Timothy nodded. "Are you in love with him?"

"Unfortunately." Because she was well aware who owned his heart, and it wasn't her. Again, she swallowed to keep it hidden.

He laughed. "So you regret it?" he wanted to know what existed inside this woman, now that she held his grandson's heart.

"I don't regret it. I just wish I could talk him out of it, and maybe save his life. Please, tell him he can't be with me, make him walk away. Tell me what I have to do to make him hate me, and I'll do it." She wanted to beg the old man to help her buy some time. Time to rethink and focus on the facts and weigh the options.

Timothy could see and feel the conflict. The woman wouldn't intentionally hurt Callen, she was a confused mess. Elizabeth had been right about her. This little woman was scared out of her mind. "So you'd let him despise you, just to save him?"

"I can face whatever is chasing me; I'll risk my own life, but I won't risk him. I would rather live without him and secretly love him forever, than risk him for a minute. I'm a horrible choice for him." The tears were falling still, as she begged the man sitting beside her. "Help me save Callen, and get him as far away from me as possible."

Timothy could feel the issues bubbling to the surface, and once again he questioned what Elizabeth saw in the woman. He had a few choices, but he decided to let fate play its hand and lead where they were all heading. Timothy could feel the half-truths and new the woman wasn't being completely honest, but this was Callen's journey. He was an old man and his time here was coming to an end. Now he needed to let the next leader of the family take her place and carry the men. "Are you willing to run from a chance at family?" Timothy patted her cheek, and wiped the tears with the palm of his hand.

It was like he saw into her and saw the truth. What she wanted most was a family of her own, and a place to belong.

"If you stay you'll have a family to protect you, Desdemona."

And he saw that too. Now she was wary of the man. He seemed to see her inner secrets. Coming here wasn't a good idea.

"If he loves you like you love him, losing you would hurt him beyond words, and if you ran he would certainly follow. Then who would protect his back from what chases you both?"

Desdemona broke down, crying and feeling completely helpless and out of control. Less than a week ago she was in FBI West doing her job and now she was going to live with a man who was insistent she marry him and have kids soon. Desdemona's brain started battling back for control and she was glad.

Timothy remembered when the other woman in his boys' lives came to him crying over Ethan. "You won't face this alone. You will be protected little doe. If you run from him, he will continually bring you back. You cannot run forever. Maybe this is your time to stand your ground and let him keep you safe."

"What if he gets hurt?" she leaned against him, as he patted her shoulder.

"The Blackhawks protect their own, and he's picked you, Desdemona. You need to just accept it, and let him be the man. You'll also have the protection of my son, myself, Ethan and Elizabeth. It's time to stop running."

She sniffled.

"Now, do you want to marry him and have a family."

"Yes," she answered semi-honestly. Desdemona would do anything to belong somewhere and be accepted. "It's my secret wish, more than anything. I love him with all my heart." What she didn't tell him was how she didn't believe he loved her with all his heart, because he was head over heels in love with a married woman.

"Then marry him and trust that this family will keep you safe. Elizabeth and Ethan won't let anything happen to you."

"What can she do?" she laughed and cried at the same time.

"Did you see the totem outside my home?"

"Yes." She didn't get the allure, but it was their culture not hers.

Timothy patted her hand. "The raven at the top is Elizabeth. She watches over all the men in this family, and I believe was sent here to do just that. I trust in her and you should too. Ethan is the other Raven and as a boy he would be the one that warned everyone of oncoming danger. The fox is Callen and his gift is that he stands out but yet can blend in when need be. He will keep you safe. I am the bear. Fiercely territorial of its cubs and children and will have the Great Spirits guide my family. Then there is my son Wyler, the bull. He is a tiny bull on the back, but mighty with his stubbornness. We will close around you little doe, and keep you safe, all you need to do is choose to believe."

"I want to believe, but this stalker is crazy. Now he's blowing up cars."

Timothy Blackhawk wiped a tear with his thumb. "Believe little doe, and you will see that anything is possible."

"If I become part of the family do I get an animal on the totem pole too?" she asked, sniffling.

"You absolutely do little doe. What is it you wish to have as your spirit guide? Is there an animal that calls to you in here," he asked, taping her over the heart. He was curious to know what she would pick as her animal. The choice would speak volumes.

"I want to be the spider. Is that possible?" she inquired, wiping her eyes.

"Why the spider?" It wasn't what he expected from her at all.

"Elizabeth shared a quote and I connected to it, and it made me relate to the spider. I don't want to be a doe. I want to weave webs and be strong and scary."

"Our Elizabeth told you this, did she?" It was always obvious that his granddaughter-in-law was astute, but he didn't think she'd be this astute. He could see her as the spider too.

All doubts fell away about Elizabeth seeing the situation. Instinctively, she already knew what was coming. There was no mistaking it now.

Desdemona told him the quote and he patted her cheek.

"If you feel you are the spider, then by all means, who am I to question it?"

"So I get to be on the totem?"

"Anyone that marries into the family gets a place on the family totem, Desdemona." He didn't tell the woman that while the spider weaved webs and could scare; it also was the most fragile of creatures and the one creature Natives considered cunning and sometimes the bringer of death. They were untrustworthy, and generally those that hid the truth. "Stay and fight and we will stand beside you and in front of you."

Desdemona stared up at him and sighed. "What is it with all of you Blackhawks? Ethan is intimidating, Elizabeth is scary as hell, Callen is stubborn and then there's you. I didn't have a snowballs chance in hell against any of you did I?"

Timothy patted her cheek. Doctor Desdemona Adare would stay and fight and now it would be up to them all to keep her safe. "Not at all little spider. Not at all."

"I guess I'm sticking." Desdemona put her faith in people she barely knew and gained a family she always wanted.

"Now, about having children," began Timothy grinning.

Desdemona Adare laughed, and couldn't help but notice the older Blackhawk had the same endearing grin Callen had too.

"Will you match Ethan and Elizabeth child for child?"

Desdemona thought about it and laughed and just gave in to appease the man sitting beside her. "Sure, why not." It wasn't like they could force her to have children or get married. If Callen asked, she'd demand a long engagement, to make sure it was right. What was the harm in that? Logical Desdemona was back in control.

Ethan walked into the 'Cup of Joe' ahead of his wife, and was pleasantly pleased to find Joe Lemar sitting behind the counter. It was time to have some fun, and he rarely was able to be the scary one. It was usually his role to stand and intimidate, and he was happy to be bad cop today.

"You," he pointed. "In the back now," he practically growled. "I hear your hand was on my wife's ass," he said it loud enough that a few patrons looked over at the commotion. It pleased him that the man went a sickly shade of gray. To make it even

386

worse, he pulled his jacket back and showed him the gun and badge.

Joe Lemar practically scurried like a rat back to his office. When both Blackhawk's had entered and closed the door he began trying to find an excuse, but the large Native man shut him right down.

"Is there a reason you felt the need to put your hand on my pregnant wife's ass, Joe?" He stood very close to the man, staring down at him. "Are you looking to die?"

"I-I-I," he stuttered.

"Now, Ethan honey, don't hit him where the marks will show. You remember what they taught us in Quantico. Only use those special places, like his testicles." Elizabeth managed to keep a straight face, and she wasn't quite sure how.

"Oh don't worry baby. Joe and I are going to take a little ride, alone. Then we're going to have a little talk, about what happens when you manhandle another man's pregnant wife. Especially when the man can make you disappear. Hear that Joe, I work for the FBI, and you won't be the first one I made disappear."

"Wait, please," he begged, looking over at Elizabeth for help.

"Stop looking at her, Joe. Or you may make me want to do something incredibly violent to the most delicate of your organs."

Joe looked down at the floor, and kept his eyes adverted from the pregnant woman to save his life.

"You have two minutes to tell me everything I want to hear, or I walk you out of here in cuffs for the last time." He stepped closer. "It won't be hard to fabricate a story about how you tried to escape, and I had to shoot you in the back of the skull, Joe. Is that how you want to end your life? Running from an Indian through the snow?"

Elizabeth actually had to hide her mouth behind her hand. She was so close to laughing at the visual in her mind, and his choice of words.

"I'll tell you anything you want to know! Don't chase me in the snow. I won't even think about touching your pregnant wife again."

Blackhawk fought hard to not break down and laugh. "I want to know about this man," he pulled out the victim's picture. "The one that had stopped in for coffee." Ethan Blackhawk slid it across the desk, to the man's adverted gaze.

"I don't know anything about him."

Elizabeth pulled out her car keys. "I'll pull the vehicle to the back door, baby. No one will see him leave." She walked towards the door.

"Wait! Maybe he got coffee." Joe Lemar was sweating profusely, and ringing his hands.

"Tell me about Wilma May, your waitress."

"What do you want to know?" he asked, still staring down at his desk.

Blackhawk straddled the chair in front of him, and pointed to the other chair. "Sit!" he barked. When the man jumped, he again fought for composure. "Start telling me about her personal life."

"She's worked here maybe ten years." He sat and wiped the sweat from his forehead before continuing, "Her old man kicked it, and she needed a job desperately."

"Her old man?" asked Blackhawk. "She's what? Forty years old now?"

"Yeah, she married some older man, and he ended up having the big one, but he never got the life insurance policy out of wife number one's name, and Wilma May got nothing."

Ethan looked over his glasses and over his shoulder at his wife. That was most definitely a juicy bit of gossip.

"What hours does Wilma May work?" asked Elizabeth.

"Friday during the day, Saturday nights, off on Sunday and Monday, then rest of the week days."

Elizabeth leaned against the door, and watched the man. "How much time did she spend with the man in the picture, and did she make a new pot of coffee for him?"

"No, I usually make the coffee when the ladies are busy."

Blackhawk stood. "I want to talk to your waitress in here. You have two choices regarding it, Joe. Comply or take a ride. Choose."

"I'll get her!" Joe Lemar started moving towards Elizabeth, and tried to get past her carefully without looking up. Last thing he wanted was the Indian man killing him.

Elizabeth closed the door and grabbed two bottles of water from her purse. They were in an evidence bag. Carefully she used a tissue, placing one where Wilma May would be sitting, and one where she would be sitting. Then she turned to her husband and grinned wickedly. "That was amazing work baby!" Elizabeth fist bumped him and winked.

"I wasn't always good cop before you became my partner. I did get to be bad cop a few times," he paused. "I hear footsteps."

Both Agents stopped smiling as the door opened.

Wilma May opened the door hesitantly. "You needed to see me?" She had wide eyes and looked nervous.

"Please have a seat, Wilma May," said Elizabeth, pointing at a chair. "Take a break, and have some water. We'll be right with you," she said, seriously.

"Oh, okay," she cracked open the bottle and took a big sip.

Elizabeth turned towards her husband and winked, as she pulled out her tablet. "Wilma May, do you know why we're here?" she calmly sat, and put on her best serious face.

"No, I can't imagine. I didn't do anything. I swear."

"Can you tell me about what time this man was in the last day he was seen alive?" Elizabeth pushed the picture towards her.

"Wilma May scrunched up her face. "I think it had to be around three in the afternoon, because he said to me it was kinda late in the day to be having coffee, but he still had a few hours to drive."

"He said nothing else to you?"

"No, really! I swear Agents. I would tell you."

Elizabeth leaned across the table, looking into the woman's eyes. "Okay, If we think of anything else, we'll be back," she said, softly.

Wilma May bolted.

Elizabeth reached into her pocket and pulled out her gloves. Once they were on, she carefully placed the top back on the water bottle and placed it in an evidence bag.

"I can't believe this worked," Blackhawk shook his head, laughing.

"Cowboy, why do you doubt me?" she asked, dropping her sunglasses back on her face. "Shall we, Mr. Blackhawk?"

He snickered and opened the door for his wife. The second they were back where people could see them, they had the FBI faces intact and both looked menacing. Blackhawk pointed at Joe Lemar, before he followed his wife out the door to their vehicle. Once inside, they both burst into laughter.

"Ethan, that was the sexiest display of bad cop I have ever seen you pull off. "

"I'm glad I could entertain you my love. I suddenly have a craving for a smoke break."

"There are days I love my job. Today is definitely one of them." Elizabeth buckled her seat belt. "Baby Blackhawk, your daddy was extra sexy today at work. You should be proud."

He laughed. "Back to the sheriff's station, daddy has more work to do yet today." Lovingly Ethan ran his hand over her belly and couldn't help but feel warmth over power him.

Damn it, he loved his life.

*   *   *

Opening the jar, she dumped out the eyes, and they slid sickly into the palm of her hand. Inspecting them, she admired her handy-work. There was absolutely no damage done to the perfect orbs. Soon he would be almost completely put back together again. Her one true love would be reconstructed.

He would be back.

She leaned over the table and looked down into his sightless face and popped them into place. "My love! They are a perfect match. Soon we will be back to the way we were before that day." She became quiet thinking back to the horrible events that shaped their future.

"Never mind my love, we need not speak of it. Accidents will happen, now won't they?"

She looked down at the body. "I think we only need a few more pieces until you are whole again, lover."

390

"Just a little longer, and we'll be together again." The sharp pain shot through her head, and she shook it viciously to regain control and push past the pain.

"Damn headaches are getting worse and worse," she said, rubbing her temples. She looked at her watch. "I think I may sneak in a nap, you know for beauty rest."

She kissed him on the cheek delicately, and headed to their bed to get some rest before her busy night ahead.

*   *   *

Callen loved his family, especially his grandfather. When his mother was gone, the man became his surrogate mom and dad all in one. This man was so vital to his life, and always would be. When he'd come inside from being kicked out, he found his grandfather comforting Desdemona. She was protectively under his arm, and she was laughing. There was no anger on his face and true to his word, he was planning on letting his grandson choose his own path in life.

They'd sat down to lunch, and his grandfather and dad had made an all vegetarian meal, of a hearty vegetable stew. Much like he remembered eating as a child. It touched his heart that they were trying to make Desdemona fit into their circle, the best that they could. Instead of questioning her choice in foods, they accepted her and made her feel like she belonged.

During dinner they joked with her, and teased her a little, but only to the point where she laughed. No one made her feel like she wasn't already a permanent part of their unit. Desdemona was accepted and welcomed into the family.

It touched his heart that his grandfather had taken to calling her 'little spider' much like he referred to his brother's wife as 'the protective raven'. It showed they were claiming her and it was more than he ever expected. Obviously she had told his grandfather about the quote that Elizabeth had shared with her. Just those words between the women seemed to heal Desdemona's heart, and he owed Elizabeth more than he could ever repay.

Desdemona was his final choice. Now he wouldn't be alone the rest of his life and could have what his brother had.

Whitefox kept updating his brother as they were still on the Rez, and part of him wished they could have more time together there to get her integrated into the family. Now that she saw she was welcome, he hoped she wouldn't run or he'd be chasing her down and dragging her back. Maybe it was Neanderthal of him, but he really didn't care. Desdemona Adare was going to stay in his life. Regardless of what she thought was best for him.

"Callen?" She touched his arm, drawing his attention back to here and now.

"Yeah sweetheart," he said, kissing her on the top of the head.

"We should be going. Ethan and Elizabeth need us there and we've been a distraction for them. I'm sure your brother is worried about you." Who was she kidding? Desdemona wanted to escape off the Rez and the Indian's stare.

He nodded. "Dad, take care of the old man, Ethan and I will be back in a couple days, and don't forget that fishing trip in spring." He hugged his father. The bond they were rebuilding was strong and he was grateful to have him back in his life. "If you need anything call me."

"I will son. Don't worry about us. Just be safe, and watch your back," he patted him on the shoulder. "Kiss Elizabeth for me, and hug your brother."

"Oh, don't you worry! I plan on it," he said, laughing.

Desdemona shook her head. After spending lunch with the eldest Blackhawks, she could see they all felt the same love Callen had for Elizabeth. She was trying to come to peace with it, and find her own niche into the family. Trying being the operative word.

"Granddad, thank you for lunch." Whitefox went to the old man, hugging. His heart ached that one day, he wouldn't get to do that. He held on a little longer this time, because he needed it, and wanted that memory to hold. "I love you, granddad," he whispered. "Thank you for setting me free."

The man smiled and patted his grandson on the cheek. "You can thank your brother's wife. She is hard to say no to, even when I have the best intention to do it." Timothy looked over at his

392

son. "Wyler, will you escort Desdemona to the vehicle? I wish to say something privately to Callen."

"Sure thing dad," said the man, as he held out his arm, and she put her hand through it smiling.

Callen watched her walk away, and must have had a completely lustful look on his face, because his grandfather started laughing.

"That is the same look your brother gets when he's staring at his wife. I'm going to also assume you'll be mauling that poor girl just like your brother does to Elizabeth."

"Hell yeah I plan on it. As for the look, it's genetic. I can't help it." He hoped his grandfather wasn't planning on telling him to forget about Desdemona. "What did you want to say to me?"

"Follow me," he led his grandson to his bedroom. "I need to ask you a few questions."

"Okay." Now the nerves were kicking up.

"Are you one hundred percent in love with that girl, with your entire heart and soul?"

Callen knew he shouldn't lie to his grandfather, so he twisted the truth to make it more palatable. "I can say without a doubt that the only other woman I will ever love other than her is Elizabeth." Then he prayed it would be good enough. There was just no way he was going to ruin the entire experience by telling his grandfather that he was in love with his brother's wife.

That just screamed 'very bad idea'.

Timothy looked deep into his eyes, feeling the lie, but holding his tongue. What he didn't tell Callen was he saw the way he looked at Elizabeth, and it wasn't with lust, but complete adoration. Again, he was going to defer this one to Elizabeth to handle. This would be the last thing he said about it all. "I have one piece of advice and you can do with it what you see fit."

"Okay, granddad."

"If it doesn't feel right, or you feel like you're rushing into something, step back and think about it. Talk to your brother or Elizabeth and get a second opinion."

Callen kept his face completely neutral. "Are you telling me not to marry Desdemona?"

"No, I'm saying listen to your heart, not your head."

393

Whitefox didn't understand the wariness, but it was evident on his grandfather's face. "Why are you worried?"

"She identifies with the spider. A spirit guide says a great deal about the person."

"Okay, and what does it mean?"

"Just watch her carefully and make sure you keep her close to you and your family. I just have this feeling that Death is looming just outside what we understand."

Whitefox was taken aback, since he knew what the stalker said on the note, but his grandfather didn't.

"I will granddad. I promise."

Timothy nodded. "If you're happy then I give you my complete blessing."

Yeah, he was going to grab his sister-in-law, dip her low and plant a big one right on her lips. She was going to be the best woman at his damn wedding that was for sure.

He stood at his dresser and pulled out a little box. It was carved with a letter B on it, and he held it lovingly in his hand. "When your brother married Elizabeth the first time, he gave her his mother's ring, because it was part of his family history," he paused, looking up into his boy's eyes. "I know you don't have that option. Your mom didn't marry, and she didn't really want to settle and plant roots."

He shrugged, unwilling to let that hurt him.

"I want you to take this," he said, handing him the little box and watching him open it. "It was your grandmother's ring. I gave it to her when we married a long time ago."

Callen didn't know what to say. "The family tradition says this ring goes to the new woman that will be married to the head of our family." He tried to hand it back. "That's Elizabeth. Plus you picked her personally over Ethan."

Timothy sat on the side of his bed. "I spoke to Elizabeth before you arrived, and we discussed this. I told her about the family tradition behind the ring, and she insisted that you use it to marry Desdemona if that was what you wanted. She wants you to have it and give you a part of the Blackhawk legacy."

His eyes filled with tears. The Blackhawk family ring was priceless to the family, and he wasn't a Blackhawk. Not by name anyway.

"I also spoke to your brother. He also wants you to have my wedding band as your own. I would be pleased if when you marry her, you'll wear it and remember me." He slipped it off his finger for the first time in over six decades and handed it to his grandson. "When you make the vows, mean them. That's all I ask. Go into it completely sure of what you are doing. Only marry for complete love."

Callen didn't have the words. He wiped the tears and couldn't believe the luck he'd finally found. His family was precious to him. Growing up he went from a mother that never cared, to a grandfather who loved completely and now a brother and sister who understood and would sacrifice their part of the family heritage to give it to him, and cement him firmly to it. They were officially declaring he was a Blackhawk with the gift of the rings. "I don't know what to say, granddad, but of course I'll wear it, and I know Desdemona will love grandma's ring."

"Remember son that your family will keep you safe and protect you when you need to be guarded over. You can always rely on your family, especially your brother and Elizabeth."

"I won't forget that," he placed his grandfather's ring in the box and closed it. "Thank you for this," he said, slipping the rings into his pocket.

"It was our protective raven's idea. Now go." He stood and patted his boy's cheek. Soon he would be calling Elizabeth to have a private conversation with her regarding everything he'd learned and felt. Something definitely wasn't right. His boy lied to him, and was hiding his feelings deep. They needed to have a family call and soon.

Callen memorized this moment for all eternity. It was burned forever into his mind and heart. Walking out of the house he stopped at his father's side and hugged him again. "Take care of Timothy, okay, dad?"

"I will son. Be safe, both of you. Kiss our Elizabeth for me and my grandson in her belly."

"Oh don't you worry! I plan on it!"

Wyler grinned.

Callen took Desdemona's hand and led her to the Denali. It was time to head back to work and protect his family.

"Are you okay, Callen?" She saw the tears in his eyes.

"I'm more than okay. Today has been an amazing day," he said, smiling gently at her, and then he just couldn't help it, he pulled her against his body and kissed her. Whitefox held her trapped to his mouth, as he kissed her deep and shared all the emotion that was in his body.

"Callen James Whitefox, you stop mauling that girl in the middle of the yard," yelled his grandfather. "You and your brother weren't raised by wolves. You let her breathe!"

He broke the kiss, and started laughing. "Unlike Ethan, I don't have the legal document authorizing a mauling. This is a preemptive mauling. I have to kiss her like this to lure her in!" He yelled back over his shoulder.

Desdemona was completely confused, but laughed anyway. This family was insane but now she felt safe and it was all worth it in the end.

To feel safe, Desdemona believed she'd sacrifice anything.

~ Chapter Sixteen ~
Friday afternoon

Ethan couldn't believe he was going to actually smoke to get DNA evidence. It still made him laugh when he thought about it. While he staked out the woman that was their subject of scrutiny, Elizabeth made sure the ash tray was completely clean of butts. Granted most of them had Sheila Courts lipstick on them, she wasn't going to take any chance. There could only be one butt in that tray, and it was going to be shipped off for DNA to FBI West.

When she peeked out the conference room they were using, he saw the woman putting her jacket on, and getting ready to go out. "Okay, I'll be back in as soon as I get the evidence."

Elizabeth put a glove and an evidence bag in his pocket. "Here," she handed him a cigarette and a lighter. "What?" The look on his face was priceless.

"Where did you get them?"

"Tech team," she smiled. "I went down and said, 'I need a smoke and lighter' and three appeared in under three seconds."

"Great, they now think you're pregnant and chain smoking," he laughed, taking the lighter and cigarette. "Okay, be back." Ethan buttoned up his wool coat, and headed for the doors. When he spotted the woman, he found a place to stand, out of the wind. This was one reason he quit. Freezing his ass off for a nicotine high wasn't fun. If his wife would have let him wear the parka, he probably wouldn't be as cold. Unfortunately for him, she insisted on his wool pea coat for this mission.

"I didn't know you smoked, Agent," she stated, staring over at him.

"Only when I'm stressed." Blackhawk started the lies. Anything to distract her from the truth that he planned on raiding the ash tray when she went inside. The things he did for his job and wife.

"Yeah, it's pretty stressful lately. I'm so freaked out about Bobby Lee that I forgot to order supplies."

Blackhawk took a long drag and felt the head rush. All he could hope was he didn't keel over from being dizzy. "Oh, is that your job?" he asked, taking another drag. If he became addicted to smoking again, he was going to force Elizabeth to help him break the habit with something else that would keep his hands busy whenever he craved a cigarette. Mainly his naked wife's body.

"Yeah, Jimmy said not to worry, but I'm a nervous wreck."

Blackhawk went the sympathetic approach, and he prayed the woman wouldn't smoke more than one. "It's tough to lose a friend," he said.

The woman started sniffling.

Oh shit. He was pretty sure his wife was watching this go down, and enjoying every second of it. Blackhawk took another drag, because this time he needed it, and then he put the cigarette out in the ash tray. "Ms. Court, it's okay." He moved closer, patting her shoulder, awkwardly.

Sheila put out her cigarette and threw herself at the sexy FBI agent. It was the perfect opportunity, and hopefully the woman would see him consoling her. His stupid wife deserved to feel the jealousy after she got Bobby Lee killed. Her and that wannabe Morticia Addams both deserved to hurt.

Blackhawk patted her back. Then he saw his way out. "You," he pointed at his tech, getting ready to light up on his cigarette break. "Please take Ms. Court inside." Ethan passed her off on him. "Thank you," he watched the tech walk away with the woman, and Sheila was completely confused as to what just happened. Quickly he pulled on his glove, picked up the discarded butt, and dropped it in the evidence bag. His mission was done, and he was going to drop it in his wife's lap and tell her he was finished playing DNA collector. His brother was going to have to handle the last two.

Elizabeth was waiting for him when he closed the conference room.

"I know you enjoyed every second of that," he said laughing, as he handed her the evidence bag. Once he began taking his coat off, she stopped him.

"Know why I love and hate your coat, Ethan?" she asked, snapping on a pair of gloves and walking towards him with tweezers.

"No." It was official. She lost her mind. The baby hormones finally won and drove his beautiful wife to madness.

"I love it because you look absolutely sexy in it, but hate it because it catches all my hair whenever you hug me." Elizabeth moved incredibly close and checked the front of his coat. "Hello there long blonde hair. Come to the very tricky Director Special Agent Blackhawk!" Elizabeth pulled the hair from the wool.

"Is that…?" He was getting excited.

"That my love was her thinking she could piss me off by throwing herself at my husband, and because I am an infinitely calm woman and knew it was coming, I get the payoff and the DNA evidence."

"That's why you insisted I wear the wool and not the parka? Unbelievable."

"Next time Cowboy, trust your partner," she winked. "This hair has a root, and we now can compare it directly to the hair that was on the victims."

"I've decided that you are definitely an evil genius." Then he thought about it. "What am I then? Do I get to be your sidekick?" he asked, rubbing his hands manically.

Elizabeth patted him on the ass, laughing. "You get to be woman bait."

Blackhawk laughed. "I feel so cheap."

Elizabeth wandered around the photo and gift shop owned by Courtney Brewer, taking in the setup. It was eclectically arranged and looked like she took a great deal of pride in her business. As she picked up the items she had on display, she wasn't really focused on it. All that she was seeking were Ethylene Glycol related items. So far she'd spotted a printer, a coffee pot that could have been used, and then a large machine she was guessing was used to develop pictures.

Ethan was across the room, wandering the same way she was, as they both examined the scene and tried to get their bearings before they pulled the woman aside. Courtney Brewster was definitely a blond, and of the four women they suspected, the only true blond. Her eyes were a pale blue and she had the freckles splattered across her nose. She suddenly wondered if they checked to see if the killer's hair had been color treated, and she pulled out her phone and sent a text message to Christina to set her on that trail. She also sent it to her husband, so he would be keyed in to what she was thinking.

Then she knew how she was going to get some evidence.

"Can I help you find something?" asked Courtney Brewer. She was watching the two FBI agents walking around her shop.

"No just looking, and waiting for you to free up yourself from your customers. Do you have a few moments to talk to me?" she asked.

"I guess I can get a few moments free."

"Do you have a room we can talk privately?" Elizabeth inquired. "This pregnancy is killing me and I would love to get off my feet for two minutes."

"Oh sure! Would you like some coffee? I just made a pot," she offered.

"That would be terrific. I'll have it however you're having yours," she stated, and looked over at her husband. He was hiding a grin; she could see the curl at the corners of his mouth. The telltale give away that he was about to laugh.

"Great, I could use a break anyway," she answered, pouring two cups of coffee in paper cups, mixing in sugar and creamer for both of them. Handing the agent a cup, she spoke, "Follow me."

Elizabeth winked at her husband, and waited for the perfect opportunity to get the evidence they needed. When he mouthed 'behave', she nearly laughed and had to work really hard to cover it.

"Is the break room okay?" she asked, leading her to a tiny room.

"It's great, thank you." Elizabeth took a seat close to the woman and pretended to sip her coffee. If Courtney was a killer, she wasn't drinking coffee that she prepared, unless she absolutely had to do it. Until then, she was going to fake it.

"What can I do for you, Agent. I'm sure this has to do with the murders, and since I don't know what's going on, I'm really curious."

"I'm just here to ask all the shop owners if they've seen any of these men before," Elizabeth said simply. pulling out the pictures. She noticed Courtney was drinking her coffee, and not wary about it, and she knew how she was going to get her DNA.

Courtney Brewer flipped through all the pictures. "No, I haven't seen any of these men in town. If I had I'd tell you." Courtney drank more coffee.

"Do you by any chance use Ethylene Glycol in your picture development?" she asked, cutting to the chase.

Courtney looked confused. "I honestly don't know. I just order the solution offline. I can give you the name of my distributer and they may be able to give you that answer," she answered, grabbing a flyer off the table and borrowed Elizabeth's pen. Writing the name of the website down and passing it and the pen to her.

"Thank you." Elizabeth rubbed her temples.

"Are you okay?" she asked, touching her arm.

"I have a wicked headache today, and I left my purse back at the sheriff's office," Elizabeth said, trying to look like she was in pain. "They don't tell you this pregnancy thing is going to be brutal."

Courtney offered the woman a sympathetic look. "I have Tylenol in my office. Can you have that while pregnant?"

"Oh God, I would love some. Thank you so much," she overzealously answered, smiling sweetly. "I'd appreciate it."

"Be right back," she stood and left the room.

Elizabeth moved fast, she took a large sip of her coffee to make the cups look even, and she prayed it wasn't poisoned. Then she switched cups. Courtney's DNA would be on the rim of the cup. Was it sketchy legally? Yeah, well it would save a life if she was the killer. Next she pulled out an evidence bag and slid the pen and paper into it, her fingerprints would be all over them, and maybe they could match them if the killer ever left a print. Standing up, Elizabeth packed up the pictures and was waiting when Courtney came back in.

"Thank you!" She willingly accepted the packet of Tylenol. "I just got a text, there's an emergency. I have to go. Thank you for the coffee," Elizabeth said, picking up the cup and shaking the woman's hand. "If I have any questions I'll stop back in."

"Oh, okay. Feel better agent," she said, watching the woman walk away. That had to be her oddest interaction she'd ever had with anyone in her life.

Elizabeth met her husband outside the shop.

"A coffee break, Elizabeth?" he paused. "I hope you didn't drink any of that!" Ethan was alarmed now as he noticed there was only half a cup of coffee.

"I had to take a sip, and then I switched cups when I got her to leave the room. This cup has Courtney Brewers DNA on it." Elizabeth told him all about it, as she sat in the Denali.

Blackhawk wasn't sure how he felt about his wife having to drink the coffee, in her little game of switcheroo.

"Then," and she pulled out the bag with the pen and paper. "Here are her fingerprints, just in case my holding this cup has ruined any of hers."

Now he was impressed and leaned over to kiss his wife. "You're pretty devious, Mrs. Blackhawk."

"Hey, all in a day's work," she grinned, carefully holding the cup. "Come on Cowboy, let's head back in and deposit the three samples. Then get something to eat. Baby Blackhawk is starving."

Now he laughed. "When isn't he? He takes after his mother."

* * *

Christina packed up the tech van, and prepped the evidence log for shipment. Inside the van they opted to stack the six victims and all the evidence they gathered. Shipping it back to FBI West would just ensure its security. Plus the make shift cooler in the morgue was backed up, and they were lacking space.

As she signed off on the inventory, Derek Williams wandered in smiling. "Hey Christina! Good morning!"

She laughed. "Derek, it's six at night."

"Well, it's morning for me," he grinned. "What's on the night shift agenda?" He couldn't help but notice that she was taking an inventory. "Are we heading home?" he asked, hopefully. He missed sleeping in his own bed with his girlfriend. The long distance assignments were hell on a relationship.

"No, we're shipping back the bodies and the evidence. Doctor Adare wouldn't want us leaving this here."

"I'm taking a road trip?" he asked, hopefully.

"Yep. Blackhawk wants me in house in case there's another body. Do you mind doing the transport?"

"Heck no, when do I have to be back?" he asked. Maybe he could sneak home and surprise his girlfriend.

Christina laughed. "By six a.m. I'm back on shift then."

"When will transport be ready?" In his mind he was already calculating the time he had to fool around with before returning.

"I can have it ready to go in the next hour or so, and then you have roughly ten hours in your shift to get back here." There was no missing what the man was thinking of doing. "When you drop off at FBI West, I need you to check in and have the tech on duty send me an email confirming sign off on evidence."

"Got it."

"Until then, the bosses brought in some DNA samples we have to prep. They won't be on the truck. I need to get them logged and started for the lab back home. Why don't you start there?"

"I love my job."

Christina laughed. "Get moving, or you won't have your conjugal visit with the girlfriend when you get home," she teased and laughed even harder when he saluted her.

Yeah, she loved her job too.

*   *   *

It was time. She stood in front of her mirror looking at herself and inspecting her outfit. It just wouldn't do for the evening's plans. She hated getting her pretty things ruined. It was hard to find things that fit her just right, since she wasn't the typical size. Those items of clothing must be kept in pristine shape, or her true love might be angry. When he got angry, bad things happened and that was never a good thing.

As she began stripping she went to his side of the closet to borrow some of his things, after all he wouldn't mind. They shared everything and it was all for him. She pulled down a shirt and a pair of well-worn jeans, and they fit, almost as if they were made for her.

Maybe it was time to head back to the gym. Oh well, she'd think about it later. Her lover wasn't complaining, and she looked the same. Or at least she thought she did. Confusion filled her mind, and she shook her head, hoping to shake it away. Pulling on a pair of boots, she was ready to begin her night.

Time to go see who she could find to help her rebuild the love of her life.

*　*　*

Friday evening

Blackhawk sat on the couch in the living room, eating pizza with his wife, as they went over tech reports that kept coming in on his phone. Christina was sending out Derek Williams with the bodies of the victims back to FBI West. As he looked at his watch, he calculated the time it would take for him to reach headquarters. Fortunately it wouldn't be too late.

"I hear a car," Elizabeth said, taking a bite of her pizza. "Thank God they're back." She'd recently just gotten off the phone with Timothy and he'd voiced his concerns regarding Desdemona's choice in spirit guides and Callen's full commitment to the woman. He wasn't the only one concerned, but they decided to let Callen live his life as he wanted.

As the front door open, and her brother-in-law carrying in a giant suitcase that had to be packed with women's things, she relaxed marginally.

Blackhawk laughed.

"What's in the bag Doc?" she asked, grinning.

"From the way it feels, a body," Whitefox answered and dropped it in the living room. "Please tell me there's more pizza. I had to eat vegetable stew for lunch."

Blackhawk laughed. "That's sheer torture."

"There's plenty of pizza, and it's your favorite too." Elizabeth pointed to the kitchen.

"Crap," he muttered. "I lost a bet. I can't eat meat for a week."

Elizabeth began choking on her pizza and she thought her husband was going to try to administer the Heimlich. "What?" she barely got the word out. "Seriously? That had to be one hell of a bet," she said, appalled. "Or this vegetarianism thing is contagious. If that's the case, stay the hell away from me!"

Callen grinned wickedly and went over and kissed his Elizabeth all over her face and then on the lips softly and tenderly. "Opps, looks like you're next."

"If I start craving veggies, I'm going to ass kick you back to granddad and her too." Now she was laughing and wiping the wet kisses from her face with her sleeve.

Ethan Blackhawk laughed at the two of them.

"You could always pick the meat off," suggested Desdemona sweetly. She didn't miss the final kiss he gave her, and it pulled more jealousy from her and she fought it down. "Or order a plain pizza with soy cheese if possible."

Whitefox took the menu his brother just held up for him and stared incredulously at the woman. "Hell no! We didn't say I couldn't eat cheese either. You do realize I'm a man, right? I'm already emasculated enough over this. I'd rather starve."

Desdemona snickered and hung up her coat and his.

Taking the menu he left the room to order a plain pizza for them with REAL cheese. When he came back, he carried the suitcase up the stairs for Desdemona. "No meat and I have to work as a pack mule. Inhumane," he muttered to her.

"I'm going to take a shower and get changed," she smiled sweetly. "Don't eat the pizza with the meat. You promised," she laughed walking up the stairs.

When she was gone, Ethan couldn't help but ask. "What was the contest because giving up meat that's harsh?"

"I'm not saying. It's too embarrassing."

Elizabeth began laughing. "Spill it, Callen, or I'll go up and ask her. She'll tell me too because of girlfriend code."

"Shooting my damn rifle."

Both Blackhawks laughed. "You're saying the ME who doesn't eat meat out shot you with a gun we've used since we were kids?" Ethan found that super funny. He walked to the kitchen for more pizza and a beer. His brother looked like he needed one too.

Elizabeth wanted to bust his ass so bad, but she could see he was actually embarrassed about it.

"Do I need to send you back in to re-qualify?" yelled his brother from the kitchen, and then followed it up with amused laughter.

"Shut up, Ethan. How was I supposed to know she handles a rifle like Wyler? I didn't know her bayou hobby was shooting gators between the eyes. Plus she was trying to distract me with sex."

Now Elizabeth was laughing. "Well that explains it then. Sex is distracting."

Ethan was still laughing.

"Hey, let's go outside and you shoot cans off a log while Elizabeth is running her hands all over your body," and mine, but he kept the last part about Elizabeth distracting him to himself out of self-preservation. The idea made his heart skip in his chest.

Ethan thought about it, and he would have missed too.

"Well she did tell us that she was good with a shotgun. You should have challenged her with the Glock," she grinned. "Callen, I beat Ethan on our yearly handgun qualify. Don't feel bad," she winked.

Ethan was grinning like an idiot. He loved the idea a woman handed his brother his ass in something. "Welcome to my world of being grotesquely inadequate in something against the fairer sex."

"Only one thing sweetheart?" she asked, smiling sweetly.

Blackhawk snorted. "Tell me about it."

Whitefox laughed and watched Elizabeth head into the kitchen to ditch her plate. "Uh, I have to do something and I hope you forgive me after the fact," he warned his brother. When Blackhawk's eyebrow lifted he grinned. "I'll explain after I make out with your wife, but I swear I won't enjoy a second of it."

"Oh well I'll just calmly sit here while you do that then." It was funny that his brother was asking permission to kiss her, since he'd just planted ten kisses all over her face and finally on her lips.

"Just don't shoot me."

"I'll try, but that's going to depend on how much you both enjoy it," he answered, laughing.

"Hey Lyzee," he yelled and waited for her to wander back into the room with a bottle of water.

"Yes?"

Callen crossed to his brother's wife, grabbed her by the waist, careful to not jostle her or the baby, dipped her low and looked into her eyes. "You saved my ass with granddad. He gave me his blessing, and I owe you this." And then he kissed her, slow and gently. His heart ached in his chest at the tenderness of the entire action. It was filled with everything in him.

Blackhawk laughed from the couch. "I decided that you're dead when you're finished because you're obviously enjoying it."

Whitefox pulled his lips from her and stared down into her eyes and they were filled with love and laughter.

Elizabeth caressed his cheek and winked at the man.

"Are you finished with my wife?"

Whitefox righted her back to her feet and hugged her, whispering in her ear. "I love you so much, and I swear I always will not matter what happens in my life. Thank you for getting granddad to give me this chance to be happy. I don't know what my life would be without you. You changed everything."

Elizabeth rubbed her hands across his back, and noticed her husband was smiling and not offended at all. She whispered back in his ear. "I told you Callen; I'd love you forever and take care of you. Now I'll take care of you both." When she pulled away from his body, she took his face in her hands. "Promise. Thank you for coming back safe."

"Ethan, come here," Whitefox motioned to his brother. "Granddad gave me the wedding rings, and told me what you both sacrificed for me."

Blackhawk went to his family and was grinning.

"We think you deserve the rings," said Elizabeth. "You didn't get the name, the least we can do is share the tradition in its place. Now there's no doubt that you're a Blackhawk."

Whitefox choked on the emotion the words brought to the surface. "I won't ever forget this."

"It was all her," he said. "Please don't kiss me like you just kissed her."

Callen hugged his brother, and whispered in his ear too. "I love you both so much!" The emotion swamped him and tears filled his eyes.

Elizabeth went to them and squeezed back between them. "Now everything is right in the world." But granddad's words of warning kept playing in her mind. Elizabeth swallowed them. She'd promised Callen, and she'd keep her promise and deal with the fallout later.

Both men laughed. "Yeah, it most definitely is."

*   *   *

Derek was going to throw up. He was dizzy and the world was spinning around him in sick vicious circles. The last thing he remembered was hitting something laying in the middle of the road, and stopping to see what it was, and that was it. The rest was completely black and hazy. He tried to lift his head and limbs and he wondered if he'd gotten hit by a car. Nothing was moving. In fact, something was over his mouth too.

Then he saw the person across the room from him, and the horror filled him. He tried to scream, as he looked into the eyes of a killer. The face looked very familiar, like he'd seen it before, even though the clothing and hair didn't look right.

Shit.

There was only one option. He had to fight and get his hands free. Using everything he learned in training he struggled against the bonds, and freed his one hand. He pulled the tape from his mouth, and fought to get off the table and to freedom. The killer obviously had other ideas. It was fight or die. Swinging, he was off balance and almost missed, stumbling forward.

The killer didn't miss. The tire iron hit him in the side of the head, and his entire body reverberated from the blow. Lying on his back on the concrete he stared up, as the world slowly bled black. The final two wishes were there'd be no pain, and that he could go back and un-volunteer for the transport assignment, and then maybe he'd still be alive.

Darkness came and Derek Williams ceased to exist.

True love had taken another victim.

*   *   *

She stood over his body after harvesting what she needed, and placing it in a jar. The mess was to a minimum, and she was heartbroken that she had to hit her date that hard in the head, but she couldn't risk him leaving. Fortunately, after she took him home, she had the sense to return home with the vehicle. Opening the back, she found the black bags, and all her lovers waiting inside. It was a sign that the man she just brought home had found them and returned them. Now she just needed to think it out and plan her next move.

Hiding the FBI vehicle wouldn't be hard, she knew the perfect place. It was just a matter of driving it there, hiding it in the brush, and then hiking back home.

"Lover, you brought them all home to me! What an amazing gift," she said, kissing him on the cheek. "I should put you with the rest of the men, but your friends at the FBI will be looking for you and me giving you back will be my gift to you. I have a special place to put you for now. I saw your friends there the other day."

"In fact, I will hide everything in the FBI van for safe keeping in case they come here and try to take me away before I'm done. At least then they won't have you. I've worked too hard reconstructing you to lose you now."

Dawn would be coming soon; it was time to get work done.

*　　*　　*

Blackhawk heard his phone ringing, and it dragged him from sleep and back awake. His wife was stirring beside him, and he hoped for whoever's sake was on the phone it was the utmost urgency.

"Blackhawk," he muttered, his voice clouded with sleep.

"Director, we have a problem," came the scared voice of Christina Hart.

He sat up fully awake in bed. "What's wrong?" Now his wife was fully awake too. They were used to calls at all time of the night. Problems came up with the staff and the assignments the agents were out on all the time.

"Derek never made it to FBI West."

"What?" He slid out of bed and began dressing. Blackhawk hit speakerphone and placed it on the bed to begin dressing. "What do you mean he never made it back? He was carrying all the evidence." There was dual rising fear in his body. One that the killer had taken Derek as a victim, and the other that he was taken because they sent him out with the evidence.

"I didn't get confirmation from the lab back home, and I started calling about an hour ago. I've called his cell and I even called his girlfriend and woke her up. He planned on crashing there before the drive back. She didn't hear from him, other than he texted her saying he had a surprise coming."

"Get all techs into the lab and double up. No one goes anywhere alone, and especially any male staff members."

"Okay, boss."

"We'll be in as soon as we're all dressed." He hung up the phone. "God damn it!"

Elizabeth went over to him and wrapped her arms around his waist. "Ethan, we'll figure it out. I'll go wake Callen and meet you downstairs."

Blackhawk nodded. Deep down Ethan was furious at himself. Had he sent Christina she probably would have arrived safely. He was well aware that men were being targeted, and he still sent out a male tech alone. Now his only hope was they would find Derek Williams alive, and that the killer wasn't aware that they knew their team member was missing.

"Please hang in there, Derek," he whispered, as he finished dressing and dialed the sheriff to alert him to be at the office.

Elizabeth tapped on Desdemona's door, and there was no answer. She pushed the door open and found the other half of their team asleep and curled around each other. Tiptoeing over to her brother-in-law she gently tapped his arm, and his eyes popped open and fought for recognition.

"Lyzee, you okay?" he asked, rolling to his back. Whitefox saw she was dressed. "Is the baby okay?" His whole body went on alert in panic.

"I'm good, but all four of us have to head in to the sheriff's station. Our tech van disappeared mid transport and our tech is missing."

"Shit!" Callen slid out of bed and began pulling on his jeans over his boxers. "Desi too?" He looked over at her sleeping.

"Yes." Elizabeth looked over her shoulder to make sure her husband didn't follow her into their room. "It was a male tech, and he went out alone. We're probably going to have retrieval."

"How's he taking it?" Whitefox knew who was going to suffer the most over this and who was going to take all the blame.

Elizabeth shook her head. "I'm afraid he's going to lose it. I'm going to need you on this, Cal," she said softly, going into his open arms. "I'm scared that he's going to blame himself and completely lose it."

"It's okay Lyzee. I promise you that we'll survive this."

Callen hugged her close and kissed her forehead. "We'll have to just help him through it." Ethan was the boss, and he'd see this as his failure. "I'll wake Desdemona and we'll be down."

"Okay."

"Beautiful, don't stress yourself or the baby. I'm here for you no matter what."

"Promise me you'll hold him up if I can't. I don't want to see this break him."

"I'll hold you both up."

Elizabeth patted his cheek and looked up into his eyes. "Thank you, Cal."

Callen turned his head and kissed the palm of her hand as it rested over his cheek and took a few seconds to let her lean against him.

"Ethan's called for a double up of all staff. You can't go anywhere alone and neither can he. Promise me, you stick with one of us at all times."

"I promise, Elizabeth." He released her body from his and watched her walk away. At the door she looked over her shoulder and his heart skipped a beat. Never had he ever seen her look that afraid. Elizabeth didn't show weakness often, and this had to have her freaked out.

When she was gone, he went to lean over Desdemona, but she was already awake. "Another one?"

"Yeah, Desi, we have to head into the station."

Desdemona heard the entire conversation between Callen and Elizabeth. They were both so open with emotion when they came together, and she hoped one day she and Callen would be more like that too. Maybe it took time, but then she knew they hadn't been together as family for that long. She tried to not fault her friend for leaning on her family, but part of her was still unaccustomed to the easy love between them.

As she rolled out of bed she put away her emotions and started dressing, her biggest hope for the day was she wouldn't be autopsying one of their own.

All four drove into town together, and no one spoke a word the entire trip. It was blatantly obvious that Ethan Blackhawk was tense and wound tight. Elizabeth wanted to take his hand, and hold it but she was pretty sure he'd push her away. When he fell into the guilt, it took him some time to work his way through it emotionally.

"We'll find him, Ethan," spoke his brother, finally breaking the uncomfortable silence swallowing all of them.

"I'm sure we will," he answered tersely. Inside him he already knew the truth about how they would find him. As he pulled into the parking lot he looked back at his brother. "You go nowhere alone, Callen. I don't want to have to look for you."

"Then I suppose it's safe to say you'll be following your own directive, Ethan?"

Blackhawk's cheek twitched at his brother's challenge. "It's a direct order, Callen. Follow it and don't give me grief."

Elizabeth touched his arm, and looked at him with calm eyes, offering her husband a little peace. As of now, he was teetering on the edge, and she didn't like seeing him this worked up about a decision he made. "Ethan."

"Come on!" He jumped out into the bitter cold, and moved towards the tech team he knew would be waiting for him in the makeshift morgue. He had to face the people that trusted him and tell them it'd be okay.

Only he knew it wouldn't be.

Sheriff Duffy met him in the lobby. "I'm sorry about your tech, Agent Blackhawk. I have my deputies out looking for the van and your guy. I called in my staff, they're downstairs making coffee for your team, and trying to offer any assistance they can."

"Thank you, Sheriff. I'll be going out too in a little while," he added, and he could feel his wife tense behind him.

"I'll be joining him," added Callen Whitefox. Not only was he not going to let his brother do anything stupid, he wasn't going to let him upset his pregnant wife while he was trapped in the haze of guilt. Elizabeth was pale and drawn and she didn't need the stress over this. Instinctively he wanted to hold and protect her.

"I'm going to go down and talk to my team," he said, nodding at the sheriff and ignoring his brother. He walked away and saying nothing more. The energy around him said it all.

Everyone else followed him, and just let him be the boss. Elizabeth could have fought him on it, but honestly, there was no point. When they rounded the corner, before the makeshift morgue, they ran into Sheila Court.

"Guess it isn't funny when it's one of your own that the killer hacks apart," she said, mockingly.

"Go, Ethan. I have this one," said his wife. If there was one thing she didn't like it was an asshole that wanted to twist the knife on an innocent man. Elizabeth waited until both men headed into the lab and she turned on the woman. "You think you're funny?" she asked, venomously.

"I find it funny that the FBI scrambles when it's one of their own. When it was our deputy, no one seemed to care."

Elizabeth felt the anger unfurling deep in her gut, and she fought hard to not punch the woman in the face. That didn't mean she wouldn't scare the shit out of her. Stepping towards her, she shrugged out of her coat and tossed it over the railing of the stairs. "If I even see you looking maliciously at my husband ever again,

413

let alone speaking to him, I swear on everything that is holy in this world I will hunt you down and show you how we Blackhawk's protect our own."

Sheila took a small step backwards, but still held her ground. "You think I'm afraid of a pregnant woman?"

"You think me being pregnant is going to stop me from handing you an ass kicking like none you've seen before? I beat the hell out of my own half-brother and put him in a coma. I killed my husband's half-brother for trying to hurt him. Do you really think I wouldn't think of twisting your head right off your fucking shoulders for insulting my husband? You a complete stranger?" she drawled.

"You can't touch me. I'll press charges," she leered.

"Elizabeth, I just witnessed her striking you, a pregnant woman," said Desdemona. "Now I believe you can kick her ass. See how easy that was?" She'd never heard her new friend break out the southern accent; it was one she had much of her life growing up, and it entertained her, as did the idea of her beating this woman into a pile on the floor.

Elizabeth stepped one more step closer, and now the woman looked scared. "I so much as see you breathe around Ethan; I will drag you outside by your bleached blonde hair, and show you how we southern girls hand out justice for our men. I will bang that empty head of yours against the biggest rock I can find. AM I clear?"

Sheila had the common sense to escape the stairwell.

"Thank you, Desdemona," she said, slipping back into her coat, and grinning over at her friend.

She offered her a fist bump, in solidarity. "All about the girlfriend code from one southern girl to another. Nice accent, Elizabeth." Desdemona tried to comfort her friend, despite the feelings raging deep within her own gut.

"Thanks Doc. I like to save it for the right times," she said, grinning. "Let's get the team through this," she said, hoping Sheila Court would test her patience just so she could beat her ass down

Blackhawk believed he worked best in chaos, only because he lived the FBI for so many years, it was second nature. Once you handed your soul over to them, you'd bleed for them too. What he thought he could handle, he found himself losing complete control over. Once he entered the makeshift morgue, there were techs falling apart, scared and looking for their boss to lead them and tell them that it was going to be okay.

Once he entered the room there were shouted questions, tears and absolute chaos, as his staff asked if they'd be bringing Derek Williams home.

When his wife had been abducted, this was most of the team that worked incredibly hard for twelve hours scouring a scene looking for anything to tie find the killer and bring her home. Now they were looking towards him to save one of their own, and he didn't even know where to begin, all because he believed it was his fault. Self-blame overshadowed his ability to think clearly.

Then the woman he married strode into the lab and took control. He felt a mix of relief and angst. Right now he didn't know how to do it the right way, and to give Derek Williams justice. Leaning on his wife was his best shot of not losing it right then and there.

Elizabeth knew he was too emotionally close to the fire on this one, and she had to step up and be the other half of the boss team. Whistling the entire room feel into complete silence, they were accustomed to her whistling and then issuing a demand. What they needed now was continuity and the ability to feel useful.

"Christina, I need a full detailed report of what went out on that tech van. I want to know the exact second it left this building, and who saw it leave. I want the report in one hour. Am I clear?"

Christina snapped to attention, and knew her boss meant business. "On it, Elizabeth." Off she scurried.

"You," she pointed at three techs. "We dropped off evidence of possible suspects yesterday. Did it go on that van?"

"No ma'am," the one answered.

415

"Then you, you and you get yourselves busy. I want it processed and I want it relayed to FBI West. If one of those people took our tech, we need to find out, lock it down and do our damn job."

They nodded. "Yes ma'am!"

Before Elizabeth could continue, there was a knock on the door.

"Agents?"

It was the sheriff.

Hell, Elizabeth hoped it wasn't going to be about Sheila Court or she would kick the woman's ass. Elizabeth strode over, her husband right behind.

"Julian Littlemoon just took the call. We found your tech, and he's dead," he said, keeping his voice low.

"Where," asked Blackhawk, the anger rising in him.

"Dumpster at 'Cup of Joe,'" he answered, softly.

"We're heading out. Have your deputy keep the scene contained," said Elizabeth. Her husband was silent, and that usually meant he was going to blow big time.

"Callen, help Doc grab her gear and get the keys for a tech van." She didn't have to tell them anything. Elizabeth looked back over at the techs and their faces said it all. When the ME had to get her kit, it meant one thing. Derek Williams wasn't coming home alive.

As the team started to move, Blackhawk shook his head. "No. I don't want any of you to have to do this." There was no way he could subject his team to retrieval of their friend and a sweep of evidence ten feet away. "We've got this," he stated, and then he walked out of the room. "I'll be down in the Denali."

Callen took the kit from Desdemona, and then caught keys from one of the techs. They were going to bring home their team member.

"Team stays in-house until we get back or I call, am I clear?" she said, and everyone nodded, and there were tears and there were looks of anger. But right now all that mattered was getting to Derek and giving him dignity. Before she walked out the door she turned to face them. "Derek's ours now. I'll get him justice, I promise," she said, looking into their faces, the faces of the people that had hope she'd return when she was lost. The belief

416

she found there propelled her forward. Now she just needed to keep her husband from losing it.

Blackhawk drove to the scene, the feeling of dread and horror overwhelming him. Here was going to be the man that he sent to his death. It was his job to keep them all safe, and here he knowingly sent a man out alone. Gabe should have warned him how crappy this job could be at times. If he could take it back, he would. He wished he could rewind the last twelve hours and give the man back his life.

"I can do this alone, Ethan," his wife said, softly. Elizabeth knew how hard this was going to be for him. "This isn't your fault," she added. It was the famous Blackhawk guilt and it now had full control of the man beside her.

"I sent him alone at night."

Blackhawk parked the Denali, and looked over at his wife and his eyes were filled with fury and pain.

"We can do this together." Elizabeth took his hand in hers, and looked into his eyes. "We are unbreakable as a team."

He nodded the fury still beating at his heart. "Let's go get Derek."

Elizabeth hopped out of the vehicle as the Tech van pulled up, and the other two members of their team exited into the cold. "Doc, you ready?" she said, knowing this man was possibly her friend too. If she could she'd spare her too.

"I want to see him before we move him, and we need to get pictures first. I prefer to not get body temp out in the elements. It's freezing out here, there won't be an accurate reading." Her real reason was that she didn't want to probe him while Ethan Blackhawk was there. She could tell he was struggling with it. "I simply want to see in situ and then bag him up for transport."

"Got it," said Elizabeth.

"We have a timeline of his last moments. That'll be good enough," she said, softly to just Elizabeth.

They all headed for the back of the building. Julian Littlemoon was standing guard at the dumpster.

As they approached he had gloves on and he lifted the lid, nothing but sympathy in his eyes. "Is this the entire team?" he asked.

"I don't want my people to have to pull his body out of here. He mattered and had friends in the lab," said Blackhawk, looking over the side at his dead tech. He didn't go peacefully into death. It looked like dried blood on the side of his head. At least he still had his eyes, and his face.

Callen began snapping pictures.

"Director Blackhawk, what can I do to help you," Littlemoon said, watching both women climb into the dumpster.

"Can you track the movements of my tech?"

"I can try, what time did he leave your location?" he asked, pulling out a pen and paper. "Do you want me to find the van?"

"Yes, but don't approach it. Once you locate it, call me."

Julian Littlemoon respected the Native man before him. It took a lot to make something of yourself when you came from a Rez. This man remade himself, and you could tell he didn't stomp on people in the process. He had a good aura. "I'll be in contact," he said, slipping off into the night.

"Doctor Adare, are you finished with the photos?" asked Blackhawk. "I want to get him out of there as soon as possible." The sight of his tech laying in the trash like he was discarded like garbage pissed him off. He deserved a better end than this, and he'd give him the dignity the killer took away.

"Yes, Director. We can move him."

Elizabeth hopped out and rolled out the black bag, and unzipped it. Her brother-in-law took her place in the dumpster, and helped the doctor move him, careful to not disturb anything that might be evidence. They lowered him into the bag and zipped him up.

"What did the killer take?" he asked, almost afraid to ask.

"I didn't look under his clothing, Director. I'll look when we get him back to the station. I don't want to disturb any trace before I collect it." Desdemona looked up at Whitefox "Can you back the tech van around for transport. I don't want to carry him around the front. He isn't a spectacle to be gawked at."

"Can do," he said, jogging off.

418

"Load him and then let's just check the area. See if we can find anything. I want to talk to the person that found the body," Blackhawk said. "Then when we make sure it's clear, I'll have the team come in for trace. I don't want them in the room while you're doing the autopsy."

Whitefox returned with the van, and hopped out, opening the back.

"The autopsy is going to be closed. In fact, I'm the only one that's going to be in the room." There was one only one reason for that, and it was the man in front of her. She had no doubt the other two agents would survive it, but Ethan looked to be a man on the edge.

"I will be in there Doctor. He was my responsibility, and I'm seeing this out until the end," he said, heatedly. That man was his fault and if he couldn't stand over his body and swallow it, he didn't deserve to be in charge.

"Director, with all due respect, because you are my boss," she paused. "You aren't going to be in there because it will be a distraction to me too. He was my co-worker, and I worked in the lab with him daily. I need to do this alone, and I need you to let me have my final moments with him. He comes first now, and my ability to do my job. That won't be doing Derek any justice if I rush and miss anything. Once I'm done, you can finish what needs to be completed."

Blackhawk stared down at her debating whether to pull rank and insist, but at the last moment he just nodded. "I'm going to talk to the person that called it in." With that, he turned and headed to the 'Cup of Joe'.

The three remaining let out a breath collectively.

"Callen, call the team in once you load up Derek. We need the entire area swept, and I need a rush on every single test that can possibly be done. If we have to hand drive the samples to FBI West, we'll get them there, or get a courier to drive them. I'll sign off on all expenses on this one."

"Elizabeth, I can tell by the lack of blood loss, he was likely dead before the killer took what she took, or he'd be covered in blood."

"You did look then?" asked Elizabeth, looking over her shoulder to make sure the coast was clear.

Desdemona dropped her voice. "Derek had a full removal of genitalia."

"Christ," Whitefox was nauseous. Just the idea that the man had been hacked at like that not only made him sick, but it freaked him the hell out. "What kind of lunatic are we dealing with?"

"A dead one if Ethan gets to her first," Elizabeth paused. "Let's keep this quiet until we can break it to him gently."

"Lyzee, there's no way to gently break that to him." Hearing it himself gave him goose bumps and the creeps. "Once he hears that the man was emasculated there's going to be an eruption of global proportions."

"I'll tell him once autopsy is done. Desdemona, don't send it via email. I'll hand deliver it to him, and break it to him. This is going to take him right over the edge, and it's going to be ugly."

"Agreed. Can you keep him out of the autopsy? Since I'm doing this one alone and the trace retrieval, it's going to take me a while to get it done the right way. I'm going to need at least six hours."

"Callen, you need to take him to interview Carly Kester at the bookstore. If we can keep him distracted during the autopsy, then he won't try to even come down and watch it."

"I'll keep him busy," he replied, as the three of them hoisted the man into the back of the van.

"Transport Derek once you make the call to Christina and the team. I'll keep Ethan occupied until you can get Derek prepped for trace removal." Elizabeth didn't want her husband anywhere near autopsy when the man's clothes were removed. She wasn't sure she wanted to even see that, but if she had to, she'd do it to keep him from witnessing it. What had her worried right now was that her husband was a powder keg and a lit match just waiting to meet and explode. The look on his face said it all; he was battling internally for control of his temper.

Elizabeth watched the van pull away, and she pulled off her gloves and stuffed them in her pocket. Now she needed to go find her husband and keep him from losing his temper on any witnesses.

Surprisingly, she found him sitting at a table talking on the phone to Gabe. Obviously, he called waking him up. Maybe that cheered him up a bit. There was nothing he liked more than rousing his boss from bed. It was a little game he liked to play. Usually it made him smile, but when he looked up at her and that wasn't the case. Ethan Blackhawk had the scary look on his face, and for the first time it even had her pretty rattled. It was like waiting out a natural disaster. She felt like a killer tsunami was getting ready to break through and sweep all the hapless victims out to sea in a wave of anger.

Elizabeth motioned to the waitress on duty for two cups of coffee and even went and picked them up at the counter, tossing down cash. "Make sure we have privacy," she said to the woman that she'd never seen before. "Hey?"

"Yeah?" answered the redhead.

"When did Wilma May leave?" she asked, looking down at her own watch.

"I came on at eleven, and I think her shift ended around five p.m. She was gone before I got here, but I can check the time cards if you want."

"Yeah, do that, please." Elizabeth carried the two coffee's over to the table, just as her husband was hanging up the phone. "Here's some coffee. You're going to need it. I have a feeling we're done sleeping until we get to go home," she said, dumping creamer in the coffee and sliding it across the table to her husband.

"Is Derek on his way back?" he asked, softly.

Elizabeth nodded. "Tech team is on the way in, and we can check on them and get them started before we head back. Until then, want to talk about how ready you are to blow?"

Ethan wasn't surprised his wife could see right through his carefully built outer facade. The rage he was feeling at that moment was so great, that he didn't even think he could discuss it with the woman he loved. If he even started discussing the situation, he'd lose it. "No, I think we best just let it go." He looked up at her and fully expected a fight or at least for her to push him to get him to open up.

"Okay. What did the manager on duty say?" Elizabeth switched the focus back to the circumstances at hand. If she could keep him talking, by the time they returned to the station the bookstore might be open, and her brother-in-law would be next up to bat on keeping her husband busy.

421

"The night manager went to take the trash out, and when he opened the lid, he looked in and there was Derek. Right after that he called it in, and then we arrived. It was only him and the redhead working. I think she said her name was Tiffany, and she confirmed the story. 'Cup of Joe' was dead at the time."

Elizabeth leaned back and sipped her coffee. "Profile this for me, knowing what we know Ethan." There had to be something they were missing.

"Female unsub, and she's removing pieces of males. One might say she's trying to collect something, or pieces of someone."

"I'm with you so far."

"We know she's blonde, and I would say that she's about your age, maybe a little younger. But I'd say around thirties."

"Okay, agreed."

"She isn't hacking them to pieces, it's controlled. It's almost like collecting organs and limbs with a definite purpose. I prefer when the killer leaves us a note, it makes it so much simpler."

Elizabeth wasn't sure if he was joking or not, since his voice was dead monotone. Oh yeah, he was holding back the tsunami.

"Poisoning is a controlled killing. You can't be hurried or rash, a part of her is enjoying the act of the drugging the victim. I want to say that the killer is using something easily found at hand. Poisoning isn't an elaborate crime. The killer makes the conscious effort to take a life, by adding a toxic substance to the coffee. There's little planning unless it's a spouse. They plan and plot," he said, drinking his coffee.

"Good to know."

Blackhawk tried to smile. He didn't want to take this out on her, but he was just tied up in knots over it all.

"How do you feel about the profile?" Elizabeth asked.

He sighed. "You know what pisses me off?" he asked, looking her right in the eyes.

"No, tell me." She took a sip of her own coffee.

"It's like you live in here," he pointed at his head. "You know for a fact that the profile has me tied up in knots, and you know I'm not buying my own rationale."

"It's the marriage thing, Ethan. I'm sorry me being a wife is pissing you off."

"I didn't mean it that way."

Elizabeth looked him in the eyes. "My job is to know people, just as much as you do. We wade through this shit everyday of our lives. If I couldn't tell the man I love is on the edge, what the hell kind of agent am I and what kind of wife?"

Blackhawk's cheek twitched.

"You and I can talk this out," she paused when he tensed. "Or how about you listen to what I have to say and then go from there?"

Blackhawk didn't want to talk it out, so that only left one option. "Ok, shoot."

"Here's where I'm having a problem, and it's probably where you're getting caught up too. You and I tend to be in sync for lots of things in our life, and especially as partners working an assignment. We're two halves of a whole."

"So you think I'm wrong too?"

"I can't figure out how this woman is transporting the bodies. I don't mean by car, I mean by lifting. I'm pretty strong, and I can lift a good deal of weight, minus now with the baby. But generally, I could carry Desdemona if I had to do it. Maybe a few hundred feet, a half a mile if it's a fireman's hold, but I couldn't carry Derek. He was my size. I might piggy back him if he were alive, but as a body? It's dead weight."

Blackhawk drank his coffee and considered her words.

"Now you and Callen have both carried me around. Just a few days ago you were both tossing me back and forth and not even breaking a sweat. At home you've carried me up two flights of stairs when I've fallen asleep, and you probably didn't get winded."

"You're not heavy." Now he did smile, when she lifted an eyebrow waiting for the word 'yet'.

"Could you carry your brother?"

Blackhawk weighed it in his mind. "Callen weighs about what I do, give or take five pounds. I can do pull ups at home and that's dead lifting my own weight, so yeah, I could carry him, but a limited distance."

Elizabeth just stared at him not wanting to say the words. The profile didn't fit for her.

"I get what you're saying, but profiling is a science. A woman is most likely to use poison, and then look at the victims. All men, which means something happened in her life that caused her to want to take the men apart. Piece by piece. Maybe she was abused by a spouse or boyfriend."

"We need to ask Sheriff Duffy for any domestic related cases in the last year."

"I get what you're saying Elizabeth. I really do, but I just think this one has us both tripped up." Blackhawk watched the tech van's start to pull in and he stood. "Why don't you head back to the station, and I'll stay here and work? It's miserably cold out here, and I don't want you freezing our baby into a Uterus-cicle."

"He's perfectly fine, he's all cozy warm and surrounded by subcutaneous fat."

Blackhawk looked over at her and gave her the look.

"I know! All that time around the doctors in autopsy is making me weird isn't it? I used to be so much cooler," she said, taking his hand and squeezing it.

"I love you, Elizabeth. Thank you for being my wife." Without her he would have been brooding, but in twenty minutes she managed to untangle some of the knots in his gut and make him tolerable again. Now at least he could carry his tech team when they needed him. His grandfather was right, without Elizabeth Blackhawk, the men in their family were screwed.

"I love you too, Cowboy. We can take care of this together," she said, zipping up her parka and slipping into gloves. "Ready?" she asked, pulling up her hood.

"As ready as I think I'll ever be."

They pushed out the door together, and once again, team Blackhawk would get through what threatened to break them.

Callen assisted Desdemona as she loaded the man's body onto the gurney and wheel him into the prep area of the makeshift morgue. Part of him wanted to get the hell out of there, but part of him couldn't leave her to do this on her own. "Need my help?" he offered.

424

"I tell you what," she said, pulling her scrubs over her clothes. "You can sit there and keep me company, and not have to look at Derek."

"I don't know how you're going to do it," he muttered. Just the idea was making his stomach roll.

"I'm really good at detaching myself emotionally and not focusing on the fact it was a person. Right now I just think of this as a mystery that I need to solve. He isn't going to be Derek any longer to me. I can't see him as a friend, or I won't be able to do this."

"You're very strong, Desi," he said, and it was the truth. It couldn't be easy to have to put your hands in death daily, and not let it crack you under the pressure. "I'd have nightmares if I had to do it daily."

She shrugged. "The dead don't judge the living anymore, and I like to believe I can help them on the last stop before burial. If their lives were stolen, then I can at least tell the story of their death. Pass it off to the people like Elizabeth and Ethan that would find justice no matter what the cost."

"I appreciate what you did for my brother, by not telling him about his injuries."

Desdemona pulled out her tools and then started looking for trace. "Your brother is a really good guy. In fact you have a pretty great family. Your grandfather was scary at first, but he reminds me of a big teddy bear."

"What did you two talk about?"

"Marriage and kids. He was pressuring me to marry you," she said, and began pulling fibers off the tech and dropping them in little cylinder containers for trace.

"And are you going to?" he asked, thinking about the rings that were back in his bag next to their bed.

"Seriously Callen?" She pointed down at the man and looked over at him. "We can't discuss getting married while I do an autopsy." Desdemona deflected the topic.

"Sure we can," he answered. "I'm not asking you right now, I'm discussing the possibility of it becoming a reality in the future. If my grandfather thought I was asking you to marry me while you were conducting an autopsy he'd kick my ass."

Desdemona laughed. "I don't know," she said honestly. "I'm scared you're going to get hurt, and lose you."

"But what if you don't marry me and I get hurt? It could go either way, since I'm an FBI agent, and I'll be out on assignments."

That was the other part of it. Could she be married to a man that wore a target on his back every day when he left the house?

"Granted, my official title is Liaison to the Native American Community. I don't know how many people will want to kill me then," he said, grinning.

"Not funny, Callen," she said, doing the fingernail scrapings onto the paper. "That's the other problem I'm having. I don't know if I can handle you being shot at daily."

"Well, I understand that, but honestly, you were shot at too the other day." Maybe he shouldn't point out the obvious, but she wore the same bulls-eye he did working for the FBI. Right now she had a stalker, and that was going to be their big issue right after this assignment was over.

"Thanks for reminding me," she said laughing, as she began removing the man's clothing and bagging it. "Callen, it may get intense from here on out. I'm going strip him and check his body for trace."

He understood what she was doing, giving him a way out of sitting there. "I'll hang in here as long as I can," he answered. "I don't want to leave you alone."

Desdemona looked up. "I'm not alone; I have Derek here to keep me company."

He lifted an eyebrow. "If he starts talking back to you, I'm getting the hell out of here and fast," he interjected.

She shook her head. "Okay, Derek. Tell me what happened to you," she said, and started inspecting his body and the wounds that were inflicted on him. Now it was time to learn all about his last few minutes of life.

Ethan was sitting in the conference room that they were using as home base, and he wasn't in a good mood. It was early in the day, and all he really wanted was the autopsy report, and to find the killer and beat the hell out of her. Everything his wife had said to him was playing over and over in his mind, and he was starting to wonder if maybe he'd screwed up the profile. How was this woman carrying these men to the boy scout camp to leave them? At this point he wanted to yank his hair out of his head in frustration. The more he dwelled, the more doubt clouded his mind.

"Stop thinking about it, Ethan," she said, reading the reports that were sitting on the table in front of them.

"I'm trying, but that niggling doubt is making me insane," he said, closing his eyes. "Do we have the trace reports back from the DNA samples of Sheila Court, Courtney Brewster and Wilma May?" he asked. The only thing he felt like they did right in the last two days was not ship those samples with Derek, or the killer would have them too. Small miracle on their end, and at least they could check them against the reports, especially since the hairs pulled from the first six victims were now all gone.

"They aren't back, and I know how you feel, Darlin'. Just try not to let it make you crazy. We've worked cases like this before, and we'll figure it out." Elizabeth dropped her boots on the corner of the table and leaned back in the chair.

"I can't believe we lost the entire van with all the trace too," he muttered. "Right now, a judge could throw it out of court as contaminated. Everything could just be useless in court."

Elizabeth looked up. "True, but we have Derek downstairs, and we don't know what trace is on him, and we still have the samples we appropriated from the women we suspect. Plus you and Callen have to head out shortly and interview Carly Kester. We need a DNA sample."

"Lyzee, how am I supposed to get a DNA sample?"

Elizabeth laughed as she sent a text to her brother-in-law. "I know how you can do it, but neither of you are going to like it," she implied, grinning.

"That smile scares the hell out of me," he said. "That means I'm going to have to do something I really don't want to do."

She winked at him. "Cowboy, you just do what I say, and that DNA sample will be in the bag." Then she described how to get it done. The look on his face said it all, and she already knew he had no intention of doing it.

"I had to smoke; I'm drawing the line on this one. I'm a married man, Elizabeth. In fact, just the mere idea that you'll promote this, makes me think you've lost your damn mind. You lost it when that woman looked at me, and now you want me to do what?"

"Uh, Ethan. You're the boss. Make the minion do it. The joy of being the boss is making Callen do whatever you ask him to do, and he can't say no."

"Elizabeth," he closed his eyes and couldn't believe he was going to go there just to get DNA, and then he thought about the deceased man lying downstairs.

Callen opened the door to the room and stepped in. "I got the text. I'm ready for the interview."

Blackhawk shook his head. It was like leading a lost lamb to slaughter. "So, Callen, we need a DNA sample. Elizabeth and I managed to get three out of four of them."

"Okay, so I'm up?" he asked, sitting beside Elizabeth and staring at her curiously, as she laughed. "What? Why do I feel all the sudden like I'm about to get hazed into the fraternity and it's going to be painful and humiliating?"

Elizabeth was laughing so hard now, that the tears were filling her eyes. "I wish I didn't dump that vegetable juice on the woman. I'd pay big money to see the Blackhawk boys in action on this one."

Now Whitefox looked wary.

"Okay, here's what you need to do," he said, and then explained it to his brother, and he was staring at him like he was out of his mind.

"You do realize that I'm trying to convince our ME to marry me. If she hears about this that may be the deal breaker."

"Suck it up, buttercup," Elizabeth drawled. "You're up and you sold your soul to the FBI. We're calling in that card. The almighty Blackhawk," she said pointing at her husband, "and his evil counterpart," she pointed at herself, "needs that DNA sample."

Blackhawk grinned, knowing his brother wouldn't be able to say no to his wife.

Whitefox stood up and didn't look happy. When he walked past Elizabeth she slapped him on the ass, and her husband snickered at the look on his face.

"Normally I would have enjoyed that, but if Desdemona finds out about this, I'm telling her my bosses forced me into it. Then she can take it up with both of you." He pulled on his coat. "Come on, let's get this over with. I don't want to leave her alone in autopsy."

"Is it bad?" asked Blackhawk.

He looked at his brother and weighed the options. "I left before the bad part began. You wouldn't want to be down there."

Blackhawk nodded. "Thanks for not lying," he said, grabbing his keys. Immediately, Callen felt bad for lying to his brother. His eyes met Elizabeths' and they shared a secret between them that Ethan missed.

Elizabeth watched them leave, waiting until she could see them getting into the Denali and pull away. Immediately, she headed down to Desdemona's room. There was no way she was letting the woman do this alone. Gruesome or not, the man on the table deserved one of his bosses to stand over him in death.

Both men observed Carly Kester walking across the parking lot to her store. In her hands were a coffee and her keys. They wanted to catch her alone, and before the store actually opened. They had thirty minutes to get the DNA and to do the interview.

"I'm really going to do this?" asked Whitefox, still surprised. "If I wasn't here to be your whipping boy, you'd actually do this?"

"Cal, I had to go outside and smoke. I risked getting re-addicted to get the sample. You can pull this off. All you have to do is flirt your ass off and get her to give you some DNA." Blackhawk was entertained.

"Okay, but this is a crazy idea. I can't see it working."

Blackhawk opened the Denali's door and looked over at his brother. "Me either, but it's going to be funny as hell to watch you do it. I almost can't wait to see what the evil genius comes up with next when it doesn't work."

"You are both sadistic."

Blackhawk grinned. "Goes with the job."

The men crossed the lot, and Blackhawk knocked on the door, and briefly thought the woman would blow them both off. When she saw them, she rushed over. Thank god, she didn't hold a grudge.

"Agent Blackhawk, I wasn't expecting an early morning visit." Carly Kester stared intently at the other man. "Hello and you are?" She extended her hand, turning on her million watt smile.

Blackhawk winked at his brother. This wasn't going to be as hard as he thought after all. The bait was in the trap and apparently the woman liked Native men.

"I'm Special Agent Callen Whitefox." He took her hand, and grinned at her with the legendary 'Blackhawk grin. If that didn't draw her in then nothing would. As teens once they managed to perfect it, they used it all the time on the opposite sex, and rarely did it fail. It was legend on the Rez.

"Well, come in," she said, then looked over at the other man. "Where's your delightful wife? Leave her chained in the cage today?" she asked, sarcastically.

It took everything in both men to let it slide. They had a job, and they'd let Elizabeth beat the woman down later, and enjoy watching.

"She's working back at the sheriff's office. We're here to talk about the victims again, and a timeline of when you saw the one man in 'Cup of Joe'," he smiled warmly, despite how he felt about the woman ragging on his wife.

Whitefox walked around her bookstore barely impressed. He'd owned most of the books in her shop, and nothing spectacular stood out. What he wanted to do was tell the woman that, especially after he just was making comments about Elizabeth. "I love your store, Ms. Kester. I happen to collect books, and have to say that you have a great selection." All lies and his brother knew it, he was hiding a grin.

"What's your favorite book, Agent Whitefox?"

"That's easy, Ms. Kester. I'm very fond of 'The Three Musketeers'."

Now his brother had to turn his back to keep the woman from seeing the full blown smile.

She was intrigued. "What books are in your collection?"

Callen rattled off a few and watched her face. Fortunately for him, he knew his books. The woman was testing him. "My friend has a first edition Shakespeare Othello that is a piece of beauty," he added, and prayed Desdemona wouldn't ever hear about this conversation.

"Wow, that's incredibly rare. What's the condition?"

"It's in a glass box, and I haven't the privilege to touch it, but it looks pristine and class A grade."

Carly Kester was impressed. That was a one hundred thousand dollar book, and obviously this man hung with people she'd like. Maybe he'd be a keeper until she could meet the owner of the book.

Callen leaned across the counter, and stared into her eyes and winked. "Maybe we can discuss it after I'm done with the assignment."

"Maybe," she smiled seductively. "But why wait?"

Whitefox stood and patted his pockets. "Damn, I don't have a card with my number on it. Do you have one with yours?" he lied, knowing his cards were tucked behind his badge. He gave her the best 'pick up' smile in his arsenal. He'd used it countless times in the bars, before Desdemona. This was its final appearance, and he was retiring it immediately on walking out the door. Well, maybe he'd still use it around Elizabeth.

"I do." Carly pulled out her card.

"I have to say, I love that lipstick color on you. It's such a great shade of red. It's very sexy and very memorable."

Carly couldn't help herself. On the back of the card she scribbled 'Callen- call me', and then kissed the paper, handing it to him. "Now you can't forget me or my lipstick." She flirted back, easily.

"Okay, we should probably get the interview over with," interjected Blackhawk. "We only have one question."

"Okay."

"When you were in 'Cup of Joe' and saw the one victim, about what time was it?" asked Blackhawk, pulling out a pen and paper.

"Oh, that's easy. Around three p.m. I ran over for a cup of coffee and then came right back here to reopen the shop."

431

Blackhawk nodded. She had just confirmed the same time Wilma May and Joe Lebar had given him. "No coffee pot here?" he asked.

"No. Unfortunately, I had one, but it broke a while back."

Both men nodded. "Thank you, Ms. Kester," said Blackhawk, as he started for the door. "We'll be in touch," he added.

"Don't forget to call me, Callen Whitefox," she said, wavinng. My my, he was a fine piece of man indeed. Carly watched him walk away and wished he wasn't wearing so many layers of winter clothes. Well, she'd have to make sure she got him right where she wanted him and naked too.

Back in the car, Blackhawk held open the evidence bag as his brother dropped it in carefully. They now had all four samples of DNA from the women in town that could possibly be the killer.

"I can't believe that worked," Whitefox said, laughing. "In fact, that went way too smoothly. I feel like I need to shower."

"I know what you mean. You should have seen her as she was flashing her chest the other day. It wasn't even worth the time of day."

"Elizabeth is going to be thrilled this worked."

"I'm telling you that my wife is an evil genius. It makes me wonder if I even wanted to marry her, or she instrumented the entire thing in Salem, and I was just way out of my league."

Whitefox snorted. "Uh, Ethan, your wife is incredibly hot and probably about three leagues above both of us. Do you really care if it was her master plan or not. You definitely won the 'sexy wife lottery'," he replied grinning.

"Come to think of it, you're right," he started laughing. "There's days I just watch her and wonder how the hell I get to sleep with her, have kids with her, and even caught her in the first place."

"Blackhawk grin?" he asked, laughing.

"Please," he said, "that grin only gets you so far. If she didn't marry me as fast as she did, I would have sworn it was mercy sex."

"Lightening doesn't strike twice, you better be very grateful to the sex gods."

432

Blackhawk knew it and debated if he should talk openly with his brother.

"What's wrong," he said, noticing his brother's face change suddenly.

"Yesterday she actually was worried I'd cheat on her. Carly Kester walked out, and she told me she felt unattractive. I jumped down her throat telling her I wasn't dad and to not stress it."

Whitefox understood where his brother was coming from. "If you ever cheated on your wife, I'd beat the hell out of you myself."

"Wow, talk about blood being thicker than water." Blackhawk laughed. "I wouldn't ever do that. Like I said before, I got really lucky catching a woman like Elizabeth."

"Yeah you did, but I understand how you always think you'll be like dad. I feel that way too sometimes. Just take it easy on Elizabeth. You're lucky."

"I told her about our conversation."

Whitefox didn't know what to say to that.

Ethan Blackhawk could read the look on his face. "Just do me a favor, Bro."

"Yeah?" Something about Elizabeth knowing about their discussion tightened his body.

"Before you commit to Doctor Adare, make sure she's the one your heart wants completely."

Callen stared out the front window. He wasn't going to lie to his brother. Both of them knew that he wanted a woman he couldn't have. "Thanks for the advice."

"If you need to talk, you can always come to me. I'll never not be here for you to guide you through anything. There's nothing you can say to me that'll make me hate you or divide us."

Whitefox nodded.

Blackhawk tried to reassure his brother. "For the record, Callen, Doctor Adare isn't too shabby herself. You definitely could win that lottery too and get very lucky."

"Yeah, well I have to seal the deal, and if she hears about this DNA, I'm a dead man."

"My lips are sealed," he answered.

"You aren't the one I'm worried about," he paused. "Two words: girlfriend code."

Blackhawk laughed as he pulled away from Carly Kester's book store. "You're so screwed."

Chapter Eighteen

Elizabeth Blackhawk sat on the counter and watched her friend autopsy a co-worker. Now that she thought about it, she should have found someone else to do it. It was clearly visible on the woman's face that she was suffering. The tears kept coming, as she removed organ, after organ and spoke into the recorder. Despite whatever Doctor Adare thought of herself, there was only one true fact. She was tough.

Her heart ached as she looked over at the face of the man that worked in the lab, and always had a pleasant cheery word for her when she came down to the morgue. Derek Williams would be missed, and then it occurred to her, they would have to notify the family.

"When will the body be ready for release?" she asked her friend.

"In a day or two, Elizabeth. I need to get the test results in, and make sure I caught everything the first time. We don't want to have to notify the family and girlfriend that we need to exhume for a second go at the body."

Yeah, that just sucked, she'd been there for her father, and she didn't want that to happen to anyone else. "I think Ethan wants to call the family today, and let them know."

Desdemona looked up.

"I'd prefer we keep the body until we can find everything the killer took," Elizabeth said, nodding her head at the obviously missing parts of the man's anatomy.

"Me too, but honestly, they may be degraded too much, and really I can only hold him for so long. Legally, he has to be released by a certain date."

"I understand," said Elizabeth. "What do you know for sure now?" Hopefully the doctor would give her something; she didn't want anyone else to end up on the table, especially like Derek.

"I think the main question is if he suffered, correct?" She started the stitches to close up his chest.

"Yeah. Please tell me that Derek didn't feel that being done to him." Elizabeth couldn't imagine the horror he must have felt if he was awake for that act. Just the idea made her stomach swim.

"He took a strike to his head, and in fact," she turned Derek's head and pointed to a sticky substance. "The killer left trace, for the first time."

Elizabeth hopped down and looked at the spot. "It looks like grease or some kind of oil product."

"I already swabbed it, and packaged it. I have a courier coming in the next hour to transport the samples back to FBI West. We should have results on this, and the evidence found under his nails in a day or so."

"We found DNA trace?" she asked, surprised.

"Epithelial cells."

Elizabeth was surprised. This would be the first human trace that the killer left behind other than the blonde hairs. She was either getting sloppy, or they were close and she was having her cage rattled. "Derek, you got a few shots in didn't you," she whispered, softly. "Good for you. I promise that I'll get a few in for you too."

Somehow Desdemona didn't doubt it. When Elizabeth Blackhawk promised payback, she got it. The lab techs talked about how she nearly killed her own brother and took out the last killer without flinching. She was very glad the woman was her friend and not her enemy.

Elizabeth's phone beeped and she looked down at the screen. "It looks like our killer isn't a real blonde," she said, reading the message from their head tech. "Christina pulled up the reports and looked at the chemicals on the hairs, and there was peroxide present."

"Bleached blonde huh? We seem to have a few of those around her."

"That eliminates Courtney Brewer, she's the only real blonde in the bunch. We'll still run the DNA in case she's helping someone commit these crimes."

"Good idea."

"I'm going to forward this over to Ethan," she said, typing up a quick email.

"Want my professional opinion on what happened to Derek?" she asked.

"I'm always open for the impression of our fine ME staff," she said, looking up and smiling at the woman. She was pretty sure she knew what had happened, but why not get the outside perspective on the situation.

"I think Derek was drugged, when he woke up he struggled." Desdemona lifted his wrists, and showed Elizabeth the abrasions. "He got free and then tried to fight off his killer. That's how the trace got under his nails. The killer subdues him with something handy. Derek gets struck this way," she demonstrated the downward strike. "It cracked his skull, and it caused intracranial hemorrhaging. Death was fast at that point. When the killer took his genitalia, he was already dead. There was very little bleeding, and he was already beginning the coagulation process."

"Thank god he didn't feel that." Finally she said it out loud.

"Exactly."

"Now I need this report in hard copy form. I have to give it to Ethan." Elizabeth wasn't looking forward to that, once he knew the wound that was inflicted, she was pretty sure that would be insult to injury, and he was going to be upset. Then again, most men would be upset, putting themselves in his place.

"I'll prep it for you now, Elizabeth. Do you want me to tell him about it? I don't mind being the one that breaks it to him. I could use some big terminology and bury it in there so he doesn't quite get the full impact."

Elizabeth laughed. "You have big word terminology for 'his penis was removed'? She felt a little better, that her new friend was willing to take the heat for her.

Desdemona thought about it. "Yeah, you're right, you better tell him."

"I thought as much. I'll tell you one thing, when I get my hands on the woman doing this; I swear I'm going to ass kick her into the next county, just for making me have to deliver this report to my husband."

Desdemona transmitted the report from her tablet to the printer. As it printed out, she washed up her tools. "Hey, where's Callen?" she asked, suddenly wondering where he'd disappeared to earlier. He'd gotten a text and then ran out, promising to return later.

"Oh, he and Ethan went to go get DNA from Carly Kester." Elizabeth pulled the report off the printer.

"Oh did we get a warrant?" she asked, drying off her tools.

"Well, not exactly."

Desdemona looked over the top of her glasses at the agent. "Not exactly?" That didn't exactly offer her reassurance. "Then how was he going to get DNA from the woman?"

Elizabeth grinned and didn't say anything.

"On second thought Elizabeth, it's probably best I have no idea what went on today. I have a feeling that it's not going to make me happy at all."

She laughed. "I knew you were a smart woman," she said, winking and then heading out of the room to find her husband and brother-in-law.

Desdemona Adare thought about it. Yeah, well now she was obligated to find out what the man she was sleeping with had done to get DNA from a suspect.

Then she just might kick his ass herself.

Saturday afternoon.

Elizabeth added another photograph to her whiteboard. Victim number seven was one of their own, and she placed his FBI photo ID on the board and for her husband's sake, didn't put the picture of him from the crime scene. Hearing about the injuries was going to be bad enough, and she still had yet to write the wounds on the board, because she needed to be the one that told him, not the board. Maybe she could soften the blow.

Hopefully.

She could hear their voices, as they walked down the corridor to the room. Elizabeth braced herself, and hoped she'd have the courage to tell her husband the truth of the situation. Plastering a fake smile on her face, she prayed for patience and the ability to stay calm if there was an implosion in the room.

Callen carried the baggie with the evidence into the room, and saw from the look on his sister-in-laws face, and knew the autopsy was complete. "Hey Lyzee, I got your DNA for you," he said, trying to keep his voice light. "You're sadistic, and I'm glad I'm the love of your life or that would have been particularly miserable," he teased, dropping the bag on the table and a kiss on her cheek. Whitefox took a protective stance at her side. He was ready for what was coming.

Blackhawk laughed, and then looked over at the Whiteboard. There was his tech's picture, happily staring back at them all. "Where's the death picture," he said, knowing exactly why it wasn't up there. His wife didn't think he could handle it. Just that alone pissed him off, and made him want to lose his temper.

"I don't want to see it," she said, lying. Immediately she prayed he'd not notice the way he was killed wasn't posted on the board either.

"Why didn't you fill in the rest of the information?" he asked, angrily.

Elizabeth knew she was going to be the target, and she wanted to get her brother-in-law out of the room before the eruption happened.

"I didn't get there yet," she said, staring at him evenly.

"Bullshit, Elizabeth." He felt rage that she just lied to him.

"Callen, can you take the DNA down to Christina," asked Elizabeth, picking it up and handing it back to him.

"Maybe I should stay." He didn't want to leave Elizabeth alone to take the heat. She was pregnant and didn't need to be dealing with his hostility alone. He'd never seen his brother this angry before at Elizabeth, and it worried him. The male in him was demanding he stay and protect her. The part of him that was in love with her was demanding it too.

"Please go, Callen," she said softly, rubbing her hand up and down his back reassuringly.

"Yes, please go, Callen. I'd like to have a discussion with my wife, privately if you don't mind. I think she'll be safe enough," he said, venomously. On a normal basis, his brother's protectiveness wouldn't bother him in the least, but right now in the moment it did.

Whitefox walked towards the door, looking back at the woman and exchanging silent looks. He was looking for any sign that she needed him to stay.

Before he could leave the room, Christina appeared, and it was apparent that she'd been crying.

"I saw you came back, Director, and I came to see if you had more trace for us to analyze."

Elizabeth and Callen both went deathly quiet. It was the worst possible moment for her to show up. Elizabeth knew what was coming, and she prayed that the woman didn't say a word.

"As a matter of fact," Ethan Blackhawk pointed at his brother. "Callen has a sample from Carly Kester. Since you're here, you can take it down with you."

Christina sniffled, and took the bag, signing off on it, and continuing chain of evidence. "I'll get it done as soon as I can," she said, looking up at her boss.

Elizabeth crossed her fingers behind her back, and she could tell Callen Whitefox was doing the exact same thing. Again, they looked at each other and braced for worst case scenario.

"Are you going to be okay, Christina?" asked Blackhawk, focusing on the woman.

"I think so," she answered. "I just can't believe how this sicko killed him," she said finally and there was an audible gasp.

Elizabeth realized it was her, and then she just closed her eyes.

Damn you, tech department for following procedures and logging the report the minute the ME had completed it.

Just for once she wished they hired incompetent idiots.

"Damn it," she muttered.

"You've seen the report?" he asked, looking over at his wife, and then his brother. Now he had confirmation that they both knew how Derek Williams's life had ended and were keeping it from him.

"Yes, a few minutes ago, when Doctor Adare put it in the file," and then she must have realized what she just did. "I'm so sorry," she looked at Elizabeth. "He didn't know yet did he?"

"I was going to break it to him now. ALONE."

"Oh my God. I'm so sorry."

"It's okay, Christina." Elizabeth had no one to blame but herself. She didn't tell Doctor Adare to sit on the report for an hour or so. This was all on her.

Christina nodded with big eyes and backed out of the room. Now she didn't know who to be more afraid of at that moment. Elizabeth looked calm, and Ethan Blackhawk looked like he was ready to murder.

Callen tried to get to Elizabeth's side, but his brother moved between them. "Get out Callen!" The look on his face was somewhere between betrayal and murder.

"Ethan, come on. Just take a break and calm down before you say anything. Go for a walk and get it out of your system," he warned, knowing this was going to be a huge blow up and it was going to be directed right at the woman he loved. "Don't hurt her."

"Get out now!" he roared at his brothers' words. The implication enraged him, as much as the man trying to stand between them protectively.

"Callen, just go," Elizabeth said, softly. She nodded at him and offered him reassurance that she'd be okay. Even this mad, she knew he'd never hurt her. He was just going to blow off steam.

He weighed the options, and if staying made his brother angrier he should leave. He wasn't going to go far that was for sure. Now he'd take sentry outside the door to be there if Elizabeth needed him.

When the door clicked closed. The sound was so loud in the silence that it could have been a gunshot. Elizabeth almost jumped.

Ethan had never been so mad in all his life. Yes, they'd had fights before, and mostly they'd been his fault, but this time, she'd purposely withheld information from her partner, and husband. The betrayal he felt whipped at him, and clawed at his heart, that she shared information with his brother and not him.

"Ethan," she started, unsure how to calm him down.

"Don't even, Elizabeth. Trust me when I say, just don't even try to justify it to me. You purposely excluded me from the loop. You know how our tech died, my brother knows how he died, and apparently our staff does too."

Elizabeth said nothing; she just stared at him with a blank stare. Her own temper was rising that after all they'd been through, he could really believe she'd hurt him intentionally.

"My own brother kept this from me too?" he accused loudly.

She was one more step closer to her own eruption.

"Where's the report?" He stepped towards her, and she stepped back from him. She only did that once before, and it enraged him further.

Elizabeth pointed at the table and watched his face as he picked it up, scanning it and then looking back at her. "So you didn't think I could handle it? Wow, you have very little faith in the man you married."

"Oh, I know well enough, that's why I did what I did," she answered, angrily. Elizabeth was mad at herself that she backed away from him, and that she was actually afraid.

He lost it. Rage ripped through him, as she admitted to keeping him out of the loop on purpose. He lost complete and total control; he rushed the table, clearing it in one shot, sliding everything off to the floor. Papers slid, reports mixed, and he found it offered him no reprisal from his anger. If anything the fire of rage just burned hotter.

Elizabeth took another step back to be clear of the rampage, as she almost fought to catch her tablet as it flew across the room and hit the floor.

Blackhawk saw her move and it infuriated him, even though it was completely rational, he still was beyond help. He turned towards the whiteboard and felt the anger at the picture of his tech on there, and how he failed completely as a boss in keeping his staff safe, and he swept all the pictures off that too, and then pushed it over.

His wife stared open mouthed.

"What's wrong Elizabeth? Never seen me this angry before?" He stalked towards her, and as she moved away from him again. It ripped him to pieces inside, and he became more volatile.

"I think you're being a total asshole, and you just ruined hours of my work." Elizabeth had a standard rule to never call her husband names, especially since his ex-girlfriend used that technique to damage him. Yet now it seemed appropriate.

"I'm an asshole?" Blackhawk repeated, incredulously.

"Yeah, this is definitely asshole behavior!" Her own temper spiked. "You want to know why I did what I did? Well, Mr. Blackhawk I'll tell you. I didn't want to hurt you. I wanted to break it to you in private, and not in front of everyone that your tech was mutilated. I was trying to be a caring supportive wife who took her damn husband's feelings into consideration. NOW I see how stupid that was on my behalf."

He stared at her.

"I didn't tell Callen anything before you. I asked Doctor Adare and she told me, Callen happened to be standing there and overheard the conversation. We decided to tell you in private, all together to be here for you and help you through it. In fact, we were going to tell you right now."

Blackhawk looked into her eyes and saw nothing but truth. Damn it! How he needed to see that she was lying so he could justify what he just did.

"Your brother and I wanted to tell you to your face, not make you read it off a fucking piece of paper. Now I see that was a huge ass mistake, because you took it as us betraying you."

Now she moved towards him angrily, and he stepped back.

"So screw you, Ethan. I'm not going to stand here and be your emotional punching bag because you're mad at a killer. I'm hurting too. While you went off with Callen to get the DNA, know what I did?" She pointed at him, tapped him on the chest and crowded his space.

"No," he answered.

"I went downstairs and stood over our dead tech, because he deserved to have one of his bosses there as he was cut open. I didn't call his parents, or girlfriend because I knew you'd want to handle that, because you're that kind of man. So I took one for the team, and watched him be autopsied."

"Doctor Adare closed the autopsy."

"She closed it to you, because we all wanted to keep you from losing it and doing," she paused, and looked around the room. "THIS!"

Blackhawk felt the rage receding.

"I'll even let you verbally slap at me because you're hurting inside, and I'll swallow it. But if you think you can tell me

443

I have little faith in the man I married, then you know nothing about me. I have enough faith in you to start a family, and I have enough faith to give you my back when we go into a dangerous situation. I shared a secret that I swore to keep for our boss. That's fucking faith, Ethan. I also know your breaking point, and this was it."

His cheek twitched.

"I knew that you'd take this personally and you'd bleed in your gut over this, because you didn't keep one of your own safe. My husband is an honorable man, and cares about people over his own feelings, so excuse me for wanting to protect your damn heart over this."

"I'm sorry," he said, finally breaking down. "I feel like I failed him. He was a boy," he whispered, as the emotion overwhelmed him. "I sent him out, Lyzee." He looked into her eyes, and found sympathy and a safe place to go when he felt broken inside.

"This isn't your fault, Ethan. This is all about the killer, and how screwed up she is." Elizabeth touched his cheeks with her palms. "You didn't kill him and this isn't on you," she whispered.

Blackhawk let out a long shuddering breath, releasing the pain and anger he felt. Now came the time where he handed it to her and trusted her with it, even though he just was a complete asshole and didn't deserve it. "Elizabeth," he said, allowing the weakness out, moving into her arms. Holding on to his wife helped heal the pain from his heart. "I'm sorry if I scared you," he said, looking at the mess. "I'm so sorry that I terrorized my pregnant wife."

Elizabeth rested her forehead against his, and held his hand. "I'm not afraid of you, Ethan. I am afraid that next time I'm going to lose my temper and kick your ass so hard you won't walk right for a long time," she whispered, and looked over when the door clicked open. There stood Callen Whitefox, and he tried to ignore the chaos all over the room, and focused only on his brother and Elizabeth.

"You okay, Ethan?" he asked, moving towards his family, no fear on his face, only concern for his brother. He threw his arms around them both, and the three of them met with their foreheads in the center of the circle. It was a family offering their wounded spirit a little support.

"I don't know if I am, Callen."

"We'll get you there," he answered. "We have you, Ethan."

Elizabeth held onto both men, and she could feel her husband shaking. "It's okay Darlin'. We can carry this together."

Blackhawk was so grateful for his brother and wife, without them he didn't know how he'd get through this. "I'm sorry I was an asshole, Callen, and snarled at you."

"Can I punch you?" he asked, grinning.

"Go ahead," he answered, his mood already lifting. Then one of them punched him. "HEY!"

Both snorted.

All three looked over as Desdemona came in and locked the door behind her. "Holy shit," she muttered, looking around the room and the wreckage. "Mom and dad are never going to go away and leave us along again!"

"I know, we're so not getting our security deposit back after this kegger," whispered Elizabeth, trying to not laugh.

Both men snickered.

"Can anyone join this party?" she asked, hoping to be part of their group, and to feel like she belonged with them.

"Yes," answered Blackhawk. He was really lucky to have all of them, and even the addition of his brother's new woman. Just the fact she too wanted to protect him from being hurt over his tech's autopsy had endeared her to him.

There was a scraping sound as a chair was being dragged over, and the doctor stood on it. "What?" she asked. "Not all of us are as tall as you three," she said, laughing. "My head can't touch yours. I come up to your chests."

All three laughed, and welcomed the woman.

"Let's reconstruct the room, I'll buy us dinner, and then we can head back to the house," said Blackhawk offering a peace offering to his family.

"Yay, dinner!" cheered Elizabeth. When they all laughed she looked at them. "Hey, anyone here ever been pregnant before? NO? Then you don't understand how exciting it is to a woman carrying a baby around."

"Okay, so how about I order from the Italian place, no meat tonight, just because," Ethan said, knowing they all saw the autopsy.

"That sounds like a plan," answered Whitefox.

"Great," said Desdemona, "and then you all can explain to me why there's a card downstairs with lip marks on it and Callen's name followed by a big heart in evidence?" asked Desdemona, staring at each one of them with the look.

"Gig's up boys, circle the wagons. Chief Cut 'Em up is about to attack. Women and children to safety first."

Ethan laughed at the reference. "Good to see that even though you turned over a new leaf, you didn't give up on the Native American comments."

"Hiatus baby, nothing more than a small break from being crass and completely politically incorrect. Besides, it feels wrong unless I'm wearing my cowboy boots. I just can't get into it. All this snow is ruining it for me."

"Hello! You both are trying to change the subject to protect him," she pointed. "Callen James Whitefox, why are there lips downstairs?" Now she was looking back and forth at all three of them in the circle.

"Oh crap, she used your full name," laughed his sister-in-law.

Callen did what he promised. "She made me do it," he retorted, laughing when she tried to object.

"Seriously? You just threw a pregnant woman who stood up to granddad for you, under the girlfriend bus?"

"I certainly did, beautiful. It's called self-preservation," he answered, kissing her on the cheek.

"Are you three always like this?" asked Desdemona laughing and deciding to stop being a spectator and join in for a change. She wanted family and here it stood.

"Always." Elizabeth snorted. "Okay, who just pinched my ass?"

"Opps, sorry, Elizabeth," said Desdemona. "Wrong ass."

"First the kiss, then the ass slap and now this," snickered Whitefox. "This has to be the best week of my life and very hot."

They all broke apart laughing, and Blackhawk objected.

"Hey! I didn't get to see the kiss!"

446

"Baby, you snooze and you lose," she answered, patting his cheek. The storms had cleared from his eyes, and she knew he'd be okay now. The turmoil had passed and the man she married was back.

"Let's clean this up, there's nothing we can do here until the DNA reports are in from FBI West."

"Come on! Just one kiss?" he begged, and then laughed when his wife sucker punched him in the side before linking arms with Doctor Adare and walking away. "The Lingerie was awesome but a kiss would make it even better."

The woman laughed.

"Wait, what lingerie?" questioned Whitefox curiously.

Now Blackhawk grinned wickedly. "You have the kiss, but I have my wife sharing sexy lingerie with the Doctor."

"HEY!" interjected Whitefox wanting more details.

Blackhawk grinned, feeling very smug indeed.

*   *   *

Julian Littlemoon knew his town well. He wished it was his exceptional Native American skills, but really it was mostly about finding all the secret spots as a kid, and remembering which ones would be big enough to hide an entire van. There weren't many places in Red River, and if the van was indeed here, he'd find it.

As for tracking his deputies last steps, that hadn't been easy. He had people see him leave the sheriff station and head south, and then that was it. Somewhere out of town he'd disappeared. He had his feelers out, and someone should have seen something. It was only a matter of time.

Crossing another location off the list, he hoped he found the van before it was too dark. If someone was hunting down men after dusk, he didn't want to be caught off guard. Moving on foot through the trees, he kept his steps steady, and his eyes open.

Julian would find the killer for Ethan Blackhawk. People of their heritage had to stick together.

Dinner was meant to be a time of socialization. It was a coming together of people to meet and discuss the day's events-Especially if you worked for Elizabeth and Ethan Blackhawk. For them, dinner was a sacred thing, and if you joined them at the table, you brought your sense of humor and no baggage from work. When you looked at death all day long, no one wanted to talk about it over food. Food should be celebrated, even when death was knocking at your door.

Callen loved his family, and he loved that his brother and Elizabeth welcomed the woman, he had every intention of marrying with open arms. It made it easier, that all of them were having a decent dinner and sliding together without issue. This is what he wanted, wasn't it? An outsider like Elizabeth to fill the void in his life.

Here sat the brother he loved, lost and loved again. A woman, who patched up the holes in his life, made everything better and held his heart. Then there was Desdemona Adare. He was still perplexed how to get her to marry him. Just the way he felt when he looked at her, the knots in his gut, and then her smile made him forget about being lonely. It was the same things he felt for Elizabeth on a daily basis. That had to mean he was making the right choice, but his brother's words kept playing into his mind over and over.

"Callen, you okay?" asked Elizabeth. He had the same look his brother got on his face when he was completely lost in thought.

"Yeah, just thinking," he said, eyes flickering to Desdemona. He was thinking about her again, and he was at a loss.

Elizabeth knew him well enough to just see how whatever it was on his mind was plaguing him. Then the eye flicker gave it away. "So, Desdemona," she started, and drew the woman's attention. "Want to help me clear the table?" she asked, trying to get the woman to join her alone in the kitchen.

"I'll do it, baby," said Blackhawk, and when she kicked him under the table he got the point. Girl talk was coming up, and they weren't included. "Or Callen and I can work on something completely irrelevant, because I just dug a hole I have no hope of recovering from. One day I'll learn to not ask my wife anything and question her motives because I am obviously out of her league."

Elizabeth pushed her chair back and leaned down to kiss him on the lips. "I married you because you're so slick and can talk yourself out of everything," she winked at him and patted his cheek.

"Don't worry, I'm coming," said Desdemona. "Far be it for me to pass up being locked alone in the kitchen with a hormonal pregnant woman with a gun."

"Good luck." Blackhawk laughed. "She leads with her right, just a warning," he yelled over his shoulder. His brother looked mortified. "Don't stress it, what's the worst that can happen? It's not like she can divorce you," he teased.

Callen wasn't amused. This was the woman he was trying to get to say 'I do' not run from him like a maniac screaming. If the plan was going to end with what his brother had, he couldn't have the woman terrorized.

"Chill out bro," he said, standing. "Let's go sit on the couch, and let Lyzee do her thing."

"Great," he muttered. Elizabeth was an amazing woman, but there were two things that she was notoriously known for, the first being her temper and the second being… well her temper. This was going to be a disaster. He just knew it.

Elizabeth rinsed dishes and put them in the dishwasher. The woman helping her was smart, pretty and funny when she opened up. If Whitefox was just jumping the girl, and had no intention of marrying her, she'd stay out of it. But this was different. This was the girl dragging her feet and looked scared shitless and someone needed to find out why.

"Are you just shacking up with Callen or do you have genuine feelings for him?" she asked, off the cuff and catching the doctor off guard. "I had to go to bat with Timothy for you to be allowed into the family, and I need to know what your intentions are with him."

"Excuse me?" Desdemona was surprised that the conversation had to do with her just sleeping with the man; she didn't think she'd lead in with that as the starting point.

"I love him, and I like you a great deal. You might even venture to say I love you too. But if you're not serious about him, you need to cut him free, and I'll make sure he heals and gets back on the horse to ride again."

"I see why he's in love with you." Desdemona hoped there was no animosity in her voice.

"Is that why you're hesitant? You think there's some chance you'll come home one day and find me in bed with your husband?" Elizabeth watched her face. That certainly wasn't it. "Because let me assure you, I like my bed and my husband a great deal."

"Now, with this bed scenario is your husband included and is there a swap?" she asked, rebounding from the surprise and coming back with the things that Elizabeth got.

Humor and sarcasm she could appreciate, but not when Callen's heart was at risk. "I don't think so doctor. I'm attached to Ethan, and you're evading the question. You'd swap Callen?" That didn't bode well for her, and granddad had already warned her about what he was feeling.

"No, I wouldn't. I happen to be crazy about him and hopelessly in love with him."

She took Desdemona's hand. "Talk to me. What has you so freaked out about being with Callen?"

"I don't want this nutjob to touch him. If he gets hurt because of me, how do I live with that, Elizabeth?" She told her about the card and the warning, but kept her intense jealousy to herself about how she believed Callen didn't just love Elizabeth, but was IN love with her. Big difference.

The woman was genuinely scared; she could see it in her face. "I won't let anything happen to him or you."

It was said with such certainty that Desdemona almost believed it. "Timothy said the same thing."

"Listen to the sage advice from the old Indian. He's wise and tells it like it is. As for both of you, I'll keep you both safe. I promise," she added. "I'm really good at defending the ones I love.

I'm ferocious; I'm like a pit bull. I can guaran-damn-tee that nothing is going to touch either of you."

Desdemona thought about that, and looked over at her friend seriously. "He hasn't really asked me, he's ordered, demanded and told me that I'm marrying him. In fact, he told Timothy that he was going to have more kids than you and Ethan. Not once was I asked. A girl wants to be asked not ordered into a marriage. Then there's the whole 'moving very fast thing' and please don't tell me it worked for you, because I'm not you."

Elizabeth picked up on the hostility, and prayed her love for Callen wasn't the source. That she couldn't remedy, but first part of the problem she could.

"He didn't ask?" That was a typical man, although, she remembered the way her husband proposed. He got down on one knee, and her heart still fluttered thinking about it. "Go take a shower, and let me handle the man issues."

"Elizabeth," she didn't know what to say. "I want him to ask out of his free will, not you holding him at gun point." What she wanted was him to tell her she was the love of his life. Maybe it was petty, but more than any other woman in the entire world.

"Damn, I can't use my gun?" She tried to keep a serious face.

"Elizabeth!"

"I promise I won't tell him to propose. I'll be so subtle no one will even know what I'm doing," she said, grinning. That scenario wasn't likely, but why freak the woman out?

Somehow she didn't buy that. "This is going to bite me in the ass, I can tell. Why am I letting you talk me into this? I'm not sure I want to get married. I'm a logical person and this is going way too fast for me."

"Love isn't logical. When he asks, decide then, and go with your heart."

"I'm a scientist, logic is my baseline. I use my brain all day."

Elizabeth shrugged. "Be Morticia or be the scientist. You have to choose."

Desdemona stared at her, and weighed the options. It was a great family, and she was lacking one. Callen was sexy as sin, and he wanted her. There was a crazed maniac after her, and they would keep her safe. Even to a logical person it was a no brainer. Did love really matter in the long run? Maybe love would grow with time. "Crap," she muttered and then left the room to go upstairs to shower. If he did ask, she could always insist on a long engagement to buy her time. If she said no, there was no guarantee he'd ever ask again.

Damn it!

What the hell was wrong with her?

Elizabeth wandered out to the couch and sat between the two men. She leaned against her husband and dropped her legs across her brother-in-law's lap. She'd found herself between them quite often at home on their couch in the same position. Callen was a fixture there, and she and her husband liked it that way. It was a comfortable easiness that the three of them found quite often.

Until now.

Callen was stirred up like a hornets nest.

"Where's Desi?" he asked, looking at Elizabeth. "You didn't upset her did you?" he asked, and then took a shot to the ribs with her fist as her reply. "I guess that wasn't a good question to ask," he said rubbing his side.

"I beat her up and she's out in the snow."

He actually tensed and earned another punch.

"Really Cal?" she asked, incredulously and a little hurt.

"I'm edgy and nervous. I'm sorry, and I don't need her running terrified from the Blackhawk family."

"Can we discuss something?"

He looked over at her nervously. "I guess we can. What?"

Elizabeth looked up at her husband and ran her fingers down his cheek lovingly. He was the sexiest man in the world, and she couldn't imagine her life without him. "Ethan, remember the day you proposed to me?"

"I certainly do. Best day of my life." Yeah, he certainly had won the wife lottery. Slowly Ethan began kissing his wife on the lips, and then a little more, and then...

"You two, hello?" interjected Whitefox, laughing.

"Sorry, too many sexy men in one house, I'm easily distracted." Elizabeth refocused, but her body was all hot and bothered by the kiss. "Can you tell your brother the correct way to propose? A little birdy told me that he missed that part of man training 101."

Blackhawk looked confused as to where she was taking this. "You get the father's permission to marry his daughter, you get a ring, you get down on one knee, you ask and then you pray she says yes," he said, smiling down at his wife. "Then you have copious amounts of sex until you get her pregnant and wobbly," he added, snickering. He took the rib shot this time.

She stared over at Whitefox. "How many of those steps did you complete?"

He looked confused, then embarrassed, and then he got it. "I have the ring."

Ethan Blackhawk reached behind his wife's head and smacked his brother. "You didn't get down on one knee and ask?"

"No, I was going to…"

"Your brother has alluded, ordered, and assumed that she was going to marry him. In fact he's demanded they have more kids than we were going to have, but not once did he beg for her hand in marriage. Please tell your brother that women hate to be ordered to do anything, Ethan, and that if he wants to get the girl there are rules to the game."

"Son, women are delicate creatures that need to be finessed," he started and Elizabeth elbowed him again.

"I get it," he said, leaning back. "I didn't follow proper protocol." His brother was all about proper procedure, apparently in life and love too.

Elizabeth laughed. "Rules are rules, boys. You show up at the girl's house, you get on your knee, you offer up a sparkly ring, and beg."

Callen smiled.

"Can I add one more thing?" asked Elizabeth.

"Sure you can, beautiful," he said, wanting to hear what she had to say, since these two people were his standard of a happy marriage.

"Callen, you need to make sure she's the one, and have no doubt whatsoever. We support your decision and will stand with you no matter what."

Whitefox stared into the icy blue pools and could feel his body flushing. It reminded him of the time on the Rez when the body turned up in his house and he had to tell her he was looking for easy sex to get over her. "I want to do this because it feels right."

Elizabeth saw the lie, being trained law enforcement, she could spot one a mile away. "Okay, Carlin'." Then she released his hand.

Blackhawk shook his head. "Okay Callen, there are candles in the kitchen in the first cabinet, a bottle of wine in the fridge. Go get out the rings, tell her the history behind them, put one on her finger, AFTER you ask her if she wants to marry you and she says yes."

"She's in the shower. You have enough time to set the mood, and get it ready."

Callen knew how lucky he was that they cared enough to help him out on this and worry that he was settling. Now he had a plan, and was going to get what he wanted.

Elizabeth watched him charge up the steps, and then he turned around and ran back down. "I love you," he said, kissing her on the lips and then resting his forehead on hers. His hand went to his brother's shoulder. "Thank you for supporting me and believing in my choices." Immediately he ran back up the stairs, the wine and candles in his hands.

"Now I'm worried," she said, when he was all the way upstairs.

"Me too," he replied. "But Callen has to make his own way, isn't that what you told granddad?"

Elizabeth hated that he was right. Now they had to sit back and wait, and support him anyway they could.

He changed the subject. "I meant what I said; asking you to marry me was the best day of my life."

"I wish you could have asked my father, he would have loved you."

Blackhawk stroked her cheek. "I did ask him. The day they exhumed him, I asked for time alone with him, introduced myself

454

and asked for daughter's hand in marriage. When you marry a girl, you ask the dad first, and since he didn't object..."

Elizabeth felt her eyes begin to well up. "You're the best thing that ever happened to me," she said, straddling his lap and kissing him. "I won't ever love anyone the way I love you, Mr. Blackhawk."

"I happen to feel the same way," he answered.

When her hands slid into his hair and she dove into his mouth with everything she had to show him her love for him, his body hardened beneath hers. Her blood started pounding in her ears, and the scent of his cologne and soap overpowered her, and she just controlled the kiss. When she finally broke away, his eyes were hazed with lust and his breath was ragged.

"That was some kiss, Mrs. Blackhawk."

"Take me upstairs, and I'll show you what goes with it, Mr. Blackhawk," Elizabeth whispered in his ear. She giggled as he was up and off that couch so fast, her wrapped around the front of him. "In a hurry?"

"Not giving you time to change your mind, or for my brother to need another lesson," he said, serious look on his face, as he bounded up the stairs and locked their bedroom door. Carefully he placed her on their bed and hopped on beside her. "Commence your plan of attack, Mrs. Blackhawk," he snickered. "I am your willing victim."

Elizabeth rolled to her side, and looked down at her sexy husband. He was all angles and hard lines, and he made her heart pound in her chest. Lowering her lips to his, she slowly, torturously began kissing him. Drawing out the kiss, and the pleasure they both found in it. "Ethan, I can't wait to get home. I miss climbing all over my husband whenever I want," she whispered, keeping her voice down, just in case Callen Whitefox was in his room next door.

"Baby, trust me when I say that I probably miss it more," he laughed, and then her hands started wandering. His wife had a voracious appetite, but an assignment put a damper on it, especially sharing a house with others.

His focus returned to his wife as already she had his shirt untucked from his pants, and her hands were running trails across his flesh leaving scorching paths that were causing him to burn with want.

Elizabeth began kissing him again, and doing really creative things with her tongue and teeth, and when he moaned, she almost shivered just from the guttural sound. It came deep and low from his chest, and made her temperature rise even more.

Ethan could feel his buttons being undone, and his control began slipping. What he wanted was to roll his wife to her back and invade her body, with abandon. "Killing me," he muttered into her mouth, and then her hand found him, and she stroked him. "I take that back, go ahead, kill me!" He closed his eyes, and she pulled him free of his dress pants.

"Like this, Ethan?" she asked, and took him in her mouth.

The heat and wet warmth were enough to almost make him lose it, and he fought to not move his hips, not grab her by the hair, and not take complete control like everything in him demanded. There was something possessive living in him since his woman was carrying his child. It was primitive, and it fought with him for complete control every time they came together for sex.

"Yeah, that's so damn good baby!" Blackhawk moaned again, and again fought for more control against her oral assault. When she broke out the teeth, he arched and prayed.

Elizabeth loved the control over her husband, and loved when she could give him so much pleasure. She took him deeper, and his body began to shake in response. In a burst of frenzy she took him hard, until he dug his clenched hands into the bedding.

"Shit, Elizabeth," he couldn't breathe. "I'm out of practice," he whispered, as she continued to torment him. Just when he couldn't handle it anymore, she stopped, and slid off the bed, to undress.

"Get naked Ethan, and then sit up against the headboard. I want to ride my Cowboy tonight," she ordered, slipping off her shirt, and dropping her jeans. Next to follow were her bra and panties.

Ethan obeyed as he slid out of bed, stripped, then jumped back into bed where his wife wanted him. All he could keep thinking was, 'beautiful woman on top', and he was infinitely happy. "Yee Haw," he muttered, as he watched his wife crawl across the bed to him, her body now lush from pregnancy, he was even more turned on and it must have said it on his face.

"What are you thinking about, Ethan?" she asked, straddling his lap.

"That I hope your breasts stay that big after you have the baby," he confessed and couldn't help but stare at them, touch them, and taste them. It was a man thing. When his hands wandered her body, he felt the overwhelming need to take his wife, claim her and what grew deep within her body, but he allowed her the control. If just for tonight, he'd fight the beast clawing at his body.

Elizabeth enjoyed her husband's hands touching her body, stroking, finding all the spots that made her crazy and turned her on. Her hands roamed his body equally, and then she found the big black Raven, her name tattooed beneath it as she wedding gift and she felt the need to be wild and out of control. Leaving kisses across it and feeling the need build in her.

"Elizabeth," he whispered at her open mouthed kisses across the raven that was now both theirs.

"I want you out of control," she whispered into his ear, as she slid him deep within her body. I want you wild, Ethan."

"Oh God," he moaned, and braced his body for the assault he knew was coming. As she started to move, and control the depth and speed, he was already shaking. This was going to be torture, as she rode him, and grinding down, each time. It tore a gasp from his lips, as she tormented him.

Elizabeth rode him, overcome with need. The pregnancy hormones were making her crave his body. Elizabeth loved feeling his body quiver beneath her. She wouldn't last much longer, her body was already over sensitized and now she was making herself crazy. When she was just about ready to break apart, she felt his hands come to her hips, and he took over, guiding her up and then pulling her down. The pure bliss was incredible, and she began to shake and finally she shattered, his name on her lips.

Now his body was in flames, and if he didn't find relief he was sure he'd ignite. His wife was breathing heavy, and then he realized it wasn't her, but him. "I need to take my wife," he whispered, while she struggled to refocus. "Ride me, Elizabeth," he ordered, his eyes met with hers as she began again "Wait for me," he whispered hoarsely, as he pulled her down at a bruising pace, fingers digging into her hips, to control her body, and force it to give him what he needed.

"Ethan," she begged, already so close again.

"More baby, I need so much more," he was on fire; the woman on top of him was making him absolutely crazy with need and lust. Blackhawk couldn't take it anymore and rolled, placing her beneath him and slid back into her body, as far in as he could. The invasion was powerful as he continued moving deeper and deeper. With his arms braced beside her, he gave her what she wanted until neither of them could take much more.

"Ethan," she moaned and arched, fighting to stay in control.

"God, I can't get enough," he whispered, and felt his wife lose her battle, she quaked and tightened around him as she found bliss again, and he fought hard to get into her body. That resistance alone and the struggle to push in was finally all it took. Blackhawk erupted so powerfully, he may have shouted her name. Falling to the bed beside her, he fought to regain his basic abilities.

Sight

Hearing

And feeling anything from his waist down.

Elizabeth started laughing or maybe it was snickering. She wasn't quite sure, but whatever it was, she had reason to be smug. "Nice one, Cowboy," she said, slapping him on the bare ass. Then she ran a hand down his tattooed back, ridged with lines and muscles that were her little obsession.

"I'm glad I entertain you," he muttered.

Elizabeth rolled to her side, and then pulled a blanket over them both. "Let's sleep." She was suddenly exhausted. "Between you and baby Blackhawk, I don't have my never ending stamina," Elizabeth yawned.

Blackhawk rolled to his side, placing her body protectively over hers and their child. Her belly was against his hip, and the motion of his child bouncing, drew his hand to her flesh. Slowly he soothed, rubbing, and massaging the spinning baby. When the motion stopped, he kept his hand there, guarding what they made together.

"I love you, Elizabeth," he said softly, as he drifted off to sleep.

458

Elizabeth opened her eyes, and tucked a strand of his hair from his cheek. "I love you too, Ethan," she whispered back, and then curled into his body, lying there and worrying about the other man in her life two doors away.

~ Chapter Nineteen ~

Callen listened to the shower shutting off and he looked around the room to make sure the scene was set. He took the time to light a fire in the fireplace, set up the candles around the bed, and pour the wine. In his pocket were the family heirlooms that he was given by his grandfather, brother and sister-in-law.

He was ready.

No he wasn't. He was scared shitless. Ordering her to marry him was easy, putting his heart out there and allowing her to reject him was going to be the hard part. What he really wanted was reassurance from Ethan and Elizabeth. Whitefox would have run back to them to make sure he was doing it right, but he already knew they'd begun their evening. While in his room he heard the evidence and smiled. The way they loved each other was the benchmark he wanted to set for himself and Desdemona. As a child he always wanted to be just like his big brother, and now was no different. He was on the cusp of getting everything he ever wanted in life, and mimicking his brother's path in life. There was the escape from the Rez, the job in the FBI and then the finding of an outsider woman to help him complete the mission in life.

When the door to the bathroom opened, fear filled him that he'd screw this up. The woman he wanted to marry was standing there with her hair pulled back, she looked so innocent. He fought to not rush to her, wrapping her protectively in his arms.

Desdemona looked around, and knew what was happening. Elizabeth Blackhawk's hands were all over this, and she smiled. Having a girlfriend for the first time in her life was a pretty incredible thing, and having Callen Whitefox, well that was just as amazing. "Hi," she said, softly. Everything in her was pounding, and she forced herself to walk towards him.

"Hey, sweetheart," he said, putting out his hand.

Desdemona took it, because she wanted desperately to be part of this man's life. Everything about him was what she wanted in a man. Kindness, a big heart, and incredibly sexy; he was the perfect package for her, and she knew it deep down on the first day she saw him. All she wanted was to have him and the family that came with him. "I like the room, are we having a date?" She went into his arms and accepted the kiss waiting for her. It was sweet, gentle and he used it to mask his nerves, but she could feel them just below the surface.

Whitefox kept the kiss light, and as he broke it, he gave her the answer, "We are." Leading her over to the bed, he lifted her up by the waist to situate her. He sat beside her and handed her a glass of wine. "I wanted to talk to you first."

"About?" Desdemona tried to look like she was confused, but she wasn't sure if she was pulling it off at all. All she kept saying to herself was 'Be Morticia', and to let her heart make the final decision. Now she just needed to trust her friend's advice.

"Us."

"Okay, Callen." The wine helped soothe her nerves as she took a healthy gulp to help calm her down. Desdemona was scared out of her mind that she was going to make the wrong decision. Inside she knew she wasn't ready but what if she asked for more time. What would happen then? Would he leave her and then would she be alone, knowing that she was too scared to commit? What if she said yes and it ended up being a mistake? Oh God! This was so stressful.

"I want to tell you about my family and the history they have when it comes to finding the women they married. My grandfather was married to my grandmother for a long time. They were an arranged marriage, as he was the oldest son, and she the oldest daughter in another tribe. They were picked to be married to unite the families," he said, beginning the story. "She was so young, and he was so stubborn that no one believed they'd make it. The fights they had that first year were talk among the tribe. My grandfather was a stubborn brave, and my grandmother, she had a wicked temper."

Desdemona listened patiently.

"It took the time to find love together. There were many fights and battles between them, but in the end they found it." He sipped his own wine. "I was told often that I had to carry on my bloodlines with a Native woman. If my grandfather could have, he would have hand-picked mine and Ethan brides. Luckily we both were stubborn as hell."

461

Desdemona laughed at that. "I hadn't noticed."

Callen Whitefox winked at her. "As a young man, growing up on the Rez, there were only a few things I wanted in life. A way out, to be like my big brother, and to find the love of my life." He looked into her green eyes and pushed forward hoping she'd believe everything he was saying. The love of his life was in the other room, but this woman could fill in the remaining holes. He was sure of it. "I think you and I are meant to be together, much like my grandfather and grandmother. We could have a really good life and fill it with laughter, love and family."

Desdemona was holding her breath waiting for him to give her what she needed in order to say yes. Just that little spark of hope and she'd let her heart win over her mind.

"In our family, the oldest son and his wife carry on the tradition of the Blackhawk clan. On our reservation, being a Blackhawk is a huge deal. They're the oldest family, and they are important. As you know, I'm missing the Blackhawk name, but I've been included in the family, given such a precious gift." He took a deep breath.

Desdemona knew how important his family was, she could see how he loved them. Letting her mind take over was a bad idea, she stayed in the moment and stared into his eyes and saw so much emotion.

She had to believe it was for her.

She hoped.

She prayed.

"When we visited my granddad and he pulled me aside, he gave me his blessing." Whitefox felt relief over the first obstacle being cleared. "He also gave me the family rings. They were my grandparents and theirs before them." Whitefox pulled out the box, but didn't open it yet. "By all rights, they should be Ethan and Elizabeth's rings. They will head the family after my grandfather is gone." Just the thought filled him with sadness. The old man was his rock as a child, his brother as a teen and his sister-in-law as an adult. "Elizabeth will be the one that keeps us together."

Desdemona knew how defining the moment was for him as well as her. Not only was he claiming her, he was being claimed by the family. That he included her in that moment of his life was precious.

"Elizabeth declined the ring, telling granddad to give it to me. She wanted me to give it to the woman I chose as my wife. That's a huge honor for me. That I get to give the ring that my family holds sacred to the woman of my choice. Ethan and I are the fifth generation to have these rings, and until just now, no one without the Blackhawk name has ever worn them. I never thought it would be my choice and for a while, I'd given up hope on love."

"She loves you a great deal, Callen." Desdemona took a deep breath and waited. "I'd given up hope too, Callen. That I'd never find love." What she felt for this man and his family was so big it overwhelmed her.

His heart skipped a beat that she indeed understood. "I'm lucky, someone will always be there for me when my granddad is gone, but I want more." Whitefox held the box in his hand and prepared to open it. "Please marry me, and fill the rest of my heart. Give me the last piece of the puzzle and make me a very happy man."

Desdemona looked down at the two rings in the box, and they looked perfect together. This is where it all came down to her making her decision. Walk away loving him and lose what she was being offered because it wasn't enough, or take the gift and try to be happy. Take the family and the friendship along with the chance that one day he'd love her with all his heart, not just a portion or live alone and afraid.

"I can't give you the Blackhawk name, but I can give you the family that I love, the people that make me alive inside," he whispered, pulling his grandmother's ring out of the box. "It's a simple ring." The stones glittered in the firelight. "Because I'm a simple man." Whitefox held the ring in his fingers, waiting for her answer. "Now I just need a simple answer of yes or no."

She laughed. "Callen, you are far from simple. You are the most complex, exasperating, bossy man I've ever met in my entire life," she said shaking her head. Now it was all up to her. Run or stay? Desdemona closed her eyes and hoped she chose correctly.

"Well that can't be good," he said holding the ring.

She channeled the inner Morticia and took that leap of faith. She wanted desperately to have a family, a girlfriend to bond with and a man that would keep her safe. Besides the sex was amazing and there was a chance it would grow into more.

"Yes."

He looked up. "Yes it can't be good, or yes you're going to marry me and be my wife?" His heart began tripping in his chest.

"Yes, I'm going to marry you." Desdemona held out her finger. "And for the record, I love the ring and that it belonged to people that found love before us. I'll wear if forever and never take it off," she said, as he slid it onto her finger.

Callen was overjoyed and the adrenaline took over. "I love you." It was the best day of his life, and he couldn't wait to tell his family that he'd sealed the deal and got the girl to say yes to him. The ring looked perfect on her hand and he felt relief and peace.

"I love you too, Callen," she whispered, looking up into his eyes searching for what she wanted to find.

"I'm going to maul you like you've never been mauled before," he warned, laughing.

Desdemona touched his cheek, and ran her fingers across his lips lovingly. "Maul away, but let's not wake the entire house," she said, giggling.

Callen kissed her like he never kissed her before. It was hard and demanding and it showed her exactly what was building in his body for her. Nothing else around them mattered at that point. It all fell away. His hands explored her, and he found himself overheating at the gentle touch her fingers were tracing against his body. The last piece of the plan fell into place, and he had finally gotten what Ethan found for himself.

Desdemona was completely hot and melting. Something in her was begging her for more and more, and she was inclined to listen to the voice pushing her forward. Deciding to just let herself go, like she did with her heart, seeing where it went. She answered his driving kiss with one of her own. Her hands quickly unbuttoned his shirt, pulling it open, and running hands lightly down his body. When he shook at her touch, it inflamed her even more, and made her want to push him harder.

"Desi," he whispered, pulling away from her lips.

The look in his eyes drove her forward, as she pushed him back and decided to show him what lived deep in her for him. Next she flicked open his belt buckle and unzipped his pants, aiming for one goal, driving him to madness. There was no gentleness when she freed him from his pants and looked deep in his eyes. "I want you, Callen," she said softly. It almost didn't sound like her voice. It was deeper, breathier and it gave her the push she needed. Desdemona was going to take what she wanted, and let him feel what she felt, and maybe she could fill his heart even more until it overflowed. Oh, there was going to be a mauling, but she wasn't going to be the one mauled.

"Christ," he muttered, when her mouth took him intimately. He shook as she did wild and insane things to him.

Stroking him, licking him, and adding just the perfect amount of pressure made his body bow, and his breath catch in his chest. "Like this, Callen?" she asked, taking a break to catch her breath and look up his taut body for an answer.

"Uh huh," He barely could think. He was too busy trying to not embarrass himself, with his lack of control.

Desdemona began her assault, and enjoyed his leg shaking and his eyes closed trying to not watch the scene unfolding across his body. She broke contact, demanding what she wanted. It was only fair, he'd been the bossy one before, and now she was going to show him what it felt like to be out of control and wild. "Open your eyes, Callen," she waited, and when he obeyed, she saw the need, the want and the wildness there.

"Can't or I won't make it," he said through clenched teeth.

Desdemona licked her lips, and continued stroking him with her hand. "Lose control, Callen," she whispered and went back to work on his body.

"Desi!" His voice shook and was full of lust. When he couldn't handle it anymore, and was on the precipice, he pulled her from his body, and stared into her eyes. There was love in her eyes, lust and a touch of amusement.

"What's wrong, Callen? Out of control?" she whispered, and then saw the instant he lost total control, right before he struck. His eyes went from lust filled to demanding.

The tenuous threads of control snapped and Callen just let it go. He pulled her into his arms, mouths crashing together brutally, and he was pretty sure the gasp was from the woman in his arms, but he could be mistaken. He rolled with her, pressing her beneath his body as he began his assault on her senses and body, beginning at her neck, and then working his way down.

Desdemona buried her hands in his hair, only to have her hands pulled away and pinned at her sides. Apparently, his hair was off limits during sex. "Callen!" She wasn't used to the rough and wild love making, but went along for the ride.

When she pulled on his hair, that feeling of betrayal resurfaced in his body. When hands ran through his hair, he always pictured them to be the hands of the woman he loved. It immediately felt wrong, and he couldn't handle the guilt.

He ignored her words, working his way down her body, finding all the spots that he knew would drive her crazy, and he worked them over, until she was moaning and squirming under his lips. He left nothing untouched, and when she shook and shattered, he paused for only a second, before moving up her body and sliding into her roughly.

"Amazing," he whispered, as she gripped his body, trying to lure him over the edge, but his control was back and before he was done she would be the one begging. The strokes were slow, and long, and as he felt her body responding to him, they became more punishing.

She stared up at him with unfocused blurred eyes.

"I want more, Desi," he stated, continuing to move into her body. A fine sheen of perspiration was on his brow as he fought for control. He was going to burn this night into both their minds for the rest of their lives for both of their sakes. His to forget and hers to remember where she needed to stay.

Desdemona could feel her body surrendering to his battering, and it was proof that Callen knew how to pleasure a woman.

He felt the quake again, and when she started he pulled completely from her body, or he wouldn't survive, giving her a second, he rolled her over and pulled her to her knees.

"Callen!" Desdemona was barely able to breathe, let alone feel more.

Sliding home, he leaned over her back and whispered in her ear. "Again for me, Desi." And he began the drive again, pushing and pulling until he was so completely lost in the bliss of it all. He was going to take her and own her completely. He needed to feel that delicious control over her body. He was determined to find happiness, even at the bruising pace he was setting.

Desdemona felt the heat building again and she was sure he was trying to kill her. Her body tingled and shook. His hands on her hips holding her in place left trails of heat on her body, and when he reached around and stroked her, she gasped and just gave it up. The man was taking what he wanted; she only hoped to survive it all.

As he Desdemona began to shake, and Callen increased the thrusts, until it took over his body too and called to him, luring him to the edge. With her moan, he slammed into her once more and allowed her body to take anything it wanted from his. He exploded in amazing bliss and poured into the woman he was determined to make fit into his life. Maybe with her he could forget the truth.

Both fell to the bed in a tangle of limbs.

Finally, he was able to speak. "You okay, Desi?" he asked.

Desdemona shook her head. "No, I am completely numb from the cerebellum down," she answered. She wasn't sure if it was because he paralyzed her with his voracious lovemaking, or if he was just lying on her body.

He laughed. "You know, when you talk Doctor to me and wear those glasses, it makes me want to do it again." Whitefox rolled off her body and pulled her to his chest. "Better?"

"No, I'm still numb," she laughed. "Give me a day or so to recover."

Whitefox laughed. "If you need that much time to recover, I obviously did something wrong."

"I think I feel my toes."

Now he was feeling smug. "I hope you regain feeling again soon."

Desdemona had other things on her mind. "I just hope Elizabeth and Ethan didn't hear how hard you went at it. That was definitely different, Callen."

Something in him heard the words, and realized that Desdemona possibly wasn't into voracious love making. He made a mental note to tone it down, she was smaller than him and possibly wasn't comfortable. "The men in our family are animals. If anything it's expected from the two of us."

Desdemona rested her hand over his heart, and looked at her ring. She was Morticia, she just kept saying it, and hoping she could pull it off.

"You should get some rest," he suggested, leaning over to blow out the candles.

"I'd give my left kidney to sleep all the way through the night," she answered and yawned. "I can't remember the last time I slept eight hours."

Whitefox closed his eyes, and enjoyed the feeling of not having to sleep alone anymore. He had his family, his brother, Elizabeth, and now Desdemona.

Life was seemingly perfect.

Except he knew the truth, and was living with the guilt.

Sunday morning.

Callen strolled into the kitchen with a big smug grin on his face, and as he looked at his brother, they shared a common expression and both knew it. The men started laughing, because they both got lucky.

"What?" asked Elizabeth, looking up from the tech report.

"Nothing," Whitefox said, whistling as he walked over and sat beside his sister-in-law.

Blackhawk couldn't help but snicker.

"I certainly hope both of you aren't talking sex in some man language I don't have privy to, because once I crack the code, I will hand you both your very fine asses," said Elizabeth.

Callen stole her coffee cup right from in front of her, and winked at her.

Elizabeth laughed and just let it go. She'd come to grips that he planned on poaching her coffee at any given chance. "So, did you seal the deal?" she asked, and had her husband choking. "I meant with the proposal!" She slapped him on the back. "Out of the gutter, Ethan. I wasn't going to ask about his sex life. Give me some damn credit. If I went there, then he'd be asking you about ours."

"Damn right I would." Whitefox laughed, leaning over to kiss her lightly on the lips. "I did, and she said yes," he grinned.

Elizabeth patted his cheek and looked into his eyes. "I'm very happy for you, Callen." She started sniffling. "Congrats."

Whitefox looked panicked as she teared up. "Elizabeth," he pulled her to her feet and hugged her to his body.

"I'm just happy that you look happy," she answered, leaning against his body. "Sorry, damn baby hormones make me weepy."

Whitefox brought his lips to her ear. "I will love you forever for what you've done for me. Thank you for loving me before any other woman did, Lyzee." He hugged her tighter reluctant to release her, and looked down at his brother over her shoulder. "Thank you Ethan for being a great role model and picking her as your wife."

Blackhawk stood up and hugged his brother around his wife. "I'm happy for you, Cal," he said.

Desdemona wandered into the kitchen and watched the three of them. She was flooded with so many emotions. Some that filled her with happiness and some that filled her with envy. It was definitely an adjustment to have to watch the man you loved kissing another woman all the time. She watched Elizabeth run her fingers through Callen's hair, and she thought back to the previous night. Obviously his hair wasn't off limits to everyone.

"Callen, did you make Elizabeth cry?" she asked, smiling at the woman even though she wasn't the smile deep down.

Elizabeth freed herself from the men and crossed to her new friend, hugging her. She whispered in her ear. "Welcome to our family." She kissed her on the cheek, and noticed she wasn't the only one that was emotional. Desdemona looked ready to cry herself. Elizabeth hugged her against her body.

"Thank you."

Blackhawk crossed to the woman that was going to be his new sister. "Welcome to the Blackhawk family." Then he hugged and kissed her, smiling at his brother. "Now I know why you're always cuddled and kissing my wife. It's nice to hug and kiss another woman that won't elbow me."

Elizabeth looked over at Desdemona.

Ethan sucked in a breath as he took an elbow from his soon to be sister-in-law.

"That would be the wrong assumption, my love. You neglected the most obvious clue."

He laughed and rubbed his side. "What's that?"

"Girlfriend code, Ethan," added Desdemona, walking to the coffee pot.

"Lyzee hits me plenty," said Whitefox grinning, as he drank her poached coffee. "I love every second of it." He wiggled his eyebrows and winked at her teasingly.

She blew him a kiss and joined Desdemona at the coffee pot, since her brother-in-law swiped hers once again, but the ease between all four of them was refreshing. "I'm just glad you picked a woman I like, because if I had to merely tolerate someone, that would just be too much damn effort," she dropped her arm around Desdemona's shoulders. "For the last bit of lovey-dovey crap for today," she said, accepting a new cup of coffee. "Morticia, I will be proud to call you my sister," she said to the woman. "I love you."

Desdemona's eyes filled with tears, and she hugged her friend tight and whispered in her ear. "Thank you and I'm the lucky one to be part of you three." She hugged her friend enthusiastically. "I love you too." Doctor Desdemona Adare got her fondest wish. She now had a circle to call her own, and honestly believed everything else she accept was worth it.

Callen was filled with so much emotion as he watched the two women interact.

Elizabeth patted Desdemona's cheek and headed back to the table, taking a seat between her husband and brother-in-law and smiling.

It was a good morning.

"Callen, I need a huge favor," he said, looking over at his brother. "Derek William's family has requested the body to be returned, and I'm going to be bringing it back to them," he said, and looked over at his wife, to make sure she wasn't going to protest. When she didn't, he continued. "Can you hold down the fort with the women folk while I'm gone?"

Whitefox nodded. "Yeah, you aren't going alone are you?" he asked, worried about his brother's well-being.

"He isn't, because he knows we'll have a big fight right here and now if he answers that question incorrectly," said Elizabeth, crossing her arms and resting them on her baby bump. "He knows that the killer got Derek while he was alone, and he wouldn't do that to his pregnant wife, because she'll go shit wild and start a rampage. He also wouldn't do that because he'd then be embarrassed as I beat his ass down right here, knowing you'd never let him live it down."

Blackhawk laughed. "I'm taking Christina with me, and the other DNA evidence that we collected." He got serious. "He should have one of his bosses escort him back, and since you three took the autopsy duty for me, I'll pick this up and do the personal notify too."

"Well Christina will keep you safe," snickered Elizabeth, and Whitefox joined her and the two of them enjoyed the look on his face. "At the first sign of rain, she'll throw her body over you to keep you dry."

Whitefox fist bumped Elizabeth. "Good one."

"Seriously you two? Maybe leaving you both here together is a very bad idea. Who's going to babysit the children," he scolded.

"Ye of little faith," she said.

Desdemona sat at the table. "I'll babysit them," she offered. "Really, Christina wants you that bad?" she asked, looking over.

"In the worst way. All that stands in her way is Elizabeth," answered her fiancé. "She has major boss-hots."

Elizabeth giggled at the phrase. "I like that, boss- hots. I think you just coined a new one, Callen," she offered him another fist bump. "It's fun to say and rolls off the tongue."

Blackhawk sighed in exasperation.

"When I started at FBI West, my first impression of Elizabeth was that she was ass kicking and tough. When I asked Christina if she was as bitchy and hard to work for as she appeared, she told me that if I admired Ethan, don't let Elizabeth catch me," she answered. "Or the shit was hitting the fan and her fist was hitting my face. No offense, Elizabeth," she apologized.

"None taken," she answered.

Desdemona noticed her fiancé took Elizabeth's hand and was offering her some reassurance. It obviously bothered her more than she let on.

"Generally, that assessment of me is true, but rarely do I beat down a woman because she looks. Now if she touches, then I get mean. I keep saying this, but I am greatly misunderstood."

Blackhawk kissed her on the cheek.

Desdemona continued. "She really had me scared that Elizabeth was vicious and mean when it came to looking at Ethan."

"You were checking out my brother?" Callen asked, sipping his absconded coffee.

Desdemona laughed at the hypocrisy of his question since he was holding another woman's hand in front of his fiancée. "Guilty as charged, but in my defense, it was before you and who in the tech lab doesn't stare at Ethan?"

Elizabeth snorted. "Between us Desdemona," Elizabeth lowered her voice and got serious. "There's some 'how sexy is Ethan Blackhawk pool' isn't there?"

"Come on!" Now he was mortified.

"Well, there's a 'when's Elizabeth going to have the baby pool'. Then there's a 'How many tats are on the boss man pool'," she said, laughing at the look on Blackhawks face.

"Twenty three, and I get half the money if you win."

"Deal." Desdemona said, bumping fists.

Whitefox snickered, sharing a secret look with Elizabeth. It was one where he thanked her for doing everything he asked of her. Desdemona was now part of their inner circle, and he found himself even more in love with her. Damn it!

"There is one more pool," Desdemona added. "But not sure you'll like this one."

Elizabeth was intrigued. "Do tell."

"There's the 'will Baby Blackhawk mellow out Elizabeth after his birth' pool."

Elizabeth laughed at that one. "I hope you didn't put money on yes."

Desdemona shrugged. "I have fifty on you getting worse. Again sorry, but it was before getting to know you, so you really can't hold me accountable."

"Nice one. She fits in already," snickered Elizabeth.

Callen was so damn happy that they were getting along, he actually kissed them both.

"Wow, you just got to kiss two women in one day. That hasn't happened in...never," stated his brother laughing.

"Awesome. You're just cranky because you know what the tech team is doing when you're off playing emperor in your big shiny office."

"Christina is easy to handle. Make her drive and she can't check you out," said Elizabeth.

"Great, so now this six hour trip will be that much more comfortable," Blackhawk sighed.

"Lead in with Elizabeth being extra bitchy with the pregnancy and her threatening to kill people more often. You'll set the bar on the conversation and she won't check your ass out once," snickered his brother.

Elizabeth saw the blush creeping up her husband's neck and she went and sat in his lap. "I love you," she said, kissing him gently, and rubbing her hand across his chest and their hidden tattoo. "You can't help you're sexy, and if you think I didn't catch the 'hold down the fort' reference before, I did, and it was very funny, Mr. Blackhawk."

Ethan hugged his wife, but his eyes were on his brother, and a message passed between them. He trusted the man to keep safe the most important person in his life, and his child. Whitefox nodded and accepted the job. No one was touching his sister-in-law.

Over his dead body.

Desdemona caught movement from the corner of her eye. "Someone's on the porch," she said, softly.

All three FBI agents pulled their guns at the same time.

Then there was a knock on the door.

"I'll get it," said Blackhawk standing and putting his wife behind his body protectively, despite her protests. When he saw who was at the door he holstered his gun and opened the door. "Julian, come on in," he said, opening the door for the deputy.

"Thank you, Agent Blackhawk," he said, nodding towards the women in greeting.

"I'm going to assume since you're on my doorstep that means you found something that I needed to know about?"

"I found your van."

Everyone in the room went alert at his words.

"Did you approach it?" Blackhawk asked, offering the deputy some coffee.

He accepted and took a sip. "It's hidden a few miles back on a deserted piece of property. It's not easy to get to with a standard vehicle, and you're going to have to have it towed out. I don't know how it got back there, but it's not coming out easily."

"I appreciate you finding it for me. You do excel at tracking," Blackhawk made a mental note of the man, and his skill. One never knew when something like that would come in handy somewhere down the line.

"We'll have to hike in, and the woman might have a problem," he pointed at Elizabeth.

"Oh no, you just didn't point at me, because I'm pregnant did you?" she accused, putting down her coffee mug with a thud. "I still run six miles every morning when I'm back home, and I can keep up with you men. Granted I don't have your superior Native American DNA, but I just may surprise you," she practically snarled, meeting Julian Littlemoons' eyes.

"You have a feisty woman there, Agent Blackhawk," he answered, grinning.

"This feisty woman is going to kick your ass back to your teepee," she said, angrily.

As she moved forward, Whitefox grabbed her by the waist and pulled her against his body and locked her against him despite her struggles to get free. "You better haul ass out to your vehicle and wait there with the windows up and door locked. She is a bit more than feisty," he said, defending Elizabeth and still finding it funny at the same time.

Desdemona cringed at her fiancés' arms wrapped around another woman. When he dropped a kiss on her cheek and she leaned back into his body comfortably, it made her want to make a comment.

"That's probably a very wise idea. We'll meet you outside, Deputy and follow you up with our vehicles as far as we can and then hike into the woods. How many miles?"

"Two miles in, and if I may say two things?" he said, looking over at Blackhawk.

"Sure," he made sure his wife was restrained against his brother, before he let him continue.

"Whoever dumped the van there, knew the area. It was once owned by the boy scout camp, same organization that owned the buildings where the bodies were dumped."

Blackhawk considered that. "Okay and?"

"I happen to like and appreciate feisty women, and in the winter I use my cabin not a teepee in case you're looking for me," he said winking, placing the coffee mug down, and walking out the door to wait for the FBI agents.

"I think that was an invite to his teepee. Now I don't know if I've been complimented or insulted," said Elizabeth, laughing at the look on her husband's face.

"I liked that man too. Now I think I have to kill him, but it'll have to wait until after we retrieve the van," muttered Blackhawk. "Doctor, you can stay here or drive into the station."

"Well as much as I like a two mile hike in snow up to my hips, I think I'll head into the station and see if I can get the lab to move a little faster on the DNA we sent."

"Alone sweetheart?" asked Whitefox. That didn't make him happy at all. He wanted her by his side at all times.

"I'll be okay, besides the killer isn't after women. I should be more worried about you, Callen," she said, going to him and kissing him. "Please be safe for me?" she asked.

"You be safe, Desi," he said, kissing her forehead.

"Oh look Ethan. See how he trusts her and doesn't fight her constantly and make her feel like she's a wounded bird?" Elizabeth grinned.

"They aren't married yet, she can still say no and leave him at the altar. He has to play nice until they sign the papers and then it's a whole new game then."

Elizabeth elbowed him in the ribs.

Blackhawk laughed. "See?" he said, rubbing his ribcage. "It's a whole different game until you tag the woman and get the paper," he laughed, dodging another rib shot.

"Let's suit up and retrieve the van. Later I'm going to show you what 'tag' really means," added Elizabeth, grinning.

"I think I like feisty women now too," Blackhawk replied, grinning lecherously.

The three FBI agents followed the deputy in his jeep up through the mountains outside Red River. They made their plans and discussed what they were going to do once they got there. This

475

was a dangerous situation, and Blackhawk knew his wife was going to insist on going, and fighting her was going to be a waste of time.

He knew her strengths and weaknesses, and he was going to utilize them to keep them all safe. No one else was going down on his team, including his wife, child or brother.

"You're seriously giving her the tactical shotgun?" asked Whitefox. In his opinion that would make her the first target if the killer was hidden and ready to strike.

"I am, because she has the best ears, eyes and reaction time. I've qualified against her, and I know how well she shoots. Out of the three of us, she's most likely to hit the target if one pops up." He wasn't going to share the secret his wife that he now protected. His wife was an excellent shot, and had a past that made her more willing to take the shot with less guilt to slow her reaction down.

Whitefox wasn't happy.

"What?" asked Elizabeth, looking back at him.

"She can't wear Kevlar, and if someone was going to pick people off in order of most dangerous to them, they take the person with the tactical weapon out first and handguns last. You know that," he said, finally. "I'm sorry, Lyzee." He didn't want to hurt her feelings, but someone had to point the obvious out to them.

"She'll be in between us and not point man. Our Kevlar will protect her from the front and back," he answered, trying to not think about what could happen.

"Callen," she reached back and rubbed his leg. "I trust you both, and you have to trust me completely too. We each bring something to the team, and I'm really a good shot and that's what we need."

Whitefox's cheek muscle ticked.

Elizabeth hated seeing her best friend this worked up, and she looked over at her husband and the look passed between him. She knew he was carrying her deepest darkest secret. "Callen, I need to tell you something and you need to never speak of it again. It has to stay in this vehicle and then die with each one of us."

He looked concerned. And took her hand that was patting his leg in his hand, leaning forward and waited for what she had to say. Immediately their fingers twined intimately.

476

"I have a secret that's so horrible that it could put me in jail and now Ethan and you too if it gets out."

"So tell me. I'd go to jail for you in a heartbeat."

Elizabeth was overwhelmed with the love she felt in the vehicle. Having family was definitely complicated. Before both of these men she never had to worry about it getting out and now she had to trust them.

"You don't have to tell me if it's too hard."

Blackhawk took her other hand. "I love you, baby," he said, offering reassurance that he supported anything she decided. He trusted his brother.

"Never speak of it," she said. "Promise? Not even to Desdemona. It's not the kind of secret you can share with a wife. This is my deepest darkest secret."

"Absolutely. I won't tell her or anyone else. I promise."

Elizabeth told him the same thing that she told her husband not too many nights ago. Because she was getting it off her chest with the two most important men in her life made it easier for her conscious to carry. There was a lessening of the guilt.

Whitefox listened to the woman he loved and didn't speak. It wasn't surprising that she had gone after the man that hurt her friend. It was completely something she would do. Elizabeth just screamed 'Justice', when he looked at the way she lived her life.

When she had finished, the pain was clearly on her face. "I can't risk the people I love and if this gets out we're all screwed now. So, I don't know if telling you was a good thing or the worst thing I could do to you."

"How many of my secrets do you keep for me?" he asked, touching her cheek. "I'll help you carry this one, and I'll stand in front of you with Ethan on this." He could see the pain in her eyes. "This doesn't change a single thing in my heart about you," he said it, and Blackhawk met his eyes in the mirror, but he kept going. He was trusting that the conversation they had the other day still stood. "If anything I just love you more because I know if someone hurt me or Desdemona you'd be strong enough to help me find justice."

Elizabeth was touched by his words, and by both men just accepting what she considered the black stain on her soul.

Blackhawk brought her fingers to his lips and kissed them. "You are an amazing woman, Elizabeth, and we're very blessed."

"I agree, and now the tactical gun makes more sense. I thought he was crazy to give a girl that gun," he snickered, trying to make her laugh.

Elizabeth gave in and shook her head. "I'll forget you said that, since I might be forced to accidentally shoot you in the ass to prove a point." She leaned over and kissed her husband on the cheek as he drove, and then leaned back and gave her brother-in-law a kiss too. "I love you both."

"I love you, baby," he said, rubbing his hand over the baby bump.

"I love you too, Lyzee."

"We're here," said Blackhawk, pulling in behind the deputy. "We'll be using earpieces; it'll make it easier to hear each other out in the wind."

Elizabeth popped in her earpiece and listened to everything her husband outlined. When it came to arranging things preemptively, he was better at it. She was sure he had thought it through a few times already and worked in any scenarios. Her job would be to keep her eyes on the surrounding area. Elizabeth was sure that her husband had already given Callen Whitefox his job, and she would bet her paycheck it involved him watching her.

Deputy Littlemoon stood watching them prep, it was interesting to watch his Native brothers shank the front and back of the woman. When he saw the head man give her the tactical weapon, he smiled. She was very feisty, and he appreciated that, but he only hoped he wasn't giving her the weapon because she needed the most protection. "Shall we begin the hike out?" he asked, pulling on his gloves. He noticed the woman wasn't wearing one glove. "You should glove up, frost bite can happen fast," he suggested.

"Thanks, but if I need to shoot someone they won't hold on while I pull my glove off," she answered, slipping her yellow tinted glasses on. They'd offer her eyes protection from the wind and brighten the area making her find any targets easier.

He shrugged. "Suit yourself." Littlemoon gave her twenty minutes before she was bitching, moaning, and having to be carried through the woods to the van.

"Which way, Deputy?" asked Blackhawk.

"Follow me and keep up," he looked right at Elizabeth.

478

It was obvious that he believed she was going to be the weakest link and that just pissed her off, made her want to kick his ass. Elizabeth heard the voice in her ear, and it was her brother-in-law.

"He's just being a dick, just ignore him. We know you could take him while in full labor, one arm behind your back and with food poisoning."

Ethan laughed. His voice came over the ear piece. "You can show him how bad ass you are later when you beat him into a pulp, but for now I need him alive to show me where the van is," he whispered into the com.

Elizabeth didn't answer them. She was too busy doing her job. All of their lives were dependent on her not missing a single thing. She scanned and followed in the tracks behind her husband. Her trigger hand was in her pocket and ready, in case she had to fire the tactical shotgun.

Through the entire hike up into the mountains, the men in her family kept talking to her, and she would just nod or shake her head, and her brother-in-law would answer for her. When they hit the last clearing, she saw it. The tech van was hidden behind the trees, the nose of it sticking out. Someone had backed it into the trees in order to hide it the best they could.

"We're going to have to call in a tow truck to pull it out, the killer did a number on it with wedging it between those trees," said Blackhawk.

"Want me to check the back?" Whitefox volunteered for the job.

"We'll both go," he didn't want to leave his wife out in the open, but he didn't want his brother going alone either.

"I'll watch her," said the deputy, sensing his hesitation.

"I don't need anyone watching me," she answered, scanning the tree line. "Just go and get it done, Ethan. We're sitting ducks out here," she turned and watched another area, scanning it quickly.

"Deputy, can you call the Sheriff and give him this location and have a tow truck brought out for retrieval? I don't want to leave this up here any longer than we have to. If our evidence is here I need to keep it as uncompromised as I can from this point out."

"Can do," he said, pulling off his glove and dialing his phone.

Elizabeth tracked the movements of her husband and brother-in-law, watching the surrounding area, to make sure they were protected. In the trees past the van she saw movement, and got low to the ground to blend with the surroundings, watching the motion and tracking it. The figure or shape was directly behind the deputy. He was too busy on the phone to notice something was creeping up behind him. Then she saw it, and her eyes got wide. Out came her hand and the gun went into place, and just at the last second, before the deputy was attacked she pulled the trigger.

The gunshot echoed, the deputy spun and looked to see what she had shot at behind him. Blackhawk and Whitefox rushed from the trees, guns drawn.

The men stood over the dead mountain lion that was less than ten feet from where Littlemoon had been standing. The kill shot was to the head, and direct center of her forehead.

"And that's why she has the tactical gun," answered Blackhawk, looking over at his brother and grinning. She was excellent at marksmanship, and really it wasn't a practiced skill. Some people just were really good at it.

Then came his wife's voice, across the snow, directed at the deputy and not on the ear piece. "That's why I don't wear a glove when I'm on the tactical gun, Chief Kiss My Ass. Had I been wearing my glove, you'd been that mountain lion's bitch." Elizabeth went back to scanning the area.

Blackhawk laughed, and patted the deputy on the back as he headed back to the van. Once to the back of the van, both men each took a door, and prepared to open it. He signaled his brother, telling him what he needed him to do.

Whitefox's heart was still pounding from the gun shot. He nodded and signaled he was ready. They both flung the doors open, and peered inside, guns drawn and waiting for someone to jump out at them.

Both men let out a breath.

"Is it clear?" Came the voice over the ear piece.

"Clear," said Blackhawk. "You can come back here now. If there was someone waiting for us, one of us would have been targeted already, especially after the gun shot."

Elizabeth trotted past the deputy, and to the tree line and her family. When she arrived at the back of the truck she looked inside.

"Looks all accounted for," said Whitefox.

Elizabeth stared in and then shook her head, checking again. "Uh, Ethan?"

"Yeah baby?" he said, walking around to the back of the truck. The front was clear, and he didn't want to enter the vehicle, until it was swept.

"We have a big problem," she said, drawing her gun back up and training it on the back of the van.

Both men pulled their guns, but saw nothing. "What's wrong?" asked her husband, worried.

"Six bodies in bags went out on transport according to Christina's log."

"Yeah," he answered, lowering his gun and looking over at his wife. Her brow was all scrunched up with a genuine look of confusion.

"We have seven body bags. Someone left us a spare."

Shit!

.

~ Chapter Twenty ~
Sunday Afternoon

Ethan Blackhawk made the executive decision to not access the bag. If the killer had indeed put someone in it, there may be trace to find and that could net them the maniac. The main goal was to transport the van back to the Sheriff's station and have the teams unpack it, redo the trace, and sweep the vehicle. Fortunately, it was winter and the bodies were staying cold out in the snow. Nothing would have degraded and made it a worse mess to deal with.

Blackhawk noted the time, as the tow truck pulled up and Randy Duffy hopped out of the vehicle. He was there incredibly fast. He came over to them, standing beside the van and shook his head.

"Wow, how'd it get stuck in there like that?" he asked.

"We think the killer put it there," said Blackhawk. "More importantly, can you unstick it and get it back down to town and the sheriff station for us?"

"If the FBI is paying, I'm trying," he said, grinning the good ole boy grin.

Blackhawk nodded and went to stand out of the way with his wife, brother and Julian Littlemoon.

"Sure we shouldn't look in the bag first?" asked Whitefox. "I don't want Desdemona getting any nasty surprises."

"There might be trace all over that bag and whoever is inside it. I don't want to go digging around in that van without gloves on, and I'd have to move the bodies to get to the field kits to glove up."

Elizabeth linked her arm through her brother-in-laws. "Don't worry, Callen. We'll be there with our guns when the van arrives back down off the mountain. We'll keep Desdemona safe."

The man nodded.

"Julian, can you ride down in the tow truck with Randy?" requested Ethan Blackhawk. He didn't want the driver to be ambushed, and that meant sending him out with an armed guard. "Just until you get down to the vehicles, and then follow him back to the station. I'll call ahead and have the tech teams wait until we arrive."

"Sure thing," he answered, nodding at them and walking away.

Elizabeth watched him walk away and didn't say a word, but her face must have said it all. Both men started laughing.

"Still pissed at him?" asked her husband.

"No, but I was thinking about letting the big kitty lick him a few times before I shot it, just to prove a point."

Whitefox laughed. "Remind me to not piss you off, Tex."

Elizabeth sighed. "Damn, I miss my cowboy hat. I can't wait until spring. All this cold and snow isn't my thing."

The three of them started the hike down off the mountain, and each one of them was a little bit curious as to who they were going to find in that bag when they got back to the station.

At the end of the excursion out, Blackhawk called back to base, warning them that Randy Duffy was in transport with the van and no one was to access it until they arrived. Next he called Desdemona Adare and gave her the same warning and instructions until they arrived.

They were closing in on the killer, he could just feel it.

Desdemona Adare watched as the van was backed into the garage of the sheriff's station and was ready with the chain. Ethan Blackhawk wanted the back doors chained shut from the outside, to prevent anything getting out, or anyone getting in to the evidence. Randy Duffy lowered it beside the second van that they were getting ready for transport. Within the next few hours, the body of their fallen team member was going to be driven back to FBI West personally by their boss. As she chained the door through the handles, Randy just watched her.

"Seems a bit extreme," he said, leaning against the van.

"The boss's orders. I'm just the ME, and who am I to question them?" she said, smiling.

"So how does someone become a Medical Examiner?" he asked, offering some coffee from his thermos. "Are you a real doctor?"

Desdemona declined. "I went to medical school, just like any other doctor. I just specialized in pathology, and finding how someone dies. I don't save them, I just give them dignity in the end."

The man nodded. "If you don't mind, Doc, I'll just hang out here and wait for the boss man to return. I'll need him to sign the paperwork."

"Sure thing," she answered, looking up at Julian Littlemoon strolling into the garage. "Deputy, where's everyone else?" Desdemona wouldn't relax until she could see her fiancé back where he was completely safe. The entire time he was gone, she was a wreck, and it made her nervous. How was she going to feel when he was out in the field alone, and she was back in house? This was something they were going to have to sit down and discuss before they got married. Yes, she knew he was an FBI agent, but she wanted to know more about what his job as Liaison to the Native community was going to entail. This love thing tied a person up in knots.

"They should be here shortly, Doctor. I'll wait here with you," he said, watching Randy Duffy with unblinking eyes. He was very aware the man was staring at the doctor like she was a tasty snack and that bothered him. The woman before him, although not a Native was taken by one of his brothers and that had meaning. Unspoken law between warriors meant he'd watch out for her, even if he wasn't asked to by Whitefox.

It didn't take long for the Denali to pull into the parking lot outside the garage. All three FBI agents hopped out, and entered where their tech van was being housed. "Doctor Adare," nodded Blackhawk. He looked over at the tow truck driver. "Need my signature?" he asked. They weren't going to open the back of that van with a civilian standing around. Just in case the killer was in that seventh bag. Hiding and waiting to ambush them. Part of him hoped it was the killer, and she managed to self-terminate in the bag and save them all the trouble of continuing to look for her.

"Yeah, thanks." He led them over to his truck, and when he opened his truck door a bottle of hydraulic fluid fell out.

Blackhawk caught it, and righted it before it hit the floor.

"Thanks, I have a leak in my line, have to carry extra everywhere," he said, and handed him the clip board, and after he signed and handed it back, he nodded and bid them goodbye. "See ya'll later," he said, winking at the doctor.

Callen didn't miss the wink, and it pissed him off. He looked down and saw Elizabeth's hand on his arm to calm him. Soothingly she rubbed her hand back and forth. She obviously didn't miss it either and knew the man was going to be asking for trouble.

When he pulled his tow truck out of the garage, there was a puddle of fluid on the floor. "He wasn't kidding, that's a big leak," said Julian Littlemoon.

Blackhawk avoided the puddle and pulled the bay doors shut for the garage. If they were going to open the van and pull out the bags, he wanted privacy, and no way for anyone hiding in there to escape.

Elizabeth grabbed a pair of gloves that Desdemona had in her pocket. "I'll go in," she said, waiting for the doctor to unlock the padlock. "Cover me," she said to her husband and brother. As the chain was pulled slowly from the door, she jumped up into the back. "They're all tagged except the top one," she said, reaching for the zipper on the top bag. Even though the bodies were in a van in the freezing cold, she could still smell death.

"Mask?" she asked, and Desdemona pulled one out of her lab coat pocket.

"Bad?" asked her husband.

"Yeah, this isn't a fresh body," she answered, putting the mask over her mouth and nose. The last thing she wanted was to breathe in the bacteria when she opened the bag. "Ready?" she asked, as Callen Whitefox and her husband pulled their guns and pointed them at the bag.

"Ready!" They answered.

Elizabeth took a deep breath, and pulled the zipper. Open enough to look down into the bag. She zipped it back up and stood, her stomach rolling sickly. She'd seen a lot of death in her time with the FBI, but this, this was the worst.

"You can holster. What's in there isn't going anywhere." Elizabeth Blackhawk wanted to vomit, and that meant it was bad. She never puked on a scene, ever.

"What do we have?" asked Blackhawk.

"I think we can end the mystery of what the killer is doing with the body parts," she said, pulling off her mask and taking in some air to clear her head. She braced her hands on her knees and leaned over shaking her head. Elizabeth wasn't sure if it was the pregnancy, the body, or the dead eyes that once belonged in someone else's skull.

"It has to be bad, because you look green," said Blackhawk. "You don't ever flinch."

"Our killer is putting a body back together, one part at a time," she said shuddering.

"Huh?" asked Whitefox.

"We just uncovered Franken-victim."

Desdemona stood in her makeshift morgue and was suited up in a protective suit, and ready to open the bag holding the body parts of the other victims. Elizabeth had told her what she saw, and she knew it was going to be particularly gruesome. Right now, the body bag sat on her table, and her tools were close by. At that moment, the tech team was removing any trace from the outside of the bag, before the work on the inside began.

Ethan Blackhawk motioned for Doctor Adare to step off to the side, he needed to speak to her quietly. The whole team practically huddled, as he spoke in hushed whispers.

"I need a favor, Desdemona," he said, looking down at the woman.

She knew it was going to be big; he used her name in the workplace. This was going to be a personal favor and she couldn't imagine what he'd want. "If I can do it, I will."

"I'm leaving to transport Derek in a little while. If his missing body parts are in that bag, I'd like to take them with me, and return all of him to his family."

Everyone could hear the emotion in his voice. He was still hurting over letting one of his own go down on his watch.

"I know that it's not procedure, and I know that it's not the norm, but I want him to go home for burial in one piece. I can make it a direct order if that makes it easier for you to make the decision."

Desdemona considered the request. Breaking protocol had repercussions. In court and also in life, wasn't that her major rule. Follow the rules no matter what?

"I'll work on his organs first, package them up and have the tech team put them in his body bag," she said, softly. "As for making it a direct order, that's not needed."

Elizabeth smiled over at her friend. The power of family was an amazing thing, and it meant one more person to love and watch over. Desdemona Adare was taking one for her husband, and that meant a great deal in her book.

"Thank you," he said, looking back over at the body bag. "I appreciate it."

"Anything for family," she said, smiling. "That is the family motto, no?"

Elizabeth shrugged. "Well, it used to be, 'Anything for a bacon cheeseburger' but that seems grossly inappropriate anymore now that he fell in love with a vegetarian," she said, pointing at Whitefox.

All four laughed.

"Okay, I have to start this, if you want out of the room, now's the time to do it," she said, double gloving and getting ready for what waited her. She put it out of her mind that this was a person, and thought about it as a science experiment she needed to find the answers with. "Ready," she said to her techs, and they unzipped the bag and even they looked horrified. Lifting out the corpse, everyone stared.

There lay a mummified looking corpse, skin pulled taut over bones, and organs harvested from the victims grotesquely placed on the body.

"Holy shit, you weren't kidding," muttered Whitefox. "It looks like Doctor Frankenstein tried to rebuild a person."

Elizabeth nodded and shivered. "We are dealing with one sick asshole," she said, finally.

Blackhawk agreed and watched as the tech's started taking the pictures. He was pretty sure he'd never seen anything quite like it.

"Ethan, give me what you're thinking," his wife said, softly. "How the hell did we end up getting that body?"

Blackhawk thought it through. "I don't think the killer thought we'd find the van," he said, finally. "If you think about it, that's her prize, and she must smell us getting closer to move it from her home or hiding place to the tech van."

"She took a shot at us when we took her bodies away the first time, now we have all the bodies and her prize. What's that going to do to her now?"

Blackhawk shook his head. "I can't answer that. Already her state of mind seems fractured that the unsub really thinks she can rebuild a person. That she's building a male- I'd venture the killer's rebuilding someone she loved and lost."

Elizabeth looked over at the corpse. "Our perpetrator is going to go shit nuts when she finds that her long dead love is gone, isn't she?" she whispered.

"I believe so."

Whitefox shook his head, as he looked at the hands and feet on the corpse. The killer had removed the skin from the victims' severed limbs and placed it over the appendages of the dried out corpse. It was a grotesque testament to the killer's mind.

Sick and twisted.

Doctor Adare began her work. Slowly she removed the added on parts, the eyes, the skin from the feet and hands, and the genitalia from their own team member. She looked over as she reached into the cut already present in the body and pulled out a well preserved stomach.

"She must have had the organs in a solution," she said finally. These parts," she pointed to the hands, feet, stomach and tongue. "They were done months ago, and they are still," she searched for a non-technical term for the three agents staring at her. "Fleshy."

"So you think she collected and placed them in jars to collect everything then put it together?" asked Elizabeth. "Ewww."

"Yes."

"I don't buy she was done," said Blackhawk. "I think she threw him together because we were getting close and she needed a safe place to put him until she was done killing."

"Could be," said Desdemona, as he had the team swab Derek's organ and then she bagged it, safely inside a non-see through bag. She instructed her tech to go out to the van and place it with Derek's remains.

"Thank you, Doctor," said Blackhawk. He looked at his watch and then motioned over to Christina. "We should hit the road. I want to get Derek to his family before it's too late, and then back here before sun up," he said.

Elizabeth went to his side and wrapped her arms around him. "Please Ethan, be safe. Don't stop for coffee, and don't do anything Cowboy to get you hurt," she pleaded softly. "We need you to come back."

"Baby, no worries." He saw the fear in her eyes and it touched him that his woman was so worried about him. Before her, there was no one to care if he returned home or not. "I'll have Christina with me. I'll be completely safe."

She started laughing, and went up on her toes to kiss him. Elizabeth didn't care that there were tech's in the room, or that everyone was staring. If she couldn't kiss him goodbye, it would bother her the entire time they were apart. The kiss was deep and slow, and she felt her own skin flush. When she broke away she looked up into his eyes and touched his cheeks.

"I love you, Ethan Blackhawk."

He grinned wickedly, and kissed the tip of her nose. "I love you, Elizabeth Blackhawk. Hold down the fort, Boss," he said, looking over at his brother as he walked away.

Elizabeth glanced over at Christina and motioned her over to her side. The look of fear was entertaining, but she had other things to worry about. "You watch his back. You make sure he doesn't stop for coffee or any other reason. You carry your gun and you shoot any blondes, brunettes or redheads that come near him."

"Got it," she said, nodding.

"Please keep him safe and back to me, and I'll forget that you were just checked out his very fine ass while you were standing behind him."

"Damn it, you have eyes in the back of your head!" she muttered, laughing. "Or wife radar."

"Both."

"Don't worry, Elizabeth. I'll stick like Cyanoacrylate."

Elizabeth didn't speak Chemical-ese, but if it was Christina, she knew she'd be all over her husband to keep an eye on him. "Ok, watch his back and for once I'm giving you complete permission to follow him everywhere he goes. You get to be his shadow," she said, then dismissed her.

Elizabeth looked over at Desdemona for translation.

"Glue," she said, laughing. "Cyanoacrylate is superglue."

Whitefox moved to Elizabeth's side and protectively wrapped his arm around her shoulders, holding her to his body. "Then why didn't she just say that?"

Elizabeth relaxed against him, twining her fingers with him. "Who knows why?"

Whitefox could hear the tension in her voice.

"He'll be okay," added Whitefox, whispering into her ear. "I promise."

Elizabeth just nodded and thought back to what her husband had said about the killer losing her mind over them having the body. All she could hope was the nutjob wouldn't think her husband was transporting the victims and go after him.

How would she go on if anything happened to him?

Blackhawk detoured to the deputy's desks upstairs. He found Julian Littlemoon sitting there doing paperwork for the end of shift. Ethan Blackhawk had a special favor to ask the man and it involved his wife.

"Julian, you off shift?"

"Yeah, in ten minutes."

"I need a big favor," he said, pausing. "I have to transport our tech back that was murdered. I need to leave Elizabeth here to run it."

"You want a babysitter?" he asked, looking up. "I don't think she really needs one. Not after watching her out in the snow today and with that shotgun."

"How about we call it, 'keeping her company'?" he said, thoughtfully. "She can handle herself, but she tends to get into trouble. How about you just find a way to keep her from getting herself abducted, shot, stabbed or killed while I'm gone?"

"Is she going to skin you alive if she finds out about this conversation?"

Blackhawk thought about it. "Yeah, and scalp me while I sleep to add insult to injury."

The man laughed. "Okay, I think I can do it for you, and forget the favor. She kept that mountain lion from chewing on me today, even though I was riding her pretty hard over her being a pregnant woman."

"Just don't piss her off, or you'll be the hairless one."

"Got it," he said, grinning. He certainly liked a feisty woman, and this was going to be entertaining.

Desdemona placed her scalpel down and shook her head. This was completely wrong and she didn't understand it at all. This new piece of information made her head spin, and she felt off balance. Everything they were assuming just got tossed to the wind. "Oh oh," she said, looking over at Elizabeth.

"Oh shit, I really hate when the ME has her hands in a body and says 'uh oh'. It always means something horrible is about to go down," she said, moving closer to the body, Whitefox following her.

"You're not going to like this at all," she said, pointing. "The corpse, isn't a male. It's a female."

"What?" Now she was shocked and surprised. "You mean our killer is a woman killing a man, and then placing the parts on a woman's body? Are you sure?"

Desdemona pulled the skin back on the mummified woman. "See these small organs and this sac like object?"

"Yeah."

"That's a uterus and ovaries."

"Well crap. I hate late in the game changeups." Elizabeth pulled out her phone and dialed FBI West. When the tech room answered on the third ring, she barked orders to light the fire under their asses and fast. "I need all the trace evidence transmitted ASAP, and if I don't get it, someone will be getting my boot where the sun don't shine," she drawled.

The tech didn't sound impressed, he must have been new. "We're working as fast as we can," he simply stated.

"Oh, well you can tell that to Director Blackhawk, he's in route to the lab now. So, when I call him and tell him you weren't enthusiastic about getting me the data, you can explain it to him. You like being unemployed?" she asked.

There was dead silence, as if he was weighing his options.

"I want it by the time I get upstairs to my whiteboard, and I don't care if it's partial at this point, I need that damn information two days ago!" she shouted, and hung up on him.

"And this is why they call you Attila the Hun," laughed Desdemona, "and have little Lyzee voodoo dolls in their lockers on standby."

"Really?" she asked, completely amused by that.

Whitefox shook his head. "I don't know if you should be amused by the voodoo doll part, Elizabeth." Whitefox dropped his arm protectively around her shoulders.

"Little do they know, Granddad did his Native mojo thing over me and the baby, I'm covered. It should cancel it out." Now her focus was back on the body on the slab. "I'm going up to the whiteboard, and need to call Ethan. This little twist has to change the profile and I need him to update it."

Whitefox debated on whether or not to follow her upstairs.

"Cal," she turned to him and wrapped her arm around his waist. "I'm sure Ethan told you to watch over me like a hawk, but I'm indoors and I'm armed. Who gets abducted from the middle of a sheriff's department?" she asked, laughing. "You have to be a special kind of unlucky to have that happen."

"Okay, but you shoot anyone you suspect that moves towards you."

Elizabeth hugged him, glancing over at Desdemona. "You two stick together. I mean everywhere," she said. "Until I get a handle on who the killer is, no one goes anywhere alone."

"Uh," she went to point out the obvious, that Elizabeth was breaking her own rule.

Immediately, she pointed to her baby belly. "I'm technically two right now," she said grinning. "But nice try. See if we can get a rush on the corpses DNA, if you can find anything viable."

Desdemona shook her head. "Will do," she said, looking through her micro-goggles, for any hair or flesh that she could use.

Elizabeth walked away, and fell deep into thought. The killer was using male parts, on a female corpse. That had to be significant. Before entering the room they were occupying as an office, she decided to swing into the sheriff's office and dig up some information. The man was completely aloof as of late, and she didn't know if he was just worried about the FBI running him down, or if he was just so busy trying to keep his people as far away from theirs.

At the knock at his door, Sheriff Duffy glanced up.

"Hey, you have a few minutes?" Elizabeth inquired.

"Sure do, Agent Blackhawk," he answered, putting down his pencil and relaxing back in his chair. "Has someone done something? I can handle it if there's a problem."

Elizabeth stood by a chair. "May I?" At his nod she took the seat, crossing her legs. Soon that wouldn't be a possibility. "Actually, your Deputy Littlemoon was super helpful today in finding our van. We appreciate his help." The man actually looked calmer, that she wasn't there to give him grief. "Sheriff, I'm sorry if we came off difficult to work with, and I can completely understand. I was once a sheriff and had the FBI roll into my town."

The man sighed. "Agent Blackhawk," he began until she interrupted him.

"Please, Elizabeth is fine."

"Elizabeth, it's not that I have a problem with the FBI or you. It's that I'm trying to keep my people from making your lives hell. They don't like you or didn't. Julian Littlemoon is an entity all his own, and then my secretary, well she's just not a people person."

"We can handle ourselves."

"So I've heard, Elizabeth. I also hear you found a corpse added to the van."

Elizabeth should probably update the man, since it was his town, even though he said he wanted to let the FBI run it and just keep him in the loop.

"We did. Our ME has determined that it's female and the killer is using male parts that she's harvesting."

493

He lifted an eyebrow. "Really? What's that supposed to mean?" he asked.

"I haven't spoken to Ethan for a new profile yet, so I honestly can't answer that, but it's a big twist in the game," she said.

"Can I interest you in some coffee?" he asked, pointing to his coffee pot. "I just put it on," he offered.

"Thanks, cream only," she answered, and then took the cup from him, sipping it. "I have a few questions, and was hoping maybe you can help me."

"Sure thing." James Duffy sat back at the desk with his own coffee.

"Have you had any women disappear in the last year or two, just up and poof?" Elizabeth Blackhawk was thinking about how to figure out who the mummy corpse was downstairs, in case they couldn't pull DNA.

Sheriff Duffy turned to his computer and began typing. "Nothing official Elizabeth, but you know how small towns are since you're from one. People come and go all the time. Unless someone reported a person missing, we have no record of it."

"Hey, it was just a shot," she said, finishing her coffee. "I appreciate it. Thanks for getting the tow truck to us so fast."

"I'm just glad dispatch found Randy for you," he replied, sipping his coffee. "For the record, Elizabeth, thank you for all the work you all have been doing. I do appreciate it. I can only imagine how hard my people have been making it."

"No problem," she answered. "I'll be in the conference room if you need me." Now it was off to find a nutjob.

Sheriff Duffy watched Elizabeth walking away and he thoroughly checked her out. Yeah, she was pregnant and married, and the FBI could arrest him for thinking about it.

After all, he was still a male.

Elizabeth sat at the table and dialed her husband's phone. Looking at her watch, she mentally calculated how far away he was from Red River. He should just be an hour away from FBI West.

494

"Hey baby, what's going on?" he asked, answering on the third ring.

"Are we on speaker phone?"

"No, why?"

"Because I was going to sexually harass my co-worker and didn't want anyone to be able to testify at my HR hearing," she purred.

Blackhawk sharply inhaled. "Well, if that's the case feel free. I won't press charges."

"How about a rousing session of really explicit phone sex?" she asked, seductively.

Now he was laughing, because he couldn't say what he was really thinking. "Always, but it'll have to be one sided for now." The laughter became nervous, because Elizabeth wouldn't think twice about it, and he knew it.

"I miss you, handsome. Can't wait until you get back so I can crawl all over you," she began. Yeah, she was buttering him up for the cold blow of the information they discovered.

"I think you know how I feel about that," he answered back. Damn, to just be alone with his wife, or even alone on the phone. They'd never been apart since getting married and this was a new avenue to pursue on his sexual bucket list.

"I love you," she said, baiting him with kisses over the phone. "I dare you, Ethan." She didn't think he'd do it and let his staff see him be a big puddle of mush for his wife.

"I love you too, Elizabeth," he said, and then laughed as there was silence, and he knew she was waiting. "Come on," he laughed and then gave in, giving her a kiss over the phone. He was sure he was blushing and could feel the heat rising up his neck to his face. When Christina looked over at him grinning, he was even more mortified, more so than if she were staring at his ass.

"Now that's my sexy FBI husband," she laughed. "I didn't think you'd do it. Wow, someone has shocked the hell out of me today," she added.

"I do try to surprise you now and again."

"Well, speaking of surprises, I happen to have one for you and I'm not sure what to do with it, and I'm dropping it in your lap."

Blackhawk didn't like the sound of that. "Elizabeth, I really hate surprises that are work related, please be gentle."

"The corpse we found in the van?"

"Yeah?" Now he was sure it wasn't going to be a good surprise.

"Well, Desdemona identified the gender," she said, cautiously.

Blackhawk didn't understand. "We have a woman killing men to rebuild a man. What's there to identify other than the man's name?"

Elizabeth twirled a piece of hair around her finger as she tried to plot out how to tell him. "Are you driving?" she inquired.

"No, why?" It had to be pretty bad if she didn't want to tell him while he was driving. "Is it that bad, baby?"

"The corpse is a woman."

"Huh?" That surprised the hell out of him. "The mummified body is a woman not a man?"

"Yes, and that means I need a new profile from you," she added. "Surprise!"

"I don't think I can even explain or rationalize it. We have a woman killing men to rebuild a man on a woman's body? I don't' think the text books teach you that at Quantico. I think we're in uncharted territory."

Elizabeth didn't exactly like that idea. "Far be it for me to put the pressure on here, Ethan, but I need your insight. Give me anything you can at this point. I have a bunch of puzzle pieces and I don't know where to begin putting them together. Anything darlin'?"

Blackhawk stared out the window at the dark landscape and thought about everything they knew about the killer. Okay, they had a woman with blonde hair, taking strangers, and removing one part off each one, and then trying to reanimate him now or later. Ethan Blackhawk the profiler knew how off the wall this was, and as the husband to the woman that had to put it all together, he was frustrated that he couldn't give his wife definites.

"Please Ethan, give me something."

"Okay, let's start with the corpse; she obviously kept it for a reason. It's going to either be a family member, a sister, a lover. It had to mean something significant. The fact that she's trying to rebuild the dead person using male parts is puzzling. People keep a body for three reasons; to hide the evidence, they loved the victim, or they felt guilty and it's punishment to see it daily. Sin atonement, so to speak," he paused. "Can I have a little while to dwell on it and call you back once we hit FBI West?" he asked. "I need to be focused on talking to Derek's family, and then I'll have a clear head."

Elizabeth could tell he needed the time to play it out in his head, and she'd give it to him and start working on what she could until he called her back. Something had to give sooner or later.

"Okay, be safe, and call me back." She hung up the phone and heard the telltale beeps. The tech reports were incoming and soon she'd have the answer to a few more questions. She hoped and not more answerless questions. There were days Elizabeth wished she did the profiling, and this part of the job was her husband's. The stress of knowing a killer was out there and you had to put it all together could be crushing at times. Her only consolation in all this was they were safe. Ethan was almost back to FBI West, and Callen whitefox was safely watching over his fiancée. For now they could just work it and try and figure out what was going on in Red River.

At the knock on her door, she looked up to see Deputy Julian Littlemoon. She wasn't expecting him to be standing in the doorway.

"Yes?" Elizabeth asked a little ice in her voice. "Can I assist you with something, Deputy?"

"I probably deserved that," he said, walking in and sitting down. "You need any help?" he inquired. "Sometimes when you can bounce things off a person out loud it helps."

"No, I'm fine." Who was she kidding? Elizabeth did like to talk it out, but it pissed her off how the man just wrote her off as a pregnant woman. Men like him made her want to kick their asses around the room just for shits and giggles.

"I'm sorry about earlier. I underestimated you, and it was rude, arrogant, and wrong of me. Please accept my deepest apology. Had I known that you were some covert native woman disguised as a mere outsider, I wouldn't have judged."

Elizabeth looked at him and started to laugh. "If that wasn't full of bullshit, I don't know what is," she added.

"Want to start over?" he asked, grinning. "Hi, I'm Deputy Julian Littlemoon. I'm Native and at your service."

"Why?" she asked, suspiciously.

"Well, one- you stopped that overgrown cat for eating me, and two- you're married to a Native man, and that means he must believe you're worthy, or he wouldn't have married an outsider."

Elizabeth thought about it. "Okay, deal. We call a truce. Wave the white flag in surrender."

He just looked at her and then began laughing. "Truce," he put out his hand to shake hers. "Now, what had you looking so damn perplexed?"

"First off, the way these bodies were carried to the Boy Scout camp. I'm a woman, and I'm relatively tall, but I don't think I could carry you or my husband through the snow and not leave trace all over you."

"Didn't you find trace?"

"We found blonde hairs. That's it."

"What if the killer isn't working alone?"

Elizabeth thought about it. "Okay, so you and I are killing people together," she began. "I'm hacking the parts off men, including PARTS," she emphasized the last part, pointing towards his groin and watching to see if he got it.

"God, that's just..." There were no words for that in his mind. He almost wanted to cross his legs.

"Yeah, I know. So, we're killing people, can you actually see a man doing that to another man?" she asked. It just didn't feel right to her. It felt more like a woman would want to hack off men parts. "Maybe I'd do it to a man I was angry with, or to rebuild a lover, but why when a man is helping? It feels off."

Her phone beeped again. "Want to help me go through these tech reports? Maybe a fresh set of eyes will catch something."

"Can do," he said, taking the tablet she was offering and picking up her husbands.

"Okay, Julian. Let's see what we can pull out of all the techie mumbo jumbo."

*   *   *

She paced her house nervously. The stupid FBI bitches had stolen her lover away again. Now she couldn't even begin to put him back together again. He was gone. She screamed in frustration and kicked the furniture around the house. She punched the wall, leaving a hole in the sheetrock, and instead of making her feel better, it only pissed her off more.

She'd hid his body in the van in hopes of getting her lover out of the little storage room behind her kitchen wall. The FBI was poking around, and digging into things they shouldn't be. It was her last ditch effort to keep him safe and with her, and now it backfired and only ended up causing more of a mess. Now she had to figure out a way to get her lover back and then it hit her. There was a way, and it was going to be easy. In fact, when she was done, she'd have the last part of her lover, the body she'd so carefully been working on, and help with bringing him back to life.

She'd seen the man and doctor in the sheriff's station. It was easy to access the place, just through the garage doors and they'd be all hers. Slipping in unnoticed was simple; it wasn't like there was a lot of crime in Red River. Sheriff Duffy didn't keep the bay doors to the garage secured.

Easy in and then easy out.

Yes, it was a perfect plan. Now all she had to do was implement it.

*   *   *

"Hey, Doctor Adare!" yelled one of the techs. "We're heading out for dinner, do you and Agent Whitefox want to join us?" he asked, peeking into the makeshift morgue.

Desdemona was just packing up the corpse and wasn't really in the mood for dinner. "No thank you, Brigit, but I appreciate the offer. All of you head out for the night. I'll just do the paperwork and head back to the house."

"Okay! Night Doc! Night Agent!" she answered, closing the door behind her.

"Wow, she's chipper," he stated, grinning. "Not hungry?" he asked.

"Not after today. I have a pretty strong stomach, but I have to say, it's a bit queasy right now," she replied. "I just have to store our friend here back in the van. Ethan wants it locked up inside where no one can get to it."

"I'll take it out while you start on the paper work," he offered, hopping off the table.

"Are you sure?" she asked, looking up as he crossed to her.

Whitefox pulled her into his arms and began nibbling at her neck and ear. "Yeah, I'm really sure," he whispered. "We can finish up, and I'll take you home and we can find something to fill our time," he suggested.

"Uh, we'll have Elizabeth with us," she answered as she leaned into him. The man had really creative lips, and she felt herself getting warm.

"Oh well the more the merrier," and then he took the elbow to the stomach. "Point taken," he said, laughing.

"I'll be right here doing paperwork." Desdemona kissed him on the lips.

"Mmmmmm. I have to stop thinking about you in those glasses, sweetheart," he said, pulling away.

"If you're a good boy, I'll bring them home for later," she offered.

"Desi, good is my middle name." Whitefox wiggled his eyebrows.

"Uh huh," she waved him off. "Go!" she laughed, as her phone beeped. The tech reports were in, and she decided the paperwork could wait. Desdemona Adare sent them to her printer, and read them as they came off. Something wasn't right, or maybe something was very right and they just missed the obvious. The DNA under Derek's nails was male. She circled it with her red pen. Then she saw the next thing. The lab results on the trace they found on Derek. The patch of greasy liquid was Ethylene Glycol, in the form of hydraulic fluid. Desdemona circled that, and thought back to the puddle in the garage after the truck pulled away.

Crap!

Callen lifted the body into the back of the van and was whistling. He was looking forward to taking the women back to the house and tucking them all in until his brother got back into town. So far so good with keeping everyone safe.

As he stood up, he heard a sound behind him, and he turned at the last minute. Whitefox saved his own life, as the tire iron slammed into his head, and knocked him out, instead of crushing his skull.

Blackness came fast, as he felt himself being rolled into the back of the truck. His last thought was for the women that he just failed to protect.

Desdemona continued to read the papers, and heard the door open. "Callen, we have to get this paper up to Elizabeth," she looked up and stopped breathing.

"Hello Doctor. If you don't come with me, I will shoot you. If you think that the agent can be of any assistance, I've already handled him."

"You better not have hurt him," she snapped, angrily.

"Oh, he's hurting. Now let's move, Doctor."

Desdemona had to leave Elizabeth a clue. Casually she slid off her engagement ring, and left it on the papers she'd just circled information on, hoping once Elizabeth saw it she'd put the pieces together.

"Now!"

Desdemona raised her hands, as the gun was pointed right at her heart. "Okay, I'll listen," she said. "I don't know why you need me."

"You doctor are going to help me bring my lover back to life."

Desdemona didn't understand what that meant, but she kept walking and weighing her options.

"You drive!"

Desdemona got behind the wheel of the tech van carrying the bodies, and prayed Elizabeth Blackhawk was as good at figuring out things like everyone continually said.

Hers and Callen Whitefox's lives were on the line.

Chapter Twenty One

Elizabeth stared at the papers in amazement. The blonde hairs didn't match any of the women that they'd gotten samples from. The killer wasn't Wilma May, Courtney Brewer, Carly Kester or Sheila Court. That surprised her, but what surprised her more was that the DNA under Derek's nails was male.

"So the blonde hairs don't match?" asked Littlemoon. "Could they have been thrown in to screw with the FBI?"

Elizabeth shook her head, and didn't know what to think. Everything was all tossed upside down. "I need to head down to see Desdemona. Maybe there was a mistake in processing, and I'm reading this completely wrong."

"I'll come with you," he said, remembering his promise to the other Blackhawk.

"I have the feeling we've been wrong from the start, and if that's the case this whole things going to implode now that we have the killer's corpse downstairs." Elizabeth hustled down the stairs, and ran into the lab room. It was empty.

"Desdemona?" she called. "Cal?"

"No one's in the cooler," he said, walking back out.

"Julian, will you check the garage? Maybe their loading the body into the van for storage," she said, hopefully.

"Can do," he said, striding towards the garage.

Elizabeth went over to the lab table and looked down, and she knew instantly something was wrong. There sat the ring that belonged to the Blackhawk family. Desdemona Adare wouldn't have taken off the family treasure and carelessly left it sit on a table where it could get lost or stolen. Elizabeth picked it up and slid it on her finger for safe keeping before flipping through the tech reports that Desdemona had been going through. She checked all the parts that were circled.

Male DNA was present under the nails of their technician. Then there was the trace evidence found on the body. The oily substance was Ethylene Glycol in the form of hydraulic fluid. Elizabeth thought back to the earlier part of the day, and grabbed the phone sitting there. She dialed the sheriff's office.

"Hello Duffy," he said.

"Sheriff, earlier you said you were glad dispatch could find your brother when we called for a tow truck."

"Yeah, he wasn't in his office at the garage."

"Can you call dispatch and find out if they ever reached him?" she asked, her heart beginning to pound in her chest. "I have a question."

"Uh, okay. I'll call you back."

"Thanks," she said, hanging up.

Julian ran back into the room. "I think there's a problem. The van is gone, and I found this," he said, holding a tire iron in his hand, wrapped in a rag he found in the garage."

"Shit," she rushed over to it.

"I think there's blood on it," he said, holding it for her to check.

Elizabeth touched it with her finger and then sniffed it. There was the scent of copper pennies, and she knew for a fact, they had a huge problem.

The phone on the lab table rang.

Elizabeth ran to it, grabbing it. "Yes?"

"Dispatch said they didn't find him, he never called in for his messages. I don't understand how he showed up without dispatch contacting him."

Elizabeth knew. He was staking out the area, and saw them hiking into the area. "Question. Is your brother gay?" she asked, waiting for the answer.

James Duffy was outraged. "Hell No he isn't! In fact, he was dating a perfectly nice girl not too long ago. She was a pretty little blonde thing and completely devoted to him. Then she flaked out and left him breaking his heart. He's never been the same since she left him. She was the love of his damn life!"

Elizabeth felt that wave of awareness and then the sick feeling. "And she left him?"

"Yes, why?"

"Just wondering," she said, trying to sound blasé. They had their killer now, and the killer had her family. "Thanks for the time," she said, hanging up.

"It's Randy isn't it?" asked Julian Littlemoon.

"If I'm wrong my family is dead. You know where he lives?" she asked, hoping she wouldn't have to ask the Sheriff and tip him off.

"I do, want me to drive?" he said, following her up to the conference room.

Elizabeth thought about it. "Shit. Okay, you get to saddle up and be my backup," she stated, ignoring the look on his face as she pulled on her coat. "We need to walk out of here calmly; I don't want to alert him that we're heading to his brother's. He will either tip him off or he'll want to tag along to prove I'm wrong. I don't know if the brother was working alone or not, so we have to do this on the down low."

"Gotcha. Okay, I'll grab my coat and meet you out at your vehicle." He strolled out casually, peeked his head in to see Sheriff Duffy. "Hey boss, I'm heading home for the night. I'll see you tomorrow ok?"

Duffy looked up from his paperwork. "Yeah, have a good night, Julian. I'm heading out soon myself."

Littlemoon grabbed his coat and watched the FBI agent stroll out before him. He was pretty sure she started running the minute she was out the door. When he followed, he hopped into her Denali and she was already dialing the phone.

"We need a location where we can creep up on him. I don't want him seeing us coming, and then hurting either one of them."

"I know where to dump the Denali, but then we have to hike in a little bit. Randy lives out of the way."

"Give me a second," she said, as she heard her husband pick up.

"This is an incredibly bad time, Elizabeth. I'm just here with Derek's parents," he whispered into the phone. There were tears and crying in the background.

"Ethan, this is a worse time for me. The killer is Randy Duffy; he's got Desdemona and your brother. I'm going in to get them back, and I just needed to advise you and tell you I love you."

"WHAT!" he practically yelled into the phone. "You sit still, and I'll get you back up. Don't you dare go in and get anyone! You're pregnant!"

Elizabeth laughed. "Thanks for the newsflash on the pregnancy. Wait for backup, Ethan? Who are you going to get for backup? You're three hours away and there's a snow storm coming. Our tech team is a bunch of nerds that like looking at bugs and things through the microscope." She popped her ear piece in and continued, "I have back up. I got me a new Native American partner on this one," she said, trying to calm her husband.

Blackhawk started cursing and Elizabeth pulled the phone away from her ear until he was done.

"Put me on speakerphone," he demanded, scared shitless that his wife was going to be playing Cowboy and he was three hours away. This was why she needed to sit her cute ass in her desk chair in FBI West. Elizabeth Blackhawk was going to be the freaking death of him yet.

"Julian, you make sure you watch her back," he said, practically shouting into the phone.

"I got it," he said, as he continued driving through the snow.

"Ethan, I have to go. We need to plan this out and get in location. I'll call you as soon as I can, but my phone's going off until this is over. I can't be distracted if I'm trying to stalk and sneak up on the killer."

"Baby, be careful. You remember that promise you made me back in Salem?" he asked, hoping she'd keep it again.

"Hell yeah, Cowboy. Don't you worry. I'll meet you back at the OK Corral for a late night dinner," she said, lightly. "Set the table for five. I'll be bringing home our family and company." Elizabeth glanced over at her new sidekick. He was going to have her back, and she hoped that wasn't a huge mistake.

"I love you, baby," he said, softly. "Do what you have to do to finish this."

Elizabeth knew he was referring to the time she had to save Livy's life. "I got this, Ethan. Baby Blackhawk and I love you too." And she disconnected the call.

"Okay, what's the plan, Boss?" asked Julian Littlemoon.

Elizabeth handed him an earpiece and miked his collar while he drove. They'd have to be going in as silently as possible; they didn't want to alert the man holding her family. "We hike in, I go in, you cover me and I bring them both out alive."

"What about Randy?"

Elizabeth just looked over at him.

"Native to wife of Native is that man walking out of there alive?" he asked, softly.

"As long as he doesn't hurt them, yes and I can neutralize the situation without shooting. I could lie and tell you otherwise, Julian, but if he even caused either one of them an ounce of pain or I have to take the shot, I'm going to do it."

"Okay."

"Is that a problem?" she asked. "If it is, drop me off, and I'll get them out myself."

He looked over at her and grinned. "You have to be the feistiest woman I have ever met in my life. Do you have a sister?"

Elizabeth grinned back. "Nope but I do try to be feisty. It keeps the marriage fresh and Ethan on his toes."

"Yeah, I can tell," he laughed, pulling the Denali into the woods and turning it off. "We hike over the clearing to the house. Stay low; he'll have a clear view of us if he looks out the back windows. We also will have a clear view of him."

"I'm going into his house, and I want you to stay out and get ready to pick him off if he gets too close to killing anyone. Clear?"

"Yes."

"Kevlar is in the back. "You can use my husband's and I'm going in without. You are my back up. Don't shoot me." She said, hopping out and running to the back to grab her tactical shotgun and handing it to him after he suited up.

"Ready, Elizabeth?" he asked.

"Ready as I'll ever be."

Whitefox felt the gray breaking up and the room stopped spinning. He had one hell of a headache, and had no clue what the hell happened. One minute he was loading up the dead body and the next…

Oh shit, that's right. He struggled to move, and found himself strapped to something hard and cold. His shirt was gone and he had that sick feeling in the pit of his stomach. Slowly opening his eyes, he turned his head, and could see Desdemona bound to a chair, hands bound in front of her and her eyes closed.

He tried to call to her, but there was tape over his mouth. Damn it, not only did the killer have him, he had her too.

Desdemona heard the noise and shook her head to signal him. Immediately, she watched him close his eyes again, and pretend he was still unconscious. She said a silent prayer and hoped someone would be in time, or they were both going to die.

"Are we ready for the party?" came the voice, as he entered the room.

Desdemona stared up in horror. There was Randy Duffy, dressed as a woman and wearing a scalp covered in blonde hair.

It looked like they were both wrong and right. It was a man masquerading as a woman. The blond scalp explained the trace.

"Why are you doing this, Randy?" she asked, trying to get some answers.

"I'm not Randy," she said. "Randy is my lover. I need to help get him better so he can come back home," she answered.

"What's your name?"

"I'm Suzan Hollister, and I'm in love with Randy, and want to make him happy," she answered. "I need to make him very happy or bad things happen."

Desdemona could tell she was dealing with a nut case. She reached back into her mind to the psychology rotation in medical school and started to piece it together.

"What happened to Randy?" she asked, hoping the killer would stay calm.

The killer looked confused. "I don't know. Just one day he was here and the next he was gone."

Desdemona could tell that Randy believed every word he was speaking, and that made it even more dangerous and troublesome. How the hell do you rationalize with someone that's lost their self in some fractured state of psychosis? "Tell me about you, Suzan. I want to know about you. How long have you been dating Randy?"

"Oh well I think we've been together for a while, but I'm not sure. Time flies when you're in love. I want to marry Randy, but he said he needs to live with me for a while. Then he'll decide if I'm worthy of marriage. Randy says you shouldn't rush into marriage unless you know it's absolutely right."

507

This may be the only time in Desdemona's life she was going to agree with a nutcase. It was funny how a serial killer knew what her fiancé didn't.

The killer played with the blonde hair. "He's very hard to please, and sometimes he has a very bad temper, but I still love him. He's a very good man and promised to take care of me for the rest of my life if I just followed the rules."

"What kind of rules do you have to follow?" she asked, trying to keep Randy's attention for as long as she could.

"Why do you ask?" There was nothing but suspicion in the voice.

"I'm getting married too, and I just wanted to know what kind of rules that I might need to follow to please my husband."

"Oh! Ok," he smiled.

Desdemona watched the man try to process the question, and she started to analyze what could possibly be the issue with his mind. It seemed fractured and split into two personalities.

"I have to make sure the house is clean and that there are three beers ready for him in the refrigerator when he comes home from work. Then dinner had to be ready and hot or he gets mad."

Desdemona nodded. "Has he hurt you when you broke the rules?" she asked, softly. There were a few mental issues that this fell under, and she needed to keep Randy talking a little bit longer until she figured it out, and then maybe she could talk Randy down from the crazy ledge.

"There was only the one time that he really hurt me. We had a terrible fight and it didn't end well."

"Why don't you tell me about it?" asked Desdemona, trying to put as much caring in her voice as possible. She needed to win the woman over to her side and maybe save Callen Whitefox's life. "So I don't make the same mistake."

"I was late with dinner, and he got angry at the way I dressed. When he came home we had a fight and he hit me," then she looked confused. "I don't remember anything after that." Randy looked confused, as if he was struggling to figure out who he was, and who he wasn't.

Desdemona knew what the problem was immediately. The corpse they recovered had blunt force trauma to the back of the skull, and she was betting that during that fight Randy took

Suzan's life, probably accidentally. The trauma of what he did, split his conscious in two, and he wasn't aware of what the other part of his mind was doing. Typical dissociative disorder and the bad news for her was that there wasn't going to be a way to talk Randy out of it. Now it made complete sense. He was killing men to recreate himself, because his mind he'd taken on the weaker personality. The day he killed the woman he 'loved' he lost the ability to deal with the emotional and psychological consequences of it. Turning into himself, he'd given himself an escape from his actions. By becoming Suzan part time, he was able to rationalize that she was still alive and he wasn't a murderer. The longer Randy went without help, the more fractured his mind would become, and eventually he'd stop being able to slip back into reality.

"Suzan, you need to listen to me. You have to let us both go, and we'll help you find Randy, and put him back together," she cajoled in an attempt to get Callen Whitefox free. If she had to fight Randy, there wasn't going to be a good outcome. He was as big as Callen and was more beefy. She'd be hurt or killed.

"I need one last part, and then Randy will come home," she said, looking over at the man strapped to the table. "I need his heart, and you're going to remove it for me. I know how delicate the heart is, and I need a doctor to help me."

Hell no! She wasn't cutting her fiancé's heart out of his chest. Randy would just have to kill her first. It wasn't happening.

"Suzan, if we cut his heart out, it won't bring back Randy, and then he'll die too. You're going to go to jail for all this killing."

Randy laughed this twisted and sick laugh. "No I'm not. They won't find my dates, and they won't trace you back to me. I just need you to operate and take out his heart."

"Randy, I need to talk to you," pleaded Desdemona.

Randy looked at her with a look of complete confusion. "Randy isn't here, I have to find the pieces of him and remake him. I already told you that."

Callen was quietly trying to get his fingers into his back pocket. Inside was a pocket knife, and if he could reach it, he might be able to saw through the restraints. He didn't want Desdemona to deal with this wackjob on her own. He listened to everything he was saying to her, and the man was completely

509

unhinged. Whitefox wished he could open his eyes, but he had a feeling if he did, the festivities of cutting his heart out would begin. He had to buy them more time, and in the back of his mind he was praying that Elizabeth had found them missing and was at that exact moment putting it all together to save their asses. He had to put his faith in the woman that owned his heart or he was literally going to lose his own.

'*Please Elizabeth, I believe in you,*' he whispered into his own mind. He trusted the woman he loved now more than ever.

* * *

The snow was falling fairly heavily, as Elizabeth navigated the tree line surrounding Randy Duffy's home. From the perimeter of the yard, she could see inside the house. Randy was nice enough to turn almost all the lights on inside.

He must not have been expecting company. His idiocy was her good luck.

Creeping up to the side of the tech van, she snuck to the back, hoping and praying that if Callen was inside, he wasn't dead. The tire iron could have ended his life in one strike.

Opening the back, she peeked inside and found blood. There wasn't enough to be a massive head wound, and that gave her some relief. Then she thought about Callen and the other victims. Callen losing any part of his body was unacceptable to her. She loved him, and wasn't letting Randy take his life. Elizabeth had made a promise to Timothy, and she wasn't going to be telling him she failed.

Moving soundlessly through the accumulating snow, all she hoped was Randy didn't look outside and see tracks. If he did, then the jig was up. Leaning against the house, Elizabeth peeked in the living room window. There was a couch, a recliner and immaculately fluffed pillows. The house was spotless and looked like it was staged for company.

Ducking under the window, she moved closer to the front door. Next was the kitchen window, and although higher off the ground, she could still see in, barely. Inside were candles lit, food on top of the oven, and three wine glasses. One held a clear liquid and the other two a murky substance. That had to be the hydraulic fluid. It looked like Doctor Adare wasn't leaving the house alive either. All she could hope at that point was if Callen had been force fed the wicked brew, they'd have time to get him medical attention. Desdemona told her twenty four hours, and that replayed over and over in her mind.

Sliding down the house, Elizabeth stood at a door. Looking in the window, it appeared to lead into a mud room. Elizabeth planned out her tactical plan. The lights were on in the garage, and that was the likely place Desdemona and Callen were being held. There appeared to be an opening that led to the garage. Elizabeth took a deep breath and paused at the door. If anyone came around the corner with a weapon, she was at a disadvantage. Whispering into the COM at her neck, she needed eyes inside the house. From Julian's hiding place, he could see in the back windows of the house and garage.

"Julian, do you have the killer in sight?" Her voice was so low; she hoped he'd hear her over the wind.

"Affirmative. I have Randy in my sights, and you're not going to believe it when you see it. Be careful. He's standing approximately at your ten o'clock when you come in the room."

Elizabeth had no idea what he meant about her not believing it when she saw it, but that would have to wait.

"Cover me, and whatever you do, don't shoot me or Ethan's going to be pissed off."

Julian's laughter came through the ear piece. "You have no idea."

Cracking the door open, Elizabeth slowly searched the room for anything that was set up to alert Randy to an intruder. Everything looked clear. Listening, she could hear the talking, and strained her ears to figure out who it was speaking.

"Julian," she called over the COM. "Can you tell me where Callen and Desdemona are?"

"Negative. I can't see either. I see Randy pacing nervously. Maybe they're restrained on the floor."

Elizabeth felt her stomach getting sick. Desdemona she could hear and Randy too, but no Callen. Sliding along the wall, she could peek around the wall and peer into the Garage. Strapped to the table was a shirtless Whitefox, a cut on the side of his head and dried blood. His eyes were closed, but she saw motion as he was struggling to get to his pocket. Callen was alive and trying to get free. If his eyes were open, she would have given him a sign. Knowing that Randy couldn't use him as a shield helped her relax marginally. Now it was going to come down to how to take down Randy and save Desdemona.

Settling in, Elizabeth waited until the right moment to make her move. If she rushed in the man could kill Desdemona. What she needed was the perfect shot. Elizabeth focused on the man's voice, had her Glock pulled and ready, and waited. Randy Duffy picked the wrong family to try and kill. Obviously no one warned the fruit loop that she didn't have a problem with pulling the trigger.

Now it was time to do her job, and protect her family.

*　　*　　*

"How did you get all your dates, Suzan?" she asked, trying to keep her talking. As long as Randy was focused on her, Callen Whitefox had a chance to get free. Maybe he could overpower the man and save them. That was their only hope.

"We had coffee, and they came home with me."

The reply was so distorted from the truth, but in Randy's fractured mind, it was absolute fact. In the mind of the man holding her prisoner, he believed it was just coffee, and didn't realize he was pouring hydraulic fluid into it, and drugging his victims.

Suddenly, the killer moved towards her.

"It's time. You have to take out his heart, and put it in my lover. I need to get him back, and this is the last part we need." Randy cut her bonds, but kept her hands tied together, and dragged her viciously over to the table.

Desdemona could see the violence in the man and wasn't surprised he killed Suzan Hollister. The temper and anger simmered in the fractured mind, and she was sure it would have been magnified in Randy before the 'accident'. He was obviously a control freak before killing his girlfriend, and now that she was dead, he was trying to control that too, but becoming mentally unhinged in the process.

"I'm not going to hurt him. The man you have there is my fiancé and I refuse to kill him," she stated, honestly.

Randy screamed sickly at the Doctor's refusal. "HELP ME do this!" All the rage was there and now focused on the Desdemona Adare. "I need his heart to save my true love!"

Desdemona shook her head in refusal. "I won't kill Callen to give you the illusion that you have any chance of rectifying what you did, Randy. Suzan is gone and you took her life. You can't put her or you back together again." Desdemona had never been so scared in her life. Her heart was pounding in her chest, and she was pretty sure this was the end for her and for Callen. So much for Elizabeth's promise to keep them safe and boy she wished she could tell them all she wasn't superwoman like they all promised. What a big letdown. Right then she wanted to scream 'I TOLD YOU ALL SO!'

"NO!" Randy wailed.

"I love you, Callen," she said, standing her ground. She was a doctor, and she wasn't going to kill him to save herself from this lunatic.

The killer lost total control at the woman's words and in that moment of anger, Randy Duffy, in his divided state of mind made the choice to kill the woman standing between his perceived goal. Wrapping the beefy hands around Doctor Desdemona Adare's throat, he lifted her from the ground and began to end her life, squeezing the life from her body.

Desdemona struggled to fight for air, but the killer was too strong, and all she could do is look into the eyes of the deranged maniac and silent say goodbye to the family she just found. It was nice to have a girlfriend for once in her life.

Callen fought hard to get free and to Desdemona. He needed to save her, and stop the killer from ending her life. His eyes filled with tears, as he watched her being picked up from the ground, and the mans' hands strangling her. He'd failed to protect her, and now she was going to die and then he was going to follow.

Then his mind flashed to Elizabeth and Ethan having to find his body and his heart ached at how he was losing the two people he loved most.

Then there was the popping noise and all sound stopped as Randy Duffy crumbled to the ground and Desdemona fell with him.

Elizabeth came through the door, her gun drawn, and talked into her mic to Julian. "Clear, come on in," she said, and then holstered her gun.

Callen had never been so happy to see her in his entire life. Tears filled his eyes, as she met his gaze and nodded in reassurance. It was over, and they were safe. Love filled his body and replaced the fear.

Elizabeth helped Desdemona stand, and wouldn't let her look at the man that lay in the growing puddle on the floor. "You okay Desdemona?" she asked, popping her ear piece from her ear.

Desdemona shook her head and watched as her new friend pulled the tape from Callen's mouth. Elizabeth Blackhawk just saved their life. Okay, so she was superwoman and she'd been wrong. VERY wrong.

"Hey handsome, you feel like getting up from that table, or you want to hang out a little longer?" she teased, as she wiped the tear that slid down his cheek.

Desdemona rushed to his side, as Elizabeth freed her fiancé from his bindings with his pocket knife she retrieved from his pocket.

Whitefox nodded unable to speak. They'd come really close to not surviving.

"Oh my God, Callen," Desdemona whispered, as he sat up. "I thought Randy was going to kill you!" She threw herself across his body when he finally sat up.

"It's okay, sweetheart," he said, holding her in his arms. "I'm okay. Is your throat okay?"

She nodded as she wept in his arms.

"I guess you both had no faith in me, huh?" Elizabeth looked over her shoulder as her new partner rolled into the room casually.

"Nice shot, Elizabeth," he said, his own gun still around his neck. "I was just going to pull the trigger myself as soon as I had a clean shot," he said, looking at the dead man lying on the floor. Agent Blackhawk made one clean shot, to the center of the forehead. Leaning down, he pulled the wig off his head. "Yeah, it's not a wig. He scalped someone," he said, dropping it.

Elizabeth looked around the room at the set up. "There should be enough forensics here to prove that Randy was the killer." Elizabeth ignored the body on the floor; she was still trying to calm her stomach. Her family was safe, and that's all that mattered. The empty mason jar filled with a clear liquid on the counter beside the table made her sick to her stomach.

"What was he planning to take?" she asked, nonchalantly, trying to keep all the emotion from her voice.

"My heart," answered Whitefox. "Unfortunately, it was already taken and he couldn't have it," he said, dropping a kiss on the top of Desdemona's head, but looking straight into Elizabeth's eyes.

Words weren't needed between them. They never were when the bond was as tight as the one they shared. Elizabeth simply nodded, smiling gently. She touched her own heart as a reply for Callen.

His whole body clenched.

"Anyone want to tell me what the killer spilled before I had to end his life?"

Whitefox replayed everything that Desdemona managed to pull from him as they were talking. The one thing that was completely evident was the man was insane.

"You both came close on this one," added Julian Littlemoon.

Whitefox knew how true those words were. He released Desdemona to go to his sister-in-law. "Lyzee," he said, opening his arms and hugging the woman that just saved their lives. He buried his face in her hair and whispered low enough that only she would hear his words. "I love you more than anything in this world. You're my Angel for sure."

Elizabeth looked up and patted his cheek. "I love you too, Cal."

"How did you find us?" asked Whitefox, taking Desdemona back in his arms, because she was shaking violently.

"Well, Desdemona left me a bunch of clues," she said, standing to block the view of the dead man on the floor. Doctor Adare looked like she was barely holding together. "And one very important one," she said, holding up her trigger finger.

It was poetic and it wasn't missed by Callen Whitefox that Elizabeth, the heir apparent to their family, had possession of the family ring again. It was sitting protectively on her trigger finger. The finger she used to end the killer's life and give them back theirs. His heart clenched in his chest at the sight of it on her hand, and he met her eyes again. He knew the truth deep in his heart and from the look in her eyes, so did Elizabeth.

"It looks better on you, Desdemona," she said never looking away from her brother-in-law, as she slipped it off her finger to give back to Whitefox. When he couldn't keep his eyes locked on hers, the little niggling doubt almost overwhelmed her. "I was just keeping it safe for you."

"Elizabeth, thank you!" Tears filled her eyes as she looked down at the ring.

"I knew Desdemona wouldn't leave that family heirloom lying on an exam table, so it led me to the printouts that led me to putting the final pieces together. Randy was the killer, the dead woman corpse was his girlfriend, and he obviously had lost his damn mind."

Callen took the ring from her hand, briefly clutching Elizabeth's hand in his, and his other going to her cheek. The love he felt was overwhelming. He knew why she was on top of the family totem, and he'd never doubt the woman again.

"Let's get you guys out of this room, call in the tech team, and let me call Ethan. Right now he's pulling out all that very sexy hair of his worried that I've gotten in trouble."

Whitefox snorted.

"Ethan is going to kick my ass. I was supposed to be keeping you out of trouble," muttered Whitefox, sheepishly. "My bad," he said, leading them out of the garage.

"Hey, I was supposed to keep her safe," replied Julian Littlemoon. "Wow double duty. He must think you're a menace to your own wellbeing."

Elizabeth shook her head. "Do I need to point out the irony on this one, boys?"

Both men laughed.

Elizabeth shook her head, and pulled out her phone. "Oh he better not have sicked you two on me as babysitters."

"I mean…" started Julian Littlemoon, trying to cover for his Native friend.

"When I get my hands on Mr. Sexy hair, I am so going to kick his ass."

Elizabeth called for the tech team, an ambulance and a back-up ME from the next town over. Then she took one for the team and called Sheriff Duffy to alert him as to what was happening. After some loud screaming into the phone from his end, she dialed her husband.

"Elizabeth!" he answered on the first ring.

"Hey sexy. I'm free for that phone sex now if you're up to it." she teased laughing, as she walked away from everyone else to have the talk with her husband.

"Jesus Christ, are you okay?" Ethan Blackhawk demanded, his voice filled with panic. "Where are you?"

"I'm fine, and I just found your brother and Desdemona," she said, trying to soothe his nerves. "I'm chilling in the den of insanity at the killer's house."

"And the killer?"

"Tax payers are going to be happy." Elizabeth's voice held no emotion. If anything she was really good at de-compartmentalizing and now she had to, since she almost lost Callen to a killer. Oh, yeah and the woman he was marrying, even though he obviously had doubts. Apparently, there was still a mess on the horizon that was going to need clean up. Hopefully it wouldn't require a gun or could wait until after maternity leave.

Ethan sighed. The last two hours of his life were a giant string of knots wrapped around his throat and chest, squeezing the life from him. "What happened?"

Elizabeth briefed him on everything that she discovered herself and all the information that Whitefox had shared with her moments ago. "I'm going to be tied up here wrapping up the paperwork, and then the Sheriff. I already called for an ME from the next town over. Doctor Adare can't handle this one."

"No problem on the ME, I'll follow up on my drive back," said her husband. "I imagine the sheriff isn't happy with you."

"He's in route, and he was downright pissed. Seems he recanted his statement about not wanting to know and just let us handle it. Funny how that changed when he heard his brother was the fruit loop doing the killing. Apparently I'm fucking out of my mind, on a witch hunt from the start, and really shitty at my job."

Blackhawk knew it was going to get ugly. "Does he know he's dead?"

"Not yet. We're waiting on a new ME to pronounce him. I don't want to make Desdemona look at him. It was a pretty ugly face shot. I'll have Callen and Doctor Adare get checked out by the ambulance crew when they arrive."

"Be careful and if he touches you I'm going to kill him."

Elizabeth softened her voice, knowing this had to be horrible for him to live through. "I'm good baby. You know how much I love my gun and how effective it can truly be. I'll see you back at the house."

"Elizabeth, we are so going to have a conversation about how damn reckless and dangerous you are. I have serious concerns when my six month pregnant wife is stalking killers in the snow."

Elizabeth Blackhawk laughed. "Oh, we're going to have a conversation too, Cowboy, starting with having your brother babysit me like I'm an invalid. See how that all worked out? I think Callen needs the babysitter."

Blackhawk sighed. "He's not going anywhere without me for a long time either."

"Then we're going to finish up the conversation with you having Julian Littlemoon babysit me too."

"Well hell."

"Oh, it's going to be," she said, before clicking off her phone, grinning.

Three hours later

Blackhawk rushed into the kitchen of the house they were temporarily renting, and found his family sitting at the table eating pizza. His wife was perched on the counter, grinning at him as he charged the door. He strode towards her, the look of sheer panic leaving his eyes, as he saw she was in one piece. Driving back to Red River was a bitch, it was snowing, the roads were bad, and he was worried about his wife, child, and family.

"You are done in the field, Elizabeth Renee Blackhawk," he whispered, taking her face in the palms of his hands and gazed deep into the icy blue. "Do you hear me?"

Elizabeth laughed. "I hear you, Boss." She saluted him and then accepted his very welcoming kiss.

Both men in the room started whistling, as the kiss was very telling about how happy Ethan was to see his wife.

Finally he broke away. "I think you're the scariest woman in the world," he admitted. "You've no sense of self-preservation."

"Oh, well next time your brother and his fiancée get themselves abducted, I'll casually weigh the pro to con risk ratio before making a decision," she retorted, laughing. "Then maybe have a coffee and ponder if you'll be in a tizzy before I save them."

Callen laughed. "Uh, trust me when I say, there will not be a next time!"

Desdemona heartedly agreed. "I can't do this again," she said. "I have no idea how you two handle the stress of it all. We're done risking our lives with field work." She wasn't kidding; they were going to be discussing a safer job for Callen when they got home.

Whitefox didn't miss what she said; he just opted to ignore it until they were alone. He just became an FBI agent, and he wasn't giving it up because of one assignment.

"Is everything at the scene handled, Boss?" he asked his wife.

"Tech team is currently sweeping the house and the ME is working on the autopsy. Ethan honey, this isn't my first rodeo. I do know how to run a crime scene. I'm pregnant not the tribe idiot."

"Good one, Lyzee," Whitefox laughed, giving her the fist bump. "A double one is very impressive."

Elizabeth winked at him.

Blackhawk took off his coat and threw it over a chair. "I really think I need a vacation, and you're coming with me too. The stress of all your antics are going to kill me."

"Well, it wasn't all me. You can thank my back up partner for the escapade, Mr. Littlemoon," said Elizabeth, directing her husband's attention at the man leaning against the wall with a beer and a slice of pizza.

Littlemoon watched the other Blackhawk storm into the room, and kiss his wife and it made him smile. The woman wasn't exactly a weak scared creature needing protection. He suspected that Elizabeth Blackhawk was tough and well trained. She'd taken that killer down with one clean shot, and still wasn't flinching about it. He was right. She was definitely feisty.

Blackhawk walked over to him and shook his hand. "You ever need anything, you just call me. It's done."

"Well, Ethan," she interjected and then paused. "Sheriff Duffy is a tad bit upset, as you can imagine. We, meaning me, killed the conductor of the crazy train, and he's kind of holding a wicked grudge against anyone involved. He thinks I shouldn't have shot his mentally deranged brother, even though he was in the act of strangling Dr. Adare. So he's proclaimed it open season on anyone involved, including my back up Native American partner here. He can't touch us, because we're the Feds, but he's already looking for payback to his deputy."

"He can kiss my ass," answered Blackhawk.

"Ethan! Not in front of the baby!" Everyone started laughing.

Blackhawk turned and grinned at his wife. "Did he give you a hard time?"

Whitefox answered for her. "Oh you could say that he tried."

"Is he dead?"

Julian Littlemoon laughed this time.

Elizabeth figured she'd tell him now and spare him from reading it in the report later. "No, but when he tried to storm the crime scene and push past me I may have had to get physical with him. But really I was just a little physical and nothing too bad."

Ethan stared at his wife. "He put his hands on you?"

Callen laughed. "He tried, and then your wife flipped him into a snow bank after she sucker punched him right in the face."

Now it was time for Desdemona to join in. "It wasn't until he got up and called her some unflattering names that he really got his ass handed to him."

"I'm glad you kicked his ass." Blackhawk pulled his jacket back on. "I'm going to go kill him, I'll be right back."

Elizabeth laughed, hopping off the counter and stopping him. "I didn't hand him his ass. Your brother did. When Callen heard him call me the names, he may have roughed him up a little bit."

"A little bit?"

"I may have punched him again but this time in the mouth. I'm claiming post-traumatic stress disorder," he said, winking at Elizabeth. "Besides we found the tooth in the snow and they can probably stick it back in the hole. I was offended and defending Elizabeth and my nephew's honor." And he always would for as long as he lived. His eyes met Elizabeths' and again they shared their own silent conversation.

Ethan took the coat back off. "Thanks, Cal."

His brother nodded. He'd always defend her, because she mattered to him on a very deep, private level.

"Anyway, as we were saying, he's gunning for everyone in this room, and can only really touch Julian."

Ethan glanced over at Julian Littlemoon. "Do you need a job? If so, you're hired."

"Yeah, I'm not really FBI material," he said, grinning. "But you can subcontract me. I think I'm going to go private and be my own boss for a while. Unless I get to be Elizabeth's partner again," he said, nodding at the woman with nothing but respect.

Elizabeth snorted.

"I like feisty and she is certainly that and much more. Wicked right hook on your woman there, Director Blackhawk. Duffy never saw it coming or the flip into the snow bank. Very feisty and extremely hot to watch going down."

Callen agreed and got an elbow from Desdemona.

"What?" he demanded, looking over.

"Don't encourage her. She's a pregnant woman and shouldn't be doing crazy things," stated Desdemona.

Callen was going to inform her that the crazy things saved their lives, but Elizabeth placed her hand on his shoulder, just over her tattoo and ran her fingers through his hair. The tension drained from his body at her touch.

Ethan redirected the subject, feeling the tension building. "If you change your mind, Julian, there's a place for you working for us."

"Thanks for the offer, but I definitely have to decline for now."

"Now, there's the smartest man in the room," quipped Elizabeth, and she laughed when her husband looked over at her, as he gave her the look.

"Julian is the only damn person here with enough sense to not sell his soul to the FBI."

Wasn't that the truth?

~ *Epilogue* ~
Three Months Later

"Ethan Jackson Blackhawk I swear to God, if I survive this, I am never having any more children until you pony up and do the next one," she said, breathing through clenched teeth. The pain was more than she'd ever thought she could feel at one time. Elizabeth Blackhawk was tough, she'd been shot twice, survived a serial killer abducting her and a lunatic masquerading as a woman hacking men apart to rebuild his twisted view of his lost love, but this could very well be her breaking point.

Childbirth wasn't for the weak.

"Come on baby! You're almost there. Keep breathing," whispered her husband, as he held her hand and watched the miracle unfolding before him, as his wife gave life to their child. Never in his life had he loved another person more. Here she was giving him something he never thought he'd have; a family of his own.

Ethan had been sitting behind his desk working on paperwork when his wife walked into his office. Just the look on her face scared the hell out of him. When she said it was time, he barely had been able to think. He grabbed his gun and keys and rushed her right to the hospital. On the way out of the office, he was going to carry her, and she objected but all of their Agents cheered and wished them well. There was even an escort with lights flashing. Before he knew it, the calls started, the alert had been sent out, and the news was traveling around their circle. Baby Blackhawk was on his way, and everyone was eagerly anticipating his arrival.

"I'm trying," she said, as the next contraction started.

"Elizabeth, start pushing," said the doctor, sitting patiently between her legs.

She obeyed, only because she didn't have her gun and couldn't shoot her husband for putting her in this position. Well, that and she wanted this monster sized child out of her body. NOW!

As she squeezed his hand, his heart skipped in his chest, as he looked down, and saw his son, almost ready to enter the world.

"Baby, I'm so proud of you," he whispered, and tears filled his eyes. "You can do this," he cheered her on, and when her icy blue eyes met his midnight blue ones, everything around them stopped, and they focused only on each other.

They were partners, even in this.

Elizabeth blocked the searing pain out, and looked into the soul of the man she loved more than anything in her life. This man may have knocked her up, and put her in this position, but she knew she'd do it over and over again, just to see that look on his face. That pure happiness of having the life he always wanted and never dared to believe could be his.

He wiped her brow, and she closed her eyes.

"I will find you the biggest, meanest, bacon cheeseburger this side of the states, if you push this baby out and give me my son," he offered, softly in her ear.

There was no acknowledgement. Just her even breathing as she knew the next wave of pain was coming and she was to the point of exhaustion. There should be an easier way to do this, and some woman should think it up, because this was brutal. How the bloody hell had her best friend Livy done this six times? This was why Gabe bought her jewelry on mother's day, and she had news for her husband, so was he. This was diamond worthy! Big, fat, shiny ring worthy in her book.

The nurse looked over at the machine, and gave her the warning. "Here comes the next one, and it's going to be huge."

"Great," muttered Elizabeth. Again, she opened her eyes and stared into the eyes of her one true love, and began to push. She started to hear him counting for her, and on three she lost tract of the numbers, blocking it all out, as she found some deep inner strength that she didn't believe even existed. As her husband hit seven, she felt the pressure stop, and the sounds came crashing back. There was her husband, staring in awe, there was the doctor congratulating her, and finally there were the screams of a newborn.

Elizabeth Blackhawk did it.

Their little miracle was here.

Lying back, she felt the satisfaction of a job completed. Their twosome had just multiplied and they were a threesome. Her son was born. Looking over at her, husband she found inner peace.

Ethan watched his child coming into the world. Never was there anything as beautiful and wonderful. In an instant he became a father, a dad. It was the most miraculous thing he'd ever experienced, next to finding his wife and getting his family back.

"Do you want to cut the cord, daddy?" asked the doctor, handing him the scissors.

He wanted to do everything from here on out. There wouldn't be a second he'd miss.

This was his boy.

The squirming, screaming, messy baby the doctor cradled was his son. Blackhawk cut the cord, and then handed back the scissors. As the nurse took the baby away, he looked down at his wife. She watched him with unblinking eyes, and smiled up at him. "How's our son?" she asked, exhaustedly.

"Baby," he whispered and then kissed his wife. "You're amazing and wait until you see him."

"Black hair?" she inquired, grinning.

"Oh yeah, he has more hair than any baby I've ever seen!" He kissed her again. "I love you so much. I don't even think those words cover how I feel about you."

"I love you too."

"Elizabeth Blackhawk, in case there was ever any doubt, you are completely badass," he admitted, grinning wickedly.

The nurse came over carrying their son all wrapped up, and in a little blue hat. "He's absolutely perfect," she said. "Congratulations mom and dad."

Elizabeth took her son in her arms, and the tears came. He was absolutely beautiful and all theirs. She kissed him on the tiny little nose, and sniffled. "I love you," she whispered, sweetly to her little bundle of Blackhawk love. "I promise I will always love you."

Baby Blackhawk stared up sightlessly, still trying to adjust to the world but recognizing the voice that soothed him for the few months.

Elizabeth needed to see one more thing. She handed the baby to her husband. "I want to see my two men in life." She watched her husband tenderly take his son in his arms, and cradle him protectively against his body. Yeah, it had all been worth it. Just for this sight alone, she'd run right out and do it all over again.

"I love you," he whispered to his child. "I promise no matter what you do in life, I will support you and be right here for you. I'm proud of you already, and now I'm going to make sure you have the best life in the world. Your tree house is built. It's just waiting in the back yard for you. Your uncle and I finished it just in time for you." Blackhawk looked up at his wife. "Make sure you only take the right woman there, it'll be well worth it in the end."

"Ethan!" Elizabeth objected and then laughed.

The nurse came over and smiled at them. "You have a whole family out there pacing. Why don't you go tell them the good news Mr. Blackhawk, before they break in the door?"

Ethan Blackhawk handed his son back to his wife, and grinned. "Up for company?" he asked. If she didn't want to see anyone, he'd kick them out of the hospital. Right then he'd do anything for the woman that just delivered him a miracle.

"I'm ready for them," she smiled, cuddling her son. Yeah, she was probably a mess, but she didn't care. The family needed to meet the next generation. "Bring in the Blackhawk tribe."

Ethan walked down the hall to the lobby where his family waited for them. There was his eighty-nine year old grandfather in full Indian attire, garnering all the attention in the room. The stares from the other waiting families were entertaining. He smiled to himself that the man that raised him was able to see his son born. His father was sitting patiently, and holding a stuffed bear. Then there was his brother and Doctor Desdemona Adare. Since helping save his brother's life, she'd become part of the inner circle. Even though they still had yet to set a date, there was hope of a wedding in the future.

Maybe.

Callen paced like he was the expecting father and Blackhawk started laughing. The look on his face was of worry and panic. There was no doubt he would have wanted to be in there with them as Elizabeth gave birth, had she allowed it.

Whitefox just knew his brother had arrived; he looked over at him in nervous anticipation and then rushed towards him "Is our Lyzee okay?" he asked, panic present in his voice. Even after finding a woman to call his own, Elizabeth Blackhawk would always be the center of his life. Your heart loved who it loved. Knowing she was his safety net through life, and the one that saved him from a killer, tied them together even more. There was no doubt what he felt for her, or the unbreakable bond they shared. Over the last four months, they'd only grown closer. She was his rock and had gotten him through the issues he'd been facing with Desdemona.

"She's doing really well and so is my son," he said, proudly. Just the word son lifted his heart, and made his soul feel overfilled with love and peace.

They started cheering and again had the stares of the other families.

"Want to see them?" he asked, noticing they had flowers and presents ready. He shook his head, at the bear that was dressed like a Native American. It wore a headdress and his wife was going to appreciate the humor.

"Yes!"

They followed him to his wife's room, and opened the door. There sat the most beautiful sight he'd ever seen in his life. His wife had changed into her robe, and was sitting on the bed holding their chubby son.

Timothy Blackhawk was the first to approach her and the baby. "Oh, sweetheart! He looks just like Ethan did as a baby." He opened his arms, and Elizabeth handed him her child. "You did well, Elizabeth. This little boy feels like a great warrior like his father and uncle."

Elizabeth watched as the man kissed him on his forehead, and started speaking in a language only Wyler and he understood. He touched him over his heart, and Elizabeth was pretty sure he was offering him a blessing and protection.

"Welcome to the family, Little Blackhawk," said the family patriarch, cradling the baby against his robes reverently.

"Lyzee, he's absolutely beautiful," said Desdemona. "What's his name?"

Ethan sat beside his wife, and put his arm protectively around her. "We'd like to introduce you to Callen James Blackhawk," he said proudly. "CJ for short, to ease up on the name confusion."

Callen was caught off guard and stared at his Elizabeth, falling in love all over again. Just when he thought he couldn't love a person more, he did.

"We wanted to give Callen's name the honor it deserves, finally as a Blackhawk." Elizabeth offered.

Desdemona just stared at the three of them, and now a baby that had the name of the man she was engaged to marry. The wave of jealousy hit hard at what the three shared so intimately that she didn't understand and never would.

Callen was touched beyond words. Not only had he a woman to enjoy life with, but his brother and Elizabeth gave him something incredibly precious.

A nephew that carried his name and a family that obviously loved him more than anything.

He went to his grandfather and opened his arms to yet another precious part of his life.

"I promise to guide you and lead you, CJ," he said to his name sake. In their heritage the uncles passed on the knowledge and past of their ancestors. Yeah, family was an awesome thing and he was going to do it right. "I will love you like you're my own. You now have part of my heart."

He kissed little CJ on the forehead and handed him to Wyler. Whitefox went to Elizabeth and kissed her softly on the lips and stroked her cheek. "Thank you for marrying my brother and giving me a life I never thought I'd have," he said softly, as he pulled her against his body. "I love you more than words."

Desdemona cringed and felt her eyes well up. She brushed it off as being happiness for the birth of the new baby, but she knew the truth.

It had been a tough four months.

Elizabeth hugged Callen. Life was good, and now she could lean back and enjoy her family.

Wyler didn't get to hold his sons when they were born. He was too irresponsible, but now he got to hold his grandson, and his heart was filled with peace and love. "Elizabeth, he is going to be a strong warrior, like his father and uncle. Perhaps an FBI agent like the men before him too."

Blackhawk looked over at his father. "Dad." He got his attention. "When Elizabeth goes back to work in twelve weeks, we're going to need someone to help take care of the baby, especially if we travel. You wouldn't be interested would you?" he asked, giving his father a chance to be part of his grandson's life, and redemption for missing out on his sons' lives.

Wyler wiped his eyes on his sleeve and nodded, unable to speak. There was no doubt he'd make the most of it. There were so many things he was going to show the child. "I can't wait to take him hunting," he finally got out.

"I'm shocked no one bought him a gun already," snickered Elizabeth, wiping her own eyes. If anyone could make her cry, it was the men in her family.

Desdemona went to the door and reached outside for the bear. "We couldn't find a gun small enough, but we did get him this." She dropped the Native American dressed bear on her bed.

Elizabeth started laughing and looked around at her family with nothing but love for each one of them.

Timothy spoke up, wiping the tears from his brown eyes. "So, now that I have my first great grandchild, will you be having more for me Elizabeth?" he inquired, grinning. "Great Grandchildren are a blessing to this old man. The more the merrier."

The pain was already forgotten, and replaced with the love and happiness. Elizabeth grinned. "Absolutely. I have no doubt there will be more Blackhawks, but give me a few weeks off for now. Growing the Blackhawk men is exhausting!"

It was a damn good day to be a Blackhawk.

THREE MONTHS LATER...

Cordelia Adare dropped the wrapped book into the mail slot at the post office. When she came across it, in the attic, she knew something was off. Just reading it gave her chills and made her skin crawl. Something horrible had happened in their mother's life, and she wasn't buying the rumors that she ran away with some man anymore. Now with the evidence she found, she was convinced their mother was killed.

Going to her grand'mere had been a dead end. She basically told her that living in the past never had a good outcome, and to let it go. She didn't understand how she could let go something that shaped her and her sisters' lives. The only thing she could think to do was get the journal out of the bayou and to her sister in the FBI. Maybe she was just paranoid, but she felt like she was being watched all the time. As she scribbled the note to her sister, she hoped she'd read it and see what she saw.

Time would tell.

Walking back into the silent house, she locked the door behind her, making sure to slide the bolt into place. Now she'd call her sister, and tell her to expect a package in the mail. Hopefully she wouldn't be too busy to help her find the demons that were chasing their family. Someone had to put an end to all of this, before more people had to die.

As she picked up her cell phone, she heard the creak, and her whole body went on alert. Walking towards the stairs leading to the upstairs, she looked around the room, and decided it'd been her imagination. The house was clearly empty. Now her imagination was running wild.

Cordelia started dialing her sister's number, and heard it again. The creak was louder. Everything in her screamed run, and she moved to the door she'd just came in through, throwing the lock open, and then the hand came around her face with the sickly sweet smelling rag. She fought with everything she had in her body, scratching, clawing and kicking, and then the room shifted, swam to a gray color that closed in on her.

The voice in her head screamed 'FIGHT', but the voice in her ear told her it was too late. There were so many regrets and wishes that wouldn't ever come to fruition as her life was being stolen from her. Cordelia Adare wished she'd done so many things completely different and now it was too late. Life was over and she wasn't getting another chance.

Darkness came and stole her away too soon.

530

Cordelia sunk into the deep darkness, knowing like her mother that her time was now up too. By the time her sister got the book and figured out what was going on back home it would be too late.

Her life was over and the only one that could save Desdemona now was Desdemona and a huge miracle.

Dear Reader,

I know right now some of you have just finished reading about Callen and Desdemona, and are seriously questioning my sanity. The relationship feels rocky and has issues brewing that may have made this an uncomfortable read for someone loving a happy ending.

You wouldn't be wrong if you read this book and thought 'God Callen! Don't do it!' or 'Run Desdemona!'. When siting down to write this book, I had a destiny planned for everyone involved. I know where it's going, and where Callen is going to end up in the next book or two. In fact, as you read this letter, I've already written the two books that follow. Deep Dark Mire and Fire Burns Hot already have their path set and written. I can promise you that there is a happy ever after in the works, and one that is outside the box.

One of my biggest weaknesses in life is true love. I believe it exists and it's out there for everyone. When I put Callen and Desdemona together it was for a reason. Sometimes you have to cross a bridge, making a mistake in order to find the path to ultimate happiness. Lessons are learned in everything we do, and the same is true for both lovers in this chapter of their story.

When my best girlfriend sat down to read this book, she nearly wanted to kill me. Reading about the clumsy relationship between the two has a point. I'm asking you the reader to bear with me and trust that Callen will have a story that ends the way he truly deserves. Desdemona will have lessons to learn and her own path to take. When you build a relationship on lies and half-truths, it won't last forever.

Fate leads you and gives you options along the way. We just have to be open to making mistakes, fixing them, and finding the way to our happily ever after.

Much love and adoration for you all.

Morgan.

Coming next: Deep Dark Mire (book 4)
&
The Blood Retribution
&
Fire Burns Hot (book 5)

Other books by M. Kelley

The Junction

Serial Sins

An FBI Thriller Series

The Killing Times (book 1)

Sacred Burial Grounds (book 2)

True Love Lost (book 3)

The Blood Series

The Blood Betrayal

The Blood Redemption

The Blood Vengeance

Visit M. Kelley at www.morgankelley.com or Email her at author.m.kelley@gmail.com

Made in the USA
Lexington, KY
04 February 2013